Gerald W. Searle was born in Cape Town. The third born of ten children. He grew up under the unjust and cruel policy of Apartheid at its worst. He finished his schooling in 1953. Gerald worked as a factory hand for three years then experienced a calling to the priesthood. He then completed his high school followed by seven years at a Pontifical University in Rome where he graduated in philosophy and theology. Gerald was ordained in Rome in 1962. He ministered as an ordained priest in Cape Town for seven years. Gerald fell in love and married Lorraine in 1971. He migrated to Western Australia in 1980. He took up writing as a way to enrich his retirement in 2001. Gerald has since published a theological work, a novel, and his memoir. Gerald lives with his wife in Wanneroo in Perth, Western Australia.

I wish to dedicate *Out of the Darkness*, to all those dedicated men and women of the first century in the CE, who gave their all, even their lives, to spread the good news, we all enjoy today. And I also dedicate *Out of the Darkness* to all those countless number of men and women, down the past twenty centuries, up to those who are presently labouring tirelessly to bring us *Out of the Darkness* and into the light; where love, peace and joy reigns, and await us.

Gerald W. Searle

OUT OF THE DARKNESS

AUSTIN MACAULEY PUBLISHERS®

LONDON * CAMBRIDGE * NEW YORK * SHARJAH

A CIP catalogue record for this title is available from the British Library.

ISBN 9781035878833 (Paperback)
ISBN 9781035878840 (ePub e-book)

www.austinmacauley.com

First Published 2025
Austin Macauley Publishers Ltd®
1 Canada Square
Canary Wharf
London
E14 5AA

First and foremost, I acknowledge and thank the four persons who were the first to write this man's story: Mark, Matthew, Luke and John. Our protagonist died in the year 30 AD. AD indicates Anno Domini (the year of the Lord), or as now classified, CE (Common Era). Mark wrote his story between 65-70 AD. Matthew and Luke around 85-90 AD, using Mark as one of their sources. And lastly, John wrote his story as a senior citizen, in his nineties, around 90 CE-110 AD. Their stories continue to be the most read even in our present era.

You will meet Matthew (Mattheus) and John (Johanan) in *Out of Darkness* as they were the first disciples of this first-century guru.

I have grown up with the stories written by Matthew, Mark, Luke and John and have read them over and over again in preparation for the writing of this story. I have spent many hours meditating and reflecting on this guru's story. I hope I have done justice to him in this novel, *Out of the Darkness*.

I have to thank the numerous authors I have consulted in the writing of this novel. They are too numerous to mention as I researched them on the Internet. Besides my main sources of Matthew, Mark, Luke and John, I acknowledge two contemporary authors whom I know and have met personally and whose works I found most useful and highly recommend. They are Albert Nolan's classic, first published in 1977, *Jesus before Christianity*. And Charles Waddell's gem, *Jesus Matters*, published in 2014.

I also wish to thank Fulton Oursler who wrote his highly successful trilogy in the 1950s, *The Greatest Book Ever Written*, based on the Old Testament; *The Greatest Story Ever Told*, based on the New Testament; and *The Greatest Faith Ever Known*, based on the Acts of the Apostles. I've read this trilogy so many times and Fulton Oursler has inspired me to write a similar trilogy, seventy years after he wrote his.

I thank the three men who read and corrected and suggested improvements to my grammar and content. Firstly, Kevin Wringe, the first friend I made arriving in Australia in 1980 and whose friendship I treasure to this day. And who is always so generous in correcting my literary attempts. I thank my eldest son, Paul, for his excellent corrections of my common and stupid grammatical and literary errors. I have learned so much. Thank you, Paul. And thanks to a dear new friend and fellow meditator, Dennis Ryle, recently retired Church of Christ pastor, who had a keen eye to Scriptural errors. Thank you, Kevin, Paul and Dennis.

I also wish to thank my daughter-in-law, Larissa, who was very much a daughter in need and who willingly gave up her precious time to guide me through the technical world, in which I so often got lost. Without her technical, secretarial and managerial expertise, I would have surely floundered in the darkness. Thank you, Larissa.

And I thank Lorraine, my dear wife of more than fifty years, for her love and patience with me and giving me the inspiration, time and space to write. Thank you, Lorraine.

Finally, I thank the Spirit that hovers over me every time I write. Without the Spirit, I have no inspiration.

Prologue

This is a novel about a boy genius who lived over two thousand years ago, who grew up to be a guru, the likes of which the world had never seen. He was a teacher, a miracle worker, a healer, a special person whose origins, life's teaching, example and ignominious death by crucifixion stunned the world and changed humanity forever. This is his story. This is a true story, inspired by his life, and as it is also a novel, fictional characters have been created for dramatic effect. Characters that are, however, true to the life and events of this greatest man that ever lived. Whether you are a believer or not, I hope you will enjoy and be inspired by this novel and the man it encapsulates.

Chapter One
The Nazarene Kids

"Yeshua, come here, I need to have a chat with you."

Oh! Oh! What have I done now? Yeshua thinks. When mothers call you to have a chat, it is usually when you have done something wrong, something of which they do not approve. *Can't she see I am trying to make a kite, to fly in the sky?*

"Sit down; I want to have a serious chat with you."

"Really, Immah, when did you last not have a serious chat with me?" Yeshua said with a smile.

"That's not true, Yeshua. I have non-serious chats with you all the time. But you are soon to be ten years old, and there are things I have to speak to you about. You will be going to upper school soon and will learn so much more about our Scriptures, about Adam and Eve, and Abraham, Moses, Joshua, Isaiah, Jeremiah, and so many kings and prophets of old. And you will also continue to improve your reading and writing, spelling and sums and all that. And I want you to be properly prepared for what lies ahead. Your father will be home soon, so I want to prepare you for what we have to tell you."

"Immah, is this the story of the birds and the bees that all young children learn from their parents? Zadok, my friend, who is twelve years old, told me all about that, I know where babies come from. And Immah, I know all about Adam and Eve and the forbidden fruit, and all those other characters you mentioned."

"I know, Yeshua, you are so bright, and have won all those awards for your learning and your religious teachers, especially Gamaliel, has told me just how astonished they are with your knowledge and grasp of our sacred writings and all the Laws of Moses and the Prophets. You have knowledge beyond your years. Gamaliel forever sings your praises and says he is simply astonished at your knowledge."

"Immah, I owe that all to you and Abba, you have told me those beautiful stories about our ancestors, and all about Adonai and his ways and laws and the meaning of all those rituals we celebrate. You and Abba have taken me to our community centre for our Sabbath celebrations every Sabbath and we have gone on pilgrimage to Jerusalem every third year for our Passover celebrations and also at times on pilgrimage for the other festival celebrations of Pentecost and Tabernacles. You taught me to pray. And Gamaliel, our teacher who is more than a teacher, more than a rabbi, has taught me so much."

"You are a good student, Yeshua, way above all the other children. You are especially gifted. And you must be so proud of all your knowledge and awards."

"Immah, I just want to make you and Abba proud of me. And I simply love to learn, all about Adonai and his creation and how he has intervened in our lives. The story of creation, and Adam and Eve and the Serpent, in the first book of our Scriptures is so captivating, and the story of the slavery of our ancestors in Egypt for four hundred years is so fascinating, and Moses' story and how he led our forefathers out of Egypt into the wilderness where they lived for forty years before entering the Promised Land. I love those stories, Immah, they are so beautiful."

Miriam sighed; she was so overwhelmed with the wisdom of her young son, his use of such big words and his skill in communication. She thought about how quickly these almost ten years have passed. She and Yosef had not told Yeshua anything about his birth. She had grown accustomed to Yeshua as her son, her only, beautiful son, whom she loved more than any other mother could. She and Yosef had pondered long and discussed when it was appropriate to tell Yeshua all about his birth. The visitor from heaven, Gabriel, who had come to her in this very house more than ten years ago, had not visited her again. He had said such mysterious words that she had pondered on for so long. But he had given her no instructions on what to do, how to prepare her son for whatever lay ahead.

What did lay ahead for him? She did not know. She had grown so comfortable to Yeshua being her son, she had seen him grow from a little babe, to a toddler, fed him at her breast, saw him crawl, stood by as he took his first tentative steps, and wept as he let go of her hand on the first day he went to school. Now he was about to go to upper school and he would grow up so fast, Miriam felt so uncertain of the future, of her son's future. But she and Yosef thought it was time he had learned about his past.

"Yeshua, your father and I want to have a good chat with you about how you were born, and about your future, and also to prepare you for your ongoing schooling and for your life ahead. You have been such a good child and such a delight to Yosef and me, and we want you to have the best preparation for your time at school, which will lay the foundation to your future life."

"Oh, is that all, Immah, I thought I was going to be scolded for something I did or forgot to do. Abba is not home yet and won't be home for a while, may I go out and play with Achim, we are making a kite which we want to fly so high that it will reach heaven, and give it to all those children up there to play with."

"Oh, that's a beautiful gesture," Miriam said with a smile. "You know what time your abba will be home, so come in before to wash and prepare for dinner."

"Okay Immah, see you in a while with a smile."

"See you later, procrastinator," Miriam replied, smiling broadly.

Miriam continued her preparation for their evening meal; a roasted chicken with all sorts of vegetables from their own garden, her and her son's pride and joy. They spent so much of their spare time in the garden and she was amazed at how much her son connected with all that grows and how fascinated he was to see them grow and bear fruit.

A half hour passed and she heard Yosef holler, "Hi Miriam, I'm home. Where is Yeshua?" He put down his bag of tools as he stripped off his outer working garments.

"He's at the field, with Achim; they have made kites from scratch, and intend to fly them to heaven for Adonai's kids to play with."

Yosef smiled. "I'm absolutely amazed how quickly Yeshua learned how to make his own kites."

"Yes, he is a quick learner and sure messed up the place with flour all over, when he made his paste. And I found so much of my tread missing as he flies his kites into the heavens and then doesn't bother to reel them in, letting them go."

"Well, he sends them to heaven," Yosef smiled.

"More like into the lake," Miriam smiled back. "I told him we were going to have that chat after supper. Are you still okay with that?"

"Miriam, I'm not really okay with that at all. I have grown accustomed to Yeshua as our son, as an ordinary child, but you and I know that he is far from ordinary, and I guess we have to prepare him for whatever lies ahead, whatever his destiny is. Anyhow, let me just clean up, and I'm so hungry I could eat a horse."

"Sorry about that, Yosef, I only have chicken, no horse. But you will have the taste of horseradish," Mary laughed out loud.

Yosef gave a playful slap to Miriam's face that missed by a mile. "Enough of your horsing around," he grinned and went out back to wash.

In the meantime, Yeshua and Achim were completely engrossed in their kite, which was sitting like a king on its heavenly throne, high up in the sky. It was becoming smaller and smaller and when it was just about a tiny dot, like a baby ant against the blue sky, they will release it to be taken up by the angels to heaven, to delight the children up there.

Yeshua and Achim were so proud of their creation, made of flower paste, bamboo, the thinnest bit of cloth they could find, and a long cloth tale, and plenty of thread, everything recycled from stuff no one longer needed, except the thread of course. They named the kite Delilah.

"Can you still see her, Achim? Can you see Delilah?" Yeshua asked.

"Just about, Yeshua, I think just a little bit more thread and she is a goner."

Yeshua tugged at the kite. It felt so heavy and so near, yet it was miles and miles in the sky, flying free like a bird.

"You know Achim, if ever we can come back when we die, and choose who we want to be, I would choose to be a bird, like an eagle, and just spend all day flying and gliding in the vast blue sky."

"That would be great, Yeshua. Me again, I would rather like to come back as a snake, like a viper, and scare the living daylights out of everyone, and no one will approach me and I can be left in peace."

"Really Achim; that would be terrible, you will be powerful and scare everyone, but you will have no friends."

"Not so, Yeshua. I will be able to choose who can be my friend and those who I don't like I will just give them a hiss and they will go away."

"And to those to whom you don't give a hiss, you will give a kiss," Yeshua retorted with a laugh.

"Yesss! A hiss, a kiss or a miss, that will be me," Achim said proudly.

"Achim, I don't think I can see Delilah anymore. She's still there, I can feel her but I definitely can't see her."

"I can't see her either," Achim said.

"You know Achim; this must be like what it is with our Father in heaven, Adonai."

"What do you mean, Yeshua? You got one of your parables again?"

"Well, we can't see Delilah, just like we can't see Yahweh. But I can feel that Delilah is definitely there at the end of our thread. All I need is a tug and I am sure, Delilah is there, and all I need is a tug, and I know Adonai, Yahweh is there."

"Really, Yeshua, you amaze me with your stories. I suppose you have a story about the thread too?"

"Not really Achim, only that the thin thread is our way of communicating with God, slim is the thread, yet so powerful, it is like our prayers, so simple, yet so powerful that it can reach the heavens and Yahweh, just like our kite."

"Okay Rabbi Yeshua, I think we can release Delilah, I can definitely not see her anymore."

Yeshua was reluctant to let Delilah go. He and Achim had spent so much time and effort in her creation, and it is a shame to let her just go. But he thought, she will be with the angels in heaven, in the palace of Adonai, so, gently he released her and she was gone.

Achim and Yeshua walked home in silence. They were in a way, grieving the loss of their tailored friend Delilah, but they knew she was happy, and would be well cared for and that one day they would see her again.

Chapter Two
The Bolt from the Blue

"So how was your day, Yeshua?" Yosef asked, as he helped himself to some chicken.

"It was good, Abba. Achim and I made a kite and we called her Delilah, she had a long tail, and we flew her so high and then let her go so she could fly to heaven and delight all the kids there," Yeshua replied.

"And what about school, what do you remember about what you learned today?"

"We listened to the story of Samson and Delilah, and that was why we named our kite Delilah, and gave her a long raggedy tail, to remind her of Samson's long hair that she cut off."

"Why did you call your kite Delilah, it would be more appropriate to the story if you named your kite Samson and not Delilah."

"Abba, where have you been, don't you know that kites are all female?"

"Really? And why is that so? Surely, they can have both male and female names. Yahweh made us male and female," Yosef retorted.

"I know, Abba, but it is only women who can fly into the sky, they have lighter beings than men. Men are too heavy and too earthly. Women on the other hand fly easily and easily connect with the heavens," Yeshua replied.

"Yeshua, you have an answer for everything. Where do these ideas of yours come from?" Yosef asked.

Yeshua tapped the side of his forehead with his finger. "From here, Abba, they just pop up from here," he said with a smile.

"More like from here," Miriam said, as she tapped the tips of her fingers on Yeshua's heart.

"Yes, you are right Miriam; our son has a heart of gold."

"Okay, Abba and Immah, enough with the inquisition, I'm hungry. We forgot to thank Yahweh, and Abba has already tucked into his chicken."

"So, I did, okay Yeshua, you say the prayers."

Yeshua bowed his head slightly, touched his forehead with the tips of the fingers of both hands and prayed, "Yahweh, we are most grateful for the food and drink, fruit of the earth that you have created so wonderfully and Immah has cooked to perfection. Bless Immah and Abba and anyone else who had a hand in bringing this food and drink to us for our nourishment and enjoyment. Amen."

"Amen!" Miriam and Yosef said in unison.

For a while they ate in silence. Yeshua was the first to break the silence. "This is yummy, mummy, and this bread is so delicious, I could eat the whole loaf," Yeshua said, grinning, and wiping his mouth with the back of his hand.

"Yeah, yeah, I agree with you, Yeshua, this is a meal fit for a king," Yosef said.

The conversation flowed freely, Miriam, Yosef and Yeshua sharing all that happened to them that day. Miriam spoke about her neighbours; theirs was one of a cluster of four homes that shared a large common yard where they prepared their meals and where they sometimes ate as a family, and where all the neighbours came together for feasts and celebrations. Miriam reminisced on how beautiful it was to celebrate Yeshua's birthday with their neighbours and how good it was for Gamaliel,

Yeshua's teacher, to be present. And of course it was always a joy for Yeshua, Miriam and Yosef to have Miriam's parents Hannah and Jehoyakim present for the celebrations. It was such a joy for the family and for Yeshua to have his grandparents living so close by, for they often dropped in unannounced with treats for Yeshua, and Yeshua often dropped in unannounced at their place. And they were always overjoyed to have Yeshua with them.

Yosef spoke about his work for the day, who he worked for and what he did. He had built a low table and a cabinet for a rich family in the nearby town of Sepphoris, where many rich people lived.

Yeshua relived his and Achim's making of Delilah, and the joy they had in flying her so high and then releasing her to the heavens.

When the meal was finished, Yeshua helped his mother to clean up. They liked to clean up right away, both Miriam and Yeshua liked things to be neat and tidy, and Miriam had no problem having to pester Yeshua to keep his section of their home tidy or the whole house tidy for that matter, except it seems when he was making his kite, for then he really made a mess in the yard. But he would clean it all up when he and Achim returned from their adventures.

Yosef went for a short stroll while Miriam and Yeshua were cleaning up. Yosef wanted to gather his thoughts for the conversation they were about to have with Yeshua. Yosef thought back to how he first set eyes on Miriam. He had seen her grow up and she had this calm and beautiful demeanour about her. He could see that there was something special about her. He was much older than her, but he watched her blossom and when she turned fifteen, an age when she could be betrothed to a man, he could hardly take his eyes off her. She was so beautiful and he felt an irresistible attraction towards her. He remembered so clearly seeing her at a wedding celebration of one of the communities of Nazareth. There were only about two hundred inhabitants and they all celebrated life's milestones together as one happy family. There was music and the community centre was packed, the young ones and not so young ones were dancing and singing, and Miriam happened to be taking a break from the dancing and standing by herself with a fruit drink in her hand. She was sipping her fruit drink. Yosef was on the other side of the crowd, holding a glass of wine. His eyes fell on Miriam and his heart leapt. He just had this inexplicable feeling that the two of them would become good friends and that in some way their destinies would combine. He felt in his heart that they were destined for each other.

Yosef thought about how he prayed for courage to approach Hannah and Jehoyakim, Miriam's parents, to seek permission to betroth Miriam. He thought about how awkward he felt when he and Miriam first started courting. He was so nervous and he recalled how calm Miriam was, and how she put him at ease. She was so different to all the other girls and women he had met. There was something about her that he just couldn't put his finger on; she was so different and so mature, way beyond her years. Yosef's heart soared as he recalled those early years with Miriam. But theirs was a relationship that had its own secret from the rest of the world. They alone knew the truth about their marriage and the birth of their son, Yeshua. He thought about Yeshua, and what a wonderful child he was, so mature and so full of goodness and kindness, like his mother. He had everything from his mother. Yosef did at times wish he had his own biological child with Miriam, but that was not to be. No one knew that he was not the biological father of Yeshua. That was a secret that only he and Miriam shared, and their relatives in the hill country,

Elisheva and Zechariah Yosef thought about those rare visits to Elisheva and Zechariah and the conversations they had about their respective sons. Elisheva and Zechariah were of advanced age, and Elisheva had been barren, not able to conceive until well past her childbearing age. He remembered the consternation that caused, and how everyone rejoiced and gave thanks to Yahweh for the miracle of their son Johanan's birth. Johanan and Yeshua did not get on very well together, Johanan was so different to Achim and Yeshua's other friends. Johanan was a strange child, a loner really, he liked to be by himself, and he would wander off exploring the fields around where he lived and be gone all day. And he came back with all kinds of insects and plants that he found. Yeshua was so outgoing, whereas Johanan was so introverted and seemed to prefer being by himself.

"Yosef! Yosef!" Yosef heard Miriam calling out to him, breaking his reverie.

"I'm coming," Yosef cried out as he walked home, a bit nervous about what he and Miriam were about to tell Yeshua.

Miriam and Yosef were about to shock Yeshua with what they were about to reveal, and they hoped it would not shatter Yeshua's world.

The three to them sat down in the living area on the three comfortable chairs with armrests that Yosef made of solid timber and that Miriam adorned with stacks of large cushions for both the seats and the backs of the chairs. Once they were comfortably ensconced, Yosef began. "My dear Yeshua, you know, and we know that you are a very special child. I don't really know what your future will be because Yahweh has a special mission for you."

"I know, Abba, Yahweh has a special mission for each of us," Yeshua interjected.

"That is true, Yeshua, but yours is extra-special. In fact, we—your mother and I—both had a vision, an angel visited us and brought us a special message about you."

Now Yeshua was very interested. He believed in angels, he learned all about angels and knew all their names, Michael and Gabriel the archangels, and Lucifer, which meant light, and how there was a war in Paradise, and how Michael defeated Lucifer who was banished from the heavenly court and now roamed the earth to destroy souls. He learned all about how the angels appeared often as messengers from Yahweh to mortals, to the prophets and prophetesses and to bring them news and messages from Yahweh. In fact, Yeshua believed that he and everyone had their own special guardian angel that watched over them. He had so many instances when he was saved from harm by his guardian angel. He thought about those times, one not so long ago when he and Achim were out playing marbles. He had walked backwards for some reason and had not seen the large hole in the ground, and it seemed like someone had tapped him on the shoulder and told him to stop and look around and he was aghast as he saw the deep hole that had he fallen into he would have seriously injured himself and could even have died. He had a number of such incidences in his young life that he could not explain, when he was saved from imminent harm by what seemed like a tap on the shoulder or a whisper into his ear. He always remembered to thank his guardian angel when he said his night prayers, he named him Eagle.

"Yeshua, you seem distracted," Miriam said, as she could see her son deep in thought. He often would be deep in thought, and she always left him to his thoughts but this time she had to have his full attention.

"Sorry Immah, I'm all ears."

"Miriam, you can carry on with what we had discussed," Yosef said, glad to hand over the reins to Miriam.

"Yeshua, you know how children are conceived and nurtured in their mother's womb for nine months before they are born."

"Yes, Immah, I know and I have seen the mothers' tummies grow over nine months and then go back to normal after the birth of their child. I always wondered what it was like for those little babies in their mother's womb. What they did for those nine months. Gamaliel explained it to us. The miracle of conception and birth, how the sperm of the male swims and searches for the egg of the woman and how the embryo becomes fertilised and how the umbilical cord connects the little baby with its mother and through which she feeds her child. Immah, I really envy you and all women. I wish I could conceive and carry a child within my womb for nine months and experience its birth, flesh of my flesh. Now that we are on this subject, Immah, what was it like for you having me in your womb for nine months? What is it like for women, to carry a child and to experience its birth?"

"As usual, Yeshua, you always have so many questions. We have something to tell you that is very important, but I will first tell you how it was for me when I conceived you within my womb and how I loved you from that very first moment. I was so happy, Yeshua, a hundred more times happier than you and Achim are when you make and fly your kites into the heavens. I knew that I was on this earth to have you, to be your mother and the experience is like nothing else. You were and are everything to me and I feel so privileged to be your mother and to have given birth to you. You gave me so much joy from the moment you started to live within me. Every day I was conscious of your presence. I felt I was not alone, that you were not alone, that we would never be alone ever. That I would love you and you would love me forever. The joy of having you in my womb and having given birth to you, Yeshua, and seeing you grow up is the greatest gift I have ever received. You have brought so much joy and happiness to me…" Tears began to flow from Miriam's eyes and Yeshua leapt to his feet and went over to his mother, and put his little arms around her before Yosef could reach her. They both stood beside Miriam and held her in their arms. They knew that the tears that flowed from her eyes were tears of joy. Yosef too had to hold back his tears. He too felt so blessed to be the foster father of this special and gifted child, Yeshua.

When Miriam had finished weeping and wiping away her tears, she shooed the two men in her life back to their seats. "Yeshua can you not ask any more questions until you listen to everything your father and I have to say to you?"

"Of course, mother," Yeshua smiled, and making the gesture of zipping his lips.

"I don't know where to really begin telling you about how you came into the world, Yeshua, but as we were talking about angels and visions and how they brought messages from Adonai, I will start by telling you that I was very privileged to have had an angel, who called himself Gabriel, come to visit me when I was betrothed to your father."

"Wow! Really Immah, the angel Gabriel came to visit you, where, when, how?" Yeshua said excitedly.

"At Grandmother and Grandfather's place and I was sitting in this very chair that Yosef had made when the angel appeared."

17

Yeshua got up and stood to the right of his chair. "Right here, Immah, right here," Yeshua said excitedly. "Man, I got to tell Achim, he won't believe me."

"Yeshua!" Yosef said firmly. "You can't tell Achim or any of your other friends. What we are telling you today is for your ears only. Do you understand?"

"Yes, of course Abba, forgive me, I got so excited. I realise this is serious, for an angel to appear on earth must be for some purpose," Yeshua said, taking on a serious face. He bit on his lip and nodded to his mother to continue.

"Gabriel was such a handsome figure, his face was so smooth and perfect and shining brightly, glowing in fact. He was dressed in all white flowing garments."

"Did he have wings, Immah?" Yeshua couldn't contain himself; he was excited.

"No Yeshua, he did not," Miriam answered.

"Angels do not have or need wings, Yeshua," Yosef stepped in. "They do not need wings to get around, they are pure spirits and only take the form of a human being, so they can be seen by humans. In fact, Yeshua, we too are angels, spirits, for we are spiritual beings having a human experience."

"Yeshua let me continue please."

"Okay Immah. I won't interrupt anymore. I now realise I have to hear the whole story of why the angel Gabriel came to visit you. I assume that was before I was born?"

"Yes, Yeshua, in fact he came to announce your birth."

Yeshua's mouth opened and he was ready to speak but instead just shut his gaping mouth and let his mother continue. He was now totally engrossed, an angel, an archangel, Gabriel came from Yahweh to announce his birth. He now wanted to hear Gabriel's message.

Miriam continued, "I was so afraid, when Gabriel appeared. In spite of his stunning appearance, I was afraid, because he came out of nowhere; he just appeared in front of me, while I was sewing a nightgown for Grandmother."

Yeshua joined his hands and raised them to his lips almost as if in prayer, but he was all ears, wanting Miriam to continue.

Yosef too was all ears. He had heard this before, a long time ago, and he had grown accustomed to the ordinariness of life, of Yeshua's life, albeit his exceptional giftedness, life just went on and they were looked upon like any other family, a couple with a very gifted child.

Miriam continued, but then was gripped by an indescribable uncertainty. Should she continue, did she really have to tell Yeshua all of this, she wondered. The angel never told her that she had to, wasn't that up to Yahweh himself? But then she thought of how she and Yosef considered this for such a long time, and had discussed this, whether to tell Yeshua everything they could. She thought about how they discussed when to tell Yeshua, and what to tell him. Yosef initially had thought that they should wait a bit longer, when Yeshua was older but Miriam had disagreed. She had seen and witnessed Yeshua growing up before her eyes, with an intelligence, wisdom and sensitivity that amazed her. He had intelligence and wisdom beyond his years and she thought he was ready. She looked at Yeshua's expectant look and felt she had to continue.

"So Immah, what did Gabriel say?" Yeshua could hardly contain himself.

"He first of all greeted me?"

"How did he greet you, what did he say?" Yeshua said excitedly.

He just greeted me like we all do, he said, "Shalom!" And when he saw how terrified I was, he simply told me not to be afraid, that he was sent by Yahweh and that he came to give me a special message. I then relaxed a bit but was still so shaken. But Gabriel was so beautiful and his eyes seemed to pierce my soul, and he had the most reassuring eyes.

"So, after he greeted you and put you at ease, what did he have to say, what was his message?" Yeshua could not contain himself.

"Yeshua, be patient, and let your mother tell you what she wants, without interruption," Yosef said to Yeshua.

"Okay Abba, I'll keep quiet, please continue Immah," Yeshua said resignedly.

"Gabriel spoke in a most gentle voice and it seemed the earth stood still when he spoke, it seemed my heart stood still, because what he said took my breath away."

Yeshua wanted to say something, but he caught Yosef's eyes, and his gesture telling him not to speak. So, he waited for his mother to continue.

"Gabriel, after greeting me with 'Shalom', he said, 'I was the favoured one, that I had found favour with Yahweh, and that the Lord is with me'. And then he told me that I was to have a child. He said I would conceive a child in my womb, and bear a son, and that I should name him Yeshua."

Yeshua's mouth opened wide. And then his lips closed tightly. His open hand went instinctively to his mouth. For the first time he was lost for words.

Yosef and Miriam let the silence continue as they saw Yeshua processing what he had just heard. After a few minutes that seemed like hours, Yeshua spoke.

"So, Gabriel told you that he came from Yahweh and that you were to bear a son and that you were to call him Yeshua. So, Adonai, Yahweh gave me my name." Yeshua thought back over his short life and it seemed like an eternity. He understood now why he felt so close to Yahweh, how he felt his presence and his angels hovering over him all the time. He recalled how he had felt as if Yahweh were speaking to him so often. In his young mind, he was trying to fathom the significance of what his mother was telling him. He knew to name someone was to give them a special mission. Yeshua knew the story of Abraham so well, how Yahweh renamed Abram to Abraham and made a covenant with him that he would be the ancestor of a multitude of nations.

"Immah, what else did Gabriel tell you?" Yeshua asked.

Miriam was glad Yeshua asked her that question, which allowed her to continue. "Yeshua, Gabriel said you will be great, and will be called the Son of the Most High, and the Lord God will give you the throne of your ancestor David, and that you will reign over the house of Jacob forever, and that your kingdom, Yeshua will never end."

"My kingdom!" Yeshua blurted and then went silent again. This was too much. What is Immah saying to me? That I am the Son of the Most High, the son of Yahweh? How can this be, Yeshua was asking himself. He looked at his mother, this time puzzled. He had to know more, he had to understand.

Miriam could see the consternation in his eyes and she tried her best to put him at ease, and yet to let him know what his mission in life is to be. She continued, "Yeshua, I know this is a lot for you to take in. When the angel Gabriel came to me and brought me this news about you, it was a lot for me to take in, and it took me a long time to figure things out, and your father was such a mountain of strength and support to me. It was very hard on him too."

"Hard on Abba? What do you mean, Immah?" Yeshua inquired.

"Well, when Gabriel told me I was to have a child, I told him that I was still a virgin and that your father and I had decided to wait a while before we started our family, it was then that he said that the Holy Spirit will come to me, and the power of Yahweh will overshadow me and that the child that I bear will be holy; he will be called Son of God."

"What! Son of God?" Yeshua blurted out; "I am to be called the Son of God? In other words, does that mean I am the Son of God? And how does Yosef fit into all of this? Is Yosef not my father? Oh Immah, this is too much." Yeshua was about to lose it.

"It's okay, Yeshua. It's okay," Yosef rose and knelt beside his son with his arm around Yeshua's shoulder. "It's okay; it must be very confusing for you, as it was for your mother and me at the time."

"So, are you my father or what?" Yeshua said, looking into the eyes of Yosef, the man he knew and believed to be his father all these years. This revelation of his mother threw him, but he knew that he wanted to know the whole story. His eyes were fixed on Yosef, wanting him to explain.

"When your mother told me she was with child, I knew I was not the father, for we were not yet living together, and we had no intimate encounter, so I was very confused, I couldn't believe that your mother would be unfaithful to me, and that she had gone with another man. But she was pregnant. I was shattered, Yeshua; I loved your mother deeply and what she told me was a great shock. At first, I didn't believe her, what she told me was preposterous. How could she conceive without the seed of a man?"

"So, you suspected mother of being unfaithful, of committing adultery?" Yeshua said in disbelief. But Yeshua sympathised with his father, for he too was stunned into disbelief. How indeed could this be, how could his mother conceive without the seed of a man? Was his mother concocting this bizarre and unbelievable story to cover her infidelity? Yeshua could not believe that of his mother. He felt he had to give her the benefit of the doubt.

"Immah this is hard to believe? How could that be, tell me is Yosef my father?" Yeshua asked with a tortured look.

"Of course, Yeshua, he is your father, your foster father, he cared for you and he loves you as no father could. But you are not of his seed." Miriam knew she had to be blunt, and that these were hard truths for her son to imbibe, but they had to be said, she had to make it absolutely clear to him.

"So, Abba, how did you react to all of this that mother has just told me?" Yeshua was curious.

"Well, Yeshua, not very well, I was tormented. I felt completely bamboozled. I could not reconcile what your mother told me and believed that she was unfaithful. I also knew the consequences if this got out, it could get her stoned, so I decided to quietly divorce your mother."

"Divorce! Really?" Yeshua blurted.

"Yes, but then an angel appeared to me and made it clear and confirmed what your mother had told me."

"How? Was it the angel Gabriel?" Yeshua asked excitedly.

"No, he was not the angel Gabriel, but he was an angel, and he did not appear as he did to your mother. I had gone to bed that night having decided to start the proceedings of divorcing your mother that next day, and during the night an angel appeared to me in a dream and spoke to me."

"What did he say?" Yeshua could not contain himself.

"He said, 'Yosef, Son of David, do not be afraid to take Miriam as your wife, for the child conceived in her womb is from the Holy Spirit. She will bear a son, and you are to name him Yeshua, for he will save his people from their sins.'"

Yeshua inhaled a deep breath and then cupped his mouth with both his hands, his mind was ticking over. This was just too much. He rubbed his forehead with the tips of his fingers as he saw Yosef do at times, and then he joined his hands and touched the tips of his lips, as if in prayer, as he saw his mother do often. He knew he had much to consider and to talk over with his mother and his father and with Yahweh, his real father. There and then he decided that he would go to his quiet spot in the nearby fields and spend some time there to pray and try and process all that he had heard. No one knew that he did this from time to time and whenever he had to work out things in his head and when something strange was happening to him. He was starting to see how everything in his life was starting to make sense, how his closeness to Yahweh made sense.

Yosef gave Yeshua time to reflect on what he had just heard. He knew it was a lot for his young mind to absorb, but he knew just how advanced Yeshua was in so many ways. He was confident that Yeshua would be able to handle it, to work things out by himself, and that he could always come and talk to him and to Miriam, as he usually did. Then there was Gamaliel, on second thoughts, he did not think it would be advisable for Yeshua to speak about any of this to anyone else. He would make that clear to Yeshua, even though he knew Yeshua would discern that for himself.

"The angel, before leaving my dream, said, 'all this that has taken place is to fulfil what had been spoken by the Lord through the prophets'." Yosef said in conclusion.

"After that day, your father came to me, and told me everything and with my mother and father's permission I moved into Yosef's place. Your father has been so good to me and he agreed to love and care for me and for you always, and he has been and is a father to you, and he loves you with all his heart, as I do."

"I know Immah, I know, and I love you both with all my heart, and I thank you and Yosef, my mother and father for the love you give me, and for all you have done for me and for telling me the truth."

Yeshua paused for a moment, as if to take a deep breath. He was taking it all in. Miriam and Yosef had their eyes glued on their son. They knew this was a lot to take in, even for him. They both knew that he was a gifted child, but that he was more than that, and they sometimes seemed to forget that he was the Son of Yahweh. Not like we are all sons and daughters of Yahweh, but that he was really the Son of Yahweh, and he has come onto this earth to do what Yahweh has planned for him.

Miriam and Yosef knew all about the Messiah, they and their people, the chosen people, descendants of Abraham, Jacob and Isaac were the promised people. They had been slaves in Egypt, exiles in Babylon and Yahweh had brought them here. They are now still captive to the Romans but they knew that Yahweh was to send the Messiah, a Saviour, who would set their people free.

Miriam in her quiet moments discerned that her son Yeshua was somehow part of Yahweh's plan, he was somehow connected with the Messiah, and maybe he was to prepare the way? The angel Gabriel had said of her that Yeshua would be called the Son of God. And Miriam knew that Yeshua could not be called the Son of God, if he was *not* the Son of God.

Yeshua's mind was racing. But now he stopped and took a deep breath. He wanted to know more, he knew there was more for his parents to tell him, so he asked, "So, what happened after the angel Gabriel left and you moved into father's house?"

"After the angel had told me that I would have you and that you would be called the Son of God, to put me at ease, to show me how this is possible, he told me that your aunt Elisheva and Uncle Zechariah were to have a child."

"Aunt Elish? And uncle Zech. They are so old, and yet they had Johanan?" Yeshua said. He had wondered about that, seeing them with their son Johanan. He had always thought that they must have adopted Johanan. He always enjoyed the infrequent visits to auntie Elish and uncle Zech, who was a priest in the temple. They were always so kind to him. He had listened to the adults speak of them and how they seemed in awe at them being parents in their old age.

"Exactly, Yeshua, the angel Gabriel told me that Elisheva who was barren all her life and now too old to conceive would have a son and he would be called Johanan. And that in fact she was six months pregnant with Johanan, for Gabriel added, 'nothing will be impossible for God'."

"Wow! Unbelievable!" Yeshua exclaimed.

"Yes, unbelievable indeed. So, I thought, Yeshua. But I conceived without the seed of Yosef. I became pregnant at that instant."

"How did you know?" Yeshua asked.

"I just knew. I could feel the beginning of something stirring within me, new life, *you* stirring within me."

"Really Immah, I can't remember anything about that time or the nine months that I was in your womb."

"For those nine months, Yeshua, I felt your every move. You were so active, always moving around, you seemed so excited and content. When I was happy you would gently move around and share my joy. When I felt sad, I felt you would snuggle up and comfort me."

"Your mother was the happiest pregnant woman I have ever met, Yeshua. She was beaming like the sun and walking on a cloud. She was so happy to be carrying you within her womb."

"And I was so happy to be carried and nurtured by you Immah. Thank you, I love you." Yeshua sighed and got up and went over to his mother and hugged and kissed her. For a long time, they just hugged, held each other and absorbed the great warmth of their love for each other.

Yosef, not to be left out, rose and came over and put his arms around Miriam and Yeshua. They held each other for a while in silence, absorbing the love they had for each other.

"Okay, that's enough," Miriam said, as she released the two men in her life and wiped away her tears. "I think that will do for now. It is getting late and we should retire soon. It is market day tomorrow and you Yosef have to get up early to leave for Sepphoris again."

"Just before I go to bed Immah, can you tell me what happened after the angel Gabriel told you about Elisheva having a child?" Yeshua asked. He wanted to hear more.

"Okay, but you get into bed, and I will tell you."

Yeshua quickly put on his night clothes and slipped into bed for his bedtime story that either Yosef or Miriam told him. They were mostly real-life stories about the Jewish people and their God and there were so many that were handed down by word of mouth. There were some texts written down and that were available at their place of prayer.

Nazareth was a very small town in Galilee. Nazareth only had about two hundred residents. Yosef who was a tradesman, mainly in woodwork and maintenance, had to sometimes go to the capital of Sepphoris to find work, or the other large city of Tiberius. He also found work on the farms where wheat, barley, vegetables, vineyards, olives, fig and other fruit trees were planted. In Galilee many of the people also fished for a livelihood because the large Lake Galilee, which was such a favourite place for people to visit, was rich with an abundance of freshwater fish. And Yosef had promised to take Yeshua soon to the lake, the Sea of Galilee to be precise, for a fishing weekend. Yeshua loved fishing, he and Yosef had fished in the River Jordan and he found it so relaxing. He and Yosef usually just sat in silence, with their own thoughts waiting for the fish to bite. Besides the true-life bed time stories about the Jewish people and their God, Miriam and Yosef also told him other stories that they knew, or made up, stories of angels and demons, good people and bad people, and stories of all the wild animals that roamed the earth. Yeshua also loved all the stories his father told him about his travels all over Galilee, Samaria and Judaea, and Yeshua himself travelled through these places on their way to their annual celebration of Passover in Jerusalem.

Yeshua loved Jerusalem, the hustle and bustle of the great city and all the sights, sounds and smells. He was fascinated with the grand Temple, it was superb, majestic and massive able to hold thousands of people at the same time. Nazareth didn't even have a synagogue or a resident rabbi for that matter. Gamaliel, while he wasn't a recognised rabbi, Yeshua regarded him as one, for he had so much knowledge of their Scriptures and he had so much wisdom, and Yeshua learned so much from him. He was more than a teacher, he was a guide, a guru to Yeshua and they often had long chats about the Hebrew nation and their history and their turbulent relationship with Yahweh. Nazareth did not have a synagogue but they did have a community place which they used for their Sabbath celebrations and for other special events like marriages and community meetings and social gatherings.

When Yeshua was all tucked in, he called out, "Immah, Immah, I'm in bed."

"Coming, coming," Miriam replied with a smile. She loved this time with Yeshua, just to see the joy in his face, as he listened and absorbed and enjoyed all her stories. He was such a good listener, so interested in everything and everybody. He wanted to know everything. He loved how Miriam embellished her fictional stories.

"Well, about Elisheva," Miriam began. "When I heard the news from Gabriel, I immediately thought that I had to go and visit her, for she was old and might need someone to help her, be with her during the remaining three months of her pregnancy."

"Was that the only reason you wanted to visit her?" Yeshua asked with a slight smile.

Miriam shook her head. She was always amazed how Yeshua could read her mind, anticipate her thoughts. He had the insight of a grown man and the intuition of a grown woman. "No, that was not the only reason, Yeshua, I also had a selfish reason, I simply had to talk to someone about my own pregnancy, someone who would understand and accept. I was so filled with joy having you in my womb but I couldn't really tell anyone about the circumstances of my conception, could I?"

"No, you couldn't, Immah. No one would believe you."

"Exactly! And do you believe me, Yeshua, that I conceived by the power of the Holy Spirit and without any seed of a man, of Yosef? Can you believe in something like this? Do you not think people will disbelieve and think the worst of me, or that I am insane? What would the people think if we told them about the circumstances of your conception, and about your identity and that you are the Son of Yahweh? Of course you know, you cannot tell anyone what I have told you until Adonai reveals the time to do so?" Miriam said, realising that this was not said in their earlier discussion.

"Yes Immah, I understand. Not fully, but I know it will become clearer with time. And as for the miracle, for it is a miracle, my conception and birth, I believe in miracles. There are miracles all around me. How the sun stays in the sky at exactly the perfect distance to give us light and warmth and energy and life without burning us up is a miracle. And as for my existence Immah, if Yahweh could create the first man, Adam from the dust of the earth, without the seed of another man or without him being carried for nine months in a woman's womb, and if God could create the first woman Eve from the rib of a man, again without the seed of a woman, why could he not create me without the seed of a man. I believe Immah that Yahweh is the Creator of all life, and he can choose how he wishes to do that."

Miriam's mouth opened in astonishment. How can so young a child, her child, have such deep wisdom, beyond his years and how clear he made it to her. She simply bit her lip and shook her head.

"Good, Yeshua. So, let's get back to your aunt Elisheva. I was so happy to go and be with her and talk to her about what was happening to her and also what was happening to me. I was keen, Yeshua, because we were in the same boat, so to speak, and I knew she would understand. I was sure she too would want to talk with someone who would understand what was happening to her. Your father accompanied me on that long journey to the hill country of Judaea and because we took the donkey, as Yosef didn't want me to walk all that way, it took us almost a week to get there. Yosef stayed for a few days and then went off to Sepphoris for work he had to do. I stayed with Elisheva for the whole three months, until she gave birth to your cousin Johanan. Your grand aunt Elisheva was so glad to see me, she had lived in seclusion since the conception of Johanan, not wanting to face anyone and having to explain what was inexplicable," Miriam said.

"Oh Immah, how awful, how sad that must have been for Aunt Elisheva, being with child and not able to share her joy with anyone," Yeshua said sympathetically.

"That's true, because she could not even talk to Zechariah, because from the time the angel Gabriel brought him the news, just like he brought the news about you, Yeshua, Zechariah, because he initially doubted Gabriel, was struck dumb and could not speak until Johanan was born."

"Struck dumb, how awful," Yeshua said, "I would die if I was not able to speak."

"Yes, you would," Miriam smiled, "so be grateful and never take for granted that you can speak, and see and hear and sleep. Now go to sleep, you have heard enough from me for today. It has been a heavy day, for Yosef and you and me.

Yeshua, we have told you so much of what has been on our minds and in our hearts for so long, and I am glad you now know everything about your birth and your past. Now for the present close your eyes and may Yahweh bless you," Miriam said, as she kissed Yeshua on his forehead, and touched his face gently. She quietly went back to her chair to rest and just debrief by herself, and also to say her nightly prayers, as she always did.

She prayed, "Heavenly Father, Adonai, Yahweh, Father of my son Yeshua, I thank you for the great honour and privilege to bear a son, and to bear and give birth to your Son, Yeshua. He is such a joy to Yosef and me and to all that know him. He radiates so much joy to all that come into contact with him. I and others have learned so much from him, just from the way he embraces all of life and all people. He is so full of love for you, for me, for Yosef, for his friends and all in Nazareth and for all with whom he comes into contact. He is an amazing child and he has brought me so much joy. I thank you Yahweh. I know hard times are ahead for him, but that is a far way off, dearest Father, I pray for your help, for the grace to be a good mother to Yeshua and I pray that you protect him from all harm."

Miriam then had her usual cup of milk before changing into her night clothes and then snuggled up to Yosef who was already fast asleep.

Chapter Three
The Explosion

The next day after the bolt from the blue, Yeshua went to school with a spring in his step. He was still figuring out all he heard from his mother and father and what it all meant. He did not feel special, he felt like everyone else, like his best friend, Achim.

He had such a normal childhood doing all the normal things young boys do. He played his childhood games. When they were younger, they played so many make-believe games, mimicking the elders, and celebrating pretend weddings and funerals. As they grew, he and Achim loved to go on long walks into the forest and watch all the different insects, and play hide-and-seek among the trees and wild plants. They loved climbing trees and sitting on them, watching the world below they felt like giants. They caught tadpoles in the pools of water just to hold them in their hands and then gently place them back to turn into frogs. They were fascinated to hear the frogs when they slept at night and Yeshua would always say to Achim the next day, "Hey Achim, did you hear our friend Taddie, he is all grown up into a frog, did you hear him call out to you in the night." And Achim would say he did not hear anything because his mother tells him he sleeps like a log, and he would say logs don't sleep, when they are trees, they are alive and when they fall off and become a log, they are dead. Then he and Yeshua would then go off into a long discussion about life and death, trees, tadpoles and frogs, the birds of the air and the fishes in the sea, all the crawling insects in the forest, and all the beautiful butterflies, and Yeshua would sing the praises of Yahweh who made all of us creatures.

After school, Yeshua wanted to be alone for a while. He wanted so much to tell Achim all that his mother and father told him the day before but he knew that he should not, could not. Achim would not understand and would think he was making up one of his stories. Yeshua felt he had to talk to someone. He will talk with his mother and father some more, he wanted to know everything. What happened to him in the past ten years and what he was meant to do with the rest of his life? He just wanted to be a normal child growing up in Nazareth but it seemed he was not a normal boy after all, he was not conceived in the normal way. He was, he is a child of God, of Yahweh, that he always knew, but he really was a child of Yahweh, in the full sense of the word. Yahweh was his real father. He wanted to speak to Yahweh as his real father. So, after school, after going home, he told his mother that he was going for a walk in the forest. Miriam told him not to wander too deep and not to stay away too long.

Yeshua would have gone to Achim and they would have wondered off together on their forestry expeditions, but today, Yeshua wanted to wander off by himself. He walked along the well-treaded paths that he and Achim had traversed so often and he greeted the trees and the grasses and sang back to the birds. He saw the fallen logs and recalled his conversation with Achim about logs and life and death and he stopped to touch the log affectionately and see how it gave so much life to the forest and its little creatures that made a home and fed themselves inside and all over the log. He found a quiet spot, and sat down on one of the logs.

Yeshua sat quietly for a while and then he whispered, "Yahweh, Abba, I know you are my real father. I know that I am different to Achim and to all other boys even though I am also like all of them. I am no different to Achim, Abba, and I just want to be a normal child and have a normal upbringing but you have created me and you have sent me into the world to do your bidding whatever that is. I pray Abba that I may have the strength to do whatever you want of me." Yeshua continued to converse with his heavenly father for a while, for quite a while, he could see the sun was already dipping behind the trees. He had to get home to do his daily chores and help prepare for their evening meal. He still had time though to pop in and chat with Achim and see what he was up to. Achim lived in a different cluster of homes not far from Yeshua, a few minutes' walk.

Yeshua was so pleased to see Achim and his mother and father. They were such nice people and treated Yeshua like their own son, and they liked Yeshua as a friend for their Achim, he was such a good influence on their son. Yeshua felt a bit strange after the bolt from the blue of yesterday. He felt he was not able to be completely open with Achim and tell him everything that happened to him, as he usually did. But he was glad he had that conversation with Yahweh and he felt that Yahweh was with him and that his spirit would guide him on how to live his life, which he felt, would still be like any normal boy for a long time yet. He decided to put aside all those thoughts about his mission in life and just enjoy being a boy and a friend to Achim and a son to Miriam and Yosef.

Yeshua knew that there was still so much more that he had to learn about himself and that there was so much more he had to learn from his mother and father. He could not wait for Yosef to come home from his labours and for them to share their evening meal and for their chats that followed, when they shared their days' escapades.

Yeshua could hardly wait. During their evening meal their conversation was all that happened to them that day, but they not only shared what they did, but how they did it, who they encountered and how they felt about everything. Yeshua spent most of his time letting his mother and father know just how difficult it was for him to keep everything they had told him a secret, especially from Achim, with whom he shared everything.

"Yeshua, I know this must be very hard for you. Your father and I pondered over this for a long time and we did not want to disturb your growing up in any way but we knew we had to tell you everything about yourself and just how special you are. We know you are so young but we were getting so used to you as an ordinary child, as our child, and so you are, but you are also extraordinary, you are so very special, you are first and foremost Yahweh's child and your father and I have prayed to Yahweh for a long time and it has been revealed to us that we should tell you now, even though you are so young," Miriam looked intently at Yeshua as she spoke and she turned to Yosef for help.

"Yes Yeshua, I and your mother prayed hard about this. We did not want to delay this news about you anymore. You are so special and so dear to us; we love you so much but you are a child of Yahweh in a special way and he has sent you for a special mission and asked us to care for you. Your mother is fully your mother, and I am your father, your earthly, your foster father. With your mother I raised you and witnessed how quickly you have grown in wisdom and how very gifted and extraordinary you are, way beyond your years. It has become clear to us that we need to tell you all about yourself now and help you to prepare for whatever it is the Father wants of you," Yosef said, looking at Yeshua and then at Miriam.

Yeshua was silent for a while. "Immah, oh Immah, how difficult then it must have been for you living with this secret, living with it, living with me, these past ten years …"

"Oh Yeshua, these past years have been the happiest years of my life, and of Yosef's too," she glanced at Yosef.

"Yes, of course, Yeshua, these ten years have been the greatest years of our lives. You have been such a joy to your mother and me. But you are extraordinary and special beyond our understanding, at least mine. As much as we want you to have an ordinary upbringing, we feel responsible for doing all we can to equip you for whatever lies ahead. Your mother has such a deep sense that you will have to endure so much for your heavenly Father and that we need to prepare you and give you the best education and formation we can. So, we have asked Gamaliel to spend an extra hour with you every day teaching you all about Yahweh, all of our Holy Scriptures, all about our Law and our Prophets and our history and our covenant with Yahweh."

Yeshua's eyes lit up. "I'd love that, Abba. Gamaliel is such a good teacher and I enjoy all our discussions," Yeshua said. "But tell me, mother; what is this deep sense you have about me, having to endure so much?" Yeshua asked. "Please tell me more, tell me everything that has happened to me so far. I cannot remember the details of my birth and what happened to me the first few years of my life."

"Yeshua that will take years for us to tell but let me begin by telling you the special circumstances of your birth, circumstances that have stayed with me and helped to make your mother and I tell you what we have told you." Yosef then began to tell Yeshua all about how he was born and the first few years of his life, before he came to live in Nazareth.

"Yeshua, at the time of your birth Octavian Augustus Caesar ruled over all of Palestine. In fact, for more than sixty years before you were born, the Roman Empire stretched far and wide and included all of Galilee, and south through all of Judaea, including our holy city of Jerusalem, and all of Palestine was only a small part of this vast Roman Empire. They ruled over us with cruelty and treated us, and continue to treat us, as second-class citizens. They have made slaves of so many and impoverished us with their exorbitant taxes on the produce of our fertile lands and sea. They have and continue to reign with punishment, terror, and beheadings, burnings of villages and peoples and mass crucifixions." Yosef drew a deep breath; he knew that Yeshua must have seen some of these signs of subjugation and oppression at the hands of the Romans, there were statues of Caesar and the Roman gods in plain sight and public monuments to their military conquests.

Yeshua listened intently. They have never really discussed the evils of the Roman Empire, but Yeshua had learned from Gamaliel how the Jewish people felt they deserved their suffering at the hands of the cruel Romans because they had sinned against Yahweh and were being justly punished. The prophets had warned them and invoked them to repent and atone for their sins, to wait for the Messiah who would be their Saviour by overthrowing Rome and they would be a free and proud people once more in this their Promised Land of Israel.

Yeshua was listening intently. He bit his lip as his mind was ticking over at the words of Yosef. They have never spoken about the evil Roman Empire and how cruel and unjustly they treated the people but they have witnessed it all around them and especially on their journeys to Jerusalem. Yeshua had learned from Gamaliel about how Rome ruled with the help of local brutal vassals, mainly Jewish, to control the Jewish people and suppress any uprisings against Rome. In the process these vassals enriched themselves by maximising the tributes and taxes for Rome and skimming off handsome sums for themselves. They were hated by their own people.

"Yeshua, at the time of your birth Herod ruled over Palestine for the Romans. He was cruel and arrogant and executed many Teachers of the Law and their disciples for attempting to destroy the Imperial Eagle of Rome that he had placed within the temple. He was mad, Yeshua, obsessed with power and fear of conspiracy even by his own family and ended up killing most of his sons, brother, mother-in-law and his own wife," Yosef continued.

Miriam wondered whether Yosef should be telling Yeshua all these gory details about this despot that ruled over Palestine. But she knew Yeshua would find out about it himself, if he hadn't already.

"Abba, he was an evil man wasn't he, I am so glad he no longer rules over us," Yeshua said.

"Indeed, Yeshua. Now I must tell you just what Herod had wanted to do to you, how he wanted to kill you too, when you were born."

"Kill me? When I was born? Why?" These questions came tumbling out. "Did you tell him about Gabriel's visit and what he said about me?" Yeshua blurted out, although knowing that Yosef would not be that reckless to tell such an evil man anything about them.

"Of course not, Yeshua, somehow, he found out about your birth, that you would be a king, and usurp his kingdom. He planned to have you killed but we fled the country. Herod didn't know and as he could not find you, he killed all newborn boys under the age of two."

"Oh no! How could he be so cruel! Oh, Immah that is terrible. How could he! And all because of me. Oh Abba, oh Immah, I am shocked. All those babies were killed because of me! How did he get to know about my birth, I thought you told me that I was born in Bethlehem and not here in Nazareth. I thought I was born in Bethlehem because, Abba, that is where you were born and we had to go there to be registered."

Yosef thought that it was time to tell Yeshua the full story of his birth and their flight into Egypt. He looked at Miriam. "Should we tell him about his birth and our flight into Egypt?"

Yosef sought Miriam's support.

Miriam nodded. "Yes, Yosef, I think it is time, for us to tell Yeshua everything. He needs to know. It is best he hears this, finds out everything about himself from us," Miriam said.

"Yes, Abba, Immah, please tell me everything, no matter what. I want to know, if I was the cause of any other atrocities or tragedies," Yeshua pleaded.

"No Yeshua, you did not cause the infanticide perpetrated by Herod. He was possessed by power and consumed by evil and extravagance and would not tolerate anyone getting in his way or being a threat to his position," Yosef said.

"Yeshua let me tell you everything about your birth," Miriam began.

Chapter Four
The Birth

Miriam heaved a huge sigh as she began. After Yeshua was born, for a long time she pondered on the circumstances of his conception and birth but she had not done so for a long time now. She just wanted to see her son and treat him like a normal child and give him a normal upbringing. She soon saw just how gifted he was, way beyond his years, a child genius. He seemed so absorbed and involved with all that was around him and he had a natural curiosity and delight in everyone and everything. He seemed to be like a sponge just soaking up the beauty and goodness of all creatures and of all creation and he had a curiosity that would have killed a thousand cats. He also had a wonderful sense of humour and a most infectious smile and laughter that sent thrills through her being. From his childhood he had such a great joy for life. Miriam knew that she got used to the way Yeshua was but she treated him as any mother would her child. She allowed him to grow up and discover the world around him, and discover his own identity. She and Yosef would do all they could to give him the best education, formation and example possible.

"Immah!" Yeshua called his mother out of her reverie. "You're supposed to tell me all about my birth."

"Of course, Yeshua, your birth; I was almost nine months pregnant with you when we had to go and register in Bethlehem. Yosef, you tell him the rest," Miriam said.

Yosef began, "the Emperor Augustus sent out a decree that the whole of the Roman Empire should be registered. This was the very first time we had to register, and we were all required to register at the place where our family was from, so I had to go to the city of David named Bethlehem, because I am a descendent from the house and family of David. And while we were there, Yeshua, you were born."

"Wow! So, I was born in the city of David. Where was I born?" Yeshua was all ears.

Yosef looked at Miriam, indicating this was for her to tell Yeshua.

Miriam began, "I was close to giving birth to you, Yeshua, and I was by no means thrilled to go on that long journey to Bethlehem, riding on a donkey. It would have taken us close to two weeks. We had to go very slow as I was heavily pregnant with you. When we arrived in Bethlehem, you indicated you were ready to come into the world," Miriam smiled at Yeshua who beamed back at her with the broadest of smiles; he was absolutely fascinated, enthralled and engrossed in what his mother was telling him.

Miriam continued, "When we got to Bethlehem, it was evening and so we sought lodging for the night at the town's inn. But there was no room, and I was desperate and in great pain as you were kicking to come out," Miriam smiled at Yeshua, who could not take his eyes off his mother. He was absolutely fascinated by this drama in the life of his family.

"So where did you stay?" Yeshua asked.

Yosef jumped in, "When the innkeeper was unconcerned about us, he simply told us his place was full and that there was no room for us."

"But we were lucky, Yeshua," Miriam interrupted. "The innkeeper's wife, Joanna, saw my condition and that I was close to giving birth, and she accompanied us to the back of the inn where there was a place that looked like a cave but was actually a place where they kept their animals. There was an ox, a donkey and a few sheep and goats around that I saw. The place wasn't too bad but it was smelly and not too clean at all," Miriam said.

"Joanna kindly told us we could stay in the stable for the night and said we could use some of the straw to sleep on," Miriam said.

"It wasn't ideal, but we were grateful and so was our donkey, because he had company of his own kind," Yosef said.

Miriam continued with the tale, "Yosef then quickly went about sweeping a section that seemed the cleanest and made it suitable for us to sit and lie down. I was so tired that I just slumped down on our straw bed, and as soon as I lay down, you began to knock on my womb and began shouting, 'let me out, let me out,'" Miriam said, smiling at Yeshua, who smiled back, imagining that that was exactly what he was doing, what he would do.

"I told Yosef to go to the innkeeper's wife and tell her to please call the midwife, as our baby is about to be born."

"I was beside myself, bag of mixed emotions, Yeshua. I ran to the innkeeper's room and I was glad that Joanna came to the door, I told her that you were about to be born and she swung into action, told the servants to hurry, call the midwife, who luckily was not far off. She was at the stable within minutes," Yosef said.

"I can see you being beside yourself Abba, all sixes and sevens," Yeshua said, laughing but prompting his mother to continue. He knew that this was a conversation that not many children his age, or any age for that matter, would have with his mother and father. We can be witnesses to the birth of animals, and maybe the birth of other babies but never our own birth, Yeshua thought and was very curious about everything, he wanted to know all the details of his birth.

Miriam continued, "You did not take long, Yeshua, after the midwife arrived, you came into the world with a loud cry."

"Like you wanted the whole world to hear, because the whole of Bethlehem must have heard you screaming, I ran in when I heard you," Yosef said.

"How were you feeling Abba, when you saw me for the first time?" Yeshua asked.

"I was so happy to hear you and see you, Yeshua, you were a beautiful baby and I was so pleased to see that your mother was okay," Yosef said.

"And you Immah, how did you feel, when you saw me for the first time?" Yeshua asked.

"I can't describe how I felt, Yeshua. I was the happiest I have ever been in my life. I couldn't believe that you were flesh of my flesh, that I carried you for nine months and that you caused me so much pain a few minutes ago and now brought me so much joy, impossible to describe. I was delirious, Yeshua. I was so happy I felt as if I was floating on air. The fatigue I felt just evaporated as I saw you and when I held you in my arms I wept with joy. You were so tiny, yet so beautiful. You were the most beautiful baby I had ever seen, and I was so proud to be your mother. And I felt that Yahweh and all the angels in heaven were smiling down on you," Miriam said.

Yeshua was beaming. It was as if he was present, witnessing his own birth. But that was only the beginning, he wanted his mother and father to tell him everything about what happened to him after that, what his first years of life were like; years that he couldn't recall, so he asked his parents to tell him.

Miriam indicated to Yosef to continue with the tale. "Well, Yeshua, we had no crib for you. I had made one, but it was at our home in Nazareth. You were born in humble surroundings, and some of the sheep and goats and the donkey had been brought in for shelter during the night. But I kept them to one side so as not to disturb you and your mother who needed to rest. I saw an old manger in the far corner that had seen better days, so I took it, cleaned it out and filled it with some clean straw, then we wrapped you in some bands of cloth and laid you in the manger."

"So, my first bed was a manger," Yeshua said with a smile.

"Yes, and you were delicious enough to eat," Miriam said with laughter in her voice.

"I'm glad that Yosef was on guard and that the animals did not come and eat me by mistake," Yeshua said laughing. "But if I am the son of Yahweh as well then, I being born in a manger, must mean something. Yahweh is all powerful, the King of Kings and if I am his child he would want only the best for me, and this is his best," Yeshua said mischievously.

"Maybe this being born in a manger, in a stable, is part of his plan, Yeshua," Miriam said.

"Thank you so much, Immah and Abba, for sharing all these intimate details with me, there is much for me to ponder," Yeshua said. He loved the word 'ponder', for it was a word his mother often used, and it was something he saw her do often.

"So, what happened next, how did we get back to Nazareth?" Yeshua asked.

Miriam nodded to Yosef, indicating that he should continue with the story.

"Well, there was quite a bit of drama and upheaval in our lives before we eventually got back to Nazareth," Yosef continued. "On the very night you were born, some shepherds came to visit you. Your mother and I were amazed at what they told us about how they got the news of your birth. They told us that they were watching over their flock when this stranger appeared out of nowhere. He seemed to light up the night all around them and they were terrified, but the stranger told them not to be afraid and that his name was Gabriel, and that he came from heaven, with a message for them and for all the world."

"Gabriel, he sure was busy, appearing to you mother, and also to uncle Zech and aunt Elish, and now to these shepherds, he sure gets around," Yeshua said smiling.

"Yes, Yeshua, and you forgot that an angel also appeared to me, albeit in a dream," Yosef said, smiling back. "Anyhow, angels put the shepherds at ease telling them not to be afraid and then gave them the news about your birth."

"So, what did Gabriel actually say to them?" Yeshua inquired, in his usual meticulous and curious way. He wanted to know the details. He was amazed with this story about his birth.

"Miriam, you tell Yeshua, you have a better memory than me," Yosef said, looking at Miriam.

Miriam took over. "After Gabriel put them at ease he said to them—'I am bringing you news of great joy for all the people: for on this night is born in the city of David, a Saviour, who is the Messiah, the Lord.' And Gabriel gave them a sign saying they would find you, Yeshua, wrapped in bands of cloth and lying in a manger. And after Gabriel had told them this news, they said that more angels, a whole multitude, appeared around them, praising Adonai and singing, 'Glory to Yahweh in the highest heaven, and on earth peace among those whom he favours'."

And then there was silence. Yeshua got up. He was overwhelmed with what he had just heard. This was too much for him, even for his young phenomenal brain to digest. He needed to get away. "Immah, Abba, I am just going to see Achim for a minute. I'll be back soon." Yeshua just wanted some normality back in his young life. What he heard cut him to the core, those shepherds got the same message that his mother got from Gabriel, except now the message was much deeper, the angels said that he was to be a Saviour; that he was the Messiah. His mother had already told him about his miraculous birth and now this news about his full identity. What did this all mean, him being the Messiah? This was just too much. He needed to be with his friend Achim.

He reached his home and called out. Achim came out. "Achim, I need to go for a walk, can you come with me?"

"Sure, Yeshua, what happened? You look like you've seen a ghost."

"Achim, don't go far and don't be long, it's getting dark," Achim's mother called out.

"Okay, Immah won't be long," Achim responded. "So, tell me, what happened to you, Yeshua?"

Yeshua was in a dilemma. He shared everything with Achim but this he just wasn't sure he should share with Achim. But he needed to speak to him. "Achim, what do you know about the Messiah?" Yeshua put the question to Achim.

"Only what Gamaliel taught us that a Messiah would come to save us, to liberate us and put an end to Rome's power over us and he would rule over us and we would regain our Promised Land, and Israel would be ours once again," Achim said, proud that he was able to tell Yeshua something he didn't seem to know, because why would he ask.

"Thank you Achim, that was good to hear," Yeshua said. He was very tempted to tell Achim everything, and maybe he would but not yet. He needed a friend and he knew Achim could not keep a secret. He would have to wait longer but the thought that one day he could share his secret with his dearest friend, gave Yeshua some courage and some peace. He left Achim's company and returned home. He wanted to know more, because he had only heard about his birth, and he wanted to know what happened in those early years of his life that he couldn't recall.

Chapter Five
Gamaliel

Yeshua had a sleepless night. It took him a while before he fell asleep. He was going over in his mind all that his mother and father had told him about his conception and his birth. He wasn't too happy about himself; he just wanted to be like everyone else, every boy his age. He got up and went through the normal morning routine as if in a trance, hardly noticing his mum. His dad was already off to work, as usual. He had his usual breakfast and then kissed his mum goodbye. He was glad that his mother was not a morning person, she liked the silence of the morning and didn't speak much, so they did not converse much, and Yeshua got used to the silence of the morning, and the limited conversation. But he had a lot on his mind. He had made up his mind to have a serious chat with his two best friends Achim and Zadok, during the morning break at school. He especially wanted to speak to Zadok; he was more worldly wise and much older than both Achim and himself. Zadok was going to be a teenager soon and he always liked to tell, not how old he was, but how old he would be this year, as if he couldn't wait to be a year older. He had more life experience for a young boy of twelve and Yeshua always liked to pick his young and fertile brain.

As Yeshua sat in class listening to Gamaliel, he changed his mind about talking to Zadok and Achim. He knew he couldn't be as open as he would like. But he had to speak to someone beside his mum and dad, so why not to Gamaliel? Gamaliel was respected in the village for his knowledge, wisdom and life experience, and his interest in the well-being of his students. They did not know much about Gamaliel. Yeshua gathered from what Gamaliel shared over the years about himself, that he was born in a little village in Samaria. And through Gamaliel, Yeshua had learned so much about the Samaritans, and their beliefs. They believed that their religion was the true one, because it was the religion of the ancient Israelites before the seventy-year exile into Babylon. That theirs was the religion preserved by those who did not go into exile and remained in the land of Israel. And they felt that Judaism, after the Babylonian Exile was amended, no longer a pure Judaism.

Yeshua also learned the irony of the Samaritans belief, for over the years they too adopted foreign beliefs and intermarried with foreigners. And this adulteration of their religion and the fact that they were of mixed race and not pure Jews, was a reason they were shunned by the Israelites. But Yeshua also learned over the years that Gamaliel was not of mixed race, as both his parents were pure Jews. Yet Gamaliel experienced discrimination in his professional life. As a young man, in his late teens, he went to Jerusalem to study law. He also became very interested in history, especially the history of the Jewish nation. When he finished his legal studies, he continued to study every written text and commentary he could, of the Hebrew Scriptures. As a young man he had learned through the oral tradition, all the great stories about Yahweh and his relationship with humanity, and this fascinated him. So, it wasn't long when he used his legal training to become a Scribe.

Yeshua now recalled all the bits of information he had learned about Gamaliel over the years. Yeshua learned that some Scribes were Pharisees but not all of them were and Gamaliel, as a non-Pharisee Scribe, found he was discriminated against professionally and racially when it became known, he was a Samaritan. When Yeshua learned about this double discrimination against his revered teacher, it shocked him, dismayed him. If the Samaritans were like Gamaliel, then he very much would like to be a Samaritan.

Yeshua also learned that the Scribes were very knowledgeable about the law and were able to draft legal documents such as contracts for births, marriages and deaths, divorce, loans, inheritances, mortgages, land sales and the like. Yeshua also learned that the Scribes could interpret and regulate Jewish laws but that they were not allowed to meddle or assume any role in the guidance of the people. And this Gamaliel found hard to take because so many people came to him for guidance, and they sought his counsel, not only in matters of the law but in religion, in matters of the spirit, and their relationship with their God. They came to Gamaliel to speak about how Yahweh was active or not active in their lives. But when the Pharisees saw this, they condemned Gamaliel and ordered him to desist as spiritual mentoring was the domain of the Pharisees, who alone could be rabbis.

So, Gamaliel's days as a quasi-rabbi were over and the Pharisees gave him a hard time professionally, so he decided to leave and returned to Samaria where he continued to do what he felt called to, and the people of Samaria came to him for legal advice and also for spiritual guidance. Gamaliel stepped back from most of his work about five years ago when he turned sixty and felt like he wanted to have some quiet time so he moved to the little town of Nazareth.

Yeshua and the people of Nazareth soon got to know of Gamaliel and it wasn't long before Gamaliel found himself involved, attending to all their legal matters, and in charge of the education of the boys of Nazareth. He loved teaching the young and they thrived under his guidance.

Yeshua felt that Gamaliel's presence in Nazareth was the work of Yahweh that he was there to help and guide him during these times. So there and then Yeshua decided to confide in Gamaliel, and seek his guidance as a spiritual mentor. He could not wait for school to be over. He told Achim that he was staying for a while more as he had to speak with Gamaliel. Yeshua usually walked home with Achim as they lived in the same direction whereas Zadok was on the opposite side of the village of Nazareth. Yeshua's mother had already asked Gamaliel to give her son extra tutoring, so it was easy for Yeshua to use the time to speak of his personal issues.

When Yeshua asked Gamaliel if he could have some time with him and that he needed some spiritual mentoring, it seemed that Gamaliel, by his smile, was waiting for just this to happen, because he simply said, "I know." And this put Yeshua completely at ease and he felt that he could be as open with Gamaliel as he wanted. And so began their relationship. Yeshua would go to Gamaliel as his spiritual guide and mentor. He told Gamaliel everything of the past night, everything that his mother and father told him.

Gamaliel listened intently to everything that Yeshua was revealing to him. He listened with complete attention, without interrupting, as the words and sentiments tumbled out of Yeshua like a flood. When Yeshua had finished revealing everything, Gamaliel simply said, "thank you, Yeshua. Now there is still so much more you have to know about yourself and your future. You are chosen by Yahweh for something unique. So, you go home now and continue to get the full picture from your mother and father. Tell them you want to know everything that happened to you. And we'll talk again. Not tomorrow, but next week, the first day of the week. We can have a regular chat every week and let your mother and father know that you are talking to me about your spiritual journey. You do not need to tell them what you are telling me because our conversations are completely confidential. I am here for you, Yeshua, to assist you in whatever way I can."

Yeshua was happy with that, very happy, he was so pleased he could talk to someone who understood what was happening to him. And that he would receive his expert advice and guidance. He raced home, skipping and jumping. He would go home, have something to eat and then check out what Achim was up to. Maybe they would go hunt for caterpillars and watch them. Maybe they would be lucky in witnessing their incredible metamorphosis and change into the most dainty, fragile and yet the most graceful and beautiful of Yahweh's creations.

Chapter Six
Yeshua, Achim and Zadok

Yeshua had a pleasant time with his friend, Achim. This time they thought they would go and visit Zadok, as they did from time to time and find out what he was up to. Yeshua liked Zadok even though he could be so crude at times. Zadok was soon to turn thirteen for which he couldn't wait, so he could tell everyone he was fourteen that year. Zadok wasn't much good at learning what Gamaliel was teaching, he was more interested in worldly matters and kept telling Yeshua and Achim how he couldn't wait to leave Nazareth for which he had the most derogatory descriptions, too vile to repeat. He saw Nazareth for what he described as the sticks, and he kept speaking about getting out of these dead woods and take off to the big cities of Tiberias and Sepphoris, where he said all the action was. Zadok wasn't very bright at school work but he was a great artist and Yeshua admired the beautiful landscapes he drew, capturing its breathtaking beauty. Zadok wasn't very interested in school and got up to all kinds of mischief, he was what Yeshua thought of as worldly wise. He was also very handsome and he liked the girls and they liked him. Yet Yeshua liked him for his candour, his truthfulness, he said it like it is, even if a bit crudely. Zadok also loved hiking and he knew all the places, the mounts and the forests and the hills. He guided Yeshua and Achim into places they would not venture on their own, for fear of getting lost and any wild animals that may be around. They always took long staffs with them for protection, just in case.

Zadok and Achim were Yeshua's best friends and they were so different. Achim was very bright and he and Yeshua got on easily, like two peas in a pod, and they had similar interests. Achim and Yeshua could spend all day in each other's company and never be bored; they often discussed what they learned and bounced things off each other and learned from each other.

When Yeshua got home from his jaunt with Achim and Zadok, he went straight to the water and splashed himself to get rid of all the dirt and grime that got stuck onto him with his adventures into unknown territory with Zadok as their guide.

Yosef wasn't too happy with Yeshua associating with Zadok, he feared that Zadok was not a good influence and would lead Yeshua astray, but Miriam thought Zadok was good for Yeshua, he was worldly wise, honest, straightforward, said what he thought, made up his own mind on things, and he was always very respectful when he visited. Miriam knew that Yeshua was mature enough for his age and be able to work things out for himself and he liked Zadok just as much as Achim, and she was happy with Yeshua's friends and was delighted when they were around.

That night Yeshua told Miriam and Yosef all about his meeting with Gamaliel. He told them that he respected Gamaliel and that he was like a rabbi, more than a rabbi, highly intelligent and so conversant with the Law and the Prophets, the history of Israel, and Yahweh's relationship with us. Yeshua told them that he would be meeting with Gamaliel every first day of the week after school for spiritual guidance and mentoring.

Miriam and Yosef were quite happy for this to happen, in fact they were thrilled. Gamaliel was highly respected and they knew that only good could come from these conversations between their son and Gamaliel.

Yeshua then wanted to hear another chapter in the saga of his life. "So, after the shepherds left us, what happened to us in Bethlehem?" Yeshua asked, to get things started.

"Well, we stayed with the animals for about a week and then were able to get some other place to rent for a short while. When the eighth day came for you to be presented and circumcised, we took you to the temple in Jerusalem, then returned to our lodgings in Bethlehem. I then found some work to keep us going, to pay for rent and food. We were staying there for another month or so, and when the forty days from your birth arrived, we had to travel to Jerusalem again, to present you in the temple once again."

"And for my ritual purification, as the law prescribed," Miriam said.

"Yes, that's about right; I was feeling quite strong by then and we planned to present you, Yeshua, in the temple in Jerusalem, and then we decided we would return to Nazareth. And as we have no synagogue in our home town, we thought it would be nice to present you in the temple in Jerusalem."

"Yes, our plan was to spend the day travelling to Jerusalem, present you in the temple, have our own little celebration, get some supplies, rest up for the night and then begin our journey home early the next morning."

Yeshua knew all about what the presentation of the newborn meant. He had learned this from Gamaliel. The parents were to present the child for the purification ceremony, as the Law of Moses commanded. Yeshua remembered well that lesson. He had quizzed Gamaliel about why that was required, why did a newborn baby need to be purified, to be purified of what? Yeshua had wanted to know.

Yeshua remembered the lesson well; Gamaliel explained that every first-born male is to be presented in the temple and dedicated to Yahweh, that was written in the Law and the purification was for Miriam, the Law required she participate in the ceremony of her purification. Yeshua had quizzed why his mother needed purification, for he saw nothing impure in the giving of birth. Gamaliel had agreed with him and explained that it was a mere ritual cleaning.

"So, I was presented in the temple in Jerusalem, wow, that was something, I wish I could have seen that," Yeshua laughed. "Of course I was there, because I believe you and Yosef, but I was too tiny, my brain was too tiny to remember such an auspicious event."

Miriam and Yosef were amused at Yeshua's sense of humour, they were always delighted in how he could make them laugh and they were astounded by his grasp of their language and all the big words he used. He was like a wordsmith, he loved words, he was a story teller extraordinaire, he made up incredible stories and always with some meaning to them.

"Please go on Immah," Yeshua said, recollecting himself.

"But before we went to Jerusalem, we had spent almost six weeks in Bethlehem. After you were born, we spent some days in the cave, and as soon as a room became vacant, we moved into the lodgings. We still used the manger for your crib. Yosef found some work to keep food on the table and pay for our room. On our last night in Bethlehem we had very auspicious visitors," Miriam said, winking at Yeshua because she could see him smiling at her use of the word 'auspicious.' another beautiful word. "Is that an appropriate word, my little wordsmith," Miriam said smiling.

"Well, I would have to find out who those visitors were, won't I, before I can tell you if your word, auspicious, or prodigious, which means more or less the same, is appropriate" Yeshua said smiling.

"Braggart!" Yosef interjected.

"Not bragging, Abba, just delighting in language and the beauty of words," Yeshua retorted. "Okay Immah, you may proceed," Yeshua said with a flowing gesture of his hand and a smile on his face.

Miriam in turn did the same gesture to Yosef, eliciting smiles all around.

"Hmm, it was our last night in Bethlehem and your last night to sleep like a little lamb in a manger. I had just come back from the markets with a few supplies for our trip to Jerusalem because we intended to leave at sunrise. It was late afternoon when we heard this noise outside in the yard. I went to look when I saw these three strangers dressed in salubrious, oh my dear, I am getting to be just like you and your mother, Yeshua, I meant to say elegant. They had long flowing garments like rich people from foreign lands. They introduced themselves as Melchior, Caspar and Balthazar, and were foreigners from the east."

Chapter Seven
Melchior, Caspar and Balthazar

"Yosef, I think you can tell Yeshua about those three strange gentlemen that came to pay homage to our son," Miriam began.

Yeshua was beaming and his eyes jumped from his mother to his father, as he listened expectantly.

"They were strange all right, definitely not from here, they were foreigners from the eastern lands. They were dressed in rich garments and elaborate head turbans. They seemed weatherbeaten and sunburnt but one of them was of very dark complexion, he was definitely not from here. His name was Balthazar, and the other two were Caspar and Melchior," Yosef began.

"What unusual names. Who were they?" Yeshua asked. He was totally engrossed in the story; this was better than the made-up stories his mother and father had told him. He loved their made-up stories but this wasn't made up, it actually happened. But now Yeshua understood some of the characters in the stories his mother and father told him, they were based on real life people and real-life events.

"They said they were astronomers," Yosef said.

"Astronomers! Real astronomers?" Yeshua exclaimed. "Gamaliel was just speaking about Greek astronomers, in one of our recent lessons," Yeshua added excitedly. "He said they studied the heavens, the sun, the moon, and the planets. So, they were actually real astronomers? Why did they come to see us and what did they have to say?" Yeshua asked, his curiosity now peaked to the extreme.

Yosef replied, "they said that they were observing your star, Yeshua."

"My star?" Yeshua responded.

"Yes, they said, they had been observing the stars, and saw a star the likes of which they had never seen before, the brightest they had ever witnessed. They said the bright star that appeared in the heavens indicated that a king has been born but this star was of such a resplendent brightness, that it was like the king of the stars, they said; they knew that it was announcing the King of Kings, the one that was prophesied to be the King of the Jews. They said they had seen and were observing the star at its rising and had been following it, and it led them to you for it stopped above the stable. They said they were overwhelmed with joy to have finally met the newborn king and that they had come to pay homage," Yosef said.

"Are all these prophecies about me, a shepherd and now a king?" Yeshua asked, somewhat perturbed.

"Yeshua, I know this is a lot for you to take in. But we wanted; we felt we had to tell you everything that has happened to you so far, to prepare you for whatever lay ahead. And you did insist," Miriam said.

"So, I did. And thank you, Immah, but this is a lot to take in," Yeshua said.

"It is, Yeshua, but do take your time. It is not clear to me what it all means and what your future will be but we are here for you, whatever that is," Yosef said reassuringly.

"Thank you, Abba, you are most reassuring. So do go on, with the visit of these foreign men," Yeshua urged.

"It was on the last night of our stay in the stable as a room was becoming available in the inn on the following day. They paid homage, kneeling down in front of you and one of them bent over and touched the ground with his forehead, as he bowed to you. And they chanted in some strange language, but such a beautiful and prayerful chant, it filled the whole place," Yosef continued. "And then they laid gifts at your feet."

"What gifts?" Yeshua asked excitedly.

"Very precious gifts," Miriam replied, "gifts of gold, frankincense and myrrh," she added.

"Gold, frankincense and myrrh; those are expensive and strange gifts. Did they say anything else, about why they brought them to me?" Yeshua asked.

"They said you were destined to be the new king of the Jews and the king of all kings, and that the gold was a sign of your royalty, your kingship, the frankincense they said was to be used in royal ceremonies, because when burnt the smoke rises to the heavens, and the myrrh they said, is a sign of suffering ahead, that as the King of the Jews you were also destined for great sorrow and suffering, and the myrrh is to be used as embalming oil," Miriam said, feeling a bit uneasy about telling her young son all these things.

Yeshua looked at his mother and father. He was stunned. His young, highly intelligent and gifted mind was ticking over. Then he smiled, and his parents broke uneasily into a smile with him. And he said, "So what did you do with those gifts those strange men gave for me," Yeshua said, grinning.

Miriam and Yosef grinned in return, feeling more relaxed. Yeshua was his usual playful and joking self. "We have kept all those gifts in our little treasure chest for you, you will need those gold pieces to give you a start when you set out on your own and build your own home and start your own family," Miriam said.

"So, you said, that these men from faraway lands arrived on the last night of our stay in the stable cave in Bethlehem, so what happened next. Did we leave for Nazareth on the next day," Yeshua asked, hoping they would relate some other interesting stories of those eventful times when he was born. As they were telling him all these things it was as if he were present.

"So, what happened to those three visitors?" Yeshua asked.

"We don't know, they said that they had been to see King Herod, and that they should seek you out and then let him know about your whereabouts for he too wanted to come and pay homage," Yosef said.

"But I didn't trust that fox," Miriam said, surprising both Yeshua and Yosef who looked at each other with expressions of joyful astonishment at hearing their mother's colourful expression of Herod.

"So Immah, what did you do to outsmart that fox?" Yeshua asked with a grin.

"As it was forty days since your birth it was time for us to present you to Yahweh, as the Law of Moses required, and as we have no synagogue in Nazareth, we presented you and had you circumcised in the Temple in Jerusalem," Miriam said.

"But as we were suspicious and did not trust that wily fox," Yosef said, emphasising the word 'fox', with a smile on his face that brought smiles to both Yeshua and Miriam. "We disguised ourselves and tried our best to camouflage you as well, carrying you in one of our bags," Yosef said.

"How exciting," Yeshua said. "Just like in those tales you tell me of the big bad wolf seeking out young innocent children, to devour them," Yeshua added.

"Yes, that fox, was a big bad wolf. He was worse than a wolf, cruel, and he murdered his own family and tortured and killed so many of the Jews and committed all kinds of atrocities to ensure he remained in power, and eliminated any threats to that power," Miriam said.

"And because those visitors had told Herod about you, that you would become the King of the Jews, we were sure he would have wanted you eliminated. So, we went about incognito in Jerusalem, went straight to the Temple to present you and then planned to leave Jerusalem as soon as possible," Yosef said.

"How exciting," Yeshua said.

"And dangerous," Yosef added.

"We had to be so careful and had wanted to have you presented as quickly as possible and then get out of Jerusalem as quickly as possible, but something happened in the Temple that confirmed what those wise men from the east had said," Miriam said.

"Wow! There's more excitement and danger," Yeshua said, intrigued. "Tell me more, what happened in the Temple?"

Chapter Eight
Simeon and Hanna

"We went as early as possible to Jerusalem and took you to the Temple to present you to Yahweh, as the Law prescribed. We had to wait a while for a priest to officiate at the ceremony," Miriam continued.

"It was forty days since your birth, the time the law states for you to be presented in the Temple. There were quite a few people in the Temple, praying, and some Pharisees, who seemed a pompous lot, strutting around like peacocks, wanting to be noticed and treated obsequiously, dressed in long robes with broad phylacteries and long tassels. If they wanted to be noticed, they were definitely succeeding" Yosef said.

"How serendipitous it was, that the Emperor Augustus called for a census requiring Abba to take us to his family's hometown of Bethlehem, so close to our holy city of Jerusalem, and the sacred Temple and we could spend time there and I could be presented in the Temple." Yeshua smiled as he spoke, enjoying using such a beautiful word as serendipitous that rolled off his tongue like music.

"Yes, serendipitous indeed," Yosef said, trying his best not to mangle the word. "So much happened at the time of your presentation in the Temple that is so important for you to know," Yosef said.

"Yes indeed, more than serendipitous, it was more like the hand of Adonai guiding us. For in the temple at the time of your presentation there was a holy man and woman, who seemed to be expecting you. They had messages for us about you that I have pondered much on, and never forgotten. Although I must confess, Yeshua, in the past ten years, I have put all those words I heard to the back of my mind, I just wanted to be an ordinary mother to you."

"You were no ordinary mother, Immah, you were, and you are extraordinary. You are the best mother in the whole wide world," Yeshua said as he leapt to his feet and went over and hugged his mother warmly.

"Okay, that's enough," Miriam said. It seemed to her that Yeshua was never to let her go. She felt she had told Yeshua everything that he needed to know.

But Yeshua persisted and he wanted to know all about the holy man and woman in the Temple.

Miriam reluctantly continued, "We arrived at the temple at about the sixth hour. But we had to wait until the ninth hour to get a priest to preside at your presentation ceremony. So, we went to have lunch, bought some supplies for our journey and got some feed for our donkey. We went to the Temple at about the eighth hour to pray and to rest and to buy two pigeons to offer in sacrifice as part of our purification ceremony. As we sat in the beautiful Temple, I felt a bit tired, and was about to dose off when this elderly man, with a most pleasant demeanour, gently touched me on the arm and told me that the Spirit had led him into the Temple at this hour and on this day for a very special reason. I looked at this man, whom I had never seen in my life. But I felt quite safe. And Yosef was there beside me," Miriam said.

Yeshua was most interested in this visitor to the Temple. "Tell me about this man who said he was led by the Spirit into the Temple, what did he say?" Yeshua asked excitedly.

"Well, he said his name was Simeon, and he was waiting for Israel to be saved. He said that he had a vision in which it was revealed to him that he would not die before he had seen Yahweh's promised Messiah. And he said that the Spirit seemed to speak to him that day and lead him into the Temple. He said the Spirit told him that this is the day of the Lord, and that he would see the Promised One, the Messiah, the Saviour of the world, and he addressed me and said that he had been led to me and my child," Miriam said.

Both Miriam and Yosef related how astonished they were, but they both felt that he was genuine and a devout man and he had a kind face.

"Simeon asked if he could hold you, Yeshua. So, I handed you over to him. Then facing the Holy of Holies, he held you most tenderly and the deepest of smiles lit up his face. Then he solemnly raised you up in his arms and prayed. He seemed to be consecrating you to the Lord," Miriam said.

"Oh Immah, can you remember what he said?" Yeshua asked.

"Oh yes, I do, for I pondered for a long time on his words, Yeshua. As he held you aloft, he praised Yahweh and then he said, almost as if in song, these words: 'Lord, now, you are dismissing your servant in peace, according to your word; for my eyes have seen your salvation, which you have prepared in the presence of all peoples, a light for revelation to the Gentiles and for the glory of your people of Israel'," Miriam said.

"We were amazed at Simeon's words. He was speaking about you, Yeshua," Yosef said. "And then he blessed your mother and me and said some strange words to Miriam." Immediately Yosef said those words, he regretted and wondered whether Yeshua should hear what Simeon said to his mother, and Yosef was also concerned for Miriam, maybe she didn't want to be reminded of what Simeon had said about her.

"That's okay Yosef," Miriam said immediately, reading Yosef's thoughts. "Yeshua needs to know everything. We must not hold anything back." She continued, "Simeon then blessed your father and I and he told us that you, Yeshua, are destined for the falling and the rising of many in Israel, and that you would be a sign that will be opposed so that the inner thoughts of many will be revealed—and then he added that a sword would pierce my own soul too," Miriam said. Those were words that she had pondered for a long time after she first heard them, but then put them aside and put her full trust in Yahweh.

"There was also another prophet in the temple at the time, she said her name was Hannah, and that she was the daughter of Phanuel, of the tribe of Asher and she told us that she had lived with her husband for seven years when he died, and she has been on her own ever since, and she was now eighty-four. She had a room adjacent to the temple and worked there spending all her spare time in prayer and fasting and waiting for the Messiah, the Promised One who would set Israel free. And she too took you in her arms and began praising God and speaking to everyone looking for the redemption of Jerusalem."

"Wow! Immah, Abba, I am astounded by those two, Simeon and Hannah and what they had to say. What happened next?" Yeshua asked.

"We had you presented to the Lord, and Simeon and Hannah participated and assisted the priest. We were so happy they took part. Simeon was such a beautiful man, so serene and joyful. And it seemed like he felt complete, that he was fully satisfied and was ready to go to Yahweh," Miriam said.

"When we had finished the presentation ceremony, your mother and I had something to eat, and as it was too late to begin our journey home, I went and found some reasonable lodgings for us and our donkey for the night. I also needed to buy more supplies for our long trek home. Our donkey needed to have a good feed and rest as well, we had to be very careful not to be detected by any of Herod's guards," Yosef added.

"What an eventful time I must have had, what both of you, Immah and Abba definitely had, so much drama. I wish I could have been conscious at the time," Yeshua said, smiling. "And so, we all went to sleep and set off the next day for Nazareth. I think that is enough for now, you can both tell me about our trip home on our way home," Yeshua said.

Yeshua was feeling tired and ready to retire, but with all the excitement of the stories he had just heard, he now had a new injection of energy, he was all ears as he lie on his stomach on the rug in their room with his head cupped in his hands.

Yeshua had a sleepless night. It took him a while before he fell to sleep. He had a dream.

Chapter Nine
The Dream

In his dream, Yeshua appeared much older, about as old as Zadok. He was alone in a deserted place; it seemed like a desert with no people or animals or houses or vegetation of any sort. This must be a desert he thought. Where am I and how did I get here? He asked himself. All of a sudden, he saw what looked like an animal coming towards him, as it came nearer, he made it out to be a wolf. Then, all of a sudden, a whole pack of them appeared and stood in front of him almost surrounding him completely. Where did they come from, he wondered. They stood there quite still, looking at him. Yeshua thought they looked like they were studying him, studying which part of him was the tastiest to eat, he thought to himself. *Get yourself together, Yeshua, this is no time for humour, you are in big trouble. What can I do? If I run, I am a goner*, he said, and he prayed to Yahweh: "Abba, you brought me onto this earth for a special mission, well, it looks like you are about to fail because I am about to be devoured by these hungry looking wolves. You better save me."

Yeshua could not believe that he was so calm and funny, he thought in his dream, but he felt that deep down he was screaming with fear, he was just so good at hiding it. He knew that if he showed any fear, or even felt it, he was a goner. Well, I am going to die; I may as well go out laughing he said to himself. But he was trembling underneath. I am too young to die, Yahweh please save me, he prayed.

The wolves began to slowly approach him, closing the circle. All of a sudden Zadok and Achim appeared beside him with their long staffs and they handed Yeshua his. Yeshua breathed a great sigh of relief. He was so glad to see his two best friends beside him. "How did you get here?" Yeshua asked.

"What are friends for, a friend in need is a friend indeed," Zadok said grinning. "Now keep your staff stretched out in front of you, very still, and now move back very slowly towards that massive tree behind us," Zadok said.

"Tree, what tree? There's no tree, there's nothing here, this is a desert," Yeshua said.

"But there is a tree," Achim said.

Yeshua turned around and there behind him was the biggest, tallest oak tree he had ever seen. The three of them walked back slowly and gingerly until they reached the tree. At the same time the wolves were also moving slightly closer towards them, it seemed. But it was clear to Yeshua that they were intent on a meal and now they had a three course, he said to himself. Humour, seeing the funny side of a hopeless situation seemed to help Yeshua to handle his fear. This was something he was just discovering, as he had never been in such a situation before. And he found how important it was to have friends close and supportive when in danger and gripped by fear.

They reached the tree. "Now very carefully, put down your staffs and then scamper the hell and as fast as you can and climb the bloody tree," Zadok said firmly.

And that is what they did, they scampered the last bit and were up the tree in a flash as the wolves realising, they were about to be cheated of their meal, charged and attacked but they were too late, the three young ones were well out of reach and high up on firm branches and looking down at them with big grins of relief on their faces.

"Outfoxed you, you stupid *** wolves," Zadok swore.

"Mind your language," Achim said.

"Thank you Zadok for saving me. Thank you Achim; if you both had not come, I would not be sitting here in this fine tree. How did you know I was here and in this predicament?" Yeshua asked.

"I have a nose for danger, call me Captain Marvellous, I respond to danger, man," Zadok said, grinning.

"A friend in need is indeed a friend in deed," Achim added.

Then all of a sudden that dream ended and Yeshua found himself alone again. This time he was in what seemed like a big city, the likes of which he had never seen. There were big houses and buildings made of material that seemed stronger than the mud houses of Nazareth. They had solid stone houses and the streets were firmer under his feet, because they too were made of stone, beautiful cobbled streets. He seemed lost in this unfamiliar city and he walked around looking for his parents, for surely, they must be around, he thought in his dream. As he turned a corner, a big group of boys, much older than him came walking towards him. He felt an ominous chill creeping up his spine, for he could gather that they were teenagers with nothing to do and looking for some excitement. These were city wolves, seeking whom they can devour, out of boredom or just for kicks, Yeshua said to himself. He looked around hoping to see Zadok and Achim with three staffs for protection but to no avail, Yeshua knew he was alone and in deep trouble.

"Hey you! shorty!" came the deep and threatening voice of the apparent leader of the pack.

Yeshua decided flight is his best option, so he turned around and ran as fast as he could. Yeshua loved walking and running, and he was very fit so he was confident that he could outrun those older boys. He ran for about a minute and then looked around and still they were coming, running after him like a threatening sand storm, so Yeshua picked up his pace and began to sprint. After a minute he looked around and he saw them standing there, like young men all dressed up with nowhere to go. They had given up and Yeshua breathed a huge sigh of relief. Yahweh, why the violence and evil in the world, why did you create animals and humans that can hurt each other, why all the violence, why do we kill each other? I know in the commandments you gave to Moses; the fifth one is "Thou shalt not kill."

In response, Yeshua heard the words, "on your own you can do nothing, with me you can accomplish everything. On your own you are weak and can do nothing, but you can do all things with the strength I give you, with me all things are possible." Then all of a sudden, Yeshua found himself in a city square, which seemed somewhat familiar, it might be a square in Jerusalem, not far from the Temple. He felt more at ease as he roamed about for a while, but what was strange, he was now a fully grown man, in the prime of his life. It wasn't long before lots of people began to gather in the square. Yeshua sat down at a well and waited to see what was evidently going to happen. He was excited for it was clear the people were too. Then from around the corner came a group of prominent looking men, with long robes, holding scrolls in their hands. Yeshua then gathered that they were holy men, maybe Pharisees, Scribes, Sadducees or priests. Yeshua made himself more comfortable, as one of the men stood in front. He was a tall man with an aquiline nose. He seemed quite pompous, Yeshua thought, but then he corrected himself and said not to judge a man by his appearance. The aquiline nosed man opened a scroll and began to read in a very loud and melodramatic voice, as if he was on stage. He was reading from Isaiah about the coming of a Messiah. While he was reading, in his dream, Yeshua's mind went back to all that he had just learned from his mother and father about his birth, about the visit by the angel Gabriel, and about how he was conceived, and the visit from the shepherds and the three wise men from the east and what they had all said about him and that he was the promised Messiah. So as soon as 'Mr Aquiline,' finished reading, Yeshua went up next to him and said, "my dear people, this text that our reverend has just read is fulfilled today, here and now, in this place, in your presence, for I am he, I am the Promised One, the Messiah, that our revered prophet Isaiah speaks."

"Blasphemy!" The Aquiline one shouted and all the people shouted in unison, "Blasphemy!" Then they quickly surrounded Yeshua and overpowered him, grabbing him and dragging him along. "Let us take him to the mountain and throw him down to the rocks as he deserves," someone shouted from the crowd.

Yeshua was terrified. Was this the end, was this the way he was to die? Then all of a sudden, he found himself on a hill outside the town of Jerusalem. It was a different time, and a different mob. This time they were huge crowds, and there were Roman guards and soldiers, and there were three tall trunks of trees standing side by side. They were bare, with no branches or leaves, just three strong, large, tall trunks standing like three sentinels. Then he saw lying in front of the large trunks, three cross beams, just as sturdy and on the ground beside them large nails, and hammers, and ropes.

Then he saw blood flowing like a river down from the hill, down into the valley below, turning the green earth to red. He was mesmerised by the sight of so much blood, then one of the soldiers walked towards him with a lance in hand, and then he woke up.

Chapter Ten
Miriam, Yosef and Yeshua

When Yeshua opened his eyes, he looked out the open window and saw that it was still dark and the sun hadn't quite risen from its sleep, so he turned over, happy that he still had some more time to sleep. He thought about how all the world was asleep and how quiet it must be when that happens. He knew that certain people got up very early, farmers to milk their cows to take their produce to the markets, the sellers getting their stalls ready, the shepherds herding their sheep and—then he just dozed off.

What seemed like a wink of the eye, a gust of the wind, a chirp of a bird, Yeshua felt the soft touch of his mother on his arm and her gentle voice, calling his name for him to wake and get up? "Just one more minute, Immah," Yeshua cried, as he snuggled and hugged his cushion. Why is it that I am not ready to sleep when I am supposed to go to bed, and not ready to get up in the morning when I am still so sleepy and comfortable, can't we just go to bed when we are tired and ready, sleep until we are no longer sleepy and we have had enough sleep, then get up and go to work or school, do what we have to do until we are so tired we are ready to drop into bed and sleep, instead of having to go to bed not really tired and get up when not really fully slept? Yeshua asked himself these questions. But Yeshua was usually so active during the day that he had no problem getting to bed and to sleep but he still had a problem getting up, especially when it was cold.

The day passed as usual, there was nothing extraordinary. Yosef was gone to work before Yeshua woke up. Today Yosef was travelling to Sepphoris again, a distance of about ten miles, where he has been working for a while. He had left very early and would be home late. Yeshua went to school, came home, did his chores, fiddled about his dad's workshop and then wandered off to find his friend Achim. They played their imaginative games of their own making. They were Jewish warriors, freedom fighters, with their own hand made swords, conquering the Romans and driving them out of Israel. They practised their skills with their wooden swords that the two of them made in Yosef's workshop. Yeshua, who spent quite a lot of his time watching his dad at work, was quite adept at working with wood and he taught his friend Achim. Besides swords, they also made shields from wood and whatever scrap they could find. They also made slings, v shaped catapults from sturdy branches they chopped off the trees. They used the catapults to shoot at birds, but intentionally missing them, they did not want to harm the birds; they just wanted to give them a scare. They played with their slings, with a pebble they had begun aiming for the thickest tree and calling it Goliath. They imagined themselves to be a young David. When they hit the tree, they ran and with sword in hand slew the evil giant. When they got bored with the slaying of Goliath they aimed for the thinnest of trees and competed to see who would strike the little critter seven times. When Zadok played with them with his big and mighty sling he would invariably win.

Today Yeshua and Achim decided to climb some pine trees and pick some pine cones, sticky cones that looked like wooden giant toads. When they got home, they laid them out on the roofs of their homes for the sun to bake them and open them up.

Once the cones opened, they would force the shell out and then crack them for the delicious pine nuts inside. They would have a feast and all the other children would know when there were pine nuts available, as if they could smell them from afar. Achim's mum, who was the champion baker of the village made the most divine little cakes with those crushed pine nuts.

When Yeshua got home after having vanquished the terrible monsters of Rome, plucking their pine cones and putting them on their roofs, Yeshua spent some time at Achim's. Achim's mother, Tamar, was busy baking some little cakes, the size of a clenched fist. Some of them were already baked and laid out on the table, when Yeshua arrived.

"Hello Lady Tamar," Yeshua greeted Achim's mother, eyeing the cakes, the aroma of which filled the house.

"Go on, Yeshua, take one," Tamar said with a smile. She loved Yeshua and was so glad her son had him for a friend. Yeshua in turn loved and adored Achim's mother. She was much older than his mother. Yeshua saw her as a saint, more than a saint, an angel.

"What about me, Immah," Achim pleaded with his hands outstretched.

"Did you wash your hands?" Tamar asked.

"Of course, Immah," Achim replied and got stuck in the freshly baked cake.

"So, what were you up to today?" Tamar asked.

"Oh, nothing much," Yeshua replied. "We only destroyed a whole legion of Roman soldiers," Yeshua added with a grin.

"I'm so glad to hear that, the way you two are going it won't be long before we are all free of those terrible persecutors," Tamar said, humouring her son and Yeshua.

"And we picked some pines, they are on the roof cooking, Immah," Achim said.

"Good, keep me a few, I can use them in the next batch of cakes," Tamar said with a smile.

"For sure, for sure, Lady Tamar," Yeshua said eagerly. He simply loved those cakes especially with crushed pine nuts. After eating two little cakes, Yeshua thanked Lady Tamar. She gave him six more cakes to take home for his mother and father and himself. Yeshua thanked her again, profusely.

Yeshua could hardly wait for his father to come home to eat dinner and to have Lady Tamar's cakes. Yeshua waited outside for his father. When he saw him in the distance he ran, hugged his dad. He was so pleased to see him.

"What happened? Did you win an award? Did you win a race?" Yosef was smiling because Yeshua did not often run down the hill to greet him and hug him so enthusiastically. Or did Yeshua have a special request, he wondered.

"Mmmmm," Yeshua was in heaven as he ate his cake, licking his lips. When he had finished, he continued licking his lips. Then he looked at his mother with those piercing, pleading eyes she knew so well.

"Okay, you can have a second," Miriam said smiling. She was still savouring her first one. She and Yosef would have a second the following day. She would most likely give hers to Yeshua.

At the end of the meal, Yosef told Miriam and Yeshua that he was finished with his work in Sepphoris. He would find work here in Nazareth, the farmers always had things that needed fixing. He said he felt like he needed a holiday, to get away for a few days before he started looking for work again.

"Oh Immah, can we go to Tiberias, its right by the Sea of Galilee and we can go swimming and fishing. You promised you would take me one day," Yeshua said, excitingly.

"Tiberias, that's almost a day's journey away," Yosef said. "But maybe, that hike would do us good. Yes, I did promise to take you there. What do you think Miriam?" he asked.

"Why don't you and Yeshua go? Have some father-son time." Miriam wasn't too keen to travel all that way on the donkey. She thought she too could have a bit of a holiday from the two men in her life, have some 'her' time, some quiet time to just relax. Miriam convinced Yosef to go with Yeshua. She knew Yosef and Yeshua loved freshly cooked fish straight out of the fresh water of the Sea of Galilee.

It was settled. Yeshua and Yosef would leave the next day, spend a couple of days in Tiberius, mainly at the Sea of Galilee, fishing and eating fresh fish. Yeshua could hardly wait. He packed his camping gear and his back pack, taking his sling and catapult with him just in case and pants for swimming. Yosef packed their little tent and all the fishing tackle he needed. He filled their water bag and something to eat along the road. Miriam gave her one cake to surprise Yeshua on the road. Miriam would let Gamaliel know that Yeshua would not be attending his class or their chats for a while.

Because Tiberius and Lake Galilee were almost twenty miles away, Yeshua had only been there once before. He was looking forward to this trip. He found it difficult to fall asleep, but eventually he fell asleep.

Miriam began baking some bread for them to take on their trip. Yeshua loved the smell of bread baking and even more the taste of freshly baked bread, baked with such love by his mother.

That night Miriam told Yosef that he could complete some unfinished business. They had not finished telling Yeshua why they had to flee into Egypt after he was born. How they survived in Egypt, their journey home to Nazareth. Yeshua needed to know this, and he would most probably want to know, Miriam told Yosef.

It was all settled. Yosef and Yeshua were all packed, and already asleep. Miriam too, was looking forward to the time alone. She thought of going to visit some of her friends in the village but changed her mind and decided to simply stay home and go for solitary walks in the forest. Have a holiday on her own.

Chapter Eleven
Miriam and Gamaliel

Miriam was up early, packing the bread, some fruit and vegetables for the road and the remaining cakes. When they were all packed, they woke Yeshua. His things for their adventure were already packed the night before. It was dark, just before the sun woke from its slumber, when Yosef and Yeshua set off.

Miriam stood at the front door. Kissed and hugged the two men in her life, which she loved. She told them to be careful. She prayed to Yahweh to keep them safe. She made sure they took their staffs with them, for protection. Yeshua had told her not to worry as he had his sling and catapult with him. No one and nothing dared seek to harm them. Ben, their donkey was all packed with their tent and camping gear, food and supplies. Miriam stood and waved at them until they turned the corner and were gone. She went inside, prepared a cup of hot milk to drink. The place was eerily quiet. It was usually quiet, early in the morning when she got up; relatively quiet when Yosef was gone to work and Yeshua to school. She loved the time of silence, by herself, but she knew she was not alone, that Yahweh was by her side and that Gabriel was watching over her. The frogs were still croaking. Soon she would hear the birds chirping.

When the sun rose, Miriam went outside, as she usually did. No one else was out and about. It was a beautiful day. She was glad, for it would be so lovely for Yosef and Yeshua as they travelled. She looked towards the sun. This morning there were only a few clouds. She knew they would disappear and her two men would have a warm sun following them, an open radiantly blue sky to look down upon them.

Every morning Miriam, after she had her time of prayer, offering her day to Yahweh, praying for Yeshua and Yosef and all those in her heart, all those in need, she prayed in silence, simply sitting still and contemplating again the visit of Gabriel those many years ago. After her prayers Miriam was accustomed to go outside and greet the day.

"Oh, brother sun, I greet you, thank you for the warmth you give us all, the warmth you will give to Yeshua and Yosef this day. Thank you for the life you give, without you we and everything would die. Thank you for the energy you give, without you nothing would grow and survive. Sister wind, I greet you, how calm and quiet you are. Thank you for keeping us cool, for the energy you supply, and for keeping us healthy, blowing away all that would harm us. Mother earth on which I stand, and father sky above, I honour you, for holding me, embracing me, embracing all of Yahweh's children, all creatures big and small. All of you trees, plants, mountains in the distance, all you, my brother and sister creations, I honour you and I love you. You my dear ones, here in our little garden, you dear plants, shrubs, trees that surround our little home to protect, feed and delight us, I honour, love and thank you."

After Miriam had finished her prayer to nature, to all of creation, lovingly stroking the foliage of the trees, plants and shrubs, she walked back inside and enjoyed her cup of milk which was just right. She thought of the two men in her life. Wondered what they were doing right now. She missed Yeshua for when he got up, she often took him outside with her as she gave praise to all of nature. Miriam then prepared bread and fruit for breakfast.

The day passed pleasantly for Miriam. She sat on the comfortable outdoor chair Yosef made. She sat under the little awning he built for shade in the front of their house and on the cushion she had made. Miriam decided to sit there today and not at the back yard that they shared with their neighbours. She was usually very sociable and friendly, loved sharing, having a conversation with her neighbours, especially Esther, next door. Esther was a widow who lived alone most of the time. She had two sons, who were fishermen. They lived in Tiberias near the Sea of Galilee where fish abounded. They made quite a good living as commercial fishermen. The two sons took it in turns to visit Esther and brought enough money for Esther to live on. They always brought a hamper of good things for her to eat and wear. She was well cared for by her two sons, but Miriam knew she needed more company. Miriam made sure she spent time with her, every day.

Miriam also loved going to the markets, where she met others from Nazareth, chatted with them, offer a smile, a kind word, a complement, inquire about their health, and if needed, a shoulder to cry on. Miriam had a pleasant and open personality. She exuded warmth and love, peace and joy to all those with whom she came into contact. She loved chatting with the babies and their mothers at the marketplace and the little children that were too young for pre-school. Today, Miriam decided to have time for herself, simply to enjoy her own company for a change. She sat on their front stoop in the comfortable chair that Yosef had made, and let the rays of the morning sun caress her.

Before the sixth hour, noon time, Miriam knew that the students and Gamaliel would be having a lunch break. She decided to take a leisurely walk to the school and inform Gamaliel why Yeshua was not in school today. She made sure she went around the back of her house, through the community back yard, to make sure Esther would see her so that they could chat. She told Esther about Yosef and Yeshua being away for a few days, camping and fishing in the Sea of Galilee. She said she was off to see Gamaliel and tell him, so she excused herself and was on her way.

When she arrived at the school, she saw Gamaliel chatting with a woman, a mother. Under normal circumstances this would be frowned upon, a single man, talking to a married woman in private. Yet no one frowned on this, and it was a frequent sight as the mothers often wanted to speak to Gamaliel about their children, at times under that guise, they would seek Gamaliel for counsel about their own lives. Miriam had heard the gossip that he had divorced his wife in Samaria because of her infidelities. He had done so privately to protect her, and they had made it known that he was called away on family business, instead he came to Nazareth. That was all gossip. Miriam had asked him once before about that story. He told her that he was never married, never found the right woman, was not really inclined to marriage, and had grown accustomed to being on his own. So, he was really a confirmed bachelor.

Miriam waited for the mother to leave Gamaliel. He was a pleasant looking sixty something old man. Miriam thought he would be a good catch for the widow Esther, or one of the other widows in Nazareth. But it was clear Gamaliel was not interested, he seemed to enjoy his privacy and dedicated himself to the learning and formation of the boys of Nazareth. The men too respected Gamaliel, regarded him as an Elder, sought his advice on men's business. He was elected to the men's council in the management of the civic affairs of Nazareth.

At last, the mother left. Gamaliel looked in Miriam's direction. He had seen her waiting in the shade of a sycamore tree. He smiled at Miriam. She approached. But then his demeanour changed, he was full of concern, "how is Yeshua, is he all right," he apprehensively asked.

"He's fine Gamaliel, he and Yosef are off camping."

Gamaliel breathed a sigh of relief. "Where have they gone?" he inquired.

"To Tiberias and the Sea of Galilee of course where Yeshua will swim, but mostly go fishing. They both simply love fishing," Miriam said.

"So do I," Gamaliel said, smiling.

"How are you, Miriam? Yeshua confided in me about all that you and Yosef told him about the circumstances of his birth. He said he would let you both know that he spoke to me. I hope that is all right. If you do not wish him to speak with me about such private and intimate matters, please let me know," Gamaliel said.

"No, no, of course, we do not mind, in fact we are so pleased that Yeshua has confided in you. He needs to be able to speak to someone besides Yosef and myself. And it seems as if it is the Lord that has brought you here, to guide our young child on his journey," Miriam said.

"It's strange that you say that, Miriam. When I decided to leave Samaria, I wanted to go to some quiet place and I was thinking of going to Capernaum on the northern coast of the Sea of Galilee, find a quiet place to live, and be able to fish and feed myself," Gamaliel said.

"Oh, so how come, you landed here in Nazareth?" Miriam asked.

"Good question, Miriam? How I landed here in Nazareth, I do not know. I had been a wanderer for a while, sleeping rough as I made my way further and further north. But when I passed through Jezreel and into Galilee I intended to follow a path all along the Sea of Galilee and on to my destination, but something stopped me— Do you want to sit down, Miriam, we are standing in the hot sun, let us go to the bench over there under that beautiful oak tree that Yeshua and the boys simply love to climb," Gamaliel said. "Would you like some refreshment?"

"I'd love some water, thanks," Miriam said.

While Gamaliel went to fetch water, Miriam thought how lucky they were to have a man like Gamaliel in their village. He was such a wise and good man, and so caring of the community, especially the children and the boys in particular, who adored him and respected him. He was such a good teacher and mentor to their boys. She was so glad that he was here and that Yeshua could confide in him.

Gamaliel returned with a cup of water and a piece of Achim's mother's cake.

Miriam smiled, "don't mind if I do," she said, as she and Gamaliel ate some of the delicious cake.

"Where were we, Miriam?" Gamaliel said, to pick up from where they left off.

Miriam wiped her mouth with the back of her hand. "You were talking about journeying along the Sea of Galilee and up to the town of Capernaum," Miriam said.

"Oh yes, I had decided to go and look at Capernaum or maybe Chorazin on the other side of Lake Galilee. Though we call it a lake, and some call it the Sea of Galilee, it is really a lake, or an internal sea if you like, with the River Jordan, connecting it to the Dead Sea, which is also an internal sea but no one calls it Lake Dead," Gamaliel said, smiling.

"What a queer name for the sea," Miriam said.

"Yes, indeed. But appropriate as there are no fish in the sea, nothing lives there, it is a marine hell, if you like," Gamaliel said.

"We are getting off track, Gamaliel. I was asking you how come you decided to settle in Nazareth, as you seemed to be bypassing us." Miriam was curious.

"Well, I was sleeping one night under the stars. I saw this shining star and it seemed to be right above where we are now," Gamaliel said. "It was as if the star was pointing the way for me, the way I should continue. I just headed in this direction. When I came to Nazareth and entered this village, something stirred inside of me, as if I had arrived home. Something inside of me just said, this is where I am to be, it is as if a voice said to me, this is where I want you to be," Gamaliel said.

Miriam's mouth opened slightly in astonishment. She immediately saw the hand of God. Yahweh had led Gamaliel to their village, to be here not only for the people, but especially for Yeshua and for her and Yosef. She began to feel so comfortable speaking to Gamaliel.

"I am so glad, we are so glad, that you came here Gamaliel, and you are doing so much good for our village and our children and the education and formation of our boys, especially Yeshua," Miriam said.

"Miriam, after Yeshua spoke to me, it all made sense. Yes, you are right, it was, is the hand of God. Adonai drew me here, wanted me here. After Yeshua confided in me, it makes all the more sense. I felt very honoured to help to prepare Yeshua for his mission. From the very start I sensed that Yeshua was destined for something great. He was the most gifted child I ever met. His intelligence and wisdom are far beyond his years. I would classify him as a child genius. He comes up with answers that astound me. I am humbled to be a teacher and mentor to him. Although he is extremely gifted in many ways, he is still a young child who has to navigate all the normal things of growing up," Gamaliel said.

"So true, Gamaliel, I am so grateful for your presence here and for your help. You asked me how I am. Well, I am a bit uneasy at the moment. After the appearance of Gabriel and the news he brought and the circumstances of Yeshua's birth, so much happened in those first few years. After Yeshua was born, we were forced to flee into Egypt as refugees from the persecution of Herod who wanted to kill Yeshua. We settled in Egypt, lived there for four years," Miriam said.

"Oh, what a hard life you all must have lived through at that time," Gamaliel said.

"Yes, it was a terrible time, but once we came back to Nazareth, we settled down quite quickly and things soon got back to normal. I pondered for a long time on all that happened in my life up to then, about Yeshua's future, but it became all too much for me. I felt so alone. I didn't feel I could talk to anyone for a while. Yosef has been so good, even though he doesn't much want to talk about what happened. He simply wants life to be normal. It has. I soon put those thoughts to the back of my mind. With time, I grew accustomed to us being an ordinary family bringing up an ordinary, or should I rather say an extraordinary child," Miriam said smiling.

Gamaliel smiled in return. "Yes, Miriam, it must be difficult for you and Yosef. But you are both doing a wonderful job. Yeshua is so smart and yet so playful, he has such an inquisitive mind, and yet he can get lost in the games that he and the boys play. He is very competitive and does not like to lose," Gamaliel said.

Miriam looked up at the sky to see where the sun had moved. She felt that she must have taken all of Gamaliel's lunch hour. "Oh, I'm so sorry Gamaliel for taking so much of your time on your lunch break," Miriam said.

"Please, Miriam, don't worry. Not at all, please feel free to speak with me at any time. Be at ease. I will do all I can to help you and Yosef with Yeshua's needs. Shalom!" Gamaliel said in farewell.

"Shalom! Peace be with you," Miriam returned his farewell, as she walked away feeling uplifted, with joy in her heart. As she walked home, Miriam thanked Yahweh for Gamaliel. Asked him to protect Gamaliel, give him many blessings. She prayed for the two men in her life, Yeshua and Yosef that they would be kept safe.

Chapter Twelve
Gone Fishing

Yosef, Yeshua and Ben their donkey had taken it easy along the way, resting often, not only for refreshment but to enjoy the changing landscape. They passed so many farms and greeted the farmers and their workers. They saw so many different vegetables being farmed on farms, small and large, including wheat, barley, maize, corn and potatoes, as well as many fruit trees, such as figs, pomegranates, berries, grapes, apples, and olives. Yeshua was fascinated by the vineyard, grapes that seemed to be hanging like willows, from the willow trees that he so liked. They also saw so many sheep, goats, donkeys, and of course cows grazing in the fields.

It was around the ninth hour, three hours after midday, when Yosef, Yeshua and Ben, arrived at Tiberias. It was a bustling city, so different to Nazareth, and Yeshua loved it. So many people were out and about, selling all sorts of foodstuffs, at the open markets, and all kinds of breads, those made of wheat that the well-to-do bought, and those made from barley that were much cheaper that the poor could afford. There were all sorts of vegetables and fruit to eat, and of course figs, Yeshua's favourite fruit. There were also home utensils and farm goods for sale, and trade seemed to be going on non-stop. People stood in little groups, and traders were shouting for people to buy their wares. And all those who were having their after-lunch nap would be stirring and ready for their afternoon refreshment. There were also so many domestic animals around, plenty of dogs, and children too, running about freely.

Yosef and Yeshua and Ben had taken it easy, having plenty of stops and refreshment along the way. Yosef bought some more refreshments and some bait for catching fish. He decided they would pass through the town and camp on its edge at the banks of the Sea of Galilee. It would be best to set up camp while it was still light. They made their way through the bustling city. Yeshua marvelled at the sturdy stone houses, cobbled streets, all the caravans, camels, donkeys, people and children, so many little children wondering the streets, playing their games. He could see why Zadok would like to live in a place like Tiberias. But as for Yeshua, he felt it was not for him. He loved Nazareth, with its couple of hundred inhabitants. Everyone knew everyone else, and it was a village, where everyone cared for each other, shared everything. They were like one big family. Yet Yeshua didn't mind coming to a big and bustling city like Tiberias, which Gamaliel had told them had more than twelve thousand inhabitants. Yeshua remembered trying to picture Tiberias and worked out that it had sixty times as many people living there. Sixty Nazareth's in one place, he wondered how they all got on, and how they got to know and care for each other.

Yosef got some feed for Ben, even though they brought some carrots, which they fed him, let him rest for a while and enjoy the company of other donkeys and animals that were around. In all they spent about two hours passing through and stopping along the way until arriving at the shores of the Sea of Galilee. When they approached and saw the sea, Yeshua ran on ahead. He was overjoyed to see this vast expanse of sea, and he burst into song.

When Yosef and Ben eventually caught up with Yeshua, they heard him singing. Yosef smiled. He was so glad they came on this trip together. Yeshua seemed to be in seventh heaven, enjoying every minute, and now the sight of the Sea of Galilee is the crowning moment. He could see that Yeshua could not contain himself, and had burst into song, singing a beautiful psalm.

"Abba isn't she beautiful," Yeshua said, as he made a sweeping gesture to the sea. "I wish I was a poet so I could sing the glory of the sea in poetry," Yeshua said.

"Why don't you, you are a poet, Yeshua, you just don't know it," Yosef said.

"You really think so, Abba? Okay, I'll give it a go. Here goes. We have to face the sea for this poem. Abba," Yeshua said as he cleared his throat and began his poem:

"Oh, to be by the sea, just the sea,
and you Abba, and me,
and of course, Ben the donkey.
Here, close to this vast expanse of sea,
we three can simply be.
By the sea,
like a bird we can soar free."
"Look Abba, look Ben," Yeshua continued as he stroked Ben,
"Look Ben, the sky, the horizon and the sea,
a blessed Trinity.
Just like you, Abba and me.
Oh Abba, how great it is to be
by the sea.
From our journey we may tire,
but here at the sea our hearts are on fire.
Here at the sea, we will not only survive,
we will thrive."

"Well said and well sung, Yeshua, the poet," Yosef said, getting into the same mood. "Go now and put your feet in the water. Why don't you put on your swimming pants and go for a swim, as I put up our tent for the night. Just don't go in too deep," Yosef said.

"That's okay, Abba, we have plenty of time to swim, I will take Ben for a refreshing walk along the sand, and in the water. He would love that." So, Yeshua took Ben and led him to the water. "Ben, you must be tired. Thanks for carrying our tent and all our stuff. You can rest now; we will be staying here for a few days at least. Come and enjoy the refreshing water." Yeshua led Ben along in the shallow water and splashed some water all over him. Ben expressed his appreciation with a flourish of exhilarating braying. Yeshua patted him lovingly as they strolled along the deserted coast line. But in the distance, he saw some other people, frolicking in the water. It seemed they too were camping. He wondered where they were from. When he thought Ben had enough, he turned around, and was happy to see their tent all set up for the night.

In the meanwhile, Yosef had made a fire for the night, to warm some milk, and their usual night cap, make some toast, and also to keep any unwelcome live stock or wild stray animals at bay. They did have their staffs with them too, just in case they had to ward off some unwelcome guests.

When Yeshua and Ben got back, Yeshua changed his mind, and couldn't wait to strip down to his swimming garment, and go for a swim. He ran in without stopping and dived into the gentle waves, which seemed to be calming down for the night. The shock of the coldness of the water jolted Yeshua for a moment, but he just kept swimming and splashing about until his body and the water became friends. He swam under the water, holding his breath. He enjoyed this so much. He had only been to the sea once before, it must have been more than three years ago, but it wasn't the sea really, it was the River Jordan. He remembered that Yosef had taken him and his mother camping at the river's edge, on one of their trips to Jerusalem. It was a distance from Jerusalem, but Yosef knew shortcuts, and how they could get back on the road to Nazareth, after a night and day at the Jordan River. And it was that day that Yosef taught him to swim. It took a while and a number of attempts but Yeshua found it easy to do, and very quickly, he was swimming. He remembered how proud he felt as he swam, like fish, first underwater and then above the water. He felt so at home in the water. He loved to swim. He thought about his friends Achim and Zadok, how they would have loved to be here with him frolicking in the sea. Zadok especially would be beside himself. After Yeshua had enough, he got out, dried himself, and had some bread to eat, and his favourite fruit, figs, and a drink of cold milk.

Night was approaching. "Red sky at night, fisherman's delight," Yeshua said to Yosef pointing to the sky to the west behind him. There was a smattering of clouds in sight and the sky lit up with different shades of red and orange.

"Yes, that is good sign, Yeshua. We better turn in if we want to get up early before the sun rises from its slumber and catch some fish for our meals for the day," Yosef said.

"Sure, Abba, I am actually feeling a bit tired now and ready for bed," Yeshua said. He changed into his night clothes and rolled out the soft camping bed that his mum had made. Anyhow the site on which they had pitched their tent was a grassy area a distance from the sandy shoreline and a safe distance from any high tide that may encroach.

"Don't forget to say your prayers, Yeshua," Yosef said, even though he knew he didn't really have to remind Yeshua. It was just what parents were supposed to do.

Yeshua, closed his eyes as he lay in bed and prayed, giving thanks to Yahweh for all that had happened to them that day. He relived every moment and gave thanks for all that he experienced. He gave thanks especially for the swim. He prayed that Yahweh would bless his mother and father, and all whom he loved and of course Ben. It wasn't long when Yeshua was fast asleep.

Yosef went outside and sat on the little folding stool; he had made. He looked ahead and could hear the faint sound of eddies lapping the shore. He missed Miriam; he would have loved her to be with him at this peaceful place. But he respected her decision to stay home, and for him and Yeshua to spend holiday time, quality time together. He thought of Yeshua, sleeping peacefully inside the tent. What a unique child he is, and what a privilege it is to be chosen to parent him with Miriam.

Yosef sat quietly listening to the sound of the ocean and the crickets punching the air. The sky was now dark, the sun had settled for the night. Yosef thought about the past ten years with Miriam and Yeshua. He thought again how nice it would have been to have one more child, his and Miriam's. This thought, this desire plagued him from time to time. But it became clear to him and to Miriam that they had this special calling to dedicate their lives to Yeshua, for he was destined to be the Messiah, as Simeon had said. The way he was conceived was beyond comprehension. No one would believe the truth, not in a million years, if they knew. When Yeshua does leave one day and go on his mission to liberate Israel, I wonder how he is going to do that. He is going to have a difficult time, as do all great leaders. But I am sure he will lead with wisdom and compassion. Yosef was so unsure about the future for Yeshua; he was different to other children, yet so much like other children. I will be there for him. I am here for him. Yosef entered into prayer, "Heavenly Father, Adonai, look upon your son, Yeshua who lies inside this tent fast asleep. I do not know what lies ahead for him. I am fearful. But I trust in you, that you will protect him from all harm. Do bless Miriam and me that we may continue to do all we can to help Yeshua grow into the man you wish him to be."

Yosef rose, and entered the tent quietly. He could hear the gentle breathing of his son. Yeshua was his son. He might not be fruit of his seed, but he was fruit of his love, his love for his mother, and his love for him. He quietly changed into some night clothes and then lay himself down on his homemade camping bed. It did not take long for him to fall into a deep sleep.

It was still dark; the sun was still asleep when Yeshua woke up. He heard Yosef breathing. He peeped outside and saw that the sun was still asleep. He had no idea how long he had slept, but they had planned to go fishing before the sun rose from its slumber, so he shook Yosef and called his name, "Yosef, Yosef, Abba, Abba, wake up, it is time to go fishing."

Yosef stirred, he gave a big yawn, stretched his arms and slowly got up. He and Yeshua both washed their faces and rinsed their mouths and drank some water. It was a cool morning but not too cold and the stars seem to be fading away. They could hear the sea lapping the shore. They were in walking distance, a matter of a minute or so. Yosef started a fire going with some branches they had gathered the day before, and kept covered during the night. Yosef warmed some goat's milk they had purchased yesterday, and kept in their cool insulated extra water bag. Along the way they had already eaten some of the bread Miriam had baked but there was still much more over, and it would last for days. The fruit would also last for at least three or four days but they also had dried figs as well, and raisins, and all kinds of nuts, and they were sure to find some fruit along the way.

Yeshua took some feed out of Ben's bag and went to feed him; he brayed his gratitude. When he gobbled down the feed, Yeshua gave him his favourite, a large carrot. "Did you have a good sleep, Ben? You can have a good rest these days; it will be a good while before we head for home. Abba and I are going fishing, after which I will take you for a walk along the beach and you can go and frolic in the water. How does that sound, Ben?" Yeshua patted Ben. Ben seemed to understand, as he brayed his approval, and shook his head up and down.

While Yeshua was feeding Ben and having his chat with him, Yosef was preparing their fishing sticks and attaching bait to the fish hooks. When he had finished, he called out to Yeshua that it was time to go fishing. They placed their earthen ware container, which was filled with water for the fish that they would catch, and they had some more bait in a smaller bag, they used just for bait.

Yosef and Yeshua waded into the water as far as they could. When the water reached Yeshua's waist, they stopped. And then they cast out their lines. They then waited in silence. It was eerily silent; the only sound that of the waves behind them gently breaking on the shore. The stars that the previous night filled the sky like a million little lights were now fading away. It was still dark but Yeshua and Yosef could see the faint lighting of the sky on the horizon at the edge of the Sea of Galilee.

It wasn't long when Yeshua felt the first tug of his fishing line. "Abba, Abba, I think I have a fish biting," Yeshua cried out excitedly.

"Good. You have to now walk backwards, and keep the fish on the line. When you are on the sand put your stick in the hole we made, and cover it with sand and the rocks lying there, and then put on your gloves and pull in the fish to the shore," Yosef instructed Yeshua, according to which they had already discussed the night before, as they had prepared everything for their morning catch.

When Yeshua had secured his fishing stick in the sand, he pulled in his line, making sure not to get it entangled so he could use it again. He pulled in a good size fish, big enough for a meal for him but not for Yosef as well. Yeshua and Yosef had decided that they would catch only enough fish they would need to feed them for the day. They would cook their first meal on the open fire and smoke the remaining fish to eat as their evening meal. Yeshua was so proud of himself in being the first to land a fish. He cleaned off all the sand and placed the fish in the container and then got his stick and line all ready to continue fishing.

"Good one, Yeshua, that was a nice size fish you caught, you must be proud," Yosef said smiling.

"I am Abba. That will be enough for me, for our lunch for sure," Yeshua said, beaming with pride and delight. He cast his line again and then waited. The sky was getting lighter but the sun was still sleeping, it was only that they grew accustomed to the darkness. But it wouldn't be long before they came out of the darkness into the light of the morning sun. Yosef was next to land a fish, much bigger than the one Yeshua had caught, and it would be enough for a meal for both him and Yeshua.

It had been almost a couple of hours and the sun was about to pop up into the sky, when Yeshua caught one more fish about the same size as his first. "Got another one, Abba, she's a beauty," Yeshua shouted proudly.

"Great, son, pull her in." Yeshua went through the same routine. They now had enough fish for the day and tomorrow, but Yosef remained fishing. He was so relaxed and part of the sea and enjoying the cool fresh morning air, and the sea lapping his legs and the sun now rising from its sleep. He could not look directly into the sun, but gazed to its far sides and shielded his eyes to admire the lighting up of the sky.

Yeshua returned to the shore. "What a beautiful sunrise, Abba," Yeshua exclaimed. "Where does the sun go when it goes to sleep, Abba?" Yeshua asked.

"I'm not too sure, Yeshua, but from what I've heard from those who travelled far and wide, it shines at different times in different places, so when it dips behind the horizon it is really just gone off to shine on other lands, that we cannot see, lands beyond the horizon," Yosef said.

"So, the earth must be curved, Abba, it can't be flat, for how then can the sun go somewhere beyond the horizon and shine on other lands, and how can the sun rise in the east and set in the west. Does it set, and then go under the earth and then shine on other lands and then rise on the other side of earth. Then those other lands under the earth must be upside down, Abba, that doesn't make sense, don't you think, Abba?" Yeshua said. "I think the earth must be round, Abba and not just curved," Yeshua added.

"Why don't you ask Gamaliel, when you get back to school," Yosef said. He was unable to give a clear answer to Yeshua's questions about the sun's disappearing and rising. Had he thought of it he should have asked Balthazar and his two friends who visited at Yeshua's birth, they were astrologers who would have studied the sun and its movements, as they studied the movement of the star of Bethlehem that led them to Yeshua when he was born. Yosef thought again about those moments and all that happened at Yeshua's birth, as they ate their fish in silence. They had enough to eat and now the sun was well up in the sky. But as it was still early, they decided to fish some more, just for fun. If they did catch any more fish, they would release them back into the sea. They did catch another one each, and they released them back into the sea. They continued fishing for about a couple of hours after sunrise, and then decided that was enough fishing for the day.

Yosef continued to think about the circumstances of Yeshua's birth, the visits of the angel Gabriel to Miriam announcing Yeshua's birth. Their adventurous journey that ended in a cave at Bethlehem, the visit of the shepherds, what they had heard and seen, then the visit of those men from the east, Balthazar, Caspar and Melchior, then what happened afterwards and why and how they had to flee into Egypt. Yosef and Miriam had discussed the night before that it would be a good opportunity for Yosef to tell Yeshua about their flight into Egypt, on this trip. But as Yosef thought more about it, he changed his mind. He and Yeshua were on holiday, enjoying each other, enjoying this holiday together, camping, swimming, fishing, why spoil it with such matters and besides, Yosef thought, it would be better if both he and Miriam told Yeshua all about that. He then relaxed, pleased that he did not have to discuss those matters alone with Yeshua; they would just relax and enjoy their time together.

Yeshua looked at Yosef. He was still enjoying the quiet, the stillness, the sound of the sea and the sea gulls now out and about breaking the silence. "Okay, Abba, I think I have had enough fishing for today. And I had enough to eat to last me for the day," Yeshua said, smiling.

Yeshua then washed his hands and face in the sea water as it was fresh water, and also cupped some sea water in his hands and rinsed his mouth. He kept on his wet clothes, knowing they would soon dry in the sun. He then went to Ben to take him on his promised walk. He would dress fully on his return. He loved to have the sun warm his open body.

"I'm taking Ben for a walk, Abba," Yeshua called out to Yosef.

"Good, Yeshua, don't go too far and don't be too long, I will clean and cook some more fish for later in the day, and will smoke some as well. See you in a while."

"Bye for now, Abba," Yeshua said, as he took Ben by the reins and led him along the seashore. They walked where the gently breaking waves could lap at Ben's feet. After a while, Yeshua released Ben, and said, "go into the water, Ben, and enjoy yourself." Ben made braying sounds in delight, as he waded into the surf. Yeshua could see he was enjoying himself. Yeshua sat on the sand and watched Ben kick up his heels and braying, with so much joy. Yeshua smiled, he felt so much at peace, here in this place, alone with Ben and his father. He did miss his mother but he knew she too would have a good rest from looking after him and his father.

Yeshua decided to say his morning prayers, a custom he learned from Miriam. He offered all of the day to Yahweh, all that would happen to him that day, all his thoughts, all he did, everything he offered to Yahweh for his glory. He prayed for his mother, father and all those at Nazareth, all those in need. He prayed that his people would be delivered from the scourge of Rome. He thought about all that he learned about the cruelty of the Romans. Gamaliel had brought it up from time to time, in their history lessons. Yeshua felt so protected from the Romans in Nazareth, even though Nazareth was so near to the capital of Galilee, Sepphoris. Yeshua had learned that all of Galilee, of which Tiberias, where they now were holidaying, was also a major city and that the whole of Galilee had over one hundred and fifty thousand people. Yeshua learned about how the Romans were cruel and merciless and greedy, that they had all the power and taxed all the produce that the people worked so hard to farm. Yeshua learned that everyone was taxed so heavily for the fruit of their labours, taxed over a third, sometimes almost half of the fruits of their labour. Yeshua felt sad when he had these thoughts, but he was on holiday and enjoying this time by the sea with his father and Ben. He put those thoughts out of his mind.

"Yeshua! Yeshua!" Yeshua heard Yosef calling his name.

"Come on Ben, time to get back," Yeshua called out to Ben, who just seem to ignore Yeshua, so Yeshua waded into the water and led Ben out, and they sauntered back to camp.

The smell of the charcoal fire and the fumes of the freshly cooked fish reached Yeshua's nostrils and he inhaled deeply and sighed. He had already eaten but the smell of the fish caused another rush of desire to eat.

They ate a bit more of the fish, with their hands.

"This is so yummy, Abba, absolutely delicious," Yeshua sighed.

"There's nothing in the world like freshly cooked fish straight out of the ocean," Yosef responded.

"That is true, Abba, Lady Tamar's crushed pine nuts cake is a close second, though," Yeshua said, which he knew they had brought along with them. When Achim told his mother about their trip, she immediately began baking a cake for him and Yosef. He thought of Achim and his mother and interiorly thanked them, for the cake he was soon to devour.

It was a beautiful day, the sun not too hot, just fine. Yeshua and Yosef enjoyed relaxing in the sun, lying in the sun until it got too hot. They then went in for a swim. Yeshua loved diving into the waves and coming out the other side. They then sought shelter under the nearby trees, to cool down.

The day passed peacefully for Yeshua, Yosef and Ben, and when the night came, they lit up the fire again and heated some more milk and ate the rest of the fish, with bread and finished off most of Lady Tamar's cake. Yeshua took Ben for another stroll along the beach and when they returned it was time to turn in for the night. Their fishing trip and the swimming, and fishing and eating and strolling along the seashore was perfect. They spent another couple of days at their camp by the sea, and then it was coming to an end. They would rise early the following day, just before the sun, and begin their journey home. Yeshua helped Yosef pack up all their belongings and be ready to take off, soon after they rose.

Chapter Thirteen
Refugees

Yeshua had learned from Gamaliel all about the life of the Israelites, Yahweh's chosen people, how they were slaves in the land of Egypt for four hundred years, how they were exiles, refugees in Babylon, for seventy years, so he was all ears, when his mother and father began telling him all about their exile as refugees into Egypt.

Yeshua and Josef had returned from their camping and fishing trip feeling exhilarated but also tired. That night soon after they arrived home, Yeshua and Yosef shared with Miriam all of their adventures. Yeshua boasted that he was the first to catch a fish. He showed Miriam just how big it was with his hands outstretched. Out of sight Yosef winked at Miriam, shook his head and mimicked Yeshua's hand gestures, but his hands were much closer together.

Miriam was so happy for she could see that Yeshua had enjoyed the trip with Yosef so much. She was well rested and was glad to have them both home and Yeshua could not stop telling her all about their adventures. Even how they met a snake along the way, and just stopped absolutely still, with their staffs ready to strike, if necessary, but the snake just slithered away to the other side of road, and into the bushes. They had not encountered any wild animals, although they did see a fox rushing through the bush. Yeshua told Miriam all about the sights he saw, the people he met, and described Tiberius in detail. And Yosef encouraged him to sing his poem to the sea that he had sung to the Sea of Galilee. Miriam loved it and clapped warmly after he had finished, and gave him a big hug and a kiss.

That night, when Yeshua was asleep, Yosef and Miriam had a good chat and she was a bit disappointed when Yosef told her that he had not discussed with Yeshua any of the matters he was supposed to, including their flight into Egypt. But on further discussion she agreed with Yosef that it would be better for them to do that together.

The next day, Yeshua went to school as usual. He was asked by Gamaliel to relate to the class all about his adventures, which he did with relish, and which the small class of boys, especially Zadok and Achim, enjoyed immensely. Zadok was totally engrossed when Yeshua described the grandeur of Tiberias and the breathtaking vista of the Sea of Galilee.

Yosef had taken one more day of holiday. He and Miriam had decided to tell Yeshua the rest of his story as they knew he would want, and raise it, if they did not. So, after their evening meal, after they had cleaned up everything, they decided to sit on the front porch, to make sure they would be uninterrupted, as neighbours usually gathered in the yard at the back. Yosef had his cup filled with wine and Yeshua and Miriam had their usual night mugs of hot goat's milk. It was a fine night; the stars were out in all their bright and shining glory. Yosef and Miriam had broached the subject during the day, and told Yeshua they would finish telling him what he wanted to know about his past, especially their escape into Egypt.

Yosef began. "Yeshua, you remember the dream you told us you had the night before we left on our camping and fishing trip?"

"Yes. The one when I was being attacked and Zadok came to the rescue, and when I ran for my life from a band of thugs that were out to get me, and then I found myself on the hill watching rivers of blood flowing down the hill and turning the green valley below into red with blood," Yeshua said.

"Yeshua, you remember we told you about the visit of those three men from the east who came to worship you as a babe, bringing you gifts?" Yosef began.

"Yes, I remember, how could I forget Melchior, Caspar and Balthazar, and the gifts of gold, frankincense and myrrh they gave," Yeshua said.

"After they left, we went to Jerusalem to have you presented in the temple. As your presentation could only take place late afternoon Yosef and I decided that we spend the night in Jerusalem and leave early the next morning for home," Miriam said.

"But on that very night, Yeshua, I too had a dream. In my dream, an angel appeared to me, he did not tell me his name, and he wasn't Gabriel. But he or was it a she, I don't know, this angel did look more like a girl, but I was dreaming, and it just seemed to me that the angel was a girl," Yosef said.

"Abba, angels are neither male nor female, they are pure spirits," Yeshua said.

"How do you know that, Yeshua?" Yosef asked.

"When Gamaliel first told us about angels, we had a long discussion and he told us that they were pure spirits and that they merely took on human form for our benefit, so we could see them, if that is what they wanted, what Adonai wanted," Yeshua said.

"I see," Yosef said. He continued, "well this lady angel that appeared to me in my dream, told me to get up and take you and your mother and flee into Egypt, and to remain there until she tells me. She told us to do this because Herod was about to search for you to destroy you."

"Really, why did he want to destroy me, Abba?" Yeshua asked.

"Because of all that those visitors from the east told Herod about you, your destiny," Yosef said.

"So that very night, in the middle of the night, your father woke me, and I wrapped you in warm clothes, and we fled like phantoms in the night," Miriam said.

"Phantoms in the night; that is very apt Immah, because no one travels in the dead of night, except the ghosts, the spooks, the dead, for that is why they call it the dead of night," Yeshua said grinning.

Miriam and Yosef couldn't help grinning as well; they were accustomed to Yeshua's fertile mind and imagination going off on tangents all the time, and in the middle of conversations, even serious conversations.

"As I was saying, Yeshua," Miriam continued…

Yeshua butted in with a spontaneous poem:

"When the spooks come out to play,
You have to stay away.
When the ghosts come out in the dead of night
and give you one almighty fright,
there is nothing else to do but take a rapid flight.
And run with all your might.
And don't stop until you see a light,
or the ghost is definitely out of sight."

Miriam and Yosef smiled. They were both accustomed to Yeshua going off with a rhyme or a poem at the drop of a hat, ever since Gamaliel read them poems and encouraged them to make up their own poems. They did not mind, and found Yeshua's poems and rhymes quite entertaining, but now was not the time. On second thought, Miriam did think it is a good time for some lightness of being, as they discuss such important and sombre events in the young life of their son.

Miriam continued, "your father and I took you and fled in the dead of night, when all of Jerusalem was asleep, and found our donkey, the one we had before Ben, and were gone like the wind." Yeshua always seemed to make her change her language, her way of expressing herself, when he came up with his precious, descriptive and colourful poetic gems.

"Gone like the wind. But Immah, we do not know where the wind comes from and to where she goes to, but we knew where we were going, to Egypt, because the angel told us so," Yeshua said.

Miriam and Yosef looked at each other. They knew it was going to be one of those impossible conversations to have. When Yeshua's fertile mind and poetic imagination was going off the rails. So, Miriam said, "Yeshua do you want to hear about our flight into Egypt or not. Because if you do, then you have to try and stay on track," Miriam said, with a pretended firmness in her voice.

"Okay, sorry, Immah, I am all ears, please continue," Yeshua said as he held his hands open beside his ears.

Miriam and Yosef couldn't help smiling. But Yosef continued, "It was dark. We packed our meagre belongings on our donkey. We walked quietly through the sleeping city, not wanting to wake anyone. It was eerily quiet except for the odd frog croaking. Once we came outside the city, I made space for your mother on our donkey, and we were on our way. We must have travelled for at least three hours before the sun started rising. It seemed to be following us and lighting up our path. We met no one on the way, for which we were grateful."

"It was scary, Yeshua, and I was quite uneasy travelling in the dark, and on lonely roads, with no one about. It wasn't long when we passed some farmers and saw some cattle, and eventually farmers were out milking their cows, and attending to their livestock, and their produce.

"We asked for directions, whenever we felt a bit lost," Yosef said. "There were signs that showed us the way and we took the well-trodden paths. At about the third hour, we stopped just outside of a little village and found shelter under a large fig tree. It seemed to belong to no one, so we helped ourselves to some fresh figs. We did not want to camp or light a fire. So, we ate the figs and some bread we still had with us. We rested for a while, making sure of giving the donkey a good feed and a good rest as well.

"We felt a bit more relaxed, as we were now quite far from Jerusalem and King Herod, and danger. It seemed, in the middle of nowhere. I rested under the tree and fed you, Yeshua. You were of course still a newborn baby feeding from my breast. That was all the nourishment you needed. You were such a good baby, you slept most of the way, only cried when you wanted some milk, or needed to be dried," Miriam said.

Yosef continued with the story, "After three days of travelling most of the day, from early morning until sunset, stopping only to eat and rest, not only us, but our donkey too, we arrived at the city of Ashkelon, on the coast of the Great Sea. We tried to remain as inconspicuous as possible and kept to the margins of the city, filled our water bags, purchased some more food, and were on our way. We only rested well away from the city, under shady trees, and where we would not be seen."

"What an exciting experience, we were escaping the evil rulers who were out to destroy us," Yeshua said. These were the kind of stories he and Achim invented when they were playing their games of chivalry, in which they cast themselves in leading roles as conquering heroes, saving the city as the protagonists, and vanquishing the enemies.

"It was by no means exciting, Yeshua, it was frightening. I was so scared. We just wanted to get as far away from Herod as possible, as quickly as possible, and get to the safety of Egypt, where the angel told us to go. Where would be safe," Miriam said, seriously.

"Sorry Immah, that was thoughtless of me," Yeshua apologised.

Yosef continued, "We then travelled south along the coast, still trying to remain inconspicuous, until we reached the city of Gaza. We were getting tired and it took us a bit more than a whole day to get from Ashkelon to Gaza. At Gaza we were able to refill our water bags, and also get some more fresh bread. We were able to pick some figs and berries. We passed through Gaza, continued on our journey, skirting the northern border of the Sinai desert, arriving at the next city of Pelusium, where we passed through quickly, just refilling our water bags and obtaining more food for our journey. It took us more than two weeks to travel from Jerusalem to Egypt."

"You must have walked all day, every day. Egypt is so far. So, what did you do when we reached Egypt?" Yeshua asked.

"That's another story for another time, Yeshua," Miriam said. "It is getting late. Yosef has to get up early for work tomorrow. And you have to go to school."

"Okay, Immah. Thank you, Immah and Abba, for telling me all of this, you two sure had an exciting, albeit dangerous, time with me," Yeshua said.

"Albeit?" Yosef said, frowning and looking at Miriam.

"Yes Yeshua, it was exciting even though it was dangerous," Miriam said, smiling at Yosef and Yeshua. They then retired for the night.

Chapter Fourteen
In Egypt

The day couldn't pass quickly enough for Yeshua. He wanted to know all about their exciting, albeit dangerous time in Egypt. He relived all he had heard and learned from his parents about his time, their time, in Bethlehem, the visit by the shepherds, the strange men from the east, the visit by angels protecting them, leading the way, telling them to flee into Egypt to escape that wily and cruel King Herod, who was wanting to destroy him.

Yeshua sat at the front of the house that evening, waiting for Yosef to arrive home. When he saw him in the distance he ran towards him, and was swept up into Yosef's arms.

"What's up, my son, I am not usually greeted with such excitement, you running towards me, what are you after?" Yosef said, curious about why Yeshua had run to greet him. He did not do this often, as he was usually at play with Achim, occasionally with Zadok too. But he usually did it when he had something exciting to share, or when he wanted something in particular. As they had just come back from the camping and fishing adventure, Yosef was sure, it wasn't going to be any similar request.

"Oh Abba, I just can't wait to hear all about our adventure in Egypt," Yeshua exclaimed, as they walked home hand in hand.

Dinner came and went. The usual cleaning up followed with Miriam and Yeshua doing the cleaning up while Yosef sat out front, sipping his usual goblet of wine. They ate their dinner in the back yard as they usually did, interacting with their neighbours, so Yeshua had to be content with small talk, about life in their village. The men spoke politics, their work, while the young children listened in silence, and the women served. But Yeshua would always put his penny's worth in, ask questions, give his opinion, which astounded the adults at the beginning, but they now were used to it, and often asked what he thought. The neighbours' children were all much younger or much older than Yeshua. He played with them occasionally, but his playing time was mostly with Achim. They got on like a house on fire. Yeshua liked Achim and occasionally they were joined by Zadok, which Yeshua quite liked as well and who was tolerated by Achim, for Yeshua's sake.

Bed time was approaching when they were finally able to have family time to themselves. Yosef, Miriam and Yeshua sat in front of their home. Neighbours respected their privacy when they sat there, knowing it was private family matters they were discussing.

All day, Yeshua had been thinking of his people as slaves in Egypt for four hundred years. He recalled with so much fascination all he learned about the great Exodus, how Moses led the Israelites out of Egypt right through the Red Sea, and how they lived for forty years in the desert, and how Yahweh fed them with manna and quail that fell from the sky. And how the people forsook God, and all about Moses receiving the Ten Commandments on Mount Sinai, and how finally Joshua led them into the Promised Land. And now they were going back to the place where they were once slaves. Yeshua wanted to know what it was like for his mother and father and for him too.

"So, what was life like for us in Egypt?" Yeshua asked.

"It was tough at first," Yosef began. "When we arrived, we took shelter in a cave, not dissimilar to the one in which you were born," Yosef began. "The next day, early, I went into the town to scout around for a place to stay, and also look for work. I was surprised to find many Jews living in the town. I found out that many of them were refugees like us. They had fled persecution by Herod. Some men wanted to know what brought us to Egypt. Some of them had taken part in rebellions and managed to escape Herod's armies. I told them that we too escaped the threat of persecution by Herod. They wanted to know what I did to warrant that. I told them about Herod's slaughter of all male children under the age of two, because he wanted to eliminate the birth of a supposedly newborn King of the Jews. I told them that we had you, Yeshua, a newborn son, and had to flee. They wanted to know all about this. They quickly took me under their wing, and invited me to their meeting that night. They wanted to know what I did for a living and when I told them I worked with wood and metal and could do maintenance work as well, they soon found me work. Within days we found a place to stay, a small home, not unlike our home in Nazareth, in a place called Farma, not far from Pelusium."

"It was there that you spoke your first words, and took your first steps," Miriam said.

"What were my first words, Immah?" Yeshua asked.

"Mah, for a long time you called me Mah, and your dad Ba, until eventually you were able to call us Immah and Abba," Miriam said.

Yeshua was smiling with delight, and absolutely fascinated with this adventure that he and his mother and father had experienced. He wanted to know more.

"After more than a year in Farma, we had still not heard from the angel about when we could return to Bethlehem. Your mother and I were thinking of settling in Bethlehem, where you were born, as it was so close to Jerusalem and the temple, and work was plentiful there," Yosef said.

"Yes, and as it was more than a year since we left, and we had not as yet heard from the angel, we decided to see as much of Egypt as we could. So, we travelled to and stayed in Cairo. We saw the great pyramids, built by the Pharaohs. You have to see them, Yeshua, we will go one day when you are older," Miriam said.

"Gamaliel told us all about the pyramids, how they were built more than two thousand years ago, and showed us drawings of the tallest one, the Great Pyramid, which is more than four hundred and fifty feet tall. The Great Pyramid must be much more than a hundred times as big as me," Yeshua said, looking up to the sky.

"So how long did we live in Cairo?" Yeshua asked.

"We lived there for about two years before we returned to Nazareth," Miriam said.

"I can't seem to remember any of those details Immah. I have a faint recollection of us travelling a lot on a donkey," Yeshua said. "So, the angel finally came and told us to return to Nazareth?" Yeshua asked.

"Well, not quite. When Herod died, the lady angel appeared again to me in a dream and told me to take you and your mother and go to the land of Israel, because those who were seeking your life were dead. So, we packed up our belongings. We made sure not to accumulate much, and had only what we needed. I made some furniture, which we left for our neighbours. We took only what we needed for our journey home, where we would start from scratch again, and rebuild our home. Our donkey was getting on and we knew we would have to put him out to pasture, which we did not long after we got home. That's when we got Ben," Yosef said.

"Your father and I had decided to settle in Bethlehem but Yosef had another dream, tell Yeshua about that," Miriam said.

"Yes, the same angel appeared to me in a dream and she told me not to go there, so we went back to Galilee and settled here in Nazareth," Yosef said. "We found out why we were warned not to go to Judaea. It was because Herod's eldest surviving son, Archelaus, took over from his father, and he wasn't much better than his father, in fact just as ruthless."

"Herod's other son Antipas ruled over Galilee but he wasn't as bad as his father or his brother Archelaus. We lived in relative peace in Nazareth, although we were still taxed to the bone," Miriam said.

"We travelled almost non-stop to Nazareth, we were so desperate to get there, and start our home all over again. We were fortunate to get our old home back. When we fled from Jerusalem, where we stayed overnight after your presentation and purification in the temple, we were fortunate to have met a family that were from Galilee. We told them of our plight, and asked them to let our neighbours know, to tell them that they could use our home while we are gone. We had no idea we would spend three years in Egypt. When we got back to Nazareth, we found the place spick and span. No one lived in there, except for our neighbours' relatives, when they visited," Yosef said.

"We were just so pleased to be back in Nazareth, in our own home once again," Miriam said.

"How long did it take to travel from Egypt to Nazareth," Yeshua asked.

"Ah, it took almost two weeks. We slept rough most of the time," Yosef said.

"We were lucky, the weather was fine, so we could sleep under the stars, although we did have our little tent with us," Miriam added.

"Immah, Abba, you both endured so much when I was little. I have no recollection really, of my time in Egypt. I do have this sensation of coming here when I was very young and it seemed so different to my life before that. I have to go back to Egypt one day, not only to see the glorious pyramids but just to see where we lived. I would also like to go to Bethlehem when next we go to Jerusalem, to see the stable in which I was born, and to thank the innkeeper's wife for letting us stay there," Yeshua said.

"We can do that, Yeshua. That is a nice gesture. Maybe take them a present to show our gratitude," Miriam said.

Yeshua was now ten years old and his family went to Jerusalem as often as they could to celebrate the Passover. But when they celebrated the Passover and their other feasts in Nazareth, the whole of Nazareth assembled in their community hall, which was fully decorated and transformed into a synagogue. Every third year many Nazarenes went én masse to Jerusalem for the celebration of the Passover, in a real synagogue, in the Temple. It was like a village picnic and camping adventure, as well as a religious pilgrimage. They travelled together as a group, slept in tents along the way, and camped together just outside the city of Jerusalem. Yeshua was looking forward to their next visit. It was so exciting. There is so much he wanted to see and experience. He loved being on the road, camping out, and sleeping in a tent. And he would have his friends Achim and Zadok for company. With Zadok he knew they would get up to all kinds of mischief. He also wanted to see where he was born. His mother and father promised they would take him, if they had time. He could hardly wait for that trip to Jerusalem when so many from Nazareth would go on this adventure and pilgrimage. It would happen a few days after his twelfth birthday.

On the night before Yeshua's twelfth birthday, a few days before the trip to Jerusalem for the Passover, Miriam was busy baking Yeshua's favourite cake, a fruit cake with crushed pine nuts and covered in cream. Yeshua simply loved being in the house when his mother was baking, using the inside oven. The aroma of the cake filled the house. What he liked about her cake was that she used so much cream and nuts, cream in the middle of the cake and cream covering the whole of the cake. When she had finished baking, Yeshua was allowed to lick the remains. He was so excited, about the party he would have, with some of his friends, Achim and Zadok of course. He also invited Gamaliel.

They all gathered in their back yard for an evening meal. The men were there as well, discussing politics and religion. Soon it was time for dessert. The children went wild. Yeshua and the children got stuck into the cake, ended up looking like wild animals, foaming at the mouth with cream.

Yeshua's twelfth celebration was a great success. It was his final year before becoming a teenager. It was a celebration that involved the whole neighbourhood. Miriam and Yosef had stored up enough for the meal, and enough wine to drink. There was music, dancing, plenty of chatting, laughter and amusement. Yeshua was in seventh heaven. He enjoyed the attention and felt so proud of attaining his twelfth birthday. Miriam was beaming. She knew just how unique he was and yet how so like any other child, celebrating his birthday, being the centre of attention. Yosef too was proud of Yeshua, also content that he and Miriam had done a good job of raising Yeshua. He was fast approaching maturity. What lay ahead they did not know. They would continue to do what they were doing, treating him like an ordinary child, a growing boy, giving him the best education they could, and teach him all the good values they could. When he reached fifteen, they would send him to Jerusalem to the best school run by the rabbis, the experts in the Law and the Prophets.

Miriam and Yosef were filled with joy as they watched their son at play with the other children, especially with Achim. They were like brothers. They wondered what lay ahead. But they trusted in Yahweh and they would continue to do so.

Chapter Fifteen
The Passover

The community meeting to prepare for the pilgrimage to Jerusalem ended with a celebration, with plenty of food, drink and music. Yeshua loved these gatherings, when there was so much joy and laughter. When everyone seemed so happy, forgetting all about their daily trials and tribulations, and the oppression they suffered at the hands of the Romans. The Nazarenes under Herod Antipas didn't fare too badly but the stories they heard of how Herod Archelaus treated those in Judaea shocked and frightened them. But as they came together and partied, they forgot all of this.

That night, Yeshua had to go sleep early, as did Yosef and Miriam. They planned to leave early next morning, before sunrise. It was the best time of day to travel when it wasn't too hot. They planned to travel non-stop until about noon, when they would stop for lunch and a good rest before taking to the road again until sunset, when they would camp for the night.

For days before people were packing up their tents and what they would take with them. The distance they had to travel from Nazareth to Jerusalem was sixty-four miles. That would take them at least six days on the road. The night before, Yeshua packed his backpack, with undergarments, and clothes for at least a week. They would wash their clothes in Jerusalem and be clean for the homeward journey. Yeshua would have his best robes for the celebration of the Passover. He also made sure he had his catapult and sling, as he was sure Achim and Zadok would have theirs. Of course he would make sure he had his water bag.

Yosef had made carts with canopies for protection from the sun for the women and elderly and very young children. There were plenty of donkeys to carry all their tents and belongings. They would have strong donkeys to pull the carts along, as they processed in convoy. Of course, the terrain was rough in places, and no one could really travel in the carts for those parts of the journey.

And so, it had come to pass, a long line of donkeys, carts, people, and children trekked like a long snake leaving Nazareth, before the sun even started emerging. They started in silence, some still shaking off their sleepiness. But the children were wide awake, including Yeshua. They were chatting excitedly. They first stopped about four hours later for some refreshment, when the sun was well and truly up but not really shining, as it was hidden behind an overcast sky but it did not look like there was going to be any rain. Everyone was warmly dressed for such an occasion. The clouds did eventually disappear and the sun beamed down upon them, and they could dress appropriately.

Yeshua loved being on the road, and setting up camp for the night. He felt like a gypsy, and he liked it. The children played hide-and-seek and there were so many places to hide, inside tents, behind trees, and bushes. They had so much fun. At their midday stop after lunch when the adults went for a nap, the youngsters had their athletic games, racing one another. Yeshua loved the competition and he was quite a runner and did well. Zadok of course always came first, and Achim struggling not to come last. They also loved to mimic the characters from Nazareth, and also the people they met along the way.

Donkeys carried all their stuff. Yeshua travelled with his friends, Achim and Zadok. They explored the territory when they had their first short refreshment stop, at about the third hour. Yeshua and his friends wandered off into the nearby forest, listening to all the birds chirping, whistling and making all kinds of musical sounds. They watched some of the birds feeding on the grass. Yeshua was fascinated.

"Achim, Zadok, looked at those birds, how beautiful they are, Adonai created them, they don't have to work or gather stuff in their barns, yet Adonai feeds them and supplies them all they need for nesting their young ones."

Achim looked at Yeshua fascinated; he had just seen the birds but did not think such thoughts, as Yeshua did. Zadok took out his sling and had a go at the birds that scampered in all directions, squeaking as they took flight.

"Zadok, why did you do that, couldn't you see they were having their breakfast," Yeshua reprimanded.

"Come on, Yeshua, I was just having some fun, they will settle elsewhere and eat to their hearts content, didn't you say that Yahweh feeds them, well they have plenty of grass all over the land, for them to feed on," Zadok said grinning.

"Zadok, it is not allowed for us to use that name for our God?" Achim said.

"That name that starts with a Y," Achim said, trembling, fearing that God would strike them all down.

"That's right Zadok, Gamaliel explained that out of reverence we do not utter God's name as you did, but use his other name, Adonai, instead," Yeshua said.

They then sought out trees that they could climb and from which they could watch their fellow Nazarenes going about their business. When the resting time was over, a horn sounded, indicating a time for all to come together at the camp. They made sure everyone was there, before they continued on their way. At about the seventh hour they stopped again, this time much longer, as they all had a hearty lunch. The men made a fire and the women prepared all the food that would be cooked on the fire. The children played their games or simply enjoyed running around and exploring the countryside. They were however warned not to go too far into the forest, make sure they could see the campsite and the smoke spiralling into the air.

Yeshua loved the forest, he marvelled at the different trees and bushes and saw some trees that had fallen over, the logs being eaten by termites and he thought how even when they are dead the trees provide life. He marvelled at the different shades of green, the different shapes of the leaves, how beautiful and different they all were. Their trunks are so sturdy and the intricate branches with such beautiful curves, Yeshua thought. He listened to the wind making music to which the branches of the trees seemed to dance, with the birds providing the orchestra in the background.

"Yeshua, Yeshua!" Yeshua heard Abba calling him. He hastened down the tree with Achim and Zadok. They had enough adventures in the forest. They were hungry and ready for a feast.

A fire was lit and food was prepared for a sumptuous meal. After the meal some of the adults had a nap, including Yosef. Miriam remained up and watched Yeshua and the children at play. After a short rest they were on their way again and would not stop until close to sun set.

As sunset approached, they set up camp for the night. They camped a short distance from the road, where there was plenty of grass, and in front of some forest. The men set up the tents for the night and got the fire going. The women prepared the evening meal. The bread they had baked the night before was still quite fresh and would be consumed by the children, with relish. After the meal they continued to sit around the fire, chatting and occasionally singing together. The men drank their wine and they too soon were singing with delight. The children had to stay in plain sight and could not wander into the nearby forest, as it was now dark.

When everyone had helped cleaning up and making sure they left no rubbish, they turned in for the night. Each family got together and slept in their tent. There were a few larger tents where some of their supplies were kept. The children had the duty of making sure the donkeys were well fed, and given the attention they needed.

The six days to Jerusalem passed in a similar way, but as the days passed, the families became more and more like one big family. They intermingled, got to share and know each other so much more. The men enjoyed their evening drinks, and they too shared more and more about themselves with each other. By the fourth night, Yeshua, Achim and Zadok were allowed to sleep together in a small tent, close to Miriam and Yosef.

At last, they arrived in Jerusalem, with so much excitement. They set up camp outside the city. Some of the men remained behind to look after their belongings, as the rest went into the city to walk around, browse and take in the sights and sounds of the great city.

Yeshua, Achim and Zadok, were enthralled with the big stone buildings, cobbled streets and bustling market places, and so many people around. Zadok was particularly fascinated with the Roman soldier's uniforms and swords that hung from their belts and their swashbuckling swagger, as they walked around the city, as if they owned it. Zadok stood admiring the Asmonean, the stately home of Herod, and dreamed of one day owning a place like that. The other building that impressed Zadok was the impressive Antonia Fortress that housed all the Roman soldiers. Yeshua on the other hand knew all about the cruelty of the Romans, recalling all he learned from Gamaliel, with hundreds of thousands killed by them in wars and rebellions, and almost a hundred thousand Jews sold into slavery.

Gamaliel, the week before they began their pilgrimage had spoken a lot about Jerusalem; its population swelling ten-fold with Jews from all over Israel coming for the Passover feast. Miriam held Yeshua's hand, not wanting to lose him among the crowds that flocked to the marketplaces. Everything under the sun was being sold, with sellers shouting their wares and trying to entice people to buy their goods. Those selling the lambs and goats, which the pilgrims were buying, were making a roaring trade.

Yeshua was fascinated with the building of the Great Theatre and would have liked to be able to watch one of the performances. Yeshua always took a leading role in the performances that Gamaliel organised in the community hall in Nazareth. Yeshua loved the stage, and while he was so outgoing, was however, more of an introvert in real life. He thrived on stage, and seemed to drop all his inhibitions, and come alive, as he also did when he was in group discussions or conversing on serious matters. He loved debating and relished the frequent debates that Gamaliel organised. Yeshua appreciated all that Gamaliel had taught them about the Roman occupation of Jerusalem. So, while they were free to move about the city for their strength lay in their sheer numbers, they were still wary of the soldiers and the Roman presence.

The time for the big celebration of the Passover in the Temple came. The Nazarenes went early to make sure they were part of the first ceremony. While the Temple compound was enormous it could not hold all the pilgrims that flocked to Jerusalem for the Passover so the ceremony was repeated several times. Yosef and the head of each family had purchased a lamb or goat to be sacrificed. When the Nazarene families arrived, each family with its animal, created a noise that was deafening. The Nazarenes were near the front of the families crowding in front of the gates to the Temple compound, so when the gates were opened, they all managed to be part of the first of the ceremonies of Passover.

Yeshua was appalled when he entered the Temple courtyard to see the trading that was going on, for the sale of lambs and goats was happening for those who did not have an animal for sacrificing. Yeshua noticed the moneychangers making a roaring trade in the temple. It was common knowledge that these moneychangers who changed the currency with which pilgrims came to pay their Temple tax, were ripping them off. Yeshua thought that these tables of traders and moneychangers should be outside the courtyard, in the porch, or better still, elsewhere and not within the Temple precinct, but instead they were inside in what was known as the Court of the Gentiles, and spilled over more and more into the outer courtyard. It was like a marketplace, with the selling of animals for slaughter, and the moneychangers handling their money, and there was so much noise.

Then what further disturbed Yeshua was the separation of the men from the women, for worship. Only the men and boys assembled in the Greater Outer Court, while the women had to assemble in the Women's Court, the Outer Forecourt. The Inner Court was reserved for the priests alone. In Nazareth when Yeshua attended the Sabbath celebrations, he was accustomed to the men being separated from the women, but it wasn't so pronounced, as the men stood on one side of the hall, and the women on the other, but they were close together, and it was only now that the contrast and the separation hit home to Yeshua. He was devoted to his faith but he was disturbed by this separation of the women from the men. But what disturbed him most was how the entrance to the Temple was turned into a marketplace. But he recollected himself, as the Passover ceremony began.

The priests read from their Scriptures about the story of the Exodus of the Jews from Egypt, how Yahweh freed them, and how he appointed Moses to lead them through the desert to the Promised Land, the land in which they now stood. Then there was chanting of the psalms, followed by one of the rabbi's, standing at the Pulpit and preaching to them on the significance of this night, and this sacrifice.

And then the sacrifice of the animals began. Yeshua was perplexed to see this happening on such a grand scale. Yosef and the representatives of each family took their lamb or goat and handed it to the priests' representatives, who handed it to the priests, so many of them in a row, who then began to slaughter the bleating animals, a deafening cacophony of animals howling. Yeshua found this spectacle disturbing and wondered why Yahweh would countenance, what Yeshua thought to be barbaric. Yet Yeshua recalled Gamaliel's teaching them about how some pagan religions performed human sacrifice to worship and placate their gods, and also engaged in cannibalism. But why would Yahweh want this kind of ceremony, and the making of such a mess in the temple that is supposed to be a place of worship and prayer. It is more like a slaughterhouse, an abattoir, than a temple, Yeshua thought.

Yeshua watched the ceremony unfold. He watched the bleating lambs and goats being handed to the priests and the slaughter of these poor animals, then the gathering of their blood, its sprinkling over the altar, dousing the altar with blood. Yeshua watched the countless dead animals being hung on hooks and watched their skin and innards being removed, taken to the altar and burned. Then he watched Yosef and the other family representatives receive the remains of a lamb or goat. Yeshua knew that these would be taken to camp and then roasted over a fire, and then the festive part of the Passover would begin, lasting most of the night.

During the ceremony in the temple, Yeshua recalled Gamaliel's words and his reference to the Book of Moses, where he writes about the first Passover, which gave rise to these celebrations that seek to remind and to re-enact the Passover of the Jews from slavery into freedom. Yeshua's mind was swirling during the long ceremony and especially as the long story of the Exodus was being read. He imagined himself to be there, when Yahweh spoke to Moses and Aaron at the beginning of that first Passover. Yahweh told them to tell the congregation of Israel that they were to take a lamb for each family, for each household. Yahweh told them that the lamb should be without blemish, a year-old male lamb or goat. And on a date established by Yahweh, the whole of Israel should assemble and slaughter the lambs and the goats at twilight. Yeshua thought of the mess and the screaming of the animals, and all the blood being shed, but at least it was not done in a Temple but in an open community space. Yahweh then told them to take some of the blood and spread it on the two doorposts and the joist of the houses where they ate it. They were told to roast the lamb over a fire and eat it with unleavened bread and bitter herbs. They were to leave nothing behind and whatever was left over they were instructed to burn.

Yeshua listened with such focus, as the rabbi read the words of Yahweh, uttered on that first Passover night. "This is how you shall eat it, your loins girded, your sandals on your feet, and your staff in your hand; and you shall eat it hurriedly. It is the Passover of the Lord. For I will pass through the land of Egypt, and I will strike down every first-born in the land of Egypt, both human beings and animals; on all the gods of Egypt I will execute judgements: I am the Lord. The blood shall be a sign for you on the houses where you live: when I see the blood, I will pass over you, and no plague shall destroy you when I strike the land of Egypt."

"This day shall be a day of remembrance for you. You shall celebrate it as a festival to the Lord; throughout your generations you shall observe it as a perpetual ordinance."

This is what we children of Israel, chosen ones of Yahweh are doing on this night of nights, Yeshua thought. He listened as the rabbi continued the long reading, but his mind wandered. How could Yahweh be so cruel as to murder innocent children and animals? He knew about how long his people had suffered at the hands of Egyptians, how Pharaoh too had slaughtered innocent children, made slaves of his people, how Moses escaped such a fate to be protected by Yahweh, for he was to lead the Israelites out of Egypt into freedom. Yeshua recalled all of Gamaliel's teaching about how obstinate Pharaoh was and how he kept changing his mind after each of the nine plagues. This slaughter of the innocents was the final straw, the final plague. Pharaoh had to be convinced of the might of Yahweh who had power over life and death. There was no other way to persuade Pharaoh. So, it did come to pass.

Pharaoh finally relented, but again changed his mind, pursued the Israelites, but again he was thwarted, and drowned in the Red Sea.

Yeshua's ruminations stopped as he listened to the words being read about how the sea was parted, how the Israelites passed through the sea untouched, then how the sea closed over Pharaoh and his armies, drowning them all. Yeshua thought about how Moses was protected by Yahweh because he was chosen to lead the people out of slavery into freedom. Yeshua thought about his own situation, how he too was protected from being killed my Herod, who slaughtered all newborn males. He thought about what his mother and father had told him about their flight into Egypt. Yeshua, as he listened to the flight out of Egypt, thought how ironic it was that he and his parents had to flee back into Egypt to escape Herod. Why was I spared, what is my destiny, what does my heavenly Father, Yahweh, Abba, want of me?

The singing disturbed Yeshua's musings. After the reading a cantor stood in front of the Temple and led the congregation in the singing of the Song of Moses. The sound of thousands of voices filled the Temple as Yeshua joined in the song:

I will sing to the Lord, for he has triumphed gloriously,
horse and rider he has thrown into the sea.
The Lord is my strength and my might,
and he has become my salvation;
this is my God, and I will praise him,
my father's God and I will exalt him.
The Lord is a warrior;
the Lord is his name.

Pharaoh's chariots and his army he cast into the sea;
his picked officers were sunk in the Red Sea.
they went down into the depths like a stone
Your right hand, O Lord, glorious in power—
your right hand, O Lord, shattered the enemy.
In the greatness of your majesty, you overthrew your adversaries;
you sent out your fury, it consumed them like stubble.
You blew them with your wind, the sea covered them;
they sank like lead in the mighty waters…

Yeshua and the throngs continued singing the Song of Moses until it ended with the words:

When the horses of Pharaoh with his chariots and his chariot drivers went into the sea,
the Lord brought back the waters of the sea upon them,
but the Israelites walked through the sea on dry ground.

Yeshua was a bit disappointed that it wasn't a woman that sang Miriam's song, as Moses wrote: "Then the prophet Miriam, Aaron's sister took a tambourine in her hand, and all the women went out after her with tambourines and with dancing. And Miriam sang to them:
Sing to the Lord, for he has triumphed

Gloriously;

horse and rider he has thrown into the sea."

But Yeshua knew that at their celebration at the camp site there were women among them who played the tambourine and with their music there would be plenty of singing and dancing. Yeshua loved to dance. It intrigued him to learn that the Israelites danced to the musical sounds of the tambourines of Miriam and the women. Yeshua would have loved to hear the tambourine being played in the temple, by women.

The ceremony came to an end. Everyone felt uplifted. They felt as if they were with the people of Israel on that first Passover night, with them as they fled, led by Moses through the Red Sea, into the desert, onto their way to the Promised Land.

The men collected the remains of the lambs and goats that were sacrificed. These would be roasted on the fire at the campsite. When they arrived back at the campsite the fire was rekindled and soon it reached into the air and smoke spiralled into the heavens. When the coals were ready, the lambs and goats were put on the spits and roasted and the smell sent everyone into a spiral. Everyone's mouth began to water.

A great feast ensued, although they still ate unleavened bread and bitter herbs as part of the meal. The unleavened bread was to recall the haste with which the Israelites prepared to flee out of Egypt, and the bitter herbs was a reminder of all that the people suffered at the hands of the Egyptians. The unblemished lamb was of course the centrepiece of the Passover celebration; it was the blood of the lamb on their doorposts and lintels that saved them.

Besides the religious significance and rituals, it was also a celebration of their freedom and their grace of being the chosen people of Yahweh. There was plenty of food to eat, with the lamb and the goats, and plenty to drink, as all the families of Nazareth gathered together around the campsite. When they all had their fill, the music filled the air, tambourines, cymbals and drums got everyone onto their feet, dancing and laughing, singing, and the whole place was alive with joy and togetherness. Yeshua was enjoying himself.

Chapter Sixteen
Bethany and Bethlehem

The next day everyone got up late, with many having a hangover. Even Yeshua enjoyed a bit of a sleep-in, but as soon as he woke, he was up. He didn't want to miss anything. He went to search for Achim and Zadok, as they had slept with their families last night. The three of them gave themselves a quick wash, drank some milk, ate some of the leftovers, and were gone. They wanted to explore the forest. Miriam was up and she told them not to go too deep into the forest, and to be careful. As Zadok was with them she felt a bit more secure, as he was much older, and had recently celebrated his fifteenth birthday.

Yeshua, Achim and Zadok walked among the trees. At that time of the morning the birds were chirping wildly. They saw some birds, wag tails and bee-eaters feeding on the grass. They climbed onto rocks and up trees, and sat admiring the view below them. Sitting high up in the trees gave them a feeling of being mighty and powerful. All three of them loved the bush, walking among the different trees and bushes that came in all shapes and sizes. They stopped to inspect a huge tree that had parts of its large branches lying on the ground but still attached to the trunk.

"Must have been a storm to knock this tree over," Zadok said, as they inspected the dead branches.

"Just look at those termites, they must be having a feast," Yeshua said.

"I can't see any termites, Yeshua," Achim replied.

"You can't see them, but you can see they are there, by their handiwork. The way the wood of the trunk is so finely chewed and almost like brown dust, is all their work. They are termites all right," Yeshua said.

"Wow, they sure are mighty little critters to chew these branches to dust. Look at that ant heap over there, gosh, isn't it amazing what such little devils, can build like that?" Zadok said.

"Truly amazing Zadok, amazing what can be accomplished if we work together," Yeshua said.

"An example of strength in numbers, hey," Achim said.

The three of them poked around among the fallen leaves with their sticks to see if there were any insects crawling around.

"Hey, the soil here looks quite damp and brown and rich, I bet there must be lots of worms here," Zadok said, "let's poke around, tickle the worms, and get them to come out and play"

They quickly looked around for branches they could use. They sharpened the ends on a rock, then they each pressed the end of their sticks deep in the ground, started twirling them round and around, singing, "little worms, little worms, come out and play, come out and dance for us this day."

"Here's one, here's one," Zadok screamed, as a little worm wiggled its way to the surface. Soon both Yeshua and Achim also had worms coming to the surface. Zadok started poking one with the end of his stick.

"Don't do that Zadok, you're hurting and frightening the worm," Yeshua reprimanded.

"I'm not, I'm just tickling the little critter, and getting it to dance," Zadok responded.

After a while of watching the little worms dance, they left them and wondered yet deeper into the forest to explore.

"Yeshua! Yeshua!" Yeshua and the boys heard someone calling.

"It's my father," Yeshua said.

"Coming Abba, coming," Yeshua yelled back.

The three friends walked back out of the forest.

"Time for breakfast. Your mother was a bit worried you might have gone too deep into the forest," Yosef said.

"You needn't have worried, Abba. We left good tracks on the forest ground. It seemed that it hadn't been disturbed for a long time, until we came along," Yeshua said.

"Shalom, shalom, Mister Yosef," both Achim and Zadok greeted Yosef simultaneously.

"Shalom, Achim, shalom Zadok, did you have a good time in the forest."

"We sure did, Abba, we sure did," Yeshua replied.

The Nazarenes planned to remain in Jerusalem for another four days before returning to Nazareth. They came all this way and they wanted to make the most of it. They had all prepared and saved up for this trip, which were both a pilgrimage and a holiday for them all.

After they had finished their breakfast, Yosef and Miriam told Yeshua that they were going to Bethany for the day, where Yosef had some cousins, he wanted to visit.

"Bethany is only about two miles, Yeshua; we should be there within the hour. We will spend most of the day there and return before sunset," Yosef said.

Yeshua was delighted; he had not been to Bethany before, and had not met that part of his family yet. He was eager to see Bethany and Yosef's cousins.

"Shalom! Shalom! Shalom!" There was much greeting and kissing and hugging as they arrived in Bethany and Yosef introduced Miriam and Yeshua to his relatives. They were a big family of nine children, seven girls and two boys. The boys were the last of the children and were two and four years old, the eldest was eighteen and it seemed that they were all born two years apart. Yeshua was thrilled to meet his cousins and so many of them in one family. He got on well with the girls. They flocked around him, taking delight to meeting their handsome cousin.

Yeshua was quite at ease among all the girls. They took him around Bethany and introduced him to all their friends. Bethany was a little town, more like a village, about a third the size of Nazareth with less than forty homes. They were poor and many were former Galileans who came here over the years to find a living in nearby Jerusalem, only two miles away.

Judith, the eldest of Yeshua's cousins, was a beautiful girl with long flowing hair. She did most of the talking. Yeshua discovered that their father was away most of the time, working, and that she helped her mother to keep all the children in line. Yeshua observed how they all respected Judith. They were a delight to be with, and Yeshua felt so different being among so many girls, who were so enamoured of him. He loved the attention and the girls were so proud to show off their cousin to their friends.

The twelve years old, the fourth born, Ruth was Yeshua's age. She was just as beautiful as Judith, with hair even longer. Her hair cascaded like waves over her shoulders. Yeshua found her so attractive and got so much delight in just looking at her. Yeshua was not accustomed to play with the girls in Nazareth, although there was Rebecca, who was his age, whom he sometimes met and with whom he chatted. Now finding himself in the company of so many girls, he found a new joy, especially being with Ruth.

Ruth in turn found Yeshua very attractive. He was her cousin, but she had never met him before and she felt a strong attraction to Yeshua. She found him so handsome and liked Yeshua instantly. And he was so clever too.

Yeshua felt something stir inside of him when Ruth was nearby. When she spoke and they accidently brushed up against each other, he had the first stirring of adolescence attraction for the opposite sex, and he was enjoying it. He felt that he loved being in their company and that they were so intelligent and wise. He enjoyed chatting with Ruth and Judith. He loved the female attention and adulation, with the girls fussing all over him.

"That's the house of Lazarus, and his two sisters Martha and Miriam. They live with their mother, their father died only last year. They are barely teenagers, yet they care for their mother, who is quite sickly. Lazarus is a bit older than them but he always seems to be away somewhere," Judith told Yeshua. Just then Miriam and Martha came back from the markets carrying groceries and Judith introduced their cousin Yeshua from Nazareth to them. Yeshua took an instant liking to Martha and Miriam. Martha was the more outgoing, whereas Miriam seemed quieter and shyer. They chatted for a while, and then parted.

"Hope to see you again, Yeshua, you are always welcome whenever you come to Bethany," Martha said, as they said their goodbyes. He watched them walk away, and then saw Miriam turn around and smile at him, and his heart melted. She had not said a word when they met as Martha did all the talking, but her smile said so much. Yeshua felt a warmth stir inside of him and a deep feeling, a premonition, that he and Miriam would become good friends.

The day passed so quickly and already it was the eleventh hour. It was time to head back to Jerusalem before the setting of the sun. They said their goodbyes and Yosef promised to see them again next time they came to Jerusalem. The girls almost smothered Yeshua as they wanted to touch him, say their goodbyes, begging them to come and visit again.

The next day, Yeshua caught up with Gamaliel, who was also on the pilgrimage with them. Gamaliel had not stayed at the camp. He stayed with some friends in Jerusalem. Gamaliel asked Yeshua about his stay so far. Yeshua told him everything that happened, his visit to Bethany and meeting up with his cousins. Yeshua spoke of his meeting with Miriam and Martha and the feelings he felt for Miriam, that they would become good friends.

Gamaliel was accustomed to Yeshua discussing matters not only of the mind but also of the heart with him, matters no young twelve-year-old would ever think of discussing with him. Yeshua had an innocence that astounded Gamaliel. Yeshua spoke of how he noticed these feelings that he now had towards the opposite sex.

Gamaliel then said, what is happening in you is quite natural, Yeshua; it is the way God created us male and female with an innate attraction for each other. When we get back to Nazareth, I think it may be a good time for us to have time in the class to discuss these matters.

"I look forward to that Gamaliel," Yeshua said.

When Gamaliel left, Yeshua approached his mother and father and reminded them that they had promised to take him to Bethlehem to show him the stable in which he was born.

"As it is not too far, just about six miles we could do it in two to three hours at a leisurely pace. If you like Miriam, we could take Ben along," Yosef said.

"Yes, that would be good. I don't mind the walk, but I think it would be good for Ben to have some exercise and a change of scene."

Yeshua was excited. Bethlehem, he learned was about the same size as Nazareth, and had about the same number of residents. But Yeshua wanted to go there simply to see and be in the place where he was born.

The family decided that they would leave after breakfast and take a leisurely walk, have time to admire the scenery along the way, and arrive there in time for their midday meal. They decided to stay the night, in the inn, where they stayed sometime after Yeshua was born, and then return to camp the next day.

Yeshua watched the farmers working in the fields, growing barley and wheat and corn, and looked at the sheep, goats and cows in the fields, either grazing or just standing about doing nothing, enjoying the sun and the gentle breeze. Yeshua also greeted all the trees as they passed, he loved trees and spoke to them as if they were persons, complimenting them on their stature, their beautiful and curvaceous stumps, branches, the luxurious display of their leaves, their vibrant and different colours and the intricate shapes of their leaves. When he came across any of the birds, he listened to their chirping, and whistled back to them, or spoke to them, greeting them. He also stopped to admire the wild flowers and grasses and inhaled their scent.

Yosef and Miriam marvelled at their child, how in tune he was with all of nature. He was their only child, so he called all the trees and shrubs and wild flowers his brothers and sisters. But Yosef knew he got this love from Miriam, for she loved nature with a passion. When Yeshua was little, she would take him out among the trees and plants and wild flowers. He shared his mother's great love for all of nature.

They stopped so many times. Walking at a snail's pace, so as to admire the changing scenery. They stopped to speak with those they encountered along the way. Yeshua loved to greet people, with his warm smile. While he was shy by nature, he somehow grew to be outgoing and engaging with children his age and all ages, and with grownups as well. He simply loved people, to be with them, irrespective of how they appeared, for in Jerusalem he spoke with the beggars and homeless people and he prompted Yosef to give them some coins or whatever food they had with them.

Both Yosef and Miriam marvelled at their young son who radiated such love, peace and joy all around him, to all of nature, all of creation and all Yahweh's creatures and all people with whom he came into contact. Yosef knew that Yeshua got this love for nature and people, and respect and love for all, irrespective of their outward appearance, or life circumstances, from his mother. Miriam had this effect on him as well.

It was well after noon when Yeshua, Yosef and Miriam arrived in Bethlehem. Yeshua was filled with excitement. "This is my town; this is where I was born. So, if the emperor ever has another census I would have to come here to register, wouldn't I?" Yeshua said.

"I suppose so," Yosef replied.

The family went straight to the inn. They were pleasantly surprised that the innkeeper was the same who turned them away on that night when Yeshua was born. He did not recognise Miriam and Yosef. Neither did he recognise Yeshua, of course, because Yeshua was just a newborn baby when he last laid eyes on him. After greeting him, Yosef introduced the family and told the innkeeper their story. Then his eyes were opened.

"Of course, of course, I thought I recognised you from somewhere. My word, after all these years, and this must be your baby, all grown up, what a fine young lad," he said with positive joy, as he laid his hand on Yeshua's shoulder and looked him over as if he was his own son.

"Joanna, Joanna!" He cupped his mouth with his hands and shouted for his wife.

Joanna, came running, almost breathless, "What's it, what's wrong?" she said, unaccustomed to such an urgency in her husband's shouting. She was expecting the worst but was so relieved when he told her about Yeshua and Miriam and Yosef.

Joanna's mouth opened wide and her hand covered it for a long while before she shut her mouth and was able to speak. She was absolutely thrilled to see Yosef and Miriam, and especially Yeshua, before whom she bent down on one knee and hugged him, as if he were her long-lost child, "you have grown into such a fine boy, and so handsome," she said, as she gazed at Yeshua. "You were such a tiny baby, when you were born," she said, gesturing his size with her hands. "Nashon, quickly, go set a table for our guests," she instructed her husband, who obeyed immediately.

Miriam smiled, at Joanna giving such instructions to her husband, and him obeying without any problem. It would usually have been the man instructing the woman of the house.

"And get a room ready for them, our best one," she called out, as he was already out of sight. "I'm so sorry, Yeshua, that you were born in such humble surroundings, but it was the time of the census and we were full and every little space was occupied in our inn. But you did stay here as soon as a room became available. I remember that night you were born so clearly. I was there helping the midwife, and saw you coming into the world, Yeshua, you were such a beautiful baby. I remember some shepherds came knocking on our door asking about where the newborn king is? They were just ignorant shepherds, so I thought they were daft, the stable was no palace and no place fit for a king.

"But it was such a strange night. These shepherds brought a lamb as a present and your father roasted it. And then sometime after, three strange men from faraway in the east came, they were definitely upper class and wore rich garments and came bearing gifts for the newborn king. That made me really curious. I thought what the shepherds were saying was ridiculous but when these fine and sophisticated looking gentlemen said the same thing, I was perplexed. If this child is a king, how come he is not born in a palace, surrounded by guards and his royal household? I just couldn't figure it out, and just dismissed it from my mind. And now I can see you are definitely not dressed like a king and you would not be travelling like this on a donkey, and without your guards and entourage," Joanna said. "Come let me show you to your room," she said with obvious joy.

She led them to a sumptuous room with a basin of water for them to wash, and clean towels were laid out on the large bed covered with fine blankets. And on the side table was a bowl of fine fruits and a flask with wine and another with water.

"Wow, what a fine room, Immah, fit for a king," Yeshua said in jest, with a broad smile on his face, which brought a smile to Miriam and Yosef as well. They were grateful for their warm reception, but glad all the adulation was over.

After they had washed and had some fruit, Yeshua asked if he could see the stable and the place where he was born. Miriam and Yosef approached Joanna and Nashon. They were most accommodating. They led them to the cave that had served as, and still served as a stable for their animals, and then left them there.

Yosef and Miriam both felt like falling on their knees, all the memories of that sacred night came flooding back. The place was still a stable and it smelled of animals. Miriam pointed out to Yeshua, the very spot she gave birth.

Yeshua cleared the spot. He just knelt there motionless and touched the spot where he was born. He was silent as he did this and Miriam and Yosef remained silent too. Then Yosef looked around for the manger, but it was nowhere to be found.

"I had cleaned this whole area here and filled it with clean straw, for you and Miriam and then found an old disused manger, which I cleaned up and filled with clean straw and your mother after feeding you wrapped you in swaddling clothes and laid you in the manger, right here," Yosef said, placing a foot at the spot.

"Right here?" Yeshua asked rhetorically, as he too placed his foot on the spot of the manger. He remained silent for a moment, as if trying to remember that moment, which of course he couldn't. He lay on his back on the spot looking at his mother and father, who were frowning and smiling at the same time.

Yeshua had his hands clasped in a fist and to his mouth and he spoke, "Immah, Abba, thank you so much for all you have done for me, since I was born in this spot. It is a sacred spot for me, and I am so grateful you have brought me here. And now I am hungry," Yeshua said with a smile, as he jumped to his feet.

The next morning Joanna fussed over them and ordered Nashon around, much to Miriam's amusement. Yeshua also found it endearing because it was so unusual to see a woman bossing a man about. They were treated to a sumptuous meal. After the meal they packed up their belongings and made sure that Ben had a good feed and were on their way back to Jerusalem.

Joanna and Nashon said their goodbyes with a fuss, and refused to take any money from Yosef. They felt something special for this family, whose child was born in such poor circumstances in their stable, and to whom both shepherds and strange men, dressed in strange rich garments, also came bearing gifts for a newborn king. What would become of that child they had wondered then, and now they saw him, and he was like any other child.

Yosef and Miriam showed Yeshua the rest of the town, on their way out. They took their time back to the camp site, as they had all day. They had another day in Jerusalem before heading back to Nazareth.

The next day, Achim asked Yeshua if they could spend the day together, he wanted Yeshua all to himself, without Zadok.

"For sure, Achim," Yeshua replied.

"Yeshua, I asked my mother if you could sleep with us, and if you could travel with us back home tomorrow," Achim said.

"I'll ask my mother and father. I'm sure that will be okay," Yeshua replied.

When Yeshua returned from his time with Achim, he approached his mother and father and asked, "Immah, Abba, Achim asked if I could sleep over with him and his mother, tonight, and also travel with them tomorrow?"

Miriam looked from Yeshua to Yosef and gave a slight nod and waited for Yosef to respond. Yosef took a moment, then said, "That's okay, Yeshua, I'm sure Achim and his mother would love you spending the night with them and travelling with them tomorrow."

And so, it happened. Yeshua packed his things in his backpack and went off to Achim's tent, which was on the other end of the campsite. He was thrilled to sleep over and to be travelling with his dearest friend and his mother.

Chapter Seventeen
Yeshua Is Lost

Yeshua and Achim stayed up late that night, sitting outside their tent chatting. Achim's mother, Tamar, was delighted, as she lay on her bed listening to them. She was so pleased for her son, to have such a good friend. She knew what a good influence Yeshua was on Achim. Without wanting to, for she wanted to see them asleep first, she started nodding and fell fast asleep.

When Achim and Yeshua eventually entered the tent, they found Tamar fast asleep, so they stopped chatting and turned in for the night.

The next day there was much commotion, as everyone was busy packing up the last of their belongings on the donkeys and getting ready to set off for Nazareth. They all had a good time but were now yearning for home. They decided to go non-stop until after noon, when they would stop for a lunch break.

"Shouldn't we go and check on Yeshua, Yosef?" Miriam asked.

"Okay, I'll go," Yosef said and headed off to the other side of the campsite and found the boys packing their stuff and ready to go. He greeted Tamar and the boys and then headed back. "They're fine, Miriam. We'll leave them alone, and catch up with Yeshua at the end of the day," Yosef said.

The convoy of people, carts, and animals snaked their way out of the campsite, which they left clean and clear of all rubbish, and made sure the fires were doused and dead. They passed through Jerusalem and had one last look at the Temple, the sight of so much activity and commotion a few days ago, when they celebrated the Passover.

When Yeshua saw the Temple, he told Achim and Tamar he would be popping into the Temple for one last time, then he would meet up with his mother and father who were further towards the back of the convoy, and then catch up with them again. And so, it happened.

Yeshua entered the temple and found it relatively empty. There was a group of men sitting in a nook to one side of the portico, in a circle, about ten of them. They seemed to be discussing serious matters, as they were deeply engrossed. As he went closer, he discovered that they were involved in serious debating on matters of the Law and the Scriptures. They must be the high priest, Pharisees and the rabbis, and the priests, for some of them were part of the Passover celebrations. Yeshua, courtesy of Gamaliel, knew all about the religious hierarchy and who wielded power among the Israelites. The elite were the chief priests, Elders and Scribes. The leaders among the Pharisees were referred to as rabbis, some of whom operated as priests. Then there were the Sadducees, who were like the Pharisees but differed from them because they did not believe in the resurrection of our bodies on the last day. Yeshua recalled Gamaliel's story about when he was a Scribe, who with his knowledge of the Law could draft legal documents, for their role was to interpret and regulate the Law but not interfere or meddle or assume any role in the guidance of the people. But many people came to Gamaliel for guidance and sought his counsel not only in matters of the law but in religion, in matters of the spirit, and their relationship with Yahweh. Because of this, the Pharisees condemned Gamaliel, and ordered him to desist, as spiritual mentoring was the domain of the Pharisees, who alone could be rabbis.

Yeshua did not have a high opinion of the Pharisees from what he learned of them from Gamaliel, and also because how they treated his beloved teacher. He approached the group and sat down near to them, listening as they debated. They were oblivious to his presence but he was totally engrossed in their debate. Yeshua was fascinated and became engrossed in all they were saying, and debating, as he listened to these men. They were so educated, knew the Law and Prophets and the Scriptures to the finest detail. Yeshua sat and listened with full attention.

Yeshua was oblivious to how long he sat there listening to these learned men. He wanted so much to pick their brains, ask questions, but he was content to listen. After what must have been a couple of hours, a chief priest, whom Yeshua learned from listening to the group, was Ananias, stood and told the group that they would disperse for refreshment, and come back for their discussion within an hour.

Yeshua remained in the Temple. He was pondering on all that was being discussed. He appreciated all that Gamaliel had already taught him, but these men were discussing and debating the finer details of the Law and the Prophets, the Kings, the Scriptures. Yeshua wanted to know more and to learn all he could. Yeshua continued to sit in the Temple, praying and reflecting and dreaming. He completely lost his sense of time. His mother and father had discussed with him about his going to Jerusalem when he turned fifteen to study the Law, the lives and teachings of the Prophets, the stories of the kings, the history of the people of Israel, their relationship with Yahweh, and all about Yahweh.

Yeshua was now more than ready to come to Jerusalem to learn, but he had to wait three more years. He knew he would learn so much more from Gamaliel and that would give him a good foundation to become an expert in the matters of Yahweh and his relationship with us. Yeshua wanted to know what his mission is, what Yahweh, his heavenly Abba wanted of him. He was reflecting on the debate the group had on the Messiah, and he recalled what his mother and father told him about the circumstances of his birth. He recalled that momentous discussions he had over several evenings with them about how he was to be a king, how his mother was told by the angel Gabriel that he would be great, and will be called the Son of the Most High, that he would receive from Yahweh the throne of his ancestor David, and that his kingdom will last forever. Those words had haunted Yeshua. He could not fully understand them. They were so farfetched that he had put them out of his mind. But listening to these men, these thoughts came flooding back.

Yeshua was brought out of his reverie by the shuffling of the feet of the men who returned to their station to continue their debating. One of the men recognised Yeshua and engaged with him, asking what he was still doing here in the Temple, as he had noticed him before they went for lunch.

"I was praying and pondering all you men have been debating, and I had so many questions I wanted to ask," Yeshua said.

"Well then, come and ask them?" he said to Yeshua. The man introduced himself to Yeshua as a Scribe named Amos. Amos brought Yeshua to the group and introduced Yeshua. The rest of the men frowned and were not too pleased with Amos for bringing this youngster to them. They had serious matters to attend to, and to discuss. But Amos told them that Yeshua had been listening to most of their morning's debating, and that he in fact had listened to their debating the ceremony of the Passover, and had listened intently to all of the discussion, and was very interested in all they debated, that he had listened intently to Ananias' talk, and all that was then discussed. The group were surprised that such a young person could and would want to listen to them for so long a time; surely what they were discussing would be way beyond his comprehension.

"Well, young man, tell us why you were sitting there all morning and listening to what we were saying," Ananias asked.

"I am Yeshua of Nazareth, son of Yosef of the house of David, and Miriam of Nazareth. I am twelve years old and we came to Jerusalem for the celebration of the Passover. When I turn fifteen, I will come to Jerusalem to study all that you learned men have been discussing," Yeshua said.

Ananias and the rest of the group were now interested and wanted to know about this young boy for it would be up to them whether he would be accepted or not. So, they questioned him about the Scriptures, the story of the Israelites, Yahweh's chosen people and his relationship with them. They were astounded with Yeshua's knowledge, eloquence and command of their language and knowledge of their history and the Law and the lives and teachings of the prophets, as well as the astuteness of the questions he asked about Yahweh and the Messiah, the kind of questions no other child his age had ever asked, no other child of any age for that matter. He had an inquisitive mind and a grasp way beyond his years. After a while, Ananias dismissed Yeshua and told him he could return to where he was sitting in the Temple, and that he could continue to listen and learn from what they were talking about and debating.

Yeshua though had to go to relieve himself and have a drink and something to eat. He was glad he had his backpack with him, for there was some bread and a pomegranate and some figs. He sat outside and watched the people go by. From the position of the sun, he only now realised how much time had passed. It must be closing in on around the ninth hour, mother, father and the rest of the Nazarenes would be far on their journey home, as they left almost nine hours ago. It would be foolhardy for me to try and catch up to them. I'll just have to stay in Jerusalem. I'm sure they will come back to find me, Yeshua thought. Yeshua was so caught up with the debates of the men, he lost all sense of time and the seriousness of his predicament. He trusted in Yahweh.

After about an hour, Yeshua then went to the marketplaces and browsed around, looking at all the household foodstuffs and paraphernalia on sale. He sat for a while on a bench and watched the people going about their business, no one bothered to talk to him, although he greeted, 'Shalom' to all those who caught his eye. What shall I do, Yeshua finally asked himself. He prayed, "Yahweh, my heavenly Abba, I am lost, my parents are far gone on their way to Nazareth, I pray for a place to stay until they come back and find me." Yeshua then decided to return to the Temple. He found the learned men still debating intensely. He sat and listened.

After a couple of hours, Amos got up and left the group. He had already noticed Yeshua's reappearance. He approached Yeshua and said, "You are still here, where are your parents?"

Yeshua then told him of his predicament. "Come with me," Amos said. Yeshua followed. "You better stay with me for the night. It is not safe to be on the streets by yourself at night time. You can bunk down with my two sons. Elijah is your age, a year older actually, and Joel has just turned eight."

Yeshua was most grateful. He gazed heavenwards and silently said, "thank you Yahweh."

Yeshua met Amos's wife, Sarah, a petite lady, who had an infectious smile. Once Amos told her of Yeshua's predicament all her maternal charms came to the fore and she made Yeshua feel at home. She prepared a hasty but delicious meal of vegetable soup and thick chunks of bread. Yeshua got on well with Elijah. Joel was rather quiet. But Yeshua found them both to be just as warm and kind as their parents. Yeshua enjoyed the evening with his new found friends and was most grateful to them, for he was a stranger, and they took him in.

When Yeshua went to bed he prayed for his mother and father, and prayed that they were safe, and he prayed to Yahweh for Amos, Sarah and the boys that Yahweh may bless them for the kindness they had shown him. Yeshua thought about his mother and father and wondered what they were doing, and how distressed they must now be for at this very time he was sure they would be most distraught at his not being with Achim or with anyone else in the community.

On the next morning Amos was up early baking bread, the aroma woke Yeshua and he got up, washed, and found Amos in the corner of the house near the back entrance where there was an inside stove, it had two sections. The top was used for cooking and the bottom oven was for baking small loaves of bread. He used straw and pine cones to make the fire. Yeshua was surprised to see Amos baking bread. He had never seen a man baking bread before. He missed his mother and father. He wondered where they were. He surmised that they would be on the road back to Jerusalem to look for him. When the rest of Amos's family were up and about, they sat down for breakfast of bread and milk and fruit.

Yeshua spent the rest of the day with Elijah and Joel. Amos went into the city centre, while Sarah his wife went about her household chores. The boys tended to the handful of goats, sheep and pigs, and quite a few chickens, and a cow, which Amos had already milked. Sarah tended to the vegetable and herb garden. Yeshua saw how self-sufficient they were and he enjoyed being a farmer for a day and attending to the animals. The day passed quickly and he was well fed simply devouring the freshly baked and most tasty bread that Amos baked.

That evening they enjoyed roasted chicken that had been prepared on the outside fire. Yeshua thought to himself that his parents could by now be close to Jerusalem, for surely, they would have discovered his absence, the night before. They would be under the impression that he was travelling with Achim and his mum, only to discover he was not.

This is now the beginning of the third day that he had been separated from his parents and Yeshua thought the best place for him to be was in the city centre. So, he told Amos.

Amos said that he was in fact going to the Temple for another day of debating. When Amos was ready to leave, Yeshua said his goodbyes to Tamar and the boys. Tamar made a parcel of chicken from the night before and some of Amos's freshly baked bread and gave it to Yeshua. Yeshua filled his waterbag and he and Amos left for the city centre.

When they arrived, Yeshua said he would go with Amos to the Temple, for he was sure that his parents would end up there, looking for him. This time, Yeshua was engaged with the holy and learned men. He had questions to ask them about the Saviour, the Messiah, and who he was and how he was to save the people of Israel.

Yeshua listened intently and then spoke, "I do not think the Messiah is the kind of person you expect him to be. He is not going to overthrow Rome, he will not have an army of men, and he will not sit on a throne or live in a palace. He will—"

Ananias interrupted Yeshua, "You are mistaken, young man, the Messiah will come with great power, a power the world has never known, and he will have men under him who will give their lives to serve him, and he will lead them against the power of Rome."

"Already there are many groups quietly preparing for that day, they are making and stockpiling weapons for when the day of redemption comes," Nathanael, one of the rabbis said.

"No, it will not be like that," Yeshua retorted. "The Messiah will be like Moses. Moses had no army. It was with the power of Adonai that he set our ancestors free from slavery and the tyranny of Pharaoh and the Egyptians."

"These are different times; the Messiah will be different to Moses. Our forefathers were slaves under the tyranny of the Pharaohs for over four hundred years, but we will not have to wait that long to be freed from the tyranny of the Romans, for the time is near," Ananias said.

Yeshua had learned something about the history of Palestine, or Israel, as it is now called by some. Gamaliel was an expert on the history of the Israelites and if Yeshua remembered correctly, it was the Roman General Pompey who conquered Jerusalem a mere fifty to sixty years ago, and the Romans had put Hyrcanus II up as high priest, but Gamaliel had made it clear that Rome still ruled the roost and Israel was a kingdom of Rome. This changed even further about five to ten years later when Herod was crowned King of Judah, and with the help of the Romans Herod seized Jerusalem. Yeshua also learned that Ananias was appointed by the Roman Legate Quirinus as the first high priest of the newly formed province of Judaism, when Yeshua was a mere six years old. So, this must be the same Ananias, right here, leading this group, and he is the high priest, Yeshua said to himself.

And so, the debate continued. The men, the religious elite of Jerusalem, the experts of the Law and the Scriptures were so impressed with this young boy, Yeshua. They marvelled at his knowledge and eloquence and debating skills and the complexity of his questions.

Amos too was so overwhelmed. Yeshua had spent an evening and a night, then the whole of yesterday with them, and this morning with them. He was just like any other boy. Like his two boys, he was such an ordinary child, and from Nazareth to boot, and here he was displaying a wisdom and understanding beyond his years.

Chapter Eighteen
Yeshua Is Found

It was nightfall of the first day since they left Jerusalem when the Nazarenes stopped for the day. They had covered good ground, hardly stopping at all. They were tired, hungry, and relieved to be stopping for the night.

"Yosef you better go and check on Yeshua," Miriam said.

Yosef walked towards Tamar and Achim's tent, hoping to find Yeshua. "Shalom," he greeted Tamar and Achim. "You must be very tired. It has been a long day."

"It sure has," Tamar responded. "I'm so glad we can have a good feed and a good rest," she added.

"Where's Yeshua?" Yosef asked, rather surprised that he did not see Yeshua in their company.

"Yeshua! We thought he was with you," Tamar said, perplexed. "When we passed through Jerusalem, he said he just wanted to pop into the Temple, and that he would catch up with you and Miriam for the rest of the day's journey."

Yosef gasped, his hands reaching for his opened mouth. "He didn't—we haven't seen him at all, all day. We thought he was with you," Yosef exclaimed, confusion and panic gripping him. He went around to all the rest of the families from tent to tent asking if they saw Yeshua. No one did. Some of the men joined Yosef in searching for Yeshua among the rest of the people and throughout the campsite. No one had seen Yeshua all day. Yosef was beside himself as he returned to Miriam.

Miriam had surmised that Yosef must have been spending some time with Tamar and Achim for he had been gone quite a long time. Yosef had told his helpers not to alarm Miriam until they were absolutely sure Yeshua was not with them. Yosef thanked the men helping him, and then with a heavy heart returned to Miriam.

"You have been gone a long time, how are Tamar and Achim?" she asked, smiling, looking for Yeshua and surprised not to see him come running to hug her.

"He's gone," Yosef said sadly.

"Gone! What do you mean gone?" Miriam exclaimed, alarm beginning to grip her.

"He did not leave Jerusalem. He had entered the temple one last time and told Tamar and Achim that he would join us. Miriam he is still in Jerusalem," Yosef said, with a heavy heart. He rushed to hold Miriam, as she was ready to collapse. He held her as she began to sob.

"Oh no, oh no, oh Adonai, please keep him safe. We have to go back to Jerusalem, Yosef" Miriam said.

"It is too dark and dangerous for us to go now by ourselves, we will leave at first light," Yosef said, as he released Miriam.

They both had a sleepless night; both wondering where Yeshua was sleeping, hoping he had a good place to sleep and that he was warm and safe. They could not wait for the light to show its first glimpse, Miriam wanted them to leave without Ben so as not to be slowed down, but Yosef insisted. A journey back to Jerusalem and then immediately on the road again would be too arduous for Mary on foot. It would be dark by the time they arrived at Jerusalem. They walked a fast pace, with urgency, urging Ben to keep up with them and without resting at all. Their hearts were heavy but their feet were light. However, it was an overcast evening as they grew nearer to Jerusalem, and darkness came early. The moon or the stars could not be seen and it began to rain. Yosef and Miriam found shelter in a cave and waited for the rain to stop. Then they were on their way again. The rain, the darkness and Ben slowed them down. When they arrived at Jerusalem it was pitch dark. They found some lodging in a dilapidated inn at the poorer section of Jerusalem. They had something to eat, washed themselves, and in spite of their deep grief they both fell asleep. They woke before the sun was up and set on their way. Very few people were up and about in the city centre, but the market sellers were setting up for the day. Yosef and Mary had something to eat. They had not eaten much all of yesterday and were now hungry. They drank plenty of water and then went around asking the market sellers and everyone they met, if they saw their boy, Yeshua, a young lad of twelve years old, taller than average, lean, darkish complexion, tanned, long wavy blackish hair, almost reaching his shoulders and wearing white clothing. No one could say if they saw Yeshua.

"I wonder if he perhaps went to Bethany and stayed with my cousins," Yosef said.

"I don't think he would do that. He would wait for us in Jerusalem, where he knew, we could come to look for him. Where can he be Yosef?" Miriam said, becoming more fearful for her son's safety. She prayed and prayed for Yahweh to protect him.

After searching everywhere and asking everyone they met if they saw Yeshua, without success, they went to the Temple. It was now about the third hour and the city was busy, with plenty of people about. They went to the Temple because that was where Tamar and Achim said he went when they last saw him. They went and found only a handful of people there and no Yeshua. They spoke to someone who was sweeping in the outer courtyard and asked him. He said that he had seen a young lad like the boy they described; he was sitting in the Temple some time yesterday when he was here, but that was yesterday, early morning.

Yosef and Miriam left the temple forlorn and continued their inquiring as more and more people began to appear and the city centre became alive. But no one saw their Yeshua, until one man said he had seen a young boy like they described, could have been him, he was walking around here at the stalls, just browsing. The man said that he noticed that the boy was on his own, without his parents. "It could have been your son," the man said.

"Where did he go, after you saw him?" Miriam asked.

"I don't know, but he headed in the direction of the Temple," the man said.

It was now getting closer to noon, when Yosef and Miriam entered the Temple a second time. They had searched and searched and inquired of all they met about Yeshua and decided to come to the Temple again to see if he was perhaps there, and because the man at the market place had told them that their son was heading in this direction. There was no service on and there were not many people in the Temple, so they walked up to the front of the Outer Forecourt. To the right was an enclave, with about a dozen men, who were talking and totally engrossed in their conversation.

Yosef and Miriam decided to approach them and inquire about Yeshua, when their eyes fell on Yeshua. He was totally absorbed in their conversation. The men were evidently teachers, rabbis, Elders, priests, for they were conversing about the Faith and Yeshua seemed so incongruous among all those mature men. Yet he seemed to be accepted by them and involved in their discussion. They seemed to respect and listen to what he had to say.

"Yeshua! Yeshua!" Miriam called. She was overwhelmed. A moment earlier she was losing hope and ready to collapse, now she was almost collapsing in exhaustion, and a mixture of joy and relief swept over her.

Yeshua turned to see his mother and father, standing there perplexed, Miriam with her arms outstretched, Yosef with his arm around Miriam's shoulder. The men looked at them and then at Yeshua. Amos realised that they must be Yeshua's parents. He had not doubted that they would come looking for him and finding him. "Go, Yeshua," he urged.

Yeshua got up from his chair, and bowed to Ananias and the men and gave Amos a hug and said Shalom and thanked him and walked towards Miriam and Yosef.

"Yeshua, why have you treated us like this? Your father and I have been overwhelmed with anxiety in searching for you," Miriam said, somewhat perplexed.

"Yes, Yeshua, this was thoughtless and inconsiderate of you to do this to your mother. How could you—"

Yeshua cut off Yosef and said, "Why were you searching for me? Did you not know that I must be in my Father's house? That I must be about my Father's business?"

Yosef felt like slapping Yeshua, he was so annoyed. He had never had any real reason to discipline Yeshua before, but now he wished he had a rod to discipline him. He thought Yeshua was uncharacteristically being really insensitive to just how much pain he had caused them, especially his mother. But at the same time the feeling of relief just took over. Anger vanished from his heart.

"Oh Yeshua, I was so frantic. I was so worried about you. Where you were, were you safe? I am so glad to hold you in my arms again," Miriam said, as she held onto him for a time and then she released him.

By now, Amos had left the group, who just continued their debating, as if nothing had happened. Amos however approached the family and Yeshua introduced him to his parents. "Immah, Abba, this is Amos, he took me in, he is a Scribe and a baker and he took me in. I stayed with him and his family, his wife Sarah, and their two sons, Elijah and Joel. Elijah is just a year older than me. I was a stranger and they took me in. And they fed me. Oh Immah, Abba, they were so good to me."

Yosef and Miriam bowed to Amos in reverence and gratitude and thanked him profusely. "Thank you so much, Amos, for keeping Yeshua safe, and for looking after him these past three days. We are so grateful," Miriam said.

"Yes, we are really and truly grateful to you for caring for our son," Yosef added.

They said their goodbyes and then walked off. Miriam had seen how livid Yosef was, and sensed how furious he was with Yeshua, especially with Yeshua's apparent lackadaisical response to their distress at having lost him for three days. He had merely said, 'why were we searching for me and did we not know that he must be about his Father's business?' Miriam was furious too, but she was just so relieved to see him safe and sound and so grateful to Amos for caring for him. Relief and joy overpowered all their other emotions. Miriam pondered on Yeshua's words. In spite of Yeshua's genius, he was at times just an ordinary child, like any other child his age, thoughtless and apparently insensitive, so she forgave him. She pondered about Yeshua's sonhood, son of Yahweh. She and Yosef had grown accustomed to seeing Yeshua and treating Yeshua as their son, like any mother and father would treat their son, their only son. They tended to spoil him and yet they did try their best not to be over-protective. But he was only twelve years old and to do what he did was really thoughtless. But…he was different, he was the chosen one, and now she was forcefully reminded of that fact. Maybe Yeshua was trying to drive that home, or maybe it was Yahweh who was driving that home to them. Anyhow Miriam was just so pleased to have her son back that she dismissed all those thoughts for her happiness overshadowed any other feelings she might have.

Yosef too calmed down, and those resentful feelings he had receded in the happiness he felt in having Yeshua safe and sound and in the overriding joy he saw in Miriam.

The family went and fetched Ben and then made their way home.

Chapter Nineteen
Yeshua, The Carpenter and the Scholar

After Yosef, Miriam and Yeshua returned to Nazareth, Achim, Tamar, Zadok and everyone in Nazareth were overjoyed that Yeshua was found safe and sound and back with them. The story circulated and everyone was amazed. Achim and Zadok wanted to know every detail. They were captivated as they listened to Yeshua as he retold those three days that he was lost and then found. Yeshua became the talk of the village, even among the children, who wanted to hear every detail of Yeshua's three days on his own in Jerusalem.

Gamaliel too was delighted to have Yeshua back safe and sound and at class again. He too was curious as to what happened to Yeshua during those three days. He let Yeshua tell the whole class. During their private lesson after school, he got Yeshua to elaborate on what he discussed and debated with the teachers. Gamaliel knew all about Ananias, or Annas, as he was called. He was the high priest and of the religious elite of Jerusalem. Gamaliel because of his expertise in the law was a member of the Sanhedrin that was presided over by Annas, the high priest. The Sanhedrin was the highest Tribunal of Jewish Law in the land. It was Annas who was instrumental in having Gamaliel dismissed.

The next year of Yeshua's life flew by. He continued with his regular schooling and his extra private tuition after school under Gamaliel, for which Gamaliel was paid, although he did not charge much. Yosef could afford it. Miriam took in some sewing to supplement their income. When Yeshua turned thirteen, they had the usual coming-of-age celebration. The whole of the village met once a year in their makeshift synagogue for the ceremony in which all the boys who turned thirteen that year would be blessed by their now acting rabbi, Gamaliel. The boys were also blessed by their own fathers, as a sign of their adulthood. Yeshua's identity as a Jew was now solidified. He would continue his studies at school until he was fifteen and after that, who knows.

The next few years passed by and Yeshua turned fifteen. The whole of Nazareth was again preparing for their pilgrimage, camping holiday to Jerusalem for the celebration of the Passover. Yeshua had completed his schooling but was still spending at least a couple of hours a day with private tuition under Gamaliel, for which Yeshua himself was able to pay because he was now officially a carpenter's apprentice. In fact, Yeshua had been an apprentice to Yosef ever since he was able to handle tools. He learned and became expert in the trade. From the age of thirteen Yosef made him officially his apprentice and taught him all aspects of his trade. Yeshua loved working with wood. He loved the feel and the smell of the different woods that he worked with and delighted to see his finished works. By the time he reached his eighteenth birthday, he would be considered ready for marriage and by the age of twenty he would be expected to venture out on his own to earn a living. But Yeshua was also very interested in continuing his studies and learn as much as he could about the history of Israel, and world history and literature and of course all about Yahweh, his laws and his teachings through the Prophets, through all of the Hebrew Scriptures. He loved having deep discussions and debates.

Yeshua's fifteenth birthday arrived and again they were preparing for the long journey to Jerusalem. Not so many from Nazareth were going this time. Zadok had turned eighteen and moved to Tiberias, working as a blacksmith's apprentice, making horseshoes and farm tools and other metal goods and fixing them. He was smitten with a girl who was only sixteen years old from Tiberias. Her name was Gadija, and according to Zadok, her family were descendants of Ishmael, the son Abraham had from his servant Hagar.

Yeshua was thrilled to have met Gadija. Yeshua had learned all about Abraham and how he was an old man and his wife barren and to have a son he slept with his concubine and had a son and named him Ishmael. But then Sarah too conceived and had a son, Isaac. While the two families had a fall out and parted ways, Yahweh promised both Abraham and Ishmael that they would be father of great nations.

Tiberias was a major city on the shore of Lake Galilee and not too far from Nazareth so Zadok often visited. He told Yeshua that once he finished his apprentice in two years' time, he was going to asked Gadija for them to be betrothed. He then planned to start his own blacksmith business, and once he could afford a place of his own, which he hoped would take no longer than a couple more years, he would then ask for Gadija's hand in marriage.

Yeshua was so happy for Zadok. "The wild child of Nazareth has been tamed," Yeshua said with a smile. He had concerns for his friend, who was so adventurous and had such wild dreams but now he was so pleased that the beautiful Gadija has won his heart. Zadok was now so different. His carefree ways seemed a thing of the past. He was now so sure of himself. Yeshua marvelled how he had these long-term plans and Yeshua prayed for his friend that all his dreams would come to fruition.

"Gadija is such a beautiful girl, Yeshua, and so smart too," Zadok said.

"I'm so happy for you Zadok. I know you will be a good husband. a good provider and you will have as many children as Ishmael," Yeshua joked.

Achim on the other hand was still single but he started cattle farming with his father in a big way. While Yeshua spent a lot of time with Achim and his mother, he seldom met Achim's father. He was always away or busy and kept very much to himself. He never went to the synagogue or to any of the community celebrations.

Achim's father bought a farm, and with time hoped to have plenty of pigs, goats, cows, which they planned to breed and sell and make a very good living. They were already on this path and Yeshua whenever he had some spare time would visit his friend Achim, who since he finished school, spent all day with his father tending to the cattle. His mother had a huge vegetable garden, where Achim also spent some time. They sold produce to neighbours and at the markets. Achim's family were doing well. Yeshua had not seen much of Achim since the day they finished school, which wasn't too long ago, yet Yeshua missed his best friend and went to see him whenever he had the chance.

And so, Miriam, Yosef, Yeshua and a group of Nazarenes set out once again on the pilgrimage to Jerusalem for the celebration of the Passover. This would be a significant pilgrimage for Yeshua as he was now fifteen and recognised as an adult. This time he would not have Achim and Zadok with him. Yeshua was not going steady with any girlfriends. It was not that he wasn't interested in the opposite sex; he just was so interested in so many things, in his learning, his friendships and growing intellectually and emotionally. He felt he was still too young to be courting and he wasn't that way attracted to any of the girls in Nazareth yet, although he knew of a few that seemed interested in him. He was always very respectful of the girls. On this journey one of the girls, Rebecca, an only child of Adam and Joanna, who was Yeshua's age showed a fancy for Yeshua. Yeshua had noticed her, seen her growing up. Although they never really spoke to each other, she stood out for Yeshua; he just felt a natural attraction for her. He liked her, and from the occasional looks they exchanged, Yeshua knew she liked him. They had seen quite a bit of each other growing up, but boys and girls their age just kept apart, until they were ready for betrothal and courting.

Yeshua liked Rebecca. She was so different to the other girls, more like a tomboy. She was always running. She would never walk if she could run. This intrigued Yeshua, as no other girls ran for that matter, and she dressed in a shorter dress for running, which would have been frowned upon in higher circles but the people in Nazareth knew Rebecca and didn't mind. She was regarded as somewhat of a wild child. Yeshua was intrigued for she seemed to be so brazen for her age and her gender, simply ignoring social mores and expectations, for she had already approached Yeshua before they came on this pilgrimage and now along the way when they had their stops, she would somehow bump into Yeshua, especially when he was alone. When they made their second stop on their journey to Jerusalem, to eat and rest, Yeshua went off to the nearby forest to explore and have some quiet time, when Rebecca appeared. This was the first time they were alone, together. Yeshua was thrilled.

"Shalom, Yeshua, how are you going?" Rebecca greeted Yeshua with a smile.

"Shalom, I'm going fine, Rebecca, what about you?" Yeshua responded, smiling in return.

"May I walk with you?" Rebecca asked.

"Sure. Rebecca. You are very bold, you are the first girl that has ever approached me on my own and the first girl to initiate a conversation with me," Yeshua said. He was now quite intrigued and interested in being with Rebecca. He found her to be quite pretty in an unusual way. She was tall, about the same height as him and she was quite fit looking, like an athlete.

"You are looking so fit and healthy, must be from all that running, Rebecca."

"I love running, especially along the lake whenever we get there, or through the forest and especially early in the morning. I love getting up early to see the sunrise. It is so beautiful to see how the sun creates all those beautiful images and patterns with the clouds. I can spend hours just watching the changing pictures the sun creates from the patches of clouds and to listen to the birds in the morning when they are so chirpy and singing like an orchestra," Rebecca said with obvious joy.

Yeshua opened up to Rebecca and found in her a kindred spirit for he too loved the mornings, and whenever he could he would get up with the sun and watch how it does indeed light up the sky and create masterful skyscapes with the clouds and sometimes the moon is still visible. He loved how the sun creates glittering diamonds on the foliage of the plants and trees from the morning dew. They chatted and chatted and the more they talked, the more Yeshua grew in fondness for her. She spoke of all the women in the Scriptures that she heard about in the few years of schooling that she had and how she wanted to know more about them. She spoke of her admiration for Ruth, remembering how moved she was when she first heard her story. She remembered Ruth as being loyal, exhibiting great integrity, generosity and self-assurance. She admired Ruth's strength and independent thinking, because she had strong convictions and spoke her mind.

"Yeshua, I remember hearing the story of Ruth, being so impressed with her story and Ruth's song moved me to tears. I'm sure you know the story well don't you, Yeshua?" Rebecca said.

Rebecca knew that Yeshua was smart, always top in his class. She wanted Yeshua to tell her the story for she had heard it so long ago and never again. She recalled just how much she enjoyed the story of Ruth. She heard about how Yeshua was regarded as a good story teller.

"I do, Rebecca, Ruth's story and her song moves me to tears as well, whenever I listen to her story and hear her song," Yeshua said.

"So, Yeshua, tell me her story again. It is such a long time since I heard it. It is a story I do not want to forget," Rebecca pleaded, as she sat down on a log.

"I can't forget Ruth's story, Rebecca, because I am connected to her by ancestry. She was the great-grandmother of David; from whose lineage I was born. My father Yosef is of the line of David. Ruth was a foreigner, of a different race and religion to us, and of mixed heritage. She lived in the Land of Moab. She was a Moabite. In the days when the judges ruled there was a famine all over the Land of Judaea and a certain man named Elimelech and his wife Naomi and their two sons Mahlon and Chilion from Bethlehem, where I was born by the way, were starving, so to survive they went to the country of Moab. But misfortune followed them because Elimelech died soon afterwards, so Naomi was left with her two sons. They eventually married Moabite women, Orpah and Ruth, Ruth marrying Mahlon. Within ten years more tragedy struck because both Mahlon and Chilion died, so Naomi, a widow, was now without her husband and her two sons. She was now alone with two widowed daughters-in-law, in a foreign land."

"But then the famine in Judaea came to an end and food became plentiful again and Naomi decided to return to Judaea. She told Orpah and Ruth to return to their people and to their former homes where they will be able to practice their own religion, worship their own gods and be taken care of. Naomi knew they would have a hard time in Judaea because of their mixed race, being of a different race and different religion with different gods, the people of Judaea would ostracise them. Naomi convinced Orpah to return to her own people. But she could not convince Ruth. She pleaded with Ruth for her own good to follow Orpah and return to her people and her gods, Judaea was no place for her.

"But Ruth refused to desert her mother-in-law. She knows that Naomi will need her. She is thinking only of Naomi's welfare and her future. Naomi is the mother of her late husband Mahlon. She will be faithful to Naomi, help her and live with her.

"Naomi insists and persists but to no avail. Ruth is under no obligation to go to Judaea with her mother-in-law, very likely facing discrimination and a life of poverty but she will not desert Naomi. She replies with her beautiful song, the one that moved you Rebecca to tears and moves me too whenever I hear it," Yeshua said.

"Please sing it to me, Yeshua," Rebecca pleaded as she continued sitting on the log.

Yeshua was taken by surprise. "Well, Ruth didn't really sing those words Rebecca, but they are so poetic and powerful that they could easily be put to song and because of its lyrics it became known as Ruth's song," Yeshua said.

"Do you know the lyrics, Yeshua?" Rebecca asked.

"I do, Rebecca, they are so beautiful," Yeshua replied.

"Then recite them to me, Yeshua," Rebecca pleaded.

Yeshua felt a bit self-conscious. He was accustomed to speaking before his class, but not to a girl in a forest, surrounded by trees and the sound of birds in the background. The sun was filtering its way through the trees. Yeshua thought what a beautiful day it was and what a beautiful place to recite Ruth's song to a girl, to Rebecca.

"Okay Rebecca, I haven't recited solo in public before, to an audience of one and a lady at that, so here goes, Yeshua cleared his throat and began to recite the Song of Ruth:

"Naomi, do not press me to leave you
or to turn back from following you!
Where you go, I will go;
where you lodge, I will lodge;
your people shall be my people,
and your God, my God.
Where you die, I will die—
there will I be buried.
May the Lord do thus and so to me,
and more as well,
if even death parts me from you!"

"Oh Yeshua, that is so beautiful. Your reciting of Ruth's song moved me so, you must put it to music, to a song," Rebecca said.

"I do not play a music instrument Rebecca, although I did play the drums with mother's pots and pans when growing up," Yeshua said smiling.

"There is more to Ruth's story, Rebecca. Naomi also has a song, but it is a depressing one. Naomi and Ruth arrive in Bethlehem and the women couldn't believe it was Naomi.

"Is this really Naomi?" they exclaimed. Naomi then responds, which becomes her song. "Do you want to hear it, Rebecca?" Yeshua asked.

"Yes, please Yeshua, I did not hear about Naomi's song," Rebecca said, eagerly. Yeshua obliged.

"Call me no longer Naomi,
call me Mara,
for the Almighty has dealt bitterly with me.
I went away full,
But the Lord has brought me back empty.
why call me Naomi
when the Lord has dealt harshly with me.
and the Almighty has brought calamity upon me?"

Yeshua continued to relate the story of Ruth, to a captive audience of one. "Naomi arrives back in Bethlehem, with Ruth her Moabite daughter-in-law, at the beginning of the barley harvest. They had to eke out a living by Ruth going to glean among the ears of grain and gather behind the reapers. And it so happens that she is doing this in the field that belongs to a wealthy landowner called Boaz. Boaz discovers she is a Moabite and learns of her story. He also learns about how Ruth remains faithful to Naomi. He becomes their protector. Boaz warns the men not to harm Ruth in any way and allow her to glean. The story has much more intrigue but in the end, it is a beautiful love story. Boaz, after some obstacles, eventually succeeds in being able to marry Ruth.

"I love Boaz, Rebecca. He is a wealthy and respected person but he both provides for the poor widow, the Moabite Ruth and her mother-in-law, the widow Naomi. Boaz looks beyond the differences of race and religion and eventually marries Ruth. They have a son, Obed who became the father of Jesse, the father of David."

"What a beautiful story of a woman's fortitude, loyalty, integrity and strength. And what a beautiful love story, Yeshua, and you tell it so wonderfully," Rebecca said with obvious joy.

"And what a powerful story of a man's integrity and respect for differences of race and religion and his indomitable spirit in doing all he did to win Ruth's hand in marriage. Boaz is an example to all men of how to treat his fellow men, especially his workers and the poor and women in particular," Yeshua said.

"Amen to that!" Rebecca said, as she got up from the log. "I think on that note we can go back to home base, I'm sure your parents must be wondering where you are?" Rebecca said.

"Yes, we better get back and I am feeling rather peckish," Yeshua said.

Yeshua walked alongside Rebecca, feeling a warm closeness to her, knowing that they would become and remain good friends from this day forward.

They walked back, in silence for a while. All of a sudden, Yeshua had a start as Rebecca grabbed his hand in hers. What a courageous young lady, Yeshua thought. He had never before held the hand of a girl and it delighted him. Yeshua was surprised that his first instinct was not to withdraw his hand. He had been intrigued by Rebecca and liked her free spirit and it gave him great joy to hold Rebecca's hand. Somehow, she had managed to find her way to his heart. He found that he liked Rebecca, her boldness and that she was like no other girl he knew. In fact, Yeshua had never before had such a long and interesting chat with a girl. They continued walking back in silence though, happy to just hold hands and feel each other's nearness and warmth. When they reached the end of the forest, before they entered the clearing of the campsite, Yeshua released Rebecca's hand, as he felt she was not going to do so.

"I think we better not come out of the forest together, or we will indeed cause a scandal," Yeshua said. "Let's split up and enter the campsite from the far ends where we won't even be seen," Yeshua suggested.

"Sounds like a good plan," Rebecca said. "See you later, Yeshua," she said, as she walked away in the opposite direction from Yeshua.

"Enjoy your lunch," Yeshua said, as they exchanged smiles.

"Where have you been?" Miriam asked as Yeshua arrived. "I have your plate of food all ready to be eaten. Had you taken any longer you might have gone hungry, as I'm sure Yosef would have devoured your portion," Miriam said in jest.

"Thank you Immah, for saving me some food from that hungry lion of a husband of yours," Yeshua responded, laughing.

Later when Yeshua was alone with Miriam, he told her all about Rebecca and what happened in the forest. Yeshua was accustomed to sharing everything that was happening in his life with his mother. He was quite at ease in speaking to Miriam. Besides he did not feel all that ease in speaking to Yosef about matters of the heart.

Miriam smiled. She was happy that Yeshua was showing an interest in the opposite sex. One day one of her kind would steal his heart and what a lucky girl or woman that would be. "That's wonderful, Yeshua. Rebecca seems a nice girl. I often see her running past our house early in the morning. Maybe you should have a chat with your father about her," Miriam suggested.

"Maybe I should, so he knows the score, in case she comes over or he sees me with her," Yeshua said. "Now that my friends Achim and Zadok are going their own ways, it seems it has just happened that my first new friend is going to be a girl," Yeshua said, smiling.

"Well, you are growing up, Yeshua, and that is natural and good that you should have both male and female friends," Miriam said.

The Nazarenes arrived in Jerusalem and had the Passover Festival, with the slaughter of the lambs, the burning of their entrails in the Temple and the feasting of their leftovers at their campsite. There was lots of gaiety, music and dancing. Rebecca sought out Yeshua and they danced together, much to the surprise of the other boys and girls around Yeshua and Rebecca's age. But it wasn't long when they too found partners and danced with great joy. Miriam and Yosef, who was already told about Rebecca, smiled at each other.

"Looks like our son and Rebecca, are starting a revolution, with such openness among the sexes," Miriam said. "And that is a good thing, for them to be free and open with their friendships, instead of our customary distances," Miriam added.

Yeshua and Rebecca were delighted to see other boys and girls their age dancing and singing and having fun together. They felt they now could be together in the open, instead of having to sneak out into the forest. And so, their friendship blossomed for all to see.

The Nazarenes were going to spend another couple of days in Jerusalem before heading back to Nazareth. Before they came on this pilgrimage Yeshua and Gamaliel had a long discussion about Yeshua's further education. Gamaliel told Yeshua about a school for advanced learning in Jerusalem. Gamaliel knew one of the teachers there, Zephaniah, an old friend, and if Yeshua liked, they could call on him. And so, it happened. Gamaliel made a lunch time appointment for Yeshua to meet with Zephaniah. They met at Zephaniah's house. Zephaniah seemed at least five years older than Gamaliel, who was now close to reaching his fifties. Zephaniah was a bachelor; he had never married.

"He is married to Adonai, Yeshua," Gamaliel had told Yeshua when he told Yeshua about his bachelor friend. "He is forever buried in the Scriptures, not only the oral tradition but whatever is written down of our history with Adonai and whatever commentaries he can lay his hands on. He is an expert in the Scriptures and its interpretation and like me he loves history. He also has a great love of literature and he writes poetry. He is able to speak both Greek and Latin."

Yeshua was looking forward to meeting with Zephaniah and finding out all about the Advanced School of Learning on the Law and the Prophets and all of the Hebrew Scriptures. And so, it happened.

Yeshua and Gamaliel were warmly met by Zephaniah. They sat around a small table in the backyard of Zephaniah's house, ate some roasted lamb and vegetables prepared by Zephaniah and drank some wine.

"So, this is Yeshua, you told me about Gamaliel?" Zephaniah said. "So, tell me, Yeshua, why do you want to do further studies?"

"Zephaniah, I have learned so much from Gamaliel. He is in charge of our school in Nazareth, teaches some of us boys. I have had some private tuition from him for a number of years now. He told me about the School of Advanced Learning here in Jerusalem and I would like to advance my knowledge and understanding of what I am learning and have still to learn," Yeshua said.

They continued discussing the school and what it had to offer. Zephaniah was quite impressed with Yeshua and thought that Yeshua would easily qualify for admission. Yeshua discovered that the fees to the advanced school were quite high. The first course would be intensive study for three years. They studied and attended lectures and debates for nine months straight and then had a break for three months. This meant that Yeshua had to live in Jerusalem for nine months of the year.

Zephaniah informed Yeshua about rooms that were available for students at the school, at a reasonable rent. Besides lodging, Yeshua knew he would have to feed himself as well. And the school was so intense, Gamaliel had already informed Yeshua that they studied and debated all day, something to which Yeshua was looking forward.

Yeshua and Gamaliel thanked Zephaniah for his hospitality and for the meeting. Yeshua and Gamaliel had much more to discuss. And Yeshua had a lot to discuss with his mother and father. "I think I will have to work hard for at least a year, to be able to pay for my board and lodging and fees for the first year. Then I have three months to work for the next year. I will have to talk with my parents," Yeshua said to Gamaliel, as they walked back to the campsite.

But Yeshua wanted; felt he needed some time to himself. He had a lot to think about. "I'd like to spend some time with Adonai in the Temple. Please tell my mother and father that I am in the Temple and will be back at camp shortly," Yeshua said.

Yeshua entered the Temple. It was quiet as the morning ceremony, worship and sacrifice was over. It was also too early for the evening ceremony. Yeshua found a spot where he sat down on the ground with his legs folded. He prayed; he felt a great love for his heavenly Father. He sat and discussed all that happened at Zephaniah's and all about the Advanced School of Learning. He also discussed Rebecca, his girlfriend, how his feelings for her were growing. He sat for a while waiting for a response from his heavenly Father.

Yeshua wanted to know what his future is. He was feeling affection for a girl, Rebecca. He was still young. They were just friends, nothing serious, like that of Zadok and Gadija. But Yeshua felt it could develop further because he liked Rebecca. Yeshua was reflecting on all he knew about his birth and what his mother and father told him about his future, but he wanted to hear it from Yahweh. "Abba, what is it that you want of me? Please make that clear to me," Yeshua pleaded. And then he heard a voice, not a human voice, and not loud, but in the silence. It was in the silence but it was as clear as if a person were speaking to him. He could not explain how he was hearing Yahweh speak but he was hearing and listening.

"Yeshua, my beloved Son, I have sent you into the world to save the world. Your mission and how you will do this will become clearer as you continue to grow. Do not be afraid, I am with you. My Spirit will guide you. Your life will be a sacrifice to me, so it will not be a long one. So, you cannot have a wife or a normal family like everyone else for I need all of your time, effort and strength for the work I have for you. I love you Son and I love all those whom I have created and they are in need of salvation, of redemption and that is why I have sent you. That is the purpose of your life, your mission. Take courage. I am with you always."

Yeshua dropped his face into his hands, slowly his face emerged as he breathed heavily and then his hands rested on his mouth. Like Moses Yahweh has spoken to me. There was no burning bush or no sound, yet I clearly heard what he was saying and wanting of me. Yeshua sat for a long while, his hands now clasped with his thumbs holding up his chin.

Yeshua exited from the Temple feeling a great peace and certainty. He also felt a certain apprehension. What the Father was asking of him was to sacrifice his life entirely, to do only his work. Now he understood what he had said to his mother and father when they found him in the Temple when he was only twelve, how he had said that he must be about his Father's business. Those words seemed to have come from nowhere at the time, as if it was not, he that was speaking them. Now he understood. This is my life, to be about my Father's business.

Yeshua felt he needed to speak to Gamaliel. But he would wait until they were back in Nazareth and have a complete session with Gamaliel to speak of his encounter with Yahweh in the Temple and what his mission is. Yeshua then felt a deep peace and joy wash over him. He felt a lightness of being, as if he was floating and not walking. A great love seemed to be emanating from him, touching everything and everyone as he walked through the city centre, the market place, and back to camp.

"Yeshua, you have been gone a long time, are you okay?" Miriam asked.

"I'm fine Immah, never been better, just had an audience with Adonai," Yeshua said light-heartedly, with a broad smile on his face.

"Oh, how nice, and what did Adonai have to say?" Miriam said, humouring her son.

"Seriously Immah, I went with Gamaliel to meet with Zephaniah at the School for Advanced Learning. I'll talk to you and Abba about that later when we get home. After our meeting I parted with Gamaliel and spent some time in the Temple to talk over with Adonai what it is he wanted of me. You are the only one Immah who would understand, for you know what my real mission in life is. I am so happy that you know and understand. I need your guidance Immah and I plan to seek guidance from Gamaliel as well. But all that serious business can wait until we get home. Let us just enjoy this time. Now if you don't mind, I think I will go and see Rebecca, and let her know that we can only remain friends," Yeshua said.

Miriam watched her son walk away. She had an inkling of what was happening with her son. While she was happy for him, she also felt a tinge of sadness. He could not experience the joys of adolescence, of growing up, of falling in love with a girl, and later with a woman and have a family of his own. It would be such a lonely life for him. He would be able to make a girl, a woman very happy, for he had so much love to give. She whispered a prayer that Yahweh might give him the strength he needed.

"Shalom, Rebecca, would you like to go for a walk," Yeshua asked when he found Rebecca, who had just come back from her run. She still had her running shoes and was all sweaty. "Let me just wash, I'm all sweaty from my run and I must smell."

"I don't mind, Becky," Yeshua said, "I love the smell of sweat. It is like the scent of a woman," Yeshua said light-heartedly.

"I do mind, Yessie," Rebecca said in return, "and you are the first to call me Becky. I like that, but only you will call me that and only in my presence," Rebecca said.

"Of course, Becky, Rebecca, I didn't really mean to give you a nick name. It just slipped out. And I don't think I will call you that again because Rebecca is just such a nice name, Rebecca," Yeshua said, rolling her name off his tongue.

"And so is Yeshua, Yessie. But I do like to wash and change. See you in a minute," Rebecca said, as she went to the back of her tent.

I was only using a term of endearment, Yeshua said to himself as he waited for Rebecca. She didn't take long. She returned looking clean and refreshed, her long black, wavy hair cascading over her shoulders. Yeshua thought she was gorgeous. He reminded himself of his time with Yahweh in the Temple and the reason why he wanted to walk and talk with Rebecca. They were to be friends and friends only. They could never become lovers; that would not be fair to her. Yeshua was uneasy about how he was to deal with this with Rebecca. But in his heart, he knew he had to tell her now, and not lead her up the garden path to nowhere. He had to give her the freedom to have other boys as friends and find the one who would and could love her completely and eventually make a life with her.

As they walked, they engaged in some small talk. Yeshua then said he had something serious to discuss with her. Rebecca was immediately attentive. "What is it, Yessie, I mean Yeshua, what's on your mind," Rebecca asked. She was thinking that Yeshua was going to ask her for them to go on being friends and more than friends, to be boyfriend and girlfriend.

"Rebecca, you know that I have been receiving private tuition with Gamaliel while I was doing my schooling and now continue to do so with him, now that I have finished with school. Well, he took me to a teacher friend, Zephaniah, here in Jerusalem, at the School for Advanced Learning. I plan to enrol in the school, in a year's time. I need to work and save enough money for the fees. I will be studying and living in Jerusalem for at least three years and maybe longer. I will be in Jerusalem for nine months of every year. I think that Adonai is calling me to be a teacher, a rabbi, or something, and I am being called to dedicate my whole life to this work of preaching and teaching and spreading the Good News of Adonai's love for us. As such I just wanted to make it clear. I very much want to remain your friend but I want to make it clear Rebecca that we can never become lovers or anything more than very good friends. I do like you Rebecca and want to be your friend even when you find the person you want to share your life with," Yeshua said, and then remained silent, waiting for Rebecca's response.

"Wow!" Rebecca gasped. "That is a mouthful and a lot to take in, Yeshua," Rebecca said, scratching her head. She rubbed her forehead. "I need to absorb what you have just shared with me, Yeshua…eh…but I am grateful for your honesty and sincerity. Mmm, so let me be honest and sincere too. I do like you a lot, Yeshua. I was hoping that our friendship would develop and we could come closer and have a future together. But I did think you were a bit too holy for me," Rebecca said, smiling.

"Too holy, wow, that is the first time anyone has described me as holy," Yeshua said.

"Well, you go to the synagogue every Sabbath, on all the feast days, you go on pilgrimage to Jerusalem so often, you are always praying and talking about Adonai and spiritual things," Rebecca said. "I don't mind that, Yeshua; I find that quite endearing but I am not so inclined. All those stories we are told about Abraham, and Yahweh asking him to kill his own son, and him having a child with his concubine, with his wife's approval, and that being, okay? And those other stories of Noah in the Ark with two of all animals, come on, Yeshua, you don't believe all that do you? And how could Jonas survive in the belly of a whale? And what about that old guy, what's his name, Mesoosalah who supposed to live for almost a thousand years?"

"His name was Methuselah and he lived for nine hundred and sixty-nine years to be exact," Yeshua said, with a smile.

"Nine hundred and sixty-nine years, really, Yeshua. How is that humanly possible, physically possible?" Rebecca asked.

"Well, Rebecca, you know that for God, a thousand years is like one day," Yeshua said.

"Yes, but Masoo—Methuselah is not God," Rebecca said, shaking her head.

"That's true, Rebecca," Yeshua said, laughing. He loved how Rebecca spoke her mind. She raised such interesting points. Yeshua would have loved debating those points with her but he felt now was not the time. He would shelve them for another time.

"That's fine, Rebecca, you raise such important points. I am so glad that you have been so honest with me and know this; I respect you and whatever you believe. I still like you and want to be your friend no matter what, so are we still friends?" Yeshua said, pleading, for he so much wanted to remain friends with Rebecca.

"Of course we are. I'll race you to that last tree, you can see from here, the one with the overhanging branch." Rebecca pointed to the edge of the forest to her right, a distance of about a mile. "You ready, ready, steady, go."

They raced, neck and neck and then Rebecca started picking up the pace gaining ground and slipping away from Yeshua. He kept up with her, just. As they approached the last hundred yards or so, she began to sprint and left dust in her wake. She dropped onto her back, panting, as she waited for Yeshua. Yeshua arrived out of breath and dropped on his back next to her, breathing heavily. They lay there for a while continuing to breathe heavily and waiting for their breathing to ease.

Yeshua reached for her hand and touched her. "You are a great runner Rebecca, like a gazelle," Yeshua said.

"Like a gazelle, I like that," Rebecca said, as she squeezed Yeshua's hand. They lay for quite a while, holding hands and letting the sun caress them.

Chapter Twenty
The School of Advanced Learning

Yeshua had turned seventeen and within six months he would be eighteen. Rebecca, while she seemed okay with what Yeshua said to her that day in the forest on their Jerusalem pilgrimage, and in fact broke up with her, in private she took it hard, and wept quite a bit. She grew in fondness for Yeshua and was hoping that would have developed, she was hoping for a future with Yeshua, but that was not to be. However, they continued to be good friends.

Yeshua had saved enough for his first year of studies at the Jerusalem School of Advanced Learning. Yosef and Miriam felt they could use the gold that they had saved, which those astronomers from the east gave to Yeshua when he was born. They had saved it for when Yeshua was ready to have a family of his own, and build his own home, but that was not to be, so they felt it would be in order for Yeshua to use it for his advanced learning in Jerusalem, for his tuition fees, board and lodging. But Yeshua refused, he wanted to pay his own way and work his way through his studies. He wanted his mother and father to have it for themselves as an investment for when they could no longer earn a living.

Yeshua packed his belongings, all the clothes and everything else he needed for his lonesome journey to Jerusalem. The last few days he spent saying his goodbyes, firstly to his grandparents, Hannah and Jehoyakim. They were so proud of their only grandson and they gave him some money, which he knew he would not be able to refuse. He thanked them profusely for all the love and kindness they had shown him over the years. They hugged and kissed him, and Yeshua asked for their blessing. Jehoyakim laid his hands on Yeshua's head and gave him a silent blessing, as did Hannah, who now had tears running down her cheeks.

"I'll only be gone for nine months, Gran," Yeshua smiled and Hannah smiled back. After visiting his grandparents, Yeshua made his way to Achim and spent a couple of hours with his dearest friend.

"Wow, Yeshua, Jerusalem School of Advanced Learning, only the brightest of the brightest get into that uppity School. Imagine that, a humble carpenter entering the Jerusalem School of Advanced Learning. You show those other students what Nazarenes are made of. I know you will do us proud, Yeshua, and I am so happy for you."

"Thanks, Achim, I'm going to miss you. We had such good times growing up, didn't we?"

"We sure did," Achim answered.

"I'm going to miss you and if you are ever in Jerusalem, make sure to visit," Yeshua said. "And Achim I am so proud of you, you and your parents have worked so hard and deserve your success. Let me now say goodbye to them."

Yeshua met Achim's father, whom he never saw much when growing up because he was always away working, but since they owned and worked the farm, Yeshua did get to know Achim's father, Josiah, much better. He was a taciturn sort of man who did not say much, but Yeshua could see beyond his cool exterior to a man who loved his son and wife greatly. Achim's mother, Tamar, was the opposite, she could not stop talking. She showered Yeshua with so much affection. She was so proud of Yeshua and heaped praise on him, and enough small cakes to last him for days.

Achim walked with Yeshua for part of his journey home. "What about Rebecca, how is she taking your going off to advanced learning?" Achim said, smiling. "I'm sure you are breaking her heart. I really thought you two would get betrothed."

"I'm off to say goodbye to her, Achim. Yeah, I am very fond of her. If I had not been going for at least three to four years of advanced study, I think I would have asked to be betrothed to Rebecca. Had it been otherwise, had his heavenly Father not asked him to give his whole life to his purpose, then he would most likely betroth Rebecca. But then Yeshua had to tell his friend, 'But to be honest, Achim, Rebecca and I had discussed this a long time ago. She knew that would not happen, and we have remained such good friends. I am so fond of her Achim. What about you, is there no woman in your life?'" Yeshua asked.

"No Yeshua, I don't know, I am not really attracted to any woman just now. And besides I have so much work on the farm," Achim said.

"I'm sure you will find a good woman, Achim, who will love you. I wish you well for your future and I'll see you in nine months. Shalom, my friend."

"Shalom, Yeshua, peace go with you," Achim said, as he turned around and walked away from a friend he would sorely miss. But he was so proud of Yeshua, he was happy for him. And he expected great things from Yeshua; he would make all of Nazareth proud.

The last person Yeshua wanted to say goodbye to was Rebecca. She was hanging out some washing on the clothesline at the side of their home, when he approached.

"Oh Yeshua," Rebecca exclaimed and ran into Yeshua's arms as soon as she saw him approaching. "The time has finally come, you are leaving me forever," she said, hugging him tightly.

"Rebecca, you are smothering me. I am not leaving you forever. I'll only be gone for nine months, and we will always be friends."

"I know," Rebecca said, as she released Yeshua. "You will most likely meet other beautiful women and fall in love, and I will never see you again," Rebecca said, feigning heartbreak.

"Don't be ridiculous, Rebecca, you know the love of a woman is something I cannot entertain, as my heavenly Father has other plans for me. Rebecca I am destined for a short life. You know that. And you will always be my first love and I will always love you as my closest and dearest friend. I wish you all the best. I know you will find a man who will sweep you off your feet."

"I don't know about that, Yeshua, you have set them all such a high bar," Rebecca said smiling.

"Come let's go to the markets and have something to drink and eat. Do you have time?" Yeshua asked. He wanted to have some quality time with his dearest friend.

"Of course, let me just let mother know and let me tidy myself, I must look a mess."

"You look like a princess," Yeshua teased, as Rebecca disappeared into their home and came out looking as pretty as a princess, with her hair combed and hanging so lovely over her shoulders. She was the only girl who never bothered to cover her hair, and Yeshua liked that. He always thought it peculiar that woman would want to cover the beautiful hair with which Yahweh had blessed them.

"You look stunning Rebecca."

They walked to the markets, holding hands for the last time. For a while they just walked in silence as they were often accustomed to but then began chatting as two young people so much in sync. They enjoyed the hustle-bustle of the little market centre and sat down for something to eat.

"So, what are you going to be studying at this Advanced School of Learning, Yeshua?" Rebecca asked.

"I'm not so sure, but according to Gamaliel, we will be debating a lot, which I rather like. We will be studying all that has been handed down in our tradition, everything that is written in our Scriptures and all of the commentaries that exist. We will also be studying and learning to speak Hebrew, Latin and Greek."

"Really, Hebrew, Latin and Greek, that's amazing, Yeshua."

"Of course I will have to be proficient in Hebrew, because most of what is written is in Hebrew, and not our dialect of Aramaic."

"So, you are going to be a linguist, Yeshua. Well, when you come back for your three months you can teach me Greek," Rebecca said.

"Sure will, that will help me as well," Yeshua said.

They continued to eat, and chat about life in general, and at times they simply sat quietly. After a while, long after they finished their meal, Yeshua said that they better get back, and so they walked again in silence for a while.

"I'm going to miss you, Yeshua. I'm going to miss beating you at races," Rebecca said, smiling.

"Well, in my spare time, I will run through the streets of Jerusalem so you better be faster when I return," Yeshua said smiling too.

It was a sad parting, for they knew their lives would be different, and that they would take paths apart, but in their hearts, they were content, they knew they would be friends forever and would love each other forever. They hugged each other and said goodbye one last time.

Miriam cried tears of joy as she said her goodbyes, and as she and Yosef watched their son leave home for the first time, off on his own to the big city of Jerusalem to study and learn. They were so proud of their son and their hearts were burning with love for him, but in Miriam's heart there was also a flicker of apprehension. For she knew that in a way she was going to lose him, as he had a mission from Yahweh, and that would now consume his life. She prayed that Yahweh would protect him.

Yeshua enjoyed the solitary journey to Jerusalem. He greeted all whom he met along the way. He arrived at the School for Advanced Learning, and was impressed with the grandeur of the buildings, and the vast open spaces surrounding the main buildings. Yeshua did think it was perhaps too extravagant and opulent. The school complex was situated at the edge of the city. He was greeted by one of the students, Amon, who showed him around the grand open fields at the back of the main buildings. It also had some shacks and Yeshua was told it was for those who managed the farm. The farm had rich fertile soil where they grew their own vegetables and there were plenty of fruit trees, figs, olives, pomegranates, berries as well as a small vineyard. There was also a huge open space with plenty of grass for the sheep and goats that were grazing, as well as cows and oxen and a few chickens. There were also some donkeys in the field.

Yeshua was amazed. "In our spare time, the little time we do have off, we help the labourers on the farm and the garden. It is meant to give us a break and to get us close to nature, to Adonai's creation, for us to be self-sufficient and fed, and save the school some wages, because we work for nothing. It is part of our formation, and besides providing our own produce the school also sells surplus at the markets. Nothing goes to waste."

Yeshua was shown the sleeping quarters. It consisted of three large halls that served as dormitories and community space, with a stone wall running down the middle of each length, like a spine, and this was divided into small cells, side by side and back-to-back, with a wooden wall, dividing the cells with a curtain in the front of each cell for privacy. Each cell was about seven square feet, held a bunk, a chair, a desk, and a small cupboard for their clothes and belongings. A part of each hall had an open space for the students to gather, debate and recreate. There were twenty-four cells in each hall, twelve back-to-back. The school catered for seventy-two boarders but could take in at least one hundred students at any time. Those over the seventy-two boarders had to find their own accommodation. They were mostly from Jerusalem itself or nearby, or were from rich parents who could pay for their private rent and board.

Yeshua met some of the other students from his section, those in the first year of the three-year course. After that, students could do a fourth year but they would have to have their own accommodation and board, and the fees were much higher.

Most of the students came from Judaea, but there were also students from Idumea south of Judaea and Perea to the east, across the Jordan River, and a few from Decapolis, north-east of Perea. Yeshua discovered there were none from Samaria; in fact, the school would not accept any Samaritans. Yeshua recalled again what he had learned about the Samaritans from Gamaliel. While the Jews considered that they are the one true religion, so did the Samaritans. The Samaritans believed that theirs is the true religion of ancient Israelites from before the Babylonian captivity, preserved by those who remained in the land of Israel, as opposed to Judaism, which they regard as an amended and adulterated religion. Yeshua again recalled that the Samaritans, who separated themselves from Judah, started to accept foreign beliefs, and also began to intermarry with foreigners. Yeshua thought it was such a pity not to accept Samaritans, whom the Jews despised. Yeshua felt the Samaritans had so much to offer and could have so many issues rich for debate. Yeshua took no part in the apparent prejudice that seemed to prevail against the Samaritans.

Yeshua was amazed at all the dialects that were spoken and for them to have a common language they all had to quickly learn to be proficient in Hebrew. As he mentioned to Rebecca, they also studied Greek and Latin as part of their course.

Yeshua was in his element. He was enthralled with the stories and lives of his fellow students who came from far and wide. And they were all so bright, of course, Yeshua knew they had to be, because the school only accepted the brightest from all over the land. Yeshua knew he would learn a lot from them all, as well as from the teachers, the best in the land. Yeshua was like a sponge soaking up knowledge. He had familiarised himself with the course content for the first year, and also for the entire three years. He was amazed at the scope of the course. He was grateful for all he learned at the school in Nazareth under Gamaliel, and now he would build on that knowledge and deepen his understanding. He relished the prospect of debating with students from all over Israel and with the teachers as well.

The entire course would take them through the history of the world and of Israel in particular, using Moses' five books of Genesis, Exodus, Leviticus, Numbers and Deuteronomy. Through those first books, Yeshua would deepen his understanding of Yahweh's saving work in the world. Yeshua knew that those five books are referred to as the Torah, which means teaching or instruction. The scroll of the course that Yeshua was reading, spelled out how the Torah reveals how much Yahweh loves all of his creation, all his creatures, and especially all of humanity. How he loves us all collectively and in an intimate and personal way. It shows how Yahweh loves us and desires to be loved by us, and desires to be in a relationship with us. Yeshua noted the lessons about the creation of the world, and the human race in the image and likeness of God, the stories of Israel's ancestors, matriarchs and patriarchs, the slavery in Egypt, the deliverance and Exodus, the journey through the wilderness, the covenant at Mount Sinai, and so on. Yeshua had learned all this with Gamaliel but here they would go much deeper into understanding the significance of it all for the present lives of all in Israel, and indeed for the whole world.

Reading further, Yeshua saw an outline of the laws that were drawn up to regulate the lives and worship of the Jews in their relationship with Yahweh and with one another. This was the area in which Yeshua was particularly interested. He was amazed at how many rules and regulations there were, for every imaginable aspect of one's personal and religious life, and one's relationship with each other and with Yahweh. There were in fact six hundred and thirteen Laws of the Torah, concerning the thirty-four areas of human and religious life, relationships with each other, and with Yahweh. From what is permissible to what is not permissible, and to what is sinful. Yeshua noticed that there are for example, twenty-four different forbidden sexual relations, twenty-five reasons for punishment and restitution, and forty-five idolatrous practices.

What was amazing to Yeshua were the hundred and one laws about sacrifices and offerings. These laws and regulations Yeshua found challenging, and he wanted to debate these, for he found them to be burdensome to the ordinary people and needed to be simplified. Yeshua would of course be studying all the intricacies of those laws. He knew he would also be studying the twelve periods in the history of Israel, from when the world began, through the time of the Patriarchs and then the time in Egypt, the Exodus, the rule of the Kings, the Divided Kingdom, the Babylonian Exile, the Return, and then the Maccabeus Revolt to the present time. There would also be lessons on great world leaders and philosophers, some of the names that Yeshua heard of but did not really know anything about their lives and their teachings. The course mentions the existence of men like Homer, Buddha, Confucius, Plato, Aristotle and Alexander the Great. Yeshua was excited about learning something about these great individuals of the past.

The first year went past like a flash. It was all study, work, lectures, debates, assignments, examinations. Working with animals, in the garden, and picking fruit was a welcome change. But it was mostly school work. When they were not engaged with the teachers and lessons and debates, they would be involved in personal study. And of course, then there was their spiritual and religious formation as well. They attended both the morning and the evening services in the Temple. The only recreation was a few hours off in the middle of the week when they could go into the city centre or on hikes or excursions in groups of six. Of course, they also had the Sabbath free, they had to attend the Sabbath celebrations in the Temple but after that they were free to do what they wished. Yeshua would cherish this private time. He would often go to visit his cousins in Bethany, which was so close to Jerusalem. He also visited Martha, Miriam and their brother Lazarus and their mother, who was still quite feeble. She seemed to be getting worse with every visit of Yeshua's. Yeshua enjoyed his visits to Martha, Miriam and Lazarus who was mostly away on his work and adventures. Going to visit Bethany, Martha and Miriam and their mother, Rahab, became part of his Sabbath. They in turn looked forward to Yeshua's visits and Martha usually prepared a great lunch for him. Yeshua would share with them all that he was learning. Miriam was especially fond of Yeshua, and enthralled with what he had to say, and Yeshua found in Miriam a kindred spirit, she reminded him of Rebecca, but she was different, quieter and reserved. But Yeshua grew to love Martha and Miriam. It was such a joy to have some female companionship for a change, as his entire week was spent in the company of men.

The first year came to an end with oral examinations. It was quite a daunting experience but Yeshua excelled. He had to face four top teachers who put questions to him, and as soon as he answered them satisfactorily, they would change the subject and the questions, trying their best to unsettle or stump Yeshua, but he thrived on their questions and strategies. They in turn were amazed at his grasp of all that he had learned and his intelligence, the depth of his understanding and grasp of all the great truths.

At the end of that first year, which simply flew past, Yeshua went and spent a few days with Martha, Miriam and Lazarus, and Rahab their mother who was now confined to bed and looked like she did not have long to live. Yeshua sat with her too, and spoke to her. She was interested in all that Yeshua had to say, and she hoped and asked that he continue to visit and told Yeshua that her daughters really appreciated his visits, especially Miriam, and that Martha too fussed so much when she knew he was coming.

"Miriam, Martha and Lazarus are very fond of you, Yeshua, I do hope you will come and visit throughout your studies. Miriam would like that very much," Rahab said. "They have been so good, looking after me, but they must look after themselves now and find a good man to love and care for them and have a family of their own," Rahab said, taking Yeshua's hand.

"I am very fond of both Miriam and Martha and your son Lazarus, Rahab, and they will always be my friends. I will always visit them, and you, for as long as you are here," Yeshua said. "I must go now. I am returning to Nazareth. I miss my parents very much, as I have not seen them for nine months. I will be back in three months' time to see you. Shalom, and peace be with you."

Martha had prepared some refreshments, biscuits she had baked, and some fruit juice she made. She also served Yeshua some figs, which she knew he liked. Yeshua spent time with Martha and Miriam, Lazarus was away, with work. Yeshua enjoyed the refreshment and said he was sorry he would not see them again for at least three months when the new year of study would begin. They both wanted to know how he enjoyed the year and what life was like at the school, and what he learned the past year. Yeshua shared his experiences and especially some of the interesting historical non-Jewish figures he learned about, who were not part of their history with Yahweh. Martha and Miriam both showed an interest.

"There were some great political and spiritual leaders, great thinkers, philosophers that had a lot of influence on humanity. Men like Buddha, Confucius,

Socrates, Plato and Aristotle just to name a few. We did not really go into depth about their lives and their teachings. That would take a whole semester and would have taken too much of the time of our syllabus, but one of our teachers wanted us to know something about these great figures of the past."

"So, tell us something about them, Yeshua," Miriam said. She wanted Yeshua to stay longer and she was genuinely interested in these men of whom she had not heard. In the meantime, Martha got up to clean the kitchen.

"It would take a long time Miriam, which I do not have. But briefly, Buddha was a great teacher, philosopher and spiritual leader and founded a movement named after him, Buddhism. He was born in India, near a place called Nepal and he lived about five hundred to six hundred years ago. In a nutshell he found a way to happiness, a kind of middle way between the severity of our religion, and what it asks of us and the lackadaisical way the Romans relate to their gods. He taught a spiritual path of good moral living and practiced and taught a way of praying in silence, without words really, a meditative practice, a kind of mindfulness that he believed would bring happiness and peace. The centre of what he taught was respect, respect for all of creation, and for all creatures and for one another."

"Sounds interesting, Yeshua, our religion could do with, we all could do with a little more respect, especially for women and the vulnerable," Miriam said.

"You are right, Miriam. Of course, Buddha did not believe in a personal God but in the ability for mankind to reach a state of blessedness which he called Nirvana."

"What about Confucius, who was he?" Miriam asked. She was fascinated and marvelled at all Yeshua was learning. She enjoyed listening to him; he was so wise and profound and explained deep things in such an easy way for her to understand.

"Oh Confucius, now he was a character all right. He was born over five hundred years ago and is the most famous teacher and philosopher of the Far Eastern Lands. He believed in the fundamental goodness of all people, and for him a teacher exists to teach us to live with integrity. He is famous for his wisdom. He is as wise as our Solomon and he has hundreds, if not thousands of famous quotes. I'll just give you a few of what I learned, and liked:

Wheresoever you go, go with all your heart.

It does not matter how slowly you go, so long as you do not stop.

Our greatest glory is not in never failing, but in rising every time, we fall."

"Oh Yeshua, how beautiful and wise, he captures such profound teaching in a few words."

"He does indeed, Miriam. The one I like most though is this:

When the student is ready, the teacher will appear."

"How true, Yeshua, you are my teacher and you came along at a time when I am so ready to learn. Who were the others you mentioned."

"Plato and Aristotle, they were both great Greek philosophers that influenced humanity's way of thinking, Aristotle was Plato's student. Plato lived just over four hundred years ago. These men wrote so much down it will take a lifetime to study and absorb, and their writing will influence us for centuries to come. They explored justice, equality, beauty, education and theology, which are humanity's relationship with God, and God's relationship with us. Plato believed that we have a soul that is eternal and explored the possibility of an afterlife and the soul has three functions, reason, emotion and desire. These great thinkers did not have the richness of our experience with Yahweh, Miriam. They were before our time, before Yahweh revealed himself to us as a Father who loves us, who wants to pour out his love for us, and wants our love in return, a Father who is compassionate, generous, and magnanimous, who has given us all of creation, and whose love for us is eternal, limitless and unconditional."

"We are indeed blessed, Yeshua."

"Miriam, I must go, it is getting late. I have to still pack, and I want to have a good night's sleep because I want to start my long walk home early tomorrow. It is so much easier to walk when it is cool, and also so enjoyable to be walking when the sun comes up and all of nature and all of Yahweh's creation comes to life, especially the birds that will accompany me along the way."

"Oh sorry, Yeshua, I have kept you. I am going to miss your visits, and so will Martha, Lazarus and mother. Shalom, Yeshua. Martha, Yeshua is leaving," Miriam called out to her sister who was with her mother.

"Shalom, Yeshua, I have prepared this for your journey tomorrow." Martha handed Yeshua a parcel wrapped in cloth.

"Thank you, Martha, you are so kind. I will see you all again in three months' time. Let me go and say goodbye to your mother."

When Yeshua returned from saying goodbye to Rahab, he hugged Martha and Miriam warmly. They came to the front of the house to see Yeshua on his way, and waved when he finally slipped into the distance.

The next day, well before the sun was up, Yeshua was on the road to Nazareth.

Chapter Twenty-One
Annus Horribilis

Yeshua's homecoming was both full of joy and sadness. Miriam and Yosef were beside themselves with happiness in seeing Yeshua again. It seemed as if he had been away for years. It was the first time they had not seen him for so long and it was a shock to their lives. But grief had descended on the household. Jehoyakim, Miriam's father, was very ill, in fact he was dying and not expected to live much longer. He struggled to breathe, his lungs giving up on him. Yeshua went to his side immediately, and remained there every waking moment.

Jehoyakim was seventy-two years old and had lived a full life; he was feeling sad because he had to leave Hannah behind. He would no longer be able to care for her but he was comforted in knowing he had his daughter and son-in-law and Yeshua close by. He knew they would love her and care for her. He motioned to Yeshua to come closer because he could hardly speak. In fits and starts he struggled to speak, "Yeshua, you… have been a good… son to Miriam… and Yosef… and a grandson to Hannah… and me. You have brought so much… happiness into our lives… I know… you will continue to love and care… for them and… for my Hannah." It caused him so much effort to speak, for he could hardly breathe. Yeshua, Miriam and Yosef took turns to be at Jehoyakim's bedside and Hannah would not leave him alone.

When Yeshua had a moment with Hannah, he asked, "How are you, Gran?" Yeshua knew that she must be suffering so much at the prospect of losing Jehoyakim. Yeshua loved his grandparents. He received so much love from them, and they spoilt him when he was growing up. He could not imagine life without his grandfather.

On the second day at about noon, Jehoyakim died, surrounded by Hannah, Miriam, Yosef and Yeshua. Tears were running down all their faces, as grief overcame them. Hannah asked Yeshua to say a prayer. He prayed, "Adonai, God of love and mercy, we recommend to you for your safekeeping our grand-abba, he was grand indeed, grand in love, goodness, kindness and we weep his leaving us, but at the same time we are comforted in knowing he is with you face to face. He is home away from home. Or rather he has been home away from home; like we still are, but now he is really and truly home, with you his heavenly Father. We pray for Hannah who grieves his loss. Heavenly Father who art in heaven, glory be to you. Your kingdom come as it is in heaven. Your will be done on this earth as it is done in heaven. Give Jehoyakim all the joy and happiness he deserves and give Hannah all the strength and support and love she needs. And forgive us Father for all our transgressions as we forgive those who hurt and offend us. In times of difficulty and temptation deliver us, and in times when Gran Immah is feeling overwhelmed, lift her up. Amen."

"Thank you, Yeshua," Hannah said, as she embraced Yeshua.

Yeshua held her for a long time, as long as she wanted and needed to be held.

The whole of Nazareth came to the funeral. Gamaliel now a recognised rabbi, as well as teacher, officiated at the funeral. Yeshua and Hannah were so glad to have him preside over the funeral of their beloved Jehoyakim.

At the gathering afterwards, Yeshua was able to meet all of Nazareth, and of course his loving friends, Achim and Rebecca and also Zadok and his betrothed Gadija who came all the way from Tiberias. Yeshua was so pleased to see how well and happy and different Zadok looked.

"You look so happy, Zadok, you seem to be radiating joy, as if you are floating above the ground," Yeshua said, smiling. He was truly pleased to see the genuine radiance on the face of his friend. "Gadija, it is so nice to see you and Zadok, and I can see you two are so happy. You must let me know when the great day of your wedding is, so I can make sure I am in Nazareth."

"We hope to marry sometime in the middle of next year, Yeshua, and Zadok and I want you to be our best man," Gadija said.

"I'd love to and am honoured to be asked." Just then Yeshua caught the eye of Rebecca. She was looking at him and waiting patiently to have some time with him. "Excuse me Gadija, I see my friend Rebecca over there. I haven't had a chance to speak with her since coming back from Jerusalem. I'll see you later and before you and Zadok return to Tiberias."

Yeshua approached a smiling and radiant Rebecca. She seemed to glow as Yeshua approached. She threw herself into his arms in total abandon, not caring for social appropriateness. She was just so glad to see Yeshua. She missed him so much; the nine months was more like nine years.

"Oh, Yeshua, I am so sorry for your loss, and at the same time I am so happy to see you again, after all these years, you look good."

"It's been months, not years, Becky, I mean Rebecca," Yeshua said smiling. "So how have you been?"

"Life has been a bit dull without you around," she said. "You must tell me all about your nine months, in Jerusalem's School of Advanced Learning," Miriam said, so obviously happy to see her loving friend. They chatted for quite some time and then Yeshua excused himself telling her he had to mingle, and that he would catch up with her later.

The remaining stay of Yeshua in Nazareth was relaxing and taxing. Everyone wanted a piece of him, they all wanted to know and hear what he had learned and experienced in Jerusalem. They were all so proud of Yeshua. He was the first Nazarene to be accepted by that prestigious school.

Yeshua spoke, or rather preached at the synagogue that Sabbath. Gamaliel had asked him to, and all the people were so impressed by his sermon. He spoke with such ease and simplicity, yet his messages were so deep and made everyone reflect on their relationship with Yahweh. He spoke of Yahweh's great love for us all, his infinite, compassionate and unconditional love, and Yeshua praised and affirmed all in the synagogue, for their faithfulness and their love for Yahweh and for each other, and he encouraged them to continue.

Before he knew it the three months had passed, and it was a full three months for Yeshua. He did his rounds of goodbyes and of course Rebecca almost smothered him with her hugging.

It was a bleak morning, the clouds threatening rain as Yeshua set out for Jerusalem to begin his second year at the School of Advanced Learning. He was looking forward to learning some more. He would now move to the Year Two classes. There would be a new batch of students beginning their first year. Yeshua was looking forward to meeting them, and all his fellow students. However, Yeshua was still grieving the loss of his grandfather. He knew the grief would stay with him for some time. His studies would help.

As usual, Yeshua left Nazareth when the town was still asleep, way before sunrise. As the weather was quite cool and the sky overcast it was good weather for walking at a brisk pace, and he prayed it wouldn't rain. By the time the sun rose, a few hours later, the sky began to clear and there didn't seem to be any rain in the clouds, so Yeshua continued to walk at a brisk pace. It was late in the day and dusk by the time he reached Sychar, a town on the outskirts of Samaria. Yeshua decided to seek lodgings in Samaria and would have liked to stay there for a day or two and get to know the Samaritans a bit better, but he did not know how welcome he would be. He shelved that idea for another time. He only stopped to eat and sleep and then was on his way, early the next morning before the town was awake. It was a lonely journey, which Yeshua didn't mind, as his three months in Nazareth was quite hectic. He enjoyed the solitude and he never felt alone, as he chatted with Yahweh as he walked. And he did encounter some travellers going in the opposite direction. He greeted them warmly but then proceeded on his own.

The second year was off with a bang. A new teacher, an expert in the Law joined the staff. Yeshua learned all about the law, and it wasn't something he enjoyed. The more than six hundred laws, he felt was way too much for ordinary people to grasp and adhere to. He felt those laws needed to be simplified, and a lot of them seemed ridiculous to him. The laws needed to be simplified and updated and suitable for real people to understand and be able to live by, without suffocating them. It was not the Law so much that mattered to Yahweh, but the spirit with which people applied them, and the spirit with which they lived their lives. Yeshua welcomed this new expert and hoped for some lively debates with him and the class.

One month into his second year, in mid-morning, Yeshua was surprised to be called to the common room because he had a visitor. He wondered who it could be and was surprised to see Lazarus. Lazarus had never been to the school before, in fact visitors were not allowed except in extenuating circumstances or for compassionate reasons. Yeshua felt a sense of apprehension.

"Lazarus, how good to see you. Is everything all right with your mother, with Miriam and Martha?" Yeshua asked hoping that they were.

"It's mother, Yeshua, she is very sick, in fact she is dying, and she is asking for you, as is Miriam and Martha, can you come?"

"Of course, of course, right away. I'll just speak to my superiors and pack my back pack and be with you shortly." Yeshua rushed off and soon returned to Lazarus, and were on their way to Bethany.

Martha ran out of the house to greet Yeshua, while Miriam stayed at her mother's bed side. When they entered the house, all was quiet. Martha took Yeshua to her mother's bed. "Immah, it's Yeshua, he has come to see you," Martha said. She had to raise her voice as her mother could hardly hear her anymore and she looked so gaunt and feeble.

Yeshua greeted Miriam briefly with 'Shalom Miriam,' and a nod, and then went straight to Rahab's bedside. He took her hand in his. She seemed to come alive briefly and gave a glimpse of a smile, but then seemed to collapse with the effort.

Yeshua's heart went out to Rahab. He was still grieving the loss of his grandfather and now he had another shock. Rahab was like a second grandmother to him. He loved her as if she was his own, and to see her now, filled him with sadness.

She was always sickly but now she was a shadow of her former self, and Yeshua could see she did not have long to live, for she was struggling to breathe. She was no longer able to eat and drink. Miriam simply soaked a feather in water, and slipped it along her tongue for some relief.

"Dear Rahab, I am sorry that you are not well. I am here. I will stay here with you, Miriam, Martha and Lazarus. We are all here with you. You know that we love you Rahab, and we are so grateful for the love you have given us. Do just rest. We are here." Yeshua continued to hold Rahab's hand. After a while she seemed to fall asleep, although she only did so for short periods but when she did, Lazarus took over from Yeshua to hold his mother's hand. They all took turns to hold their mother's hand, until about an hour before midnight, when she died.

Yeshua noticed how she seemed to come alive at that very moment, as if she was seeing a beautiful sight or a beautiful person, for a radiant smile lit up her face. It seemed as if she was a young girl again, and then she breathed her last. Tears flowed from Miriam, Martha and Lazarus' eyes. Yeshua wept, and was filled with compassion and love for his dearest friends. He reached out and touched them. Miriam leapt into his arms, and wept on his chest. He held her with all the love in his heart. They all remained so, still and weeping. Yeshua's grief was intensified. This is the second person whom he loved that has died. "Adonai, this is more than I can bear," he prayed. "But how much more Martha, Miriam and Lazarus must be suffering, do hold them in the palm of your hand."

Yeshua stayed with them for the funeral and the gathering afterwards. He decided to stay a couple of days with them, to grieve with them and to comfort them. The two days stretched into four when Yeshua thought he could finally leave them. It was a sad parting but they were so grateful that Yeshua shared his time with them, and he brought them so much comfort.

Before going back to the school, Yeshua spent some time in the Temple to pray for his friends in Bethany but also for himself to ask for strength to bear the grief that seemed to be weighing him down. He felt so depressed. His whole world seemed dark. After finding some peace in the Temple, he headed to the school with a heavy heart.

It took a while for Yeshua to settle in again, but he was glad for the studies and the busyness of life in the College, especially the working breaks he had tending to the animals and the farm. But in the midst of so much activity and surrounded by so many students and teachers, Yeshua felt a deep loneliness and sadness. He was still grieving for the loss of his grandfather and his second grandmother, Rahab. He just couldn't seem to shake the heaviness of heart and darkness in his soul. How Yeshua wished he was with his mother, and Gamaliel and Rebecca, he could talk to them, unburden his soul with them. Here in Jerusalem, at this school there was no one he felt he could really confide in, someone who would understand. Yeshua gave himself over to his studies, his work in the fields and threw himself into his debates. He was still grieving the two losses of two of his loved ones, when a third shock would rock his world.

It was barely a month since he left his friends at Bethany and now, he got a message that he had a visitor in the common room. Yeshua surmised it would only be bad news, just like the previous visit. But his eyes lit up and his heart leapt when he saw Gamaliel. They greeted and embraced.

"Oh Gamaliel, it is so good to see you, let's go outside and walk and talk. Or better still just wait here, I will go to my superiors and ask for some leave to go to the city centre with you for a bite to eat and maybe a cup of wine." Yeshua dashed off and was back within minutes, his heart racing and uplifted, so pleased to see Gamaliel. He thanked Yahweh for sending his friend.

"So, what brings you to Jerusalem, Gamaliel? It is so good to see you," Yeshua said, when he returned. Yeshua was beside himself with joy. He so much needed to see someone from Nazareth, his mother, or Rebecca or Gamaliel, and Yahweh had answered his unuttered prayer. He has sent Gamaliel, Yeshua thought.

Yeshua was oblivious to the real reason why Gamaliel was in Jerusalem but he knew that Gamaliel often came to Jerusalem during his school breaks, so he surmised he was on one of those breaks. They chatted about all the people and the happenings in Nazareth and at Gamaliel's school and Yeshua chatted about all his experiences here at the School of Advanced Learning. Yeshua wanted to know how grand Immah was doing, and his mother and father. Gamaliel put Yeshua at ease and told him that he often visited them, and that lightened Yeshua's heart.

When they finally sat down for a light meal and some wine, Gamaliel asked how Yeshua was holding up after the deaths of both his grandfather and Rahab. He knew of her death, because Yeshua had already written to him.

For the first time, Yeshua was able to pour out his heart and he told Gamaliel how heartbroken he was to have lost his grand abba and Rahab. They died in such a similar way and they were of about the same age. Gamaliel and Yeshua were able to talk about Hannah for Gamaliel knew her well and Yeshua was able to tell Gamaliel all about Rahab, who was like a second grandmother to him. He told Gamaliel all about his friendship with Lazarus, Martha and Miriam, and his home away from home, for he often went there whenever he could. Gamaliel listened and allowed Yeshua to speak and pour his heart out. Yeshua felt a dark cloud lifting and his heart felt a release.

"Oh Gamaliel, it is so good to see you and speak to you. You are looking well, what about you, how are you doing?" Yeshua asked.

Gamaliel looked at Yeshua and knew that it was time to tell him the real reason why he was in Jerusalem. "Yeshua, I know you have been to hell and back with the loss of two people you greatly loved, but I have some more really bad news, your father Yosef is very ill and I have come to take you back to Nazareth. I went and visited him and Miriam. She asked me to get word to you, and I suggested, offered to come and tell you in person, and accompany you back to Nazareth," Gamaliel said, his heart going out to his friend and student.

"Oh no!" Yeshua cried out. "Oh Adonai, please no, this is more than I can endure. Please keep Yosef safe, and make him well again…we must go at once," Yeshua then said, and practically jumped from his seat. They hurried back to the school and Yeshua took his leave.

Gamaliel and Yeshua left immediately. It was now about an hour after noon and they travelled throughout the day and only stopped to sleep along the way. The distance from Jerusalem is just over ninety miles and usually Yeshua would walk it in four days, but this time he and Gamaliel did it in three and a half days. They arrived at Nazareth at nightfall, exhausted but Yeshua and Gamaliel went straight to Yeshua's home.

Miriam and Hannah were so happy to see Yeshua. Hannah had already moved in with Yosef and Miriam after Jehoyakim had died. "Oh Yeshua, it so good to see you," Miriam cried as she hugged her son.

Yeshua held his mother for a while before releasing her and going to his father's bedside.

"Abba, it is good to be here with you. I am here now, to stay. I am so sorry, Abba, that you are not well." Gamaliel had already filled in Yeshua on all of Yosef's symptoms. It was felt that Yosef had picked up an infection while he was away in Tiberias working. It seemed to have attacked his lungs and spread throughout his body. It first began with Yosef breaking out into night sweats, shortness of breath, and Yosef complained of chest pain. The doctor gave him some medicine to ease the pain.

Yeshua took the cool cloth from Miriam and continued wiping Yosef's brow. Yosef was struggling to breathe. Yeshua was shocked at how quickly his father had deteriorated from the time he last saw his father, before leaving for Jerusalem. Yosef was only in his mid-fifties and he was robust, strong and healthy. But now he was a shadow of his former self. Yeshua who was at the bedside of both Jehoyakim and Rahab knew the signs and knew that Yosef was dying. He prayed, silently, "Oh Yahweh, this is too much. Mother has lost her father. Please do not let her lose her husband too, and so soon. I pray that this fever and this infection leave him." Yeshua took his father's hand in his. "Father, I am here; I will stay with you at your side and I am praying for you." Yeshua was at a loss of how to comfort his father and his mother. He could just remain at his father's side, stroke his forehead with a cool rag and hold and stroke his hand. He stayed there for a long time, until Miriam took over and Yeshua went outside and wept. He wept for his father, and his two grandmothers, and his mother, and for himself.

After a while Gamaliel, who was still there, came outside and comforted Yeshua, putting his arm around Yeshua's shoulder. He said nothing, simply stood beside Yeshua in silence, holding him for as long as Yeshua needed him. After a while, Yeshua dried his tears and went to take over from his mother and found that Grandmother was now beside Yosef, holding his hand. Yeshua was glad for he wanted to comfort his mother.

He went straight to her and held out his arms and she rushed into them and wept. Yeshua held her. "Oh Immah, you suffer much, your father and now Yosef. I am here Immah, I am here, and I am here to stay," Yeshua said, as he continued to hold his mother as long as she needed to be held. When she released her arms from around Yeshua, she went straight to take over from her mother to be beside Yosef. Within an hour Yosef died.

Again, Yeshua noticed the radiance on Yosef's face at the moment his spirit left his body, radiance so deep and joyful, like Moses' face when he came down from Mount Sinai after he had seen the Lord, Yeshua thought. He immediately went to hold his mother again as she wept. They remained motionless in their sorrow.

The whole of Nazareth attended the funeral. Yosef was admired and loved by all. He had done so much work for them, and they now treasured all of these. Their friend and carpenter were no more.

Yeshua stayed another two weeks. Miriam was so pleased but she knew that Yeshua would need to go back to Jerusalem, to continue his studies. Yosef would have wanted that. But Yeshua had other ideas. He had spoken to Gamaliel and said he would quit his studies in Jerusalem, and continue his private tuition with him. He did not want to leave his mother and grandmother alone. And he needed to support them by taking over his father's business, as a carpenter. Miriam, as much as she loved Yeshua staying, she wanted him to continue his learning. But Yeshua would not be persuaded. In the end Miriam was really pleased to have her son home with her and mother. He brought so much comfort to her and made her endure her losses so much easier.

Chapter Twenty-Two
The Carpenter

Yeshua was still grieving three great losses in so quick a succession. It was too much for such a young person to endure. But Yeshua prayed about it, often, expressed his feelings to Yahweh, and wept in private. He also spoke to Gamaliel, who was a great listener, and a comforter. Rebecca too was a great support to Yeshua in his time of grieving. At the same time Yeshua made sure he listened to and comforted both his mother and grandmother, for they too were still grieving the loss of the men in their lives. Yeshua became quite busy, as the people of Nazareth gave him more and more work. He was good at his work, for he loved carpentry, working with wood. But Yosef had also worked with stone and even dabbled in working with metal. Yeshua had learned some of those skills too, so he also had stonework to do, on the homes of the community. He also maintained the community hall, which was used for both the synagogue, and school activities.

When Yeshua visited Zadok, he learned a bit more metal skill. So, Yeshua was busy for this first year and did not need to go outside of Nazareth to find work. Yeshua also did work for many of the poorer residents of Nazareth, and they, if they could not afford to pay him, he accepted the produce that they gave him instead. Miriam continued to do sewing and earn an extra amount for the household.

The next three years flew by and Miriam, Hannah, and Yeshua were now well into the phase of acceptance in their grieving. They had been a strong support to each other and not having to grieve alone helped. They also had their faith and a supportive community. All this had helped to finally accept their losses. Yeshua, having been so busy with work and study, also helped him a lot. He loved his work and the people he worked for, and they loved him in return. Yeshua saw his work not only as a means of income and support for himself and his mother and grandmother, but also as a service and as a prayer, a sacrifice to Yahweh. For him work is prayer and prayer is work. By the work of our hands, we give glory to Yahweh. Yeshua knew that work is good for the soul, and to love one's work and the spirit with which one worked is important. Even in the most banal of work, like cleaning their home, or doing the laundry, Yeshua felt that to do these tasks with a good spirit made it easier and also gave glory to Yahweh, as well as satisfaction to his mother and grandma, to see the place so spick and span. Yeshua did the heavy cleaning and kept the house clean inside and outside as well. He also kept the common outside community area in good shape, and this gave great pleasure not only to Miriam and Hanna, but to the neighbours as well.

Yeshua still took his long walks or short walks into the forest whenever he could. Occasionally he joined Rebecca on her morning run. He could do so because she liked to run early in the morning when most of the town was still asleep, or at least just waking up. Yeshua worked five days a week and took at least one day off beside the Sabbath. He sometimes joined Rebecca on those days for her run. And on his off day they sometimes had breakfast together. Rebecca was not a regular attendee of the Sabbath ceremonies but since hanging out with Yeshua, she had changed her attitude somewhat, and now attended more often. And she liked Gamaliel's sermons.

He was so down to earth and did not preach to the converted or to people who were not there. He spoke to those present, and did not only emphasise that they are sinners and warn them or frighten them with hell and damnation, as she had heard other rabbis, on the rare occasions when she happened to be at a service. Rebecca felt that the rabbis were forever warning people of the dangers of the devil and of their sinfulness and need for repentance. It was all fire and brimstone, and they made her feel as if Yahweh was a vengeful and overbearing Lord, who watched and waited for one to slip up, so he could punish. Gamaliel instead was so affirming and encouraging and spoke of the goodness of people, and of the love, compassion and forgiveness of Yahweh.

Yeshua was always pleased to see Rebecca at the Sabbath service, and would always chat with her afterwards. During this time, Yeshua no longer wanted to give any sermons at the synagogue services, and refused Gamaliel's invitations. He felt Gamaliel was so much wiser and more experienced, and the people were getting so much out of him. And besides he was now a full-time carpenter.

While Yeshua enjoyed Rebecca's friendship, and the time they spent together, he prayed that she would find a man and fall in love, and betroth, and have someone who could love her as a husband and have children with her. He trusted that Yahweh would hear his prayer. Yeshua also prayed for himself that he may remain pure and spotless in the sight of Yahweh and be faithful in the life of celibacy, which Yahweh has called him to. Yeshua would have loved just being like everyone else, fall in love, with Rebecca, build a home with her, have children with her, love her and love their children, and be like everyone else, but that was not to be. Yahweh had made it clear that day in the Temple in Jerusalem when he was just fifteen. That conversation with Yahweh, the voice of Yahweh speaking to him was still so clear, as if it was yesterday. It was not a human voice; it was a divine voice but a voice he heard deep within his soul. It is something he could not explain, and no one would understand, unless they had the same experience. *It must have been like that for Moses on Mount Sinai*, Yeshua thought. *Well, I had my Mount Sinai experience, when the Lord had spoken to me and gave me my mission*, Yeshua mused. *Mother had already told me so much about my birth that is like no other, but I did not fully understand, even when I had that experience in the Temple, but it has become clearer and clearer. Yahweh has a special mission for me and I am destined to suffer and die for that*, Yeshua thought.

These thoughts about his life and mission seemed to come to the fore on the Sabbath when Yeshua attended the service and listened to readings from Scripture and listened to Yahweh's relationship with his people and with all humankind, and Yahweh's boundless love for us all. Yeshua became more and more conscious of his divine sonship. He was the child of Miriam and Yosef but also the child of God. He was both fully human and fully divine. How these two traits in his being would be fully expressed he trusted that Yahweh's Spirit would be his guide.

Sabbath was a day of the Lord and for the Lord, and the people kept the Sabbath holy by refraining from work and of course by attending worship in the synagogue. Yeshua enjoyed the Sabbath, being able to spend most of the day with his mother and grandmother and with his friends. He would at times visit Achim and his parents. And they were always delighted to see him. On his other non-Sabbath day off, Yeshua would sometimes take a walk to Tiberias and visit his friend Zadok who was now married to Gadija and they were expecting their first child. They had got married at around the same time that Yeshua was called to the bedside of his friend at Bethany, and actually got married on the day that Yeshua attended the funeral of his friend. So, Yeshua missed the wedding and being the best man. They could not change the date and Yeshua was so sorry he missed their great day, but now was so pleased to see them. And it was such a joy for Yeshua to spend time with them and both Zadok and Gadija were overjoyed to have Yeshua with them. It did make Yeshua envious in a way. He could imagine, himself and Rebecca in that situation but he dismissed the idea immediately because he knew it was never to be. He was called to love no one person in particular in this way but he was to love everyone in a special way, he was to bring Yahweh's unfathomable love to all of humankind. Yeshua at times like this felt himself weaken, and he prayed to his heavenly Father to give him the strength to live his mission, and to spread Yahweh's love to all of humanity, and to all with whom he came into contact and here and now to Zadok and Gadija.

Yeshua's life took on a routine of work, five days a week, a run once a week with Rebecca, attending of the Sabbath celebrations, solitary walks with Yahweh, community celebrations, and now only twice-weekly sessions with Gamaliel on the Sabbath and on his day off. He had to forfeit the other days as he had to work from dawn to dusk, to support his mother, his grandmother and himself. Yeshua took pride in his work and was admired for his fine craftsmanship. And every third year, Yeshua joined the Nazarenes on their pilgrimage to Jerusalem for the celebration of the Passover.

As Yeshua had now been working three years without a break, he thought it was time for a holiday. He had always wanted to walk, all around the Sea of Galilee, which was really the Lake of Galilee. He had already seen so much of Jerusalem and it's surrounds that he wanted to explore elsewhere. As spring was approaching between the third and sixth month of the year, Yeshua thought the weather and the time was right for his first holiday. Ever since Yeshua first went on a fishing trip with Yosef to the Sea of Galilee, he had a desire to walk around the lake. And for this first holiday that is what he was now planning to do. It might take him at least a week to walk around the lake. He was excited as the time arrived for him to set off on his first adventure on his own.

"Yeshua, you sure you want to do this trip, walking all the way around the Sea of Galilee, that will take you forever," Miriam said. She knew that he could take care of himself and that he was fit and strong, yet she was worried him travelling these paths that he had not travelled before, and on his own. "What route will you be taking, Yeshua, are you going to head straight for Tiberias, and will you go north first, or head south around the Sea of Galilee?" Miriam was curious and she wanted to know where Yeshua would be over these next days and weeks.

"Immah, the distance around the Lake of Galilee, is less than forty miles. I will be starting early each day at sunrise and walk until midday, for five or six hours a day and then remain in whatever place I find myself. I don't want to rush but enjoy the walk and the sea and the people and all it has to offer. There are about six to seven towns around the lake where I will definitely stop for the day. As the weather will be fine, I will find a place in the fields to sleep, there are also plenty of caves about. While I would like to explore the mountains and valleys on this route, this time I just want the experience of going all around the sea and familiarising myself with the terrain, and enjoy the walking, and enjoy the scenery and of course the people I will meet along the way. There is of course the city of Tiberias and at least six or seven towns around the sea where I will stop and rest. I am looking forward to this walk Immah. And don't worry, I will be all right, and I will be careful."

"So will you be heading for Tiberias, which will take a long time as well?" Miriam asked.

"No, Immah, I did that fishing and camping holiday with Abba at Tiberias, so I will be heading for the town of Magdala, north of Tiberias. I will first pass through Cana, which is not far, about four or five miles and continue on to Ziddim which is about half way to Magdala, and rest up there. I should be able to walk to Magdala on the coast in about three days, allowing stops along the way. It does look like I will most likely need more than a week Immah to get to the lake, go all around it and then get home. I'll most likely take at least two weeks. But I am going to take a good break, and not rush, and so you can only start worrying if I am not home within three weeks," Yeshua said, smiling. "Please don't worry Immah, I will be okay, Adonai will be with me. He has a big job for me, so he will have to keep me safe," Yeshua said, smiling even more broadly.

"You are right, Yeshua, don't worry, leave all the worrying to me," Miriam said, still smiling. "You better get a good night's rest now." She hugged her son and kissed him.

"Goodnight, Immah. Don't get up in the morning. I will be leaving very early, before you get up. So goodbye for now and see you next year," Yeshua joked. "See you in four weeks' time," he added. Yeshua had already said his goodbye to his grandmother, who was already asleep. Yeshua then made sure his backpack was packed with all he needed, and then retired.

The next morning early, while the whole of Nazareth was still asleep, except for the insects and the odd birds and little animals of the night, Yeshua was on his way. The early morning air was crisp, but it was spring, so it wasn't chilly at all, and once the sun was up, it would be most pleasant walking. Yeshua enjoyed the stillness and the quiet of the early morning. He was looking forward to this walk and he felt like an explorer. His first stop was to be Cana, which he would reach in about a few hours, so he would simply pass through as most of the town will still be asleep, or just waking up.

It was the first hour after sunrise when Yeshua arrived at the sleepy town of Cana. Most people were already stirring and farmers were out and about tending to their goats and sheep and milking the cows. Yeshua waved to those that saw him, walking past their farms. He saw smoke spiralling from fireplaces, most probably women baking bread or warming milk or cooking for the day. He saw some women, outside their homes doing the washing. Yeshua greeted those who were close enough, and he waved to those who were far off. They all greeted him warmly with a smile.

Yeshua stopped in the centre of the town for a drink of water. He was not yet hungry, only thirsty; he would walk another hour or two and then have breakfast. His mother had baked bread for him the night before, and that would last for at least three days. He also had some fresh figs and berries and they would not last long in the warm weather. He also had some dried figs with him and he would be able to find fresh fruit to eat along the way. Yeshua was enjoying the solitude, as he left Cana, and continued on his way towards the town of Magdala on the lake. His only stop would be about half way to the town of Magdala, at the town of Ziddim. Yeshua walked for another hour and a half when he stopped for a bite to eat. The bread was still fresh, and the figs ripe. He sat down against a tree in the field. Across from where he was sitting, he saw farmers out in the fields tending to their crops and there were sheep and goats grazing, as well as cows and some donkeys. A few travellers past by on foot and they stopped and greeted Yeshua and they chatted for a while. They were interested to know that Yeshua came from Nazareth, and that he was on his way to Magdala and then walking all the way around the lake. They wished Yeshua well and went on their way.

Yeshua sat for a while, just enjoying the pleasant morning sun, and a slight breeze. "Good morning brother sun, I greet you," Yeshua said, as he looked towards the sky. "You are great indeed brother Sun, without you there is no light, or warmth, or energy or life itself, thank you. And thank you Yahweh for Brother Sun. Abba, heavenly Father, it is time I call you Yahweh. You are my father; you have work for me. All of creation is our kin, like family, brothers and sisters. Sister Wind, thank you for the soft breeze that caresses my face and that makes the leaves of the trees dance to your tune. Thank you for the refreshment you give us, by keeping us cool. And Brother Tree, thank you for the support and the shade you give me and the birds that nestle among your branches. Mother Earth and Father Sky thank you for embracing me and Mother Nature, I thank you for all the beauty with which you surround us. I thank you Yahweh, for your beautiful creation. I look at the birds in the fields, they do not sow or reap yet you feed them. Yahweh, I offer you my day and I offer you myself, all that I am I give to you. Your will be done on earth as it is in heaven."

After Yeshua felt fed and rested, he continued on his solitary walk. He walked at a leisurely pace. It was warm, not unpleasantly so, and a slight breeze, in fact the weather was perfect, so Yeshua took his time. He wanted to enjoy the walk and the sights and sounds, He often stopped to take in the scenery, the distant mountains and valleys, the beautiful landscapes, the cattle grazing, the birds flying about, singing, croaking and showing off as they glided through the sky, mostly in small groups of two or three, sometimes more, and sometimes a lone bird would glide close past him as if to say 'shalom'.

It was late afternoon when Yeshua arrived at Ziddim, which is half way to Magdala. Yeshua decided to rest in the town. He greeted those whom he encountered and they would notice that he was not of their town and they welcomed him warmly and engaged in conversation with him. They were warm and inviting when hearing that he had come all the way from Nazareth and that he was on his way to Magdala and then all the way around the lake. They were intrigued because none of them had dreamed of walking all the way around the Sea of Galilee. They thought he was crazy, but some of the teenagers thought it exciting. Yeshua rested at the fountain where he drew some water to drink and filled his water bag and continued chatting with all those who came to draw water. The water was so fresh, Yeshua enjoyed the drink. Yeshua talked to a blacksmith, and they could converse about the trade. Yeshua told the man, David, about his friend Zadok, who worked as a blacksmith in Tiberias. David was very interested because he was thinking of going there to live for a while and see what the work was like. Yeshua told him to find Zadok and mention that they met.

"Where are you staying for the night?" David asked.

"I don't know yet, I will find a spot in a cave somewhere, or wherever I can find some cover of sorts," Yeshua said.

"You can stay with us for the night. I'll make a spare bed for you," David offered.

"You are so kind. Thank you, I accept your offer." Yeshua was delighted. He was prepared for sleeping rough and now Yahweh has provided a place to sleep and some genial company to enjoy. David was married to Phoebe and he had two sons and two daughters. The youngest were the two girls, who were identical twins, and they were about ten years of age. The two boys were around Yeshua's age. They were like all country people, friendly and welcoming of the stranger in their midst. The girls were especially fascinated with Yeshua when they learned that he was going to walk all around the Sea of Galilee. Phoebe was a woman of few words but she made Yeshua welcome, and got bedding for him and made sure he would be comfortable for the night. They had a meal of stew with plenty of vegetables and bread. Yeshua was grateful and thanked Phoebe for the most welcome and tasty homecooked meal. Yeshua wasn't sure when he would have a homecooked meal again.

One of the great things about hiking Yeshua thought was the people he would meet on the way, and the new friends he would make. Already he made new friends with David, Phoebe and their four children, Judah, Yosef, Rachel and Lydia. Yosef was quite a common name and Yosef was pleased to hear that Yeshua's father's name was Yosef, but sorry to hear that he had died more than three years ago. Yeshua spoke about his father and his work as a carpenter and the boys were impressed with Yeshua when they discovered that he was a skilled carpenter and that he also worked with stone and metal.

Yosef worked as a labourer on a nearby farm and Judah was following in his father's footsteps as an apprentice to his father in his blacksmith trade. Yeshua also mentioned Zadok to Judah and said he could call on Zadok if ever he was in Tiberias, and just mention his name. Judah said he would, for he was actually thinking of visiting Tiberias on his next break from work. The girls wanted to know what it was like in Tiberias, and Yeshua, the boys and their father discussed Tiberias. Sepphoris was the capital city of Galilee and with Tiberias it was where most of the people lived, while under a thousand people resided both in Nazareth and here in Ziddim. Thousands of people lived in Tiberias and Sepphoris, more than ten thousand for sure.

"The elites live there," David said, "the government and tax officials lived there in their mansions built with the taxes ripped off from hardworking people like us," David added.

"The religious elites as well," Yosef said. "And they lord it over the people and work hand in glove with the government officials. And the tax-collectors are the worst, Jews like us, yet they rip us off, taking a cut for themselves, and they live in style and luxury," Yosef added angrily.

"Many people in Tiberias also fished for a livelihood, as the Sea of Galilee has lots of fresh water fish," Yeshua said. And he told them about the time he and Yosef had spent time fishing there. "And Tiberias is named after the Roman Emperor Tiberias, who now rules over us. He is the stepson of Caesar Augustus," Yeshua told them.

The girls were so impressed with Yeshua's knowledge of history. Yeshua told them all about the school at Nazareth, and also his teacher and Rabbi Gamaliel, in

Nazareth. The girls wanted to know if girls also attended the school. Yeshua told them they did, but only for a few years to learn the basics of reading and writing, and they learned religion at Sabbath school, which Gamaliel gave to all children, who remained after the Sabbath service.

"I suppose the river that runs through Rome the Tiber must be named after the Emperor Tiberias," Rachel said, wanting to pick Yeshua's brains.

"Actually, it was named after Tiberius, who was a Tuscan king who supposedly drowned in the river. The Tiber is over two hundred and fifty miles long and runs through Rome and into the Great Sea," Yeshua said.

"Okay girls, that's enough history, it's time for bed. Yeshua needs a good sleep, as he wants to leave early in the morning on his journey," David said.

The girls were reluctant to go to sleep, they were so enchanted with Yeshua and his knowledge and they thought he was so handsome too. They said goodnight to Yeshua and wished him a safe and enjoyable journey and told him to call on them on his way back. He promised he would. Yeshua continued chatting with the boys and David and Phoebe for a little while longer, and then sought his leave and thanked them profusely for the fine meal and their hospitality, their kindness, for he was a stranger and they took him in. Yeshua then said his goodbyes. He said he would leave early before they awoke, and he would be quiet.

But when Yeshua awoke about an hour before sunrise, Phoebe was already up and about preparing for their morning meal. She had prepared a breakfast for Yeshua, hot milk, bread she had baked the day before, and two eggs. Yeshua was not accustomed to eat that early but he did not want to disrespect Phoebe, so he tucked into the breakfast and was glad he did. It was a while since he had fresh eggs for breakfast. Phoebe had also packed him some food for the road, dates, nuts, and dried figs, for which Yeshua was most grateful He ate in silence as he and Phoebe did not want to wake anyone. After Yeshua had his meal, he thanked Phoebe profusely and was on his way. The town was asleep and it was still and quiet and a beautiful spring morning. Yeshua felt fortified and thanked Yahweh and asked him to bless David, Phoebe, Judah, Yosef, Lydia and Rachel.

Chapter Twenty-Three
Walking Around the Sea of Galilee

Yeshua began his day as he usually did in prayer. It was more like his morning chat with his heavenly Father and the offering of his day to Yahweh. "Heavenly Father, Yahweh all mighty, powerful and loving. You know me, my rising and my falling, my strengths and my weaknesses. I give you thanks for giving me life. I thank you for all of your creatures, all of creation that surrounds me, all of humanity, that gives us so much pleasure, joy and that nourishes us all. Abba, you have a special mission for me. This is not all that clear to me, but I trust in you and in your Spirit that will guide me on my way. I offer myself to you this day, all that I am, all that I have, think, say, do, feel, desire, suffer, experience. I offer all to you heavenly Father for your greater glory and for the salvation of all humankind. I thank you for this beautiful day and for the family of David and Phoebe that I have met. I ask you to bless them truly, with peace and joy. I pray heavenly Father for the grace to know and love you evermore and to make you known and loved. I pray for the grace of peace, love and joy, that is all I desire, and to spread your love, peace and joy into the world, into all of creation, to all your creatures and to all with whom I come into contact today, and every day. Amen."

As Yeshua continued on his journey, he chatted with his heavenly Father about all that had happened so far. He spoke to the trees as he passed, and whistled to the birds, and greeted them as he passed them while they were feeding on the grass. He said his favourite prayer for the birds, "you do not toil or spin or gather into barns, yet our heavenly Father feeds you, for you are precious in his sight." Then he saw some lilies and he continued with his prayer, "Oh lilies of the field, how beautiful you are, how your heavenly Father and Creator loves and feeds you, endows you with life, and with so much beauty. Yet you are here today and gone tomorrow. If our heavenly Father clothes you thus with so much beauty and love, how much more will he not do for us, clothe us with his beauty and his love." Yeshua continued his morning conversation with Yahweh and with all of nature, and he felt so close to the Creator of all.

Yeshua delighted in seeing the effects of the sun rising from its sleep, the beautiful haze on the spattering of clouds, and it's beginning to light up the sky. The birds were chirping heartily and Yeshua responded by imitating their sounds in greeting. He stopped to watch them flitting in and out of the branches and singing to their hearts content. He watched as they flew, showing off their prowess, as they glided for as long as they could before flapping their wings again. Yeshua enjoyed the experience, the waking of the day and the people, the farmers going about their business, the smoke spiralling into the sky as the baking and cooking began. He had not seen any wildlife; antelopes, wild ox, wild goats, deer, fox or such, but he had his staff with him just in case. But they did not come out into the open and stayed deep within the bushland. Yeshua also knew that there were venomous snakes that would still be hibernating for the next few months or so, but he was still vigilant and kept to the well-trodden paths.

After his morning prayers and his conversations with nature and the birds and animals, seen and unseen, Yeshua walked along in silence. His thoughts would return to Nazareth and his mother and grandmother and he whispered his love for them. He thought of Rebecca and prayed that she would find her soul mate, someone to give her the love she deserved. But then Yeshua began to simply enjoy the pleasure of walking alone. Yeshua was often alone, but never lonely. He always felt the nearness and presence of his heavenly Father in all of creation. He always felt he was being loved by Abba, by so many here on earth, and he had so much love in his heart for all those dear to him, and for all humankind. As he walked, he felt joy in his heart and a peace that no one could take away. And he was grateful.

Yeshua had walked in silence for almost five hours more before he sat down against a tree for a rest and a bite to eat, of what Phoebe had prepared for him. He still had enough water to last him until he reached Magdala. He ate the boiled eggs first, it was hardboiled and still feeling good to eat with his bread, which was still quite fresh. He dipped the bread in the olive oil that Phoebe had given him. He ate some of the fresh figs and berries and kept the dried fruit for later. As he ate, some birds came close looking at him with pleading eyes and watering beaks. Yeshua smiled at them. "You go and find your own food to eat, there is so much around for you that your heavenly Father and Creator gives to you, go!" But they would not go and just stood there pleading with Yeshua, so he relented and threw them some crumbs, which they relished and fought over and made such a big noise. "Don't fight, I've got plenty here," Yeshua said, smiling at them and enjoying their company. When he had stopped feeding them and they realised their free meal was over, they flew away.

Well-fed and well-rested, Yeshua was on his way. He had not passed anyone so far on the road. But as he rose, a man and his donkey appeared. Yeshua greeted him. "Shalom, my good Sir, and what brings you on this way?"

"Shalom, I am from a little village near Magdala and I am on my way home. I have been visiting relatives in Ziddim," the man said.

"I am Yeshua, and I am from Nazareth. I have just met some new friends in Ziddim, David and Phoebe and their four children, twin girls and two boys; do you know them?" Yeshua asked.

"I sure do, I know David the blacksmith quite well, he has done work for me. They are a fine family, and by the way, I am Joshua, and I am pleased to meet you. What takes you to Magdala; you are going to Magdala, are you?" Joshua asked.

"I am. I am Yeshua and I am a carpenter from Nazareth. This is my first holiday since I took over from my father Yosef when he died almost four years ago," Yeshua said.

"I'm so sorry to hear that. So are you staying in Magdala, there are some great fishing spots there, and it is a fine town," Joshua said.

"I will most likely stay the night there, but I am planning to walk around the Lake of Galilee. It is something I wanted to do ever since I visited Tiberias with my father," Yeshua said.

"Where are you staying in Magdala?" Joshua asked.

"Any good caves nearby the town?" Yeshua asked, smiling.

"Oh no, you must stay with us. We will be only too pleased to give you a bed for the night," Joshua offered.

Yeshua sighed and quietly thanked his heavenly Father for caring for him. How fortunate he is to meet such kind and hospitable people on the way. Yeshua was prepared to sleep rough; he did not mind that, but he welcomed the hospitality. "Thank you so much," he said.

Yeshua continued the rest of his journey with Joshua and his donkey for the next couple of hours when Joshua turned into a side road that led to a farm. "I will be dropping in on some friends here, for an hour or so, just to rest the donkey and give him a good feed and then I'll be on my way. Would you like to join me?" Joshua offered.

"Thank you so much, but I will continue on, and catch up with you in Magdala," Yeshua said. While he enjoyed Joshua and his donkey's company, Yeshua yearned for solitude, and silence and he did not want to presume on the hospitality of Joshua's friend, although he knew he would be welcomed. So, they parted ways.

"Joshua told Yeshua to just ask around to where he lived. It was about two miles outside of the town, to the north, it would be on his way of going around the lake, it is a little farm with a little house on the top of a hill," Joshua said.

Yeshua thanked Joshua and patted his donkey, as they parted. Yeshua walked for another couple of hours before he sat down and rested, and had another bite to eat. It was quite warm, as it was a few hours after noon. Yeshua estimated that he should be in Magdala within in a couple of hours. He had rested for a while and thought he would walk more slowly and enjoy the scenery and allow time for Joshua to hopefully catch up. And it worked because as he was coming close to Magdala he saw a figure and his donkey in the distance. Yeshua then stopped and waited until it became clear that it was Joshua, who smiled when they met up again.

"Good timing, Yeshua, it won't be long now." The two men and the donkey continued on until they arrived at Magdala. It was about the tenth hour, about three more hours before sunset. Yeshua was still feeling okay. He was fit and accustomed to walking long distances, and his work and his running with Rebecca kept him fit.

They arrived at Magdala, so close to the Sea of Galilee. "What a beautiful mountain over there," Yeshua said, as he gazed on the mountain overlooking Magdala.

"She is beautiful, isn't she, Arbel, Mount Arbel. We often go there to picnic, and I have climbed to the top. To be a Magdalaean, you have to climb Mount Arbel," Joshua said.

As they entered the town, everyone greeted Joshua as if he was one of their families. And Joshua introduced Yeshua as they engaged in chitchat. Joshua had a little farm, just big enough for his family's needs and that of his few animals. Yeshua was glad that Joshua had some business in the town before heading for home, as Yeshua wanted to see something of the town.

Magdala was like a small Tiberias, a fishing village, little stone and mud homes and a busy marketplace, where people bought and sold produce, household items and clothing. Joshua introduced Yeshua to his two daughters who were selling garments. They were both in their late teens and lovely girls. They were delighted to meet Yeshua. Joshua told them that Yeshua is from Nazareth, and that he would be staying with them this night. The girls, Ruth and Orpah, smiled at Yeshua and it warmed his heart. Yeshua was pleased to meet Ruth and Orpah and he smiled back at them. He thought of Rebecca, she would be pleased to meet Ruth and Orpah because he and Rebecca had been talking about, Ruth and Orpah, the two Moabite women, and daughters-in-law of the widow, Naomi a Judaean woman. Yeshua surmised that Ruth and Orpah were most likely named after those two Moabite women. It was arranged that Ruth and Orpah would accompany Yeshua to their home. Yeshua then took his leave of Joshua and his daughters and arranged to meet up with Ruth and Orpah in a couple of hours. Joshua left the donkey with his girls. The donkey would be used to carry their unsold goods back home.

Yeshua saw some nice scarves at their stall, and he bought two for his mother and grandmother. The girls said they would wrap them and hold them until he returned. They were so pleased to have made the sale. Yeshua said goodbye and went on his way. He browsed around the rest of the stalls, and chatted with the sellers who tried to sell him some of their goods. He bought some dried figs and fruit juice and sat on a bench and had some figs and drank his berry juice, and watched the people going about their business. After a while, Yeshua got up and walked around the rest of the town. He walked towards the lake, and when he got there, he encountered some youngsters who were fishing in a little dinghy not far from the shore. They seemed to be having a lot of fun for Yeshua heard much laughter. Yeshua thought of his father and the time they went fishing in Tiberias.

After a stroll along the seashore, walking barefooted, and letting the eddies lap his feet, and greeting those he met on the way, and watching fishermen or just residents in their little boats on the lake enjoying themselves, Yeshua sat on a sand hill and watched the waves come in and break gently on the shore. He felt so peaceful listening to the sound of waves breaking, it was like music. Yeshua sat in silence and rested and was starting to feel refreshed. As he sat looking out towards the horizon, he could see the effects of the sun descending behind him in the west and he got up and returned to the town centre to meet up with Ruth and Orpah. On his way he came across a little synagogue, and the evening service was in progress, Yeshua went inside and joined in the prayers. They were singing a psalm, Yeshua was surprised to see so many men, of all ages standing and singing the psalm, and he came in when they were singing the last two verses:

O Lord, I love the house, in which you dwell,
and the place where your glory abides.
Do not sweep me away with sinners,
nor my life with the bloodthirsty,
those in whose hands are evil devices,
and whose right hands are full of bribes.

But as for me, I walk in my integrity,
redeem me and be gracious to me.
My foot stands on level ground,
in the great congregation I will bless the Lord.

A lector then went to the lectern and began reading from the Book of Moses. He read about Moses' encounter with Yahweh, and how the Lord asked Moses to remove his shoes for they were standing on holy ground. The rabbi then asked the men to do likewise because they were standing on holy ground. And they all did. Yeshua too removed his sandals. The rabbi then spoke about the presence of Yahweh here in the synagogue, and that all the earth was his sanctuary, and all the earth was sacred, and to walk this earth is to walk on sacred ground. He continued, "The earth is sacred. We need the earth and the earth needs us. We need to look after the earth, as the earth looks after us. Without the earth and all that it produces we would not be able to live. But we need to work with the earth and respect the earth, as we respect its Creator."

Yeshua listened intently and liked what the rabbi was saying.

"For too long," the rabbi continued, "man regarded himself as the master of the earth, when instead he was to be a good steward and care for the earth. Besides being stewards of the earth and all she produces and all her creatures, as Yahweh commanded us to, we are most of all, essentially kin with the earth, we are interdependent, related, like members of one family. The sun, the moon, the sky, the wind, the sea, the earth, the trees, the plants, the birds, the fish, the animals and all humankind are interrelated and interdependent and we are one family who need to care and nurture and love each other."

Yeshua concurred with what the rabbi was saying. Yeshua believed we are not meant to dominate the earth and all its creatures, but care for Mother Earth as we care for our biological mothers, for the earth too is our mother, and mother of all creatures whom she nurtures. We are not superior in the sense of having to dominate but as the rabbi said, we are kin, relatives, related, connected, and interdependent. These thoughts ran through Yeshua's mind as he listened to the rabbi.

Yeshua left before the service had ended, as it was getting late, and he didn't want to keep Ruth and Orpah waiting. When he arrived at their stall, they were busy packing up their goods on the donkey. They were pleased to see Yeshua, as he was pleased to see them.

Yeshua enquired how their day was, and they told him that it was a good day. They had sold quite a few garments. They asked Yeshua about his day, and he told them about his time on the beach, and his visit to the synagogue, and what he heard the rabbi say.

Ruth and Orpah spoke highly of their rabbi, Lamech. He spoke with such conviction and depth, and he was greatly admired and respected.

Yeshua was pleased to hear about Lamech, and Yeshua in turn told them about Gamaliel and sang his praises.

Yeshua, Ruth, who was the older and more talkative, and the rather shy Orpah became more at ease with each other, and Yeshua felt like he was one of the family, and Orpah too opened up more. When they arrived at their little farmhouse, they were chatting away amicably as if they had been friends forever.

Joshua was all refreshed and welcomed Yeshua and introduced his wife, Emzara, and his three sons, Shem, Japheth, and Ham.

Yeshua expressed his pleasure at meeting them all and thanked them for their hospitality in welcoming him and taking him in for the night. "I see you all have good Scriptural names," Yeshua said, smiling, "Ruth and Orpah, the Moabite daughters-in-law of Naomi and Shem, Japheth and Ham, the sons of Noah," Yeshua said.

"Yes, we wanted our children to learn and love our stories, the stories of our ancestors, our prophets and patriarchs and Adonai's relationship with us, and our relationship with our heavenly father," Joshua said.

"Ruth was King David's great-grandmother. My father Yosef is of the line of David. So, Ruth, we have a connection," Yeshua said, smiling and looking at Ruth, who smiled back.

"So, what do you do for a living, Joshua?" Yeshua asked. He did not ask that of Joshua when they walked together because Yeshua made a habit of not asking people what they did, as if that defined them. Yeshua preferred people to speak of their family, where they came from, what their likes and dislikes and aspirations were. But now that he was their guest, Yeshua was curious. They seemed to be comfortable, with a neat home and solid furniture, which Yeshua admired.

"I am a fabric worker, I design and cut garments, outer and inner garments, robes, tunics and the like. And I make turbans and headwear, and scarves, sashes and girdles and that sort of stuff," Joshua said.

"And for both men and women," Ruth added.

"I'm impressed. Those two scarves that I bought; did you make them?" Yeshua asked.

"Yes, he did," Ruth interjected. "Father does all the designing and the cutting, and mother, Orpah and I do the sewing. We do work for people here in Magdala, and also sell our garments at the markets," Ruth said.

Yeshua then noticed some garments on a table in the corner and went and inspected them. He felt the softness and admired the design, "It is beautiful work," Yeshua said candidly.

"It's time for dinner," Emzara said. "Yeshua, would you like to freshen up before we sit down for our evening meal? There is a tub with water out the back, if you wish," Emzara added.

"Thank you, Emzara, that would be most welcome." Yeshua then went to the back of the house and found a towel and a wash rag and a tub full of suds. He removed his outer garments and gave himself a good bathing. He felt refreshed. He thought about Joshua and his family. What an unusual family, and so gifted. He was amazed at Joshua's skill. He marvelled at meeting men with skills usually associated with women, first David who was the family baker, and now Joshua a garment maker, who designs garments for both men and women. Yeshua was amazed. He surmised that Joshua would be around forty years of age, and Emzara a few years younger, but she was about six inches taller than him, which is unusual, for usually the men are taller than their wives. They were a loving couple and evidently had devoted children. Yeshua wasn't sure what the boys did, most likely they looked after the farm and the cattle, Yeshua thought.

The family sat down to a hearty meal of fish and lots of vegetables including lentils. "I caught the dinner," Shem said proudly. "It was this big," he said in jest, stretching his hands out wide. The boys spoke about fishing and farming and life in Magdala.

Yeshua in turn told them about his family, friends, life in Nazareth, and his experiences at the School in Jerusalem. "I had to cut short my learning because of the deaths, first of my friend, Rahab of Bethany, mother of my dearest friends, Lazarus, Martha and Miriam. Then within months the death of my grandfather, Jehoyakim and shortly after him, my father, Yosef," Yeshua said. All of a sudden, he felt a lump in his throat. Tears started, which he could not control and burst into tears, sobbing like a child.

Emzara, Ruth and Orpah rushed to Yeshua and put their arms around him, smothering him with their compassion and love. They said nothing, just held him and let Yeshua cry. He wept for some time. After his weeping subsided, Ham brought him a towel and a cup of water. Joshua went to a side table and poured Yeshua some wine, which he gratefully sipped.

The family were at a loss for words to comfort Yeshua. Three deaths of three loved ones in such quick succession, was more than anyone could endure.

"How long ago did your father die, Yeshua?" Joshua asked.

"It's almost four years ago. I thought I was well over grieving the loss of my father and grandfather and friend, who was like a third grandmother to me. But it seems that I still…"

"It's understandable, Yeshua, losing three loved ones like that, and so quickly is a heavy burden to bear," Emzara said. "Let's have some dessert. I baked a cake full of figs and berries. I don't usually bake cake in the middle of the week, but I don't know why, it was as if someone was telling me to bake because we were going to have a special guest," Emzara said, smiling, and there was laughter all around.

When the evening came to an end, Yeshua felt so close to Joshua and Emzara and their family. He thanked them profusely for their hospitality, their kindness in taking him in, the delicious meal and cake, and for the compassion and comfort they gave him. They sat outside for a while around the fire chatting and Yeshua had another cup of wine. By the time he went to bed, he fell into a deep sleep.

Yeshua slept in and did not get up early as he had planned to but instead got up when he heard the rest of the household up and about. He had a quick splash outside and then dressed and packed his backpack for his onward journey. Emzara had already prepared breakfast. Yeshua wasn't really hungry but he did have some bread dipped in olive oil and a cup of warm milk. They indulged in the usual quiet morning talk inquiring how each other slept. Everyone it seemed slept like logs. The boys were out already, milking the two cows, tending to the other animals and working in the field attending to their farming duties. They made sure their fox proof fences were secure. Yeshua found his way to them to say his thanks and goodbyes. He then returned to the house to do the same. Joshua was already busy with cuttings, and the girls were busy packing their garments and other clothing for the market, onto their donkey.

Emzara brought Yeshua two beautiful robes. "Yeshua, this is for your mother, Miriam and your grandmother, Hannah. And this is for you for your journey. She handed him a parcel containing bread, some olive oil to dip his bread, some berries and dried figs.

"Thank you, Emzara, they're lovely, thank you so much; Mother and Gran will love it. And thank you for the parcel to sustain me on the way. Thank you." Yeshua was deeply touched. He then thanked Joshua and the girls for their kindness, and then was on his way. As the girls were heading to the town centre and Yeshua was heading in the other northerly direction, Yeshua said goodbye to everyone.

It was another pleasant spring day. The birds were out in their usual noisy fashion. It was sweet noises though, music to the ears. Yeshua greeted nature, as he usually did, the sun and wind, the earth and the sky and all of nature's delights. He then walked and prayed his morning prayers as he usually did, offering himself and the day to Yahweh. He then recited his favourite psalm, which was so appropriate for his journey and his surroundings:

The Lord is my shepherd; there is nothing I shall want.
He makes me lie down in green pastures.
He leads me besides still waters.
He restores my soul.
He leads me in right paths
for his name's sake.

Even though I walk through the darkest valley,
I fear no evil
for you are with me;
your rod and your staff
they comfort me.

Yeshua walked for about an hour and a half when a gang of youths, in their late teens, came towards him on the road. There were eight of them, and they looked bedraggled. But Yeshua was not one to judge people by their appearance or the way they dressed. Half of them had the usual length staffs and the other half had short thick sticks, more like clubs. Yeshua felt some apprehension. He sensed he could encounter some danger.

"Hey you," a deep voice came from the oldest looking one. "What you got on you, what in your backpack, man," he croaked.

"Shalom to you, gentlemen, I am Yeshua from Nazareth, and I am on my way to Gennesaret. I assume you are on your way to Magdala. I do hope you have a good day," Yeshua said, trying to keep calm and calm the youth.

"Well, if we can have what you've got on you, then it will indeed be a good day," the leader laughed, and his pack roared along with him.

"Oh, so you are robbers, thieves, then. And you are eight to one. So, I don't have a chance, do I?" Yeshua said, still trying to make sure he would not be harmed and hoping small talk would somehow placate them.

"Now, enough of your talk, empty your backpack," the leader commanded sternly.

"I only have some clothes and some food for the road," Yeshua said, as he handed over his backpack. One of the leader's handlers took the bag, opened it and threw it on the ground. Some of the contents, including the food that Emzara prepared, fell on the ground, as well as the scarves Yeshua had bought for his mother and grandmother and the two outer garments that Emzara had given for them.

"Oh ho, look at this," the gang member said, laughing, as he held the two women's garments aloft for all to see. "Is this yours, are you one of those sissies who like to dress in women's clothing?" he guffawed. The rest of the gang laughed raucously.

"Please, those are for my mother and grandmother. My father and grandfather have both died recently, and these were given as a present to my mother, Miriam, and my grandmother, Hannah, from Emzara and Joshua of Magdala; you know them, do you?"

"That odd couple, we know them, and what great girls he's got," another of the gang spoke, continuing to laugh. They were enjoying themselves, toying with Yeshua before depriving him of his goods.

"Give us your money," the leader then said in a stern voice.

"Sorry, I don't have any money," Yeshua lied. He kept his money in an inside pocket of the sash he wore inside his outer garment. He needed the money for he still had a long way to go on this journey. And he wasn't going to part with his hard-earned savings.

"Really, I don't believe you. You look well-to-do. We'll take all those garments and all your money and don't waste our time. Or we will have to just beat you up and take everything you've got," the leader said sternly.

"I thought the people of Magdala were all like Joshua and Emzara and their daughters Ruth and Orpah and their sons Seth, Japheth and Ham. I'm sure the family will be very upset to know that you gentlemen took the garments they gave for my mother and grandmother, and also the parcel of food that Emzara prepared so lovingly for me," Yeshua said. "I will of course be passing through Magdala again on my way home to Nazareth and will visit and report my experience to them, and to the police of course," Yeshua said firmly.

"Hey, Jake, I think we better leave this guy. We are already in trouble with the law, and he will be going back to Magdala. I don't want any more trouble with the law or with Joshua and his boys. They're a tough lot."

"Yeah, Jacob, I think we better go, I don't want to mess with Seth, Japheth and Ham," one of the others chimed in. And the others agreed.

"Okay, let's go," Jacob commanded and they all just left, leaving Yeshua's stuff lying on the road.

Yeshua breathed a sigh of relief. It was like the dream he once had of being surrounded by a gang wanting to do him harm and when Zadok came to his rescue. How he wished his friends Zadok and Achim were with him, they could take them on. Yeshua whispered a prayer of thanks to his guardian angel. And prayed the verse of his favourite psalm again:

Even though I walk through the darkest valley,
I fear no evil
for you are with me;
your rod and your staff
they comfort me.

Yeshua soon settled his nerves, from what was a scary encounter. He had tried to remain as calm as possible but he was scared. A pack of youth on the prowl and looking for trouble can end badly. "Yahweh, I'm sorry I lied about not having money, there was no other way to make sure they would not steal it," Yeshua said aloud, trying to justify his lie.

Yeshua continued walking for the next couple of hours, at first the encounter with the gang occupied his mind but gradually it faded into oblivion, as Yeshua engaged in the sights and sounds of the birds and the wind whistling through the branches of the trees. He continued walking for another couple of hours and then found a spot and rested in a field against a tree. He had a bite to eat of what Emzara had prepared.

Then his encounter with the gang of youths returned. He thought about the lie he had said in telling them he had no money. Yeshua then recalled the lesson he and the class had with Gamaliel about the Eighth Commandment, 'You shall not bear false witness about your neighbour.' Yeshua recalled the debate that went on for quite a few lessons on lying and the truth. He remembered Gamaliel quoting from their laws, "Yahweh's faithfulness endures to all generations. Since Yahweh is 'true' the members of his people are called to live in the truth." Yeshua recalled how the debate focused on the need to tell the truth always, and especially when to lie would cause harm to another in any way whatsoever, especially to another's life, property or reputation. Yeshua debated with himself, trying to justify the lie he told to those young thugs. *I did not cause any harm to any of them in any way, instead I prevented them from doing harm to me and in that way to themselves, for they would be displeasing Yahweh*. Yeshua enjoyed this internal debate with his conscience.

Yeshua continued his walk but the incident with the gang kept recurring in his mind and the lie he had told. He did not want to succumb to scruples of any kind. With the way the many laws of his faith was taught and inculcated in the minds of the people, Yeshua thought how easy it was to succumb to scruples. It could become like living in a straightjacket. In his mind, Yeshua relived the debate they had in class about whether it is ever okay to tell a lie.

It went like this: 'The Torah says that we have to distance ourselves from words of falsehood and not to kill an innocent and righteous man. We are forbidden to lie in a way that causes death or harm to another. So, what do you think class, is it ever okay to tell a lie?' Gamaliel had asked the class. 'Are we breaking the Eighth Commandment whenever we tell a lie, no matter the circumstances, even if telling the truth meant we could suffer harm and even death?' Gamaliel had put the question to the class.

Yeshua began to relive the debate in his mind: 'In a court of law one has to tell the truth, the whole truth and nothing but the truth,' one of the students, Barakil, had answered. 'But in real life, we are not in a court of law, so to save our skin or someone we love, we can and have to lie,' he had added.

'I agree,' Zadok had chimed in. 'If my life is in danger or that of my family, I will lie through my teeth to save them, never mind the Law of Moses, this is the Law of Everyday Living. It is common sense and the natural desire to survive and protect that kicks in,' he had added.

'Well said, Zadok,' Gamaliel had replied. 'You raise an important truth; besides the Law we have also been endowed by our Creator with common sense and a conscience. Before Yahweh gave Moses those Laws, the Ten Commandments, and before they were written on stone, they were already written in the hearts and souls of all of humanity. It was common sense and conscience that was our ancestors guide to good living,' Gamaliel had answered.

'But I was told we can never lie. We have the Law of Moses and it is clear we have to always tell the truth, the whole truth and nothing but the truth, not only in a court of law but in everyday life,' another student, Solomon, had said.

'True, Solomon, you are indeed wise,' Gamaliel had said with a smile. 'And we justify telling of half-truths by using our reasoning, common sense and conscience. To put it more precise, we use philosophical and theological reasoning. Take this example, let's say, your father is unwilling to associate with a person for some good reason, and the person comes to your house and asks you if your father is home, can you lie, to protect your father, and say he is not home?' Gamaliel had asked.

'Yes, we can,' Yeshua recalled what he had said. 'We are bound by the truth. But philosophically, we can restrict the truth. If we told the truth without restrictions we would have to say—no, my father is not home, to you, because he does not want to see you, because you are a pest,' Yeshua recalled what he had said with a smile.

'You are correct, Yeshua. You would be using what is called a 'mental restriction' of the truth, to save hurt to the visitor *and* your father. It is true that your father is not home, not home to the visitor. Does that make sense?' Gamaliel had said.

Yeshua came back to the present from his reverie of the debate they had in class about the truth and lying. The debate had gone on and on, and it had ended with much mirth. Yeshua then got up, and continued on his walk to his next stop, Gennesaret.

It was noon when Yeshua arrived at Gennesaret. He had taken a leisurely pace. It was quite hot and it seemed that most people were indoors to escape the heat at its peak. It was a small fishing town and Yeshua engaged with the few people he met who were out and about. He took a stroll along the beach and spoke with a man, Magog, who had come out of the water where he had gone for a swim. From him Yeshua found out that the people of Gennesaret called the Sea of Galilee, Lake Gennesaret.

"Just like the people of Tiberias calls the Sea of Galilee, Lake Tiberias, so it seems the people of Gennesaret have named the Sea of Galilee, Lake Gennesaret," Yeshua said aloud.

Yeshua then continued his walk along the beach, but it was too hot, so he decided to go for a swim. There was no one else in sight so Yeshua removed his robes and kept his undergarment on, and then ran into the water splashing. He enjoyed the cool waters and dived into the low waves. After he had cooled off sufficiently, he sat on the beach, and waited for the sun to dry him. Then he dressed and continued to walk along the beach. He continued his walk until he found some adjacent grassed area with some palm trees planted for shade. He sat up against one of the trees and soon began to nod off. He must have slept for at least half an hour when he stirred. A slight breeze caressed his face, so Yeshua got up and decided to continue on his journey to Capernaum. Capernaum was also a coastal town and not too far away. Joshua had told him it would be about three hours walk. At the pace he was going Yeshua thought it would take him four hours. He decided that he would sleep over at Capernaum.

When Yeshua finally arrived at the town of Capernaum, it was still hot and he headed to the beach again, to cool down. He swam around for a while, and then came out and waited for the sun to dry him. He got dressed and stood looking out at the lake. All of a sudden, a mighty wind came out of nowhere and blew across the lake. The sea was angry, upset, making a boisterous noise, fuelled by the wind and whipping up the waves. Luckily there were no fishermen on the lake, as far as Yeshua could see, because they would be in big trouble. Yeshua later found out from the inhabitants that what he had experienced was something that occurred from time to time. A mighty wind could suddenly and unexpectedly appear, and cause havoc to fishermen on the lake. The fishermen had to be careful because a storm could suddenly arise unexpectedly on the calmest of days.

Yeshua then continued to walk around the town as people came out of their homes, as the temperature dropped slightly. Yeshua went to the synagogue for the evening service. This time he listened to the story of the exile into Babylon, all about King Nebuchadnezzar, his successors, Daniel's role in interpreting the writing on the wall, and the predictions about future kingdoms. The rabbi, an elderly gentleman, with a long white beard was quite knowledgeable and spoke for a very long time. But Yeshua had plenty of time and at the end of the sermon, the rabbi asked everyone, "If Adonai had to write on the wall of your heart, what would he write; would it be words of condemnation or would it be words like, 'Well done, good and faithful servant, you have been faithful in big and small things, enter into the kingdom prepared for you'?"

Yeshua stayed for the singing of the psalms, and the final prayers, then strolled back into the city centre, where people were still out and about, as it was still a warm evening. As the dark started to blanket the town, Yeshua decided to head for the beach. As it was such a balmy night, Yeshua decided he would sleep on the beach. He walked a while and listened to the melodic sounds of the gentle waves lapping the beach. There were a few people still walking along the beach. Yeshua eventually found some sand dunes and a good spot between them for him to lie down and sleep. He used his backpack for a pillow.

It was such a beautiful night on the beach, listening to the sounds of the sea, feeling the soft sand beneath his body and gazing at the myriad of stars twinkling in the sky above. He turned his thoughts first to Nazareth, to Miriam and Hannah, and wondered what they were doing. He missed them and said a prayer for them. He thought of his life in Nazareth, its people and prayed for them. He also gave thanks for the day and for his adventure so far and thought of all the people he met who showed so much kindness to him. He prayed that Yahweh would bless them all. Yeshua then just lay there gazing at the heavens and being lulled to sleep by the sound of the waves.

Chapter Twenty-Four
The Other Side of the Sea of Galilee

Yeshua woke to the chirping of the birds and the faint sound of little waves gently breaking on the shore. He lay for a while, waking to the day, slowly rose to his feet, stretched and yawned widely. He looked out to the sea. It was quiet, gentle, and seemed to be waking as well. He saw some fishing boats in the distance, and fishermen fishing, what seemed, with nets. The shore where he stood was deserted, except for sea gulls standing to attention and looking out to the sea as if they were watching the fishermen or studying the sea to see from where their next meal was coming. Yeshua went to the water's edge and splashed his face, arms and legs. He then wiped his face, arms and legs with fresh water from the lake and slid his hands through his hair, which now reached well past his shoulders. His beard was also growing quite long and shaggy. I should have had a haircut and a beard cut too before I left Nazareth, it seemed my hair and beard has grown a lot on the road, Yeshua said to himself. I will have to search for a barber in Capernaum and trim my hair and beard to a much shorter length, Yeshua said to himself.

It was still early and the sun was just lighting up the edges of the sky. Yeshua, did not yet feel hungry but did feel like his usual morning cup of warm milk. He still had some berry fruit juice, which he drank. Yeshua decided to remain on the beach for a while longer. He sat on the top of a low dune and looked out to the wide-open sea. Yeshua estimated that he was quite near to the upper end of the Sea of Galilee, maybe two or three miles to where the River Jordan flowed into the sea. He sat quiet for a while, absorbing the silence of his surroundings and then began his morning routine of silent prayer. He closed his eyes and simply became aware of the sensations in his body, the slight breeze on his face, the sounds of the waves and the birds in harmony with each other. He listened to the rustling of the wind in the nearby trees and he felt the sand beneath his feet. He became conscious of being one with the earth, his Mother Earth, and one with his heavenly Father, the Creator of all. He sank into a deep and mysterious silence, became one with nature, and one with Yahweh. Yeshua often started his day in this way, simply entering into the silence, into union with nature, with all of creation and with Yahweh the Creator of all. Yeshua remained in the silence for quite some time. When he finally came out of his silence he looked out to the sea and then gave thanks to his heavenly father for another day of living. He gave thanks for all the gifts and graces and blessings he had received so far on this journey, and he prayed for all those he met on the way, including the gang of youths. His mind turned as he usually did at the beginning and the end of the day to his mother, Miriam and his grandmother, Hannah and prayed they were well.

He then made his usual morning offering, offering himself, all his thoughts, words, deeds, desires to his heavenly father for his greater glory and the salvation of all on earth. And he ended his prayer with a spontaneous prayer to his heavenly Father, "Heavenly Father, my Father, our Father, may your name be revered by all. May your kingdom exist on earth, as it does in heaven. Give me Father and give to all of creation and all your creatures this day, all we need to nourish our bodies, minds and souls. And Father forgive us all the harm we do to your creation and to one another and help us Father to forgive all those who harm us. Amen."

The sun was lighting up the sky, so Yeshua decided he would go to the city centre and find a barber to cut his hair and beard and give it a good trim. He found a place where a very elderly gentleman had a small booth with a single chair, and all his haircutting implements on a table in a corner of the booth.

The barber was pleased to have a customer so early in the day. He was just setting up and giving his booth a sweep. "Come in, Sir. Have a seat." When Yeshua was seated, he threw a large cloth over Yeshua's shoulders and began his cut, after asking Yeshua how much he wanted cut off his hair and his beard. Yeshua indicated how much he wanted trimmed.

"My name is Yeshua; I am from Nazareth and just passing through Capernaum. Have you been living here long?" Yeshua asked.

"My name is Methuselah, no, I'm only joking," the barber laughed. "That's what the kids call me, because I am the oldest man here in Capernaum, and I have been here all my life. My real name is Job, but I am nowhere near having the patience of Job. My mother told me that I was so impatient to come into the world that I came so early they did not expect me to live, so they decided to call me Job," Job laughed out loud.

"So, you were impatient to come into this world and it seems you are not impatient to leave this world, how old are you Job, if I may ask," Yeshua asked, light-heartedly.

"What do you think?" Job asked, with a glint in his eye.

"Mmm, I'd say you are in your top seventies, maybe around seventy-seven years of age," Yeshua guessed.

"No, I wish I was. I am actually ninety-two," Job said proudly.

"You're joking, Job, really? You sure look young for your age. I suppose most strangers will ask what your secret is," Yeshua said. "How do you manage to age so gracefully Job?"

"I have quite a recipe for that, Yeshua; good food, a good night's rest, a daily walk and a prayer, a cup of wine a day, a good wife and children, love in my heart, living in the present, and having a sense of humour. These are some of the ingredients to a long life," Job said, laughing heartily.

"You sure have a sense of humour. and an infectious smile Job, and I must remember your ingredients for a long life," Yeshua said, but he recalled his encounter with Yahweh in the Temple in Jerusalem when he was fifteen and how it became clear to him that his life was to be cut very short. How short, Yeshua did not know. But he thought it was an impetus to him to live his life to the full.

"I am a carpenter. I live with and care for my mother, Miriam. My father died four years ago. My grandfather, my mother's father also died soon after and his widow, my grandmother, Hannah, lives with us as well. I am on holiday for the first time since taking over the business from my father. I passed through Cana, Magdala, Gennesaret and my next stop is Bethsaida on the western coast of Lake Capernaum."

"Lake Capernaum? There's no Lake Capernaum, Yeshua, this is the Sea of Galilee, the Sea belongs to all Galileans and not just Capernaum's," Job said, laughing, and displaying a few gaps in his front teeth.

"I know, I was just teasing. The people of Tiberias and Gennesaret name the sea, Lake Tiberias and Lake Gennesaret and I thought the people of Capernaum might want to do the same," Yeshua said light-heartedly.

"Nah, it is the Sea of Galilee, it is a lake really, but for us it is the sea, the Sea of Galilee, and so it will always be, for everyone, for you and for me," Job said, laughing loudly.

"Besides cutting hair, I see you are also a poet," Yeshua smiled.

"A poet, I dunno about that. But sometimes I just feel like bursting into poetry," Job said.

"I'm the same, Job, I am not a poet, but I love poetry, and sometimes like you I just burst into poetry too. So, Job, give us a poem, to lighten up my day," Yeshua said cheerfully.

"A poem, mmm... let's see. Oh, I know, I thought up this one not so long ago, and most appropriate for the moment. I've entitled it 'Growing Old by a Young 92-Year-Old'. It goes like this:

Growing old, what is it like?
I do not know.
Am I old?
Or am I too old to know?

What is 'growing old'?
I do not know.
When I am in my eighties,
Will I know?
I do not know.

Maybe when I enter my nineties
But I am in my nineties
I still do not know
What growing old is?

Or maybe when I am
Over a hundred
Who knows?
I do not know.

I feel the aches and pains in my joints.
When I walk up the steps
Or they stiffen when I
Sit too long.

But even some young
Experience this
There is much I cannot do physically.
So, my body grows old
But my mind seems
To be growing young.

So, what is growing old?
I do not know.
Maybe I'll know
When I can no longer
Move or think
But then will I still
Be able to love
And be loved?

If I am no longer
able to love
or be loved
That is growing old

But I will always love
Experience love
Always be loved
So, I can never grow old."

"That's great, Job, you are indeed a poet. What a lovely poem about growing old gracefully. I won't be growing old, but if I did, I would reflect on your poem."

"You are looking fit and healthy, and you have a most pleasant personality. You seem to exude joy, and you have a sense of humour, so I think you will live to a ripe old age, and maybe the kids will call you Methuselah too," Job laughed. "Well, I'm all done. Let me just brush you off."

Job completed his cutting, removed his cloth and brushed Yeshua's shoulders and around his neck. "Let me get the mirror so you can have a good look at my handiwork," Job said, as he went to the side table and brought a circular bronze mirror. "I gave the bronze a good polish this morning, so you should get a good image of the new you," Job said, smiling and pleased with his work.

Yeshua took the mirror by its metal handle and moved his head from side to side and had a good look at the cut and also his beard. The image was hazy but Yeshua could see his black hair and beard. He ran his hand through his hair and beard and it felt good. "Great job, Job," Yeshua laughed. "Your name says it all, Job," Yeshua said, smiling broadly. "And I look and feel ten years younger."

"The girls will be falling over their feet for you, Yeshua. Or do you have a woman at Nazareth? I'm sure the girls must be falling over their feet for a handsome guy like you," Job said, grinning.

"I do have a girl that I am very friendly with, her name is Rebecca. I am very fond of her and her of me." Yeshua left it at that. He knew that he and Rebecca would never become lovers or a couple, get betrothed, marry and have a family. Whenever the subject came up about his relationships; the thought of never being with a woman and being allowed to love and be loved by someone, by Rebecca, and having a family of his own, with her, hurt deeply. He wished he could simply be an ordinary man, able to love and be loved and share his life with someone he loved. But it was not to be. Jesus felt a sadness when such thoughts and feelings came to him. He simply sighed and put it out of his mind and whispered, "Thy will be done."

Yeshua thanked Job and paid him, and said his goodbye. "It was good meeting you, Job, I will tell my friends about you, so that if they do pass through Capernaum they will know where to come for an excellent cut," Yeshua said sincerely.

"So, where are you off to now?" Job asked.

"I will have something to eat and then I will be heading for Bethsaida, on the other side of Lake Gennesaret, I mean the Sea of Galilee," Yeshua grinned. "What is the best way to get to Bethsaida?" Yeshua asked.

"There is a boat, a ferry that goes across during the day. You can't miss it at the pier. There are also some residents who are fishermen, and they too take people across but be careful, they will rip you off. The ferry is quite inexpensive, depends how many people cross at one time."

"My plan is to walk around the lake, the sea, so I will walk up to where the River Jordan runs into the sea and cross somewhere around there. I would like to cross the River Jordan. Is it safe and is it possible. Is there a place where I can walk across, maybe a bridge somewhere close," Yeshua asked.

"There's no bridge, I'm afraid. And the River Jordan is quite deep, between a hundred and two hundred feet, so you won't be able to cross by walking," Job said.

"I believe I've heard there are some shallow spots, fords, with good footing where one can cross safely by wading across," Yeshua said.

"You're right. The river is very wide at places, almost two miles and narrows at some sections to just about a quarter of a mile. If you walk upstream from the mouth, it won't take long for you to reach a narrow section with a ford clearly marked, where you can cross on foot. Good luck and enjoy your crossing, and think of our patriarch Joshua who crossed the Jordan near Jericho, with all our people, to the Promised Land, so many generations ago."

"Yes, I will, it is on my list of things to do, to visit Jericho and cross the Jordan at that very place where Joshua crossed with the people of Israel. It was just like Moses's crossing of the Red Sea. What a sight that must have been, Job, after all the years of bondage in Egypt, and then forty years in the wilderness and finally, Joshua, and not Moses, leads our people across the Jordan into the Promised Land."

"Indeed, it was a glorious day for all our ancestors. Free at last, home at last. While all of Israel were crossing over the Jordan on dry ground, the priests who bore the Ark of the Covenant of the Lord, stood on dry ground in the middle of the Jordan, until the entire nation finished crossing over the Jordan, what a sight that must have been," Job said, with a most pensive look, as if it was an event of a few weeks ago.

"I must go now, Job, thank you once again. Unfortunately, I will not be crossing the Jordan in such a spectacular fashion as Joshua and the people did, but I will walk across to the other side. And I will think of you Job, as I think of Joshua and our people of old, and I will give glory to Yahweh."

Yeshua gave Job a hug; that surprised him, but he liked it. He couldn't think when he had last received a hug from anyone. He waved as Yeshua went on his way, feeling like a new person with his hair and beard trimmed to perfection. Yeshua sat on a bench near the water fountain, where he had a drink and filled his water bag, and where he had something to eat of what he had bought; some fresh fish and bread and he kept some of the bread and some nuts and fresh figs, berries and olives for the road.

Yeshua liked Capernaum; close to the Sea of Galilee and he had a good feel about the place, even though it was also a garrison town housing a detachment of

Roman soldiers under a Centurion, along with government officials. He somehow had a sense that he would visit this place again, spend time here. Maybe it was simply because of the friendship he had made with old man Job. Yeshua spent another hour or so in the town and then walked in a north-easterly direction towards the place where the River Jordan flowed into the Sea of Galilee. His next stop was Bethsaida, on the other side of the River Jordan and the Sea of Galilee. Bethsaida was quite close to where the River Jordan flowed into the Sea of Galilee. Yeshua was excited about this part of his adventure. He walked feeling fed and refreshed, with a spring in his step. He started whistling a tune. He thought of his mother and grandmother and also of Rebecca, how exciting it would have been if she was with him on this adventure, she would have loved every minute. But it was not to be and Yeshua dismissed the thought immediately. While he would have loved to have Rebecca as company, Yeshua liked his own company, he never felt lonely, never felt alone. Yahweh always felt close. And he felt close to all of creation and to all whom he encountered on life's journey.

Yeshua was excited about reaching the River Jordan and where it flowed into the Sea of Galilee. How great it would be, Yeshua thought, if he could sail all the way down the river from where it started at Mount Hermon, in Iturea, and all along its course into the Sea of Galilee, right down to where is flows into the Dead Sea. What a trip that would be, Yeshua thought. I might do that some time, Yeshua said to himself. He loved the sea and he loved the mountains and the forests, the bush, all of nature. There was so much to see and experience and enjoy of Yahweh's creation. These thoughts milled around in the mind of Yeshua, as he walked along the river to where it flowed into the Sea of Galilee.

Yeshua left Capernaum quite early, well before noon, as he wanted to reach Bethsaida before sunset. And he was uncertain of the way and how long he would have to walk along the river before finding the ford where he could cross. So, he wanted to give himself plenty of time. It only took Yeshua a couple of hours when he caught sight of the River Jordan gushing into the Sea of Galilee. He sat on a rock and rested and watched as the River Jordan flowed into the sea. It was a wondrous sight, to see the river merging with the sea.

I better get a move on, Yeshua said to himself, *I have to find a place to cross on foot*. Job had said there was a sign about a mile from here, but Yeshua was aware how inaccurately people, especially people from the country, estimated distances, a mile could easily be two or three miles. So, Yeshua set out to find the ford where he could walk and wade his way across. Yeshua knew that the river was as wide as two miles in places but there were spots where it narrowed considerably, as much as a quarter its width, and at places even to a half of that. Yeshua walked along the river, listening to its sounds as it meandered its way to the Sea of Galilee.

After a couple of hours, Yeshua was pleased to see it narrow considerably and then his face lit up as he saw the sign where it was safe to cross. Yeshua immediately descended into the waters of the river, holding his back pack aloft. The river wasn't too wide, and Yeshua sunk to waist height in water, he trusted that the sign did not delude him, but he walked on tentatively. The water level fluctuated a bit but never went above his chest. It didn't take Yeshua too long to get to the other side. He climbed up a gentle slope and then put down his back pack and jumped up and down to let the water shake off. He was glad the weather was fine. Yeshua took off all his clothes. There was no one in sight. He had a spare undergarment, which he put on and then hung his clothes on a branch of a nearby tree, for it to dry. He then sat down in his undergarment and then helped himself to some bread and fruit. It was still, except for the sound of the river meandering downwards towards the sea.

Yeshua estimated that he would need the same amount of time to go back down following the path of the river to where it flowed into the Sea of Galilee, and from that point Yeshua knew it was only a couple of miles to Bethsaida. Looking at the sun Yeshua estimated it was around the eighth hour, if he left now, he would make Bethsaida, before sunset. His garments were not quite dry, but dry enough, and Yeshua knew it would dry soon enough as it was quite warm. He dressed himself, said a prayer of thanks to Yahweh and continued his journey back to the mouth of the river, and then on to Bethsaida.

Yeshua arrived at Bethsaida late afternoon, before the sun began its final descent. Yeshua began to feel at home around this upper end of the Sea of Galilee, on both the western and eastern side. He was now on the east of the river, and he had the same feeling he experienced in Magdala, Capernaum and now in Bethsaida. He just felt he would be back to these places in the future.

When Yeshua reached Bethsaida, he was close to the sea and saw quite a number of fishing boats close to the water's edge, and several rugged and tanned fishermen repairing and cleaning their fishing nets and boats. Yeshua greeted them, and found out that it was a good day's catch, and they had sold most of their fish, and had enough for themselves.

Yeshua spoke to a big fisherman named Jonah; he was cleaning his nets. Jonah was a big man with muscular arms and legs, and a ragged and tanned face from a lifetime on the open sea. Yeshua found out that Jonah was a professional fisherman. He pointed to his two sons, Shimon and Andreus that were on the boats, cleaning them. Shimon, Yeshua thought was about his own age, maybe a year younger and his brother Andreus, maybe a couple of years older. Andreus waved back, but Shimon just ignored Yeshua and kept on doing what he was doing. Yeshua was feeling hungry and asked about purchasing a small fish that he would like to have for dinner. When Jonah heard Yeshua's story, of his journey from Capernaum, crossing the Jordan and walking all day, Jonah simply gave Yeshua some of the fish left over that he and his sons had just cooked on a charcoal fire and eaten, before cleaning up. Yeshua was most grateful. He took out some bread and devoured the fish.

"Aah, there is nothing like eating fresh fish just caught and cooked on an open charcoal fire," Yeshua said, licking his lips. His mind went back to his father, when the two of them were on that camping trip, and were eating fish on the seashore at Tiberias, after having just caught some fish.

"Sure is," Jonah said, smiling at Yeshua. When Yeshua had finished his meal, he thanked Jonah and went on his way, waving to Shimon and Andreus, and again Andreus waved back but Shimon merely looked up and ignored Yeshua, and went back to his work on the boats.

Again, Yeshua had this strange feeling that his path with this family would cross again in the future. Yeshua had relished the meal and felt satisfied as he walked into the city. And as he walked, he could see the imposing mountainous cliffs and caves. Mmm, I think I have found my sleeping place for tonight, Yeshua thought, as he gazed on what looked like a deep enough cave.

Yeshua, while feeling well fed, began to feel the need for rest. So, he did not stay long in the town but made his way to the mountainous cliffs and found a cave. He sat down at the entrance to the cave and looked across to the sandy shore and to the open sea. He turned his thoughts to what had transpired this day and gave thanks to Yahweh. Yeshua then began his conversation with Yahweh as was his custom at the beginning and the end of each day and often during the day. He gave thanks for all he had experienced and asked Yahweh's blessing on Job, Jonah and his two sons Shimon and Andreus, and especially Shimon, who from afar seemed such a grumpy person.

Yeshua had a restless sleep. He had strange dreams about being lost in a forest and not being able to find his way out. He felt cold and miserable and hungry and thirsty, and then he heard the sounds of wild animals that seem to be closing in on him. He had no weapons with him, and he knew that his life was in grave danger, and the wild animals were getting closer. He had nowhere to run, and there was nothing he could do but face them like a lamb to its slaughter. And then he woke up, relieved. What was that dream all about, I wonder. Anyhow Yeshua just shirked it off. How strange dreams are, he thought, we are in worlds of our own creation and encounter beings and creatures we create. Yeshua thought about the ingenuity of his dreams. I suppose that is what it is, an outlet to our creativity, and when we are deep in our sleep, we enter our dream world and create our own world; or rather what is there deep down in our subconscious surfaces. Yeshua shook off his wondering of the mind, and then turned to his heavenly father, Yahweh for his morning prayers of thanksgiving and offering of himself and all his experiences to Yahweh. He drank some water, and longed for his hot mug of milk. And he ate some bread and dipped it in the olive oil that he had purchased.

It was still early and only the usual morning creatures greeted him with their chirping and flying about. The other sounds were that of the wind rustling the leaves of the trees. Yeshua found his way into the town and the fountain where he washed his face and refilled his water bag. My desire was simply to walk around the Sea of Galilee, Yeshua said to himself. I have lost track of time. I think it must be at least five days since I left Nazareth. I will continue this walk. I have visited all the main towns I have heard of, and am unfamiliar with the rest of the towns, so it will be interesting passing through places I have not been to, and not even heard of.

Yeshua walked a couple of hours at a leisurely pace and arrived at the town of Gergesa. It was like most of the towns and villages along the shore; he stopped for just a while, filled his water bag and washed his face. He needed to bathe, so he found his way to a quiet spot at the lake and stripped and gave himself a good wash. It was still warm, and he had bought a hand towel on the way, which he now used to dry himself. He felt refreshed, had a bite to eat and was on his way again. His next stop was at the town of Hippos. It was mid-afternoon when he arrived there. The town of Hippos is located on a hill overlooking the Sea of Galilee. It is just over a mile from the shore. Yeshua found a high spot and got a great view of the Sea of Galilee. He sat there for quite a while, admiring the vast expanse of sea that appeared quiet and tranquil from a distance. Yeshua looked as far as the eye could see and calculated that he must be somewhere in line with Tiberias, and further on with Nazareth. His mind went back to his hometown. He had not thought much of Nazareth, except for his mother and grandmother and Rebecca at times. But now he visualised his town and felt the absence, all the familiar faces, sights, sounds and smells. But he was not homesick. He was enjoying this time on his own, and this journey around the Sea of Galilee. He had seen such wonderful sights and met such great people along the way. He loved the sea and its shoreline. And when he has to move out on his own one day, he would definitely settle on the coast, and Capernaum was the town that sprung to his mind. After about an hour of just sitting and looking out to the sea and thinking all kinds of thoughts, and wondering what his future held for him, Yeshua was on his way again.

Yeshua had no idea when he would reach the bottom end of the sea and then had to find a crossing over the Jordan River again, to get back to the western side of the Sea of Galilee. He strolled for the next two hours and the sun was beginning its downward journey and disappear for another night, and light up other places. Yeshua had often wondered about the journey of the sun. He recalled the discussion he had with his father about this, when they were camping on the seashore at Tiberias. Where did the sun go, when the darkness arrived? Yeshua recalled his discussions with Yosef. The darkness was actually the result of the sun disappearing from view. At the end of every day, the sun set in the west and then rose the next day in the east. So, it must travel during the night under the earth, but that is the place of darkness, does the sun not lighten up and warm and give life to all that is under the earth? These thoughts sprung up in Yeshua's inquisitive mind. He had pondered this before and chatted with his father about this. It would be a topic he would discuss with Gamaliel when he got home.

When darkness began to descend, Yeshua was in the middle of nowhere, and no town or village in sight. He found a protected spot in a bushland and camped for the night. He lit a fire to warm up. He still had some bread and olives that he had purchased at Hippos and figs and a pomegranate, which he now devoured. He thought he must be quite close to the southernmost point of the Sea of Galilee. He let the fire burn out and then curled up to sleep. It wasn't long when he fell into a deep and peaceful sleep.

Yeshua woke to the sound of the birds and the rustling of the wind in the trees. The wind was quite gusty and there was a nip in the air. *It would be okay once I get walking*, Yeshua said to himself. Yeshua noticed that he was now talking to himself. *Must be going crazy, I guess, that is what life must be like for those living on their own, they will talk to themselves*, Yeshua thought.

Yeshua wiped his face with some water, gargled inside his mouth, and was on his way. He did not feel hungry, only missed his early morning drink of hot milk. It was then Yeshua saw, to his left, on the way he was to walk, a wide expanse of daisies and wild flowers, as far as the eyes could see, an array of flowers like that of a wide endless rainbow, reds, whites, yellows, orange, purples, it took Yeshua's breath away. He stood still, simply to take in a deep breath, and to take in the sheer vastness of the beauty of flowers unfolding before him, like a magical carpet. Oh, how mother and grandmother and Rebecca could see what I am seeing here and now, they would be overjoyed. If only I could capture this sight and take it home with me, to show them. Maybe we can come here one spring.

Yeshua then found a dead log, and sat down, and just rested to take in some more of this wonderful sight. "Oh God, O Yahweh, how great thou art," he whispered, and then Yeshua with tears in his eyes sang of the beauty of Yahweh. He softly entered into his morning prayers of praise, and offering of himself to his father, and asking his blessing, and he thanked Yahweh for his creation. It was indeed a sight to behold.

It was only then that Yeshua realised it was the Sabbath. It was a day of rest. Yahweh commanded us to rest on the Sabbath day, because after he created the world, he rested on the seventh day. How busy Yahweh must have been creating the world, the mountains. I have not been working these past six days, walking is not really working, is it, Abba? Yeshua conversed with his heavenly Father.

Yeshua realised that when on his own, he was now calling Yahweh 'Abba', the term he had used only for Yosef. But Yeshua felt so much like a child in the midst of all this floral beauty and grandeur, and he felt so close to his heavenly Father that the expression 'Abba' simply arose from the depth of his heart. "Abba," he said again, "from now on, you are my Abba," Yeshua said again. "I will stay here this day, and rest, rest in this beautiful place, in this Garden of Eden." Yeshua then walked into the midst of the array of wild flowers and lay down on his back, and simply breathed in the beautiful aroma that surrounded him.

In seven days, the Lord created the earth, all its creatures, including the first man and woman. Yeshua recalled the story from the first Book of Moses about God's creation of all that exists, inanimate, animate, the sky, the sea, the mountains, the plants and all animals and fish in abundance, and all the beauty I now see, and man and woman to enjoy, and be part of this creation.

Yeshua's mind went back, to the discussions he had with Gamaliel, and then again with the teachers at the School of Advanced Learning in Jerusalem about the creation of the world. Yeshua recalled the debate he had with his teachers. "How is it possible that Yahweh created all that exists in seven days? Did He not just first create an army of angels, and then send them out to spread the seeds all over the land, and let the earth and all life, on the earth and the sea, evolve from there?" was the question or rather the statement Yeshua made to the class, and to his teacher.

Yeshua recalled his reasoning in those lectures on the first Book of Moses about creation that were debated for days on end. Yeshua relived those moments; he had said, 'I believed for most of my life that Yahweh created the world and all living creatures, animate and inanimate, in seven days. I took the account in the first Book of Moses, literarily, but I believe it is not to be taken so literally. It is Moses using poetry, an allegory, a metaphor, a parable for what actually happened. No one was there, and I do believe Moses was inspired, for he was the chosen one of the Lord to set his people free, but what he wrote, he wrote to make us believe in the greatness of Yahweh and his creation, his great love for us, his magnanimity, his endless love for us.'

We will never be able to fathom the creation of the world, in all its beauty and magnificence. It will be a mystery that the human mind will never be able to fully fathom, Yeshua said to himself.

After his internal discussion, Yeshua stood up to admire the beauty of creation all around him. He bowed to the sun and the sky and the wind and looked down onto Mother Earth and father sky and listened to the birds and the music of the wind rustling the branches of the trees. And Yeshua recalled the writing of Moses, on which he reflected.

'In the beginning God created the universe. The earth was a formless void and darkness covered the face of the deep. Then God let light appear. He then put some order into what he created. And God named the light 'Day' and the darkness, 'Night', and the dome, 'Sky'. He then continued separating his creatures and named the land

'Earth' and the water that he brought together, 'Sea'. He filled the sea with countless creatures and the sky with numerous birds. Then God created all kinds of animals. Then God made us humans, according to his own image. He took some soil from the ground and formed a man out of it. He breathed life-giving breath into his nostrils and the man began to live. And while the man was sleeping God formed a woman out of the man's rib.'

Yeshua prayed, "Yahweh, God, Abba, you did all this grandiose work of creation in seven days. At the end you looked at everything you made, and you were very pleased. And then you rested."

What a beautiful story, Yeshua thought. In a nutshell, it speaks of Yahweh's great love, power, and generosity, his wanting to share all of himself with us, and his wanting to shower on us his goodness, and his beauty.

"We are, I am still discovering more and more each day of the wonder and beauty of what you, Abba, have created for me, for us, to have and to hold, and to enjoy to the full. Thank you, Abba."

Yeshua then recalled the class discussion on whether it was seven days or seven years or seven thousand years that it took Yahweh to create everything. And Yeshua recalled mentioning that a day is like a thousand years to Yahweh and with Yahweh there is no time, no past, or future only the present. Yeshua then recalled the psalm he had then learned and now as he lay among the daisies, Yeshua sang this psalm:

Lord, you have been our dwelling place
in all generations.
Before the mountains were brought forth,
or ever you had formed the earth and the world,
from everlasting to everlasting, you are God.
You turn us back to dust,
and say, 'turn back you mortals.'
For a thousand years in your sight
are like yesterday when it is past,
or like a watch in the night.
You sweep them away; they are like a dream,
like grass that is renewed in the morning,
in the morning it flourishes and is renewed,
in the evening it fades and withers.

Yeshua then lay down on his back with his hands cupping the back of his head as he rested. He felt so at peace. He was alone, yet he did not feel alone; he was in the midst of all of creation, of his friends, of his family, of his God. Yeshua lay still, his eyes began to close and then softly he fell asleep, as if in the arms of his mother.

Yeshua was not aware of how long he had slept, but when he woke up, he was hungry. So, he had something to eat, and then walked towards the sea, which was not too far away. As he walked, he passed some trees and wild plants and shrubs of all shapes and sizes. He could not fail to recognise a mighty sycamore tree by its massive dome like shaped canopy, and its massively fat trunk and its brittle bark with patches of green, tan and white, and its branches so strong and sturdy. *Oh, how*

I wish Achim and Zadok were here, they would be climbing this tree in a flash, Yeshua thought.

"Why not!" he said aloud, as if they were there with him. Yeshua put down his pack and started climbing the tree that must have been at least a hundred feet tall. Yeshua climbed as high as he could, and then sat down on a strong branch, and admired the carpeted earth of plants, shrubs and the unfolding wild flowers he had left behind. It was a sight to behold. "What do you think, Achim, Zadok, Rebecca?" Yeshua said aloud. If Rebecca were with them, she would be up the tree with them.

Yeshua recalled his Nazarene friends and imagined them to be sitting with him on this branch of this majestic sycamore tree. Yeshua sat there for a while contemplating the beautiful surrounding sights, and the Sea of Galilee in the distance. I can remain here forever, he thought. But he had to descend. He had a drink of water then continued his walk towards the seashore. When he arrived at the sea it was quite warm, so he decided to go for a swim. There was no one in sight, and he had met no one since he woke up, and as it was the Sabbath, he knew there would be no one up and about or travelling this way. He enjoyed the quiet and the peace and having the sea all to himself.

So, Yeshua stripped naked and ran into the sea. He splashed about and swam and felt so happy and filled with joy and peace. He floated on his back and swam under water, and over the gentle waves. He stood in the water for some time and gazed into the distance from where he had come. He got out, sat for a while and let the sun dry his body. He then got dressed, had a snack and a drink, and then decided to go back to the sycamore tree and sit in its shade. He had decided as it is the Sabbath that he would rest and spend the day in these beautiful surroundings. And so, he did.

Yeshua walked back to the wild flowers to admire them some more, and then back to the beach, and then took a long leisurely stroll along the sandy shore, letting eddies lap his bare feet. He walked for miles before he made a u turn. He thought he would camp under the sycamore tree for the rest of the day and sleep there. When he got back to the spot he was still on the beach and hunger pangs started to assail him. He looked into his backpack and there were only a few dried figs and a handful of the berries left over that he had picked along the way, and some bread that was still edible. He needed something more substantial because he was going to be here for the night and would only be able to obtain more substantial food the next day. He really felt hungry and then the thought came to mind, why not fish, the Sea of Galilee abounds with fish. He immediately got to work.

Yeshua walked towards the bushland and found a long enough stick to use for spearing a fish. It already had a sharp end and Yeshua sharpened it further on a rock. He then needed to get some bait.

Chapter Twenty-Five
Back Across the River Jordan

Yeshua wondered if bugs or grasshoppers would do for bait, but then he thought about worms, fish would go for them. His childhood games with Achim and Zadok of using sticks to bring worms to the surface came to mind and brought a smile to Yeshua's face. He found a small stick, with a sharp enough tip and then pressed it as deep as he could into the fertile soil. "Round and round you go, round and round you go, come on little worms, give us a show," Yeshua sang the little ditty they did as kids, as they moved the stick in circles and tickling the worms to come to the surface. It didn't take long for the worms to appear. Yeshua gathered them up and when he had enough, he stripped and went into the water, with his fishing spear. He waded into the water and when he was deep enough up to his waist, he opened the leaves that held the worms and let them down into the water as deep as he could and then released them. It worked. It wasn't long when several fish were fighting over the worms, and Yeshua struck. He couldn't miss, as his sword pierced one of the fish. It was just the right size for a hearty meal. Yeshua felt elated to have succeeded so quickly. "Thank you, Lord," he whispered.

Yeshua changed into dry underwear and then dressed and went about gathering some rocks to enclose the fire and some dry leaves and dry sticks and branches to start a fire. At home in Nazareth, a fire never went out, the community kept a fire going all the time, or at least kept embers alive, for it is such a tedious exercise to start a fire. The community had some flint, a very hard, greyish black stone that was struck with a piece of steel that produced the sparks to light a fire. And the fire was never fully extinguished so that the embers remained to start a fire again and again. Yeshua knew that it was forbidden to light a fire on the Sabbath, and all over, fires were kept burning at least from the night before the Sabbath. But Yeshua knew Yahweh would understand. And lighting a fire with two sticks is work, but the Sabbath is for man, not man for the Sabbath, Yeshua said to himself. I need to be nourished, and the only way is to start a fire.

Yeshua knew it requires super human effort to start a fire without flint and steel but he had done it before and it was the only way to light a fire out here in the bush. So, he got his two sticks and started rubbing them together furiously with the driest of leaves that he crushed into an almost fine dust. He had to use speed and his hands worked furiously, he thought of the effort of racing Rebecca and his hands became his legs, he rubbed and rubbed furiously and as fast as he could without pausing for quite a long time until some sparks flew and he continued until enough began to ignite the dry leaves, and the semblance of a fire began. He knelt down and blew gently on the tiny flame, and what a joy, what an accomplishment to finally see a fire. He fed the fire with some more dry leaves and then some very small thin sticks, once the fire grew, he gradually added larger and thicker branches until he had a fire big enough to cook his fish.

All the effort of finding fuel for the fire and starting the fire and keeping it going was worthwhile as Yeshua held the fish at the end of his spear over the fire, turning it from side to side, until it was cooked. Yeshua's mouth was dripping as he waited for the fish to cool just enough for him to eat. He still had the last of his bread and olives in oil. He ate the olives and dipped his bread in the oil, and ate the bread with the fish. It was a meal fit for a king. Yeshua relished the meal. "Mmm, nothing on earth, like fresh fish, freshly caught and cooked on an open fire and eaten with bread dipped in olive oil, out in the open, in such a beautiful place," Yeshua sighed once again, licking his lips.

Yeshua in all his efforts and hunger and anticipation of the meal made him forget to give thanks before his meal, but he remembered and prayed, "Thank you, Yahweh, for the fish you have created and filled the sea, for our nourishment and enjoyment. Abba, I would usually pray that you bless the fishermen and all who brought this meal to me for my nourishment and enjoyment, but I am the fisherman, so I thank me and ask you to bless me, but then I thank too all those who had a hand in the planting and picking and packing and handling of the olives and the making of the oil and the baking of the bread, so many hands, bless them all, Abba, all who had a hand in bringing this meal to me. Thank you."

As Yeshua was in a lonely place, he had to extinguish the fire and all his hard work. But he decided he would keep it going and sleep here for the night. When Yeshua had finished his meal, he walked to the sea again and rinsed his mouth and washed his hands and face with the fresh water from the sea. Yeshua then made a comfortable bed on the ground from the leaves from the surrounding trees and bushes. He would feed the fire some more when it got dark and he was ready to sleep and the fire would also protect him from any wild creatures of the night.

And so, night came, and Yeshua added some more thick branches to the fire, and lay down on his earthy bed with his back pack with all its clothes inside as a soft pillow. He looked up at the sky, it was so clear and bright, and so many stars, twinkling in the sky. Lying on his back and looking up at the sky and a full moon was a spectacular vision to behold. "Hi brothers and sisters stars, and sister moon how bright you are and thank you for lighting up the sky, and delighting us with your beauty." Yeshua then said his usual prayers of thanks for the day and his petitions for his mother and grandmother and all his loved ones. He then continued looking up at the sky and after a while fell fast asleep.

It was at sunrise on the eighth day when Yeshua woke. It was quite light and the full moon was still visible in the sky, but not as bright as at night. Yeshua greeted the moon, "good day to you, sister moon, how beautiful you still are, although your brightness fades as brother sun begins to light up the sky." Yeshua continued to lie still for a while and took his time to completely wake up. Yeshua made sure the fire was completely extinguished. He then tidied up his camp site, and was on his way. He decided to walk along the shore line as far as he could in a southerly direction and then find the well-trodden paths to where the River Jordan continued its path southwards through Decapolis and through the divide between Perea, and Samaria and Judaea, and into the Dead Sea. Yeshua walked slowly along the seashore, there were no fishermen around but he could see a few fishing boats in the distance. He thought of Jonah and his sons Shimon and Andreus; they would most likely be out on the waters, for it was a fine day for fishing.

It only took a couple of hours for Yeshua to arrive at the southernmost point of the Sea of Galilee and from where the River Jordan continues to snake its way south into the Dead Sea. Yeshua had now to again negotiate his way across the River Jordan by finding another ford where he could walk across the river. He began his long walk and the river soon seemed to be sinking deeper into the ground, as it was now about fifty feet below the river bank. Yeshua hoped to find a ford where the descent would not be too steep. He was sure to find a well-trodden path down the slope to where people would cross the river on foot. And so, it was as he had envisaged. A clearing and a sign consisting of huge boulders and an arrow made of large stones showed the way to the ford. And it was well-cleared and well-trodden, unlike the other sections along the river.

Yeshua climbed slowly down the lengthy embankment. It took quite some time and was slippery in sections, and he had to move slowly, so as not to slip. When he finally arrived at the river's edge he removed his sandals, and all his outer clothes and put them in his backpack, and then with his staff in hand he waded across the river. Yeshua estimated the distance to be less than half the usual width of the river, so he reckoned he would be wading somewhere between three and four thousand feet. Yeshua thought of counting his steps but dismissed the idea. He had to concentrate on his footing and take his time to make sure he didn't fall into a dip. It took Yeshua more than half an hour to get to the other side. He then had to climb another fifty feet or so to the eastern bank of the river. He first changed his undergarment tying the wet one to his backpack to dry and kept the rest of his clothes in his back pack, as he climbed the embankment. He was feeling some fatigue but he was eager to be on solid ground so he continued without stopping until he finally arrived on level ground. He felt as if he had climbed a high mountain and a sense of exhilaration and all his fatigue just left him. He then dressed; and went on his way.

Yeshua had to back track his way up the river again and arrived at the town of Philateria at the tip of where the river leaves the Sea of Galilee. Yeshua knew that the town of Philateria was on the southernmost point of the lake just on the western side of the River Jordan. It was an ancient Greek city and Yeshua had learned that the city was named after the sister of a great Greek historical figure, whose name Yeshua could not recall. Yeshua liked the idea of the naming of a city after a woman. Philateria is such a beautiful name, "and if I was that Greek nobleman, I would name this city Rebecca."

Yeshua was interested to know more about this once Greek city. His curiosity was soon satisfied for he met an elderly gentleman, Obadiah, who had a wealth of knowledge about the city of which he was so proud to tell anyone who showed the slightest interest. And when he heard Yeshua's story of his travels from Nazareth and all around the Sea of Galilee, he found a kindred spirit. Obadiah offered to act as a guide and took Yeshua to some Greek ruins.

"I know that your city was named by a Greek nobleman, to honour his sister," Yeshua said.

"Yes, he was Ptolemy the Second who named the city, using his sister's name, Philateria, to honour her. These ruins here, are most likely his mansion, it measures sixty-six feet by thirty-six feet consisting of eleven rooms, that were decorated with marble and mosaics, which have all been lost, but you can see some of the colonnades. One entered this magnificent home, through a colonnaded courtyard."

Obadiah had a wealth of knowledge and he loved his town and was so proud to show it off to Yeshua. Yeshua however had seen enough. He wondered about the opulence, and wondered how many people lived in such a stately home, with eleven rooms. Yeshua thanked Obadiah for his kindness and sharing his knowledge and then took his leave. He wanted to reach Sennebris before nightfall.

The city of Sennebris was a distance from the shore of the Sea of Galilee so Yeshua's path veered further and further away from the sea. It was around the ninth hour when Yeshua arrived at Sennebris and the town was still abuzz with people. Yeshua found a well and splashed his face and had some water to drink and filled his water bag. He then went to the city centre and the markets where there were crowds. Yeshua enjoyed the milling around and the crowds, after days on his own. He purchased some freshly cooked fish, bread, oil, olives, and figs and grapes and sat on a bench and ate some of the olives, bread dipped in the oil and the fish and watched the people going about their business of living, buying and selling, and chatting and laughing. The children were running about and a few of them were annoying their parents. Yeshua saw a father slap his child on the backside and reprimanding him with a wagging finger. Yeshua could not hear what the father was saying but he knew the proverb that everyone knew, especially fathers, and was regularly quoted to justify corporal punishment of their children, 'spare the rod and spoil the child'.

Yeshua remembered the reading and lessons on the Book of Proverbs that he had learned during his time at the Advanced School of Learning in Jerusalem, as well as with Gamaliel. The Book of Proverbs is a treasure trove of wisdom that gives advice and guidance to the common problems and issues of everyday living. Yeshua learned that it was purported to have been written by Solomon. Yeshua recalled that for most, Proverbs were addressed firstly to young people and a shorter part addressed to all and sundry. Yeshua recalled the lectures and debates that took place on the Proverbs, relating to such common place issues like: laziness, cheating, pride, laughter, gossip, visiting neighbours and being a good wife and of course the training of children. In his education and training Yeshua was encouraged to often consult the Book of Proverbs for it tells of the rewards of living a virtuous life and the dangers of vice.

The sight of a father spanking his child in public brought to Yeshua's mind the whole Book of Proverbs. He had committed several of them to memory and of course the one that now sprang to mind, 'spare the rod and spoil the child.' Yeshua had learned a deeper meaning to this proverb, which correctly is written as, 'Those who spare the rod hate their children, but those who love them are diligent to discipline them.' Yeshua remembered his discussions with Gamaliel about this very issue. He had done so when he was twelve, after he had returned from Jerusalem, after being separated from his mother and father for three days. Yeshua recalled how furious Miriam and especially Yosef were when they saw him, seemingly so unconcerned in the temple, engrossed in debating with the teachers there. Yeshua recalled how relieved his mother was but how very angry Yosef was, more so for the grief he had caused Miriam, and if it was not in the synagogue Yeshua wondered if Yosef would have given him the deserved spanking of his life.

This was one incident in his youth that Yeshua regretted. To have put his mother and father through that living hell was most inconsiderate and insensitive. Yeshua had tried his best to make up for that misdemeanour of his. He simply lost sense of time and all reality. Yeshua knew his parents loved him, and that whatever they did, when they disciplined him, it was because of their love for him, because they loved him. But to hit someone, especially a child is not an act of love, even in the cause of discipline, Yeshua thought.

Yeshua's parents never hit him. There has and there are other ways to discipline, to make the child understand his or her error and mend their ways. These were thoughts and memories mulling around Yeshua's mind, as he saw the father spank his child. Yeshua recalled this subject in classes in Jerusalem and Nazareth. Yeshua was grateful that his parents did not inflict corporal punishment on him, although they did discipline him, they did use the rod in the right way, and as intended by the proverb. A rod is made of wood but a rod more powerful is that of the spoken word, words of wisdom, spoken with love. The rod of correction is something that shepherds used when the sheep strayed from the path. A good shepherd, like a good parent, would use a rod to steer sheep away from danger towards green pastures and clean water, it was never used to beat them.

Yeshua's recollections made him recall again the first words of the psalm:

The Lord is my shepherd, I shall not want,
He makes me lie down in green pastures;
He leads me beside still waters.
He restores my soul
He leads me in right paths
for his name's sake.

Yeshua whispered a prayer, "Yahweh, you are the Good Shepherd, you have indeed shepherded me these past days. I have not wanted. I have lied down in green pastures and still waters. You have through all those whom I've met, restored my soul. You have saved me from danger and led me in the right paths. I am grateful O Yahweh. And Abba Yosef and Immah Miriam, you have been good shepherds to me, you have loved me so, and led me on right paths, and I am grateful."

Yeshua was deep in prayer, communing with his Lord, right here in the centre of the town, in the midst of the crowd. It was a prayer without words spoken not out loud, but with words of the heart and the mind.

Yeshua spent a couple of hours in Sennebris and then found his way to a synagogue and joined in the evening service. He was a stranger and they noticed him, and one of the ushers made him welcome. Yeshua prayed the psalms with the worshippers and listened to the reading, of all the books of Moses and the others in their Testament. How uncanny that the rabbi was reading a section from the Book of Proverbs, Yeshua thought. The rabbi stopped after reading the words, "Whoever belittles another lacks sense, but an intelligent person remains silent. A gossip goes about telling secrets, but one who is trustworthy in spirit keeps a confidence."

The rabbi, a very elderly man, then spoke about gossiping, "When I was a young man, I loved to gossip, and now that I am old, I like it even more." Yeshua and those present were immediately interested in what the rabbi had to say. Was the rabbi condoning or excusing such an everyday occurrence as gossip? Surely gossip is evil and sinful as the Book of Proverbs makes so clear. Everyone knew it was bad to gossip, and forbidden by Yahweh, yet everyone did it.

The rabbi continued, "Gossip gives us pleasure, because somehow gossiping about others can be fun, and for those in that circle of gossip it can give an importance of superiority, of being better than the victim of gossip. Never mind if what is being said is true or not and never mind how hurtful it is to the person's reputation. What would the victims of gossip say and feel about what is being said about them? When we gossip, we raise ourselves up by putting others down. Because we are losing the art of communication, we resort to spice things up with gossip. When you are in company and you hear gossip, I pray you keep your mouth shut. I know that if you speak up for the victim and correct your friends you will lose all your friends. But if that is too much to ask of you then at least keep your mouth shut. And when someone tells you a secret, seal it in your heart. Gossip makes us feel important to tell it to our friends. But take heed of the proverb, of what Yahweh desires, 'whoever belittles another, lacks sense, and an intelligent person remains silent.' So please do not lack sense, gossip makes no sense, be an intelligent person and keep your mouths shut."

Yeshua felt like clapping. He had never heard a rabbi in all the times he attended the synagogue read this section of Proverbs on gossiping or comment on it in such a forthright manner. After Yeshua left the synagogue, he chatted with the other men, who were then joined by their womenfolk outside the synagogue. And Yeshua asked a group, "What did you think of the rabbi's talk?"

There were plenty of smiles, and glib remarks, and laughter. Most people openly agreed with the rabbi and felt that they needed to take more care in gossiping about others, but Yeshua wondered whether they would return to gossipmongering, for it was so ingrained when friends got together. Yeshua resolved to be more careful and watch his tongue.

It was now time for the evening meal, but Yeshua had already eaten and wasn't hungry. It was quite a distance from the lake and Yeshua didn't feel like sleeping rough tonight so he sought and found the inn and a room. He was feeling a bit tired and as he lay down, he milled over the words of the rabbi and thought about how easy and how commonplace and yet how destructive gossip can be. Yeshua was not one to gossip but he resolved never to take part in gossip, even if it lost him friends. Gossipers might regard it as harmless, but it is by no means harmless, it destroys not only the victims of the gossip but it destroys the souls of those who engage in gossip. There is so much that can engage us in fruitful conversation than to gossip about another, were some of Yeshua's ruminations.

Yeshua then turned his mind to Nazareth and to those dear to him and he prayed for them. He had only been gone eight days, and he was starting to miss their presence and their company. It didn't take long for Yeshua to fall asleep.

Yeshua slept late, he wanted to have his money's worth of a comfortable bed, which he was allowed to have until the fourth hour. He got up at about the second hour after sunrise, feeling quite rested and hungry, and went to the eatery for breakfast. After having something to eat Yeshua felt refreshed and decided to leave the inn and continue on his homeward journey. It was now nine days since he left Nazareth and he had told his mother and grandmother that he would be back in about two to three weeks and it looks like he was on target to reach that deadline. He didn't want to take more than three weeks, as he didn't want to cause his mother any undue worry.

Yeshua was lucky he had fine spring weather all the way but today it was rather cool and overcast. It didn't look like rain clouds, but there were some dark and ominous patches in the sky. Yeshua left Sennebris at past the third hour. The sun was starting to make its presence felt from behind the dark clouds. Yeshua saw the thick silver linings at the end of the dark clouds in the east. His next stop was the village or town of Tarichaea. Yeshua loved the towns that bore Greek names, they sounded so poetic. He had studied a bit of Greek during his time at the School in Jerusalem. The route from Sennebris led back towards the Sea of Galilee, as Tarichaea was right on the coast. Yeshua was pleased to be close to the sea again and his heart quickened as he saw his first glimpse of the Sea of Galilee. It was now mid-afternoon and the sky was much clearer and the dark clouds were gone, and there were plenty of blue sky around. Yeshua sought out and found the well and was able to give himself a splash and have a good drink of water and refill his water bag.

In his studies of Greek, Yeshua recalled the teacher speak of Tarichaea. The Romans invaded this little town more than fifty years ago and completely destroyed it. Like the town of Philateria, Yeshua saw the ruins of those wars. Yeshua spent a few hours in and around the town, simply watching the townsfolk going about their daily living. He greeted and chatted to those he met. It seemed that these cities alongside the Sea of Galilee were accustomed to strangers, to people visiting from elsewhere. The sea and its coastal towns were a drawcard for all those who lived inland. Everyone it seemed wanted to spend their spare time, to holiday along the coast, to swim and fish and simply laze on the sea sand or walk along the beach, especially during the warmer months.

Yeshua was now in his ninth day of hugging the coast, and he felt like he belonged here, he belonged to the Sea of Galilee. Once he left home, he knew that time would come, he would definitely make his home somewhere along the coast, most likely the town of Capernaum, which is only twenty miles from Nazareth, a day's walk away. It would soon be dusk and Yeshua decided he would walk to Tiberias, which was only about three miles distance, it would only take him less than a couple of hours and he would be there before nightfall. He could easily find a place to sleep there.

Yeshua arrived at Tiberias and even though it was dark, people were still milling around the town centre. Yeshua found lodgings. He recalled his first camping visit to Tiberias with his father, Yosef. How he enjoyed that time together. The memory brought a tear to his eye and he remembered his father, now deceased for more than four years. Yeshua thought about so many people around the world that were grieving the loss of loved ones, to illness, to wars, to crime and simply to old age. So much grieving around the world and he knew that for everyone it was different, and here he was four years after the loss of Yosef, Jehoyakim, his grandfather and Rahab, mother of his dearest friends from Bethany, Lazarus, Martha and Mary. How he grieved these losses and yearned to be with his friends of Bethany. It is four years now and still I grieve. At the same time, Yeshua reflected on how many children are being born around the world, and how much joy that brings to parents, families and the community. Yeshua thought of his childhood friend Zadok and his wife Gadija. It has been a while since he last saw them and Gadija was then expecting their first child. He would visit them tomorrow. Yeshua turned his thoughts to his heavenly Father and said his usual nightly prayers and soon fell asleep, with joy in his heart as he thought about visiting his friends here in Tiberias.

Yeshua had bathed before he slept the night before, so he simply washed his face and rinsed his mouth and had a bite to eat. He chatted a while with some of the other lodgers and they were fascinated with the stories Yeshua had to tell, and the fact that he had now almost circled the Sea of Galilee on foot. "That is very impressive," a visitor from Jerusalem, a forty something gentleman, Abijam, said. And when he heard that Yeshua had been a student at the School of Advanced Learning in Jerusalem, he was even more impressed.

Yeshua eventually had to leave the lodgings at the fourth hour, which was the time to vacate the rooms to be cleaned for the next guests. Yeshua said his goodbyes and was on his way. Yeshua headed straight to the city's blacksmith workplace, at the other side of the city. Zadok was clothed in a large apron and totally engrossed in what he was doing. His back was turned to Yeshua.

"Shalom Sir, I have a problem with my hoof, could you please repair it," Yeshua said with a chuckle.

Zadok turned around and looked at Yeshua, but he had already recognised that melodious voice. "Yeshua," he cried and dropped his implements and hugged Yeshua warmly, evidently so pleased to see his friend. They chatted for a while and Zadok was just as impressed as the guests at the inn who heard of Yeshua's exploits. "So, you walked around the sea, wow, when did you start?" Zadok asked.

"I began nine days ago. Set out from Nazareth through Cana and then Magdala, went north to Gennesaret and Capernaum, crossed the River Jordan and then stayed at Bethsaida, then on to Gergesa, Hippos, and all the way down the east coast and crossed the River Jordan, wading across again at Philateria, then on to Sennebris, and Tarichaea and now here."

"Yeshua, that is such a great adventure, you must tell me and Gadija all about it. You are staying in Tiberias," Zadok insisted.

"No, Zadok, I really have to get home," Yeshua teased. "Of course, how can I come to Tiberias and not visit its number one resident!" Yeshua said. They both laughed.

"I have to finish a few jobs for today and then I will be free. Should be a couple of hours, and I will close up for the day. Gadija will be so pleased to see you and so will our little one, Ahijah, he just said his first words," Zadok said proudly.

"What was that, 'Abba'?" Yeshua asked.

"No, it was Imm, not yet the complete Immah," Zadok said.

"Congratulations, Zadok, I am so thrilled for you and Gadija. I'm sure Ahijah must give you so much joy." Again, Yeshua felt that tinge of sadness that he would not have a wife and children of his own. *Is this not too much Yahweh is asking of me*? He whispered again, "Thy will be done."

"What was that you said?" Zadok heard the whisper.

"Nothing, actually, something, I just whispered to Yahweh, how envious I am of you and Gadija, and how much I too would love to have a wife and a child to love and care for," Yeshua said.

"Your time will come, Yeshua; you're a handsome guy and the ladies love you," Zadok said with a smile. "What about Rebecca," Zadok added, "I have seen the two of you together, and I can see she's sweet on you, Yeshua, and you like her, don't you?" Zadok added.

"Okay, that's enough of you, Mr Matchmaker. Get your work done so we can get out of here; I am dying to see Gadija and especially your little one, Ahijah," Yeshua said.

"Okay, my apprentice will be here in a minute. I'll let him finish this work. He's good enough now, almost fully apprenticed, and I will employ him, there is enough work for both of us."

"Well, I'll leave you to it, Zadok, I do want to browse around a bit, let's say I meet you back here in an hour."

"That's perfect. See you in an hour." Zadok then got back to his work.

Yeshua went to the city centre and browsed around the markets. And as usual he drifted into the synagogue. As there were no public services going on, he spent some quiet time, praying for Zadok and Gadija and their little one, Ahijah.

The hour passed quickly and when Yeshua arrived back, Zadok was giving instructions to his apprentice, a big lad in his late teens.

"Ah you're back. Yeshua, meet my apprentice, Hosea. Hosea, this is Yeshua, my dearest friend from Nazareth."

"Shalom!" Yeshua greeted Hosea with a slight bow and with his hands clasped together. "I'm very pleased to meet you, Hosea, your boss speaks very highly of you," Yeshua added.

"Shalom, Yeshua, I'm pleased to meet you, you are very kind. I have heard of you before from Zadok, he called you the brains and the goody-two-shoes from Nazareth."

"Did he now and we called him the Hercules and dreamer of Nazareth," Yeshua said with a smile.

"Okay now, Hosea, you know what to do, I leave you in charge for the rest of the day. And you know what to do tomorrow. I won't be in, so just finish what I gave you to do and then you can close up for the day. I won't be in, I have an important guest from Nazareth to entertain," Zadok said, smiling. He took off his apron, washed his hands in a bucket filled with water and suds, and he and Yeshua were on their way.

"Oh Yeshua, how great it is to see you," Gadija cried out as soon as she lay eyes on Yeshua. She was so thrilled that she impulsively ran into Yeshua's arms, surprising Yeshua. This was so uncharacteristic of Jewish women but then Gadija wasn't really Jewish; her parents were merchants originally from Egypt and they loved Tiberias and built a home here.

"Shalom, Gadija, it is so good to see you and you are looking so good. Is Zadok treating you well? If not then just let me know and he will have to answer to me," Yeshua said smiling. "But you are looking so well and happy, so I guess he must be treating you well," Yeshua added.

"Yes, very well indeed, he is a great husband and a wonderful father," Gadija said, looking from Yeshua to Zadok, who was smiling broadly.

"Okay, that's enough of my two only admirers in the whole wide world," Zadok joked.

"So where is your little one, Ahijah, I am dying to see him," Yeshua said.

"He is asleep but should be awake soon, he will cry for some milk." Gadija had barely said the words when a cry came from the next room, first faintly and then firmly.

"The boss calls," Zadok said, as Gadija left the room and returned with her bundle of joy, Ahijah. She showed him off to Yeshua, who beamed with delight, but Ahijah showed no interest, now he was howling for his mother's milk.

Zadok and Yeshua surrounded Ahijah being held in his mother's arms. Yeshua reached out to Ahijah, who grabbed Yeshua's finger and wanted to put it in his mouth. "Looks like he is hungry alright," Yeshua said.

"Yes, he is really cranky, until he has his feed," Zadok said.

"Do excuse us, I will give him some milk," Gadija said, as she returned to the next room. And it wasn't long when Ahijah was completely quiet.

"He is a beautiful boy, Zadok; you must be so proud and so happy."

"I sure am, Yeshua, it was the happiest day of my life when Ahijah was born. And he is such a good boy, except when Gadija takes too long to feed him."

"I guess in that way, he takes after his father," Yeshua said, smiling.

"Forgive me, Yeshua, there is a bowl with water out back if you would like to wash. And while you are doing that, I will get you a towel. Would you like some wine before our dinner?" Zadok asked.

"Thanks, Zadok, that will be great." Yeshua went out to the back yard and found the water and washed. Zadok came out with a towel and then disappeared inside.

When Yeshua came back into the house, a jug of wine and two cups were on the table. Yeshua felt refreshed and was glad to have a cup of wine. It had been a while since he had imbibed. Zadok filled both cups. They lifted them to each other and then drank.

Gadija then entered the dining area with Ahijah in her arms. She brought him to Yeshua. "Would you like to hold him, Yeshua?" she asked.

Yeshua put down his drink and took Ahijah in his arms. This was the first time Yeshua had ever held a baby in his arms. He felt so protective and something just stirred inside of him, a feeling of such warmth and love, the likes of which he had never experienced before. He sat down and just held Ahijah and stared at him, and Ahijah seemed to be staring back. Yeshua reached out to him with his one hand and again, Ahijah grabbed Yeshua's finger and just held on to it. Yeshua was absolutely enthralled and in another world. *If I experience such an indescribable joy in holding a baby in my arms, what great joy it must be for Gadija and Zadok.* Yeshua could understand why his childhood friend with his harsh and fierce ways had become so soft and tender.

"What a beautiful child, Gadija and Zadok, I am sure that Ahijah must give you a lot of joy," Yeshua said.

"He sure does, except when he howls in the middle of the night for a feed," Zadok said.

"He is a very good baby, we are fortunate," Gadija said. "You must be hungry, Yeshua. I have some beef stew prepared and did bake some bread today." Gadija then went about preparing the table.

When the table was laid and prepared with the food, Gadija took Ahijah from Yeshua and laid Ahijah in a cot nearby. They then said prayers of thanks and ate their meal. The conversation flowed easily and Zadok and Gadija listened with delight as Yeshua related the stories from his travels around the Sea of Galilee.

"Yeshua, you have such an enchanting way of telling stories about the places you've been and the people you've met," Gadija said.

When Yeshua told them about the time, he was confronted by those youths from Magdala, Zadok was all ears. "I was thinking of you, Zadok and Achim, and I had said to myself, if the two of you were with me, we could have taken them on."

"But that must have been frightening, Yeshua, but you seemed to have handled it well," Gadija added.

The three of them ate their meal, drank wine, ate some cake and chatted for hours.

"Zadok, you must be tired and you have to be up early, maybe it is time to retire," Gadija suggested.

"No, it's okay, my love, Hosea is minding the place tomorrow, I am taking the day off to entertain our distinguished guest," Zadok said, making a sweeping gesture towards Yeshua.

"That's good, Zadok, you have not had a day off for a very long time," Gadija said, pleased to have him home with her, and to have Yeshua with them.

"I think we can go on a picnic by the lake tomorrow. What do you think, Gadija? You are going to spend the day with us, Yeshua," Zadok commanded.

"A picnic by the lake, with my two…my three best friends, how can I refuse? Can we fish? It's been a while since I caught some fish," Yeshua said.

"For sure," Zadok replied, beaming for he too loved fishing, and it had been a while.

"You two can go out back and put some wood on the embers and start up the fire if you like, while I clean up and take care of Ahijah," Gadija said.

Zadok and Yeshua retired to the backyard. Zadok fed the embers and the fire soon lit up the place and warmed them. Zadok brought the jar of wine and their two cups with them and they drank some more. They chatted for some time until Gadija joined them.

Yeshua enquired about her parents, and were told they were both in good health.

"I was five years old, when we came to Tiberias from Egypt," Gadija answered in reply to Yeshua's question.

"Where about in Egypt did you live and do you remember anything about Egypt?" Yeshua asked.

Gadija was pleased to talk about Egypt where she was born, and about her visit there with her parents about five years ago. She was enchanted to hear about Yeshua's flight into Egypt with his parents and that he lived there in exile for the first three years of his life. Of course, Yeshua did not mention that he was the person that Herod was trying to kill.

It was now about two hours before midnight and Gadija said goodnight, and left Yeshua and Zadok to continue their conversation. She brought them some snacks. Yeshua and Zadok continued chatting till well after midnight. They finished the jar of wine and that made them all the chattier.

"I don't know when last I chatted so much, Zadok said, it's so good to see you again, Yeshua. Would you like some more wine?" he asked.

"No thanks, Zadok, I think I had enough and maybe it's time for some sleep. I sure enjoyed our time together. Thank you and Gadija so much for a wonderful evening. I'm ready for bed now."

"Me too, I am feeling a bit tipsy. Good thing I won't be working tomorrow. You sleep in as long as you wish, Yeshua. And we'll be off to the lake after breakfast. Goodnight Yeshua."

"Goodnight Zadok."

Zadok doused the fire. Then they went to bed. Yeshua lay for a while reflecting on the day. And he had such warm feelings for his friend and so pleased how Zadok's life had turned out. He always knew that the bravado exterior of his friend had a soft centre. Yeshua said his prayers of thanks to Yahweh and was soon fast asleep.

Chapter Twenty-Six
The Last Leg Home

Yeshua spent a memorable day with his friend Zadok, his wife Gadija and their child, Ahijah. They chatted, laughed, fished, ate, drank wine, and entertained young Ahijah. Yeshua had not enjoyed himself so much for a long time. He spent hours with Ahijah, taking him on long walks, letting his feet feel the water. Yeshua built a big sand castle for him, chatted so much with him, it seemed that Ahijah was taking it all in with his constant smiles, which simply warmed Yeshua's heart. Again, that nagging feeling, I will never have a child of my own. But again, the only way out, "Abba, thy will be done." And as Yeshua was an only child, he never had the joy of holding a baby brother or sister in his arms.

Zadok and Gadija, it seemed, enjoyed the break from their son, Ahijah, who occupied all their waking and a lot of their sleeping moments. They enjoyed watching Yeshua at play with Ahijah.

"Yeshua will make such a good father," Gadija said, as she and Zadok watched Yeshua building the castle for their child.

"I know he will, but it seems that he will never marry," Zadok said.

"Why, what do you mean, he will never marry?" Gadija asked, perplexed.

"I don't know; there is just something about Yeshua. There is just such a goodness and kindness and lovingness in him, for everyone. I don't know, I don't think he is destined for a family of his own. I just feel that he will be a great person one day and that he is going to make a difference in the lives of so many, and that his life is to be dedicated for the good of so many, that he will not have the time for a family of his own," Zadok said.

"Really Zadok, you're a prophet now, are you?" Gadija said, smiling.

"Gadija, I grew up with Yeshua, and I just know he is destined for great things," Zadok said.

"So, what are you two gossiping about?" Yeshua said, as he approached Zadok and Gadija, who were deep in conversation, and did not notice him approach with Ahijah.

"Aah, how great a husband and father you will be one day," Gadija said, looking from Yeshua to her husband, and giving him a shaking of the head gesture.

"It seems that Ahijah wants a feed," Yeshua said, as he handed the baby to Gadija.

"I think it's time for us to work for our lunch, let's go fishing," Zadok said.

Zadok and Yeshua left Gadija with the baby. Zadok walked with Yeshua a little distance from where they were. "I can see some fish over there," Zadok pointed out to the sea.

"Where?"

"Over there." Zadok pointed.

"I don't see anything over there, but I bow to your fishing prowess, oh Mighty Zadok," Yeshua joked.

The two friends engaged in light-hearted banter as they walked deeper into the water to cast their fishing nets as far as they could for a catch.

"This is the life, Yeshua, mmm, isn't it?" Zadok sighed. He was feeling so contented to be at the sea side with Gadija and their newborn baby, and his best friend.

"It sure is, my friend, heavenly bliss. Now we have to be quiet if we are going to net any fish," Yeshua said, putting his finger to his lips.

"Okay," Zadok whispered. It wasn't long when they felt a movement in the net. They quickly pulled it towards them as quickly as they could and admired their catch, a couple of fish wiggling and trying desperately to free themselves from their entanglement, at the bottom of the net.

Zadok brought some flint and a piece of steel to start a fire on the beach. Yeshua minded the fire to make sure it kept burning in the breeze. It was a beautiful spring's day, as it was now nearing summer. And as it was now just past midday, they were grateful for the breeze.

After Zadok had prepared the fish, they laid it on the grille that Zadok had made, and let it cook to perfection. Zadok then poured some wine for Yeshua and himself. Gadija did not drink alcohol but she had brought some berry juice. She spread some mixture of oil and crushed olives on the bread and lay it on the large plate in the middle of their picnic table cloth spread out in front of them.

Yeshua was pleased that Ahijah was sleeping peacefully and looking so contented. It meant that Gadija could enjoy the fresh and delicious fish they were now eating in silence. Yeshua was enjoying it so much, licking his lips and sipping his wine with every mouthful.

After the meal, Gadija took out a flute from her bag and surprised Yeshua as she began to play a melody he did not know and had not heard before. He sat with his hands clasping his knees and listened, enchanted by the music.

"That was beautiful, Gadija, and you play the flute superbly," Yeshua said. "I did not recognise the tune," Yeshua added.

"It's a song about friends sitting around a fire at the seashore, it's from Egypt. My mother taught me to play the flute and the song that I thought is most appropriate for the moment."

"It sure is. Thank you for that," Yeshua said.

"Do you play any instrument, Yeshua?" Gadija asked, as she put her flute back in the bag.

"Only the drums and the cymbals, I never took lessons, just taught myself with mother's cooking pots and implements, much to father's annoyance when he wanted peace and quiet" Yeshua said, with a grin. "I always wanted to learn to play the harp though. I know it is mostly women who play the harp but I think it is such a beautiful instrument and gives such delightful music."

"It sure does," Gadija said.

"Gadija plays the harp, and the lyre and other instruments, even the organ, she is a musical genius," Zadok said proudly.

"Both my mother and father are musicians and they love music, and we always had music in our home," Gadija said.

"That is wonderful; music is such a precious gift. It sure delights the soul and you sure delighted us Gadija, thank you," Yeshua said.

The rest of the day passed peacefully. By mid-afternoon, the wind was picking up more strongly and Zadok decided it was enough for the day. Zadok and Gadija's home was not far from the beach, a ten-minute walk, so they did not bring the donkey for Gadija to ride on, but Yeshua offered to carry Ahijah in his arms.

Yeshua thought of his mother, Miriam, and his father, Yosef, as they carried him on their long journey to Egypt when he was a newborn baby. He witnessed the love and caring that Zadok and Gadija displayed for their newborn baby, Ahijah. And the love that Yeshua felt for his mother and deceased father, and the love he received from them, now flooded Yeshua's heart.

Yeshua had not intended to spend another night in Tiberias, but it was late afternoon and Zadok and Gadija insisted he stay the night.

Yeshua thanked them. "I have to leave in the morning though. I know Tiberias is a more direct and shorter route to Nazareth, but I started my journey around the Sea of Galilee from Magdala so I have to end my journey there. And I have some new friends that I met there and I would like to call on them."

After a light dinner of the leftover fish, Yeshua and Zadok sat outside again, with a cup of wine. It was a perfect night and the end of a perfect day. Gadija joined them after she had put Ahijah down to sleep.

"As you have to work tomorrow, and it has been a full day, I think we should have an early night and not talk till the early hours of the morning," Yeshua said.

"Yes, I have lots of jobs lined up," Zadok said.

They sat for a little while longer. Yeshua had a nightcap of another small amount of wine. And they then all retired for the night.

Yeshua stirred as he heard movement in the house. Gadija was busy preparing the table for their morning meal. Yeshua got up, dressed, went outside to wash and came in. Zadok appeared dressed for work. He had already eaten and was ready to go.

"You're off to work, and I'm off to Magdala," Yeshua said to Zadok. "I hope you have a good day, Zadok, and thanks again for everything. I really enjoyed my time with you and Gadija but most of all with little Ahijah. How is he today?"

Yeshua went over to the crib and saw Ahijah, awake and playing with a rattle. "Oh, there you are, Ahijah. How are you, did you have a good sleep? I had a very good sleep. Thank you, Ahijah, for the great time I had at the beach, and thank you for spending time with me." Then turning to face them Yeshua thanked Gadija and Zadok for such a wonderful stay.

"It was good having you with us, Yeshua. But I must be on my way now. Do have a good time on the rest of your adventure. And give my regards to your mother and your grandmother," Zadok said.

"I will. And you have a good day." The two of them hugged and Zadok kissed Gadija and Ahijah and was on his way.

Yeshua then had something to eat and Gadija prepared some food for him for the road. "It was good having you here, Yeshua, and thank you so much. Zadok really enjoyed you being here and it was good for him to have a break, he works so hard."

"It was a pleasure to spend time with him and with you Gadija, and of course with Ahijah."

When Yeshua was finished the meal, he packed his things, said goodbye to Gadija and Ahijah, and was on his way.

Magdala is just over five miles from Tiberias, so I should do it in about two hours at the pace I'm walking, if I don't stop along the way, Yeshua said to himself. But Yeshua knew he would stop to smell the flowers, admire the scenery and stop to chat with whoever he met along the way. It was now about the third hour so Yeshua calculated he would be in Magdala by noon. He was now delighted to be so near to home and to be reaching the end of his encircling of the Sea of Galilee.

It is now the eleventh day. I only have three more days before I have to get home. I told mother that I would be home within two weeks, three at the most. Even though I told I could be away for up to four weeks, I don't want to take longer than two weeks, otherwise she will worry. I'm also looking forward to visiting Joshua and his family in Magdala.

It was a pleasant day. Yeshua was fortunate he had such fine weather all the way, and he gave thanks to Yahweh. As he walked, he talked with Yahweh. He gave thanks for the fine weather and for all the good things that happened to him along the way and he asked Yahweh to bless all those whom he met and especially those who gave him hospitality, and he prayed especially for Zadok, Gadija and Ahijah, and asked Yahweh to bless them.

The birds were singing heartily as usual. And the wind was making its usual music rustling the branches of the trees. "Thank you, sister wind, your caress of my face is so refreshing in this heat." Yeshua was feeling refreshed and so happy to have spent such quality time with his friends in Tiberias, and he was so pleased with how Zadok has matured.

It was almost noon when Yeshua arrived at Magdala. He sought out the water fountain or well and found both. He drank some water at the well and then had a splash with the water from the fountain, at the city centre, which was abuzz with people. And the markets were full of buyers, sellers, and people just browsing. Yeshua was about to buy some fruit, when he opened his backpack and the parcel Gadija had given him. It had bread with some slices of lamb and his favourite, figs and berries, and a couple of apples. Yeshua was about to look for a spot to sit and eat when he changed his mind, and thought he would search for Joshua's daughters and see if they were at their stall. He found them.

They were so excited when they saw Yeshua. "Oh Yeshua," Ruth cried out loud, as she rushed instinctively into Yeshua's arms, and then quickly withdrew as she realised its inappropriateness. She had presumed familiarity only reserved for close kin.

Yeshua smiled and was not in the least embarrassed, although he could see that Ruth was. "It's okay, Ruth, I am so grateful for your warm welcome, it is so good to get a hug from a good friend," Yeshua said, with the warmest of smiles, and he opened his arms and Ruth responded with a hug, and it succeeded in putting Ruth completely at ease.

Just then Orpah appeared and she greeted Yeshua warmly but without the exuberant hug of her sister.

Yeshua greeted Orpah and winked at Ruth and smiled.

"What's going on with you two?" Orpah said, as she saw Yeshua wink at her sister.

"I can't lie, Orpah, your sister Ruth, not realising that I am not close kin, ran into my arms and gave me the biggest of hugs," Yeshua said with a grin.

"Ah, now why didn't I think of that," Orpah said, as she clicked her fingers.

"Okay, Orpah, let's do that again. Orpah, it is so good to see you, may I give you a hug," Yeshua said mischievously.

"You may indeed, Sir," Orpah said with a smile. They hugged. Orpah had been so withdraw and shy when she first met Yeshua, but with his first visit she had got to know him more intimately, and felt so much more relaxed around Yeshua, which delighted both Yeshua and her sister.

Yeshua felt so much at home with Orpah and Ruth after that encounter. They chatted and Yeshua told them that he had now finished his walk around the Sea of Galilee and must now continue on his way home.

"Oh, but you must come and see Abba and Immah, they will be so pleased to see you, and hear all about your adventure around the Sea of Galilee, as we too would be," Ruth said.

"Oh yes, definitely," Orpah chimed in.

"Okay, I did of course intend to visit your mother and father; I couldn't pass through Magdala without greeting them and your brothers. Are your parents at home?" Yeshua asked.

"Yes, they are, working of course," Ruth said.

"Good then, I just want to browse a bit. I was thinking of buying a present for a girl friend of mine, Rebecca, in Nazareth, are there any stalls with fine jewellery, and not too expensive," Yeshua asked.

"Rebecca, is she your girlfriend, Yeshua, are you betrothed?" Ruth asked.

"No, she is just a very good friend, we have grown up together," Yeshua said.

"You are not betrothed to Rebecca and you are going to buy her jewellery," Orpah said frowning.

"Yes, I am, is there anything wrong with that?" Yeshua said.

"If a man gave me jewellery, I would think he has serious designs," Orpah said.

Yeshua did not want to pursue further explanations of his friendship with Rebecca, but Ruth and Orpah does make a valid point. Yeshua reflected on the fact that he and Rebecca had that serious chat and she knew the score. Yeshua decided he would nevertheless buy some jewellery for Rebecca.

"Thanks for your caution, girls. I will be off now and I'll see you later, say around the ninth hour, and I'll go home with you," Yeshua said, and was on his way.

Yeshua found a stall at the end of the market, a lady very fashionably dress, with large earrings and a necklace full of precious stones and bracelets bedecked with charms and beads, was serving at the stall. The table and the entire stall, was strewn with jewellery of all kinds.

"Shalom, good Sir, welcome to my store," she said.

"Shalom, my good lady, I'm Yeshua, I'm from Nazareth and I have a good friend, Rebecca, living there and I would like to buy her a present, what do you suggest? I have never bought jewellery for anyone before."

"You are the first man who has done so in a while. Tell me about your Rebecca. By the way, I am Jasmine."

"Well, Jasmine, Rebecca is a couple of years younger than me, she is a feisty girl, more of a tomboy, loves the outdoors and is a keen runner, she's not really into women's fashion as far as her dressing goes. But I did notice her wearing a silver-coated bracelet with a single charm on it."

"Can you describe the charm?"

"It is…eh…a ladybird, red, with black dots," Yeshua said.

"She has fine tastes. You could buy another charm for her, or you could purchase one of these beautiful silver necklaces with a charm," Jasmine suggested, as she showed Yeshua a tray of necklaces with all sorts of charms and trinkets on them.

"I'm afraid I cannot afford any silver jewellery, Jasmine."

"These are not pure silver, Yeshua; they are nevertheless silver-plated, as are the charms, and are quite reasonably priced, and no one will know the difference."

"I like these," Yeshua saw one chain with a silver Star of David and one with a silver butterfly with multicoloured wings.

"Good choice, now which one do you think Rebecca would like on her neck chain, the Star of David or the butterfly?" Jasmine asked.

Yeshua recognised the sales technique Jasmine was using; he had seen just how effective it was and commonly used by the sellers. *She is giving me a fatal alternative, no matter what one I choose, she has made a sale*, Yeshua mused.

"The Star of David is beautiful, such a striking symbol of our faith. But I think a chain with the butterfly will be a perfect match for Rebecca's ladybird bracelet and more to her taste," Yeshua proclaimed. "It's perfect."

"A good choice, Yeshua, she will love it, and you are right, it is a perfect match for her bracelet."

Jasmine wrapped the neck chain with its butterfly in a tiny silk bag and thanked Yeshua for the purchase. "Go well, Yeshua, and be sure, Rebecca will love the present you have bought her."

"Shalom," Yeshua said again, and was on his way, satisfied with the present he had bought for Rebecca. He was now feeling hungry, he found a bench at the outer perimeter to the market stalls and sat down to eat, while watching the people going about their business of living.

Yeshua no sooner opened his parcel lunch when pigeons came swarming in. Yeshua knew if he fed them, he would be inundated with a huge flock. "Go on now, my friends, and go find your own food, you have plenty of food to eat, you do not sow or reap or gather into barns, your heavenly father feeds you, go now and eat to your heart's content. This food I have here is not good for your constitution, these are manmade, and yours are divine, go now."

Yeshua spoke to the birds and they seemed to be listening to him because the moment he had finished speaking, they flew away, leaving Yeshua to eat his lunch in peace.

After lunch, Yeshua tossed up whether to visit the synagogue for some private prayer or to go to the beach for a walk. He decided on the beach. It wasn't a difficult choice because after a heavy meal Yeshua never felt like praying. He felt like a leisurely stroll after that tasty lunch. He walked to the beach, not too far away, and there were quite a few people, lying on the beach and soaking up the sun, and a few families having a picnic. Yeshua greeted all those whom he passed.

Yeshua must have walked for at least an hour, without realising it. It was so peaceful and delightful walking at the water's edge, and listening to the waves lapping onto his feet. Yeshua looked up at the sky and the position of the sun. "I better turn around now, as brother sun is well on its course westward," Yeshua said aloud. Yeshua estimated it to be around the ninth hour, he could take a leisurely walk back and arrive in time before the girls will be ready to head for home.

When Yeshua got back to the marketplace, he found Ruth alone, packing up for the day. She was pleased to see Yeshua again, looking quite sunburnt.

"Where is Orpah?" Yeshua asked.

"Oh, she has gone to fetch our donkey, she should be here in a minute."

"Shalom, Yeshua," Yeshua turned around to see a smiling Orpah. "Looks like you've been on the beach and added more sunburn. You have to be careful, Yeshua, and use some protection against the sun."

"I've been on the road for two weeks with brother sun following me all the way, so I guess I must be somewhat sunburnt," Yeshua said. "Shalom Orpah, and where's the donkey?" Yeshua asked.

"He's tethered just on the outside. We have to carry our bags to him."

Yeshua helped the girls carry their big bags of fine clothes to their donkey that brayed as soon as they approached, evidently happy to be going home.

Joshua and Emzara were thrilled to see a sunburnt Yeshua. They welcomed him warmly.

Joshua and Emzara wanted to know all about Yeshua's adventure. Ruth and Orpah had already heard quite a bit of Yeshua's exploits for they had questioned him all the way home. They disappeared for a while to wash and brighten their appearance. And it wasn't long when Seth, Japheth, and Ham arrived, looking well-worn after a day's work in the fields. They greeted Yeshua and then disappeared to remove their work clothes, wash and get ready for the evening meal.

It was now quite cool with a fresh wind when they finally sat down for their evening meal.

"Aah, this barley soup is delicious," Yeshua said, as he dipped his bread in the soup and slurped another mouthful. Yeshua ate the fresh fish with great delight. And of course, there was the wine to cap it all.

Yeshua spent the evening in the company of Joshua, Emzara and their two daughters and three sons, and it seemed as if he was one of the family. Even the boys opened up more to him, as he recounted all of his exploits.

When they had finished their meal, Ruth and Orpah wanted some more quality time with Yeshua alone, and Yeshua noticed their desire.

"Ruth and Orpah, I would like to show you the present I bought for my friend Rebecca, to hear what you think," Yeshua said, and walked to his backpack, which he had left at the back door, so the girls followed him. They went outside and had a close look.

"It's beautiful," Ruth exclaimed. "Your Rebecca will love it."

"It sure is, Yeshua. You have good taste in jewellery, for a man," Orpah said with a smile.

Ruth and Orpah had some quality time with Yeshua. Their parents could see what was happening and they left them alone.

"Yeshua would make a fine husband to one of our girls, Joshua," Emzara said.

"He sure would," Joshua responded.

"Let's leave them alone for a while, so they could get to know each other more. Who knows what the Lord has in store," Emzara said.

The boys had already said goodnight to Yeshua, as they were off to meet up with some of their friends for the evening. Joshua and Emzara left Yeshua with Ruth and Orpah.

Yeshua was enjoying the company of both Ruth and Orpah; they were now both very comfortable and at ease in his company, as Yeshua was in theirs. Yeshua had so much to share; they wanted to know all about his journey around the lake, and also about his life in Nazareth. They were especially fascinated to hear about how Yeshua escaped the wrath of the evil King Herod, who massacred thousands of infants in order to kill a newborn king.

"So, if your mother and father had not fled into Egypt on that very night, you would have died with all those poor children," Orpah said.

"I would have."

Ruth and Orpah were fascinated with the details of Yeshua's life so far, and Yeshua made sure that he listened to them as well, what their life has been, what their dreams are. They both wanted to continue to make fine and fashionable garments, not only for the people of Magdala, and all those who passed through Magdala, but also for the rich and famous in the big cities of Tiberias, Sepphoris and of course Jerusalem. They were working on designs that they knew would become fashionable in the near future.

Yeshua encouraged and affirmed them in their aspirations, and they were only too pleased to show him the designs they were working on.

"I am not rich or famous, and never will be, but I will make it my business to buy one of your designer garments when next I pass this way," Yeshua said.

"For Rebecca?" Ruth said with a mischievous smile.

"Depends, or my mother, she's not really into fashion, but she loves to dress well. And she is still young," Yeshua said.

"How old is your mother, Yeshua?" Orpah asked.

"She was only fifteen when she was betrothed to Yosef, and I was born in that year. I am now twenty years of age that makes her thirty-five, but she looks much younger," Yeshua said.

Ruth then disappeared and returned with a beautiful shawl with fine tassels. "This is for your mother, Yeshua, from Orpah and me. It is one of our designs."

Yeshua thanked them. They continued chatting for more than a couple of hours. Ruth and Orpah were so surprised at how Yeshua could converse with them, he was so different to the other young men they knew. And they felt so at ease in his presence, and it seemed that he too was so much at ease, in theirs.

It was getting very dark and late when Joshua finally came out and told the girls to say goodnight to Yeshua. They reluctantly did so, but were contented for the time they spent in Yeshua's presence. He was like no other man they had ever met. And he exuded such gentleness, kindness, joyfulness and peacefulness about him, and he was such a wonderful story teller, they could listen to him all night.

Yeshua shared a nightcap with Joshua, during which time Emzara joined them for a while and then said her goodnight to Yeshua. Yeshua thanked her for the superb meal.

Yeshua did not want to detain Joshua for long because tomorrow was a working day. The boys were still out. So, Yeshua said his goodnight and thanked Joshua once again for his hospitality, and then went to sleep.

Chapter Twenty-Seven
Leaving the Sea of Galilee

Yeshua was up with the rest of the family. They had breakfast, except for the boys who were already out in the fields attending to the cattle and the farm. Before breakfast the girls had already loaded up the donkey with their garments to take to the markets. Yeshua said good bye to Joshua and Emzara, thanking them once more for the food and lodging, for their warm hospitality. He then accompanied the girls to the city square, saying good bye to the boys on his way.

At the markets, Yeshua said his goodbyes to the girls, who hugged him warmly. It was now going to be the way with Yeshua and them. The other people in the marketplace, mostly sellers at so early in the day, looked at Yeshua and the girls, embracing so warmly in public and were not taken aback but rather intrigued, for it was not a commonplace occurrence. And they knew that Yeshua was not of their family, but even if he was, it was not proper for women to display such gestures of affection, especially to men not of their family. Some though, especially some of the women, had smiles of approval.

Yeshua decided to go to the synagogue for morning service before leaving Magdala. After the community prayers Yeshua remained for about an hour for his own personal time with Yahweh. He had lots to talk about and he prayed especially for Joshua, Emzara, Ruth Orpah, Shem, Japheth and Ham, and thought how easy it was going to be for him to remember their names, such famous people from their Scriptures. It was now twelve days since he left Nazareth and he had told his mother that he would most likely be back within two weeks. Yeshua was pleased. His next stop was Cana, about three hours walk, and then from Cana to Nazareth about another four hours or so. I suppose I could head for home right now and walk non-stop and get home before nightfall, Yeshua said to himself. Yeshua decided otherwise, he would take his time, stopover in Cana and arrive home on day fourteen, as he had predicted. And his mother would not have time to worry.

Yeshua decided to give Ruth and Orpah one more surprise by turning up at their stall, as he had to pass that way out of the city. When he arrived, they were chatting to a girl in her late teens, she had a scarf over her head but couldn't cover all of her hair that was long and flowing.

"You're still here, Yeshua," Ruth exclaimed excitedly, when she saw Yeshua.

"I went to the synagogue for the morning prayers, and as I had to pass this way out of the city, I thought I would just greet you one more time, I don't know when we will meet again," Yeshua said.

"Oh Yeshua, I'm so glad to see you again, I was starting to miss you already," Orpah exclaimed with a smile, as she hugged Yeshua once again.

The girl with them was astounded at the familiarity and public display of affection between Orpah, Ruth and this man they called Yeshua.

"And who is your friend?" Yeshua asked, as he gestured to the girl.

"Oh, this is Miriam; we have been friends since we were little. She lives here and sometimes joins us at the stall," Ruth said.

"Shalom, Miriam, I am so pleased to meet you, a friend of Ruth and Orpah is a friend of mine," Yeshua said, with a smile.

Miriam was extremely shy and nervous and kept her eyes downcast. "I must hurry, my mother is waiting for me," Miriam said, and left in a hurry.

"Oh dear, I hope I didn't frighten your friend Miriam, she sure left in a flash," Yeshua said.

"Miriam is a troubled soul, Yeshua. Some days she is a delight to be with, full of vigour and enthusiasm and bubbly, and then on other days she is the complete opposite, down in the dumps, sad and dreary. We never know what mood she is in. Like today she was so fearful of you and dashed off. If she was in her more joyous mood, she would be all over you like a rash. She can be very temperamental and unpredictable and her parents are beside themselves to relate to her and at times to control her because she can also become very violent. Everyone says she is possessed of demons," Ruth said.

"At times she is so bad, and almost goes into a fit, and people are saying she is possessed of several demons. I wish there was a doctor who could treat her properly, so she could be more stable. But she has a heart of gold, Yeshua, and we love her," Orpah said.

"Oh, I'm so sorry to hear that about your friend Miriam, do give her my regards," Yeshua said. "I better get going now. I have to be home early on the day after tomorrow, which is two weeks since I left Nazareth, and the day I told mother I would be home. I want to arrive early on that day so as not to allow too much time for mother to worry," Yeshua said. "And thanks again for the presents you gave for Mother and Grandmother, they will love it. Well, until we meet again, Shalom."

They hugged once more and Yeshua was on his way, feeling so much love for Ruth and Orpah and thinking of their friend Miriam, whom somehow, he felt he was destined to meet again in the future.

"Goodbye, Sea of Galilee, until we meet again," Yeshua said out loud as he turned around after his last sight of the sea, now disappearing into lower ground and the distance, and hidden from sight by the hills and trees and homes and other manmade constructions.

Yeshua felt a bit of sadness that his adventure was coming to an end. He had seen and enjoyed so much of the scenery but most of all he had enjoyed the people he met along the way, and the friendships he had made. He had recalled all the people he met and said a prayer for them, especially for Miriam of Magdala, the troubled soul who had dashed off so soon after they met. He gave thanks to Yahweh for all his experiences and for keeping him safe. The feeling of sadness evaporated quickly as the joy of nearing home, hit home. He was now longing to see his mother and grandmother and encounter all the familiar sights and sounds and smells of his home, and Nazareth.

Yeshua paced himself and walked more slowly than usual. He had decided to sleep rough on this last night somewhere along the way, near to Cana, and then leave early and arrive home on the following day before midday. It was still afternoon and at least a couple of hours before the sun would begin its dip when Yeshua arrived at Cana. He remembered that his father Yosef had some distant relatives living here in Cana, but Yosef did not seem very close to them, and Yeshua had never met them, at least never went there with Yosef. So, Yeshua left it at that. He would most likely meet them at some time in the future, for now he was just focusing on getting home.

Yeshua stopped at Cana as he did in all the towns and villages he had passed in the past two weeks, to meet and greet the places and the peoples. And as Cana was so near to Nazareth, only about three hours or so away, he knew he would be here again, sometime in the future, as he would definitely be visiting the Sea of Galilee again.

Yeshua simply stopped for water to drink, and to refill his water bag, and to have a splash on his face, and wash his hands, arms, legs and feet. He often washed his feet, as it gathered so much dust from walking on the dusty roads, as he wore the customary open sandals.

For the first time the weather looked like rain. Yeshua had seen the dark clouds in the east that had begun to gather not long after he had left Magdala, knew he would encounter a down pour on his way home, and it now looked like the clouds were ready to give birth and shower the earth. Yeshua knew he had to find shelter quickly. He found a fairly deep cave not far out of Cana, and prepared to camp there until the rain had passed, or maybe I should just stay here for the night, the weather should be better, tomorrow, hopefully, Yeshua thought.

It wasn't long when the darkness covered the earth. Yeshua wished he had a fire going but it would be near impossible to light one in this weather, as the lightning flashed across the sky, and the thunder roared like an army of wild beasts. "Well, Yahweh I have been lucky with such fine weather and now thank you for this wet and dreary homecoming. But it is rather a wild and delightful homecoming," Yeshua sighed.

And then the sky opened and it poured out its sea of water that pounded the dry and thirsty earth. The earth and all of nature must be delighting in this downpour of water, Yeshua said to himself. Yeshua sat near the entrance to the cave and watched the water drench the earth outside. He found just watching and listening to the downpour of water from the heavens to be intriguing, intoxicating and relaxing. It rained for quite some time. Yeshua simply sat, watched and listened to the downpour, until it finally reduced to a whimper and then silence. Yeshua then had something to eat. He spent the next hour in prayers of thanks for the day and for all those he met along the way and all his loved ones in Nazareth, and for all those in need, especially people like Miriam of Magdala and all those homeless people and beggars that he had met along the way. Yeshua always stopped and gave what he could to the beggars he met along the way, so many of them, and most people just ignored them and gave them a wide birth, for they were unkempt and smelled of the poverty that consumed them. But Yeshua found time to not only give them something of what he had, but he would take time to chat with them, and they all seemed so appreciative of the chance to chat and be treated like a human being.

After Yeshua calmed down and spent an hour in silent prayer, he was ready for sleep. It wasn't really that cold but he went deeper into the cave and found a little nook that looked a comfortable place to bed down for the night. During the night, Yeshua heard the rain again, it was not as loud as before because Yeshua was now deep into the cave. But the sound was relaxing. Yeshua was appreciative of the rain; it was a good homecoming. But he hoped it would be gone when he got up the next morning.

Yeshua's hopes were fulfilled when the rays of the rising sun lit up the entrance to the cave, and caused Yeshua to stir. He got up, took a handful of water to splash wipe his face and rinse his mouth. He cleaned up the place where he had slept to leave it as it was, and then was ready for the last few miles home. Yeshua recalled the time he took from Nazareth to Cana, a distance of just of about ten miles, he had taken about four hours but if he walked fast or ran part of the way, he could be home in far less than that, but as it is the first hour of the day, as the sun is rising, he could be home before noon. Yeshua slipped on his backpack, and was now determined to reach home by noon, so as not to cause his mother any undue worry.

Chapter Twenty-Eight
Home at Last

It is such a good feeling to be nearing home. It seems like I have been away forever, Yeshua said to himself. *I will take a day to recover and spend time with Mother and Grandmother before I get stuck into my work again.* By now the rain had passed and there was just a smattering of clouds in the sky, and no rain in them. It was cooler than usual but that didn't bother Yeshua, it was perfect for walking. Yeshua passed a few people on the way. He greeted them with Shalom and a smile, as they crossed paths. And Yeshua noticed how, whenever one was greeted with a smile, one felt there was no option but to smile back, it was just something human, and so natural. Just a fleeting moment with two complete strangers, exchanging smiles that for a moment and sometime after that, who knows how long, lights up their day.

There were a few people that Yeshua thought of in Nazareth that never seemed to smile. They forever had a stern look on their faces, as if they were carrying the world on their shoulders, and even when Yeshua greeted and smiled at them, they would not or could not smile in return. Yeshua wondered about that. Maybe those people are carrying some past or present heavy burden. Yeshua prayed for those individuals, and all who were heavily burdened so much so that they were unable to smile, that Yahweh may grant them peace.

Yeshua often had these thoughts as part of his morning prayers. He would, as he did now, ask Yahweh to walk with him, and talk with him. "Heavenly Father, Almighty and all loving, walk with me and talk with me, as you do with all those who see you face to face. Talk to me, Lord, as you talked to Moses on Mount Sinai, and as you talked and walked with Adam and Eve in the Garden of Eden. I am walking now, in the Garden of Eden, here in nature, on Mother Earth, this beautiful and wonderful earth that I have traversed these past two weeks; I have admired your beauty all around the Sea of Galilee. I have been enraptured by sunrises and sunsets, and the beauty of the forests with all its grandeur, with all its inhabitants and natural beauty. I have walked on the seashore and swam and fished in the Sea of Galilee, and have met so many wonderful and beautiful people along the way.

"Yahweh, I am so grateful. I say to you walk and talk with me, and I do not hear your voice, as Moses did, but Lord, you have been walking and talking with me, for you are everywhere, in every living creature, for in you we live and move and have our being. Thank you, heavenly Father, who art in heaven, hallowed be your name. Your kingdom come on earth, as it is in heaven. Amen!" Yeshua continued to pray as he walked but now, he walked in silence, in silent union with Yahweh.

Yeshua's heart skipped a beat when he had a first glimpse of Nazareth in the far distance. It looked so small in the distance. Nazareth was not as big and beautiful and exciting as the bigger towns, cities, he had passed on the way. When he was in Jerusalem, he had endured unkindly sneers and snubs from others, who looked down on Nazareth, as if nothing good can come from Nazareth. Yeshua thought of Achim and his parents and family, and Rebecca, and Zadok and his family, and Gamaliel and several others, and of course his own mother and father and knew that so much good has come and does come out of Nazareth. And he thought of the greatness of his own mother, Miriam, surely, she must be the greatest woman on earth, for an angel, angel Gabriel, appeared to her in person to ask her to be the mother of the Son of God. *What greater deed could come out of anywhere on this earth?* Yeshua said to himself.

And I am the Son of God. How can that be? Yeshua asked himself. I am flesh and bone, I am human, I have to sleep and eat and work like all other human beings. I experience fatigue and fear and anxiety and hunger and thirst and a desire to love and be loved, like everyone else, how can I, then be the Son of God? How can this be, mother must be mistaken. I am a human being like everyone else. I feel and hurt and cry and love. I love Achim, and Zadok and Rebecca, my childhood friends, and I love all those with whom I grew up, and who are now part of my life, and I love all those people who I met along my journey these past two weeks, and not only these past two weeks but these past twenty years of my life. How can I, who am flesh and bones and weak and ignorant of so much, be at the same time the Son of God? Yeshua pondered these truths and sighed and then stopped, lifted his eyes to heaven and prayed, "Father in heaven, Abba, my father, father of us all, be with me and through me may your will be done."

Yeshua ended his prayer, but he never really ended his prayer, for he always felt to be in the presence of Yahweh. He walked along, whistling, touching, greeting the branches of the trees as he passed, stopped to watch and greet the birds, as he usually did, as they feasted on the grass of the fields or as they rested on the branches. He stopped to speak to the trees, as he usually did, as well as the birds and of course any persons he encountered on the way.

Yeshua was feeling content and uplifted. He always felt so strengthened after his morning prayer. But he was now feeling the need to feed and nourish his body as well. He was close enough to Nazareth but he stopped nevertheless and sat against a tree, shaded by the morning sun, and ate the last of the bread and drank some water. I should be home within the hour, Yeshua said to himself, as he rose and continued his walk home.

It was now almost noon and people were out and about and Yeshua was greeted by all and sundry, some not even conscious that he had been gone for two weeks, others so glad to see him again. Some knew he was gone, others did not know, but Yeshua felt the warmth and goodness of his fellow Nazarenes. Some stopped to ask him how his holiday went. Yeshua stopped to chat briefly with them, but he was now eager to get home, and be with his mother who would now begin to worry.

"Immah, I'm home," Yeshua called out, as he entered their little home.

"Oh Yeshua," Miriam cried out and came rushing into Yeshua's arms. They stood like that frozen in time. Yeshua held his mother for as long as she wanted and needed.

"I'm glad I only went away for two weeks, Immah, just imagine if it was longer, I would never be released from your embrace," Yeshua said, smiling broadly.

"Oh Yeshua, it is so good to see you and you look so good and handsome with your tan. How was your holiday, you must tell me all about it. But wait till Grandmother comes home from the markets. She loves to do shopping for the little things we need, it gets her out of the house, and even if we do not need anything she will go, even if it is just to talk to those she meets.

"Mother, I met a beautiful family in Magdala, when I stopped there on my way to the Sea of Galilee; they took me in and showed me such kindness and I stayed with them on my way back as well. The parents are Joshua and Emzara and they have five children, Ruth, Orpah, Shem, Japheth and Ham."

"How nice of them, and such beautiful and meaningful names the children have, Yeshua."

"They are a beautiful family, mother, he is a maker of fine clothes, he designs, cuts them and his wife and daughters sew them. Their clothes are in high demand by the people of Magdala and their daughters have a stall in the marketplace as well to sell to those passing through. I have some, a shawl for you and Grandmother that they have given to you." Yeshua took out the shawls.

Miriam took them in her hands, touched them, and spread them out to have a good look. "Oh Yeshua, they are beautiful and so soft. I will keep this for festive occasions. And Grandmother will love this," Miriam exclaimed with delight.

"These are my gifts, Immah, I bought these scarves for you and Grandmother. I bought them from Ruth and Orpah. I hope you like them."

"Oh, thank you, Yeshua, they are lovely," Miriam said, as looked at the scarves, touching them and placing one on her head, before taking it off. She kissed Yeshua on his cheek. "Oh Yeshua, they are lovely. Gran will love hers. Oh Yeshua, I am remiss, you must be hungry, can I get you something to drink, I have some berry juice."

"That will be fine, Immah, but I can get it myself, don't fuss, Immah, I am your son, not the king of Israel," Yeshua said laughing.

"Of course, you are my son, but you are also my king," Miriam said, laughing along with Yeshua, but in her heart, she knew what she was jesting about was indeed the truth.

When Hannah returned home, Yeshua went through everything he experienced with his mother once again. Gran held him so tightly; Yeshua was surprised by the strength of her grip. "Grandmother, you are smothering me," Yeshua said at last, as it seemed that Gran was never going to release him.

As Miriam predicted, Gran was over the moon with her scarf and shawl.

"Yeshua, it is so good to see you and looking so bright and tanned. But you must be exhausted walking all around the Sea of Galilee. You must tell us all about your adventures," Hannah said.

So, the rest of the day, Yeshua had to recount every detail of his two weeks. When dinner came, he was ready for a meal and some idle banter. They continued their chitchat and then when dinner was over, Yeshua excused himself and made his way to see Rebecca.

Rebecca was thrilled to see Yeshua, and she rushed into his arms, ignoring their pact.

"I must be the only man in the whole of Jerusalem that is so enthusiastically hugged in public by women," Yeshua said, "why is that so, Rebecca?"

"It's because you are so lovable and huggable, Yeshua, and the women feel it. You are like no other man I know; you are so gentle, sensitive and understanding and you are such a good listener that is why we women can relate to you so easily," Rebecca said.

"Thank you for that, Rebecca, now I am feeling really self-conscious," Yeshua said. He felt good to be so complemented, albeit a bit uncomfortable to hear such things about him. But he knew how a kind word, a word of affirmation can be so uplifting and he encouraged any such behaviour.

"I met some good friends in Magdala, and they gave you this as a present." Yeshua explained again his encounter with the family in Magdala, and Rebecca was delighted with the shawl they had given her.

"And I got you this present," Yeshua handed her the little bag with the necklace and the butterfly charm.

"Oh, Yeshua, it's beautiful." Rebecca leaned forward and kissed Yeshua on the cheek. "You see, no man has ever given me a present, and jewellery at that. You see, Yeshua, you are so sensitive and understanding of us women, that is why women like you, that is why I like you Yeshua," Rebecca said, smiling.

Yeshua stayed for a while, chatting with Rebecca, and then left. Yeshua was now ready for bed. The excitement of coming home, the exuberance of his mother and grandmother and Rebecca was overwhelming. When he got home, his mother and grandmother were still up. They continued to fuss over him for a while, and when things quieted down and returned to normal, they all decided on going to bed.

Yeshua first went outside for a while, even though it was quite cool. He needed to unwind completely. He spoke to Yahweh, said his end of day prayers. He gave thanks once more and prayed as he did for his loved ones, his new friends he had made on his adventure, and all those in need. Yeshua then entered his home and laid himself down to rest.

Chapter Twenty-Nine
Life Goes On

The next day came and went and the day after, Yeshua was back at work. He had a list of customers who had indicated they needed some work done in their home or on their farms. Yeshua decided to spend the day visiting them and see if they were ready for him. He would then make a list and a time to do the work for them. Some wanted house furniture made, doors made or fixed, and cupboards to store household goods and sheds built to store stuff, and for their animals, farmers needed fences to be made or fixed, and some of the implements repaired. There was always maintenance work to be done in the homes, on the farms and Yeshua had plenty of work lined up. As usual some were poor and not able to pay Yeshua but he would still do what they required, and they would pay him in kind, with produce from what they grew.

And so, life went on; working five days a week and then resting on the Sabbath and participating in the Sabbath services in the synagogue. Yeshua had already met with Achim and his family and told them all about Zadok. And Yeshua had also spent time with Gamaliel. Yeshua needed to talk with someone, with Gamaliel, about what was happening to him spiritually, and Gamaliel, and his mother, were the only ones who knew about his situation, his birth and his future. Yeshua continued to pick Gamaliel's brains, but he also more and more needed spiritual guidance and someone to accompany him on his spiritual journey and Gamaliel was the perfect person to fulfil that role.

Gamaliel invited Yeshua to talk to the students at the school about his adventure around the Sea of Galilee. He did so and the students were absolutely enthralled with what Yeshua related and they had plenty of questions to ask him. Yeshua spent a lot of time telling his family, friends, and fellow Nazarenes all about his two weeks journey around the Sea of Galilee. Yeshua did not mind, he was able to relive all those precious moments, and to appreciate even more all that he had experienced and all the people he had met.

And so, life went on for the next five years and Yeshua was now twenty-six years of age. He had been working quite hard and supporting his mother and grandmother and also putting aside some savings for when he had to one day leave home. The family, together with the Nazarenes, continued their now annual trips to Jerusalem for the celebration of the Passover.

When Yeshua had turned twenty-seven, Gamaliel asked if he would like to preach at the Sabbath celebrations. Yeshua had grown up debating and speaking in small groups, to the students, but he had also spoken at community gatherings of Nazarenes, as he did on Gamaliel's invitation, after his walk around the Sea of Galilee. Yeshua knew he had the gift of speech, of being able to communicate in a way that people understood. He accepted Gamaliel's invitation and so began his ministry of preaching the Word. People were so impressed and surprised by his wisdom, and enjoyed the way he brought the Scriptures to light and to life. They enjoyed his parables, the stories he told about the great truths of their faith. Yeshua spoke with such depth and understanding and the people were surprised that their carpenter had all this knowledge and wisdom. Yeshua spoke with such authority. But some were not all that impressed with the way Yeshua sometimes seemed to deviate from the strict observance of the Law.

And so, life went on. Yeshua worked and prayed and went to the synagogue and at times he preached. Not all the time. Yeshua did not want to take over from Gamaliel, who was now their established rabbi, but Gamaliel was ageing and could do with an assistant, who could give him a rest from his Sabbath duties.

Yeshua had been working without a long break, since he walked around the Sea of Galilee seven years ago and he once more needed to have a break from his daily grind and take some time off and away from his usual surroundings and refresh himself. Yeshua had developed the custom of spending a few days at the end of each year, away by himself in a lonely place to pray and reflect on his life and especially the past year. He had been going on this annual private retreat for many years but now he wanted to go on an extended trip somewhere, like the one he had done around the Sea of Galilee, which was now a distant memory.

Yeshua had not gone to the west coast, to the Great Sea at all. The immense land mass of Phoenicia covered the whole western boundary of Galilee and stretched for miles further north hugging the shoreline of the Great Sea. Yeshua was aware of the contempt his people in Galilee and all over Palestine held for the Phoenicians. He was interested in visiting the two most important coastal towns of Tyre and Sidon sometime in the future and get to know these people for himself. He had also never visited the town of Caesarea further south on the coast of the Great Sea in Sharon.

Yeshua had lived a fairly protected life in Nazareth but he had kept abreast of all the political manoeuvrings, the civilian uprisings and rebellions and the cruelty and the wielding of the might of Rome, and the hopelessness and submission of the Jewish religious leaders, working hand in glove with the powers that be.

While Yeshua lived all his life in the backwater town of Nazareth in Galilee, the whole of Palestine was crushed by the power of Rome. Nazareth and the whole of Galilee and the whole of Judaea, including the holy city of Jerusalem and all of Palestine were firmly in the grip of Rome. There were statues of Caesar and Roman gods everywhere, and the mighty power of Rome was felt through their military conquests, by all, even the poor, through the heavy taxes and tariffs on all they produced. Rome reigned with terror and reduced many to slavery and there were mass crucifixions, beheadings and burning of villages, and slaughtering of its inhabitants.

Yeshua learned and heard all about Herod, who ruled over Palestine. He was an arrogant ruler who lived luxuriously in a lavish palace. He persecuted and burned to death Jewish Teachers of the Law. He was ruthless in his obsession with maintaining power and killed most of his own family, his brother and his own sons, and even his wife and mother-in-law out of fear of conspiracy. Yeshua came to understand why his father and mother fled to Egypt to save him from the wrath of this infamous king.

Herod however did also start to rebuild the Temple in Jerusalem but he infuriated the people because he hung an image of the Roman eagle over the entrance of the Temple. This caused religious dissent, which Herod crushed by burning several of the protestors.

Herod also built up the city of Caesarea by the Great Sea to ingratiate himself with Caesar and to serve as a port to facilitate the docking of Roman legions that came to quash any rebellions. Yeshua had never met this evil king Herod, for he died when Yeshua was only about two years old.

There were so many rebellions after the death of Herod but they were brutally and mercilessly put down by the might of Rome. Yeshua had learned all about this history of his people and how thousands of them were crucified around Jerusalem. All this was happening while he was still a young child. Yeshua also knew that his father and mother returned to Nazareth when Herod died and Herod's son, Herod Antipas became the tetrarch of Galilee as well as Perea and Iturea. Unlike his father Antipas, he had no power in Judaea, for Rome wanting to maintain the peace put the area under its direct control. And Annas, whom Yeshua had met just once when he sought admission to the Advanced School of Learning in Jerusalem, became the high priest of the temple. Annas, was a Jewish aristocrat and became the chief mediator for the Jews with Rome. When Yeshua first met him, they were calling him Ananias, but it seemed the shortened version of his name to Annas, had stuck.

As Yeshua grew up, he learned and heard more about the politics of the land. When he was nineteen, just a year before he had completed his historical walk around the Sea of Galilee; Caesar Augustus died and was succeeded by Tiberius. And four years later, when Yeshua was twenty-three years of age, Yosef Caiaphas, son-in-law to Annas, was appointed by Rome as the new high priest. Yeshua had never met Caiaphas but had seen Caiaphas when he was on his trips to Jerusalem. Yeshua did not feel ingratiated to the man. Yeshua saw him as pompous and aloof who strutted around like a peacock. Yeshua abhorred the pomposity of Caiaphas and the Pharisees who wore elaborate clothing and walked around with their noses in the air and seemed to regard themselves as superior, and Yahweh's gift to mankind, and expecting everyone to show them deference. They were sticklers for the minutiae of the Law and went about observing everyone, like police waiting to catch someone breaking the Law. And Yeshua observed and detested how they kowtowed to the Roman authorities.

Yeshua was quite happy to live in, what those in Judaea and especially in Jerusalem, regarded, as insignificant Nazareth. He grew up away from all the hustle-bustle of politics, power-plays, and the religious leaders working hand in glove with Rome. They preached about a promised Messiah who would free the people from the power of Rome, yet they succumbed to and kowtowed to the power of Rome. And above all, Yeshua observed how they did not practice what they preached.

And so, life went on. "I am now twenty-eight years of age, I am still single, and so is Rebecca, she says she is waiting for me to change my mind, and she says she can never find anyone to match me, what am I to do, Yahweh?" Yeshua prayed in the synagogue, way past the end of the Sabbath service, when everyone had already rushed out of the synagogue after the service. Yeshua was unsure what was to become of him. He knew he had a special mission, and that he was different, and he had grown in wisdom over the years. He was physically fit, thanks to his manual labour, and his frequent walks and occasional running with Rebecca, and he was also mentally alert, constantly improving his mind, and above all he felt spiritually fit, spiritually alive, living a life in the Spirit, daily communicating with Yahweh, his heavenly father. And he still had regular meetings with Gamaliel, who was still accompanying him on his spiritual journey, and he also had lengthy discussions with his mother. Yeshua had lost his grandmother, Hannah who died a year ago. He experienced once again some of the grief he endured so long ago when his father, his grandfather and the mother of his dearest friends of Bethany, Lazarus, Miriam and Martha, had died.

He thought of his friends at Bethany. He still visited them briefly whenever he was in Jerusalem with his mother and the community of Nazareth for the celebration of the Passover. And it was always such a joy for him and for them. If he did have to marry someone, Yeshua knew it would be either Rebecca or Miriam of Bethany. He felt so close to these two women, one near and one so far away. But Yeshua knew it was not to be.

"Yahweh, what am I to do, please let me know." But Yahweh was silent. Gamaliel had told Yeshua to be patient that Yahweh would let him know when his time would come and when he would have to leave home and go on spreading the news of salvation and redemption. So, Yeshua left the synagogue and walked home by himself, as everyone had already left the synagogue precinct.

Yeshua did eventually go to the coast of the Great Sea and spent a couple of weeks walking to the coast then all along the miles and miles of sandy seashore. The walk from Nazareth to the coast and the town of Tyre was over forty miles and from Tyre to Sidon another more than twenty miles, so it took several days. He stayed some time in Tyre on the seashore and walked as far as Sidon, also on the Phoenician coastline. Yeshua was keen to visit Phoenicia and to get to know what the place and the people were like. Yeshua knew of the prejudices of the people of Palestine, the Israelites, towards the Phoenicians. Yeshua was uncomfortable with any kind of prejudice or discrimination. Palestinians regarded themselves as superior to the Phoenicians. The Israelites knew that they were the chosen people of Yahweh, and they believed in, worshipped and served him alone. Yahweh was the one and only true God.

The Phoenicians on the other hand believed in several gods and goddesses; Elohim, which Yeshua discovered could refer to Yahweh, the one true God but to the Phoenicians Elohim was more of a generic term, and could refer to many gods, and then they also worshipped other gods such as Baal, Asherah, Astarte, and they had different customs and ways of worship to the Israelites.

The Palestinians looked down upon the Phoenicians because they were Canaanites, the descendants of Noah's second son Ham, who was the disgraced and cursed son of Noah. Yeshua found the Phoenicians to be an enterprising, industrious, hardworking and seafaring people, who had ports for ships to dock. At the same time, they were a people who still knew how to relax and enjoy life, especially those who lived along the coast. Here the waves were different to the Sea of Galilee; they were mightier and could reach great heights when the sea was stirred up by the winds. Yeshua loved spending time along the beach and practically spent most of his time relaxing on the beach and soaking up the sun and the sound of the mighty sea beating up on the shore, after all this was his holiday time, and what better way than to soak up the sun and the surf.

On the beach, people were relaxed and communicative, but in the cities, they seemed so preoccupied and intense, going about their business. But they could also party. Yeshua had made friends with some of the residents of Sidon and they invited him to a party. Yeshua loved parties, loved the company of people, enjoying themself, letting their hair down so to speak, and especially so, as he was on holiday. There were the finest foods to eat and fresh fish and plenty of wine to drink, and there was music and singing and dancing and much laughter.

Yeshua in his studies had learned about Noah's curse of his son Ham. Noah was the first to plant a vineyard, he drank some of the wine and became drunk, and he lay uncovered in his tent. And his son Ham, father of Canaan, saw the nakedness of his father and told his two brothers outside. When Noah awoke and found out what Ham had done, he cursed him and in the same breath he blessed his other two sons, and cursed Ham to become a slave to his two brothers, Shem and Japheth. Because of this curse, the Palestinians looked down upon the Phoenicians who were descendants of Canaan, the son of Ham.

Yeshua witnessed their religion and their customs of putting out food for their gods and the images they had of their different gods. Yeshua thought about Yahweh's appearance to Moses on Mount Sinai, giving him the Ten Commandments. From childhood at home and at school Yeshua learned these commandments by heart and they were embedded in his psyche. The very first one makes clear that there is only one God and him alone are we to worship, love and serve. Yeshua recited to himself that first commandment when he became aware of how the Phoenicians worshipped several gods, "I am the Lord your God, who brought you out of the land of Egypt, out of the house of bondage. You shall have no other gods before me. You shall not make for yourself a graven image, or any likeness of anything that is in heaven above, or that is in the earth beneath, or that is in the water under the earth, you shall not bow down to them or serve them."

Yeshua somehow knew that his mission was to make Yahweh, the one true God, known and served and loved. But how he was to do this, he had no idea. Maybe he would simply continue what he was doing, giving the occasional sermon in the synagogue in Nazareth. Yet Yeshua felt in his heart that there was more to his life and mission. When he thought about the circumstances of his birth, as told by his parents and his being spared from the slaughter of the newborn babies by Herod, he knew that the hand of Yahweh was in all this, and that He would make it known what to do. Yeshua was now fast approaching his time to leave home. He felt it was time. He prayed to Yahweh to let him know what he wanted of him.

Life continued its cycle of work, eat, sleep, rest and recreation, prayer, worship, fellowship, loving and being loved. Three more years passed. Yeshua was now just beginning his thirtieth year of age, it was time, time for him to settle down, have a wife and begin a family, move out of his family home to start a family of his own or do what he was born for, what Yahweh wanted of him, whatever that was.

Chapter Thirty
A Blast from the Past

This time, Miriam decided not to go on the annual pilgrimage to Jerusalem for the celebration of the Passover. She wasn't feeling too well. She wasn't really ill, just feeling tired, but still Yeshua did not want to leave her alone, but Miriam insisted; besides, she had such good neighbours whom she could call on if she needed them. When the day came to leave for the Passover, Miriam was feeling much better but not in the mood for the long trip to Jerusalem.

"I'm just getting too old, Yeshua, for these long trips," Miriam said.

"Too old, Immah, you are not yet fifty, you are still a young chicken, and even more sprightly. But you work too hard, going about helping everyone, doing good. When I am away, do take things easy, and have a good rest," Yeshua said, pretending to be stern.

"Oh, I'll have a good rest, with you away and not bothering me with all your silly questions," Miriam said in jest. "And I hope this time in Jerusalem, Yahweh will answer all your questions about what you are meant to do, so that you will stop pestering me for answers," Miriam added.

"He better, Immah. If he doesn't, I am coming home and proposing to Rebecca, and put her out of her misery," Yeshua said, smiling.

"Put her out of her misery, more like Rebecca putting you out of your misery, if she marries the likes of you," Miriam said, continuing the jesting vein of their conversation. They loved to tease each other in this way.

"Okay, Immah, you win. Now it's up to Yahweh to finish me off," Yeshua said, laughing out loud.

Yeshua decided that on this occasion, in Jerusalem, he needed some space, some private time, there was much on his mind, and he felt that this was an important trip for him, the turning point in his life; he just felt it in his bones. So instead of sleeping rough, in a tent at the usual campsite with the rest of the Nazarenes, Yeshua sought and found lodgings on his own. As he was on his own, he was fortunate to find a single room at a dodgy looking place, but Yeshua didn't mind, all he needed was a bed. He registered and paid for the room and then went straight to the Temple.

But as he was about to enter the Temple a group of men came out and they were chatting. "I think, he is the Messiah, the Promised One," one of the men in the group was saying, and Yeshua overheard him.

"Excuse me, good Sir, Shalom to you, I couldn't help overhearing you speak of someone as the Messiah, who is he?" Yeshua asked.

"You are not from here, I can see, as you would know of Johanan, the hermit, a great prophet who speaks with the voice of God," the man replied.

"No, I am not of here, I am Yeshua from Nazareth, and I have come to Jerusalem for the celebration of the Passover."

"Welcome to Jerusalem, Yeshua, and I am Mattheus, and these are some of my friends, Judas, Micah and Nahum," Mattheus said. "I suppose you could say we are followers of Johanan; we have all been baptised by him in the River Jordan," Judas said.

"I can see, or rather I can hear that you, Judas, are from Judaea, but Mattheus your dialect is Galilean, is it not?"

"Yes, I am from Galilee, you are right, I came to Jerusalem some time ago, and I listened to Johanan, was baptised by him, and now am his disciple," Mattheus said.

"We too," Judas, said, gesturing to the other two men of the group. "Micah, Nahum and I are all from Judaea, and we are also disciples of the prophet, Johanan."

"So, who is Johanan, what do you know about him?" Yeshua asked, now curious about this prophet whom Mattheus and his friends think, is the Messiah.

Yeshua like all Jews was waiting for the Messiah, the Promised One, who was to set them free. But free from what? Yeshua had several discussions and debates over the years with his teachers and with Gamaliel, about the promised Messiah. Most Jews thought that the Messiah would come in triumph and power and free the people, the Jews, from the tyranny of Rome. But Yeshua had thought otherwise, for him the Messiah is the one who would save the people from the scourge of sin and evil and death, and give them the Good News of Yahweh's great love and compassion and care for them.

"So, tell me about this prophet, Johanan," Yeshua asked.

"What we know is that he was born here, in the hill country of Judaea, in the days of King Herod, his father was a priest named Zechariah. All we know is that his father belonged to the priestly order of Abijah," Mattheus said.

"And his mother, what was her name?" Yeshua asked, excitedly.

"I think his mother's name was Elisheva," Judas answered.

"I believe they were both very old when they had Johanan," Micah added.

"The story goes that Elisheva was in fact barren, and had been way past childbearing age when Johanan was born," Judas said.

Yeshua's heart skipped a beat, he was now certain this man Johanan, this prophet, was indeed his long-lost cousin about whom his mother, Miriam, had told him. He continued to listen to what these men were saying about Johanan.

"So, from his very birth, Johanan, was touched by Yahweh and destined for great things," Nahum said. "Johanan was living here, in the wilderness of Judaea for a long time, surviving on locusts, and grasshoppers and wild honey. He is like no other prophet. He wears a camel hair coat with a leather belt, and he is a fiery preacher, and calls us all to repentance. People from all walks of life, go and listen to Johanan. I am a Pharisee, and even though he had some harsh words about us Pharisees, I still am drawn to what he has to say," Judas said.

"And for the likes of me too, for I am a tax-collector," Mattheus said. "But his words have moved us all. We are all filled with expectation of the coming of the Lord. And we have all repented and been baptised by Johanan in the River Jordan," Mattheus added.

"Hundreds, thousands, have been baptised, as a sign of repentance for our sins, and as preparation for the coming of the Lord," Judas said. "You must come, in the morning. Johanan preaches from about the third hour, after which the people repent of their sins, and enter the Jordan, and Johanan baptises them, washes them of their sins," Judas added.

"The place where he baptises is the very spot where Joshua had first crossed the River Jordan, leading our forefathers, the chosen people of Yahweh into the Promised Land," Micah said.

"We know that Johanan, is a prophet, a man of God, a servant of Yahweh, he might even be the prophet Elijah come back to life, to prepare us for the way of the Lord," Mattheus said.

"Thank you so much for telling me about Johanan. I will definitely go out to see him and to listen to him," Yeshua said.

Yeshua and the group then parted ways, and Yeshua entered the Temple. Yeshua knew that the meeting with those disciples of Johanan: Mattheus, Judas, Micah and Nahum and their mention of Johanan, of the priestly order of Abijah, was not only serendipitous, but had the hand of God in it.

Yeshua sat in the temple and his mind and heart was racing. He had come to Jerusalem and the Lord had arranged that he meet with Johanan.

Yeshua learned all about the mysterious circumstances of Johanan's birth from his mother and father. He knew that Johanan's father, who was a priest of the order of Abijah and his mother, Elisheva, who was a descendent of Aaron, was Miriam's aunt, and that makes Johanan, my cousin, Yeshua said to himself. He continued to reflect on all his mother had told him about the birth of Johanan. Both Zechariah and Elisheva lived righteous lives but they were without children, because Elisheva was barren and they were both getting on in years.

Yeshua heard how Zechariah had entered the sanctuary and an angel of the Lord, Gabriel in fact, appeared standing at the right side of the altar of incense. Just like mother was terrified when Gabriel appeared to her, Zechariah was overwhelmed with fear. But Gabriel put him at ease and told him that Elisheva was to bear a son, and he was to be called Johanan. The angel told Zechariah that he will have joy and gladness, and many will rejoice at his birth, for he will be great in the sight of the Lord. He will be filled with the Holy Spirit, and he will turn many of the people of Israel to the Lord their God.

Yeshua sighed; all that his mother had told him about Johanan has now come to pass. Yeshua recalled the rest of the story. Zechariah did not believe what Gabriel was telling him and as a result he became mute, unable to speak, until all Gabriel had said came to pass. When they were going to name the child Zechariah after his father, Zechariah asked for a tablet on which he wrote, 'His name is Johanan.' Zechariah then regained his speech.

Yeshua also recalled what his mother told him of what Zechariah prophesied when he regained his speech. Zechariah blessed the Lord God of Israel and prophesied that Yahweh was going to raise up a mighty Saviour from the house of David, a Saviour that would save the people from the hand of all who hate them. Of his son Johanan, he prophesied that he would become a Prophet of the Most High, for he will go before the Lord and prepare his way, to give knowledge of salvation to his people by the forgiveness of their sins.

Yeshua relived his fascination, when he first heard this story about his cousin Johanan. It was after the incident when he remained in the Temple for three days, and his parents searched for him. When they got back to Nazareth, his mother told him all about Johanan.

After he learned all about Johanan from his parents, Yeshua had then said that on their next trip to Jerusalem, he would like to meet his cousin, Johanan. But that did not eventuate.

Yeshua recalled how distraught he was when he was told that Zechariah died soon after Johanan's birth, two years in fact, and they moved away to live with

Zechariah's brother. Elisheva died when Johanan was ten years old. Johanan remained living with his distant relatives in a far away and isolated place, miles away from everyone, and Yeshua's mother had lost touch with them. But Miriam had heard that Johanan left home, at a very early age, and everyone lost touch with him.

And now I have come into touch with my long-lost cousin Johanan, once again. Yeshua couldn't wait to meet with Johanan. So, Yeshua went early the next morning to search for Johanan, wanting to have some private time with him but he could not find him. Eventually, crowds gathered at the site on the banks of the Jordan River, waiting for Johanan to appear.

Yeshua's heart raced as he caught a first glimpse of his cousin Johanan. He was as they had described. He was rugged with olive-coloured skin from exposure to the sun, and he was dishevelled, like one living in the wilderness for a long time, surviving on locusts, and grasshoppers and wild honey. He was wearing a camel hair coat with a leather belt, as Mattheus and the others had said.

Yeshua listened, engrossed by the words of this fiery preacher, and his call to repentance. After Johanan had spoken for about an hour, people began asking him questions. Yeshua listened to some of Johanan's answers, "Whoever has two coats must share with anyone who has none, and whoever has food must do likewise," was what Johanan said in answer to one of the questions.

Then a number of voices cried out, "Johanan, are you the Messiah, the Promised One?"

Johanan answered all of them by saying, "I am not the Messiah. I baptise you with water; but one who is more powerful than I is coming; I am not worthy to untie the strap of his sandals. He will baptise you with the Holy Spirit and fire."

When Johanan had answered all their questions, some of the people approached to be baptised and Johanan went with them into the water and baptised them. When Johanan eventually sent the people away and walked into the direction of the wilderness, Yeshua followed him.

"Johanan, forgive me, I know, you now wish to be alone, but I must speak with you, I am Yeshua of Nazareth, son of Yosef of the house of David, and of Miriam. Your mother Elisheva is my mother's aunt, and that makes us cousins," Yeshua said.

"Praise the Lord," Johanan exclaimed, raising his arms above. "I have heard of my aunt Miriam and uncle Yosef and you, Yeshua, when I was very young. All I can remember is mother telling me that you and I were very special to Yahweh, and that an angel gave us both our names," Johanan said, becoming quite excited.

"Is that all she told you, Johanan?" Yeshua asked.

"I was very young, Yeshua, when father died and mother not long afterwards. When I got older, I regretted her not telling me more, for I felt there was more, for she always spoke about me doing great things. But I was only ten years old when she died. What I do remember though is her telling me that you, Yeshua, and I would meet one day and that our paths were destined to cross," Johanan said.

"Johanan, I lost my father and grandmother within months and it took me years of grieving to get over those losses but I cannot begin to understand what it was like for you to lose both your father and mother by the time you were ten years of age," Yeshua said.

"It was terrible, Yeshua. It was a hard life," Johanan said.

"So how long did you stay with your relatives, Johanan?" Yeshua asked.

"When I was seventeen, I left home, and drifted from town to town, and eventually came to Jerusalem, and I found the hustle and bustle of city life hard to take. The people seemed to be drifting away from the way of the Lord, and lax in keeping the Law of Moses. They seemed to be hypocrites, pretending to be religious, yet secretly many were living lives of sin, and no better than the people of Sodom and Gomorrah. I worked as a labourer, and after some time I became so completely disillusioned with the way of life of the people, who seemed so far from the ways of God, and then I heard about the Essenes who lived out in the wilderness, I sought them out, and I found in them a community in which I felt at home."

"Why was that, Johanan?" Yeshua asked. He had heard of the Essenes, who lived in the desert, and their rigorous ascetic lives in their quest to live a life dedicated to Yahweh. Yeshua had heard that they lived as a closed community, in the desert, and committed to lives of celibacy, and the strict observance of the Law of Moses.

"I had observed just how lax the people in Jerusalem and the other cities were in observing the Laws of Moses. And I found in the Essenes a community that were meticulous in observing the Law of Moses, the Sabbath, and I found their way of life and their rituals meaningful. They have a ritual of Baptism of Repentance that is a ritual washing of the soul; it's performed after one renounce sin. With the Essenes, I studied the Scriptures daily, and we worked and prayed all hours of the day. I grew closer to Yahweh and in knowledge of his ways. But I left the Essenes many years ago and have lived by myself in the wilderness ever since."

"Why did you leave the Essenes, Johanan?" Yeshua asked. He was curious.

"While I grew in knowledge of the Scriptures, and in a life of prayer, and the ways of the Lord, I found the Essenes to be too, how can I put it, inward focused, self-centred, a closed community, suspicious of outsiders, and they held that the study of the Scriptures were to be kept within the community, and we were forbidden to be outside of our settlement. The Essenes were not outward looking at all, and kept their beliefs to themselves, and the few who sought them out, like me. I became disillusioned with its secrecy, and they prized obedience and loyalty to the group as paramount. I found them more and more stifling because I began to believe that the Good News of Yahweh's love and compassion, and forgiveness of sin, was something to be spread to all the people. They were the ones who need repentance and God's mercy and forgiveness and love. I believe all people are called to repentance and need to prepare themselves for the coming of the Messiah," Johanan said.

"I am so glad that you found your own way, Johanan. The people have great respect for you, and you are doing a great work of spreading the Good News of God's love and compassion to the people," Yeshua said.

"During those years alone in the wilderness, the silence, especially in the night, was so overwhelming, yet so peaceful. I was alone all day and all night, yet I never felt alone, Yeshua. I felt the closeness of God, I was getting closer and closer to Yahweh; He was by my side every moment. And I could hear his voice in the silence. One day it was so clear. He told me to leave this place and to go back into the world and to preach the Good News of his love and compassion, and his sending of the Messiah, who will teach the people the ways of God, as it should be. The Messiah was coming, to bring redemption and salvation to all. Yahweh told me to go and preach repentance of sin, and to baptise the people as a way of preparing them for the coming of the Messiah, and for judgement. I know that the Messiah's coming is imminent, and that I will see him before I die," Johanan said.

"Johanan, I thank you for sharing all of that with me. I will leave you now, to have your rest. I am in Jerusalem for the Passover celebrations, and will remain for a few days, so I will see you again; I appreciate your preaching, and will come and listen to what you have to say. Shalom, and peace be with you."

"Shalom, and peace be with you cousin. It has been a joy to meet with you. Until we meet again, may the Lord be with you," Johanan said, as they parted ways.

Yeshua went to the campsite of the Nazarenes. He wanted to have a chat with Gamaliel. He wanted to talk about his meeting with Johanan, and what it all meant. Yeshua felt the hand of God at work in him, and through his meeting with Johanan. Where to from now? Yeshua wondered.

Gamaliel listened intently and then simply told Yeshua to let things be; that his time will come when Yahweh will make things clear to him. "Be patient Yeshua, Yahweh has called you to do his work, his work of redemption and salvation. We all need to be redeemed and saved, saved from sin; we need to turn away from our sinful ways, and give our lives back to God, and live in ways of goodness, kindness and innocence. We have become worldly and self-centred and self-occupied, we are called to be other-centred, other-occupied and that starts with being God-centred," Gamaliel said. "Yeshua, just let the Spirit guide you."

"Okay, thanks for those words, Gamaliel. I do believe that in everyone there is the spark of other-centredness, of God-centredness, of goodness, of love, of kindness and I simply have to ignite, to light up that spark, that it may become a fire to consume us all," Yeshua said.

The next day was the day before the beginning of the Passover celebrations, so Yeshua decided to go and listen to Johanan again.

Chapter Thirty-One
A Dove from Above

As promised, Yeshua returned the next day to the banks of the River Jordan to listen to Johanan. He stood amongst a throng of people, as Johanan stood on a raised level of ground and preached to the people.

"You must know the Word of God, understand the Word of God, love the Word of God, and live the Word of God. And at this time, the fifteenth year of the reign of Tiberius, and the governing of Pontius Pilate of Judaea, and Herod ruling over Galilee and his brother Phillip ruling over the region of Ituraea and Trachonitis, and Lysanias ruling over Abilene, and Annas and Caiaphas ministering to you as your priests, I come to you, to announce the coming of the Lord, the coming of the ruler over all rulers, the King of Kings, the one and only true high priest, the Lord of Lords, the Messiah. He is already here amongst us and Yahweh will make him known to us, he is the one we must obey above all those I mentioned. He will teach us the Laws of God, he will teach us the way, the truth and life. He is here and has come to save us from sin, death and meaninglessness and show us the way to live and to die."

Johanan was astounded by the words that were coming from his mouth. They were words that came from deep within his spirit. They were words that were not prepared or rehearsed; they were words that were inspired by the Spirit within him.

After his exhortation, the people repented of their sins, and some of them, who had not yet been baptised, approached Johanan for baptism, and he entered with them into the waters of the River Jordan. And then Yeshua, moved by the Spirit, walked into the River Jordan to be baptised by Johanan.

Since his meeting with Yeshua, Johanan had reflected and he had wondered about Yeshua. He had been told by his mother, Elisheva that their paths would cross, and that they both were special to God and they both had special missions to perform for Yahweh. And it seemed that the Lord had spoken to me and told me that the one I was waiting for has come, could it be Yeshua of Galilee, Johanan wondered.

As Yeshua approached Johanan to be baptised, Johanan felt a stirring within the very depths of his soul, and out of nowhere the words came tumbling out. He said, "You come to me, Yeshua, to be baptised, but I think it is I who need to be baptised by you."

Yeshua too was being moved by the Spirit and he said in reply, "Let it be so for now, for it is proper for us to fulfil all righteousness."

Johanan, still being moved by the Spirit, consented and baptised Yeshua, and as Yeshua came up from the water, suddenly the heavens were opened, all the clouds moved away and disappeared, and the sun seemed to become brighter and the sky bluer. Everyone then saw a dove descending and resting above Yeshua. And then everyone heard what sounded like a voice out of nowhere, "This is my Son, the Beloved, with whom I am well pleased."

The people were overwhelmed, wondering what was happening. They had never before heard such a voice, a deep, powerful voice, a soothing voice, coming from nowhere. Is it the voice of God, or is it some trick, someone playing, somehow amplifying a voice, or was it some form of magic? Some assumed that the voice was referring to Johanan, for many still believed him to be the Messiah, and some still thought he was Elijah come back to life, in spite of Johanan making it clear that he was neither, and that he was simply a voice crying in the wilderness, preparing a way for the Lord, for the coming of the Messiah. But Johanan knew that the voice was not of this earth, and it was the voice of God, and the dove was a symbol of his Spirit, and it was descending on Yeshua.

Both Johanan and Yeshua knew what was happening to them both. Johanan was now certain that his mission is now accomplished, that this man, his cousin, Yeshua, is most likely the One, the Chosen One, the Son of God. God has spoken, and God's Spirit rests on him.

And Yeshua knew now that his time had come, that he has been exposed in a way never before, in front of all these people who seemed perplexed and unable to make out what had just happened. They were all murmuring among themselves. Yeshua said farewell to Johanan and left. He needed to be by himself. He headed straight to the wilderness, and there he stayed for the rest of the day, in prayer and reflection, and the Spirit of the Lord was with him.

"Abba, heavenly Father, you have spoken, I am your beloved Son. You have spoken in front of all the people, and made me known. Father, here I am, show me, let your Spirit, our Spirit guide me from this day forward." Yeshua was bewildered about how he was to proceed, but Gamaliel's words came back to him, be patient and let the Spirit guide you. I must go home first, and speak to mother, it is time for me to leave home for good, and to do what the Father wants of me.

Yeshua, after all the Passover celebrations, made his way home on his own, not waiting for the Nazarenes, who travelled back as a group. He had a talk with Gamaliel, who let everyone else know that Yeshua had to hurry back home.

Miriam was surprised to see Yeshua, earlier than she expected. "You are early, I did not expect you for three more days, and you are alone, are you alright? Is everything okay?" Miriam asked with concern.

"Everything's fine Immah, just fine," Yeshua said, and then he proceeded to tell Miriam all that had happened to him, his meeting with cousin Johanan, and all about Johanan, and his own baptism by Johanan in the River Jordan, and the dove descending, and the heavens opening, and the Father acknowledging him in the presence of the people.

"Immah, I have decided to spend some time with Johanan, be a disciple, learn from him and be guided by him. I have come back to make arrangements to leave again. I will first complete all those jobs I am working on, and not take on any new work, and then I must go back to Jerusalem. But Immah, I am loathe to leave you alone," Yeshua said.

"Don't worry, Yeshua, I will be fine, you must do what Yahweh requires of you, what you were born to do, you must go. I will be okay. I have enough sewing to support me financially, and we have our own little patch of vegetables to keep me alive," Miriam said.

"Mother, I have some savings, which I need to support myself at this time, but you can have most of that, Yahweh will provide. If I am to do his work, then He will provide," Yeshua said. "And please, mother, you must make use of that gold you have saved, I have no need of it now," Yeshua said. "I have spoken to Gamaliel, and he will look in on you, and please, if you are in need in anyway, he said he will be only too willing to do what he can for you, so mother, please, if you are in need in any way, do call on Gamaliel, you promise?"

"I promise, Yeshua, do not worry, I will be fine. I have such good neighbours and so many friends here in Nazareth. Do not worry about me, please, I will be okay, you must give your full attention to the work Yahweh now wants of you," Miriam said.

The next day, Yeshua went to see Achim and his parents and to let them know that he was leaving for Jerusalem and would be in fact leaving home for good, as he had some special work to do, and he also told them to keep an eye on his mother. Achim assured Yeshua that he would drop in from time to time.

"Don't make it too conspicuous, Achim, as mother will know I had a hand in it, she is so independent, and I know she will make ends meet and care for herself, but I am concerned to have to leave her on her own," Yeshua said.

After his visit to Achim, he went to see Rebecca. "Rebecca, I am finally leaving home, I will be going to stay in Jerusalem, and live there for a while. Do call in on mother, you can give the excuse that you want to know how I am, for I will get news to her," Yeshua said.

Rebecca, hugged Yeshua, and the tears began to roll down her cheeks. She knew now that her hope of a life with Yeshua was never going to happen. "I'm going to miss you, Yeshua, I wish you well in whatever your life throws at you," Rebecca said.

After a week, since his return from Jerusalem, Yeshua was ready to return and to become a disciple of Johanan, and prepare himself for whatever Yahweh wanted of him. It was early in the morning, he had some breakfast and then said goodbye to his mother. She held onto him for a long time. She had prepared some sustenance for the road. She knew that Yeshua was all grown up, and that he could care for himself, but to her he was her only child, her only son, whom she treasured and loved with all her heart. She knew this day would come, and she resigned herself to it. But she could not hold back the tears streaming down her cheeks.

Yeshua too felt the intensity of these moments. He loved his mother so dearly and she had been such a good mother to him. "Immah, forgive me all the pain I have ever caused you. And thank you for all the care you have given me, all the joy you have given me, I am going to miss you mother. But we shall meet again. I have a feeling I am not going to remain only in Jerusalem. For now, I will spend some time with Johanan. Goodbye, mother, I love you, and Yahweh is with you." With those words, Yeshua kissed his mother and left.

Chapter Thirty-Two
The Next Phase

When Yeshua returned to Jerusalem, he found the same dingy lodgings. It was an improvement on sleeping rough in caves and whatever protection he found along the way. He then went to the city centre intending to go to the Temple for prayer, and hoping to find one of Johanan's disciples, to learn what has happened since his own baptism.

It so happened that Yeshua met Micah. "It's so good to see you, Yeshua; many people have been talking about you. I have bad news, Johanan has been arrested," Micah said.

"Arrested, when, why?" Yeshua asked, full of concern.

"Annas and Caiaphas, the priests and Levites, our religious leaders and teachers, and some of the Pharisees were concerned with Johanan, because the people were flocking in droves to listen to him. They were not happy because Johanan had abandoned much of the Temple and ritual purification rites that they practised. They were particularly concerned, upset with Johanan, because of the way he does the purification ritual. As you know it is our custom to be purified by the priests in the traditional pools of purification, but Johanan does it in the fast-flowing waters of the River Jordan. And in the rite, we are accustomed to wash ourselves, but Johanan totally immerses us in the waters. But I think they were just jealous that people were flocking to listen to his teaching, rather than to theirs," Micah said.

"So, what happened when they arrested Johanan?" Yeshua asked.

"Those that were sent by the priests and Levites came to where Johanan was preaching, and in the presence of all the people, they asked Johanan: 'Who are you?' Johanan answered, 'I am not the Messiah.' They then asked him if he was Elijah, to which he answered, emphatically, 'I am not.' They then asked him if he was the Prophet, and he again answered that he was not the Prophet. So, in frustration the messengers asked Johanan, 'Who are you?' They said that they wanted an answer to give to those who sent them. To this, Johanan said, 'I am the voice of one crying in the wilderness. Make straight the way of the Lord'."

Yeshua was totally engrossed in what Micah was telling him. "What happened next?" Yeshua asked.

"They asked Johanan why he was baptising if he was neither the Messiah, nor Elijah, nor the Prophet. Johanan answered, words we have heard him utter before: 'I baptise with water. Among you is one whom you do not know, I am not worthy to untie the cord of his sandal.' And he added, 'He is the Lamb of God, who takes away the sin of the world! He ranks ahead of me, because he was before me. I, and many others, saw the Spirit descending from the heavens like a dove, and it remained on him, and it had become clear to me, that he is the one who baptises with the Holy Spirit. I myself have seen and have testified that he is the Son of God.'"

Yeshua listened with overwhelming interest. Micah was recounting Yeshua's baptism and encounter with Johanan in the River Jordan. Yeshua had a strange feeling. So many people had witnessed what happened in the River Jordan, but it was as if they had not understood, and even though they were mesmerised by what was happening, it was as if their minds were closed. And here Micah was speaking to Yeshua about the same incident, and it seemed even Micah was blind and unseeing, for if what had happened is the truth, then Yeshua, standing before him, is the Son of God. Yeshua himself was processing all that had happened with him and Johanan in the River Jordan. Things were beginning to crystallise in his mind. He needed to process them further. I am flesh and blood, I am like any other man, I work and sleep and think and feel and hurt and cry and hunger and grow weary and have my fears and dark moments. I am fully human, so how can I at the same time, be the Son of God. These were thoughts that were swirling around in Yeshua's mind, before, but now they were so forceful, and crying out to be answered.

"So did they arrest Johanan there and then?" Yeshua asked.

"No, they did not, it was Herod's guards who came and arrested Johanan a few days later," Micah said.

"Herod!" Yeshua exclaimed with surprise.

"Yes, Herod, he had Johanan put in chains and in prison," Micah responded.

"But why?" Yeshua asked.

"Johanan had for a long time castigated Herod publicly for marrying Herodias, even though she was the wife of his brother Phillip. Johanan kept telling Herod that it wasn't right for him to be married to his brother's wife," Micah told Yeshua.

Yeshua thanked Micah for informing him of what had happened to Johanan, and then said, "We have to make sure that we continue the good work that Johanan has been doing. For now, I have a lot to think about, so I will be going into the wilderness, like Johanan did, and spend some time there," Yeshua said.

"Shalom, and God go with you, Yeshua," Micah said. Later in the day, Micah met with his friends, Mattheus, Judas and Nahum, and told them about his encounter with Yeshua and their discussion.

"Do you think Yeshua is the one that Johanan spoke about, the Promised One, the Prophet, the Messiah?" Mattheus asked.

"I was wondering about him, thinking about him quite a bit. His baptism by Johanan was like no other. Those signs, the coming down of the dove upon Johanan and Yeshua and the voice, did you hear that voice saying that this is my beloved Son, with whom I am well pleased. I think most of the people who heard the voice felt it was referring to Johanan but I think it was about this Yeshua," Judas said.

"I think you are right Judas. Johanan always made it clear he was not the one, and that one greater than he was to come. And now that Johanan is in jail, and this Nazarene, Yeshua, has appeared, was baptised by Johanan with such miraculous signs, maybe he is the one," Mattheus concurred.

"But he is a mere carpenter, and from Nazareth of all places. Do you really think Yahweh would call such a person to do his great work, to be the Messiah to set us free?" Judas asked.

The four of them parted, still unsure about the future, about their teacher and prophet, Johanan, and now this new disciple of his, Yeshua. They went together to the temple for the morning prayers, praying and hoping for the deliverance of Johanan from the clutches of Herod.

Chapter Thirty-Three
Temptations

Yeshua had always gone on personal retreats, whenever he was to begin any new project or period in his life, and now he decided that what he was about to embark on was the greatest he would ever be asked to do. He felt so uncertain of himself, so out of his comfort zone, and so alone. He needed to find his inner strength, and the Spirit within him. He needed time with Abba. Yeshua decided that he would spend forty days in the wilderness, in memory of and in celebration and solidarity with his ancestors who, led by Moses, spent forty years in the desert, where they were sustained by Yahweh, with manna from heaven and water from a rock.

It was on his thirtieth birthday that Yeshua entered the wilderness. And for forty days and forty nights, Yeshua spent his time in a little cave in the wilderness. He spent his time in unceasing prayer, fasting and surviving like Johanan on locusts, grasshoppers and wild honey, which he ate every now and then, breaking his fast only in order to sustain his body. During this time, Yeshua felt so alone and yet not alone, because the wilderness was full of wild trees, and other wild flora and of course wild animals who made their presence felt during the night. But Yeshua kept a fire going to make sure they kept a safe distance.

For a long time, the silence was hard to endure and seemed deafening. He prayed and prayed for Yahweh to speak to him, but all he heard was the din of the silence, the sounds of the wilderness, the creatures of the night, the smouldering fire, and the fireflies that gathered around. At night, the stars shone brightly, but all was silence, deep, enduring silence. Only after the first week did Yeshua begin to hear the voice of God. It was in the depths of the silence that he heard that voice, not like the booming voice that spoke from the heavens when he was baptised in the River Jordan, but a soft, gentle voice, not a human voice, but a divine voice, a spiritual voice, that spoke not even in words, but in something inexplicable, deep within his heart.

It became clear to Yeshua that his time is close for him to go out and proclaim the Good News. It became clear that he was to continue and to perfect what Johanan had proclaimed and done. He was to awaken in the minds and hearts of all humanity that Yahweh, that Abba is a fatherly, a motherly God, who loves us all as a mother and father loves their children, that we are indeed children of God, who is Abba. No longer are the children to wait for redemption and salvation, they are already being redeemed and saved from the evil in the world. Abba, God, is already redeeming and freeing us all from being enslaved by evil and death. He is overcoming sin, evil and death forever.

It became clear to Yeshua, what he always believed, that God would triumph over evil not so much as a judge, as even Johanan preached, nor as a king, like Caesar, but as a loving, merciful and compassionate father, who loves us, desires us, cares for us, as a father and a mother, with a heart that is full of love, unending love, infinite love, eternal love. Men and women would still have to repent and turn away from evil as Johanan preached, but not so much to prepare for judgement, but to enter into, and to embrace the reign of God, of Abba, and his forgiveness and his love. Yeshua just felt his Father's love and that the Good News that he was to preach to the world is that we are all the beloved children of God, our Creator and loving Father, who loves us with a love that is infinite, unconditional and eternal.

When the forty days came to an end, Yeshua was understandably famished, and yearning for something substantial to eat. And a thought came into his mind. If I am the Son of God, I have the power to change these stones before me into loaves of bread. And in his imagination, he saw this miraculous changing of stones into bread. I can do this, I have the power from my Father, I am the Son of God, and I can do this, and satisfy my hunger. Why not, no one is around, no will see this, why not. These thoughts began swirling around in his mind.

Yeshua shook his head. What is happening to me? This is the work of the tempter, Yeshua said to himself, almost as if he were speaking to the devil, the tempter, who spends all his time tempting people to evil and selfish deeds. No, I must not succumb to this temptation of pride and greed and selfishness and boastfulness and be wanting in integrity and fidelity to why my heavenly Father has sent me into the world. "Get behind me Satan," Yeshua said out loud. "One does not live on bread alone, but by every word that comes from the mouth of God."

Yeshua still felt hungry and weak though, and almost delirious. He caught some more locusts and grasshoppers and found wild honey and ate. It was time for him to leave the wilderness. I will make it clear; that people will no longer need to go into the wilderness or the desert to find God, and repent, for I will bring God to them, for Yahweh Abba is already with them, he desires them and seeks them. He is near to them, dear to them, desires to be one with them.

After Yeshua had some light sustenance, his imagination ran wild and, in his mind, once again, in his imagination, as if in a dream, he had this image, of himself in Jerusalem, on the pinnacle of the Temple. How he got there he did not know. But in dreams anything happens in a flash. And Yeshua felt as if he was in a dream state. And in his imagination, he heard a voice whispering in his ear. It was as if he was awake and having a dream at the same time. It was a weird feeling. Deep in his imagination, the same voice said, "If you are the Son of God, throw yourself down, for it is written: 'He will command his angels concerning you,' and 'On their hands they will bear you up, so that you will not dash your foot against a stone'."

This is the tempter at work again, he never leaves us in peace, especially when we are close to and love Yahweh, and he knows when to strike, when we are at our weakest, when we are vulnerable, Yeshua said to himself, and then prayed, "Abba, my body is weak, give me the daily bread I need and forgive me my sins, and deliver me from this temptation."

In his imagination, in his dreamlike state, Yeshua responded to the tempter, "You wish me to show off, to presume in God's goodness and power, and want me to assert my position, but I say to you that again it is written, 'Do not put the Lord your God, to the test'."

It seemed to Yeshua that he was in a daze. Oh, why am I plagued with these futile thoughts? Now that I am weak and tired, does the tempter see an opening, a way to bring me down, to destroy the work of Yahweh, "Abba, please deliver me from these temptations that now plague me," Yeshua prayed.

But it seemed the temptations would not cease, for again in his mind, in his imagination, as if in a dream again, Yeshua found himself on a high mountain. He did not recognise the mountain, but it must have been the tallest mountain in the world, for it almost touched the sky. Yeshua found it such a beautiful sight, and he wished to remain in this dreamlike state but then the thoughts, the voices returned and came into his mind, like another temptation. He heard a voice that said to him, "Yeshua, just look at all the kingdoms of the world, and their splendour. All these I will give you, if you will fall down and worship me."

Yeshua knew it was the voice of the tempter, and he shouted out loud, "All these are not yours to give, Evil One, away with you Satan! For it is written, 'Worship the Lord your God, and serve only him'."

Yeshua dropped his head in his hands, rubbed his face and sighed. *Am I going insane, are these voices real, or are they the fruits of my imagination, or are they the words of the tempter, of Satan?* Yeshua felt tired, and wanted no more of these futile yet subtle temptations. The kingdoms of the world belong to the Father and not to Satan. "Father, Abba, deliver me from all evil. And give me the strength to do your will in all things."

Then it seemed a deep peace came over Yeshua and it seemed as if angels were surrounding him, and holding him in their arms. He experienced a peace like he had never experienced for a long time. And he felt his strength return. He was now ready to face the world.

Because Johanan was now in prison, Yeshua thought it wise not to stay in Jerusalem, as he had planned. He was to follow up on the mission, work and message of Johanan. But Yeshua knew it would be foolhardy to do so in Jerusalem, while Herod was losing his mind. So, Yeshua decided to return to Galilee.

While Yeshua was in the wilderness for forty days, word had spread in Jerusalem about him. Matthew, Judas, Micah and Nahum were responsible for spreading the news about Yeshua; a disciple of Johanan, who it seemed, would carry on his work. They spread the story of Yeshua's baptism, and the appearance of the dove, and the voice from above. So, when Yeshua returned to Galilee, the word had also spread there about him all around the surrounding country side. Yeshua had no idea of his growing reputation, but he first went home to Nazareth under cover of darkness because he wanted to spend some quality time with his mother, before going on the road again, because he knew that this time, it would be for good.

Yeshua spent that night and all of the next day alone with his mother. He told her all that had happened to him in Jerusalem, his meeting with Johanan, his baptism and what happened then, and Johanan's imprisonment by Herod. Yeshua also shared with Miriam his time in the wilderness, and the temptations he experienced.

Miriam listened; she was so happy to have Yeshua home again. Yeshua was planning to go out and begin to carry on the work of Johanan, the work of Abba Yahweh, to announce the full story of what Johanan began. He will tell the people that the reign of God, of Abba, Yahweh was not coming sometime in the future; it was already here in our midst.

While Yeshua was sharing all these deep insights with Miriam, she had other things on her mind—a wedding of a relative in the town of Cana to which she and Yeshua were invited. Yeshua had planned to tell Miriam so much more of his experiences in the wilderness and his plan to go on the road and proclaim the Good News but he could see his mother's excitement. She had been alone for so long, while he was away. She was in need of some serious socialising, and she seemed so excited about going to this wedding.

So, Yeshua decided to postpone, suspending his plans to after the wedding. In fact, on second thought, Yeshua found that he too was delighted to have some down time, some socialising. He loved parties and missed them and hadn't really attended any festive celebrations for a while, and there was nothing bigger than weddings that went on for a whole week, during which time relatives and friends stopped by to celebrate. So, the next day, Miriam and Yeshua went to the market place to buy a present for the bride. They found some beautiful jewellery, a necklace and earrings, adorned with big gem stones. Yeshua and Miriam then had some lunch together in the town. People came up to greet them and several of them were pleased to be able to greet Yeshua, and to welcome him back. Many had already heard about Yeshua. The news of Johanan's arrest, and also the story of the dove from above, and the voice of God had circulated, and the name of Yeshua of Nazareth had spread. Yeshua felt a bit uneasy. He did not want the attention.

"Relax, Yeshua, you are a curiosity in Nazareth because of your association with Johanan and his arrest, soon after your strange encounter with him, and I'm sure the news has spread all over Galilee. But let us just enjoy this lunch, and our time together, and the forthcoming wedding. Let it also be your send-off, Yeshua," Miriam said with a smile.

"My send-off, I'm not going off to war, Immah," Yeshua said, smiling.

"Ah, it's going to be a war, Yeshua, a war like no other, between you and the world, between good and evil, between you and dark powers of Satan, and his worldly followers," Miriam said. "You have to bring the people out of the darkness and into the light," Miriam added.

"I guess you're right, as always, Immah. Let us just forget all of that for a while and enjoy this lunch, shall we, my last days of freedom before the WAR," Yeshua said, grinning broadly.

"Yes, let's just do that," Miriam responded with a smile. She was happy to see Yeshua now relaxed and contented and in a jovial mood. She needed this quality time with him for she knew she would not see him again for a long time once he left home this time. She wanted to enjoy his presence, and his company. They chatted amicably and enjoyed teasing each other, as they also enjoyed their meal.

On the next day, they set out on the road to Cana. Yeshua knew that on his own he could walk there in less than four hours, and although Miriam was also a fit walker, he decided they would take Ben the donkey with them this time, so she could ride in comfort, and also because the wedding was not for a couple of days yet. They could therefore take their time and enjoy the ride, the scenery, and each other's company. Both Miriam and Yeshua were so happy to be going on a sort of holiday together, for one last time. Miriam especially was so happy to have Yeshua all to herself for these few days, and to enjoy a wedding celebration, and catch up with some relatives and friends. She was looking forward to the wedding and the celebrations, and so was Yeshua.

As they journeyed to Cana, it brought back memories to Yeshua of his trip around the Sea of Galilee, such a long time ago now. He had not stayed over in Cana, so this would be a first for him. They went immediately to the home of the bride, Deborah, who was about to marry Zedekiah. There was so much excitement in the place, and the women were all fussing over Deborah, and inspecting her wedding dress. Yeshua left his mother and the women to chat about women's business, and he enjoyed some men's company, who were out in the backyard enjoying a drink.

Yeshua met the father of the bride, Samuel, and some of the men from Cana. They greeted Yeshua and offered him a drink. They stood around the smouldering fire and enjoyed the wine and chatted amicably.

"This must be quite an expense for you, Samuel," Yeshua said.

"It sure is; we have been saving a whole year for this. But it's not too bad, as we are sharing the expenses with Zedekiah's family, and they are not too badly off. The wedding dress and all that goes with it costs a fortune, and that is all *our* expense. Deborah and her mother, Susannah, went all the way to Magdala for fittings, the dress and accessories were all made by a man, believe it or not, I can't think of his name," Samuel remarked.

"I *can,* believe it. I actually met him, the dressmaker from Magdala, his name is Joshua and he has two lovely daughters, Ruth and Orpah."

"Ruth and Orpah, really, and is his wife's name Naomi?" Samuel said, laughing out loud.

"No, actually, she is called Emzara, and they have three sons and guess what their names are?" Yeshua asked.

"Mmm, three sons," one of the men, Barakil, thought out loud, "the only three men, three brothers I can think of, are the sons of Noah—Shem Japheth and Ham," he said.

"You are right; they are his sons indeed and fine lads too. I met all of the family about, eh…ten years ago, I'm just thirty years now, and I remember I had turned twenty when I went on that trip, walking all around the Sea of Galilee. And I met Joshua, the dressmaker and his family. They actually took me in, and I stayed with them, they were so kind to me."

The mention of Joshua and his family and his walking around the Sea of Galilee led to Yeshua having to tell them all about his adventure. Yeshua actually relished retelling his story, it seemed so long ago and now telling it to these men brought it all back. It seemed as if it was just yesteryear. The men were all agog, as they listened. None of them had done such a walk or even considered it.

"You must do it sometime, it is worth it, and the scenery is breathtaking. There is plenty of forest, with all kinds of trees, flora and fauna and lots of little villages along the way, and bustling towns and cities with plenty to see and do, and the people are the highlight really, such great people to meet," Yeshua said. "And also, a great place to fish," Yeshua added.

"So, what are you doing now, Yeshua?" Samuel asked.

"I am a carpenter, but now I am leaving Nazareth and on my way to Capernaum and not sure what will happen to me there," Yeshua said, not wanting to elaborate.

"Wait a minute; you are the carpenter from Nazareth, were you in Jerusalem recently, with Johanan the hermit baptiser. I heard all about Johanan, who is now in prison, arrested by that cruel despot, Herod. And there was talk of a man, who was baptised by Johanan in the River Jordan, they said he was a carpenter from Nazareth, and people said that the sky just lit up like fire, and doves came flying out of nowhere, and rested on Johanan, and this man from Nazareth, and everyone heard voices, and a voice was heard saying that these two men were blessed and sons of the Most High," another of the men, Lamech, said.

"That's close enough, Lamech. But the sky did not light up like fire, but the clouds did disappear, and a voice was indeed heard," Yeshua said, he did not want to say anything more, simply to correct the finer details.

"So, you were there when that happened?" another of the men, Ziezl, said.

Just then, Susanna, mother of the bride came out and called to her husband, "Samuel, get that fire going, and you men, make yourselves helpful and come fetch the meat and corn to put on the fire." Yeshua was pleased for the interruption; he did not want to elaborate or elucidate on the incident with him and Johanan. It seemed to Yeshua that the men did not think he could be that person. The men stoked the fire and fuelled it with more wood and it didn't take long before they had a solid fire going. And it wasn't long afterwards when the men and women and the bride to be, sat outside around the open fire enjoying their meal.

The night came, and the men and women and friends of the family were ready to leave for their homes.

"Miriam and Yeshua, we have prepared a bed for you both. Come, let me show you," Susanna said, as she led Miriam and Yeshua to an adjacent room. The smallish room was divided down the middle by a curtain. "This is your bed, here Miriam, and this is yours Yeshua. I've put clean linen on, and there are some spare blankets in the cupboard over there, if you need them." She pointed to a cupboard in the corner of the room.

Yeshua instinctively went to touch the cupboard and inspect the wood and the workmanship.

"I hope it is all right, Yeshua," Susanna said, as she saw Yeshua run his hand down the side of the cupboard.

"It's fine, Susanna, thank you, and thank you for the meal, and don't mind Yeshua, he can't help himself in the presence of wooden furniture," Miriam said, smiling.

"Such beautiful wood and such fine workmanship," Yeshua said, "who made this cupboard?"

"I don't really know, Samuel just came home with it one day, all tied up on the cart. He said he bought it at a workshop at a small village just before Magdala," Susannah replied.

"It's beautiful, and thank you too for your hospitality, Susanna and I sure enjoyed the company of your friends. And I had plenty to drink, so I am going to sleep like a log tonight," Yeshua said, smiling.

They said goodnight to Susanna, and Yeshua went immediately to Miriam and took her in his arms. "Oh Immah, it is so good to be with you. I missed you so, during those forty days in the wilderness," Yeshua said.

"Yeah, more like you missed all my cooking, and do let me go, you smothering me, I can hardly breathe," Miriam said laughing, as Yeshua released her.

"Immah, so much happened during those forty days in the wilderness. I had never spent so much time alone in one place, and living on locusts and grasshoppers and wild honey, like Johanan did for years."

"I don't know how Johanan and you could survive on snacks such as locusts and grasshoppers, Yeshua. And you sure lost a lot of weight in the process," Miriam said, as she sat on her bed and began to unpack her night clothes. "I will have to fatten you up when we get home, and before you leave for wherever you are going," Miriam said, a tinge of sadness in her voice.

"Well, I started that fattening up process already Immah, after that meal tonight, and I'm sure I'll put on some more pounds during these wedding celebrations," Yeshua said, grinning while rubbing his stomach.

"Immah, so much happened in the wilderness," Yeshua sat down beside his mother and continued. He had not really finished talking to Miriam about all that had happened. She was in no frame of mind to hear of those things, but Yeshua just wanted to, needed to let her know, what had happened to him during those forty days.

Miriam was now feeling relaxed and she seemed recharged after the time spent with Susanna, and the bride to be Deborah, and all the ladies. The women's company and conversation revived her. So, Yeshua proceeded.

"Immah, at the end of those forty days, I went through a most horrible time, I was plagued by all sorts of temptations, hearing a strange and sinister voice, which was definitely the voice of Satan, mother, and he was tempting me to do all sorts of things," Yeshua said, and then continued to tell his mother of the temptations he experienced.

"You must have been very close to Yahweh after forty days and forty nights in retreat, in silence, alone with the Lord. The evil one would do all in his power to bring you down, Yeshua, so you have to be on your guard at all times," Miriam said.

"You are right, Immah. I felt so close to Abba Yahweh, and He spoke to me, he encouraged me, and he sent his Spirit to enlighten me, and his angels to comfort me, and I felt his power enter me. It was a strange experience mother; everything about me became so clear. I discovered who I really am. You told me about my birth, but it didn't really register with me. At first, I thought that was what mothers told all their children that they were little angels. And I didn't really understand or fathom the depths and significance of who I am, and what Abba Yahweh wants of me, and why he sent me into the world."

Yeshua had already told his mother about his experience in the River Jordan, when he was baptised by Johanan. "And Immah, when I was baptised and the heavens opened up and a voice came out of nowhere and saying, 'This is my beloved Son, in whom I am well pleased, listen to him,' I was overwhelmed, and the full significance of those words didn't fully register with me, until I had been in the wilderness for more than a week."

Yeshua continued to open his heart to his mother, "Immah, I came out of the darkness and seemed to be surrounded by a bright light and all became clear. I am the incarnation of Abba Yahweh, and his Spirit. We are three, but we are one. Abba is love, his love is supreme, boundless, infinite, unconditional, and eternal, and there are simply no words to describe how much he loves all of his creation, all of us creatures. Abba, Yahweh is our Creator and Nurturer God, he is Love Supreme, and I am his Son, his only beloved Son. He and I are one and the same, I am Love Incarnate, I am here on this earth, flesh and blood, I am God visible, divine and human, all powerful and all loving, and at the same time totally human, totally vulnerable.

"Immah, so many faiths of peoples in the past have believed in their god taking a human form, and some rulers believed they were gods, was this some subconscious desire of us all to have a god, who is above us but still near to us, like us. So Immah, I now understand fully the circumstances of my miraculous birth, the presence of the power of my heavenly father. God is my abba in the sense that Yosef was my abba, more than that, more than Isaac was the son of Abraham. And as Yahweh asked Abraham to sacrifice his son, so he is asking you to sacrifice me, to sacrifice your son. I am one with my Father in heaven. I am the presence of Yahweh in the here and now, but I have existed before all eternity. Mother, who will accept this?"

Miriam had pondered much on this time, when her son would fully discover and understand his true identity and mission. "Yeshua, many will believe, and many will laugh and ridicule those who believe, they will say it is a fable, fulfilling some kind of unmet need. When it becomes known how you were born, they will laugh and ridicule even more, they will think those who believe this as childish. They will regard your birth as ridiculous."

"I know, Mother, but I have thought of this. If Yahweh Creator created the human race out of dust from the earth, the earth that he brought into being, out of nothing, then surely, he can let me be conceived in your womb through his creative power. Oh, Immah, what I am and what I have to reveal to the world will be hard for many to accept."

"Do not be alarmed, Yeshua, you have the Spirit with you, who will guide you and sustain you. And I am here for you, always, Yeshua my son."

"That is a great comfort, Immah. I am here to show all of humanity Yahweh's love, that boundless and magnanimous love. I am here to spread his love, his peace, his joy, to make him known and loved throughout Judaea, Galilee and beyond. For too long have the people seen Abba Yahweh as a stern judge, watching and waiting for us to sin, and then to punish us. He is not like that Immah, he is a loving father, a loving mother, Abba and Immah wrapped up in one.

"You love me so, Immah, yet Abba Yahweh loves me a million times more. All Abba Yahweh wants is for us to know of his boundless love for us, and his willingness to forgive us whatever wrong we have done. Oh Immah, all this became so clear to me during those forty days in the wilderness. I must now go and proclaim this Good News wherever I can. As soon as we get back home, I will leave you Immah, and I am not sure when I will see you again. I have decided to find a place to stay in Capernaum, for now. I have always felt that is where I would make my home."

"Oh Yeshua, I am so pleased and so happy for you. I can see that you are filled with the Spirit of Adonai, of Yahweh, of Abba Yahweh." For the first time Miriam too, now, and only in the presence of her son feel she could call God, Yahweh. She felt such an intimacy with Yahweh and his beloved Son, her son. "I love you son with all my heart and I will be praying for you every day. What you are going to embark on will be a difficult road and you will experience great wonders and great joy and accomplish much but you will also encounter opposition and hardships and suffer much. You are now so ultra-sensitive, you are now Abba incarnate, with a love that I and no one else can ever understand or fathom its depths. I am with you my son, wherever you are. Now it's time for you to rest and for me to rest. We will simply put all these matters behind us for the next few days," Miriam said, as she leaned over and kissed her son. "Goodnight, my son, sleep in peace."

"Goodnight Immah," Yeshua said in return and kissed her on her cheek and hugged her one more time. "Thank you, Immah, for listening and for understanding and have a good night's sleep. And yes, I will put all these matters in that cupboard over there for the meantime," Yeshua said, pointing to the cupboard, and smiling.

"And I will lock it in there, for now. Go sleep now my son. Goodnight," Miriam said, as she crept into bed. But as she lay there, hearing the sounds of Yeshua, as he too slipped into bed behind the curtain, tears were welling up in her eyes, and as she turned, they flowed down her cheeks. They were a combination of tears of joy and tears of sorrow, she was filled with the joy of God and the joy of what her son was now going to embark on, he would change the world as never before. But while she shed tears of joy, she also shed tears of sorrow, as she somehow knew that he would pay a great price and that it would cost him his life.

Chapter Thirty-Four
"They Have No More Wine."

And so, the big day arrived for Deborah. Everyone was up early. Susanna, Samuel, and others were all fussing around, and getting everything ready for the big celebration. The preparations had already started way before Yeshua and Miriam had arrived. But now the outside area was set up for guests.

The main celebration after the wedding ceremony was to be held at the home of the groom, Zedekiah's parents, where there were tables and chairs, and benches everywhere, for those who needed to sit, and in a place of honour, a long table covered with a white cloth and festooned with decorations and flowers for the bride and bridegroom and the best man and bridesmaid. And close by, a specially decorated table for the parents of the bride and the groom. But here at the home of the bride, the fire was all ready and a whole lamb was on a spit above the flames, the first of more to be roasted for sure, and taken to Zedekiah's parents' place. And there would of course be several jars filled with wine, bought and collected over several weeks, if not months for all the guests who would turn up, for the week-long celebrations.

When Yeshua and Miriam helped carry containers to the home of the groom's parents, they saw more lambs being roasted, and besides lamb there was also roasted duckling and all sorts of good things to eat, including olives, sardines, grapevine leaves, dried apricots and dates, almond nuts, raisins, pomegranates, and Yeshua's favourite, figs, fresh and dried. For those who did not drink wine, there was grape and berry juice. Wedding celebrations was a time of great feasting and a great expense to both the groom and bride and their families.

The wedding ceremony was celebrated with great pomp in the synagogue and everyone was dressed in their best Sabbath clothing. Miriam and Yeshua were so pleased to see Deborah wearing the necklace and earrings they had given her. They had decided to give it to Deborah earlier, as they thought she might just want to wear them. And they were glad they did, it looked superb on her, looking like a queen in her beautiful wedding dress made by Joshua with the help of his wife Emzara and their daughters Ruth and Orpah.

And so, the wedding celebrations went on. Miriam and Yeshua had attended the celebrations on the day. They had decided to stay a couple more days, but kept away from the celebrations, as so many other guests came streaming in. Miriam and Yeshua decided they would spend some time at the celebrations on the third day, and then head back home, early the following day.

It was early afternoon on the third day, and the place was still filled with guests. Miriam noticed some consternation among the servants around the jars of wine. She observed them approach the head steward, who in turn approached Zedekiah and Samuel, and they then went and had a look at the jars themselves. By their actions and expressions, Miriam surmised what was happening. She approached the head steward and her fears were realised, they had run out of wine. This happened partly because there were so many guests and several from faraway had turned up and the place was full. This was going to be a great embarrassment and humiliation to the bride and the groom and their families, if they had no more wine for their guests.

Miriam went across to Yeshua, He was holding a cup of wine, must have been the last, and he was chatting amiably with some of the guests who came all the way from Magdala. Yeshua was just talking to them about Joshua and Emzara and their family. And as he was in conversation, he thought of Miriam, the friend of Ruth and Orpah. He had the vision of the beautiful Miriam. She came to his mind, and his heart went out to her, for she had looked so depressed and forlorn and troubled when she had slipped away from them, in the marketplace.

"Son, can I have a word?" Miriam said, as she tugged on his sleeve. Yeshua excused himself from the company and stepped aside with his mother.

"What is it, mother, I don't like the look on your face, is anything wrong?"

"Yes, Yeshua, a lot is wrong. They have no more wine," Miriam said, with a look that said, *do something and save the family this greatest of embarrassment.*

Yeshua looked at his mother; he frowned, and for a moment, felt helpless to do anything. But the look on Miriam's face said it all, it said, 'you *can* do something, and you *must* do something.'

For a fleeting moment, Yeshua had the vision of himself in the wilderness and the temptation of the tempter, telling him to change the stones into bread. And here his mother was doing something similar, telling him to use his divine power and fill the empty jars with wine. But in the wilderness, he was not enduring any extreme embarrassment. It was not about him, but about the bride and the groom, Deborah and Zedekiah on the biggest days of their lives. *And about their families and all these guests, who have come from afar. Abba, Yahweh, with whom I am one, you poured down manna in the desert, and supplied water from a rock. How am I to supply wine to these guests. And if I do, the consequences will open for me the floodgates. I will have to…*

"Well, Yeshua, did you hear me? I said, they have no more wine," Miriam repeated, as she interrupted Yeshua's wandering mind. She knew he was pondering the situation and what she was asking of him would cause consternation and have repercussions that would launch him into the future, his purpose in life.

"Mother, what is that to me, my time has not yet come," Yeshua said the first words that came to mind. He knew his time was near, but he would postpone it as long as he could. And to do something miraculous, to somehow supply the bride and groom with the wine for their guests would propel him into his mission in a big way. He looked at Deborah and Zedekiah and the torturous look on their faces. He decided to save them.

When Miriam saw the expression on Yeshua's face change, she breathed a sigh of relief. She then went to the servants and said to them. "Whatever Yeshua tells you to do, do it," she said emphatically. She had no idea what Yeshua was going to do, how he was going to show this kindness and concern but she put her trust in him. She knew the consequences of whatever he would do, would be massive. She did not think it through meticulously at all. There was no usual pondering, she just responded instinctively.

Yeshua then walked towards the servants. He said to them, "Follow me." He led them to the six stone water jars, which stood near the entrance of the house. Three of the jars held about twenty gallons each and three larger ones, about thirty gallons each. The stone jars were used for the Jewish rites of purification. Yeshua then said to the servants, "Fill all these jars with water."

The servants did not know what Yeshua had in mind. Was he going to perform some ritual of purification, now at this time, during wedding celebrations? They looked at Miriam, who simply nodded and they recalled her telling them to do whatever Yeshua instructed. So, they filled the six stone jars with water, a total of one hundred and fifty gallons. It took them quite a while.

At the same time, the head waiter, Arpachshad was frantic, and chatting with Samuel about what to do. They decided to send some of the servants to go and purchase some wine, at least a supply for the rest of the day, but that would take hours. But they need wine now, and still need more wine for the rest of the week, and especially on the last day, when everyone would turn up. Some of the guests came; looking for refills of wine and Arpachshad stalled them, telling them more wine will be available soon.

Arpachshad approached the servants and saw them filling the stone water jars with water. "What are you doing?" he inquired.

They told him what had happened. He then approached Miriam, and she told him to be patient, and that Yeshua was about to solve the problem.

Arpachshad was only too glad that someone else was going to solve the problem. When some of the guests came looking for more wine, when Arpachshad told them that there would be some available in a moment, they were satisfied.

Arpachshad had heard rumours about this Yeshua. He did not believe all that nonsense about the sky on fire and doves descending on Johanan the baptiser, and a certain carpenter from Nazareth, named Yeshua. And when he first met Yeshua, his disbelief was confirmed, there seemed nothing extraordinary about this man Yeshua. He was like any of the other guests, he loved a cup of wine, and chatter, and laughter. He couldn't be the prophet, the one who is to come. But he was hedging his bets and he let the servants do what they were told to do.

When all the jars were filled, Yeshua said to the servants, "Now draw some out of the jar and take it to the chief steward." The chief steward was now mingling with the guests. And when the servant approached with a cup filled with what he thought was water, Arpachshad took it and sipped from it, and his eyes lit up, and he licked his lips, and cried out, "Zedekiah, Samuel, what have you done. Everyone serves the good wine first, and then the inferior wine after the guests have become drunk," he laughed. And the guests laughed with him, still unaware of what had just transpired. Arpachshad continued, "But you, Zedekiah and Samuel, have kept the good wine till now. Gentlemen, wine is served." There followed a dash towards the waiters, who now stood beside the six stone jars serving the guests, who were bewildered by the presence of so much wine. And when they tasted the wine, they agreed with Arpachshad, because they had not tasted such good wine, ever.

The whole place was abuzz. Everyone was amazed with so much wine, of such superior quality. They all wanted to know where the wine came from. Even the servants were amazed and incredulous. How could this be, and who is this man, who has accomplished such magic. When the word spread about what had happened, Yeshua and Miriam had already left. Zedekiah and Deborah had thanked Miriam and Yeshua before they left. And it was Yeshua who asked Miriam for them to leave.

By the time Yeshua and Miriam left Cana the next morning, the whole town was abuzz with the great miracle that had taken place. Some believed it to be the work of a great magician but others believed it was the hand of God. Everyone wanted to meet the man who did this great deed, change one hundred and fifty gallons of water into the finest of wines. But Yeshua had already left the town.

As a result of that miracle, many came to hear about Yeshua as a great miracle worker, and when it became clear he was also the same person on whom the dove descended when he was baptised by Johanan in the River Jordan, and there were great signs in the heavens and the voice of God, proclaiming him as a prophet, a man of God, Yeshua's fame spread far and wide, like wild fire. He was now the talk of every city, town and village throughout Galilee.

Chapter Thirty-Five
And So, It Begins

Yeshua and Miriam were supposed to go onto the road back to Nazareth; instead they changed their minds and Miriam decided to go with Yeshua to Capernaum, she wanted to see him settled, or at least where he would stay. No amount of protests by Yeshua would make her change her mind. So off they went, the two of them, with Miriam sitting on Ben.

But this time, Yeshua decided to venture off the main and well-trodden roads, and to go to the out of the way places, and stop at every village he could find, along the way. Yeshua wanted to reach the smallest of villages, where the poorest of the poor lived, those despised by the elites and the city-dwellers. He knew of these discarded people, treated like scum of the earth, just like the lepers in the leper colonies. They were hungry, ousted from their land, day labourers, often unable to find work, and having to go hungry. They were the sick, the blind, the lame, the incapacitated, the dispossessed and those regarded as possessed, the fallen and unwanted women, and all of them regarded as sinners by the rest of society. They were the outcasts and it was to these first and foremost that Yeshua wished to go and bring the Good News of salvation and redemption, and of Abba, Yahweh's great love. These poor, incapacitated, destitute people, were regarded as sinners, and shunned by the rest of society, but to Yahweh, they were first, and wanted and loved, and it was to these first and foremost Yeshua wanted to go to proclaim the Good News of Yahweh's love for them.

Besides the cluster of villages where the outcasts lived, where Yeshua stayed and spent time, Yeshua also planned to stay in other small and insignificant villages. Where there were rabbis, or religious leaders, Yeshua decided to meet with them first. And so, it happened at the very first little village just over an hour from Cana. Yeshua and Miriam found out where their religious leader lived and went and paid their respects.

"I am Yeshua, from Nazareth, and this is my mother, Miriam. We are passing through your village, and would like to find some lodgings, and stay here for a while," Yeshua said.

"Yeshua, I have heard about you, only last night. A couple from our village had been in Cana, and they heard about you, and the great miracle you worked at a wedding feast. Is it really you, Yeshua? And are you also a disciple of Johanan the baptiser, and are you the one that was baptised with such great signs from the heavens," the rabbi asked.

"Yes, he is," Miriam said. "And it is here that he is coming to proclaim the Good News of Yahweh's day of salvation and redemption," Miriam added.

"I am Zimri, and I have been the synagogue leader here, for several years now. I used to preach in the synagogues at Tiberias, but I contracted a severe illness, a terrible rash all over my body, and I was proclaimed unclean and a sinner, and dismissed. My face is okay as you can see, but my whole body is covered with a rash. People here, do not mind, they cannot see my malady, and they are in need of a pastor, a rabbi. We do not have a synagogue but we have built a little hall for our

Sabbath and festive celebrations. Will you come and preach tomorrow, Yeshua, as it is the Sabbath," Zimri asked.

"I will be most happy to do so, Zimri. But first can you tell me where we can find some lodgings in your village?" Yeshua asked.

"Oh, you can stay here, Yeshua and Miriam. I have a spare room and some camping beds, if you don't mind them," Zimri said.

"That will be fine, Zimri. Thank you so much," Yeshua said.

"You must be hungry, I will make us something to eat," Zimri offered.

"Thank you, Zimri. We have been eating enough these past three days in Cana. I am inclined not to eat for the rest of this day. Some water will be fine," Miriam said.

"The same goes for me, Zimri. What time do you have your Sabbath service?" Yeshua asked.

"We usually gather around the second hour. I usually preach for an hour, and then we do the rest of the service. If you will preach, I will lead the rest of the service," Zimri said.

"That's fine," Yeshua responded.

Zimri, Yeshua and Miriam conversed for quite some time. Yeshua listened, as Zimri related his story. "I grew up in Tiberias, and from an early age I felt Yahweh calling me to do his work, so I became a rabbi, to teach and to preach. But when I got sick, I was dismissed. But I am quite happy here in this village. The people have accepted me, for most of them are in the same boat, discarded, looked upon as the dregs of society. All of them are poor, or sick, or incapacitated in some way, and we all have been regarded as sinners, because of our condition," Zimri said.

"This is the first place that the Spirit has sent me, Zimri. And I come to bring Good News to the poor and the discarded, I come to tell them of Abba's great love for them, his special love for them," Yeshua said.

It was getting late and when the darkness descended on the village, Yeshua and Miriam retired to their sleeping quarters.

"Immah, are you okay, with us staying here. It is clear to me now. I am sent to preach the Good News, to the poor, the discarded, to those whom society rejects and abandons, and to let them know that Abba, Yahweh, does not reject them, and does not abandon them, but loves them with an indescribable love, and that they are precious in his sight."

"Son, I am happy to be here, to be with you. I will stay with you for now, like Ruth said to Naomi, where you go, I will go," Miriam said, with a smile.

"Immah, please don't think you have to care for me. I can look after myself. I am a big boy now. I lived for forty days and forty nights in the wilderness remember, among wild beasts and the heat and the cold, and lived on locusts and grasshoppers and wild honey, so I can care for myself," Yeshua said, grinning.

"Yes, I know, Yeshua, and look how thin you got. You are just starting to pick up a bit, more flesh on your bones, and I want to make sure you have a healthy diet and look after yourself; you can't live on locusts and grasshoppers. You have to have proper and healthy food, if you are to do this heavy work," Miriam said, pulling a face and grinning from ear to ear.

"Okay Immah, you win, as usual. I will be stopping at all the villages on our way to Capernaum, and then once we get there, we can make arrangements for you to get back to Nazareth. Or rather I will go with you back to Nazareth. Does that suit you, Immah?"

"That's fine, Yeshua. I will stay with you, and feed you, and do your washing, and keep an eye on you, and make sure you do the right thing, and not neglect your health," Miriam said.

"Thank you, Immah. You have taught me well, I do look after my health though, and feel in good shape. I walk every day and at times I even go for a run," Yeshua said. "When I was in the wilderness, I would go for walks and spend a lot of time catching those darn grasshoppers and locusts. They are tasty morsels, especially with the wild honey, and quite nourishing in fact. And I walked at least an hour in the morning and an hour in the afternoon, so I had plenty of exercise."

Yeshua chatted some more about his time in the wilderness. "Immah, I learned how to really be silent. It took a number of days though. For the first six or seven days, the silence was deafening. I couldn't enter into the silence. I had so many distractions; thoughts and doubts running through my mind. But I soldiered on, and after the first week the silence came more easily. It wasn't as if I didn't have those distractions any more, but I just kept returning to the silence, and to help me enter into and remain in the silence, I simply said, Abba, Abba, over and over again. I called Abba's name over and over again, not out loud, but silently, in my heart, and after some time, I just drifted into deep silence, and the sound of Abba seemed to be repeating itself on its own deep within my heart, and in the depths of the silence, I communed with Abba. Abba spoke to me, without words, he communicated his love and his care for me. I felt a great peace out there in the wilderness, Immah," Yeshua said.

"I am so glad, Yeshua, that you had that experience. I know that Yahweh is with you. He has been with you from the moment I conceived you in my womb," Miriam said.

Miriam then shared with Yeshua how she felt about him as her son, "Yeshua, when I first conceived you, I was so young and immature. I couldn't understand why Yahweh chose me, a young girl from Nazareth, of all places. And then we had to go on that trip to Bethlehem. I was heavily pregnant with you and we had to go slowly. And then we could not find a place to stay in Bethlehem. And the only lodgings were a stable where the animals were kept. And so, Yeshua, you were born in a stable and laid in a manger, and I wrapped you in swaddling clothes. You had such humble beginnings, Yeshua, and it is so appropriate that you are beginning your public ministry here in this village, among these people," Miriam said. "And now, we will close our eyes on these humble camping mats, and go to sleep. Goodnight, Yeshua," Miriam said, ready to fall asleep.

"Goodnight, Immah, sleep tight, don't let the critters of the night bite," Yeshua said with a chuckle.

It wasn't long when Yeshua was breathing heavily and fast asleep. Miriam too soon fell asleep.

On the next day, the word had gone out early that they had a guest preacher, Yeshua from Nazareth, and that he and his mother, Miriam had spent the night with Zimri. All people of the village heard the news being spread through a most prolific grapevine. Yeshua is the carpenter from Nazareth, baptised in the Jordan, with great signs from Yahweh, and this same Yeshua had changed water into wine at a wedding feast in Cana, just yesterday. There was great excitement in the village and the hall which served as a synagogue was packed, like sardines. Every man, woman and child were present.

Yeshua had entered the hall that was already converted into their synagogue. It had the Star of David and the Menorah; all the seven candles alight with flames glowing, and in the centre, the table of sacrifice. On a table to one side of the sanctuary there were a number of scrolls containing portions of the Scriptures. Yeshua had entered their synagogue at sunrise. He spent the time in prayer, in silence and had taken one of the Scrolls that contained the writings of Isaiah. He read and reflected and prepared in his mind what he wanted to say. But Yeshua was not sure exactly what he would say. He had his theme, and selected the Scripture that would inspire his words, and he trusted in the Spirit to inspire him with what he would say.

When Yeshua had finished his time of prayer, the people started entering the synagogue. And within a short space of time the whole place was filled to capacity. Yeshua sat at the back of the synagogue and watched as the people streamed in, men, women, children, babies on arms. Many of the people were clearly poor, poorly dressed and several were ill and incapacitated, the lame were brought in, with the help of others, and the blind led in by family or friends. Several could hardly walk, but they all wanted to come and hear this new prophet from Nazareth, from their own province of Galilee.

Zimri introduced Yeshua, "My dear friends in the Lord, we are blessed to have Yeshua with us today, to address us. You have all heard of the great signs that have accompanied him in the River Jordan, with Johanan, the great prophet and baptiser, and only yesterday, at Cana, you all know what took place. Yeshua, please come forward, we are ready to listen to you."

A hush descended throughout the building as all eyes were on Yeshua. He began with a prayer. "Abba, Adonai, you have sent me here to this village, with no name, to these people, who have been rejected by society because they are poor or ill or incapacitated. You know them all by name. Before they were conceived in their mother's womb, you knew them, and loved them. From all eternity you have loved them and for all eternity you will love them. Your love for them is endless, boundless, unconditional and eternal. They are regarded by all as sinners and punished by you for their sins. Abba, Adonai, let them know that is not true, that in your eyes they are special, and favourites, and loved. Let them know how much you love them and care for them and hold them forever in your heart. You know their pain, their cries, their sorrow, and your heart, Abba goes out to them, and you bless them with riches beyond compare."

Yeshua then opened the scroll that contained the writings of Isaiah that he had prepared, and read a passage to the people:

"The Spirit of the Lord God is upon me,
because the Lord has anointed me;
He has sent me to bring Good News to the oppressed,
to bind up the broken-hearted,
to proclaim liberty to the captives,
and release to the prisoners;
to proclaim the year of the Lord's favour,
and the day of vengeance of our God;
to comfort all who mourn;

to give them a garland instead of ashes,
the oil of gladness instead of mourning,
the mantle of praise instead of a faint spirit.
They will be called oaks of righteousness,
the planting of the Lord, to display his glory."

Yeshua then rolled up the scroll and all eyes were upon him. He looked around the packed synagogue, where men and women were not separated. They were all seated together. Yeshua thought how right it was that they should have the wisdom and goodness to display their love and affection through the simple act of sitting together. These people were united in their poverty, in being ostracised by the rest of society. Yeshua's heart went out to them.

"My dear people, I have been in many synagogues and always the men are in the prominent places, and the women separated in places of less prominence, where they are not even seen. But here you are all in one place, you are all equal and so it should be. You are all equal in the eyes of Adonai, who is the father, Abba of you all. Those words I have just read from the prophet Isaiah are being fulfilled right now in this place. The Spirit of the Lord is upon me, and He has anointed me to bring you the Good News of his unfathomable, boundless and special love for you. You are the ones Isaiah speaks of, you are the oppressed, the broken-hearted, captives, prisoners. I proclaim to you the Lord's favour. You are indeed his favourites. He gives you, his comfort. Instead of ashes he gives you a garland of roses, the oil of gladness. Instead of mourning; he praises you for though others seek to crush your spirit, he covers you with the mantle of praise. You have shown to be as solid as oaks; you will be called oaks of righteousness."

Yeshua paused and allowed a few moments for his words to sink deeply into their hearts and into their consciousness. He could see their faces light up. Some had tears streaming down their cheeks. He continued:

"My dear people, Abba, Adonai has sent me to you, to let you know how pleased he is with you, how much he loves you. He knows how hard it is for you, how difficult life is for you, the pain and suffering you bear in your bodies, but more so in your hearts, and in your souls, as you feel ostracised, separated, segregated, ignored and looked down upon. Know this, the Lord does not look down upon you, he does not ignore you. He listens to your pleas and your mourning, and he feels and suffers with you in all your sorrows. He is with you, close to you, he knows you by name, and he will never abandon you, no matter what.

"Do not despair, do not wallow in your sins, repent of them, he understands and forgives, he is not a harsh judge, watching and waiting for you to fall and to fail, and to step outside the law. He is there to sustain you and give you the strength you need, and no matter how many times you fail, or you sin, he will never, never, never, condemn you. He will be there right beside you to pick you up and hold you in his arms. He loves you my dear brothers and sisters."

Again, Yeshua paused to allow his words to sink into their hearts. He needed to give them time to digest what he was saying. For too long have they been told how displeased Yahweh is with them, for too long have they believed that their maladies, their misfortunes are the result of their sins. He has to correct them, and to free them, to save them, to redeem them. As he gazed around the synagogue, he could see their eyes light up, and their souls gladden. He could still see tears of release and joy streaming down several faces.

"My brothers and sisters, I see among you several mothers, holding in their arms their infants. Dearest mothers, there is nothing that you will not do for the child you have carried in your womb for nine months and brought into this world. Mothers, fathers, can you recall that moment when you saw your little one come into the world. Take a moment to recall your concern, your anxiety, and your thrill of anticipation as you waited for your child to be born. Mothers, recall the pain you endured in bringing your child into the world, a pain like no other. Yet recall the indescribable joy and happiness that flooded your whole being, as you held your newborn child in your arms."

Again, Yeshua paused, allowing them time to reflect on those precious moments in their lives. He saw pregnant women smile and touch their babies, in their wombs. And he saw mothers smile and look at the babies in their arms, and the little children beside them with a glow of unbelievable tenderness and love. And fathers too glanced at their babies and touched their children.

"My dearest brothers and sisters, I have been sent by Abba, by Yahweh, by your heavenly Father, to tell you that that moment of joy and love that flooded your hearts and your entire being as you gave birth to your child, that is the kind of love Abba has for you, not just for a moment, not just for a while, but for all eternity, and that love is incomparable and unceasing. We were all once babes in our mother's arms, loved with an indescribable love. Remember that always. Can a mother ever not love the child of her womb? Can a mother ever forsake the child of her womb, but even if she did, I, Adonai says, will never abandon you. Adonai's love for you is like that of all the mothers of the world combined and that moment of love poured out at our birth, such is that love of Adonai for you, and that love is not for a while and conditional on what you do or become, that love of Adonai for you is unconditional, boundless and eternal."

And Yeshua paused once more. He wanted his message to sink in. He wanted his listeners to realise the depth of his Father's love for them, and his love for them.

"My dear brothers and sisters, you all suffer much, in your bodies and in your souls. Some of you have endured the loss of a baby that has died in your womb, a child you have miscarried, or a child that has died young. You mourn that loss; your sorrow and your grief are indescribable. Your Father in heaven, Abba, wants you to know that he grieves with you. Death and suffering are simply part of the natural cause of the cycle of life, and is not caused by anything that you have done or might have done. Your grief, your losses are not the result of sin, they simply are. What Moses wrote in his first book about the creation of the world and how Abba created us, men and women, he used a beautiful story, a parable to simply try to make us understand that Yahweh is the all-powerful, who created all that there is, who brought us into the world. I know suffering and death, is a mystery to us all. But the Father has sent me to share your suffering and your losses; he has sent me to suffer and to die, to let you know just how much he wants to let you share in his life and his love.

"I will suffer, I will die. But through all of the vicissitudes of life, know that God our Father is close to sustaining you, to give you the strength to bear whatever comes your way. But I have been sent not only to suffer and to die and to show you how to suffer and to die, but I have been sent to live among you, to be with you in all you endure. I have come to show you life, to show you how to live your lives, to be close to you, to imprint in your minds and hearts how close Abba is to you and how dear you are to him and how much he loves you. I have come to give you life and life to the full. I have come to give you the love of Abba, for Abba our God is love."

Yeshua stopped again. He knew what he was saying were profound truths, and words they might not have heard before, or not often enough. He allowed time for those listening to him to ponder and digest what they had heard. Then he continued:

"My dearest brothers and sisters, mothers, fathers, single people, children, we are all God's children, and he loves us with a boundless and unconditional love. Abba Adonai is love, and who abides in love, abides in Adonai Abba, and Adonai abides in him and her. None of you have seen Adonai, the one and only true God, but if you live a life of love, then you indeed abide in God and God abides in you. And if God is love and loves you with certainty so too you are called to love one another. My dearest friends know that I who am sent by God, I love you too. And if we are so loved, then let us love one another.

"Let us live every day in love with God and in love with one another. And let us show our love for God and for one another in the way we treat each other, the way we greet each other, the way we comfort each other. Let us go about not with dreary faces and consumed with our own needs and desires but let us reach out to others in love, in whatever way we can, with a kind word, a listening ear, a hug, a smile, a greeting, a visit, just with our loving presence. Every day in every way let us spread love, peace and joy into all of God's creation, to all God's creatures, to all with whom we come into contact. May God bless you all."

With those words, Yeshua ended his talk. He sat down next to Zimri in the sanctuary in silence. Yeshua whispered to Zimri, "Before you continue, could you please let us remain in silence for a while?" For a while, the silence allowed the words that Yeshua uttered to sink deep into their souls, into their hearts. And when Yeshua thought the time of silence was enough, he nodded to Zimri. Zimri then led the people in prayer for the rest of the service. Afterwards, Zimri and Yeshua stood outside the synagogue and people came to meet and speak with Yeshua. After most of the people had left, a young boy, a teenager, was brought to Yeshua by his mother.

"Yeshua, my boy is tormented by fits, he goes into convulsions and sometimes foams from the mouth, it is happening more and more often and more severe. Doctors can do nothing for him, and many tell me he is possessed of an evil spirit."

Yeshua looked at the mother and saw the sadness and anguish on her face. And then he looked at the boy, a teenager. "What is your name, son?" Yeshua asked.

"My name is Jonathan," the boy answered.

"Please Yeshua, can you cure my son, can you release him of this evil spirit?" his mother, Josephine, pleaded.

"My dear Josephine and Jonathan, my heart aches that you had to suffer so much for so long. What would you like me to do for you, Jonathan?" Yeshua asked.

A number of the people who were still around now gathered around Yeshua and the boy.

"Yeshua, please take away my sickness and rid me of this evil spirit," Jonathan pleaded.

Yeshua's heart went out to the boy and his mother; he felt their pain and their misery. "Dear Jonathan and Josephine, you have suffered much, and my heart hurts to know this. But you are not possessed of an evil spirit, and your illness is not a curse or a result of your sins. It is an illness; it is part of our human condition. Jonathan, do you believe I can cure you?" Yeshua asked.

Yeshua was now in a whole different place, similar to when he was at Cana and responded to his mother's request. Somehow, he felt a power rise within him. A certainty he was only feeling for a second time, a power he could not fully comprehend, he just felt it within. He felt himself being filled with the Spirit and the power from on high. He had already worked his first miracle, he had revealed his power as the Son of God, he had revealed his divinity and there was no going back. And now here before him are these two people, a mother and her son, who have suffered much and his heart went out to them. He looked at Jonathan with love in his heart and then laid his hand on Jonathan's head and said, "Jonathan, your faith has cured you. Go in peace."

Josephine at that moment just knew, she just knew in her heart that her son was cured. "Thank you, Yeshua, thank you, Yeshua," she cried out. Immediately, Jonathan felt something stir within his body. It was something he had never felt before in his life. It wasn't painful, in fact quite pleasant, and he smiled at Yeshua, and at his mother, who was beaming. They then went home.

Yeshua remained in the village for the next week. And he preached in the synagogue every day. At the end of the week, at the end of his preaching, Josephine, with Jonathan beside her, stands up in the synagogue and cries out, in a loud voice, "Praise the Lord, praise to you, Yeshua, you are indeed the Promised One, you have come to save us. You have cured Jonathan, for he no longer has any more fits, he is cured."

The people responded in spontaneous applause and praising God for sending his Promised One to them. This was revealed on the last day that Yeshua was in that village and the word spread throughout the village. People then flocked to Yeshua, bringing their sick, their maimed, their incapacitated, and Yeshua cured them all. There was so much rejoicing and the people pleaded with Yeshua to stay with them, and they showered him with gifts, the little they had, but Yeshua told them to keep everything for themselves. So overwhelming were their pleas that he stayed one more day and then left. He told them that there were others who needed to hear the Good News. Reluctantly they let Yeshua go. The whole village saw him leave.

Yeshua and Miriam left that day. But the news spread like wildfire beyond that village. Yeshua and Miriam continued their journey towards the town of Ziddim, but again they went off the beaten track and found another village, and again discovered that many of the villagers were the outcasts of society, the homeless, the poor, the sick, the maimed, those with disabilities and incapacitated. They were led to believe that it was because of their sins that this plight had befallen them. And because of their illnesses and their disabilities they had not been able to work, so they lost their employment and their homes, and some of them their farms, and their land. With their inability to work and not earn an income, they still had to pay their taxes and tariffs, and their land and possessions, even their homes were taken from them. Here they lived in poverty eking out a living off the land. Some of the members of some of the families were able to go to the towns and find work as day labourers. Many went into the towns to beg for a living.

Yeshua remained in that village for another week. Word had reached the people and one of the leaders of the people, Jehu, asked Yeshua to preach to them. They gathered in an open space, as they had no synagogue and no community hall. The word had spread about Yeshua and that he was to address the people in their open gathering place, and everyone was there, men, women and children. There was a buzz in the air. They felt so important, that such a person would deign to visit them. They were also regarded as unclean because of their infirmities, and this man, a devout Jew would know that he would as a result of his contact with them, make himself unclean. But he did not seem to think about this, or even mention this. It did not matter to him. He just seemed so pleased to be here with them. And they discovered that his mother was with him as well.

Yeshua stood on a slightly raised piece of ground and began to speak. "My dear friends, I come to bring you Good News, of God's love for you." Yeshua then went on to repeat what he had said in the previous village. Yeshua continued, "I know there is a lot of bitterness in your hearts, and maybe even hatred because of how you have been treated, and discarded by the rest of humanity. And some of you may even have turned away from God, and blamed him for your plight. You, my dear brothers and sisters, can justifiably feel anger at the injustice you have endured. It is not right that you have been discarded, that your properties have been taken away from you, and that you are ostracised because of your maladies. It is not right; it is not just. And we all need to stand up and do all in our power to right what is unjust, what is not right and decent and humane.

"But at the same time, you have heard how it was said in ancient times, 'You shall not murder' and 'whoever murders shall be liable to judgement.' But I say to you, if you are angry with a brother or sister, or if you insult a brother or sister, or if you call him a fool, you are no better than him and will be judged accordingly. No, I say to you, work for justice, but do not stoop to the level of those who inflict injustices on you in the first place, that will make you no better than them."

As he usually did, Yeshua paused and allowed some time for his words to penetrate in the minds and hearts of his listeners. He knew what he was saying was hard for his listeners to accept. But he continued.

"My dear friends, I bring you the Good News of our heavenly father, of God's love, salvation and redemption. You have heard that it was said, 'an eye for an eye, and a tooth for a tooth. But I say to you, do not resist an evildoer. If anyone strikes you on the right cheek, turn the other also, and if anyone wants to sue you and take your coat, give your cloak as well, and if anyone forces you to go one mile, go also the second mile. Give to everyone who begs from you, and do not refuse anyone who wants to borrow from you."

The crowd started murmuring, these were not words that they wanted to hear or that they expected from this Yeshua they had heard so much about. Is he really the Chosen One, the Messiah who has come to set us free from our misery and the wrath and cruelty and domination of Rome? He is telling us to kowtow to those who persecute us. These were sentiments that they whispered to each other.

"Yeshua, your words are hard to understand and accept," Jehu said on behalf of all those present.

"Yes, they are, Jehu, especially for you and all of you present, who have suffered so much and continue to suffer, but bitterness will not lessen your suffering, it will only increase it a hundredfold. You have heard that it was said, 'You shall love your neighbour and hate your enemy.' But I say to you, love your enemies and pray for those who persecute you, so that you may be children of your Father in heaven, for he makes his sun rise on the evil and the good, and sends rain on the righteous and the unrighteous. For if you love those who love you, what reward do you have? Do not even tax-collectors do the same? And if you greet only your brothers and sisters, do not even the Gentiles do the same? You must rise above all bitterness, anger and desire for revenge, for that will destroy your soul. Your heavenly Father knows what you suffer at the hands of those who persecute you and vengeance is for the Lord, not for you, not for us. You are better than that, your heavenly Father, knows all you have suffered and continue to suffer, he loves you, he wants you to be perfect, as he is perfect."

"Yeshua, your words are challenging, *and* discouraging. How can we rise to those heights of perfection you preach, we are mere mortals, not gods," a person from the crowd yelled out.

"You speak right, my friend. These are indeed a challenge for us all. Bitterness, revenge, anger, and hatred kill the soul, and bring even more suffering to oneself and to others. For hatred spreads hatred. Without the grace of our heavenly Father, it is not possible, but with Him all is possible. Let us now pause for a moment and pray for the strength to bear only love in our hearts for all on this earth, all living creatures for we are all interrelated and interdependent."

Yeshua then allowed time for silent prayer. After some time, he began a prayer he now began to pray whenever he was with people. "Our Father, who art in heaven, hallowed be your Name. Your kingdom come; your will be done in heaven as it is done on earth. Give us this day our daily bread, and forgive us our sins, as we forgive those who hurt us, persecute us and cause us all kinds of sufferings. And in time of temptation, give us the strength we need to be strong, and to have only love, and nothing but love in our hearts for all. Amen."

The crowd now calmed down from the uneasiness they were feeling when Yeshua was speaking and they began to see the wisdom in his words. For so long they have carried bitterness and desire for revenge in their hearts, and it has brought them no solace. Yeshua was asking them to rise above all of that. In a way Yeshua was setting them free.

Yeshua continued to mingle with the people after his talk. They had questions for him. They wanted to know about what happened in the River Jordan, when he was baptised by Johanan, for they too had heard all about it. And they wanted to know about all that happened at Cana at the wedding, and also at the neighbouring village, for some of them had followed Yeshua and had spread the word.

A while after the gathering, some went away and returned with their sick and incapacitated, wanting Yeshua to heal them. Yeshua laid his hands on them all and they were healed, and there was much joy and praise to Yahweh, and the news of what happened spread throughout the village and beyond. People who after their encounter with Yeshua, left on their search for some day labour, spoke of this Yeshua, the carpenter from Nazareth, and all were wondering, is he the Promised One, the Prophet, the Messiah who is come to save us, to set us free? The expectation filled all with great hope and promise, and the news of Yeshua spread far and wide.

Yeshua and Miriam were well looked after. And they were grateful. The people, who were so poor, brought gifts. And they would not allow Yeshua to decline their offers. Yeshua and Miriam took what they found they needed for their journey onwards, and gave the rest to Jehu to quietly make the best use of them.

Yeshua and Miriam and Ben were on their way. Miriam was glad that Yeshua insisted they bring Ben along, for Miriam was beginning to feel the toll and now enjoyed being carried by their donkey. And he was well looked after and spoilt by the villagers.

Yeshua's next stop was the town of Ziddim itself. He told Miriam about the friends he had made on his trip so long ago, ten years ago, in fact. "I wonder if they are still in Ziddim, shall we go and visit them, Immah?" Yeshua asked. "I am a bit overawed by all the adulation I have been subjected to. I find it rather burdensome and it simply drains me, Immah, when I heal those who suffer, it is as if all my strength is being drained from me. There is so much suffering and I cannot heal them all."

"Yeshua, you will heal those who need it and those who have faith. The healing is part of Yahweh's plan to make you known, and to let people know that you are his Son, who has come into this world as its Saviour. Trust in your heavenly Father, Yeshua. And yes, it would be a good idea for you to catch up with your friends in Ziddim."

As Yeshua and Miriam came near to the home of David and his wife Phoebe, they met one of the sons, Judah, who was attending to the cattle in the field. Yeshua and Miriam approached. At first Judah did not recognise Yeshua, as Yeshua's beard was now longer than when they met, ten years ago.

"Yeshua, the carpenter from Nazareth, my word, you look different," Judah said.

"And you look the same, haven't aged a bit," Yeshua said with a smile. "And this is my mother, Miriam," Yeshua added.

"I am pleased to meet you, Miriam. You are lucky, Mother and both the girls and their children are at home, but Father and Yosef are in the town on business. Rachel and Lydia are both married and live close by, and today is the day they usually visit mother. Do go, I will join you later, they will be so pleased to see you Yeshua," David said, and then went about his work.

Phoebe and her two daughters, Rachel and Lydia, were overwhelmed with joy to meet Yeshua. They each had two young children who were playing out in the backyard. Phoebe, Rachel and Lydia too had heard all about Yeshua, his reputation was now all over Galilee, and everyone knew about the River Jordan and Cana, and in the villages. Anything unusual, any news, was passed on from mouth to mouth. It was the only way people knew what was happening. And this news about this man Yeshua was unusual, spectacular. His words and his deeds now became The News, and people were speaking about it all over the land.

Yeshua was hoping they would not have heard, so he could have some quiet time and just unwind with some friends, but it seemed that was not to be. Phoebe and the girls fussed all over them.

Yeshua introduced Miriam and told them that they had met Judah on the way.

"David and Yosef will be so pleased to see you again, Yeshua, it has been such a long time," Phoebe said.

"It has, ten years in fact. And the time has gone by so quickly. Tell me all about the family, how have things gone for you, what has happened in your lives," Yeshua asked.

"Ah Yeshua, so much, but first things first, tell us about yourself while we get you and Miriam some refreshments," Phoebe said, as she busied herself getting some snacks and warm drinks for Yeshua and Miriam.

"Our whole family, when we heard about you, Yeshua, and all the signs and miracles that were associated with you, we were amazed and so proud that we had met you, Yeshua, in person, and could claim you as a friend."

Yeshua and Miriam then proceeded to tell them about the wedding at Cana. "After the wedding, we stayed for three days and then Yeshua had finally decided to abandon me, and leave home and settle in Capernaum," Miriam said, tongue in cheek.

"Oh, and she was so pleased to get rid of me, and live in peace for a change," Yeshua said playfully.

"I can see you like to tease each other," Rachel said.

"Mother is the one who does the teasing, Rachel, and I am the one who has to bear the brunt," Yeshua said, smiling.

Yeshua and Miriam fitted in so well with the family, and it wasn't long when they felt so much at home. When David and the two sons, Judah and Yosef, finally arrived, there was much jubilation and hugging.

Dinner was served and they all sat around a large table, and the conversation flowed, all sharing about their lives over the past ten years. The boys were still single, too much engrossed in their businesses. But Rachel and Lydia were both happily married, which pleased Yeshua. They invited Yeshua to come to meet their husbands, and Yeshua agreed.

Chapter Thirty-Six
The Itinerant Preacher and Miracle Worker

The next day, David took Yeshua to the residence of Rabbi Joram, who was extremely pleased to meet Yeshua and felt thrilled at the prospect of Yeshua preaching to the people on the Sabbath, in a couple of days' time. Joram had heard all about Yeshua, as had everyone else. Yeshua was the talk of the town. Word had spread from Cana, and from all the villages that Yeshua had visited. And people, who had met and witnessed Yeshua's baptism in the River Jordan, also spread the news about Yeshua. Yeshua became renowned as a miracle worker, the likes of whom, they have never encountered before. And the people from the villages where Yeshua spoke spread the word about him as well.

When the people of Ziddim heard that Yeshua was in their town and staying with David and Phoebe, the excitement was contagious and spread to families and friends outside of Ziddim. People from elsewhere made their way to Ziddim to see and listen to this Yeshua, this great prophet and miracle worker. Some brought their sick family and friends with them, hoping for a cure.

Yeshua was glad he had a day by himself and also to prepare his talk for the Sabbath. He knew he could repeat what he had already said at the villages he went, but he had already been here in Ziddim, and knew some of its residents, had a feel for the community, and wanted to speak to them in response to what was on their minds and in their hearts. Several people from out of town passed through Ziddim, on their way to Cana or Magdala on the coast of the Sea of Galilee, but many had not met Yeshua in person, and it was ten years ago since he was last in Ziddim, so Yeshua knew he would not be recognised by the locals, even though they would recognise him as a visitor and not from the town. So, Yeshua tried to be as inconspicuous as he could as he walked around the town, just observing the people going about their business. But he became aware of the buzz around the town, and the talk about him.

Yeshua decided to walk into the bushland on the edge of the town, and spend time by himself. Miriam had remained with Phoebe for the day. Yeshua walked among the trees and nature, something he loved doing. The birds greeted him and he stopped to greet them and to watch them feeding on the grass, as he was accustomed. As he walked through the forest watching the birds, he saw a large tree that had been uprooted and lying on its side, most likely the result of a storm. Yeshua always stopped at these dead trees, as if mourning with them. He felt for the dead tree, but he saw, as always, how the dead tree was being eaten by termites, providing nourishment for them, and all the tiny creatures of the forest, that were foraging, feeding and finding shelter in the tree. He had seen fallen trees before in the forests and he always stopped to simply look at the way it took on a new life, as it became a haven and a food fest for little creatures of the forest.

Yeshua stopped and prayed, "Dear Brother Tree, in your life, you gave life, and shade, and beauty to so many, and now even in your death, you continue to give life and shelter to so many. I mourn your death, and I rejoice in what you continue to do, you came from dust and eventually to dust you will return," Yeshua thought of the image of the birds and the trees and the luxuriant nature all around him, and it gave him some inspiration for what he was going to say to the people of Ziddim.

Sabbath came, and the synagogue was packed to the rafters. In the front, there were a few people on stretches and in the assembly some with crutches. Yeshua could see that many came hoping to be healed. Yeshua was aware of the seating arrangements, the men folk on the right and the women on the left. Yeshua had liked how in some of the villages where he went, among the destitute, they did not separate by gender, people sat where they wanted. And Yeshua thought that is how it should be, all are equal before Yahweh.

Yeshua was introduced by Rabbi Joram, and a hush filled the packed synagogue. "My dear brothers and sisters, adults and children, I thank you for your friendship and your hospitality. I was a stranger here once, ten years ago, and you took me in, and took me to your hearts, and I thank you. David and Phoebe, and your children, Judah, Yosef, Rachel and Lydia, you gave me a place to stay and accepted me and my mother and gave us a place to stay and we became part of your family."

Yeshua rested his gaze on David and the family, and their faces lit up and glowed with appreciation and pride.

"I found in all of you people, good hearts and a good nature. Yesterday, I walked about your town as you went about your daily grind. Some of you were so intense, with worried looks on your faces, you were all going about your business, and I walked through your marketplace and witnessed the chatter and the joy of many, the smiles, the conversation, and the delight friends were having in simply being in the presence of each other. And children, I saw you enjoying your games and being with your friends. And all of you adults, I saw many of you greeting each other with a smile on your face, but I also saw several of you in your alone moments with a frown on your faces and worried looks, some as if the whole world was on your shoulders. And unfortunately, I did also witness some of you being rude and rough to each other and treating each other unkindly.

"My dear brothers and sisters, we are all brothers and sisters, with one father, Abba, our heavenly father. I am his son and he has sent me to bring you the Good News of his love and salvation for you all. And I now say to you, come to your heavenly father, and come to me, whom my father has sent and learn from me for I am gentle and humble of heart and you will find rest for your souls. Come to your father, and come to me whom he has sent, you who are heavily burdened and you will find peace in your hearts and rest for your troubled souls. Take your burdens, the yoke that you bear on your shoulder and I will give you rest and peace in your heart. Every moment of every day, your father is with you, beholds you and loves you, and wants you, and wants you to know of his love and peace, and his care for you.

"Yesterday I walked through your bushland, the forest teeming with such life. And I watched the birds of the air, down on the grass feeding, and I said to myself, as I say to you, look at the birds of the field, they do not grow or reap or gather into barns, yet your heavenly father feeds them, are you not more precious than they are. And I saw so many beautiful trees and plants and flowers and some lilies, radiantly white, and I said to myself, as I say to you, look at the lilies in the field, how beautifully your heavenly father adorns them, clothes them, and if he does so for the lilies of the field, that are here today and gone tomorrow, how much more will he adorn you and care for you. You are all lilies in the field, and your beauty is forever.

"Of course, our natural beauty may fade as we age," Yeshua said with a smile. "Some of us our God has endowed with great outward beauty, and some of us are not so pretty, and not endowed with outward beauty. We may not all be beautiful lilies in the field, outwardly, but inwardly, we are all beautiful beyond compare, our souls, our spirits are beautiful in the eyes of God. In our spirits, within us, we are all indeed beautiful. And true beauty is within. If God adorns the lilies of the field with such beauty—lilies that are here today and gone tomorrow—how much more will he adorn and sustain your inner beauty? And my friends, as I look at you all, I see that inner glow, that beauty that radiates from within you. And the way you let others see that beauty is by the love and care that you have for each other."

Yeshua then shared of what he saw of the trees in the forest and on the open spaces and the fruit-bearing trees on the farms and around people's places. "When I walked through your town, I saw several fruit-bearing trees and helped myself from a huge fig tree, the branches of which reached out onto the road, and I picked a fig, my favourite fruit, as I am sure all those passing by must do the same. I thank whoever's fig tree that is. It has abundant fruit and you must really care for it."

Several people turned and looked in the direction of a man sitting at the back of the synagogue, who was smiling, and Yeshua gathered that he must be the owner of the tree.

Yeshua continued, "A tree is known and admired and plucked for its fruit, a tree is known by its fruit, like that fig tree. It is admired and loved for its fruit. When I was a young boy, my friends and I would often sneak into a neighbour's place and climb into his fig tree and have a feast. We loved that tree, its look, its smell, and its nourishing and delicious fruit. A tree is known by its fruit. You have it in your power to plant, care, and nurture and make a good tree or you can through ignorance, neglect, make a bad tree; for a tree is known by its fruit.

"A person, who is evil, cannot speak of good things, and cannot do good things, for out of the abundance of the heart, the mouth speaks, and actions flow. The good person brings good things out of a good treasure, and the evil person brings evil things out of an evil treasure. And I tell you, that on the day of judgement, you will have to give account for every careless word you utter, and deed you perform, for by your words and deeds you will be justified and by your words and deeds you will be condemned."

Yeshua could sense the mood of the people, their reaction to what he was saying, and he continued, "I can see what you are thinking as I speak to you about Judgement Day. We will be judged by our fruits. And I say to you do not be afraid. Your heavenly Father does not want to overburden you or make you miserable, thinking of Judgement Day, and worrying and fearing judgement by a just God. Be assured, while I tell you, you must give account of every evil word and deed, you must also give account and God will take account, of all your good deeds. Adonai already knows of all the good words you have uttered, and all the good deeds you have done.

"So do not fret, do not worry, if you have said evil or hurtful words, or entertained evil of sinful desires or perpetrated them, know you have a compassionate and loving and forgiving Father. He also takes account of all the good you have done that by far outweighs the bad."

Yeshua continued, as he saw the people were still with him. "But our heavenly father is also a just judge, I hear you say." Yeshua was aware of just how focused people were on their sinfulness and how ultra-aware of Judgement Day and the justice of God, the Judge. He sought to put them at ease.

"My dear friends, do not fear Judgement Day. Do not fear God, the just judge. He is a truly a just God and at the same time an understanding and merciful judge. For when he judges you he metes out true justice, he does not only look at the times, the occasions when you sinned in word and deed, as earthly judges do, he looks at your entire life, and all the times you uttered good words and did good deeds, the good you have done and continue to do by far outweigh the evil that you do, and the evil does not live on after you, it is the good that does, and that outweighs the bad.

"Take heart, the Father does not take for granted all the good you do, so neither should you. You have twenty-four hours in the day and most of those hours, and minutes you utter good words and perform good deeds, words and deeds of love and kindness, care and sacrifice for those near and dear to you, and to others in the community. Mothers and fathers, how much time a day do you spend in work, in honest labour, inside and outside your home. Many of you toil from sunrise to way beyond sunset, to earn a living, to feed and house your family, while many toil all day in the home in loving care for the family. You mind your sheep and goats and work in your farms and vineyards, and some of you toil all day under the hot summer sun and cold winter, to feed your family, to serve your community.

"All this is the good you do and take for granted. Adonai does not take it for granted. He sees you toiling under the hot sun and winter's chill. Your work is a prayer, a sacrifice pleasing to him. He sees and he blesses. So, I see, and I bless you. You are good people and you live good lives and you work hard and suffer much and you all have such love in your hearts for one another. And you have shown such love for me, and I am most grateful. What you do for me and for one another is what the Lord God sees and what pleases him. On the occasions when we do fall into sin, our God is there, to pick us up, simply turn to him, with sorrow in your heart, repent and he forgives you. Our God is a merciful and forgiving God. Let us now have a few minutes of silence to reflect together on what we have heard."

The synagogue was quiet, a cough here and there, a slight shuffle of feet, but silence. Even the babies and young children were silent. Yeshua too sat in silence, in communion with Abba. After a while, he prayed to the Holy Spirit to continue to give him the words to say. He then continued to speak.

"My dear friends, dear children, our God is a loving father, a forgiving father, a merciful father, who loves you all with an indescribable love. Let me tell you a story to illustrate his great love for you. There was a man and a woman who had two sons. The younger son was the more adventurous of the two, the older one was more focused on the family business and toiled in the fields all day. One day the younger son approached his father and spoke, 'Father, give me my share of the property, my inheritance, for I want to go and explore what is out there'."

Yeshua could see the shock on the faces of his listeners. This was something unheard of. For a son to ask his father for his inheritance, while the father was still alive, was tantamount to saying 'Father, I want you dead.' Yeshua noticed some fathers gasp, holding their hands over their mouths.

"The father asked, 'You sure you want to do that, son?'

"'Yes, I am sure,' the son replied.

"The mother pleaded with her son not to leave, but she could not convince her son to stay. So, the father gave his son, all that was to be his. And the son, rich with the money given to him as part of his inheritance, went and quickly sold his property as well, and gathered up all he had, and went on his way. He travelled to a distant country in the northern area of Phoenicia and lived as if there was no tomorrow. Soon he squandered all his money on gambling, extravagant and immoral ways of living.

"When he had spent everything, a severe famine took over all of the country where he was staying. He was now living in extreme poverty, begging for food. He lost all he possessed, and only had the clothes on his back, that were now reduced to rags. So, he hired himself out to one of the citizens of that country, who sent him to his fields to feed the pigs. On the day he started working, feeding the pigs, he was so hungry he was tempted to eat the pods that the pigs were eating for no one gave him anything to eat. And then he came to his senses and said to himself, 'How many of my father's hired hands have bread enough and to spare, and here I am dying of hunger. I will leave this place and go back to my father.' And when he had finished his day's work and paid his pittance of a wage, he began his long walk home."

Yeshua let his eyes wander across the synagogue and let them rest on his listeners, he did this to gauge if they were with him, or switching off. He could see and sense that they were fully engaged and interested to hear how this story was going to pan out. Yeshua knew they could identify with what he was telling them, they knew such people as that young son, and rich farmers who exploited the poor and the vulnerable and made them do all the degrading work and paid them a pittance.

Yeshua continued, "When he arrived at the town where his father and mother and brother lived, he was filled with trepidation. And he was tired and hungry and depressed. As he walked through the town, people did not even recognise him, and regarded him as a beggar, because he was dirty, barefooted and dressed in rags. However, one of his friends recognised him. 'Please do me a favour,' he asks his friend. 'Go to my father and tell him that you met me, and that I would like to come home. And tell my father, if he will have me back, to please give me a sign, place a white cloth on the front of the roof where I can see it.'

"The friend agreed. Later on, as the son was walking towards his father's house, he was rehearsing what he would say to his father, 'Father, I have sinned against heaven and before you; I am no longer worthy to be called your son; treat me like one of your hired hands.'

"After giving his friend enough time to speak with his father, the young son began his walk up the hill to his father's house. He felt miserable. He was penniless, and feeling lost and depressed, if his father would not take him back what would he do. He was downcast, not daring to look up towards the house, in case he did not see a white cloth on the roof. But he had to face the truth. Slowly, he lifted his eyes and prayed that his father would let him come home and work as his hireling.

"As the vision of his father's house came into view, he was mesmerised and stopped in his tracks, and tears began to well up in his eyes and came streaming down his cheeks. For not only did he see a single white cloth on the front roof but the entire roof and front of the house was covered and draped with white sheets. He gasped, fell on his knees in the dirt, and wept like a child.

"The father, who with the mother took turns every day to watch and pray and hope to see their son return, was overjoyed with the news. And as soon as the father and mother saw their son far off down the hill, they were filled with compassion and love and relief. The father caught hold of his robe and ran down the hill. When he arrived at his son, still on his knees, he lifted him to his feet, and hugged him.

"Then the son said to him, 'Father, I have sinned against heaven and before you, I am no longer worthy to be called your son.'

"But the father took him by the hand and led him home, where his mother welcomed him home with open arms and tears running down her cheeks. The father then said to his servants, 'Quickly bring out a robe—the best one—and put it on him; put a ring on his finger and sandals on his feet. And go get the fatted calf and kill it, and prepare a feast and let us eat and celebrate; for this son of mine was dead and is alive again, he was lost and is found.' And they began to celebrate."

Yeshua stopped. There was another part to this story, there was another son, but he wanted the people to concentrate on the father and the compassion he shows for his son. Yeshua wanted the people to focus on the love and compassion and forgiveness of the father. So, he sat down and asked for silence, once again, and time to reflect on this prodigal son and his loving, forgiving and compassionate father.

After some time, while everyone in the whole synagogue was wrapped in stillness and silence and reflecting on this story, which they had never heard before, they were left in wonder. Never before had any of their rabbis told stories like this, their stories were all of Moses, and David, and the Prophets and the kings, wonderful stories indeed, but this story of Yeshua was not in their Scriptures, and they were fascinated and now wanting to hear more.

"My dear brothers and sisters, I tell you this story to instil in your minds and hearts how much our heavenly Father loves you, and how much compassion he has, and no matter how badly and for how long you have sinned, he waits for you to come home. See the Father, running down the hill, see God our Father run, impatient to see you, to hold you, to love you. Note that the Father is not interested to listen to what his son has done, to hear of his sins. He is not judging his son in the least, he is not interested in the sins he has committed, he is just so happy to have his son home, and he can see by his son's actions and expressions that he is sorry, and that is all that matters. All that matters is that his son who was dead is now alive, who was lost is now found. And notice his great joy, and he wants the whole world to celebrate. My friends, there is more joy in heaven over one sinner that repents than a multitude of others who remain faithful… I have said enough for now. Joram will now lead you in the rest of the service."

When the service ended and Yeshua stepped out of the synagogue and into the front courtyard, people crowded around him and wanted to hear more. But Joram intercepted and told the people that Yeshua would preach again, as he would be staying for the next week. The people were thrilled and now some of those who had afflictions and their carers came forward and pleaded with Yeshua to heal them. There were among the afflicted, a cripple, a blind man and a mute woman and several who had no visible malady, but Yeshua laid his hands on all who approached him, and they were healed. And everyone was amazed and wondered about this Yeshua. No one had ever done such deeds, he makes the blind see, the deaf hear, the mute speak and the lame walk. And never before has anyone spoke like this man, he speaks with authority, and he speaks not so much of the stern and judging God, they were accustomed to hearing about, but a God of boundless and incomprehensible love and compassion.

Yeshua and Miriam stayed in Ziddim for another week, and Yeshua preached many sermons and healed many, for many came from far and wide to listen to him and to be healed of their afflictions. The whole of Ziddim and beyond were abuzz with news of Yeshua and his reputation soared. Yeshua and Miriam stayed another week but then decided it was time to continue on their journey to Capernaum. But the next stop on their way was Magdala, on the coast of the Sea of Galilee.

Chapter Thirty-Seven
Magdala

"Immah, I have some good friends in Magdala as well. Remember I told you about them, they befriended me when I took that hike around the Sea of Galilee ten years ago. Shall we call on them first, hopefully they can give us lodgings or suggest some for us," Yeshua said.

"Sounds good, Yeshua, it seems that trip of yours around the Sea of Galilee was meant to happen and prepare you for the work you are doing. Yeshua, I always knew you were destined for greatness. The day I conceived you, in such an extraordinary and miraculous way, I knew you would be different, different to any other man who ever lived. After the creation of Adam and Eve out of the dust of earth with the breath of Yahweh, no one has been conceived and born in the manner you were. Listening to you speak, and seeing all the wonderful deeds you are doing, and the power you have to heal people, just leaves me breathless. I am so overwhelmed.

"With time, I came to forget or rather I put aside the circumstances of your birth and wanted you to be just like all other children, and the child of Yosef and me. But now it is all coming back. I am now resigned to who you really are, that you are not only here to be my child but to be much, much more."

"Immah, please don't go awry on me now. I need you to treat me as you always have. I am your son. Yes, I know now that I am the Son of Yahweh too, I am his incarnation on this earth, and as your son I too am overwhelmed with what is happening to me, and I too am amazed by the works that I am doing in the name of the Father. But mother, please continue to treat me as you always have, I need to remain grounded."

"Okay Yeshua. I will. I need to, for me too to remain with my feet on the ground. I still am so moved by what I am witnessing. You are destined for greater things Yeshua. At Cana, when they ran out of wine, it was as if a voice out of nowhere spoke to me and told me to approach you and tell you. But for now, let's just stop and have something to eat, I am hungry," Miriam said with a smile.

"Now that's more like it, Immah. I forgot to eat," Yeshua said, returning the smile.

They stopped on the side of the road, near some trees and sat down on the grass and ate what the people of Ziddim had given them. After the food and the drink, they just sat there for a while, breathing in the freshness of the air and the green surroundings.

"Let us now get up and go, or I will simply sit here in this peaceful place, fall asleep and never wake up," Yeshua said laughing.

"Yes, it is peaceful here, but duty waits," Miriam replied.

Yeshua and Miriam proceeded and went straight to the home of his friends, Joshua and Emzara and their children. Yeshua noticed several more houses on the large property owned by Joshua and Emzara. Outside of one of the properties, Yeshua saw a woman, about his age; she was hanging out the washing. Yeshua could not be sure because of the distance, so he walked towards her, and then it became clear, it was Ruth.

"Ruth, Shalom, how are you, it is so good to see you."

For a moment, Ruth did not recognise Yeshua, but then she did, he had been on her mind for a while now, for people all over Magdala had been talking about Yeshua and the signs that accompanied him. "Yeshua, oh, it is so good to see you." She leapt forward and embraced him. "Do come in. I have my mother with me; she and father still live in the main house on top of the hill. But she is here now with me, inside. Do come in."

"Yes, I would love to meet her," Yeshua said. "And Ruth, this is my mother, Miriam."

"I am so pleased to meet you, Miriam, do come in. I am married now, Yeshua, to a lovely man, and we have a son, we have called him Yosef, after your father. When we were to name him, I remembered how you cried in our arms when you spoke of your father Yosef, so that's what we named him."

"Oh Ruth, I am so happy for you, and your husband and Yosef, and my father Yosef is honoured," Yeshua said.

Miriam was also so touched when she heard this. A tear rolled down her cheek. They then all entered the house.

"Isaac, my husband will be thrilled to meet you Yeshua, he was excited when we told him that we had already met and are good friends, and that you stayed with us. You know, Yeshua, you are like a celebrity here in Magdala, everyone is talking about you, your preaching and the miracles you perform and the people you heal. Is this all true, Yeshua?"

"Ruth, I am your friend, Yeshua, the carpenter from Nazareth. For now, can I just be that?" Yeshua said.

"I will go and fetch mother, she is out back, and she will be so delighted to meet you." Ruth disappeared then returned with her mother, and her son, Yosef.

As they approached, Yeshua and Miriam were delighted to see Ruth with her son, whose hand she held; he looked to be about six years of age.

Miriam had been quiet all this time, just taking in these good friends of her son, but now she spoke, "Ruth, I am so pleased to meet you, Yeshua has told me all about you and the family, and this must be Yosef, so pleased to meet you, Yosef," Miriam said, as she looked at a shy little boy. And they all greeted Ruth's mother, Emzara, who was so pleased to see Yeshua again and also to meet his mother, Miriam.

They went and sat outside, and Ruth offered refreshments but both Yeshua and Miriam declined as they had just eaten, but were pleased to have some water.

"So, tell us about yourself, Ruth, I can see you are happily married, with a charming son, Yosef." Yeshua looked at Yosef and smiled. Yosef was now more at ease and smiled back.

"Well, as you can see, Jacob and I have moved into our own place, which Jacob built with the help of father and our brothers. The same was done for Orpah and her husband as well, she lives next door with her husband, and she has two children, a boy and a girl, she will be ecstatic to meet you. I'll go and fetch her."

Ruth left and Yosef followed her, and they soon returned with an ecstatic Orpah and her two children, the girl was the older of the two, and the son was about Yosef's age. Orpah greeted Yeshua with open arms and they hugged.

"This is my mother, Miriam," Yeshua introduced his mother.

"Miriam, I am so pleased to meet you and your son, you have a wonderful son and we have heard such amazing things about him," Orpah said, she was bubbling over with excitement.

"And who are these handsome children?" Miriam asked.

"This is Isaac and his sister, Miriam," Orpah said.

"I am so pleased to meet you, Isaac and Miriam," Miriam said, "and I am delighted that we have the same name," Miriam added, as she held Miriam's hand.

"And so have thousands of women all over Galilee, Mother," Yeshua said with a chuckle. "I too am pleased to meet you, Isaac and Miriam, we are good friends with your mother," Yeshua said.

"Okay now, children, go out back and play," Ruth said, and the children obeyed, pleased to leave the adults and to go out and play.

After introducing his mother to Orpah, Yeshua said, "Orpah, it's so good to see you, do tell us about yourself."

"As you can see, I'm married to Noah, and we have two children. Noah and Jacob both work on a farm; they have become partners in a business and farm all kinds of animals and also lots of fruit trees and olives," Orpah said.

"What a coincidence that you married a Noah, seeing you have brothers named Shem, Japheth and Ham," Yeshua said, "how do your brothers feel about that?"

"They got ribbed a lot at the beginning, us telling them that they now had to keep in line, because they now had two famous and great people around, Joshua and Noah, and they better behave themselves. But everything's normal now," Orpah said, laughing.

"And how are your mother and father?" Yeshua asked.

"They are fine, Yeshua, father is busy all the time, and he is creating all new designs and the elite ladies from Tiberias are all agog with his creations. Orpah and I still work for him and mother, with our sewing," Ruth said. "We don't work at the marketplace anymore, we have two ladies employed to do that," Ruth added.

"It looks like you all are doing well, I am so pleased," Yeshua said.

"And tell us about yourself, Yeshua, is it true all the things we hear about you?" Ruth asked.

"Ruth, Orpah, I don't know what you've heard, people tend to exaggerate, but it is true that there were great signs when Yeshua was baptised by Johanan, the hermit prophet, in the River Jordan, the sky did brighten and a dove did descend upon Yeshua at that moment and a voice was heard by Yeshua and by all present, which said, 'This is my beloved Son, listen to him," Miriam said. "I wasn't there at the time, but I have reliable sources who told me all of this," Miriam added.

"So, what does that mean, Yeshua?" Orpah asked, unable to figure what Miriam was saying.

"Yeshua, you have to explain this," Miriam said, for she too needed to and wanted to fully grasp the significance of that event.

"I…eh…don't really want to talk about that right now, Orpah and Ruth. Suffice to say that God spoke to me and to all in the River Jordan as clearly as he spoke to Moses on Mount Sinai. It was the first time he has acknowledged me so publicly. You know that many other nations believe in several gods and that they also believe in a god of theirs taking on our human nature. We the chosen people of Israel have always believed in one God but now here I am, his son. I have come to know that I have been sent, that my father in heaven has sent me. his son, into the world, to become as all humans are. The Father has sent me to bring his Good News of salvation and redemption to all, the Good News of his love for us. That is as far as I can tell you at this time," Yeshua said. "For now, at this time, please just treat me as the son of Miriam, for I am also her son. I would now very much like to just be Yeshua, the carpenter from Nazareth," Yeshua said with a smile.

That evening Yeshua and Miriam were treated to a feast. The entire family was present, Joshua and Emzara, their two daughters, Ruth and Orpah and their husbands and children and the three sons, Shem, Japheth, and their wives and children. Shem had three, and Japheth, two and Ham was still single. Shem and Japheth also now had their own home on the other end of the property but Ham, still lived at home with his parents.

Yeshua and Miriam wanted to know all about them, what they were interested in, what has happened in their lives, their experiences, but they were more interested to know all about their friend Yeshua, the prophet, the miracle worker, the one whose words were stirring up the people. Why were people flocking to him in droves?

Yeshua was reluctant to speak about himself, in this setting. He was comfortable about speaking about, proclaiming the Good News of redemption for humankind, salvation for humanity, about the boundless love of the Father for all. He did not want to speak about what has happened since he left Nazareth. But Miriam was pleased to speak about her son. But instead of speaking about all that happened at the villages where they stayed and at Cana and Ziddim, she spoke of Yeshua growing up like a normal child in Nazareth.

"When Yeshua was twelve years old, we went from Nazareth to Jerusalem for the celebration of the Sabbath, the whole of Nazareth went there together. When the celebrations had finished, we all began our long trek home together. Yosef and I believed Yeshua to be with a family from Nazareth, and after a day's journey when Yosef went to check on Yeshua to our dismay, we discovered that Yeshua was not there, nowhere to be found, it then dawned on us that we left Yeshua behind in Jerusalem."

"Oh no, that must have been terrible," Emzara said.

"It was my worst nightmare. I could not sleep that night, waiting for the dawn so that Yosef and I could return to Jerusalem to look for Yeshua." Miriam then told them the whole story of how they searched for Yeshua and after three days since he went missing, they found him and she described their relief and consternation to find him in the Temple talking to the teachers there.

"Yeshua, how could you have done that to your mother and father?" Ruth exclaimed.

"I don't know, Ruth; thank you, mother, for reminding everyone of just what a brat I was as a child. I just got lost in the moment." Yeshua then explained how he was simply drawn to the Temple and how he got drawn into the conversation with the teachers' discussion.

"Mother never lets me forget that incident, neither do I, it was very thoughtless and inconsiderate of me, and I was lucky my father didn't discipline me severely as I deserved. All I can say about that is that I was only a child and that Abba, my heavenly father drew me into the Temple and to the circle of teachers there," Yeshua said.

"Yeshua, did you really change six jars of water into wine at Cana. I heard you changed water into something like one hundred and fifty gallons of wine. That must have caused quite a stir and enough to keep the whole of Cana drinking forever," Ham said, grinning.

"Well, you know weddings, people expect to eat and drink and celebrate for a whole week. And it is such an expense for the families of the groom and the bride," Ruth said.

"I wish you were at our wedding, Yeshua, the wine cost me a fortune," Japheth said, laughing.

"Boys, show some respect. What you did, Yeshua, was most considerate, and I know that it was not simply to save the bride and groom and their families an embarrassment but a sign, like what happened in the River Jordan. I believe, Yeshua, that you are the One we have been waiting for and we are so fortunate to have you as our guest," Emzara said solemnly.

"Thank you, Emzara, for those words. I do have a mission, and am sent by the Father to bring the Good News to all, of his boundless love for all. I have been sent to redeem all from slavery to sin and death. And the Spirit of the Father guides me in all I say and do. And that sign in Cana was a sign of God's great love and care for us in our everyday lives. He did not want that couple to endure any embarrassment. He is not a distant God, a distant judge but a loving Father, like a loving mother, friend, brother, sister and he wants to be near us and be part of our lives, and wants us to know and experience his nearness and his boundless love for us, and his generosity and magnanimity," Yeshua said, words just flowed out of his mouth. "But for now, I am among friends, while I am sent by my heavenly father to do his work, I am also the child of Miriam and Yosef and fully human, flesh and blood, so let me and us get stuck into this lamb, which is absolutely delicious, thank you, Emzara," Yeshua added, smiling broadly.

"Anyone for more wine?" Ham said, and everyone laughed.

The rest of the meal, Yeshua was pleased to be treated like anyone else, a normal human being, without all the adulation that was now part of his existence. The conversation covered the life of the people, Rome's might and enslavement of the people, the burdensomeness of so many laws and regulations, and also sport, the games of Greece that were causing quite a stir. Yeshua spoke about how he and his friends Achim and Zadok raced all the time when they were kids, and he spoke of his friend Rebecca and how fast a runner and competitor she is and how he too has taken to running as a way of exercise.

"Joshua, I would like to meet your rabbi and ask if I may speak to the people on this coming Sabbath," Yeshua asked.

"I will speak with him, Yeshua, I have to go into the city tomorrow, and I am sure he would be most delighted to have you speak; as a matter of fact, if he knew you were in town, he would have searched you out to ask you to speak, for he too has heard about what you were preaching and all the signs that have been accompanying you," Joshua said.

"Thank you, Joshua, let the rabbi know, I will see him on the eve of the Sabbath. Until then, I would like to remain incognito. If mother and I could further indulge your hospitality, I would be most appreciative."

"Of course, Yeshua, you are most welcome to stay as long as your wish," Joshua replied.

The women, including Miriam, started cleaning up, and the men went outside. They reignited the fire from the embers, and soon there were flames licking the air.

More wine was poured. The men continued discussing politics, and complaining about the ever-rising taxes and tariffs, and about how many people are losing their properties because they are unable to pay their exorbitant taxes and tariffs.

"I've met quite a number of those families who lost their land, and their houses like that, and are now living, barely existing in the faraway villages, mother and I have visited," Yeshua said.

"Yeshua, your reputation has spread far and wide. People are flocking to come and listen to you. Your fame as a miracle worker and healer is known all over Galilee and in Judaea, and this can be dangerous for you, with the authorities. I am concerned for you," Joshua said. "Herod has put Johanan, the baptiser in prison, and I fear for his life. We now have another new Roman governor, Pontius Pilate; he has just arrived in Judaea and lives in a palace in Caesarea Philippi. Caiaphas of course has taken over form his father-in-law, as the high priest. He was appointed by Rome; a while back actually, must be at least seven years ago. I think you have to be careful, Yeshua. What they did to Johanan could happen to you," Joshua warned.

The womenfolk joined the men, while Joshua was speaking, and they heard what he was saying, warning Yeshua of danger. Emzara then spoke, "Yeshua you should be careful, not only of Pontius Pilate and Caiaphas but all the other religious leaders as well. For too long have they lorded over the people, and they will not take kindly to you, stirring up a following," Emzara said.

"Yes, they do not like you stealing their limelight, and already I have heard murmurings of discontent among the Pharisees, Sadducees, Elders, Scribes and the Teachers of the Law, they are not happy with your teaching, and they say you are not a man of God, for you cure on the Sabbath, and you associate with sinners and with the unclean," Ruth said.

"Maybe you should return to Nazareth, Yeshua, and don't go anywhere near Jerusalem, or anywhere in Judaea for that matter," Joshua said.

"Mother and I are off to Capernaum after we leave Magdala, and I will be staying there for the foreseeable future," Yeshua said. But Yeshua knew he had to go to Judaea some time, for his mission is to spread the Good News of God's love for all, and Yahweh's desire to be loved in return, and to bring peace into their hearts.

The conversation ebbed and flowed between the Roman governance and that of the religious leaders, and Yeshua spoke to his friends about all that happened in those out of way villages that he and Miriam had visited.

"It is getting late, I think Yeshua and Miriam will need their rest now," Emzara said. She could see the conversation would not cease and they could go on all night listening to Yeshua.

"Yes, I do think I need some sleep," Miriam said.

They all then adjourned to their sleeping quarters. Yeshua and Miriam chatted for a while, before they parted and went to the separate rooms they were given for their stay.

Yeshua was up early the next day, the eve of the Sabbath, he walked into the nearest bushland he could find, and found solace among the trees and nature and the birds. He spent time in prayer as he walked and talked with Yahweh. He thought about what he was to say to the people of Magdala. Yeshua did not have a problem speaking about the reign of God, about the Kingdom of God; the words simply flowed from his heart. But he always spent time in preparation, gathering together some theme or other.

Miriam spent the day relaxing and she decided to spend some time with Ruth and Orpah and their children. When Yeshua returned from his morning walk, he found only Joshua and Emzara in the house. "Where is mother?" Yeshua asked.

"She has gone to visit Ruth and Orpah, said she wanted to spend some time with the children," Emzara said.

After Yeshua had something to eat, he told Joshua and Emzara that he would join Miriam and the girls and also spend some time with their children.

Ruth and Orpah were pleased to see Yeshua again. He spent time with their children and they seemed to be engrossed in the stories he was telling them. When it came time for the mid-morning refreshments, they all sat outside, while the children played their games, chasing each other, and hide-and-seek.

Yeshua enjoyed the time with Ruth and Orpah and his mother. "Tell me, how is that girl, Miriam that I met such a long time ago, when I was last here. She is of course all grown up now. I remember you telling me that she was suffering a lot, at the time," Yeshua said.

"Yes, she was, Yeshua, and she still suffers. She is getting worse and her spells are more frequent and more severe. She becomes so severely depressed and won't eat or sleep and her moods are getting more extreme, and sometimes we fear she won't come out of them. When she is in her jovial mood she can't stop talking and is highly active and joyful but we know that it is just a prelude to her long periods of crashing into deep depressive states, from which we fear, she will one day not return. And her mother is really fearful of her when she is in one of her foul moods because she can also become violent and harm herself, and even her mother. It is so sad to see her so, Yeshua, she seems to be spiralling out of control and getting worse and worse, and injuring herself, and shouting and screaming, and harming herself really, and none of the doctors seem to be able to help her," Ruth said.

"Everyone says she is possessed by demons; in fact, they say she is possessed of seven demons. How they came to that figure, I do not know," Orpah said.

"She lives not far from here, in a big house. She is the only child. The family are quite well-to-do. Her father owns a big vineyard and winery in Capernaum, and he spends most of his time there, so Miriam's poor mother has to deal with Miriam. I feel so sorry for her. We visit them, whenever we can," Ruth said.

Yeshua's heart went out to Miriam; he felt her suffering and that of her parents and all those who loved her. "Can you take me to her?" Yeshua asked.

"For sure, Yeshua," both Ruth and Orpah said simultaneously.

"Okay, Ruth, you take Yeshua, Miriam seems to relate best to you, and we'll look after the children," Orpah offered.

Yeshua and Ruth then set off to meet Miriam.

Chapter Thirty-Eight
Miriam of Magdala

They did have a big house on the top of a hill, and Yeshua saw lots of cattle and workers with them. When they approached, they saw Miriam's mother, tending to a little flower garden near the entrance of their house.

"Lydia, Shalom, I've brought a visitor, Yeshua, from Nazareth, we spoke about him when I was last here. He has come to visit you, and to see Miriam," Ruth said.

"Peace be to you, Lydia, I am so pleased to meet you. I have heard of Miriam's long suffering, and I have come to see her," Yeshua said.

"She is out back, quiet at the moment," Lydia said.

"I'll find my way," Yeshua said.

For some reason, both Lydia and Ruth left Yeshua to meet with Miriam on his own. They sensed that was what he wanted.

Yeshua found Miriam sitting on a bench beneath a huge fig tree, she was eating a fig.

"Peace be with you, Miriam, I am Yeshua, a visitor from Nazareth and am staying with your good friends, Ruth and Orpah and the family, I have come to visit you. I met you when I was last here, about ten years ago, I met you at Ruth and Orpah's clothing store in the town centre, do you remember?" Yeshua asked.

"No, I don't," Miriam shook her head.

"May I join you, Miriam?" Yeshua asked gently.

Miriam seemed to relax, for reasons she could not fathom. She had never been alone with a man, alone in his company, a stranger at that. It was not the expected thing for a man and a woman who was not betrothed or married to be alone with a man, and a stranger at that. But she was not alone, her mother was here, and so was Ruth. For some unfathomable reason, Miriam felt completely at ease with this stranger, to be alone with this man, Yeshua. She could not remember when last a man had come to visit her or speak with her, except the doctors, who could not help her. But he wasn't really a stranger to Miriam, because Ruth and Orpah could not stop speaking about him, especially of late. Miriam began to relax and feel at ease with Yeshua, as if she knew him and he was her friend.

"So, you are the carpenter from Nazareth, the One people are saying is the Promised One, the Prophet, and you can work miracles and cure people. Can you cure me?" Miriam said, not believing that he could, she was sceptical and dismissive.

"Miriam tell me about yourself, your life, how has it been for you, how are you feeling now?" Yeshua asked.

For some reason, Miriam felt immediately at ease and opened up to Yeshua. "I am in hell on earth, Yeshua. I believe I am indeed possessed of several demons, as people say I am. I feel as if I am seven different persons, who take turns in ruling me. I am so tired of being like this Yeshua. I do all kinds of strange things and when I am lucid and myself, I can't remember what I've done. I have caused so much grief and suffering to mother. And to father, when he is home, which is seldom, as he spends most of his time at his vineyards and winery in Capernaum."

Yeshua listened, as Miriam shared her story, the loneliness she felt, how no one understood her and thought she was mad, and how she hated the way she lived and wished she was dead, and often thought of ending her life.

"Miriam, do you wish to be better, to be healed of your illnesses?" Yeshua asked. "And do you believe, Miriam, I can heal you?"

Miriam looked at Yeshua, and she saw his eyes, which were moist, tears at the ready. She saw the compassion in his eyes, and she spoke from the depths of her heart, no longer with sentiments of despair, but filled with hope. She said, "Yes, Yeshua, I want to be healed, and yes, I do believe you can heal me."

Yeshua then took both Miriam's hands in his, and he gazed heavenwards, and then there was a deep silence, as Yeshua communed with his Father in heaven. "Go now, Miriam, your mother waits for you, go in peace, and let your illness no longer plague you."

Miriam got up and walked into the house. "Ruth, how nice it is to see you and thank you for bringing Yeshua."

Both Ruth and Lydia knew at once what had happened. There was a glow all over Miriam and she seemed to be radiating a peace and a joy they had never seen on her before. She seemed so relaxed and at peace and so self-assured.

"What happened to you, my daughter?" Lydia asked.

"Mother, I am cured," Miriam blurted out spontaneously. "Yeshua has cured me. He held my hands and prayed and I felt a warmth come all over me, the likes I have never experienced before, and I felt as if those seven demons were leaving me, once and for all. Mother I have never felt the way I feel. And it is all because of Yeshua, I do believe he is the Prophet, the Promised One, the Messiah," Miriam said.

Lydia burst into tears and hugged her daughter, and Ruth joined in a group hug, and tears were rolling down both Lydia's and Ruth's eyes. But Miriam was smiling, she felt like a new person. And her heart went out to Yeshua.

"Where is Yeshua?" Lydia asked.

"He is still out back, he told me to come to you and bring you the good news," Miriam said.

Lydia was overwhelmed. She had heard of Yeshua's miracles, of the many people he had healed in the villages where he went, and in Cana, and Ziddim and now here in Magdala, and in their home. She was overjoyed and rushed out back and found Yeshua sitting on the bench. She fell on her knees before Yeshua, and began kissing his feet, "Oh Yeshua, oh Yeshua, thank you, thank you," she cried out.

"Lydia, please, get up," Yeshua stood up and lifted Lydia to her feet. She then hugged Yeshua and would not let him go.

Ruth and Miriam came, and saw Yeshua lifting Lydia to her feet. Lydia then took Yeshua's hands in her hands. "Yeshua, if there is anything we can do to repay you, if there is anything you need, then please do not hesitate to let us know," Lydia said.

"Yeshua, there is something I would like to know. I hear that you have been travelling from village to village where you stay and preach, and heal those in need, and that you were in Ziddim and now here in Magdala. Is this where you will stay, or are you going elsewhere?" Miriam asked. She was so appreciative of what Yeshua had done for her, she wanted to do something for him in return.

"Miriam, I usually stay about a week or two, wherever I am made welcome. But I intend to set up home in Capernaum, after I leave Magdala. And then I will wait and see where the Spirit leads me, but I have been sent to preach the Good News to the poor, to set prisoners free, to heal the broken-hearted and those whose spirits have been crushed, to make the blind see and the lame walk and to bring all I meet out of the darkness and into the light of God's glory, love and compassion."

"Yeshua, in this work that you do, how are you supported?" Miriam asked. "Where do you stay and do you have to work to support yourself or do you have the funds for board and lodging wherever you go?"

"I have been blessed Miriam. Wherever I go, I have found nothing but love and hospitality and Yahweh has provided me with loving friends who have provided me with a place to stay. Again, as if moved by the Spirit, Yeshua felt at ease in addressing God as Yahweh, with Miriam. But I do not at this time have a fixed abode, and if needs be, I am willing to sleep rough. I was thinking of purchasing a tent, and I am a carpenter and if needs be, I will find work to support me in the work the Father has sent me to do," Yeshua said.

Miriam, with a new lease of life, was being moved by the Spirit. "Yeshua, we, I, would like to support you in what you are doing. I would like to support you in your work. We have funds, I have funds, and I would like to put that at your disposal. May I accompany you and see to your daily needs, so that you can focus entirely on the work you are doing?" Miriam asked. She was so grateful for having been cured of her tormented life that she was thinking of ending. Now she had a new lease of life, and she was drawn so strongly to this man, this Yeshua, she wanted to support him in his endeavours.

"So, you wish to support me, Miriam, I am most grateful, that will be a great help. I accept for you to follow me," Yeshua said, impulsively. And at that moment, Yeshua realised that he would have followers, like Miriam, who would want to be his followers, especially now that Johanan was in prison. Followers who would want to follow him, not simply to support him materially, or out of curiosity, or to witness his miracles, but followers, like Miriam, who would care for him, for his welfare, and be more than that, be his disciples, and follow him, to learn everything he has to teach them.

"Yeshua, do come in for some refreshment," Lydia said.

"You have to excuse me," Ruth said. "I have to get home and get lunch ready for the children." But what Ruth really wanted to do was to tell her mother and Orpah the good news of Miriam's healing and all that had happened. She was overjoyed for her friend. And now Miriam was to be his disciple and she will support him wherever he went.

Miriam set the table and brought bread and fish to eat and fruit and grape juice to drink. "Would you like some wine, Yeshua?" Miriam asked.

"It is rather early for a drink of wine, but I will have one. I feel so drained," Yeshua said.

"Drained, Yeshua, you must be tired, going from place to place and preaching and teaching and the crowds all wanting a piece of you. And not having any rest," Miriam said.

"When I touch anyone and heal them, as I did with you, Miriam, I feel the power of Yahweh going out of me, I feel so drained afterwards, that I need rest and recovery, so I think a glass of wine is most welcome," Yeshua said. "Mmm, this is fine wine, Miriam, Lydia, is this from your father's vineyards in Capernaum?" Yeshua asked.

"It sure is. I will take you to our vineyards, Yeshua, and you can meet father. We have a house at the vineyards, and also cottages for the servants and some for workers who need a place to stay," Miriam said.

"And Yeshua, you and your mother can stay at our home, if you are able to put up with father, he can really be a pain in the neck at times, but I can take care of him," Miriam said.

"Yes, Yeshua, you are most welcome to stay. There are a number or rooms in our house there and you will be comfortable, and there are plenty of servants to care for my husband, Elijah's needs," Lydia said.

"That will be helpful and I am most grateful, Miriam and Lydia. You are so kind. I will be preaching tomorrow, at the synagogue and will stay for about a week and then be off to Capernaum," Yeshua said.

Yeshua enjoyed his meal and the company of Lydia and Miriam. Lydia then said she would clean up and that Yeshua and Miriam could go out back and relax. Miriam was grateful, she wanted so much to speak with Yeshua and thank him for what he had done for her, and she wanted to talk to him about his work, and how she could be of help to him. She was so excited, as if she had found her real vocation in life, to be a disciple and assist Yeshua in his work.

"Thank you so much, Yeshua, I feel like a new person, as if I have been reborn, it is as if I was in prison all my life and have been finally released. It's as if I was dead and now for the first time I have come to life, you have brought me out of the darkness and into the light," Miriam said.

"I am so happy for you, Miriam, you have suffered much. And I am so grateful for your kindness and that of your mother. And the offer of accommodation in Capernaum is most generous. Miriam, I see that you will be more than just assisting me in my material needs, I need your counsel. I need a woman's perspective. We live in a very patriarchal and male dominated world, and even our way of faith and living discriminates against women," Yeshua said.

"Yes, Yeshua, I felt that deeply, I was looked down on, so much, because of my illness and doubly so because I am a woman. I have grown up with these superiority attitudes of men towards us women. We are regarded as inferior by men. We are expected to kowtow to the needs of men and even the rules of our religion are male orientated, which downgrades us women. God made us male and female and he made us equal, not one superior and the other inferior," Miriam said.

Miriam poured her heart out about how she felt about being a woman in today's society, and the way she felt being a woman in her own Jewish religion. And Yeshua listened intently. He had grown up with a male superiority complex, but his friendship with Rebecca and the many strong women he met in his life, had taught him much and now he was so glad to have Miriam, as a friend and not only a disciple but a confidante, especially in the needs of women.

More than an hour must have passed and still Yeshua and Miriam were deep in conversation. Lydia came to the back door and saw them, and decided to leave them to continue. She was so pleased to see how radiant and alive, Miriam was, she was a new person. She just couldn't stop the tears of joy that kept streaming down her cheeks.

Yeshua began to share with Miriam some things about himself. He did not think she needed to know the circumstances of his birth but he did tell her how he spent three days as a twelve-year-old in the temple in Jerusalem, and already then realised he had a mission from Yahweh, to spread his word. Miriam already heard about Yeshua's baptism in the Jordan, and his miracle at Cana and all the other healings.

But Yeshua shared with her how much he wanted to bring everyone out of the darkness and into the light of Yahweh's great love and compassion for all of God's creatures, without exception. He wanted to bring Yahweh's love, peace and joy into the world. They spoke about the world order in which the poor became poorer and the rich richer, and how that had to change.

Yeshua and Miriam had no idea of how much time they spent together, but in those hours they bonded deeply. And Miriam made it clear, she wanted to follow Yeshua and learn from him, and support him in his work. In effect Miriam was the first of Yeshua's disciples but there would be many more that would follow Yeshua. Many would follow simply like sheep follows the shepherd, but there would be those who would follow Yeshua as his disciples to learn from him and to grow and to assist and support him in his work. And because of Miriam there would be lots of women too, who would also become Yeshua's disciples.

When Yeshua was about to leave, Lydia invited Yeshua and his mother to dinner, she planned to begin roasting a lamb. "Elijah, my husband, will be here, he usually comes home for the Sabbath and the weekend." Yeshua gladly accepted and then left.

When Elijah arrived home, he was out back washing himself when Miriam approached. "Shalom, Father. How was your week? Father, I have something to tell you." Miriam then told her father about Yeshua's visit and the healing she had received. "I am cured, Father. Those demons are no longer."

Elijah dried his face and looked at his daughter. He could see the change. She was radiant, glowing, with a peaceful and joyful look. He believed her. He was so happy. He took Miriam in his arms and held her. "I am so happy, Miriam. Where is this Yeshua now?" he asked.

"He and his mother, Miriam, are staying with Joshua and Emzara. Ruth brought him to us and he stayed here this afternoon, and that was when he healed me, Abba," Miriam said.

"I must go and see him and reward him for what he has done," Elijah said.

"Father, we have invited him and his mother for dinner, they will be here soon," Miriam said, and she told her father of her plans to accompany Yeshua and tend to his needs, and that she had offered him and his mother lodgings at their house in Capernaum.

Time came for the dinner. Yeshua met Elijah. He was a tall man, with a well-groomed beard and short haircut. His face was tanned from the sun, and his arms muscular from hard work.

"So, this is the famous Yeshua that is the talk of the town, and all of Galilee. Now I hope, Yeshua, that you are not going to pull that stunt that you did in Cana, changing all that water into wine. You will be putting me out of business," Elijah said, with a loud guttural laugh.

"Elijah! Please behave yourself. Yeshua, Miriam, please forgive my husband, he can be so uncouth at times," Lydia apologised.

"No need to apologise, Lydia, and I won't pull that stunt here or in Capernaum, for I am sure no one will run out of wine, here, as I must say you do make the finest wine," Yeshua said, with a smile.

"Thank you, Yeshua, on that note excuse me as I go and fetch some wine in the cellar, and Miriam, put some wine cups on the table," Elijah said, as he left the table and soon returned with a jar of wine.

"Yeshua, I must thank you for what you did for my Miriam. I am so pleased for her. She tells me of her plans to accompany you, and that you will be staying at our home at Capernaum. I will be most happy to receive you there, and you can visit our vineyards," Elijah said proudly. He was happy for Miriam to accompany Yeshua, he thought he would be a good catch for his daughter, and it was time she had a man in her life.

The meal was most tasty and the conversation was congenial as Yeshua let Elijah speak of his winemaking ventures. But Elijah too was interested in what Yeshua wanted to accomplish, and how he got all those powers. Elijah was not a religious man, like his wife and daughter, and what happened to his daughter Miriam impressed him and he agreed to her plans to accompany Yeshua. He was a man of the world, and he did not think of women as most of his fellow males did, he would judge a person male or female by what he or she thought and of what they were capable.

It was a most pleasant evening and it was late when Yeshua and Miriam left and were accompanied by Elijah back to the home of Joshua and Emzara.

Chapter Thirty-Nine
Still in Magdala

As usual, Yeshua was up early, and he found the woods and spent some time among nature and the birds. He always felt this most soothing and a perfect start to his day, and a perfect place to pray and to prepare for the day ahead, and today, for his Sabbath preaching. *What am I to say to these people, Abba? Why have you sent me here, to meet with and heal Miriam, and for her to be the first to follow me, and support me in spreading your word? These are good people here in Magdala, industrious, but among them are also the poor, the disadvantaged, the sick and handicapped, and those who have drifted far from you Father, and from their faith. There are those who are without hope or joy or peace in their hearts, and who live in darkness, and the shadow of death.*

Yeshua had been in the woods for about an hour when he finally came out, and waiting for him at the entrance to the woods with a warm glass of milk was Miriam.

"Good morning, Yeshua, I had gone to Emzara and she told me you were here in the woods, and your mother had mentioned that you love to start the day with a cup of hot milk, and a fresh fig. You left for the woods more than an hour ago, so I thought you would be ready to break your fast with some warm milk and fresh figs," Miriam said. "I hope I am not disturbing you from your morning routine, and your time of prayer, Yeshua," Miriam apologised.

"Not at all, Miriam, the milk and figs are most welcome, and so are you. I have been thinking of what to say to the people of Magdala. I will try my best to convince them of Yahweh's love for them and the Good News of redemption and salvation that is theirs. But tell me about your people, Miriam, you have lived here all your life," Yeshua said.

"Yeshua, there is a wide variety of people here, poor and rich, young and old, kind and cruel, those faithful to our laws and the teachings of the prophets and those who have drifted far from the faith. There are many who suffer all kinds of afflictions, some lepers who are cast out to live outside of the town, and there are destitute women, including widows who have turned to prostitution to support themselves. I have been fortunate to be blessed with material goods but there is so much poverty and many of the rich treat the poor with disdain and downright cruelty. Many have become poor because they were not able to pay their rents, or if they did have property, they were unable to pay the exorbitant taxes and tariffs to Rome, and as a result have lost their properties. There is much bitterness and the rich are becoming richer and the poor becoming poorer. Many have given up on their faith and drifted far away from the ways of our faith," Miriam said.

"Miriam, you paint a dismal picture of life here in Magdala, and I think of perhaps all over Galilee and beyond. How am I to give hope to the people, how will they embrace the message I bring of Yahweh's love and care for them?"

"Yeshua, I am sure you will find the words, the Spirit is with you," Miriam said.

"Miriam, in the synagogue I will be talking to the crowds, but during the week I would like to meet and talk to those you mention, the outcasts, and marginalised and those who are steeped in poverty and have lost all hope. I would like to meet them, the vulnerable, and the afflicted and hopefully bring them some solace, and let them know that Yahweh knows and cares for them, and loves them, and does not forget them but holds them all in his heart."

"Yeshua, I am most willing to take you to those people. I know some of the women who have turned to prostitution to survive. They have been divorced and abandoned by their husbands and their families, and there are a few widows who have also become destitute and turned to prostitution to survive."

"Miriam, it is to these that I have been sent. I appreciate that you can take me to see them."

Yeshua and Miriam continued walking back from the woods, chatting about Yeshua's work and his mission and Yeshua spoke to Miriam more and more about his own problems, doubts and fears. He spoke of his desire to be like everyone else, not to experience this heavy burden of giving his life to spreading the Word of God. He yearned for a close relationship, for intimacy, for someone to love and to be loved, to have children of his own, but it was not to be. "Miriam, I love Abba, Yahweh, with all my heart, and I have been sent to be his presence and utter his word on earth, and I accept this with all my heart, but I am flesh and bone like you and everyone else, and my heart yearns for the happiness we all yearn for, and to have someone close and intimate in my life."

Yeshua was so grateful that he could open up to Miriam in this way, about matters close and personal. He had Rebecca in Nazareth, with whom he could speak about matters of the heart and Gamaliel with whom he could speak about matters of his mind, and his mother of course and now Miriam. In his heart, Yeshua thanked Abba for giving him these people in his life to support and love him.

"Time is moving on, Yeshua; soon you need to be in the synagogue. Shall we return to Emzara first?"

"Yes, we will, I would like to freshen up a bit."

As expected, the synagogue was full to overflowing. Not only was it full of the people of Magdala but people from far and wide, from surrounding villages and even people from as far as Ziddim and Capernaum, and they brought with them their sick and incapacitated.

Yeshua began, "Peace be to you all. May the love of God our Father in heaven and the communion of the Spirit be with you all. My dear brothers and sisters, I wish to begin with a reading from the prophet Micah. You are all familiar with the great prophet, Isaiah, who, although he was a member of the upper class; he defended the rights of the poor, whereas Micah was a poor person, yet suffering with the poor and the dispossessed. That is why Micah speaks so passionately about the mistreatment of the poor. His words are very graphic and send shivers up my spine when I read them. Listen to Micah and take heed, he writes: 'Listen you heads of Jacob and rulers of the house of Israel! Should you not know justice?—you who hate the good and love the evil, who tear the skin off my people, and the flesh off their bones, who eat the flesh of my people, flay their skin off them, break their bones in pieces, and chop them up like meat in a kettle, like flesh in a cauldron. They will cry to the Lord, but he will not answer them, he will hide his face from them at that time, because they have acted wickedly.'

"Micah speaks passionately about the mistreatment of the poor, of the have nots by those who have. Many of you are poor; many of you have lost everything you toiled for, being dispossessed of your land because of the greed of the rich and powerful. To all you who suffer from dispossession, and for all you who live in poverty, know that our heavenly Father hears your cries, as Micah prophesies, 'when I sit in darkness, the Lord will be a light to me. He will bring me out to the light, I shall see his vindication. Then my enemy will see and shame will cover the faces of them who said to me, 'where is your God?' My eyes will see their downfall, now they will be trodden down like the mire in the streets.

"My dear friends, neither wealth nor poverty will give us true happiness. We all want to be rich. We regard poverty as a punishment from God. It is not so; poverty is nothing to be desired but it is not punishment for sin or disfavour from Adonai or anything that should cause shame. Neither are riches the result of God's favour, it can be the result of ingenuity, industriousness, hard work, intelligence, luck, or inheritance. Riches do not give us happiness. There are so many rich people, who are not only unhappy, they are downright miserable. And then there are rich people who have become so through evil means, and on the backs of the poor who were exploited. And there are the rich whose hearts are pure and who do so much good to so many and for so many.

"Let me offer a word first to the rich and then a word to the poor. There are rich among you, and I have encountered many rich folk. Some have become rich through exploitation of the poor, and through other dark and evil means, and through cruelty. To these I say, Woe to you, for you have received your consolation. Woe to you who are full now, for you will be hungry. Woe to you who are laughing now, for you will mourn and weep. Woe to you when all speak well of you, for that is what their ancestors did to the false prophets.

"To these rich, who have become so on the backs of the poor, and exploited the poor, and who are consumed by their wealth, and have no regard for the needs of those whom they continue to exploit, and who become richer while those they exploit become poorer and poorer, the Lord God sees, and their day of judgement is imminent.

"To these rich who have no regard for the fate of the less fortunate, and those whom they continue to exploit, I say to you that it easier for a camel to enter through the eye of a needle than for a rich man to enter into the Kingdom of Heaven.

"To these rich I say, no one can serve two masters; for a slave will either hate the one, and love the other, or be devoted to the one and despise the other. You cannot serve God and wealth. I say to you, do not store up for yourselves treasures on earth, where moth and rust consume and where thieves break in and steal; but store up for yourselves treasures in heaven, where neither moth nor rust consumes, and where thieves do not break in and steal. For where your treasure is, there will your heart be also. I say to you, what does it profit a man if he gains the whole world and loses his immortal soul?"

Yeshua paused. There was a hush all over the synagogue. Yeshua had learned from Miriam that her father did not go to the synagogue except at the Passover and Festival of the Harvest but he was now present, for he was curious and wanted to hear Yeshua speak, and he was also curious, hoping to witness for himself, a miracle.

The people in the synagogue were a mix of rich and poor and Yeshua could see the different expressions on the faces of those listening to him. Yeshua knew that some of the rich would be feeling uncomfortable with his words, while others will take them to heart. Yeshua's eyes rested on Elijah, and Yeshua could see that his words were disturbing Elijah to some extent. After a short silence, Yeshua continued.

"Now, let me say a word to the poor. You are Adonai's favourites. You have a special place in his heart. Your plight is not the result of sin, it is not punishment; it is life. Know this; that you are precious in the eyes of God, our Father. and he hears your cries, and knows your distress and your suffering. I say to you, Blessed are you who are poor, for yours is the kingdom of God. Blessed are you who are hungry now, for you will be filled. Blessed are you who weep now, for you will laugh. Blessed are you when people hate you, and when they exclude you, revile you and defame you. Rejoice in that day and leap for joy, for your reward is great in heaven. I have come to bring you the Good News, the day of salvation is here, and the day of redemption is here. I have come to set you free from all that binds your heart and souls."

Yeshua paused. His eyes fell on Miriam, sitting next to her mother, and he saw her smile and her encouragement. He continued, "Remember how the Lord your God led your ancestors for forty years in the wilderness, to humble you, to test you, and to know your inmost heart—whether you would keep his commandments or not. He humbled you, he made you feel hunger, and then he fed you with manna from heaven, to make you understand that you do not live on bread alone but that you live on everything that comes from the mouth of the Lord. It is the Word of God that gives true nourishment, and true riches, and I am to bring to you the Word of God. Listen to what I say."

Yeshua continued speaking to the packed synagogue for over an hour. Religion was something that was central to these people's lives, it was front and centre, and they were accustomed to long talks and intense discussions. After the service, the people continued to gather around Yeshua, outside in the courtyard, and they asked him all sorts of questions. Their questions related to the Torah; the Laws of God given to Moses. The number of laws and commandments and regulations that they had to adhere to were innumerable and insufferable.

"Yeshua, there are so many laws that regulate our lives, it is impossible to remember them all, let alone uphold them, what do you say about this?" one of the crowd asked.

"You are right; the number of laws is innumerable, six hundred and thirteen to be exact. The Lord God gave Moses only ten; if you live by these, you are pleasing to Him. In fact, only one Law is supreme, and if you live by this Law, you are saved and pleasing to God and it is this; you will love the Lord your God, with all your heart, with all your mind and with all your strength. And the second is this; you shall love your neighbour as yourself. So, in everything, do to others as you would have them do to you, for this is the fullness of the Law and the Prophets," Yeshua exclaimed.

"Is this a new commandment you are giving us, Yeshua? And on whose authority do you do so," one of the crowd called out.

"He is a Pharisee," Miriam whispered in Yeshua's ear.

"What is your name, my friend?" Yeshua asked.

"I am Levi, and I have studied all the Laws of Moses and the Prophets, and I have adhered to them all my life, so, I ask again, is this a new commandment, and on whose authority do you proclaim it?" Levi said in a stern voice.

"Levi, I say this to you, and I say it to all of you present here, do not think that I have come to abolish the Law or the Prophets, I have not come to abolish but to fulfil. Therefore, whoever breaks one of the least of these commandments and teaches others to do the same, will be called least in the Kingdom of Heaven, but whoever keeps them and teaches them will be called great in the Kingdom of Heaven. For I tell you, unless your righteousness exceeds that of the Scribes and the Pharisees, you will not enter the Kingdom of Heaven."

"Yeshua, you have not answered my question," Levi retorted with a tone of aggression.

"I say to you, this is no new commandment, but an old commandment that you have from the beginning, the old commandment is the word you have heard. But it is now new, in that it is in me that the Father has sent, and is now in you, because the darkness is passing away and the true light is already shining. Whoever says, 'I am in the light', while hating a brother or sister; is still in the darkness. Whoever loves a brother or sister lives in the light. But whoever hates another is in the darkness, walks in the darkness, I am the true light that has come into the world, to bring you all out of the darkness and into the light."

The people were astounded with the words of Yeshua but Levi and a group around him did not seem to warm to what Yeshua was saying, and they were mumbling and grumbling among themselves.

"Yeshua, have pity on me," a voice cried out loudly from beyond the crowd. The people turned around and saw the man, and saw that he was a leper and they moved even further away from him.

Yeshua steered a path through the crowd and approached the man. All eyes of the crowd were upon him. Yeshua went up to the man and took him by the hand and raised him up for he was kneeling down and stooped over, with his face on the ground. He was covered in leprosy.

Levi and his friends were aghast. "He is touching a leper, he cannot be from God, he has made himself unclean," Levi said, to those around him. But everyone was more interested to see what was happening with Yeshua and the leper.

"What is your name, young man?" Yeshua asked.

"I am Baruch and I have been cursed with this leprosy for several years now. Lord, if you choose, you can make me clean," Baruch pleaded.

"Do you believe I can cure you, Baruch?" Yeshua asked.

"If you choose to, Yeshua, I believe you can, I believe that you are the Promised One sent by God; please, Yeshua, make me clean," Baruch continued pleading.

"I do choose, Baruch. Be made clean." Immediately, the leprosy left him, disappearing like dead skin from his body. And the crowd was amazed and in awe of what they had just witnessed.

"Baruch, go now and show yourself to the priest, and, as Moses commanded, make an offering for your cleansing, as a testimony to them."

Elijah stood with mouth open in awe and disbelief. The words that Yeshua had uttered about the rich had disturbed him, but now that was all forgotten, as he witnessed the power of Yeshua. *Yeshua is definitely a man of God; no one can work such miracles. So, all that was being said about him is true*, Elijah said to himself.

Several others came forward with their sick and Yeshua cured them all. And now Yeshua felt the need to withdraw to the woods again. He told Elijah and the family and Miriam and his mother that he would spend some time in the woods.

"Don't be too long, Yeshua, lunch should be ready within the hour," Lydia said.

Elijah, Lydia and the two Miriams walked home together, deep in thought for a while, until Elijah broke the silence.

"Miriam, your son is special, he has great gifts, but I think he is headed for trouble," Elijah said.

"Why do you say so, Elijah?" Miriam asked.

"You saw Levi and his cronies there, the Pharisees and the Scribes and the other hotshot religious leaders. They are not going to be happy with Yeshua, stealing their limelight and their power over the people. I can see Yeshua's reputation spreading all over Galilee and Judaea and even in places like Samaria and Phoenicia and to the other side of the Sea of Galilee," Elijah said.

"Elijah is right; Yeshua's power of persuasion and his teaching is different to that of the rabbis, the priests and the religious leaders. And he speaks with authority and is down to earth, and speaks the language of the people, and champions the rights of the poor, the outcasts, the vulnerable, the dispossessed and the marginalised. He even touched a leper, which is unheard of, he made himself unclean, and you saw how Levi and those with him reacted to that," Lydia said.

"And he has this incredible power to heal the sick, the blind and lame and the incapacitated. None of the other priests or Pharisees, Sadducees, or Scribes can do what Yeshua does, and they are already exhibiting signs of jealousy," Elijah said.

The two Miriams were deep in thought.

When they all arrived home, the servants were busy roasting lamb on the fire outside and cooking vegetables and they could smell the aroma of the roast, and when they entered the house the smell of freshly baked bread, delighted their senses.

The next day, after breakfast, of bread and honey, Miriam was ready to accompany Yeshua to meet those they already spoke about. Yeshua's mother decided to remain and spend the time with Lydia. The two had become close.

"Yeshua, I will take you to the lepers, first, they were six and now there are five of them." Miriam had visited them before, to bring them food, but she always kept her distance. But now she was not afraid, she was with Yeshua and she knew, she felt, that she would not be in danger.

As Yeshua and Miriam approached the cave, voices cried out, "Unclean! Unclean! Unclean!"

"It is okay, this is Miriam, and I have brought Yeshua. He wishes to visit you." The lepers too have heard of Yeshua, even before he had healed one of them. They were aware that Baruch was missing; he had said he was going to meet with Yeshua. They wondered what happened to him.

"My friends, Yeshua has healed your friend, Baruch, and he wishes to meet you." The five, three men, and two women, tentatively came out of the cave. They were dressed in rags and had their hands and most of their faces covered. Yeshua and Miriam's hearts went out to them.

"Yeshua, if you have healed Baruch, then heal us too," one of the group, cried out.

Yeshua then approached them, Miriam followed. Yeshua then touched them all one by one. "I bless you, my friends. You have been shunned, cast out, ostracised, and suffered much. I bring you the Good News of God's love and compassion for you. He has heard your cries and he has sent me to you. You are now cleansed. Go and show yourselves to the priest and make an offering as the Law of Moses requires."

Within moments, they were all transformed. They were still dressed in rags, but their skin was restored to their former beauty. They looked at their hands and lifted their rags to inspect their legs and they touched their faces and they cried out in joy. "Oh, thank you, Yeshua, oh blessed one, you are indeed the Promised One, the Anointed One, our Saviour, praise to you Yeshua." They were overjoyed.

"Here you are; some money for food and clothing and for your offering to the priest. Go, my friends, and be at peace," Miriam said, sharing in their joy. She was overcome, and gazed at Yeshua, his face was glowing.

The lepers hurried away; a new life awaited them.

Miriam and Yeshua walked for a while in silence. Then Yeshua stopped and had to sit on some grass and rest. So much power had gone out of him. They sat for a while in silence. Yeshua was so pleased to have someone, to have Miriam beside him, to be part of his experience, part of his work.

When Yeshua got to his feet, Miriam said, "Yeshua, I will now take you to the house where the prostitutes live. Are you sure you want to go there?" Miriam asked. She was concerned for Yeshua's good name and people would misconstrue Yeshua's visit. It was early in the day and Miriam did not think there would be any men there. So, they walked in silence for a while. It seemed to Miriam that Yeshua needed the silence. She recalled how he had said that when the power of healing came out of him, it drained him. And she witnessed that after he healed all those lepers. They now walked along slowly.

"There it is, Yeshua." Ahead, Yeshua saw a grey sombre-looking stone building. They approached, and when they arrived at the front door, Miriam knocked and called out, "Bethsheba, Jezebel, it's Miriam, I have brought you a visitor, Yeshua, the Nazarene."

Immediately, Bethsheba and Jezebel appeared; their hair long and flowing and they were dressed in exotic, graceful garments, and adorned with jewellery and smelling of sweet scent. "Miriam, how nice to see you and Yeshua, do come in. Yeshua, we have heard so much about you, and all the miraculous signs that have accompanied you." The ladies were overawed and could not believe that Yeshua would come to visit them. They did not for a moment believe that Yeshua had come for their services. They knew Miriam, she was a friend and they sensed the bond between Miriam and Yeshua. The other ladies had already joined them. Jezebel introduced them to Yeshua.

"I am pleased to meet you all ladies," Yeshua said.

"Yeshua is staying with us. He is preaching in the synagogue, and outside the synagogue he has healed many from the town. We have just been to the leper cave, and all of them were cleansed, and healed," Miriam said.

The women were in awe, some of them with mouths agape. They could not believe this man of God would deign to visit them, here at this place.

"Yeshua, thank you, you honour us with your visit, can we get you something to drink or some refreshment," Bethsheba asked.

"A drink of water will be fine, Bethsheba," Yeshua said.

Yeshua then sat down and chatted with the women. He asked them about their lives, what brought them to this place, and he listened to their stories. Some were abused, others divorced, some widowed, but all ill-treated, cast out, ostracised. They had to fend for themselves, and turned to this way of life.

Yeshua listened and his heart went out to them. He did not condemn them or preach to them but said, "My dear ladies, you are more than friends to me, you are my sisters. I have been sent by Abba, my Abba and your Abba, to bring you the

Good News of his great love for you. He knows of your plight. He has seen all that you have endured. He does not condemn you; he loves you, just the way you are. You are dear to him. He wants you to know that he understands and does not condemn, or judge, he is your father and your friend and he loves you as we do, Miriam and me. More than we do. He is your friend, not your enemy. He wants your salvation. He loves you with a boundless and unconditional love and he will never stop loving you, no matter what. I want you to remember that always," Yeshua said. His heart went out to these ladies, and he prayed in his heart for Yahweh to bless them and give them the graces they needed.

Yeshua and Miriam spent quite some time listening to the stories of all these women, and they in turn wanted to know all about Yeshua, and he spoke to them of his relationship with Yahweh and why he was sent, to bring Good News to the poor and downtrodden and to set all those enslaved in any way, free. With these women too, Yeshua felt at ease addressing his father as Yahweh. He told them that the time has come for all to repent and to turn to Yahweh, who has sent him to bring peace, freedom, salvation, redemption and love to all.

The women listened and Miriam could see how deeply impressed they were with Yeshua, and how his visit affected them. She could sense how overawed they were and surprised that this man of God, this holy one, would even look upon them, let alone visit them and befriend them, and speak such loving words to them.

When Yeshua and Miriam left the ladies, as they were walking away, two men were approaching the house. They looked at Yeshua and recognised him. Miriam noticed their look of surprise. She knew that they would spread the news all over the town that they saw Yeshua at the house of prostitution.

The next day, after Yeshua's talk on the need not to judge, that judgement is to be left to God alone, the people gathered outside the synagogue as usual, and one of the Pharisees, surrounded by his peers, priests and Scribes pointed to Yeshua and cried out, "this man is an impostor, he does not respect the Sabbath, he performs healing on the Sabbath, he is unclean, touches the unclean, he is immoral, he visits the house of prostitution and associates with prostitutes and sinners, he cannot be from God."

Yeshua did not reply, but Miriam spoke up, "I took Yeshua, to the house of prostitution. He wanted to visit the ladies there. To let them know of God's love for them. I was with Yeshua. We spent the time listening to the ladies, listening to their stories of ill-treatment, abuse at the hands of men. We listened to their stories of how we all have abandoned them and cast them out and left them to rot. Yeshua came to bring them comfort and to let them know that Adonai hears their cries, and knows of their plight, and that he loves them unconditionally, as he does for all of us," Miriam said, in Yeshua's defence.

The crowed were amazed as they listened to Miriam speaking so eloquently in defence of Yeshua. They all knew of her, the mad one, the one possessed of seven demons, and here she was speaking with such clarity, and wisdom and persuasion. They were all in awe, especially the women. For a woman to speak so, publicly, is unheard of. Some of the women, came later, and spoke to Miriam, and wanted to hear more.

Magdala was abuzz with what happened. Word had spread of Yeshua's visit to the lepers' cave and how he had healed them all, and also his visit to the house of prostitution and Miriam's defence of Yeshua.

Yeshua spent the rest of the week in Magdala, preaching to the people, not only in the synagogue but in open places, for people sought him out, and he continued to visit the elderly, the sick, the lonely and the outcasts and the vulnerable, and he healed many.

The time came for Yeshua to move on. He now planned to go to Capernaum. He had planned to set up home there, but he was glad that Elijah had agreed for him and his mother to stay at their place in Capernaum. Yeshua decided he would stay there for a few days, and then scout the terrain for a place to set up home, and then head back to Nazareth with his mother. Miriam was glad, she was beginning to pine for Nazareth, and the familiar people and sights, sounds and smells of the place.

Chapter Forty
Back in Nazareth

Yeshua only spent a few days in Capernaum. He was eager to take his mother back to Nazareth, for she was pining too much for home. He and his mother enjoyed their stay in the big house, and the rooms that Elijah made available to them. Yeshua decided not to begin preaching in Capernaum, he would leave that when he returned. He was glad to have Miriam of Magdala to accompany and assist him, and he would need others to support him in his work, and also to be coached to carry on after him, for Yeshua had a sense of the opposition and danger he would face. Elijah was right to warn him.

The sight of Nazareth tugged at their heartstrings and even Ben hee-hawed his delight. They had been gone a long time and it was a joy to be home. Yeshua no longer sought or took any more carpentry work, he was now a celebrity even in Nazareth, and the place was abuzz when news spread that Yeshua was back in Nazareth. But there were many Nazarenes who were sceptics and refused to believe in what was being said about this lad they saw grow up before their eyes, putting paid to the saying that 'a prophet is never accepted in his own country'.

Gamaliel had been seriously ill while Yeshua was away, so ill that he no longer was able to teach or preach or fulfil his duties as pastor and preacher of the word. The religious leaders in Jerusalem had moved swiftly against Yeshua, they orchestrated a replacement for Gamaliel, a rabbi from Jerusalem. The rabbi brought a team of Pharisees, Sadducees and Scribes with him. The hierarchy of Jerusalem wanted to keep an eye on Yeshua the Nazarene, who was stirring up the people. And many other people from all over Galilee and even from Judaea flocked to Nazareth. They all wanted a glimpse of Yeshua; they were curious and hoping to see him work his wonders. But there were also those who came with great hope, hoping he was the Promised One, the Messiah who would set them free from the bondage of Rome.

Yeshua's hope of returning to Nazareth for some quiet time to refresh was soon shattered when he realised the situation. The place was full of strangers. Yeshua, when he discovered that Gamaliel was ill, immediately went to visit his friend and confidante. Gamaliel had a lady who was caring for him but he was bedridden.

"Gamaliel, I am so glad to see you, but not so glad to see you so sick," Yeshua said.

"Looks like my heart is saying it has had enough, Yeshua. But I am glad to see you, tell me all about your travels," Gamaliel said eagerly and seemed to perk up in Yeshua's presence.

Yeshua related all that had happened starting from Cana and all the way to Capernaum and back. And Gamaliel informed Yeshua of the situation of the new regime, the new religious leaders in Nazareth, and how the place is overflowing with visitors all wanting a glimpse of him.

Gamaliel had heard of Yeshua's power of healing but he did not ask to be healed. He was resigned to his fate, whatever that was. "I'm sure the chief rabbi, Jerome, will be in touch with you soon. He has a whole contingent with him, some all the way from Jerusalem, they are here to keep an eye on you, Yeshua, so be careful," Gamaliel said.

"I will, my friend."

"Yeshua, Gamaliel has to rest now," Gamaliel's carer announced.

Yeshua said goodbye to his friend. He then went to visit Achim and his family and they too were overjoyed to see Yeshua, especially now that he had become famous. Achim was still single and from what Yeshua gathered he did not seem to be interested in the opposite sex, so Yeshua did not inquire if he was courting anyone. When Yeshua left Achim and his family he went to see Rebecca, and she too had not yet been betrothed to anyone. Yeshua had hoped that she would by now have found someone. They went to the forest and walked and talked for a long time. Rebecca wanted to hear all that had happened in Yeshua's life and he was most willing to talk with her. He told her especially about Miriam of Magdala, and her parents, and how good they have been to him and his mother. And about them giving him a place to stay, in Capernaum, where he was going to return to continue his mission, the work that the Father had for him and for what he was sent.

When Rebecca heard that Miriam of Magdala was going to accompany Yeshua on his mission and support him, it was like a light came on in her mind. She decided that she would also be a disciple of Yeshua's; she too would follow him, wherever he went and support him in his work, in whatever way she could. She believed that Yeshua would never be completely hers, but she would be completely his, she would give her life in following him, accompanying him, supporting him in whatever way she could. She told Yeshua so.

"Are you sure, this is what you want to do, Rebecca?" Yeshua said.

"Yes, Yeshua, I have never been surer of anything in my life."

Yeshua was pleased and happy to have Rebecca, not only as his disciple but as his friend and confidante and support, together with Miriam of Magdala. And he knew she and Miriam would get on well together and it would be good that they had each other. And he also knew that they both would be good for him, as confidantes, and counsellors for him. He now had two disciples who would help him in his work and they too would carry on his work when he was no longer there. Now that he had Miriam and Rebecca as disciples, Yeshua sensed that he needed to call more, have a band of followers, of disciples, whom he would teach in a special way, so that if anything happened to him, they could carry on his work of spreading the Good News of redemption and salvation for all.

In Nazareth, Yeshua kept to himself, but when the Sabbath came, he went to the synagogue hall as he usually did. There were many religious leaders there, whom Yeshua had not met before, and the whole of Nazareth were present, as well as many visitors from far and wide. Rabbi Jerome presided over the service. He realised that the synagogue was more packed than usual, with no more sitting or standing space and he knew they all came to listen to Yeshua. He had no option but to invite Yeshua to speak. He handed Yeshua the Scroll with the Book of Isaiah. Yeshua looked for and found a text he wanted, one he had commented on before, and began to read:

"The Spirit of the Lord is upon me, because he has chosen and anointed me to bring good news to the poor. He has sent me to proclaim release to the captives and recovery of sight to the blind, to let the oppressed go free, to proclaim the year of the Lord's favour." Yeshua then rolled up the scroll and gave it back to an attendant and sat down. And all eyes were fixed on Yeshua, full of expectation on what he was going to say.

Yeshua got up and began by saying, "My dear fellow Nazarenes and all visitors to Nazareth, today this Scripture has been fulfilled in your hearing." As Yeshua spoke, everyone in the synagogue listened and was impressed and amazed at the gracious words that flowed from his mouth. Those from Nazareth had heard him speak before, but never like this, and they now saw him with different eyes and listened with different ears. He was one of them, and now he is famous, he is renowned as a great preacher and a miracle worker, yet he has not shown any of these signs here in Nazareth, he has not healed anyone, not even his old friend Gamaliel, who is now severely ill, and may even be dying.

When Yeshua came out of the synagogue, people continued to gather around him and they were all astounded by his wisdom and some were murmuring among themselves, "where did this man get this wisdom, and the power to heal that we have heard of, yet have not seen for ourselves, for not a single person has been healed here in Nazareth. Is he not the son of the late Yosef and Miriam? Where did he get all this power?" And stirred on by those sent to keep an eye on Yeshua, they took offence at Yeshua, especially because he had worked no wonders here in his own hometown of Nazareth.

Yeshua sensed what they were thinking, so he said to them, "Truly I tell you, no prophet is accepted in his hometown. And I know what you are thinking, 'do here, also in your hometown, the things you have done in Cana and Ziddim and Magdala and all the way to Capernaum'."

Yeshua continued, "There were many widows in Israel in the time of Elijah, when for three years and six months there was a severe famine all over the land. Yet Elijah was sent to none of them except to a widow, a Canaanite in the Phoenician town of Sidon. There were also many lepers in Israel in the time of the prophet Elisha, and none of them were cleansed, except Naaman the Syrian."

When they heard this, the religious leaders were enraged, and they stirred up their supporters, filling them too, with rage. They hurled false accusations against Yeshua, and they made Yeshua to be an impostor, and that he did all those signs through the power of Beelzebub. Many were surprised, and shocked, never before has anything like this happened in their town, and in their synagogue. They were confused, and pandemonium ensued. The crowds followed, wanting to see what was going to happen. It was becoming like a blood sport.

Rebecca was at a loss on what to do, she felt so helpless. Yeshua too was in shock, and taken by surprise. Was this a sign of things to come? The mob, stoked on by the religious leaders, took Yeshua by force to the brow of the hill, on which Nazareth was built and took him to the cliff's edge, intending to hurl him off the cliff. But Yeshua, knowing his time had not yet come, simply disappeared from their sight. This was the only sign that Yeshua did in Nazareth, and it was the talk of the town. But the religious leaders and their followers continued with their vilification of Yeshua, and repeated their cry that Yeshua was possessed, and that he did what he did through the power of Beelzebub.

Later in the day, Rebecca felt lost, and she wondered where Yeshua was. He had disappeared into thin air. She went to see Miriam, his mother, and found Yeshua there, sitting inside, having something to eat, and unperturbed, as if nothing had happened. She was so pleased and relieved to see that Yeshua was alright.

"Yeshua, I sense that danger awaits you. If people from your own hometown of Nazareth did what they did, what can you expect elsewhere?" Rebecca said. "Yeshua, I think we should leave Nazareth," Rebecca added, with urgency in her voice.

"We shall, Rebecca, we shall. A prophet is never accepted in his own hometown," Yeshua said again, with a tinge of sadness. "We shall leave tomorrow at first light and head for Capernaum."

Chapter Forty-One
Capernaum by the Sea of Galilee

Yeshua and Rebecca left Nazareth way before sunrise, and Yeshua intended to walk non-stop to Capernaum. Rebecca was still feeling so uneasy about what happened in Nazareth. She could not believe that her own people would do that to Yeshua. But she had noticed how Nazareth had changed, since Gamaliel was replaced.

Yeshua sensed Rebecca's uneasiness. "Rebecca, fear not, the Lord is with us. We have work to do, his work, and He will not let anything happen to us until all is accomplished."

Rebecca began to feel a bit more at ease.

Yeshua planned to stop at Magdala only to fetch Miriam. She would be ready to leave, for she was waiting for him, to follow him and take him to their home in Capernaum. He planned to skirt around and by pass the towns of Cana and Ziddim. Yeshua had walked this journey a number of times now, and he estimated that it took him between five and six hours and with Rebecca who was able to match his pace, they would do so now. They had left an hour before sunrise that meant they could be in Magdala around the fifth hour. That would be a good time to stop for lunch, and that would still give Miriam most of the afternoon with her mother, and to get ready to leave. It would only take a little more than an hour to Capernaum and Yeshua wanted to arrive there under cover of darkness.

Miriam was overjoyed to see Yeshua. They embraced warmly. She could not forget what he had done for her, he had changed her life forever, and now she wanted to give her life to love and serve him and the One who sent him. She wanted to live close to him and learn all she could from him and support him in his work. Yeshua introduced Rebecca.

"So, you are Rebecca, Yeshua told me so much about you. You are his dearest and closest friend. I am so glad to meet you," Miriam said.

"And I have heard so much about you too, Miriam. As we walked together from Nazareth, Yeshua told me all about you, and like you, Miriam, I also intend to be a disciple and follow Yeshua wherever he goes and assist him in any way I can," Rebecca said.

"I am so glad, Rebecca, that I am not alone, we are now two disciples," Miriam said proudly.

"Lydia, it is so good to see you again. Meet Rebecca," Yeshua introduced Rebecca to Miriam's mother.

"Rebecca, so good to meet you at last, I feel as if you are one of my daughters, Yeshua speaks so highly of you and you have been such a good friend to him in Nazareth, and I am so pleased that my Miriam won't be alone in accompanying Yeshua," Lydia said.

"Miriam would not have been alone, if Rebecca had not come too, Lydia," Yeshua said with a smile.

"I know, Yeshua, but you would be busy with your work, and you would be surrounded by, swamped by crowds wherever you go," Lydia said. "I am so glad that Rebecca will be a friend to Miriam too," Lydia added.

"Yes, mother, I am glad too," Miriam said, as she and Lydia exchanged smiles.

Yeshua was so pleased that Rebecca and Miriam took an instant liking to each other. Miriam then excused herself as she went into her room and asked Rebecca to join her. It wasn't long, when Rebecca shared with Miriam, what happened in Nazareth.

"Really Rebecca? How awful! I would not have expected that from the Nazarenes. I do fear the Pharisees and the other religious elite, especially in places like Jerusalem. We have to be ready for whatever happens," Miriam said. The two then shared their stories, and Rebecca was amazed by Miriam's story and how Yeshua had cured her. And Miriam in turn was touched and could understand what Rebecca told her about her true feelings for Yeshua. After some time, the two of them joined Yeshua and Lydia.

"Elijah was here until a few nights ago, but he is now in Capernaum and is prepared for you to come, Yeshua. Your old room is all ready. And Rebecca, you can have the room that Yeshua's mother, Miriam, had," Lydia said.

"I would like to leave just before sunset, and not be seen by anyone here in Magdala and we should be in Capernaum before it really gets too dark," Yeshua said.

"I can show you a way to skirt around the town, Yeshua," Miriam said.

Miriam had her bag all packed. And as sunset approached, she said her goodbye to her mother. "Mother, I am not sure when I will see you again. I will tell father to come home every night while I am gone. It is only a short distance and he can do it, without much effort," Miriam said.

"Don't worry about me, Miriam, I will be all right, you take care and care for Yeshua, peace go with you, my love, stay safe," Lydia said as she hugged her daughter.

"I love you, mother."

"I love you too, my child. God go with you," Lydia said.

"He does, mother, he does," Miriam said, as she and Rebecca exchanged knowing smiles again.

And then they were on their way. Yeshua walked on ahead, he wanted the silence for reflection and prayer, and he wanted to give time and space to Rebecca and Miriam so that they could get to know each other better. Yeshua prayed for his two friends and his first two disciples. He knew he would have to find more to accompany him, and be with him and learn from him to carry on his work, when he was no longer around. Yeshua was aware of what had happened to Johanan who was still in prison, and he had no illusions of what might happen to him, for what Johanan preached he would continue and fulfil. Yeshua knew that he would incur the wrath not only of Herod but of the Pharisees, Scribes, the Sadducees and the priests, the religious leaders whom Yeshua had observed and found them wanting in what they preached and how they lived. And then there was Rome, who would come down quickly on anyone who stirred up the people in any way. Yeshua knew that the people had a false idea of the Messiah; that he was going to come in triumph and power and overthrow Rome and set them free.

They arrived at a locked house that was in darkness. Rebecca was impressed with the fine-looking building, and how big it was. Miriam went out back to where the fire had now become almost extinguished but where there were still some hot embers, enough to light a large lamp, large enough to light up the front of the house. They then entered the dark place that lit immediately with the flame from the huge lamp. Miriam put the lamp on a large lamp stand standing in the corner of the front room. Next to the lamp stand on a table stood four more lamps, which Miriam lit and gave one each to Rebecca and Yeshua. She then led them to their rooms, and when she left them, she lit a fire in the fireplace to warm up the place.

After a while, Yeshua and Rebecca joined Miriam and she offered them something to eat. "I have brought some bread with honey and some fruit and dates and nuts with me, or would you like me to make us some soup," Miriam asked.

"The bread will be fine with me, Miriam," Yeshua said.

"Me too," Rebecca added.

The three sat and chatted like old friends for a long time. Then Yeshua told them that he wanted to find some more people who would accompany him, be his disciples, and carry on his work, if he had to endure a similar fate to Johanan. "It is urgent that I call some more, Miriam and Rebecca, to join you. I want you and them to be more than just my disciples. I want to endow you with the authority and the power to carry on my work in the event of my being taken by the authorities. We have the power of Rome to contend with and they have their spies and even the religious leaders in Jerusalem are working hand in glove with them. So, we have to be careful. It is urgent I speak openly and boldly. This could cause me some harassment but I trust in Abba, his Spirit is with me and will guide and protect me," Yeshua said.

Early the next morning, Miriam had gone to the chief rabbi, Malachi, who was in charge of the synagogue and the services and she told him that Yeshua was staying with her and that he was making his home here in Capernaum, and he sought permission to speak to the people in the synagogue, on the Sabbath, which was the next day.

Malachi was not too pleased for this to happen. But he had heard of Yeshua, the carpenter from Nazareth, who was stirring up so much interest, with his preaching and his miracles of healing that the whole of Capernaum was talking about him, and hoping he would come to their town. And if they knew he was here and he was not given permission to speak in the synagogue, Malachi knew there would be hell to pay. So, he acquiesced. In a way though, he too was curious to see if all that was being said about this man from Nazareth was true or whether he was an impostor.

The word then spread like wildfire. And when Yeshua, Miriam and Rebecca finally arrived at the synagogue, it was filled to the rafters. The murmuring ceased as Yeshua was seen for the first time.

"There he is."

"Is that him?"

"He looks so ordinary."

"He looks like a carpenter."

"Can he really be the Promised One?" were some of the murmurings among the people.

Yeshua was aware that the people when attending the synagogue were accustomed to hear about the power of Yahweh, the need for them to obey his commandments or suffer severe consequences. Yeshua was aware of how the people were reminded over and over again of their wickedness and their need for repentance. But he wanted to give the people hope and encouragement, so he began his preaching.

"My dear brothers and sisters, I come to you from my Father in heaven, he is our Father, and hallowed be his name. His kingdom has come; his kingdom is with you, within you. Your Father knows not only all that you do, he knows you intimately, from the moment you were conceived in your mother's womb he knew you and loved you and he knows you by name. So, fear not, he is not a harsh judge or one that keeps account of every weakness. When you stumble, he is there to pick you up. All you have to do is to call on him for his forgiveness and his love. But he sees not only your weaknesses; he also sees your strengths. And this gives him so much joy. Mothers, fathers, sons, daughters, he sees the work you do, the way you honour and sacrifice for each other. He sees your love and care for those near and dear to you and for the less fortunate and your reward will be great in heaven."

Yeshua then paused and looked around the synagogue and could see that the people were hanging on his every word, he now wanted to encourage them to greater heights, so he continued, "You are the salt of the earth, but if salt has lost its taste, how can its saltiness be restored. It is no longer good for anything, but is thrown out and trampled underfoot. I come to restore that salt in your life, to bring out the flavour of goodness in you. You are no longer living in the dark; for I come to bring you out of the darkness and into the light. You, my dear friends, are now the light of your city, the light of the world.

"Last night, when my friend Rebecca from Nazareth came here with me, we were shown such hospitality by one of your own, Miriam, daughter of Elijah and Lydia, who you know was someone that some of you found wanting and looked down upon because of her illness, some of you believing she was possessed of the evil one. But the power and love of Abba has touched her and made her whole, and she is now not only my dearest friend but the first of my disciples; listen to her and learn from her, the Spirit of Adonai is upon her, and upon Rebecca, who with her are both now my disciples and who accompany and support me in spreading the Good News of God's boundless love and compassion. The Spirit now rests upon them, so listen to them."

Miriam and Rebecca were seated together in the court of the women, out of sight of the main assembly. They looked at each other with surprise; they did not expect Yeshua to mention them at all, no other religious leader ever made such mention of women, in such a way. They were there to accompany him and see to his needs and support him, make sure he was well fed, wash his clothes, find him lodging, befriend and comfort him, and see to his material and emotional needs, but it seems that he was expecting more, or rather blessing them with the power of the Spirit and something stirred within them.

Yeshua continued, "When we arrived at Miriam's home, here in Capernaum, it was in darkness. Miriam disappeared to the back of the house and left Rebecca and I standing in the darkness but when she returned with lamps for each of us the whole place lit up. As we entered the darkness of the house it lit up too, and we could see our way forward. And from one lamp we passed on the light to other lamps and the house was filled with light. To you, my brothers and sisters of Capernaum, and from other parts of Galilee, I have come to bring you light, to bring you out of the darkness and into the light. You have been living in darkness, but now you are living in the light. You are called to be the light of the world, so let your light shine and light up the darkness all around you.

"Like Miriam lit those lamps, I now light your lamp. Never let your light go out, but let it shine and light up the world around you. Light up your city of Capernaum. Remember a city built on a hill cannot be hid. Miriam after lighting the lamp put it on the central lamp stand and it lit up the entire house. No one after lighting a lamp puts it under a table or under a bushel basket, but on the lamp stand, where it gives light to all in the house. In the same way let your light shine before others, so that they may see your good works and give glory to your Father in heaven.

"My brothers and sisters, I bring you peace, the peace that comes from Abba, who wants you to live in peace and harmony with each other. This is the way people of the light live. All evil deeds are done under the shield of darkness. But you are children of the light, and you no longer live in darkness.

"I challenge you, my friends, to excel in your efforts to live in the light. You know the Law of Moses, 'Thou shalt not kill'. You have heard how it was said to those of ancient times, 'You shall not murder and whoever murders shall be liable to judgement.' I am sure I do not have to exhort you in this way. For I am sure that among you, no one is a murderer, even though at times you might feel like murdering someone who has harmed you or your loved ones in some way.

"But I say to you, that if you are angry with a brother or sister, you will be liable to judgement. And if you insult a brother or sister, or call them a fool, you will be liable to the Council. So, in future before you come to the synagogue on the Sabbath when you are offering your gift at the altar, if you remember your brother or sister has something against you and you have something against them and harbour ill will, and anger against them, leave your gift there before the altar and go, first be reconciled to your brother and sister and then come and offer your gift.

"Hold it!" Yeshua smiled at his listeners and raised his hand. "I do not expect any of you to now rush out and go and reconcile with your brother or sister who has harmed you, insulted you, or called you a fool, or to whom you have done these things, you can do so afterwards, but in future, do so before you come with your gift to the Lord. That is the gift he wants; he is pure spirit.

"My dear friends, I know there is good reason at times for us to feel anger rising within us. It is part of our nature. But to feel that emotion within us; is not displeasing to our God. He did not create us with evil or anger in our hearts. That has been of our own doing or rather our undoing. I have come to lead you out of the darkness of anger and into the true light of forgiveness and reconciliation with those who hurt you in any way. And to give you the strength not to do likewise. To feel anger when you have been unjustly treated is part of being human, and one needs to stand up to injustice but with real justice and with mercy and compassion. It is what we do with our anger, how we react that pleases or displeases our heavenly Father, who is full of compassion, love, mercy and forgiveness for us all."

Yeshua paused again; there was so much to ponder on what he was saying. "Therefore, I say to you, do not judge, so that you may not be judged. For with the judgement you make, you will be judged, and the measure you give, will be the measure you get. Why do you see the speck in your neighbour's eye, but do not notice the log in your own eye? Or how can you say to your neighbour, 'Let me take the speck out of your eye,' while the log is in your own eye?"

Yeshua continued, the words and thoughts seem to be gushing like a torrent from his heart and his lips. "The eye is the lamp of the body. So, if your eye is healthy, your whole body will be full of light but if your eye is unhealthy, your whole body will be full of darkness. So, I say again to you, you are the light of the world, so let your light shine and light up the darkness all around you.

"My dear friends, I have come to bring you the Good News of God our Father's great and undying love for you. This is the message I bring you and to the entire world. God is love and who abides in love, abides in God. Let me then conclude on the word of love, the real challenge of love. You have heard that it was said, 'you shall love your neighbour and hate your enemy.' But I say to you, love your enemies, and pray for those who persecute you, so that you may be true children of your Father in heaven, for he makes the sun rise on the evil and on the good, and sends rain on the righteous and the unrighteous. For if you love those who love you, what reward do you have? Do not even the tax-collectors do the same! And if you greet only your brothers and sisters, what more are you doing than others. Do not even the Gentiles do the same? Be perfect therefore, as your heavenly Father is perfect."

Yeshua then sat down, allowing for time of silence, time for reflection. There was silence. The people were astounded at his teaching. He spoke with such authority and depth and wisdom.

All of a sudden, the silence was shattered as a voice from the crowd shouted in a loud voice, "Let us alone! What have you to do with us, Yeshua of Nazareth? Have you come to destroy us? I know who you are, the Holy One of God."

The entire congregation was aghast, they all turned towards the man, who was shouting. The people recognised him as unclean and possessed of a demon, and those close by moved away, not wanting to be made unclean themselves. "He is possessed, stay away, he is unclean," someone uttered close by.

There was consternation in the synagogue; the man should not have been there; they were all afraid of becoming unclean. And they were terrified of his mere presence and overcome with fear as they heard him shouting such words. They then turned to Yeshua, who now stood up and began walking towards the possessed man. The crowds parted, making way for Yeshua. As Yeshua approached, the man continued with his protestations, "Let us alone, let us alone, what have you to do with us, Yeshua of Nazareth, I know you are the Holy One of God!"

As soon as Yeshua reached the man, he rebuked him, "Be silent!" and then he commanded, "I say to you, come out of him!" All of a sudden, the man shook all over, as if in a fit, and he was thrown to the ground. The people watched in terror, and then the man went limp and still and all could see a complete change, a metamorphosis. The man looked at Yeshua and Yeshua reached out his hand to the man. The man, who seemed unharmed, rose to his feet, still holding Yeshua's hand. "Go in peace, my dear man, and may God the Father be with you now and forever."

The man thanked Yeshua and said, "You are indeed the Promised One, the Messiah, who has come to set us free. You have freed me of these demons that have possessed and tormented me all my life, I thank you, Yeshua." And with that, the man left the synagogue.

The people were all amazed. One man said, "What has just happened here, with his words, with his authority and power, he commands the unclean spirits, and out they come!"

This incident spread like wild fire all over Capernaum and beyond. But Malachi, the rabbi, and those around him did not seem all that impressed or pleased. "This man cannot be a man of God, he cannot be the Holy One of God; he does not respect the Sabbath, for he healed this man on the Sabbath and here in this house of God."

Yeshua then left. He let Malachi complete the Sabbath service. The people were amazed at what they had just witnessed. But they feared Malachi and his cohort, so they remained in the synagogue for the rest of the service. When Yeshua came outside, he was feeling drained, and was glad to see Miriam and Rebecca waiting for him.

"Would you like to return to the house, Yeshua, for some refreshment, perhaps?" Miriam asked.

"Thank you, Miriam, maybe later. Let us go to the Sea of Galilee for a walk on the beach, I need to revive my spirits." So off they went to the beach. Yeshua took off his sandals and walked along the sandy shore, with his feet in the water. As it was the Sabbath, and most of the people were in the synagogue, there were not many people at the seashore.

Yeshua wondered about these people. Religion was central to the lives of the people of Galilee. Yahweh was never out of their thoughts. They feared his power and his judgement. And they were all waiting and hoping that he would send the Messiah who would save them from the tyranny of Rome and all their oppressors. But these people here on the seashore did not seem to bother, for they were not in the synagogue on the Sabbath, and they were enjoying the day of rest with a picnic on the beach. Yeshua, Miriam and Rebecca greeted them and they greeted in return, not a bit surprised to see a man with two women walking and talking.

"These people, Miriam, Rebecca, are like sheep without a shepherd. But even those there in the synagogue are also like lost sheep, like sheep without a true shepherd. The Father has sent me to seek out all that are lost and to bring them back into the fold."

Yeshua, Miriam and Rebecca continued walking for about an hour, when Yeshua stopped and turned around. "I think I would like for us to go home now. I would love some of your father's grapes and maybe a cup of wine," Yeshua said. "But I want to come back here tomorrow," Yeshua said.

Chapter Forty-Two
The Big Fisherman and the Roman Centurion

The next day, very early when most of the town was still asleep, Yeshua went to the Sea of Galilee for a walk, for his morning prayer and reflection, his time with Yahweh. He was alone, walking along the shore, deep in thought when he was disturbed by voices and looked up to see two men, fishermen, who were washing their nets. They must have finished fishing all night. They seemed to recognise Yeshua, but Yeshua did not at first recognise them.

"You are Yeshua, the carpenter from Nazareth. We are from Bethsaida, but we heard about what happened in the synagogue here in Capernaum. We heard that you were staying here in Capernaum and that you spoke to the people and healed a man of an unclean spirit," one of the men said.

"We actually met you, well, never really met you, we were on the lake when you met our father Jonah; we were fishing at Bethsaida, on the other side of the lake. You won't remember, Yeshua. My brother and I were still young then, must be about ten years ago. My name is Shimon and this is my brother, Andreus," Shimon, the taller of the two, said.

"Yes, I do remember your father, Jonah. He was very kind to me and gave me some fish to eat that he had just caught and cooked on a charcoal fire; it was the tastiest fish I ever ate. Yes, I do remember you both, Andreus, you waved to me from the boat, you were a distance from the shore, and you Shimon just ignored me, or rather you were so totally engrossed in catching fish that you barely acknowledged me."

"We heard some of the things you said in the synagogue and all about your cleansing of the man possessed with demons and what the evil spirits cried out when the possessed man approached you," Andreus said.

"Did you have a good catch?" Yeshua asked, changing the subject.

"No, not at all, it was a bad night, we fished all night and caught nothing," Shimon said.

"What a pity, I was hoping for some fresh fish to eat," Yeshua said smiling.

"We also heard about what you did at a marriage feast in Cana, and what happened when you were baptised by Johanan," Shimon said.

"Have you heard anything more about Johanan?" Yeshua asked. "He is my cousin, you know. He was born a mere three months before me, and we lost touch until that time when I met him and listened to him and was baptised by him in the River Jordan."

"We were both baptised by Johanan too, Yeshua, when we were in Jerusalem long before Johanan was arrested. We remained in Jerusalem and were with Johanan almost every day, we also went into the wilderness with him as one of his many disciples, and there he spoke to us, about the Kingdom of God, and about the coming of the Messiah, and our need to repent our sins in preparation of the One who would bring us Good News of salvation and redemption," Andreus said.

"Well, it is Andreus, who was really the first disciple of Johanan; he was the first to follow Johanan into the wilderness and live with him there and learning from him. Others then followed and became Johanan's disciples too. I also went into the wilderness with Johanan, and became part of the community but only for a short while, my father needed me in our family fishing business," Shimon said.

"Among those born of women, no one is greater than Johanan, yet the least in the kingdom of God is greater than he," Yeshua said.

"Yeshua, we live in Bethsaida, just across the Jordan, you have been there of course, and will you be visiting Bethsaida again?" Shimon asked.

"Shimon, yes, I will. Shimon, you were a disciple of Johanan, I now ask you, invite you, will you follow me too, and be with me in my work," Yeshua asked.

"Yes, I will," Shimon said immediately. Ever since he was a disciple of Johanan's for a short while, and listened to him and heard about the imminent coming of the Promised One, the Messiah, who was to bring peace and freedom to all of Israel, Shimon was very interested in knowing more. And after hearing all that happened when a carpenter from Nazareth was baptised by Johanan and what Johanan had said about him, Shimon was most interested in this Messiah. And here he was in the presence of this very person, the carpenter from Nazareth, the One the whole of Israel had been waiting for. Without hesitation, with his usual impulsiveness, Shimon responded, "Yes, I will, Yeshua, I will follow you wherever you go."

"Good, Shimon, you will no longer be only catching fish from this sea, you will now be catching men and women, bringing them to the new shore of freedom, of salvation and redemption," Yeshua said.

"Andreus, I ask you too, will you follow me, as you followed Johanan and work with me to spread the Good News of Yahweh's love for all of humanity?" Now again, Yeshua speaks the name of Yahweh to these two fishermen, he now calls to be fishers of men.

"Yes, I will, yes I will, Yeshua, I will follow you to the ends of the earth," Andreus said.

Andreus had been a disciple of Johanan right up to the time he was arrested. He had remained in Jerusalem for a while, hoping that Herod would release Johanan, but when all hope had failed, he came back to Capernaum and to the family business. He was now thrilled to be with the man that Johanan spoke to them about, especially just before he was arrested.

"Yeshua, I will go now and speak with my father and my wife, Eva, and get whatever I need for the road, and I will be with you from now on," Shimon said.

Before Shimon was about to leave, Yeshua said to him, "Shimon, you will find me at the home of Elijah, the winemaker, I am staying there for the time being until I find a place of my own. And with me are the first two of my disciples, Miriam from Magdala, and Rebecca from my home town of Nazareth," Yeshua said.

Shimon was surprised. He did not expect that Yeshua would have women disciples with him, but he said, "Good, Yeshua. I have heard about Miriam of Magdala and what you did for her. I have not heard of Rebecca." He was surprised to know that Yeshua had women disciples. He had not expected that. All of Johanan's disciples were men. The Pharisees, the Scribes, the Sadducees, the priests, as far as he knew were all men. Women were not allowed in their ranks and here is this Prophet, this Teacher, the Messiah, the Promised One, and the first disciples he calls to accompany him and learn from him and be part of his mission, are women. Shimon wondered about that.

Shimon was about to sail across the Sea of Galilee to Bethsaida when a large crowd were approaching, and the crowd grew bigger and bigger. They were all coming to Yeshua, they had with them people who were clearly incapacitated or suffering from some illness. They were hoping for a cure.

Yeshua saw the swelling crowd and knew he would be swamped so he said to Shimon. "Shimon put out a little way from the shore. I would like to speak to the people."

When the boat was a short distance from the shore, Yeshua sat down on Shimon's boat and gestured to the crowd to sit down. They all sat down on the seashore. Then Yeshua spoke to them.

"Why are you following me? Why are you here? Why am I here? What is the meaning of life? What do you know? What do you believe? Who are you following? These are questions, I am sure you have. Some of you are Pharisees, and your very name means 'the separate ones, the holy ones,' yet only Adonai is the Holy One. You Pharisees teach that life is a matter of reward and punishment, that God loves those who keep the law and punishes those who do not. But you do believe in the resurrection of the dead, and in a future Messiah, whom Yahweh will send to liberate us from the Romans. Dear brothers and sisters, you have eyes to see, can you see that the time has come, the Messiah is in your midst. But I have not come to liberate you from the Romans. I have come to liberate you from yourselves, from your self-love and your self-loathing. I have come that you might have life and life to the full. The salvation I bring is the salvation of your immortal souls, for what doth it profit you, if you gain the whole world and lose your immortal souls? I have not come to liberate you from the Romans. The Spirit of Yahweh is upon me, he has anointed me to bring Good News to the poor, to proclaim release to captives, and recovering of sight to the blind, to let the oppressed go free, to proclaim the year of the Lord's favour."

Yeshua let his eyes roam across the crowd and continued, "There are among you, disciples of Johanan, the baptiser, the prophet. No greater man has existed. What did Johanan teach? Did he not say, 'whoever has two coats, must share with anyone who has none; and whoever has food must do likewise.' And to the tax-collectors who are here today, what did Johanan say to you? What he said, I say to you, stop over burdening tax payers, and lining your own pockets, collect no more than the amount prescribed for you.

"To the Pharisees, Sadducees, Scribes, priests, Elders, all you religious leaders, who lead and teach, I say to you; do not overburden the people with the minutiae of the Law, overburdening them. I have come to bring Good News to the poor, to set prisoners free, to mend the broken-hearted. I have not come to over burden you; you already have enough daily burdens to bear. I have come that you may have life and life in all its fullness. Learn of me for I am humble and gentle of heart, and you will have peace in your hearts. We all have crosses to bear, some heavier than others, I say to you, learn from what Johanan have taught you and what I now teach you, I do not come to add to your burdens, my yoke is easy and my burden is light."

Yeshua paused for a moment and then continued, "To whom have I been sent to bring God the Father's message of peace and salvation? To all, but especially to the poor, the so-called sinners, I have come to bring peace and freedom especially to the poor, the blind, the lame, the crippled, the prisoner, the thirsty, the hungry, the prostitute, the sinner, the possessed, the leper, widows and orphans, the lost sheep of the house of Israel. These poor, these little ones are not sinners, they are the ones we have ostracised, cast out from among us, but they are the ones dearest to the Father's heart and it is to these that I am sent."

Again, Yeshua paused for a moment, to let his words sink in, then he continued, "Fear not, my dear friends, my peace I bring to you, my peace I give you, a peace that the world cannot give, a peace that not Rome or any power can take away from you. If you would only this day, recognise the things that give you this peace. But now they are hidden from your eyes. Do not let your hearts be troubled, do not let your spirit be crushed. Recognise your visitation from the Lord, your God. My peace I bring you, my peace I give you, a peace the world cannot give, a peace no one else or nothing else can give you. This peace is yours."

"Teacher, how do we get this peace?" a voice cried from the crowd.

"Empty your hearts of all that is not peaceful. Empty your hearts of evil, of vice, of all that is not of God, and pray to your Father in heaven to fill you with the peace that I bring to you. There is enough evil in the world, we do not have to add to it by harbouring any evil in our hearts. You were born to love; you were created to love. God is love and who abides in God, abides in love, and God abides in him and her. It's as simple as that my dear brothers and sisters, simply empty your hearts of all that is not of God, and you will empty yourself of all that is not of love. And let your hearts be filled with love of God. And you will have the peace that nothing or no one on this earth can give you. This is where your true treasure is. God is love and who abides in love, abides in God, and the peace of God will fill your souls."

As Yeshua was ending his speaking to the people, a commotion arose among the crowd, as a group of Elders came to the fore and to the water's edge. One of them spoke up, "Yeshua, Longinus, the centurion who abides here in Capernaum with his regiment, has a slave, whom he values highly, who is ill and close to death, he has sent us to ask you to come and heal his slave."

"Yeshua, he is worthy of having you do this for him, for he loves our people, and it is he who built our synagogue for us," another Elder said.

Yeshua listened and immediately he got out of Shimon's boat, and followed the Elders and the crowd followed as well; wanting to see what was going to happen. Would Yeshua, heal the slave of a Roman soldier, a Centurion?

When Yeshua and the Elders were not far from the house some friends of Longinus appeared and stopped Yeshua and one of them said, "Yeshua, I bring a message from Longinus. He instructed me to say these words to you on his behalf: 'Lord, do not trouble yourself, for I am not worthy to have you come under my roof; that is why I did not presume to come to you. But only speak the word, and let my servant be healed. For I also am a man set under authority, with soldiers set under me; and I say to one, 'Go' and he goes, and to another, 'Come' and he comes, and to my slave, 'Do this,' and the slave does it'."

When Yeshua heard these words, he was amazed, and he turned to the crowds that followed him and cried out, "I tell you, not even in Israel have I found such faith."

Yeshua then sent the crowds away and went on his way. But the crowds did not disperse; they followed the Elders to the house of the Centurion. When the Elders arrived at the house to report to Longinus, with the crowd in tow, Longinus came out, and exclaimed to all. "Go home, my servant is healed, he is now in good health. Go and listen to this man, Yeshua, he is indeed a man of God."

Later that day, Longinus found out that Yeshua was staying at the home of the winemaker, Elijah, and as night approached and under cover of darkness and in disguise, he found his way to the home where Yeshua was staying.

Miriam answered the door; she did not at first recognise Longinus, as he was not in his usual attire. "I am Longinus, the Centurion, Yeshua had cured my servant, I have come to thank him personally. May I come in?" Longinus asked.

"Yes, sure, come in," Miriam led Longinus inside.

Everyone who was at table, just having finished their evening meal, looked up at the stranger that had just entered. But he was a stranger only to Yeshua and Rebecca, the rest all knew him; he was highly regarded by the people of Capernaum, for he had built their synagogue for them. Of course, he still represented Rome, to whom all of Israel was subjected. Rome that ruled with an iron fist and with cruelty, Rome that had prosecuted and persecuted so many of their people, put them to death, crucified thousands. But Longinus, who was to keep law and order in Capernaum and beyond, was not like the others, he respected the religion of the Jewish people, under his authority, and he respected the one God they worshipped.

"Yeshua, this is Longinus, he is the Centurion, whose servant you had healed. He is in charge of his regiment here in Capernaum and he has built our synagogue for us," Elijah said.

"Yes, I know that, I do commend you Longinus, and I am pleased to meet you. You are highly respected by the people of Capernaum, and I am honoured to meet you, and this is Rebecca, from Nazareth, my home town, one of my disciples, and you met Miriam, the first who wished to be one of my followers," Yeshua said.

"I have met Elijah before, and drank lots of his wine," Longinus said, with a smile. "His wine has done much to keep the morale of my troops high and makes my job so much easier," Longinus added, still smiling broadly.

"I thank you for the business, Longinus. This is my wife, Lydia," Elijah said.

"I'm pleased to meet you, Lydia," Longinus said, nodding to Lydia who nodded in return.

"I have come to personally thank you, Yeshua, for healing my servant, Onesimus. He is well again," Longinus said. "Please accept this as a token of my appreciation." Longinus handed over a pouch with gold coins to Yeshua.

"Thank you, Longinus, that is very kind, but I do not accept any monetary gifts, you have already given me a great gift, the gift of your faith. I have not experienced such faith as yours in all of Israel, and you have been an example and an inspiration to the people, and your words, your faith, will echo down the generations to come," Yeshua said.

"But we will accept the gift, we will use it for the poor and those in need," Miriam said.

"Thank you; that will be good. And thank you, Yeshua, for your kind words, and once again thank you for healing Onesimus."

"Would you like a cup of wine, Longinus?" Elijah offered.

"I thought you would never ask," Longinus said, grinning.

Miriam, Rebecca and Lydia cleared the table and cleaned up and then disappeared. They decided to leave the men to their business. After another couple of cups of wine, Elijah said, "That's enough for me. Please excuse me, I have to be up early tomorrow and it is a busy day for me. Please stay as long as you wish, Longinus," Elijah said, and then disappeared.

Longinus and Yeshua remained seated. "Tell me, Yeshua, about your God. We have many gods, and I only hear of one of your gods, Yahweh. And I don't know much about your people and their god," Longinus said.

"For four hundred years, we Jews were persecuted, lived as slaves under the mighty rule of the Pharaohs in Egypt. But Adonai, the name we use for the Yahweh you mention, raised up a great prophet and leader, Moses, who with great and powerful signs, set our people free, but not without great suffering and hardship. For forty more years our people were wanderers, living in the desert. And finally, another great leader, Joshua, led our people into our Promised Land, Israel. But it looks like we are still not free," Yeshua said. "But I hear good things about you, Longinus. You are not cruel, and you are fair in your dealings with our people, and you are a man of compassion, you treat your slaves and your servants with great respect, and I admire you for that, and you will be blessed," Yeshua said. "And your faith astonishes me, I have not seen such faith in all of Israel," Yeshua said again, deeply moved by Longinus's faith.

"Tell me about your gods, Yeshua," Longinus said, now interested to hear more.

"Moses wrote five books, the first is about how Yahweh created the earth and all that exists and how he created the human race. His words go something like this: In the beginning Yahweh created the universe. The earth was a formless void and darkness covered the face of the deep. Then Yahweh let light appear. He then put some order into what he created. And Yahweh named the light 'Day' and the darkness, 'Night', and the dome, 'Sky'. He then continued separating his creatures and named the land 'Earth' and the water that he brought together, 'Sea'. He filled the sea with countless creatures and the sky with numerous birds.

"Then Yahweh created all kinds of animals. Then Yahweh made us humans, according to his own image. He took some soil from the ground and formed a man out of it; He breathed life-giving breath into his nostrils and the man began to live. And while the man was sleeping, Yahweh formed a woman out of the man's rib," Yeshua said.

"Your Yahweh did all that?" Longinus was surprised and impressed.

"Yes, Longinus, and we have only one God," Yeshua said.

"You have only one god, but we have many, Jupiter is king of the gods, and the god of thunder and lightning. And Juno, his wife, is the goddess of women and fertility. And Jupiter's son, Neptune is god of the sea. And we have Bacchus, that Elijah would be pleased to know, is god of wine," Longinus said, smiling. "And I am sure Bacchus would be pleased with this fine wine," Longinus said, continuing his smiling and lifting his cup. He was beginning to feel the effects of the wine.

"We have only one God, Longinus, who created all that exists and all life on earth, out of nothing," Yeshua said again.

"Your God, Yahweh, is he male or female? We have both gods and goddesses," Longinus said.

"Language does restrict us as human beings in trying to describe our God. He is neither male nor female, Longinus, for he is a pure spirit and does not have a body like you and me or like Miriam and Rebecca. He is therefore neither. At the same time, he is both male and female, for a Creator, cannot create what is not from within. Our Yahweh is both Abba and Immah, his love and care for us in boundless, without limit and unconditional. All that is good and beautiful within the male and female nature is found in abundance and without limit in Yahweh. And all that exists on this earth, he made out of love for us, to have and to enjoy and to care for. Our God calls us to love and care for one another, especially the vulnerable, those most in need of our care. Like you care for your servant Onesimus, Longinus," Yeshua said.

"I am amazed at your God, Yeshua. But he seems a distant God, for he is not flesh and bone like us. We have Hercules, also a son of Jupiter, he is the son of a mortal mother, he is therefore half god and half man," Longinus said.

"In a similar way, Longinus, we too have our God, who has taken on a human form, who was born of a woman, and lives among us," Yeshua said.

"You do, who is this god, this half god and half man," Longinus asked, with great interest.

"First of all, Longinus, this man is not half man and half god, he is fully God and fully man, fully divine and fully human," Yeshua said.

"How is that even possible, Yeshua?" Longinus asked.

"With man this is not possible, Longinus, but with God all things are possible. It is the perennial paradox to the question of what came first, the chicken or the egg. God created the first humans from nothing, without the help of man. From the dust of the earth, he created them all. And everything that exists he planted the seeds, and he ordained that all should increase and multiply and fill the earth."

"Yeshua, that still does not answer how this god of yours, has taken on the form of man and as you say is not half man and half god but fully man and fully god," Longinus said, wanting to understand. And he wanted to know how this god was conceived.

"I just told you, Longinus, how the first humans were created without human seed. The Son of God was in a similar way created without the seed of man. The Spirit God, who is equal with Yahweh, came over a maiden, and she conceived and bore a son, and in her God has taken on our human form."

"And this person, is he now living among us, where is he, that I may see him and touch him and do him homage," Longinus said.

"Longinus, he is here, he who speaks with you, is the Son of Yahweh, the Messiah who is come to liberate the Jews and give new life to all humankind." For the first time Yeshua enunciated the truth about himself, to anyone. For the first time the Spirit endowed him with the understanding of his true nature, that he was both fully man and fully God.

"You, Yeshua, you are he. I am overwhelmed. When I heard about you and what you do, the powers you have to heal, the way you healed my servant, Onesimus, I said to myself, you must be a god, or the son of a god, and I was right. I am honoured to be in your presence," Longinus said, and he stood up, with clenched fist beat the left of his chest in salute and then fell on one knee and bowed his head. "Lord, God, I am not worthy to be in your presence. I ask your blessing."

"Rise up, Longinus, I do bless you, you are blessed, continue to maintain law and order and continue to show the kindness you do to the people."

Longinus sat down again, and caught his breath. He did not want to leave, he wanted to prolong this visit and he wanted to know more. "Yeshua, so there is

Yahweh, who is Father god, but as you say both Father and Creator god, and then there is you, the Son of God, the Messiah, God become man and living among us, and you mentioned the Spirit God, who came over the maiden in Nazareth. That will be your mother, so there are in fact three gods," Longinus said.

For all his life, Longinus believed in so many gods, and now here is a god made man in front of him, and he is the one the Jews, and he has powers only a god can have, and he is one of three gods, yet he says and the Jews speak of only one god. "Yeshua, I am confused, I have learned that you, the Jews believe in only one God, so how can you explain your existence and the presence of three gods?" Longinus asked, seeking some clarity.

"Another paradox, a mystery that is unfathomable to the human mind. Longinus. No human can fathom the mystery of God, the one true, infinite God, who created all that exists out of love. Abba, Immah, Yahweh God, is one person, and I, the Son am one person, and the Spirit is one person. We are a Trinity of persons, but one God. We have only one nature, even though we are three distinct persons. This is beyond the grasp of the human mind Longinus, you have to accept it on faith, and the Father, the Spirit and I are one. We are three persons, with one divine nature. And I am divine and human; I am one person with two natures."

"Yeshua, I do not understand, but I believe. I believe that you are God made man, and now living among us. I want now to leave what I am doing and follow you, and be your disciple, like Miriam and Rebecca," Longinus said.

"You are my disciple, Longinus, but I do not want you to follow me, you have your duties and responsibilities here, to maintain law and order and to care for the people as you have, the people respect you and you are kind to them. You can do more. You have built a synagogue, go now and build a home for widows and orphans and care for the poor and the sick, those who are discarded by society, it is to these that I have come, and you are my disciple if you care for the poor and the outcasts," Yeshua said.

"I will do that, Yeshua. I am honoured to be in your presence, and to have learned from you. I go now." Longinus got up and gave Yeshua the Roman salute and went down on one knee and Yeshua laid his hand on Longinus' head and blessed him. "You are a good man, Longinus; go now in peace, my peace I give you." And then Longinus left.

Yeshua prayed to his Father, "Abba, you have sent me to the lost sheep of the tribe of Israel, but there are others too who need redemption, lead me where you will, your will be done." Yeshua blew out the lamp on the centre lampstand and, taking his lamp, he made his way to his room. The house was eerily quiet, as all were fast asleep.

Chapter Forty-Three
Yeshua's Manifesto

The next day, very early when most of the town was still asleep, Yeshua went to the Sea of Galilee for his morning walk, a time for prayer, to think and reflect. He saw Shimon and Andreus. They were cleaning the fishing nets, after fishing all night. They were expecting Yeshua to come and they had others now employed to carry on to do their work and assist their father, Zephaniah in the business.

Zephaniah was not too pleased with both his sons Shimon and Andreus leaving him with all of the business. He could understand why Andreus would leave and follow this man, but Shimon, his impetuous and bumbling son, he wondered, but then he was nevertheless good at heart and good at catching fish, but above all he would miss Andreus. Andreus was his right-hand man, the eldest of his sons. Andreus was good at organising things and managing the business and the workers. Now he had to make do with these new men that Shimon and Andreus had asked to step in to do their work. At least they were experienced fishermen and been in the business for a long time.

Zephaniah was glad that he was in partnership with Zebedee and his two sons. He would discuss matters with old man Zebedee later this day. Zephaniah heard all about this Yeshua, but he had no time to go about listening to him like his sons, he had a business to run, a business that he shared with the Zebedees.

"Peace be with you, Shimon; peace be with you, Andreus," Yeshua greeted them.

"And peace be with you too, Yeshua. Do look around, see the crowds are approaching," Shimon said.

Yeshua turned to look. He was not expecting people to come to him, so early in the day. But he was prepared. "Shimon, Andreus, move the boat out a bit from the shore as you did before and then get the people to sit on the seashore," Yeshua said.

Yeshua saw that the people brought with them their sick, people suffering all sorts of afflictions. His heart went out to them. As they gathered around, Shimon and Andreus asked them to sit down. Yeshua addressed the people. He spoke to them.

"My dearest brothers and sisters, men, women and children of Capernaum, of this beautiful town of Galilee, in the territory of Zebulun and Naphtali, which I now call home, I greet you, my peace I give you, a peace the world cannot give. I have come here to make what the great prophet Isaiah had prophesied about you and your great city, he said, 'Land of Zebulon and land of Naphtali, on the road by the sea, across the Jordan, Galilee of the Gentiles—the people who sat in darkness have seen a great light, and for those who sat in the region and shadow of death, light has dawned'."

"Yeshua spoke to the people at length about the kingdom of God likening it to a treasure that a man found in the field and went and sold all he had and bought the field. And he went on to repeat himself saying: 'The Kingdom of Heaven is like a merchant in search of fine pearls, on finding one pearl of great value, he went and sold all that he had and bought it'."

After Yeshua had been speaking to them for a while about the kingdom of God and asking them what they treasured most in life, and saying to them, "where your treasure is there, your heart will be also," the people brought to Yeshua all the sick and the afflicted.

Among the sick were many with various kinds of diseases. Yeshua was full of compassion for them as he saw their plight and his heart went out to them and he laid his hands on each of them, and they were healed. And demons also came out of many of them, shouting, "You are the Son of God."

When Yeshua had healed all the sick and cast out the demons from many, he sent the people away. He was now feeling drained and hungry, so he said to Shimon, "Sail out further into the deep, Shimon, and put down your nets for a catch."

Shimon said to him, "Master." This was the first time anyone had called him Master, but Yeshua did not correct Shimon. Shimon continued, "Master, we have worked all night long but have caught nothing. Yet if you say so, I will let down the nets."

When they had reached the deep waters and let down their nets, they caught so many fish that their nets were beginning to break. So, Shimon and Andreus signalled to their partners, James and Johanan, in the other boat to come and help them. And they came and filled both boats, so much so that they were close to sinking. When Shimon saw what was happening, he was overcome, as were Andreus, and James and Johanan and the other four fishermen with them. Shimon was so overcome, that he fell on his knees before Yeshua and cried out, "Go away from me, Lord, for I am a sinful man!"

Then Yeshua said, "Shimon, get up off your knees and do not be afraid; from now on you will be catching people."

Shimon, Andreus, and their partners Johanan and James, sons of Zebedee and their co-workers were all amazed at their catch; they never experienced anything like this in all their years of fishing. When they arrived at the shore, they sent one of the men to fetch more helpers to bring in the fish. Several men came, and they too were amazed, they had never seen anything like it.

James and Johanan, sons of Zebedee, with their father had been in partnership with Shimon and Andreus and their father for a long time. The Zebedees had heard of Yeshua, of the great miracles he had done, but this was just too amazing for these fishermen.

Yeshua then approached Johanan and James. "Johanan, James, I have heard that you both were also disciples of Johanan the baptiser. Will you also be my disciples, and join Shimon and Andreus, I need men like you to assist me in the work I have been sent to do, to bring Good News to the poor and the suffering, and to set all who are captive in any way, free," Yeshua said.

James spoke first, "Yeshua, Shimon and Andreus, told us how you have invited them, called them to be disciples, as they were of Johanan, the baptiser. My brother Johanan and I have already discussed this, and yes, we are willing to join Shimon and Andreus and assist you in whatever way we can in your work, and to learn all we can from you. We lived with Johanan in the wilderness and he taught us so much of the kingdom of God, and spoke so much of the Promised One, the Messiah, that was to come and save and redeem us all from the tyranny of Rome," Johanan said.

Yeshua was aware of the general thinking about the Messiah. The people all thought that the Messiah was to bring the reign of God on earth and topple the power of Rome. Yeshua seemed to possess great power and it filled them with hope. Yet Yeshua knew he had to change that thinking, he is not such a Messiah. He came to bring the reign of God on earth that is true. But it is not like that of military kingdoms or worldly kingdoms, it is the reign of the Spirit of God over evil and sin and death.

Then Yeshua gathered the four around him and spoke to them. "I have to make it clear to you, for you are now my disciples and must know my mind. I will need your support. I have not been sent to liberate Israel from the yoke of Rome, in a military sense, I have no weapons, no military or worldly powers, as you can see. I have no army and have no intention of having such. There have been many rebellions against Rome, and they were all quashed with terrifying consequences. But I, we will indeed wage war, but it will be a spiritual warfare, for the hearts and minds and souls of all. I have come to bring hope, the hope that Isaiah prophesied when he said, 'the day is coming when the deaf shall hear the words of a scroll, and out of their gloom and darkness the eyes of the blind shall see. The meek shall obtain fresh joy in the Lord, and the neediest people shall exult in the Holy One of Israel. For the tyrant shall be no more, and the scoffer shall cease to be; all those alerts to evil shall be cut off. Then the eyes of the blind shall be opened, and the ears of the deaf unstopped, then the lame shall leap like a deer and the tongue of the speechless sing for joy.'"

"Yeshua, we will go with you and spread this Good News all over Israel," Shimon said, and the others agreed.

"Yeshua, I have taken to heart the words of our great prophet, Isaiah, as you speak, and having seen this great miracle of the abundance of fish we have just caught, and having heard from Johanan the baptiser about the coming of the Messiah, and having heard about your great miracle in Cana and in Magdala and now seeing you healing the sick, I can see that it is indeed you that Isaiah speaks of," Johanan said.

"What does Isaiah say of the One that is to come?" Yeshua asked.

Johanan replied by quoting the words of Isaiah. "Isaiah prophesies about the one who will bring the Good News of deliverance with the words; The Spirit of the Lord God is upon me, because the Lord has anointed me; he has sent me to bring Good News to the oppressed, to bind up the broken-hearted, to proclaim liberty to the captives, and release to the prisoners; to proclaim the year of the Lord's favour, and the day of vengeance of our God."

"Well said, Johanan, you have been right in quoting Isaiah. It has been a taxing morning for us all. Let us go on our way now, have some refreshment and some rest. There is still much to be done. This afternoon, Shimon, Andreus, James and Johanan, I want you to spread the word and to tell the people to assemble at the base of that northern mount, in the Korazim plateau, there is plenty of grassland for the people to be seated there around the hill from which I would like to speak to the people. I have important words to say to you and to them."

Looking up towards the sky and seeing that the sun indicated noon, Yeshua said, "Assemble the people in three hours' time, around the ninth hour." Then Yeshua left them.

Miriam and Rebecca had been with the crowds. They had not witnessed the miraculous catch of fish, but Yeshua had brought a bag of fish enough to last them for days. "From Shimon, Andreus, and the two Zebedee sons, James and Johanan, they had a great catch," Yeshua said.

"Good I'll go and clean and prepare them and we can have fish for dinner tonight," Lydia, said.

"I'll clean and prepare that Lydia," Yeshua said, "you have enough to do, looking after Rebecca and me," Yeshua said.

"I'll help," Rebecca offered.

"Yeshua, please, it's okay, Miriam, Rebecca and I will do it, you go and have a rest," Lydia insisted, speaking to Yeshua.

"Thank you, Lydia, I don't mind if I do. I have told Shimon and the others to gather the people at the base of the mount, in the Korazim plateau, where there is plenty of grassland for the people to be seated around the hill from which I would like to speak to them. I have important words to say to you and to them. I told Shimon and the others to gather them at around the ninth hour, so I will rest for an hour or so. Do wake me at the eighth hour, please," Yeshua said.

Yeshua told Miriam and Rebecca that there were now four more disciples that had responded to his invitation—Shimon, Andreus, sons of Jonah; and Johanan and James, sons of Zebedee. Miriam said she knew of James and Johanan because they were from Capernaum, and she also knew of Shimon, the big fisherman, and his brother Andreus. They were from Bethsaida but they were often in Capernaum as they were in partnership with the Zebedees.

When the time came, Yeshua, Lydia, Miriam, and Rebecca walked together to the mount. When they arrived, there were thousands of people gathered and more were streaming in. Shimon and the others were organising the seating to bring the people as close as possible to the mount so they could hear Yeshua. Yeshua had a strong voice, and he needed to really project his voice if all were to hear him. But the place he chose was a good place for his voice could travel well around here.

"Shalom, peace to you all," Yeshua began. "I thank you for coming. What I have to say to you today is the core of the message I bring from the One who sent me. Moses went up Mount Sinai, and there he heard the voice of God, who gave him Ten Commandments, for the people to follow. Those commandments he wrote on stone, but they had from the very beginning been written in the hearts of us all. When Moses stood on Mount Sinai, and God spoke to him, from the burning bush, God told Moses to remove his sandals, for he was standing on holy ground. My dear friends, this is your, our Mount Sinai, just as Mount Sinai is forever etched in our minds and hearts because of what happened there, and because God's presence made it holy ground, so too this mount is now, at this time, holy ground, from here I will speak God's words to you. So, I ask you, to forever remember this place and what you hear today, I ask you to remove your sandals, for this is indeed also holy ground."

The people, the children, all began to remove their sandals, and the buzz of low voices could be heard. There was a quiet excitement and anticipation in the air. After a while Shimon and the other disciples, including Miriam and Rebecca, sought to quieten the crowd.

Yeshua looked out across the vast crowd and his heart was filled with love. They were like sheep without a true shepherd. He had come to be their shepherd and now he had Miriam, Rebecca, Shimon, Andreus, James and Johanan, to help him to shepherd the people. Yeshua loved them all. He then began to speak.

"My dear friends, Yahweh loves you with a boundless love, and wants you to be happy, to be blessed. He made you so, that is why we all desire, we all want to be happy, to be blessed, and we do what we do because we want to be happy. But at the same time, we often make poor choices and embrace what will not really give us true happiness, but only the illusion of happiness. Through Moses, Yahweh gave us the Ten Commandments, to guide us through life and to the attainment of what will make us truly blessed and happy. Today I give you New Ten Commandments, not really commandments, but Invitations, Blessings, I give you Ten Beatitudes." Yeshua then paused, he could touch the silence and expectation that hung in the air, the crowd were fully attentive, sensing the importance of what they were about to hear.

Yeshua spoke in a loud voice for all to hear: "Happy are you. Blessed are you who are poor, and poor in spirit, and know that you are totally dependent on the mercy of God, for you are highly favoured by God, who loves you with a special love. The Kingdom of Heaven is yours.

"Happy are you. Blessed are you who mourn now, who weep now, for you will be comforted.

"Happy are you. Blessed are you who are meek, and humble of heart, for you are the ones who inherit the earth.

"Happy are you. Blessed are you who hunger and thirst for righteousness, for you are filled with God's love.

"Happy are you. Blessed are you, who are merciful, for you, will receive God's mercy in abundance.

"Happy are you. Blessed are you who are pure in spirit, pure in body, mind, heart and spirit, for you see God. You see God, in all of creation, in all creatures, and in all with whom you come into contact.

"Happy are you. Blessed are you who are the peacemakers, who live in peace with all, who spread only peace to all, who work for peace, you are called, you are, the children of God.

"Happy are you. Blessed are you, who are persecuted for righteousness' sake, for yours is the Kingdom of Heaven.

"Happy are you. Blessed are you, when people revile you and persecute you and utter all kinds of evil against you on my account.

"Happy are you. Blessed are you. Rejoice and be glad, for your reward is great in heaven, for in the same way they persecuted the prophets who were before you."

Yeshua, as usual, paused, giving people time to digest the words he had uttered. There was a long silence before Yeshua continued.

"The Ten Commandments and the Ten Beatitudes you have just heard, my dear brothers and sisters, stand side by side, two sides of one coin, of one loving God. The Ten Commandments command us mostly what not to do, whereas I bring you the Beatitudes telling us *what* to do, how to live. Together they form our Way of Life, the Don'ts and the Do's. They complement each other and do not contradict. This is what I mean when I said to you that I do not come to destroy the Law but to fulfil it, to perfect it.

"Moses simplified all of this when he wrote in Deuteronomy and Leviticus what I say to you now, 'You shall love the Lord your God with all your heart, with all your soul, and all your mind, and with all your strength, and you shall love your neighbour as yourself'."

Yeshua paused one more time, and then he continued his teaching. He taught them much, affirming them in many ways; repeating what he said to them before: "You are the salt of the earth, do not lose your taste, for if salt loses its taste, how can its saltiness be restored. You are the light of the world; let your light shine to all in the house. Let your light shine before others that they may come out of the darkness and into the light and that they may see your good works and give glory to your Father in heaven."

Yeshua continued teaching them many things, about everyday matters, challenging them to resist anger, with compassion, and on adultery, teaching that if a married person looks upon another with lust, they have already committed adultery in their hearts. He taught, concerning retaliation, about turning the other cheek, and repeating his teaching about loving one's enemies. And about almsgiving, he said to the people, in colourful language, that brought a smile to people's faces, "Whenever you give alms, do not sound a trumpet before you, as the hypocrites do in the synagogues and in the streets, so that they may be praised by others. Truly I tell you, they have received their reward. But when you give alms, do not let your left hand know what your right hand is doing, so that your alms may be done in secret, and your Father who sees in secret will reward you."

Yeshua ended his lengthy Sermon on the Mount, as these words he had spoken, were to become known, with a teaching on prayer. "Whenever you pray, do not be like the hypocrites, for they love to stand and pray in the synagogues and at street corners, so that they may be seen by others. Truly I tell you they have received their reward. But whenever you pray, go into your room, and shut the door and pray to your Father, who is in secret, and your Father, who sees in secret, will reward you.

"And when you are praying, do not heap up empty phrases as the Gentiles do; for they think that they will be heard because of their many words. Do not be like them, for your Father knows what you need before you ask him."

"Master, Teacher, I do not know how to pray, teach us to pray," a voice shouted from the crowd. And a chorus of voices followed, "Yes, teach us to pray."

Yeshua's heart went out to them; he was filled with love and compassion for them. So, he taught them a prayer that was to become a prayer they would pray every day, and a prayer they would teach their children to pray, and a prayer that would rise up from the hearts of followers of Yeshua all around the world. He taught them what they would call the 'Our Father or the Lord's Prayer'. He taught them what he had taught others:

"Pray then in this way; Our Father in heaven, hallowed by your name. Your kingdom come. Your will be done, on earth as it is in heaven. Give us this day our daily bread. And forgive us our debts, as we also forgive our debtors, and do not let us be tempted beyond what we cannot endure, and to trials, beyond our strength, but rescue us from the evil one."

And Yeshua concluded the prayer by saying, "For if you forgive others their trespasses, your heavenly Father will also forgive you; but if you do not forgive others, neither will your Father forgive your trespasses."

The people could relate to the prayer and to what Yeshua was saying for they all experienced and continue to experience indebtedness. Many lost possessions because they were unable to pay their debts, and many lost out to Rome because they were not able to pay their taxes and tariffs, and their goods and even property was confiscated, handed over to swell Roman coffers.

Yeshua felt he had said enough for the day. So, he sent the people away. He told them he had much more to say. But he asked them to go home and think about what they heard today, and that he would be back here for a continuation of his teaching at the same time in three days' time.

But before they left the people brought their sick to Yeshua for healing. Shimon, Andreus, James, Johanan, Rebecca and Miriam organised the people and the sick as they lined up in front of Yeshua. Yeshua had dismissed the crowd, but they all hung around wanting to see what was going to happen.

Yeshua cured many. And they brought to him a paralytic, for they knew he had already cured a person who was paralysed. Yeshua said to the paralytic. "Take heart son, your sins are forgiven." Now Yeshua knew, that it was common knowledge or rather belief that all sickness that people suffered, and even poverty was the result of sin, the person's sin, or the sins of their parents or parent's parents. Yeshua knew otherwise. He knew that his Father in heaven is a God of compassion and love and would not so treat his loved ones. But Yeshua knew he had his work cut out to change this erroneous way of thinking of the people, a teaching that was inculcated by the Scribes and Pharisees, and the religious leaders and teachers of the people. This teaching was so deeply imbedded in the psyche of the people. Yeshua was sent to change all that and to let the people see the glory of Yahweh and experience his love, mercy and compassion. So, he said to the man again, "Take heart, son, for your sins are forgiven."

Then some of the Scribes and Pharisees standing close, said among themselves, but loud enough for those standing around to hear them, "This man is blaspheming."

But Yeshua, perceiving their thoughts that only Yahweh can forgive sins, said, "Why do you think evil in your hearts? For what is easier to say to this man, 'Your sins are forgiven,' or to say, 'Stand up and walk.' But that you may know, that I am sent by Yahweh, and I have authority on earth to forgive sin," Yeshua then said to the paralytic, "Young man, stand up, take your bed and go to your home."

The man stood up, and took his bed and began walking. He thanked Yeshua, as did his friends that brought him, Yeshua could see the joy in their faces and he was filled with admiration for their faith and compassion. He said to them, "Your faith and above all the faith of your friend, has made him whole, go with him, and celebrate and give glory to God."

The cured paralytic and his friends were overcome with awe and joy, and bowed to Yeshua and then went on their way, rejoicing. And the crowds standing by who witnessed what had just happened were also filled with awe, and they gave glory to God who had given such authority to this man. And the word spread throughout the town and beyond to what had just happened, especially Yeshua forgiving the man his sins.

Chapter Forty-Four
The Sermon on the Mount Concludes

Three days later, the crowds were back at the Mount of Beatitudes, which the mount would become known as. By now Yeshua's reputation had spread all over Galilee and beyond. People came to Capernaum from every town and village in Galilee, and from all over Judaea, even from as far as Jerusalem, from the territory of Idumaea, from the territory on the east side of the River Jordan, and from the region around the cities of Tyre and Sidon in Phoenicia.

Shimon, Andreus, James and Johanan, Miriam and Rebecca were on hand to help settle the crowds around the hillside. Yeshua stood on the mount and looked across at the huge crowd, and his heart went out to them. He began to speak, "The Spirit of the Lord, is upon me, because he has anointed me to bring Good News to the poor. He has sent me to proclaim release to the captives, and recovery of sight to the blind, to let the oppressed go free, to proclaim to you, the year of the Lord's favour.

"From this hill, I had proclaimed to you, the words, 'Happy are you. Blessed are you who are poor, for yours is the kingdom of God.' This is the Good News I bring to the poor. You are blessed by God, loved by God, he hears your cries and it is the poor that is dearest and closest to his heart, and he calls on all of us to give up the quest for riches, for wealth, for prestige, for power over others, for position, for popularity, and to seek to be poor, divested of worldly riches, and poor in spirit, depending entirely on the mercy of God.

"To you who are rich, who have an abundance of this world's goods, who strive to accumulate more than you need, at the expense, and on the backs of the poor, I call on you to give away your excess, your surplus, to the poor, to those in need. Do not accumulate excess, for what does it profit you if you gain the whole world and lose your immortal soul.

"Woe to you who are rich, for you have received your consolation. Woe to you who are full now, for you will be hungry. Woe to you who are laughing now, for you will mourn and weep.

"Seek no longer the prestige, honour, status, to be first, to be admired, and given the place of honour. Seek first the kingdom of God. Woe to you, when all speak well of you, for that is what their ancestors did to the false prophets.

"Do you not notice how invited guests choose places of honour at feasts and celebrations? When you are invited by someone to a wedding banquet, do not sit down at a place of honour, in case someone more distinguished than you have been invited by your host, and the host who invited you, may come and say to you, 'Give this person your place,' and then in disgrace you will have to take the lowest place. But when you are invited, go and sit down at the lowest place, so that when your host comes, he may say to you, 'Friend, move up higher,' then you will be honoured in the presence of all who sit at the table with you. For all who exalt themselves will be humbled, and those who humble themselves will be exalted.

"Take care! Be on your guard, against all kinds of greed; for one's life does not consist in the abundance of possessions. Let me tell you another story; the land of a rich man produced abundantly. And he thought to himself, 'What should I do, for I have no place to store my crops?' Then he said, 'I will do this, I will pull down my barns and build larger ones, and there I will store all my grain and my goods. And I will say to myself, *soul, you have ample goods laid up for many years; relax, eat, drink and be merry*.' But God said to him, 'You fool! This very night your life is being demanded of you. And the things you have prepared, whose will they be?' So, it is with the rich, with those who store up treasures for themselves but are not rich towards God. Where your treasure is, there your heart will be also."

Yeshua paused for a moment and looked across the faces of the crowd; there were among them many poor and dispossessed, and there were also the rich, the tax-collectors and Pharisees, Scribes and Sadducees and the elite Elders who have come up from Jerusalem and all over Galilee and Judaea and elsewhere. Yeshua could see they were not taking kindly to what he was saying, for they had places of honour, people looked up to them, and they were rich. They taught that riches were blessings from God to those who upheld his Laws and lived upright lives, and the poor were poor as punishment from God for their breaking of the Laws of God, given to Moses, and for their sinful lives. Yeshua knew that his message would rile many. But this was the core of his message. *This is what the kingdom of God is all about.*

So, Yeshua persisted, "My dear friends, in our world, the rich and powerful become richer and more powerful at the expense of the poor, and the poor become poorer and with less power. Greed consumes the lives of the rich, who seem to have little or no regard for the poor, and exploit the poor so they can become even richer. We are all called to alleviate the plight of the poor. Let me tell you one last story.

"There was a rich man who was dressed in purple and fine linen and who feasted sumptuously every day. And at his gate lay a poor man named Lazarus, covered with sores, who longed to satisfy his hunger with what fell from the rich man's table, even the dogs would come and lick his sores. The poor man died and was carried away by the angels to be with Abraham. The rich man also died and was buried. In his Hades, where he was being tormented, he looked up and saw Abraham far away with Lazarus by his side. He called out, 'Father Abraham, have mercy on me, and send Lazarus to dip the tip of his finger in water to cool my tongue, for I am in agony in these flames.' But Abraham said, 'Child, remember that during your lifetime you received your good things, and Lazarus in like manner evil things; but now he is comforted here, and you are in agony'."

The people delighted in Yeshua's colourful stories, and this one, especially the poor. They looked at the rich to see them squirm. The poor felt they had a champion in Yeshua.

Yeshua thought he had said enough, there was much to digest and reflect on. He said, "Let me conclude by letting you all know that Yahweh loves you rich and poor alike, and that he cares for you and wants you to experience his love and compassion. You all, rich and poor alike, are beset by many daily anxieties. For the poor especially it is often a matter of survival. To rich and poor alike I say to you, do not worry about your life, what you will eat or what you will drink, or about your body, what you will wear. Is life not more than food, and the body more than clothing?"

Yeshua repeated his favourite images that resounded so forcefully with him—growing up in Nazareth and when he took that hike around the Sea of Galilee. "Look at the birds of the air; they neither sow nor reap nor gather into barns, and yet your heavenly Father feeds them. Are you not of more value than they? And can any of you by worrying add a single hour to your span of life? And why do you worry about clothing? Consider the lilies of the field, how they grow, they neither toil nor spin, yet I tell you, even Solomon in all his glory was not clothed like one of these. But if God so clothes the grass of the field, which is alive today and tomorrow is thrown into the fire, will he not much more clothe you—you of little faith? Therefore, do not worry, saying, 'What will we eat?' or 'What will we drink?' or 'What will we wear?' For it is the Gentiles, who strive for all these things, but strive first for the kingdom of God and his righteousness, and all these things will be given to you as well. So do not worry about tomorrow, for tomorrow will bring worries of its own. Today's trouble is enough for today.

"Everyone who hears these words of mine and does not act on them will be like a foolish man who built his house on sand. The rain fell, and the floods came, and the winds blew against that house and it fell—and great was its fall. But everyone who hears these words of mine and acts on them, will be like a wise man who built his house on rock. The rain fell, the floods came, and the winds blew and beat on that house, but it did not fall, because it had been founded on rock."

When Yeshua had finished speaking, the people brought their sick to him so that they could be healed. Yeshua was moved with compassion for them all, he laid his hands of them and they were healed. There were among them a person who was lame, a cripple, a person who was blind and another who could not speak. Yeshua healed them all. He then sent everyone away.

When all had left, Yeshua was alone with Shimon, Andreus, James, Johanan, Rebecca and Miriam. "Thank you all so much for all your help. It has been a heavy day for you all. Shimon and Andreus I would like to cross over to the other side of the lake, and speak to the people over there. I would like to visit all the towns and villages on the other side of the lake, beginning at Bethsaida. Do you have a place there for all of us, I would like Miriam and Rebecca to come as well," Yeshua said.

"Rebecca and Miriam could take the passenger ferry in the morning," Shimon suggested.

"I've been on fishing boats worse than that of yours' Shimon, so we can sail with you all," Miriam said. Rebecca also said she was ready to sail across the sea; it was something she had not yet experienced.

Shimon and the others were surprised; they had never had women as part of their working team, and never on their boats. "Yeshua, the Sea of Galilee can be very rough, and without warning," Shimon said.

"Shimon, we have weathered more than rough seas in our lives, we are ready and able to sail across the sea, aren't we, Rebecca?" Miriam said, turning to Rebecca with a nod and a look that sought her agreement.

"Of course, a piece of cake, we have weathered storms and upheavals of all sorts. And we have Yeshua with us, we have nothing to fear," Rebecca said, looking at Yeshua and smiling.

Yeshua returned the smile. He knew he had made a good choice to call Miriam and Rebecca to be his first disciples. They were gutsy women and he thought that he needed to add to their ranks. And it would be good to have more disciples, from the eastern side of the Sea of Galilee and the River Jordan.

It was settled. Shimon and Andreus got the boat ready, and cleaned a bench for Miriam and Rebecca. While they were preparing the boat, Yeshua invited Miriam and Rebecca to walk with him along the seashore.

"Rebecca, Miriam, I am grateful for your being with me, and learning from me, for when I am gone, I want you to continue to spread and teach my message. Human beings are not living the way Yahweh intended. Power, greed, avarice, cruelty, abound. The poor are exploited and the rich get richer, while the poor get poorer, this gap is growing and will continue to grow, it has to be lessened or we will all perish. There is so much poverty, suffering and misery in the world, I want to bring comfort to the poor and the suffering, and reach out to the marginalised, ostracised, exploited, and the vulnerable, and I need your help. When we get to the other side of the lake, I want to visit all the outlying villages where the poor, forgotten and marginalised live. And I need your help and that of the others. And I will seek and find more men and women to assist me, and learn from me, so that they can carry on the work when I am no longer here," Yeshua said.

"Yeshua, you are still young and healthy, you will be here a long time," Rebecca said, sensing Yeshua was indicating a short time with them. He had hinted at this before, and it was a reason he said he could not marry her.

"Rebecca, Miriam, I will be going to Jerusalem soon, and I fear things will not go well there. Johanan is in prison and I could easily follow him. Time is short and there is much to do. I want you to look out for women, who can become my disciples. It is unfortunate that we live in a male dominated, and a patriarchal society, with so much inequality and domineering attitudes of men over women. Yahweh made us male and female; he made us different but equal in dignity and worth in his sight. He does not intend men to dominate women and treat them as inferior, that has to stop, but I am afraid it will take a long time to change. I want to make a start. I am glad to have you both with me. I need to learn from you. We need to learn from you. While you are my disciples, I too need your counsel, your feminine perspective. As a man, and brought up as a man, I know I can be insensitive and misunderstand women, so I want you to let me know, when I fail in my treatment of women," Yeshua said.

"Yeshua, I have never found you treat women with any disrespect or inequality. As long as I have known you, you have always treated me as a human being, the way you treat everyone you meet," Rebecca said.

"Yes, Yeshua, you have called us to be your disciples, and made us part of your followers, your inner circle, your confidantes, and I have never met a person, a man like you before. You are full of love, and compassion for all, and your wisdom and understanding surpasses all, and you have powers like no other man. I believe you are the Promised One, and I am so privileged to know you, and to be with you, and to be your disciple," Miriam said.

"Thank you, Miriam, thank you, Rebecca; your words are so comforting and encouraging to me," Yeshua looked up to the sky, the sun was starting its daily dip towards the horizon. "I think we better turn around. I am sure the boat will be ready. And it will be dark soon."

"Let us walk back in silence, Miriam and Rebecca, I wish to discuss some matters with Yahweh," Yeshua said.

The three of them walked together in silence.

When they joined the others, the boat was ready, and they began to sail across the lake.

Chapter Forty-Five
The Other Side of the Lake

"Shimon, is there enough place for me, Miriam and Rebecca to stay in Bethsaida?" Yeshua asked. "We will be there for a while."

"Shimon and I have plenty of space for all of us to stay, Yeshua," Andreus said.

When they arrived at Bethsaida, it was dark. Yeshua was tired and so was everyone else, it had been a heavy day. They had something to eat and then all went to bed.

Andreus and Shimon had extra cottages on their family property. They made one of the cottages available to Yeshua, and another for Miriam and Rebecca. James and Johanan, who had their home in Capernaum, usually stayed at one of their own cottages, when they were in Bethsaida. Shimon invited them all to come for breakfast the next morning.

Everyone was feeling tired and went directly to their cottages, where they retired soon after they had some refreshment. Yeshua fell into a deep sleep. He had a dream. In his dream he was taken by soldiers and imprisoned in a cell next to Johanan. Johanan was dishevelled and looking much older than when last Yeshua saw him. He was also much thinner. "How are you doing, Johanan?" Yeshua asked. "Have you been tried yet? And what have you been charged with?" Yeshua asked.

"I have not been formally charged with anything. I am here because I told Herod that what he is doing is wrong..."

Just then, Herod with a retinue of people and guards appeared. "So, you are Yeshua, from Nazareth, and a worse trouble maker and rabblerouser than Johanan here. I think you, Yeshua, are going to have a much more terrible fate than Johanan here," Herod said. "But I have come to bring you both to a feast, I want to see for myself the magic you are supposed to be able to do that astounds everyone," Herod said. "Unlock their cells and bring them to me," Herod commanded and walked off. The guards then began to unlock Yeshua's cell and the noise woke him.

The next morning everyone assembled at Shimon's place for breakfast. When Yeshua, Miriam and Rebecca got there, James and Johanan were there already. Shimon's wife, Sarah and their daughter, Petronella were preparing breakfast. Shimon introduced Sarah and Petronilla to Yeshua, Miriam and Rebecca. Sarah and Petronella were thrilled. They had heard so much about Yeshua. Shimon had told them all he could, and that he and Andreus were invited by Yeshua to be his disciples. Sarah was open to that and knew it could be good for her husband. She was accustomed to Shimon being away, fishing or busy with the business.

Petronella was especially thrilled to meet Yeshua. She was only ten years old, but she had listened to the adults talking about Yeshua, and also listened to her father, speaking about Yeshua and his calling to be his disciple. She was especially impressed to discover that Yeshua also had women disciples, Miriam and Rebecca, and she made up her mind that as soon as she could leave home, she too would be a follower of Yeshua, and be his disciple like Miriam and Rebecca. She hung around Miriam and Rebecca, like a little sister, which both Miriam and Rebecca found endearing, for they both grew up without any siblings.

Shimon told Yeshua that his mother-in-law, Deborah, was so sorry she could not meet him. "She was so looking forward to meeting you Yeshua, but she has a very bad fever and needs to stay in bed. We have had the doctor come and he has given her something for her fever, but it seems she is not getting any better," Shimon said.

Yeshua's heart went out to Deborah. "Take me to her, Shimon," Yeshua said.

Shimon took Yeshua to the adjoining room. Deborah lay in her bed, looking sick and weary. She seemed to be having problems breathing. A female servant was there, keeping watch, and keeping her cool with a wet cloth and fanning her as well.

"Shalom, Deborah and shalom to you, you are?" Yeshua said, greeting the servant.

"My name is Sheila," the servant girl said timidly, surprised because no stranger had ever asked her for her name. She too had heard of Yeshua and that he was a man of God, and she was thrilled to now meet him and to have him talk to her, she would be able to boast to her friends.

"Thank you, Sheila, for all you are doing for Deborah. Let me have a moment with her." Sheila stepped back.

"You can leave us now, Sheila," Shimon said. He was the only one with them at the moment. The others were still in the common room of the house.

"No, it's okay, Shimon, let Sheila stay. Deborah will need her," Yeshua said.

Yeshua then knelt down next to Deborah's bed so that he was at eye level with Deborah. He then took her hand and said, "Deborah, you have suffered enough. I command this fever to leave you." Immediately, Yeshua felt the power go out of him. Ever since his first miracle at Cana in Galilee, he simply knew who and when he needed to heal, and that he had this power from his heavenly Father.

Immediately, Deborah felt the fever leave her, it was as if she was receiving an injection of sorts for her strength seemed to come rushing back to her with power. She smiled, her face radiating freshness and joy. And both Shimon and Sheila knew that Deborah was without fever and well again. They both rejoiced and, in their hearts, gave glory and thanks to God.

"Thank you, Yeshua," Deborah said, as she rose and embraced Yeshua. "Let me now tidy and freshen myself and I will come and serve you all."

Yeshua, Shimon and Sheila returned to the others and by the looks on their faces, they knew that Yeshua must have driven the fever out of Deborah, and they all gave glory to God.

And very soon afterwards, a jovial and youthful looking Deborah joined them, and with Sarah, served them.

They ate and then Yeshua said he would like to go to the synagogue. By this time, news had leaked that Yeshua was in town and staying with Shimon, the big fisherman. So as soon as Yeshua appeared, walking towards the synagogue, someone cried out, "There he is, it is Yeshua, the miracle worker."

Another cried out, "He is going to the synagogue." Soon, a crowd was swelling and following Yeshua and his disciples.

When Yeshua arrived at the synagogue, there was a huge crowd and they filled the place. Shimon and the others had to protect Yeshua from being crushed. When Yeshua reached the front of the synagogue, he spoke to the people.

And as he usually did, he healed all those who were brought to him. When he had finished, he told the people that he would be leaving Bethsaida for a while, because there were other cities, towns and villages to which he must go and spread the Good News of salvation, redemption and freedom for all.

Later that day, Yeshua was walking through the town, Shimon and the others formed a ring around Yeshua, so he could be left alone for a while. As Yeshua was walking, he saw a tax-collector, sitting at the tax booth. Yeshua stopped to speak with him. The disciples were surprised to see Yeshua speaking with the tax-collector. Tax-collectors were scum of the earth, as far as the people were concerned. They collected all of Rome's taxes and tariffs. And they earned their living through commission on what they collected. So many of them were unscrupulous and overcharged some of the people and skimmed from the rest, pocketing it all. And there was nothing anyone could do. Rome needed these tax-collectors and all they were concerned with was getting their money.

"What is your name?" Yeshua asked.

"I am Mattheus, and you are Yeshua, the carpenter from Nazareth, I know of you, and have heard of all the mighty deeds you have done. And I met you Yeshua, in Jerusalem, not so long ago," Mattheus said. "I was with Judas; we were disciples of Johanan." Mattheus was surprised that this Yeshua, who now had such an exalted reputation, would stop and want to talk with him, especially right here where he was sitting collecting taxes. Mattheus knew of the reputation of tax payers and how despised they, the tax-collectors were, and he had heard of Yeshua's message of righteousness, of justice and all that, and he felt a bit uncomfortable in this man's presence.

"What do you want with me, Yeshua; have you come to pay some taxes?" Mattheus asked.

"No Mattheus, I need you, I want you to follow me and assist me to spread the kingdom of God here on earth, will you follow me, Mattheus?" Yeshua asked.

Mattheus was surprised and overawed. It was the last thing he expected, a visit from Yeshua, the Prophet, the Anointed One, the Promised One, the great Teacher and Healer. How could he refuse?

Mattheus was overcome, but something stirred within him that made him respond, "Yeshua, I will hand in what I have collected. And I will resign my position immediately." Without considering, Mattheus was moved to have Yeshua as a guest in his home. "Yeshua, I would like to invite you to dinner. Could you come this evening?" Mattheus said.

"I gladly accept, Mattheus; I will bring my five disciples with me. You must know some of them, four fishermen, Shimon, Andreus, here from your town, and James and Johanan, sons of Zebedee, also fishermen from Capernaum, and Miriam from Magdala and Rebecca from my home town of Nazareth," Yeshua said.

"They are most welcome, Yeshua. Shall we say around the tenth hour, late afternoon? We could have some drinks before dinner." Mattheus then gave Yeshua directions to his home.

The disciples kept a distance from Yeshua and Mattheus, still keeping people away from Yeshua, and they were not able to hear the conversation between Yeshua and the despised Mattheus. They saw Mattheus pack up his belongings, lock up the tax booth, and leave in a hurry. They wondered what had happened.

Yeshua returned to the group and told them that Mattheus was now one of them. He was now a disciple, and Yeshua asked them to make him welcome. They were all astonished. To associate with tax-collectors, and to have one of them as one of his disciples, would tarnish Yeshua's reputation and his message. But none of them questioned Yeshua.

"By the way, Mattheus has invited us all to dinner at his place, around the tenth hour. So, I am going to go for a walk on the beach until then. You all may do as you wish, and we will meet at Mattheus' place. It is a house on the hill overlooking the Sea of Galilee," Yeshua said.

"We know where it is, Yeshua, you can't miss it. It is the biggest house in town, a mansion, built on the money he skimmed from the collection of taxes from the poor," Shimon said, with contempt in his voice. That was as far as Shimon would go in expressing what he really thought, he loathed to be seen in Mattheus' company, and he was reluctant to let Yeshua know exactly what he thought and felt about Mattheus. Was this what it meant by loving one's enemies, which Yeshua so often said in his teachings? Shimon wondered. But then Mattheus had been a disciple of Johanan's, the prophet, so he could be an exception. Still, Shimon would not give him the benefit of the doubt.

When they all arrived at Shimon's large house, the place was abuzz with activity, with servants dashing about. The disciples were waiting outside for Yeshua to arrive. Mattheus came and invited them inside, but they said they would wait for Yeshua to come.

They did not wait long, Yeshua arrived looking fresh, having had his hair and beard trimmed. "You look nice, Yeshua, and refreshed," Rebecca said.

"I needed a haircut and my beard trimmed; it was getting much too long. I had meant to get a cut and a trim at the barber in Capernaum. I remember getting one there by Methuselah, I mean Job. He was over ninety, if I remember. Is he still around?" Yeshua asked James and Johanan.

"Unfortunately, Yeshua, Job did not reach Methuselah's age, he died about three years ago, at the age of ninety-nine," Johanan said.

"He had a beautiful funeral, the whole of Capernaum was there and many from beyond," James said.

"Come now; let us go in for dinner. Do enjoy yourselves; let your hair down for a bit. Tomorrow, we leave for the town of Gergesa," Yeshua said. Yeshua was pleased to be at this dinner, he was hungry, and felt the need to relax, and be away from the crowds and from teaching and healing for a while. He needed to refresh and recharge and he was looking forward to a good meal and some wine and of course relaxing with his friends.

But the place was packed. Mattheus was a chief tax collector, so he had several tax-collectors and staff under him. They were all present. Many Pharisees and Scribes and the elite of Bethsaida, as well as the religious leaders and prominent landowners and business people, were present. Some Pharisees, friends of Mattheus heard of the dinner and they imposed on Mattheus to invite them. Mattheus only invited a couple of Pharisees, but they brought a whole gang of other Pharisees, Scribes and religious leaders, with them. They would not normally have accepted an invitation to Mattheus' place, but when their confreres told them that Yeshua was to be the guest of honour, they fought to be there.

However, when the Pharisees were there and saw Yeshua, with a cup of wine in his hand, and chatting amicably with several tax-collectors and their staff, they were appalled. They approached Shimon and Andreus and the other disciples, and one of them, speaking on behalf of the other Pharisees with him said, "Shimon, Andreus, why does your teacher eat with such people?"

Yeshua heard them, they wanted Yeshua to hear them, so Yeshua said to them, "Why do you criticise me for associating with tax-collectors, when you are here in the home of Mattheus? Those who are well have no need of a physician, but those who are sick. Go and learn what this means, 'I desire mercy, not sacrifice.' For I have come to call not the righteous but sinners."

"Dinner is served. Please take a seat at one of the tables," Mattheus announced, diffusing what looked like an argument brewing.

Everyone scrambled for a seat, watching where Yeshua was sitting, as they all wanted to be near him. The servants came in with tray after tray of fine food and the wine flowed freely. Yeshua and his disciples were enjoying the feast, and everyone present forgot where they were, and that their guest of honour was the One who was causing such a stir all over Galilee and beyond. They were fully engrossed and enjoying the food and the wine. And the place got noisy with chatter. Yeshua made sure that Miriam and Rebecca were present. And Mattheus, when he learned about Yeshua's disciples, that two of them were women, he invited some of his female friends, the wives of his staff, and the other tax-collectors and they were all thrilled to be guests with Yeshua present. It would be something, an experience they would be able to talk about, and maybe they would witness a miracle of sorts, up close. The women were also fascinated with Miriam and Rebecca, whom they were told were the first of Yeshua's disciples. There was so much intrigue with this man Yeshua.

In the meantime, the servants, against the orders of Mattheus, had spread the word that Yeshua and his disciples were dining at Mattheus' the tax-collector's place. The guests had finished their main course when there was a commotion from outside the house.

Mattheus went outside and saw a swelling crowd outside. They had sick people with them, wanting to ask Yeshua to heal them.

Yeshua heard the commotion and followed Mattheus and when Yeshua saw the crowd, his heart went out to them. Mattheus wanted to send them all away, but Yeshua said, "Mattheus, let them be. We have eaten enough, let them in, I will talk to them."

Much to the consternation of the guests, the crowd came into the house and filled every spare seat, and every spare standing space, and Yeshua addressed them. After Yeshua had spoken to them, one of the crowd spoke up. "Yeshua, I am a disciple of Johanan the baptiser, and I have with me some of his disciples." He then questioned Yeshua, "Yeshua, why do we, and even the Pharisees fast often, but you and your disciples do not fast?"

"I am so pleased to meet you, disciples of Johanan, no greater man than he has ever lived. I hope to meet with Johanan when I go to Jerusalem. And we will do all we can to get him released," Yeshua said, and continued, "And in answer to your question about fasting, I say; Wedding guests cannot mourn as long as the bride and the bridegrooms are with them, can they? The days will come when the bridegroom is taken away from them, and then they will fast. No one sews a piece of unshrunk cloth on an old cloak, for the patch pulls away, from the cloak, and a worse tear is made. Neither is new wine, put into old wineskins; otherwise, the skins are destroyed; but new wine is put into fresh wineskins, so both are preserved."

Before Yeshua could continue, a man came forward and addressed Yeshua. "Yeshua, I have with me my son here, he is suffering badly, he can hardly walk and he is going blind and can barely speak. He is so sick and weak, Yeshua, if you will, you can cure him," the man cried out.

Yeshua's heart filled with compassion went out to the man and his son. He had already cured young men, similarly possessed. "Bring him to me," Yeshua said. The crowd parted and left a pathway for the man and his son. The boy was no more than twelve years old and Yeshua cried out in torment and then asked the boy, "What is your name, son?"

"Timothy," the boy said timidly.

Yeshua took the boy by the hand, and with love in his heart for the boy and his father, Yeshua said, "Timothy, do you wish to be healed of your illness?"

"Yes, Yeshua," the boy said softly.

"Timothy, do you believe that I can cure you?" Yeshua asked.

"Yes, I do believe, Yeshua, I believe you are the Son of God and you have the power to heal me," Timothy said, astonishing all those around hm.

Yeshua then took Timothy's hand and spoke, "Father, be glorified in this boy Timothy. You have sent me to heal the broken-hearted and to set captives free, Timothy and his father and their loved ones are broken-hearted and they are held captive by this illness. Timothy your faith and that of your father has made you whole and set you free. Go now in peace."

A smile came over Timothy's face. He rushed into Yeshua who opened his arms and held Timothy who was now weeping tears of joy. Timothy's father too, was weeping tears of joy. Everyone present could see that Timothy was healed.

Several more, sick people came forward, and Yeshua healed them all.

The Pharisees and their cohort could not help but be amazed at what they were witnessing. But some of them were filled with envy, and shut their eyes and minds to what was happening. This man cannot come from God, he ignores so many of our Laws and associates with prostitutes and sinners, and he does not observe the Sabbath. He shows no respect for the Sabbath. These powers of his cannot come from God.

One of the Pharisees spoke up, "Yeshua, you and your disciples have been seen walking through the cornfields on the Sabbath. And your disciples plucked some heads of grain, rubbed them in their hands and ate them. Why are you doing what is not lawful on the Sabbath?"

Yeshua looked at the Pharisee and those around him. His heart went out to them too; they were like blind people leading the blind. They have just witnessed faith of the simple people, who brought the sick boy to him, believing. And they saw the power he had from his father, and they have shut their eyes, their minds and their hearts. He wanted to open them, so he said, "Have you not read what David did when he and his companions were hungry? He entered the house of God and took and ate the bread of the Presence, which is not lawful for any but the priests to eat, and gave some to his companions?" Then Yeshua said to them, "The Son of God is Lord of the Sabbath."

Some of the Pharisees and Scribes and the others with them only shut their minds all the more. They were furious, and wanted to discredit Yeshua. They thought that by showing how Yeshua disrespected the Law of God to keep holy the Sabbath, they would expose him for what he is, a fraudster, a trickster, a son of the devil. So, they persisted.

Their spokesman turned to the crowd and pointing to Yeshua said, "This man cannot be a prophet, a man of God, not only does he not respect the Sabbath but he also shows no respect for the holy Temple. On a Sabbath, he was in the synagogue and there was a man with a withered hand. He made the man stand in front of all and used his power to heal this man. He cannot be a man of God."

Yeshua looked at the Pharisee and those around him, and shook his head in disbelief. Mattheus was not too pleased, he did not want a big argument to happen in his home, and while he was entertaining Yeshua.

Yeshua knew they were trying their best to undermine him. He spoke, "you forget to relate the full story of what happened on that Sabbath when I restored that poor man's withered hand, you do not mention what I said before I healed the man." Then Yeshua looked at them and around the room at the crowd who seemed to be enjoying the debate between Yeshua and the Pharisees and the Scribes and the religious teachers. In fact, Yeshua also seemed to be relishing the debate. He had been doing that since he was a child, he recalled the debates he had with the teachers in the Temple at Jerusalem. But now it was really serious. These teachers needed to open their eyes and their hearts; the Sabbath is for humankind and not humankind for the Sabbath.

So, Yeshua said to them, "I asked those who questioned me then, what I ask you now, 'Is it lawful to do good, or to do harm on the Sabbath, to save life or to destroy it?' If one of you had your ox fall into a pit on the Sabbath, and injure itself and was in danger of dying, would you leave it there to die, or would you seek help and lift it out of the pit? Worse still if your child fell into a deep dark pit on the Sabbath, and you heard your child crying for you to save him, would you leave your child there or would you not seek help and do all you can to save your child and lift him out of the darkness. I say to you again, the Son of God is Lord of the Sabbath, and the Sabbath is for humankind not humankind for the Sabbath."

"That is enough. Yeshua, I think we need to go now," Shimon said. He did not want the debate to get nasty and he knew that whatever Yeshua said, he would not sway these Pharisees and Scribes who were just out to discredit Yeshua.

"Yeshua, thank you for coming, you have honoured me; you have honoured us all with your presence," Mattheus said. He was disappointed how things developed and said, "Please forgive some of my guests, Yeshua. We have seen the power of God and we believe that you are the one that Johanan the baptiser spoke about." Turning to all present, Mattheus said, "I say to all of you, you all know me, I have been a tax-collector, for a long time and chief tax collector for some time. I have cheated you all. I will recompense you all. Yeshua I will recompense all whom I have cheated and pay back double. I will give all I own, all that I do not need to the poor and follow you."

Yeshua had already asked him to follow and be his disciple, but Mattheus wanted to make it public, he wanted his fellow tax-collectors and all his friends and acquaintances to know of his conversion and that he is now a disciple of Yeshua.

Yeshua was pleased and smiled at Mattheus, and knew what he saw in Mattheus was now being revealed. Yeshua then said, "Mattheus, you are blessed. I thank you for this fine meal, for your gracious hospitality. And I am grateful for your generosity and for you to be with me and the others to spread the Good News of the Father's love and compassion. I have come to bring peace, justice, and freedom to all," Yeshua said. "I take my leave now," Yeshua added and then he left and all his disciples with him.

"Friends," Yeshua said to his disciples while they were walking home, "tomorrow we will leave Bethsaida and go to the surrounding villages and speak to the people, and then we will go to the town of Gergesa."

Chapter Forty-Six
From the Tombs to Over the Cliff

The next day, Yeshua did as he had said. They left the town, early in the morning and went to all the surrounding villages, where the poor and outcasts lived. Mattheus had left everything, and was now one of Yeshua's disciples. The village people were all pleased to meet Yeshua and make him welcome and they were overawed that he would even think of visiting them. And there were no crowds around, only the village people. Shimon, Andreus, and Mattheus made sure no one knew where they were. That is what Yeshua wanted of them. But even if they did, the disciples knew the townspeople would not be seen dead in these outlying places, where the so-called sinners and unclean lived.

Yeshua brought them the Good News of Yahweh's love for them. He told them of the Father's great love for them, that He heard their cries and was aware of their great suffering. Yeshua healed all their sick and brought comfort to all who were suffering, and there was great rejoicing among the people, and they shared the little they had with Yeshua and his disciples. And Yeshua made sure that they too shared some of what they had, of what people had given them along the way, and that was much more than what they needed.

Andreus and Miriam were put in charge of all the gifts and money people gave them. Wherever they went people who were cured or touched in any way by Yeshua and who wanted to show their appreciation, offered gifts. And there were those who just wanted to support Yeshua in his work, and they had the money to do so. Elijah was one of them. He quietly gave his daughter Miriam a large sum of money for her and for Yeshua and his work. Andreus was in charge of the money and Miriam and Rebecca in charge of all the gifts received. But now that Mattheus, who was formerly a chief tax collector, joined their band of disciples, Andreus was only too glad to hand over the managing of their funds to Mattheus, whom he thought had all the expertise needed in managing money.

After spending some days in the villages, Yeshua and the disciples went to the town, under cover of darkness, way before sunrise and then headed for the nearby town of Gergesa, the county of the Gerasenes, on the coast. When they arrived at Gergesa, the sun had risen, and on their way to the town, as they were passing the town cemetery, and as soon as they were in the vicinity they heard howling coming from the nearby mountains. It was eerily and frightening sounds. Then all of a sudden, they heard the same howling coming from the cemetery. It was terrifying. Then they saw some men approaching. They looked like wild men, dirty and dishevelled, and making obscene guttural sounds.

When they came close, the disciples were overcome with fear and with revulsion at not only the look of the men, but the way they smelt. The disciples were scared, and they moved closer to Yeshua. Miriam and Rebecca were clinging to each other. From the noises the men were making and their strange behaviour and the piercing look in their eyes they knew the men were possessed of unclean spirits. The disciples were petrified.

And then they heard voices. The spirits spoke, with deep guttural voices that sent shivers up the disciples' spines; they knew they were in the presence of evil, of demoniac possession, the likes of which they had never before experienced.

"Why have you come, to restrain us? No one can. We live among the tombs, and no one can control us. They all come often and try to restrain us with shackles and chains, but we simply wrench the chains apart and break the shackles into pieces, and no one on this earth has the power or strength to subdue us, so don't waste your time, leave us and be gone," the possessed men shouted in deep, guttural sounds.

Yeshua knew he was in the presence of demons of the worst kind. But he did not fear. He knew that the power of Yahweh was in him and with him. He spoke in loud voice to the possessed. "Come out of these men, you unclean and evil spirits."

The possessed then shouted on the top of their voices, "What have you to do with us, Yeshua, Son of the Most High God? We adjure you by God, do not torment us."

Then Yeshua asked them, "Who are you, what are your names?"

One of the possessed replied, "My name is Legion for we are many."

The other then replied as well. "I too am Legion, for we are many more."

They then begged Yeshua earnestly not to send them out of the country. "You have them with you," one of the possessed men pointed to Miriam and Rebecca, who froze with fright, "send us into them, let us enter them and make our home in them."

Their speech sounded so menacing, like it was not the men speaking, and not just two of them, they sounded like an army, it sent shivers throughout Miriam and Rebecca, and they held onto each other.

"That will not happen," Yeshua, said.

Now it so happened that there on the hillside a great herd of swine were feeding, and the unclean spirits begged Yeshua. "Then send us into the swine, let us enter them."

Yeshua saw how terrified his disciples were, and especially Miriam and Rebecca so he commanded the evil spirits. "Go out of these men and enter the swine, as you wish."

And then it happened, a horrible, loud and frightening noise came out of the possessed men, and then they went limp and fell to the ground, as if lifeless. And then the disciples heard a most terrifying cacophony of noises, coming from the swine, and it was clear to the disciples that the evil spirits were entering the swine. There must have been more than two thousand swine, and their roar filled the air and was deafening and horrifying. The disciples had never heard or seen anything like this.

The swineherds tending the swine were out of their wits, they were completely bamboozled and had no idea what was happening and they too were terrified. They looked on helpless as they watched their herd rush madly down the steep bank into the sea and drowned. The noise was deafening and continued for some time and then just stillness. The possessed lay there lifeless, as if they were dead.

And then there was silence. The disciples were still in shock. They had witnessed Yeshua, cast out demons before, but nothing like this. It scared them.

"Do not be afraid," Yeshua said to them. "As long as you have faith, and know that I am with you, you can fear nothing from the evil spirits. But do pray regularly and be on your guard, for the devil goes about like a roaring lion, seeking whom it may devour. What you have witnessed is the power of God, the power of good over evil; the kingdom of God is now among you. In curing people of their illness and driving out of demons I am showing to you and the world that the kingdom of God is here among you. You have witnessed God's power, and his love for you, so fear not and trust in me."

Yeshua's words help settle his disciples. In the meantime, the men from whom the evil spirits had gone out had been lying limp on the ground, and now they began to stir. Yeshua reached out and took them by the hand and helped them to their feet. They seemed a bit disoriented at first, and then it seemed that all became clear.

The men looked at each other, looked at their hands, and felt their faces, and then saw their tattered clothes. Then Yeshua spoke to them. "My dear friends, what are your names."

One of the men spoke up, "I am Saul."

"And I am Josiah," said another.

"Saul and Josiah, and all of you have suffered much, the evil one has taken hold of you, but you are now free. And the Spirit of Yahweh is now with you."

While the swineherds saw all that was happening, when they saw the swine hurl themselves off the cliff, they were terrified, and they saw the men whom they recognised as the demoniacs from the tombs, with Yeshua, and seeming to be in complete control, they ran into the city telling the people what they had witnessed. And the people rushed off to see for themselves. Soon a crowd was surrounding Yeshua and his disciples and the formerly possessed men. They saw Yeshua in deep conversation. They saw the formerly possessed men, listening to Yeshua.

They stood and saw the men, they were different, and in full control of their senses and they were calm and without shackles. And Yeshua then blessed them and sent them off.

But the two men, Saul and Josiah pleaded with Yeshua that they might be with him and be his disciples as well. But Yeshua sent them away, saying, "Return to your home, and declare how much God has done for you." So, they went and all that day, they went all around that city, proclaiming how much Yeshua had done for them.

The people had followed the men into the city and saw for themselves the wonder of the Lord. But they had seen these men, living in the mountains and in the tombs, and just how dangerous they were, they had seen them shackled and shouting obscenities and living like wild beasts, and they could not believe what they were now seeing. The people were divided, some were asking, could this man be the Son of David, the Anointed One. But others were fearful and among them were the Pharisees, who were against Yeshua, for they did not believe him to be from God, because of what he taught and the way he lived. He did not respect the Sabbath and their Laws and he associated with tax-collectors, prostitutes, the unclean and sinners. The Pharisees told the people that Yeshua is not a man of God, and that it is by the power of Beelzebub that he casts out demons.

During the day, the people came to Yeshua and their spokesman, a Pharisee, asked Yeshua to leave them. "I have planned to leave today. But tell me why you are giving me such an ungracious farewell. When we arrived you were so welcoming, and so hospitable to me and my disciples. What has changed?"

The Pharisee spoke up, "Yeshua, we have heard from two of the demoniacs and from the swineherds what had happened on the hillside. And it is our firm belief, that it is only by the power of Beelzebub, the ruler of the demons that you cast our demons."

Yeshua shook his head in disbelief. And so did his disciples. Yeshua then spoke, "Every kingdom divided against itself is laid waste, and no city or house divided against itself will stand. If Satan casts out Satan, he is divided against himself; how then will his kingdom stand? But if it is by the Spirit of God that I cast out demons, then the Kingdom of God has come to you."

Then another person in the crowd, not one of the Pharisees, spoke up. "Yeshua, I have seen those two men, Saul and Josiah, I grew up with them, they were my friends, then both of them became possessed of an evil spirit, and over the years they got worse and worse until the city banished them to the mountains. Now they are changed, how do we know they will not return to their former selves?"

"That is a good question, young man," Yeshua said. "When the unclean spirit has gone out of a person, it wanders through waterless regions looking for a resting place, but it finds none. Then it says, 'I will return to my house from which I came.' When it comes, it finds it empty, swept and put in order. Then it goes and brings along seven other spirits more evil than itself, and they enter and live there; and the last state of that person is worse than the first. So, it will also be with this evil generation."

A woman from the crowd yelled out, "Yeshua, Blessed is the woman who bore you, and the breasts that nursed you."

Yeshua replied. "Yes, she is indeed blessed. But even more blessed are those who hear the Word of God and take it to heart, and live accordingly. That is what Saul and Josiah and the others will now be doing, with your help and support. Those demons that possessed them are now buried in the depths of the sea and they will no longer have any power over them. But the power of darkness is around, as I told you before, the devil and his demons, go around like roaring lions seeking whom they may devour. So be alert, be on your guard, watch and pray that you do not enter into temptation. And support each other with love and kindness and do to others as you would wish to be done unto you."

But then the Pharisee spoke up again. "We cannot trust you. What recompense do you provide to the owner of all those swine? And we see how you and your disciples live, you overindulge your senses with food and wine, and you have women travelling with you, and you are known for associating with sinners, with tax-collectors, why you even have Mattheus here, that scoundrel, the chief tax collector as one of your disciples. How can you be a man of God, if you would accept a man like Mattheus as one of your disciples?"

Then another Pharisee spoke up. "Yes, if you are from God, then give us a sign."

Yeshua shook his head in disbelief; did not they at least hear from the swineherds what had happened, had they not seen for themselves the transformation of Saul and Josiah. Even Yeshua's disciples were amazed at their incredulity in the face of what had just happened in their town.

Yeshua said to them. "You will know the Son of God by his fruits. A tree is known by its fruits. You brood of vipers! How can you speak good things, when you are evil? In your heart are pride, envy, and maliciousness. Out of the abundance of the heart the mouth speaks. The good person, the loving person, the humble person, the compassionate person, the kind person, brings good things out of a good treasure, and the evil person brings evil things out of an evil treasure. I tell you on the day of judgement, you will have to give account for every careless word you utter, for by your words you will be justified, and by your words you will be condemned.

"You ask me for a sign, an evil and adulterous generation asks for a sign but no sign will be given to it, except the sign of the prophet, Jonah. For just as Jonah was in the belly of the sea monster for three days and three nights, so the Son of God will be in the heart of the earth. The people of Nineveh repented at the proclamation of Jonah, and see, something, someone, greater than Jonah is here. The queen of the South will rise up in judgement with this generation and condemn it, because she came from the ends of the earth to listen to the Wisdom of Solomon, and see, and listen, something greater than Solomon is here!"

With these words, the Pharisees and their followers had no more to say. Yeshua then left and told Shimon and his disciples to tell the people to go to their homes and to go about their business.

The news about Saul, Josiah, and the other possessed that lived among the tombs, and the swine going over the cliff was all that people spoke about. Some were uneasy with such a display of power but others believed that this man is indeed from God, and maybe he is the Promised One, the Messiah who was to set them free.

Yeshua spent the morning and part of the afternoon in Gergesa, speaking to the people in the market place and healing those who came to him. He then decided to leave Gergesa and to go back to Capernaum on the next day.

As Shimon's boat was still in Bethsaida, they walked to Bethsaida. Yeshua said he would spend a quiet day in Bethsaida and on the following day he would like to sail back to Capernaum. He told his disciples they could do what they wanted and that he would be spending some time in the woods. Yeshua's reputation was now so widespread that he had little private time, for people followed him wherever he went, and wanted to hear him teach and also wanted him to heal them of their illnesses or the illnesses of their loved ones. Yeshua was human and all of this tired him, sapped his energy, and he needed time to rest and recuperate and regain his strength and also time alone with his heavenly Father.

Yeshua was well supported in his work and sought and received guidance from Miriam and Rebecca and Shimon, Andreus, James, Johanan and Mattheus. But he knew that his time was short and there was so much that he needed to accomplish, so he needed to call some more disciples who would support him in his work and carry on after he was gone.

Yeshua spent a few hours in the forest, and then went for a walk along a lonely and deserted stretch of beach. Yeshua, now feeling refreshed, walked back to the town. It was past noon and the place was busy. As he was walking towards the town, a man approached him; it was clear that the man recognised Yeshua immediately and he greeted Yeshua and said to him.

"Yeshua, I am Phillip, I was in the synagogue, praying, and I can't explain it, but it was as if someone had tapped me on the shoulder and told me to walk this way and that I would encounter my destiny," Phillip said.

"Phillip, it is the Spirit that has brought you to me. Come with me. Do you know Shimon and Andreus, they are also from here in Bethsaida," Yeshua said.

"Shimon, the big fisherman and his brother, of course everyone knows them," Phillip said.

"Shimon and Andreus are two of my disciples who are supporting me in my work, the work that Yahweh has given me; will you come and follow me too, Phillip?" Yeshua asked.

Phillip was overcome. "Yes, Yeshua," he cried out. "The Spirit has sent me to you, Yeshua." Then Phillip blurted out, "Yeshua, I have a friend; I would like to go and speak to him, and tell him I have met you, because we were both speaking about you," Phillip said with excitement.

"Go to your friend and you will find me at Shimon's place. We will be there tonight and then we sail for Capernaum the following day. At Capernaum we are staying at the vineyards of our friend and supporter, Elijah. His daughter, Miriam, is also one of my disciples. Do you know them?" Yeshua asked.

"Everyone knows, Elijah, we drink his wine and quite a few from Bethsaida work at his vineyards or at his winemaking plant," Phillip said.

"And here in Bethsaida, we are staying at Shimon's place. You can meet me there tonight," Yeshua said.

"I will be there tonight, Yeshua," Phillip said.

Phillip found Nathanael sitting under a fig tree, eating some of the figs he had picked. "Shalom Nathan, I have such good news to tell you, I have found the Anointed One about whom Moses in the Law and the Prophets wrote about, Yeshua, son of Josef and Miriam from Nazareth. The One we have heard about, who has been preaching and teaching all over Galilee and now here in Bethsaida, the one we had been talking about. So many signs have accompanied him wherever he goes. I have met him, Nathan, and he has asked me to accompany him, to be his disciple. Come and see him, Nathan," Phillip urged his friend.

Nathanael kept on eating his figs. He then wiped his mouth with the back of his hand and said to his friend, "Phillip, can anything good come out of Nazareth?"

But Phillip urged him, "Nathan, come and see for yourself."

"Okay, okay, I'll go and see and check him out," Nathanael said.

They found Yeshua, in the market place surrounded by a crowd. But it wasn't Yeshua that was speaking but Shimon, the big fisherman. Nathanael and Phillip joined the crowd and listened to what Shimon had to say. The people were astounded and ready to listen to Shimon. They all knew him as a rough and ready fisherman, and astute businessman who spoke his mind boldly and without fear. But they also knew him as impetuous and bumbling at times. So, they were intrigued to now listen to him speaking with eloquence and ease. Shimon himself, was taken by surprise, when Yeshua asked him to address the crowd. Shimon was not used to public speaking. He surprised himself by the words that were coming out his mouth as if it was someone else that was doing the speaking.

"My dear friends from Bethsaida, you all know me, I am honoured to know this man Yeshua and to be called by him to be one of his disciples and to assist him in his work. My brother Andreus and I were disciples of Johanan the baptiser, who is still languishing in Herod's prison. I give you the testimony of Johanan when the priests and Levites from Jerusalem were sent to question him. When they asked Johanan, 'who are you?' he confessed, 'I am not the Messiah.' His inquisitors persisted and asked Johanan, 'What then, are you Elijah or the prophet?' and he answered 'No.' They were exasperated and they said to him. 'Who are you? Let us have an answer, for those who sent us. What do you say about yourself?' To this question, Johanan said, 'I am a voice, crying out in the wilderness; make straight the way of the Lord, as the prophet said'."

Shimon continued speaking. The crowd, including Phillip and Nathanael, were hanging onto his every word. And they were amazed to hear Shimon speaking with such eloquence, ease and conviction.

Shimon continued, "Now the priests and Levites had been sent by the Pharisees, and they continued their questioning of Johanan. They asked Johanan, 'If you are neither the Messiah, nor Elijah, nor the Prophet, then why are you baptising?' To this question Johanan answered, 'I baptise with water. Among you stands one whom you do not know, the one who is coming after me; I am not worthy to untie the thong of his sandal.'"

Shimon concluded, "My dear people of Bethsaida and all visitors to our town, this man Yeshua who stands here before you, he is the one Johanan spoke about, listen to him for he has the words of eternal life."

Yeshua then spoke, "Shimon, I thank you. My dear friends, I have come to bring you the Good News of Yahweh's great love for you. I come to also warn you, to be watchful and to read the signs. When you see a cloud rising in the west, you immediately say, 'it is going to rain,' and so it happens. And when you feel and see the south wind blowing, you say, 'there will be scorching heat,' and it happens. You know how to interpret the appearance of earth and sky, but why do you not know how to interpret the present time?"

Then Yeshua told them a story. "A man had a fig tree planted in his vineyard and he came looking for fruit on it and found none. So, he said to the gardener, 'See here! For three years I have come looking for fruit on this fig tree, and still, I find none. Cut it down! Why should it be wasting the soil?' He replied, 'Sir, let it alone for one more year, until I dig around it and put manure on it. If it bears fruit next year, well and good; but if not, you can cut it down.'

"Listen to what I am saying to you; a sower went out to sow and as he sowed, some seed fell on the path, and the birds came and ate it up. Other seed fell on rocky ground, where it did not have much soil, and it sprang up quickly, since it had no depth of soil. When the sun rose, it was scorched; and since it had no root, it withered away. Other seed fell among thorns, and the thorns grew up and choked it, and it yielded no grain. Other seed fell into good soil and brought forth grain, growing up and yielding thirty and sixty and a hundredfold."

"Yeshua, you speak to us in parables, please explain," a voice came from the crowd.

Yeshua replied, "I am the sower of the seed, the Word of God. I bring to you the Word of God; the Word is love. God is love, and God so loves the world that he has sent me into the world, to proclaim the Word, to proclaim the day of salvation and redemption for all. God is love and who abides in love, abides in God and God abides in him. I come with the seed, which is the Word. I am the sower, sowing the Word among you. There are among you, some on the path where the Word is sown, for those, you hear the Word, but Satan immediately comes and takes the Word that is sown in you.

"Then there are those among you, sown on rocky ground; when you hear the Word, you immediately receive it with joy, but you have no roots, and endure only for a while, then when trouble or persecution arises on account of the Word, you immediately fall away. And then there are others among you, sown among thorns.

These among you, are the ones that hear the Word, but the cares of the world, and lure of wealth, and the desire for other things the world has to offer come in and chokes the Word in you, and you yield nothing. And then there are the ones among you, sown on the good soil; you hear the Word and accept it and bear fruit, thirty and sixty and a hundredfold."

Yeshua knew that many of them listening to him would relate to what he was saying; many of them farm the land. He continued to speak to them in parables. He said, "The kingdom of God is as if someone would scatter seed on the ground and then would go to sleep and rise night and day, and the seed would sprout and grow, he does not know how. The earth produces of itself, first the stalk, then the head, then the full grain in the head. But when the grain is ripe, at once he goes in with his sickle, because the harvest has come."

Yeshua continued speaking to them in parables. Parables that the people could relate to and that made them think. He told them the parable of the mustard seed. "With what can we compare the Kingdom of God or what parable will we use for it? It is like a mustard seed, which, when sown upon the ground, is the smallest of all the seeds on earth; yet when it grows up it becomes the greatest of all shrubs, and puts forth large branches, so that the birds of the air can make nests in its shade."

Yeshua spoke to them in many parables about the Word and the Kingdom of God. He sought to open their ears, their minds and their hearts to the message he was born to bring to them and to the whole world. No longer are they to live in fear of an overbearing God, a cruel God, an exacting God, who watched them like a hawk waiting for them to do wrong, to commit sin, and then to record, and punish them. No, he was a loving God, a compassionate God, a forgiving God, who loved them with a boundless love, a generous love, a magnanimous love, an unconditional love, an eternal love.

"Yahweh is our Abba; he does not record any of our weakness or our faults and failings. All he wants of us is our love in return, all he wants is that we love one another as he loves us, that we forgive one another as he forgives us."

When Yeshua had finished speaking, the people brought their sick and afflicted to him for healing. Shimon and the other disciples, including Miriam and Rebecca, stayed with the sick as they waited their turn for Yeshua's healing touch. Miriam and Rebecca brought so much comfort to the women who were there, those that were sick and the mothers and sisters who accompanied their sick. The women felt so reassured to know that Yeshua had women as disciples with him. The women could also speak to them of what was burdening them, burdens that only women could understand.

When Yeshua had finished healing everyone and Shimon and the others sent all the people away, Phillip approached. Shimon and Andreus recognised Phillip by sight, but they were not really friends or acquaintants. They and the other disciples were curious at what Phillip wanted with Yeshua.

"Phillip, good to see you," Yeshua said, with a broad smile.

"Yeshua, I have brought Nathanael, whom I told you about," Phillip said.

When Yeshua saw Nathanael coming towards him, he said to him. "Here is truly an Israelite in whom there is no deceit."

All the disciples looked at Nathanael. Who is this man, of whom Yeshua speaks so highly? Even Phillip was taken aback by Yeshua's comment about Nathanael because Yeshua did not know Nathanael and they had never met. And Phillip thought, if only Yeshua knew what Nathanael had said when he had spoken to him about Yeshua; he had some derogatory things to say about Nazareth.

Nathanael too was surprised at Yeshua's comments, for he had never met Yeshua before. Nathanael asked Yeshua, "Where did you get to know me?"

Yeshua answered, "I saw you under the fig tree before Phillip called you."

Both Nathanael and Phillip were astonished. Nathanael was overcome and moved by the Spirit, he exclaimed, "Rabbi, you are the Son of God! You are the king of Israel."

Phillip and all the disciples were astounded and in awe of what Nathanael had said.

Yeshua answered Nathanael, "Nathanael, do you believe because I told you that I saw you under the fig tree? You will see greater things than these." And Yeshua said to Nathanael, and meant for all his disciples, "Very truly I tell you, you will see heaven opened and the angels of God ascending and descending on the Son of God."

Yeshua continued to move all around that side of the Sea of Galilee for months, preaching and teaching and comforting and healing all those in need. He spent time with the poor and the outcasts in little outlying villages and brought them so much comfort. He spent days with them listening to them and teaching them and answering their questions, and comforting them, and giving the Good News of Yahweh's great love for them. And he reassured them that their suffering was not, is not the result of their sins. He reminded them over and over of Yahweh's love and compassion and readiness to forgive and forget. After spending months in the towns and all the villages along the eastern side of the lake with the poor and the outcasts and healing their sick, he and his disciples returned to Bethsaida. There they remained for a few weeks more. Shimon, Andreus, Phillip, Nathanael, and Mattheus, were given time to be with their loved ones. After two weeks Yeshua took all of his disciples into a lonely place for a week's retreat. He spent time with them, teaching them, and listening to them and they had some time, to get to know each other more and more.

After the retreat, Yeshua felt it was time to leave Bethsaida. It was late afternoon when he and his disciples sailed across the Sea of Galilee, heading for Capernaum.

Chapter Forty-Seven
What Manner of Man Is This?

It was getting dark and they were in the middle of the lake. It was calm. Yeshua was tired so he lay down with his head on a cushion at the stern of the boat, and soon fell into a deep sleep. The sea was calm when they left Bethsaida, and they were now about half way to Capernaum. All of a sudden gusts of wind started blowing, and then it increased and increased, and the wind began howling like thousands of wild animals. Sudden wind storms on the Sea of Galilee were common and the fishermen's worst nightmare and it could come suddenly and without warning. But now the wind was howling more and more fiercely and the sea became wild and the waves increasing in height and ferocity, the likes of which Shimon, Andreus, James and Johanan had never experienced before. Everyone held onto something on the boat that was fixed. But Yeshua slept through it all. Water was coming into the boat and it was being swamped and there was a great danger that they could all drown.

Shimon manoeuvred himself towards the stern holding onto whatever he could to remain grounded, to see if Yeshua was safe. The others were cowering down and holding onto parts of the boat to keep them from being tossed overboard. They were all terrified. The men helped Miriam and Rebecca and made sure they too were safe. They were getting drenched to the core from the waves. Shimon eventually got to where Yeshua was sleeping. He was amazed to find Yeshua still fast asleep. How could he sleep through a storm of this magnitude? The others were also concerned about Yeshua.

Andreus shouted, "How is he?"

"He is asleep!" Shimon shouted back.

They were all terrified and they all shouted to Shimon to wake Yeshua.

Shimon touched Yeshua, then shook him and shouted, "Yeshua, Yeshua, wake up!" but to no avail, so he shook Yeshua more fiercely, and then Yeshua woke up.

"Yeshua, we are being swamped by the winds and the waves; we are in grave danger of drowning. Master, do you not care that we are perishing?" Shimon cried in desperation.

Yeshua then stood up, and raised his arms wide open and commanded the wind, "Peace! Be still!" And then all of a sudden the winds became calm and still and the waves subsided and the sea became still. The disciples were amazed.

Yeshua then said to his disciples, "Why are you afraid? Have you still no faith?"

The disciples were filled with great awe and said to one another, "Who then is this, that even the wind and sea obey him?"

They then all quietened down and remained silent. They were all occupied with their own thoughts and with Yeshua. They had witnessed his great power. Yet he was still a human being like them, he felt fatigue and needed sleep and rest, so much so that he slept through this ferocious storm. And yet with a word and a gesture he calms the wind and the waves. They knew that he was indeed sent by God. And they were in awe of him and felt so honoured to be in his company and to be called to be his disciples.

They arrived at Capernaum. Shimon and Andreus tied down the boat, which seemed to be okay, and without any damage from the storm, which amazed them both. Yeshua and the rest went to their base, Elijah's place to clean up and refresh themselves, and have something to eat. The day was now calm and the sun was shining and not a breath of wind in the air. Everyone now had fresh and dry clothes. Shimon and Andreus arrived and found all of them having something to eat, of what Eva had prepared.

The next morning, after they had breakfast, Yeshua asked them to go with him to the synagogue to pray. When Yeshua arrived at the synagogue a crowd was there waiting for him outside of the synagogue. They already got the news that Yeshua was back in their town, and they all gathered outside the synagogue waiting for Yeshua to appear.

Yeshua greeted them all warmly and they had heard that Yeshua and his disciples were on the Sea of Galilee during the violent storm, and they were all amazed at how suddenly the storm had ceased and the winds abated. They were all amazed that Yeshua and his disciples survived that storm at sea, and they wondered if Yeshua had anything to do with it.

"Yeshua, how did you and your disciples, manage to survive that terrible storm last night when you were sailing across from Bethsaida," a person from the crowd asked.

"With faith in Adonai, you can survive all of life's storms. With faith, you have nothing to fear," Yeshua said.

As he was speaking, a man came and approached Yeshua and fell at his feet. "It's Jairus, leader in the synagogue," a person in the crowd called out.

Yeshua heard the man's name and he stooped down and lifted Jairus off the ground, and said, "Jairus, what is it that troubles you?" Yeshua could see the anguish on Jairus' face and he was filled with compassion for him.

"Lord, I have an only daughter, she is only twelve years old, and she is dying."

Yeshua saw the anguish on Jairus' face and also the faith he had, for he did not ask Yeshua anything, he merely told Yeshua that his daughter was dying. Yeshua admired his faith, and so he said, "Take me to your daughter."

Jairus seemed so relieved, although he was still worried. He led the way and Yeshua and his disciples followed, as did the crowd who was pressing all around Yeshua. Shimon and Andreus had trouble protecting Yeshua from the crowds.

All of a sudden, Yeshua stopped and said, "Who touched me?"

Shimon looked at Yeshua dumbfounded and said, "Master, the crowds surround you and press in on you."

But Yeshua insisted, "Someone touched me; for I felt that power had gone out from me."

Shimon, and the disciples and the crowd were astounded, and all eyes were on Yeshua, for he had stopped and waited to see who it was that touched him.

A woman standing close by realised she could not remain hidden, so she came forward trembling and fell on her knees before Yeshua, but Yeshua immediately helped her to her feet. And she spoke for all to hear, "Master, I have been suffering from haemorrhages for twelve years."

At the mention of this, a number of Pharisees in the crowd stepped back aghast— to touch a woman who was issuing blood would make them unclean. If Yeshua was the Prophet, the Promised One, he would have known this and not allow this to happen, and prevent himself from becoming unclean. They were waiting for Yeshua to reprimand the woman.

Instead, Yeshua listened with full attention and compassion to what the woman was saying. She continued, "Master, I had spent all I had on physicians but no one could cure me. And when I heard you were in our town again, I thought to myself, if only I could touch the hem of your garment, I would be healed." Then she declared for all to hear, "When I touched the hem of your garment, I knew, I felt, I was immediately healed."

The crowd gasped. The disciples were overawed. They had witnessed so many healings and just witnessed Yeshua's power over the wind and the sea and now this.

Yeshua on the other hand was amazed at the woman's faith and he said to her, "Daughter, your faith has made you well; go in peace."

Just then, someone came from Jairus' house, looking sad, came to Jairus and said to him, "Jairus, your daughter has died; do not trouble the Teacher any longer."

Jairus burst into tears and fell on his knees, sobbing like a child. Yeshua's heart went out to him. He lifted Jairus onto his feet and said, "Jairus, do not fear. Only believe, and she will be saved."

When the crowd heard this, they were bewildered. They had seen him heal the sick, give sight to the blind, make the mute speak, the lame walk, but can he raise a person from the dead? The girl must be in a faint or unconscious, some of them thought. The Pharisees among them scoffed at the very idea; no one can raise a person from the dead. Even the disciples wondered. They had just witnessed him calming the winds and the sea, and curing a woman suffering haemorrhaging for years, but raising someone from the dead!

They all followed Yeshua and Jairus. Yeshua and the disciples had to keep up with Jairus, who was almost running. The crowd still followed.

When Yeshua and Jairus arrived at the house, Yeshua asked only Shimon, Johanan, James, Miriam and Rebecca to enter with him, and accompany Jairus and his wife. He asked Andreus and the others to keep the crowd from entering into the house. When they entered the room, there was a group of people, relatives and friends, including several women mourners, who were weeping and wailing.

Yeshua was moved with compassion and he said to Jairus and his wife and the people weeping around the child's bed, "Do not weep, for she is sleeping."

Some in the room could not contain themselves and burst out laughing, for they knew she was dead. Shimon, looked sternly at them with a fierce frown on his face, and they all became quiet. But all wondered if Yeshua was out of his mind. The doctor had pronounced her dead. She had no pulse or heartbeat. And they have seen dead people, she was dead alright. Did Yeshua know something more than the doctor and everyone else?

Then Yeshua approached the girl and he took her hand and called out, "Talitha cum!" which meant, "Little child, get up!"

All at once, the child stirred, her spirit returned and she got up, as if she had been simply sleeping. She looked at all the people around the bed and was filled with surprise. Jairus and his wife rushed to embrace her, and they were sobbing as were all the mourners around her, but they were tears of joy. The disciples were in awe, and asked themselves again, what manner of man is this that he even raises the dead to life.

The girl was now standing up, somewhat confused and wondering why everyone was crying. She remembered being very sick, and her parents and servants around her, but why so many, and so many strange women, dressed in black.

Yeshua embraced the girl, and smiled, and told them to give her something to eat. And Yeshua ordered everyone in the room to tell no one of what had happened. But to no avail, the word got out and the news of what happened spread all over the country.

Yeshua continued preaching and teaching in the synagogue and all over that country preaching the Good News of the Kingdom of God, and he healed all the sick and handicapped. Wherever he went crowds followed. When he eventually sent them away, he and his disciples rested at a quiet spot outside of the town.

Yeshua had gone off into the woods again, saying he would return in an hour. The disciples had something to eat, and they started discussing all they had experienced in the last twenty-four hours. They needed to debrief. Shimon spoke of how terrified he was during the storm at sea. "I was so scared, because Yeshua was on the boat, and there would have been hell to pay from the people, if Yeshua drowned at sea."

"What about us?" James said, with a smile.

"Of course, all of you as well. It was my boat and I am the skipper, so I would be blamed," Shimon said.

"What about Yeshua raising that little girl from the dead?" Rebecca said. She had known Yeshua all of her life. She had loved him, still loved him, but now with a love so pure, she would do anything for him. To see him work such wonders and listen to him preach with such eloquence and wisdom and loved by so many, filled her with such joy, and she was so happy to be so close to him, to be one of his disciples, and to follow him, learn from him, and support him in his work.

The disciples continued to talk about Yeshua and all they had experienced since following him, especially the events of the last few days.

Chapter Forty-Eight
More Labourers for the Harvest

As the disciples were talking, a woman approached them. Miriam recognised her immediately as the woman that had touched the hem of Yeshua's garment and was healed.

The woman spoke, "Shalom. I am so glad to see you all. I am Lucia. I was the one Yeshua cured when I touched the hem of his garment."

"Lucia, welcome, what brings you here?" Miriam asked.

"I have come to speak to Yeshua. I feel I have not thanked him enough for what he has done for me. He has taken away my suffering. For twelve years, no one would come near me, I was snubbed and ostracised, as if I was a sinner. And I was blamed, and told I must have sinned grievously to have been stricken with this problem of mine. Yeshua has cured me and everything is changed. Now I have so many friends, everyone wants to be my friend, and to hear me tell of what happened to me."

"Yeshua is in the woods, having some quiet time. He will be there for a while," Shimon said. "We will tell him you came to thank him, when he returns."

"I'm sure Lucia wants to thank Yeshua in person, Shimon," Miriam said.

Rebecca nodded her agreement.

"Yes, I would like to thank him in person. But I also want to ask him if I too could follow him and become one of his disciples as you all are. I want to learn more, know more, to listen to him, and to assist him in his work, and to support him in every way I can," Lucia said.

Miriam and Rebecca immediately reached out to Lucia. They engaged in conversation with her and she questioned them about Yeshua, and asked for their support in her request. They reassured her they would. And then Yeshua appeared.

Miriam and Rebecca brought Lucia to Yeshua.

"Lucia, how nice to see you and you are looking so well. What brings you out here to us?" Yeshua asked.

"Yeshua, I want to thank you again, with all my heart for what you did for me. I was so overcome when you healed me and felt so overwrought with the attention of the crowds of people that I felt I did not thank you enough. My life has been so different since you healed me. I feel so healthy and alert and energetic, and I have come to ask to accompany you on your mission, to assist you in your work. I am prepared to learn from Miriam and Rebecca in what ways I can assist," Lucia said.

"Lucia, I can see you are keen to learn and help me spread the Good News. In the place I have just been before you came, I prayed for the Spirit to send me more disciples to assist me in my work. I need more disciples to help me, for the harvest is great but the labourers are few. I need to prepare disciples to do what I do, to preach and teach and heal. That time is coming soon, and you are an answer to my prayers, Lucia," Yeshua said.

All the disciples were listening intently. They had been learning so much from Yeshua and his mission. But what he was now saying about them teaching and healing, about that they were not so sure. We are after all mostly humble fishermen, how are we going to become teachers and healers, they wondered. But they put their trust in Yeshua.

Yeshua gave the disciples a few days off. He wanted them to go to their families and spend some quality time with them, and to those from Bethsaida, he said, "go fishing or something. We will meet again, at Miriam's place after two days. See you then."

Yeshua then sought a deserted part of the coastline and went for a walk on the beach. He was feeling refreshed but wanted more time alone with his heavenly Father. He felt he had so much to do, and so little time to do it. He had come to change the world forever, no longer can power, greed, avarice, lust, cruelty, exploitation, selfishness, rule in the world. People need to change. Humanity was not made for the rich to get richer and the poor to get poorer. The chosen people, his people are to see the light, for they too still live in darkness. They are called to lead the way, but they too are blind, like the blind leading the blind. Their eyes need to be opened, and they all need to see what the Kingdom of God is truly like, and that it is here now, it is here to stay and they all have a part to play to establish God's Kingdom on earth.

Yeshua knew he would pay a great price. And that it would happen soon. He would call some more men and women to assist him and to carry on his work when he is no longer with them. His time was short and urgent. He now had seven men and three women disciples, Shimon, Andreus, James, Johanan, Mattheus, Phillip, Nathanael, Miriam, Rebecca and now Lucia. I need at least twelve men and at least the same number of women to be my disciples and carry on my work.

Yeshua reflected on the state of the world in which he lived, a male dominated world. For too long have women been sidelined and ill-treated as mere property. That can no longer be. But that will take forever to eradicate. That has been happening since Adam and Eve. Yeshua thought about the story, written by Moses about the Garden of Eden and the fall of Adam and Eve and how men have blamed the woman for humanity's woes. For most men have wielded power and power over women ever since. But Yahweh created men and women equal and meant them to be equal, different but equal, complementing, completing each other.

Yeshua was so glad to have Miriam and Rebecca with him and now Lucia. Shimon and the others are learning from them too, from their mere presence, and from their female wisdom as well. And I am learning, Yeshua thought. I too am part of this male world, male domination. I can no longer be that, men can no longer be that, lord themselves over women, treat them like chattel. All these thoughts and reflections occupied Yeshua's mind, as he walked along the deserted stretch of beach.

As Yeshua was approaching, he saw a solitary figure walking towards him. As they came nearer to each other, the man stopped, and immediately recognised Yeshua.

"Yeshua, what a coincidence it is, us meeting like this! This morning, I got up and was about to go to the synagogue to pray when a voice seemed to tell me to go the beach. I went, but instead of walking on my usual stretch of beach, for some unexplained reason, I was drawn to this stretch of beach," the man said.

"Peace be with you. What is your name?" Yeshua asked.

"I am James, son of Alpheus," the man said.

"James, son of Alpheus, the Spirit of Yahweh has sent you to me." Yeshua was amazed at the work of the Spirit and the answer to his prayers, first Lucia and now James.

"James, I have been sent to preach the Good News that God's Kingdom of love, peace and justice for all, is come, and is to be established on earth. Will you help me to do this?" Yeshua asked.

Immediately, James, fell to his knees, and bowed low. "I will Yeshua, I will. I ask for your blessing."

Yeshua laid his hand on James' head and blessed him, and then helped him to his feet. "Go now and meet with me again later today. I am staying at the lodgings of Elijah, the big property at his vineyards, you know where that is, I'm sure," Yeshua said.

"Yes, I do, Yeshua; I will see you there later today."

With that, James left the beach and headed for home. When he arrived home, he met his twin brother, Thomas, who was just about to leave their dwelling. He said to his brother, bubbling with excitement, "Thomas I have met the Promised One, the Great Prophet; the man of God who has been preaching and teaching God's Word all over Galilee and healing the afflicted. I met him on the beach and he has asked me to be his disciple. Will you come with me?" James said.

"I have heard of this Yeshua, but it is all hype, James. Exaggeration. It is impossible for a mere mortal to do the things that are being said about him," Thomas said.

"Will you at least come with me, you can meet him and see for yourself," James insisted.

James and Thomas were twins but complete opposites. They came from a humble and struggling family, and they lived together in a small cottage and eked out a living as day labourers doing what work they could find. James was a dreamer and a believer, whereas Thomas was a sceptic and slow to believe all that was being said about this new prophet. But he had nothing better to do so he agreed to go with his brother to meet Yeshua.

And so, it happened. When James and Thomas arrived at Elijah's place, all of the disciples were there. They were both surprised to discover that there were already seven men disciples and above all, three women. That surprised and intrigued Thomas. James introduced Thomas to Yeshua.

Yeshua introduced James to his disciples. "Friends, this is James, he is joining our community. Now that we have two of you named James we have to use your family names as well, to avoid confusion, is that all right, James of Zebedee and James of Alpheus?" The two James nodded their agreement.

The disciples greeted James and made him welcome. James then introduced his twin brother, Thomas.

"So, this is Thomas, the doubter, the searcher, a true Israelite," Yeshua said with a smile.

Thomas was surprised at Yeshua's comments, as was his brother James, for Yeshua had not met Thomas before, yet he summed him up in a few words. Yeshua then welcomed James and his twin brother Thomas, as his new disciples.

"Oh, I have not come to be a disciple of yours, Yeshua," Thomas said. "I have just humoured my brother. He told me that you have asked him to be a disciple and he has asked me to meet you, that is all," Thomas said. However, Thomas spent the rest of the day and the following day in the company of Yeshua and his disciples. Urged on by his brother, he went with Yeshua and the disciples to the synagogue and the surrounding towns and listened to Yeshua preaching and witnessed his healings. After a week of accompanying Yeshua, Thomas finally acquiesced and in the presence of all the disciples said, "Yeshua, may I too be your disciple. May I too learn from you and help you in your work?"

Yeshua smiled and said, "Thomas, I thought you would never ask. Of course you have already been my disciple. Welcome to our community. Peace be with you." With those words the other disciples were all smiling, for they could see what was happening to Thomas these past days, and they could predict that this would happen. They all welcomed Thomas and made him one of them.

Yeshua then told them of his plans to have at least twelve men and an equal number of women to accompany him, and learn from him, and assist him in his mission, and to carry on after he is no longer with them. They listened and did not really let the words sink in about what he said about when he would no longer be with them. They all thought he would be with them for a long time. But Thomas thought otherwise. He witnessed the adulation of the crowds around Yeshua this past week, but he also saw the opposition of the Pharisees, Scribes and Sadducees who were also part of the crowds, and how they sought to undermine Yeshua at every turn.

Yeshua now had nine men disciples and three women, he wanted at least another three men and nine women; they would be more than disciples. When the time is right, he would endow them with the power of his Spirit, to preach and teach and heal and to do all that he is now doing.

"Yeshua, I know a person whom I think would make a good disciple. His name is Thaddeus. He is a good and kind man, of few words, but he is seeking for the coming of the Messiah. He lives outside of the town, but I'm sure he must have heard of you. I will contact him, so you can meet him," James said.

"James of Alpheus and Thomas, we are a community who live together, pray together, learn together, and work together to spread the Kingdom of God on earth. We own nothing; we share everything, all our resources. So far, we have wanted for nothing. I have friends all over Galilee, and so have all of us. And we receive so much hospitality and kindness wherever we go. People from the towns and villages open their homes and hearts to us. Although I have nowhere to call home, or to lie down my head, I and all of the community have never wanted for shelter or for nourishment. Wherever we go, we greet the people in peace and we remain there if we are made welcome. If we are not made welcome, we simply remove the dust from our feet and move on. Whatever resources we have or receive, we pool them and Andreus manages the money people give us. And Miriam, Rebecca, and Lucia look after the produce given to us for our meals."

"Yeshua, I have handed over the managing of our funds to Mattheus, remember, I mentioned that to you," Andreus said.

"Oh yes, so you did. Well, Andreus, I hereby appoint you as managing, no longer our money, but the men, and Miriam, you will take care of the affairs of all our women disciples. I know, you and Rebecca have already taken this to heart, and now you have Lucia to care for as well," Yeshua said, smiling at Lucia.

"Thomas, although he had been going about with Yeshua and his disciples, he had not been living with them; he merely wanted to observe at arm's length. But now that he had made known his intentions, he was ready to stay with Yeshua.

"Thomas, you are most welcome to stay with us at my father's house. We are living in our family house here in Capernaum. But now that our community has grown, I think maybe it would be better for us to stay in the cottages on the property. There is one for us ladies and two large ones for the men. Yeshua you can continue to stay in Father's house," Miriam said.

"No Miriam, I will stay with the men in the cottage. That will be perfect." And so, it was arranged. James of Alpheus had brought Thaddeus, who joined the group and were made welcome and soon blended in with everyone. Yeshua and the disciples made their home base in Capernaum and remained there for a long time, at least six months, preaching, teaching, healing the sick, and comforting the poor in all the towns and villages.

Then one night, Yeshua said, "We are going to leave Galilee for a while. It is time for me to go to Judaea. The Passover is six months away; we will celebrate the next Passover in Jerusalem.

"Yeshua, are you sure you want to go to Jerusalem? I don't think it is very safe there," Shimon said. "Herod still has Johanan the baptiser in prison," he added.

"Yes, Yeshua, I think it would be unwise for you to preach about the Kingdom of God in Jerusalem. Herod would not take kindly to your words," James Zebedee said.

"The Kingdom of God is not a kingdom of this world," Yeshua said.

The disciples were still not absolutely sure, what the Kingdom of God is, and what it entails, the idea of a kingdom that would usurp and replace Rome, and therefore the kingdom of Herod, still lingered in their minds. They did not think it was wise of Yeshua to go to Jerusalem, just yet.

"Yes Yeshua, the Pharisees, Scribes, Sadducees are strong in Jerusalem, and the high priest lives there and they wield great power and have authority over the people, and you have already experienced the opposition from their kind here in Galilee, it will be ten times worse in Jerusalem," Thomas said.

"Yeshua, you are well known here, in Galilee, and you have a lot of supporters and the authorities would not dare to arrest you, but in Jerusalem, you would be seen as a rebel, stirring up the crowd, and your fate could be the same as that of Johanan, the baptiser," Johanan said.

"I hear what you all say, but I must go to Jerusalem as well, I have to bring the Good News to all of Judaea," Yeshua said. "We leave Capernaum tomorrow and we will go to Jerusalem," Yeshua said.

Chapter Forty-Nine
The Journey to Jerusalem Begins

When the time came, Yeshua spoke to the disciples, "We will go along the lake to Magdala, Miriam's home town, then on to Tiberias, then west to the town of Nain, and on to the coast at Caesarea, and then south, and stop at all the towns and villages on the way, skirting Samaria, pass through Arimathea, Emmaus, and then on to Jerusalem. So have a good rest tonight. We leave early tomorrow at sunrise. And will be on the road for the next six months," Yeshua said.

They were all about to retire when a servant of a well-to-do citizen of Capernaum came, and asked for Yeshua, saying his master, Hezekiah, invites Yeshua and his disciples for a meal at his house.

Shimon answered the door; he and Andreus, Philip, Nathanael and Thomas were still in the common room and about to retire. "Tell your master, Hezekiah, that Yeshua is leaving Capernaum tomorrow early and that he won't be back in Capernaum for at least six months."

Yeshua, lying in bed in the adjacent room, heard the conversation and he called out to Shimon. "Shimon, who is it?"

Shimon stood at the opening to the room and said, "Yeshua, it is the servant of Hezekiah, he is a prominent man in the city, and a Pharisee, a leader among them, he is inviting us to a meal. I told the servant that we are leaving Capernaum early and won't be back for at least six months."

"Shimon, tell him, we accept. We will be there at noon for lunch and then be on our way after that. Go now and then have a good sleep and let the others know of our change in plans and let them know that we can all have a sleep-in tomorrow. I know I will," Yeshua said.

Shimon returned and spoke to the servant. "Tell Hezekiah, Yeshua accepts and we will be at his house at noon. We are thirteen disciples in all, who will be with Yeshua."

The servant bowed to them all and left in a hurry. He too was overcome to be in the presence of the disciples of Yeshua, and excited about Yeshua coming to his master's house. They would have to get up early to prepare for the feast.

Yeshua was up at about the second hour, and that was late for him, a sleep-in really. Johanan, James Zebedee, Andreus, Philip, Miriam, Rebecca and Lucia were up as well, the others were still fast asleep. Yeshua greeted them all, had some warm milk and a slice of bread and then left for a lonely place, where he could be by himself.

Yeshua felt well rested. He was in a good mood. He felt at peace. He prayed to his heavenly Father, "Abba, I glorify you. I thank you for sending such great men and women to surround and support me. I have much to teach them. And they have much to teach me, about life. They will have to carry on the work that you sent me to do. I know I do not have a lot of time to do what you ask of me. I sense the powers of darkness gathering. Abba, we will be leaving Capernaum tomorrow, and then visit many towns and villages as we travel to Jerusalem. I pray Abba for your blessing and protection on all of us. And I pray for Johanan, still languishing in prison. I hope to see him in Jerusalem and that he will be set free." Yeshua then prayed for all his disciples and spoke to Yahweh about them. Yeshua then walked among the trees and the wild bushes and wild flowers and the lilies in the field and watched the birds feasting in the grass and flying around joyfully, without a care in the world. And Yeshua's heart soared. He was full of love for all of his Father's creation, for all of creation, for all creatures and for all his brothers and sisters on earth. All Yeshua wanted was to spread the love, peace and joy of Yahweh to all.

It was about an hour before noon when Yeshua returned to the house, and all the disciples were up and about. Shimon had gone fishing early, without anyone knowing but he had returned with some fish. "I will smoke this fish, which we can have for the road," he said, holding up a bunch of fish.

Yeshua and the rest all smiled at Shimon. Yeshua realised how much Shimon missed the sea and the fishing. And he was glad that he had some time to indulge his passion. They waited for Shimon to clean up, and then were on their way to Hezekiah's house.

Hezekiah's house was just as impressive as Elijah's. It had a large common room with a large table in the middle of the room filled with a meal fit for a king, roasted lamb, fish, and the freshest of vegetables, lots of nuts, grapes and fresh fruit, including Yeshua's favourite, fresh figs. And even though it was in the middle of the day, wine was being served, no doubt from Elijah's winery.

Besides Yeshua and the disciples, all of Hezekiah's family and friends were there, as well as the upper-class citizens of Capernaum, and of course all of the Pharisees, Scribes and Sadducees.

Yeshua's disciples were amazed at Yeshua. He had such harsh words for the Pharisees and their ilk. He ridiculed them for their ostentatious way of dress, and condemned their behaviour and rigidity in applying the Law, and creating unnecessary burdens for the people. They inculcated fear in the hearts of the people and preached a harsh judgement on them for their sinful ways, by a ruthless God. And they were completely at odds with Yeshua's teaching about Yahweh. Yet Yeshua showed them such respect, and he was mingling with them all, and chatting with them amicably, and even ready to dine with them.

By now, a crowd had gathered outside of Hezekiah's house, with their sick and afflicted wanting Yeshua to heal them. Never before had anyone had such prolific powers of healing, for this man healed so many, all those who came and showed faith, were healed.

When they had finished their meal, Yeshua asked Hezekiah to let the people in for he would like to talk to them. The crowds then streamed in, filling the room to capacity. Andreus and Shimon stood at the door and had to stop people for there was no more room in the house. Yeshua then spoke to the people about the love and compassion of Yahweh. He used the term 'Abba' for Yahweh. No one had dared to address Yahweh in such a way, it was an endearing and intimate and familiar term, used by young children when addressing a loving father, as they would address a loving mother with the term, Immah. That was the way Yeshua had always addressed Miriam and Yosef his father and mother, and it is how he often addressed his heavenly father, and how he encouraged the people to address Yahweh in such a way, with such familiarity and trust and confidence that Yahweh is a loving and caring father.

After Yeshua had spoken for a while, people brought their sick and afflicted to Yeshua, and he healed them all.

All of a sudden, they heard a commotion coming from above. Everyone looked up and saw a hole in the roof getting bigger and bigger. It was clear that there were people on the roof removing parts from the roof and making a hole in it. What were they up to everyone was thinking. Then someone near the front door of the house, said in a loud voice. "It is Josh the paralytic and his friends, they were stopped from entering the house, so they took Josh up onto the roof."

Everyone was amazed, as well as Yeshua and the disciples. Hezekiah was not too pleased with his roof been damaged, someone will have to pay for this, he said to himself.

The place was abuzz with excitement and anticipation at the spectacle that was unfolding before them. Then slowly the men, looked like there were at least four of them, began slowly and carefully lowering Josh down from the roof, his mat tied to ropes. Shimon and Andreus and the brothers Johanan and James and the others made a circle around Yeshua and a space for Josh to come down on his mat. Hezekiah and his Pharisee, Sadducee and Scribe friends were looking on with great interest.

Then the man came to rest in front of Yeshua. He looked up at Yeshua. He had not seen Yeshua before. He had heard about him, how he has healed all kinds of maladies, including a paralytic. He did not have anyone to take him to this Yeshua. He did not have many friends. People ignored him, as if he was unclean and a sinner to have been born this way. Some blamed it on his parents, saying they must have sinned grievously for Yahweh to curse him so. And now he heard of this man Yeshua, a prophet, the people say, a Man sent by Yahweh, who also has the power to heal. He did however, have a few friends. They were scoundrels really, parasites, petty criminals, who stole and cheated to make a living. They were the only ones who had any time for him, stopped and chatted with him, and did not treat him like dirt, and shared their stolen goods with him.

One of his scumbag friends told Josh about this man Yeshua, and Josh had then asked them to take him to this Yeshua.

Josh kept his gaze on Yeshua; he was oblivious to the crowd around him, who had their eyes on this man Yeshua.

Yeshua looked at the man, and his heart was filled with compassion for him. Josh could not believe what he was experiencing, here was a man, everyone says is a man of God, and yet he is not looking at me as if I am a piece of dirt, instead he looks at me with eyes full of compassion and respect for me.

Yeshua then looked at the men gawking through the opening in the roof, at the scene below, their friend Josh before the man Yeshua, the centre of attention. "Old Josh, he must be lapping this up, he's never been the centre of attention before, having crowds fixing their eyes on him," one of the men said.

Yeshua was looking up at them, and he saw their love and friendship for Joshua, and also their faith and his heart went out to them too.

Yeshua then bent down to Josh and said to him, "Joshua, your sins are forgiven you."

Josh immediately felt a relief throughout his body. This man of God is forgiving him his sins, the very cause of his paralysis. He is now already feeling a heavy burden being lifted off him. He continues to look at Yeshua with great hope.

The Pharisees, Scribes and Sadducees, were murmuring among themselves, "who is this man, who is speaking such blasphemies? Who can forgive sins, but God alone?"

Yeshua heard their murmurings and questioning, so he said to them, "Why do you raise such questions in your hearts? Which is easier, to say, 'Your sins are forgiven you,' or to say. 'Stand up and walk'? But so that you may know the Son of Man has authority on earth to forgive sins"—he said to the paralytic—"I say to you, stand up and take your mat and go to your home."

Immediately Joshua stood up before them, and took up his mat. He could not believe what was happening to him. His legs and all his limbs felt like they had life in them all of his life. He was filled with such great happiness and joy, the like of which he had never experienced ever before in his life.

Joshua's friends were looking down at what was happening to their friend and they were astonished. They could not believe their eyes. They scampered down the roof, forgetting to replace the parts they removed, they were filled with excitement and happiness with what had just happened to their friend Josh. When they came to the front door, the people had already made way for Joshua to pass through them, and they were staring at him with astonishment. They were all spellbound.

When Joshua saw his four friends he ran and hugged them one by one. His tears were flowing down his cheeks. They then went off dancing and skipping to celebrate what has just happened.

Yeshua and his disciples left Hezekiah's place and thanked him and his wife and servants for the feast they had received. They then all returned to base, to fetch what they needed for the road. They travelled lightly, with only one extra bit of clothing to change and what they needed for personal hygiene. The disciples shared among themselves what the people had given them for their journey. And Mattheus had quite an amount of money that ordinary people gave them for their work, and in appreciation for what Yeshua had done for them.

It was now mid-afternoon and they headed for Magdala, where they would stay overnight, at Miriam's. As they were leaving Capernaum, a young man came running after them and calling out to them. Yeshua stopped and so did the rest and turned around to see a young man, about Yeshua's age, panting. He caught his breath and approached Yeshua.

"Yeshua, my name is Shimon. I am one of Joshua's friends, who had let him down through the roof. I came to thank you. Yeshua, I have done many things for what I am not proud, but I would like to be with you, and be part of your community. I heard, and now see the community you have around you. I want to learn from you, and follow you wherever you go, and help you in your work, in whatever way I can."

James and Johanan of Zebedee knew Shimon and James spoke, "Yeshua, I know Shimon, he belonged to the Zealots, and was part of rebellions in Jerusalem, and they believe in taking up arms and going to war and using violence in their efforts to overthrow and conquer Rome.

"Yeshua, yes, I am not proud of what I did, I did believe in taking up arms. But I have heard a lot of what others had said about you, you want change through peaceful means. I became disillusioned with my Zealot community; there was so much hatred and anger among them. I want to learn from you, Yeshua, to bring about change, the change you speak about," Shimon said.

Yeshua looked at Shimon with love and said, "Shimon, I can see you are sorrowful for what you have done, all is forgiven. You are now one of us. Come and meet the others," Yeshua said to them all, "Now we have two James and now we also have two named Shimon," Yeshua said.

"I am Shimon, and I can be called Shimon the Zealot," Shimon said, "That's what my friends used to call me," Shimon said.

"I don't think that would be very wise," Nathanael said. "If we called him that, he would be in danger from the Roman authorities, not only in Jerusalem but all over Judaea and Galilee, for they have garrisons everywhere and spies as well," Nathanael added.

"Mmm, what about Shimon Cananean? Cananean is the term for zealot in our Aramaic dialect," Rebecca said. "No one will know," she added.

"I don't know," Thomas said. "Why not just call him Shimon the Canaanite? That would be safest; what do you think, Shimon, are you okay with that?" Thomas asked.

"Anything rather that Zealot would be okay and safer, but not Canaanite. I'll go with Cananean," Shimon said.

"Okay then, everyone, meet our new recruit, Shimon Cananean," Shimon, son of Jonah said, laughing.

Everyone welcomed Shimon Cananean. As they went on their way, the disciples wanted to hear from Shimon Cananean, what life was like for him when he was one of the Zealots.

"We were hell bent on using whatever means we could to overthrow the Roman power in Judaea. We made and stole weapons but we were just outnumbered and did not have the weapons to defeat Rome. Every uprising was squashed and several died. There were mass crucifixions of many of us. Many were victims of beheadings and there was burning of whole villages.

"Herod, Rome's puppet was just as cruel; he slaughtered several innocent firstborns, thirty years ago, because he was told of the birth of a newborn King of Kings. And he ruthlessly, with the Roman soldiers, and his own, put down any uprising. I did not think we would do better against Herod's son. Antipas wasn't much of an improvement on his father, and though he no longer had any real power in Judaea, Rome ruling Judaea, directly, with an iron fist. And they appointed Annas, as high priest and he worked hand in glove with Rome," Shimon Cananean said.

"Thanks for the history lesson, Shimon. Why did you leave them then?" Thaddeus asked.

"We were waiting for a Messiah, who would lead us, with great power and authority and overthrow Rome, but no such person seemed to be appearing in our midst. And I heard about Yeshua, how he was influencing the people, changing their thinking, and promoting a more peaceful way of bringing about peace, and a better way of life for our people. And I've seen for myself the power of Yeshua and I believe he could be the Messiah, we are all waiting for, to set us free," Shimon Cananean said.

"Unless we all change, we will all be destroyed. Shimon Cananean has realised that we cannot overthrow the Romans in a war, a military battle, they are just too powerful and we are too weak. There has to be another way to conquer them, to free ourselves," Yeshua said.

"But how, what is this other way?" Shimon Cananean asked.

"Through peaceful ways, through inner conversion, through reconciliation with our enemies, through giving to Caesar what belongs to Caesar and to God what belongs to God. In a nutshell, through love, love is our strongest weapon, love conquers all, even loving our enemies, wins them over. This is a war against hatred, greed, lust for power and control. But for us it is a war within ourselves, to harbour no hatred for anyone, even our enemies and even to go further by loving our enemies and doing good to those who hate us and harm us. This is our way, the only way to bring true and lasting peace in the world," Yeshua said.

Shimon Cananean listened and he was still not convinced. He did think that Yeshua might still be the Messiah and that he would with power overthrow Rome and liberate them all. The rest of the disciples were also not fully convinced of what Yeshua was saying, especially about loving one's enemies, and doing good to those who hate us.

"I know what I am telling you, is not easy and contrary to what we all have come to believe and many still believe, of an eye for an eye, and seeking revenge, and hating one's enemies. But this has to change or we will never know true peace," Yeshua said.

Yeshua had a sense that the power of Rome would rule for years to come, and that Israel would fall, and that the Temple would be destroyed again, and the people would lose all hope. People need to find strength in Yahweh, have a change of heart, and have the inner strength to survive whatever destruction Rome may mete out. Rome could destroy their Temple but they could not destroy the Temple within them, within their hearts, minds and souls, where Yahweh truly dwelt. Yeshua's heart went out to his people; they have and continue to suffer so much at the hands of their enemies, both Roman and within. And their hearts are troubled. They are like sheep without a shepherd.

"We better go on our way, if we wish to get to Magdala by nightfall," Andreus said, as they had stopped to listen to Shimon Cananean, and had a long discussion.

"Before we proceed, let us join hands and pray a psalm of David," Yeshua said.

They stopped in the middle of the road and joined hands, the men laid down their staffs, and all of them formed a circle, and Yeshua lead them in one of his favourite psalms:

"The Lord is my shepherd, I shall not want
He makes me lie down in green pastures;
He leads me beside still waters,
He restores my soul.
He leads me in right paths
for his name's sake.

Even though I walk through the darkest valley
I fear no evil;
for you are with me;
your rod and your staff—
they comfort me.

You prepare a table before me.
In the presence of my enemies;

You anoint my head with oil;
my cup overflows.
Surely goodness and mercy shall follow me
all the days of my life,
and I shall dwell in the house of the Lord
my whole life long."

They took up their staffs again and in silence proceeded. They walked in silence for quite some time, before they began to converse with each other once again. Yeshua walked in front. They left him alone; they could see he wanted that. After some time, Yeshua stopped and called Miriam to him. She joined him and he spoke to her.

"Miriam, we will be staying at your place for a while. We are quite a big number now. We are now eleven men. And I would like to have twelve."

"Why twelve Yeshua?" Miriam asked.

"It's a good number, Miriam. And I guess, I'm thinking of the twelve tribes of Israel. The twelve will be future leaders when I am no longer with you. I would like twelve women too, if that is possible," Yeshua said. "Be on the lookout for more women, Miriam. Maybe women from Judaea would be good, for all of the men and women of our group are from Galilee. We are enough for now. We need to get to know each other better and learn more and bond more, for there are tough times ahead, especially when we get to Jerusalem," Yeshua said.

Miriam felt troubled at Yeshua's talk of him not being around. She sensed he was telling her that he would not be around for long. How long she wondered. She knew about the cruelty and the power of the Roman authorities, and also of Herod and now Caiaphas, the high priest, as well. They were all powerful leaders who sought to hang onto their power at all costs. Yeshua would have lots of powerful enemies in Jerusalem. But Miriam put these thoughts aside and she and Yeshua continued to walk on in silence.

Yeshua broke the silence, "Miriam, thank you for being with me, my soul is troubled. I have so much to do, and so little time to do it in. I need all the help I can get. I am so grateful to you and the others. We need to continue to pray continuously to Yahweh to let his Spirit guide us in all we do. Miriam, call the other women, I want to talk with them," Yeshua said.

Miriam stopped for the rest to catch up with her and she said, "Rebecca, Lucia, come with me, the Master wants to speak with us."

Shimon and some of the men were still not comfortable with women travelling with them and being disciples. Yeshua seemed to be putting them on equal footing with them. And it was not a good look. People would be drawing the wrong conclusions. Yeshua did not seem to realise this. I will have to have a chat with him, Shimon thought.

Yeshua slowed down so the women could catch up with him. Miriam walked to his right and Rebecca and Lucia to his left.

"Miriam, Rebecca, Lucia, I am so pleased you are accompanying me, us, on our mission. How are you doing, are the men treating you right?" Yeshua asked.

"They're okay, Yeshua. I have no problems. Some are friendly, others keep their distance. Shimon seems a bit suspicious. I don't think he's comfortable with us women as part of your disciples," Rebecca said.

Miriam and Lucia, agreed.

"Give him time, he'll come around," Yeshua said, smiling. "Miriam, will it still be alright for all fourteen of us to stay at your place," Yeshua asked.

"It would be okay, Yeshua. We can make another cottage available for the men, and the three of us women can still use the same cottage as before," Miriam said. "Yeshua, are you sure you do not want to stay in the house, it is so much more comfortable there," Miriam said.

"No Miriam, it is okay, as it is. And thank you. Look, Magdala is in sight," Yeshua said.

Chapter Fifty
Magdala Lost and Found

It was soon nightfall, so they all met for a short while at the main house to discuss what they would be doing the next few days and beyond. Yeshua usually did not plan far ahead. He was more led by the Spirit. After having something to eat they sat around and Yeshua spoke to them.

"We have come a long way. Some of you have been with me for a while now. We will stay at Magdala for some time. I will preach and teach at the synagogue. I am known to the rabbi there; Miriam will prepare the way. After time in Magdala, we will travel to all the outlying villages. Miriam has taken me there once before; I will visit them again, and bring them some comfort. They are the outcasts of society and very poor, so we will take them what we can. Do any of you have any questions at this time?" Yeshua asked.

"Is this all we are going to do, Yeshua. Go to the cities, towns, villages and you preach and teach the people and heal their sick, what about the Romans, those in power, and Herod, and Annas, and the political and religious leaders, are we not to engage with them. Are we not going to rise up against them, in any way?" Shimon Cananean asked.

"Shimon, the time will come. For now, we have a lot to teach. The people have been walking in darkness for a long time now. We have to be a light, to light up their darkness. You are to be that light to them; you have to lead them out of the darkness. They have lost their way, they have lost all hope; we are going to show them the way, to bring them hope. I am the Way, the Truth and the Life. They are all overburdened and anxious and fearful of an all seeing and harsh God, who is out to get them, to punish them. They are consumed by their sins, and fearful of eternal damnation. They are consumed by material and worldly issues, and they fear a God whom they see as distant and harsh and out to get them. We have to change all that, we have to turn their hearts from hearts of stone, to hearts most pure. They are all heavily burdened and go about their days, heavily burdened with life's responsibilities, with earning a living for themselves and their loved ones. There is so much sickness and suffering and heartbreak, and they feel that they are great sinners to have all of this heaped upon them. They feel that God has forgotten them. We have to change all that. This is a mammoth task and I am only a short while with you, so watch and pray and learn from me," Yeshua said.

Shimon the brother of Andreus, whom the others seem to look towards as their leader, looked at Yeshua. He was perplexed by Yeshua saying he would not be with them much longer. So were the other disciples. Was he going away? He couldn't be predicting that he would befall a similar fate to Johanan, and end up in prison. Shimon and the others thought this a possibility, and they had already tried to dissuade Yeshua from going to Jerusalem, but without success. Yeshua made it clear that they had to learn from him and learn quickly.

Yeshua could see their minds ticking over, he continued, "I know you are all concerned about the poor getting poorer, and the rich getting richer. And the powerful getting more powerful and you want us to be doing something about the injustices and heavy toll placed on the people by our Roman lords. You would like me to lead an army and for us to conquer Rome, and throw them out of Israel forever. The people seek freedom, liberation from the yoke of Rome. They want to be free of the burdens Rome places on them. But before Rome and without Rome, and after Rome, even if Rome did not rule here anymore in Israel, we would still not be free, there would still be those who lord over others, who subjugate the poor, who think themselves above everyone else, and who wield power over the poor, the sick, the unclean, and the sinners. There are those who still think they alone are God's chosen ones, and they look down on the rest as sinners and cast them out. We all still believe that suffering and illness is the cause of sin and the result of God's displeasure and punishment. Your religious leaders preach a strict, severe, distant, a vengeful and unforgiving God. That must all change. The real oppression is not at the hands of the Romans, but in our minds and hearts and it is in our hands, the way we treat one another. The way we think of and relate to one another, the way we think of and the way we relate to Yahweh," Yeshua said.

Yeshua continued talking in this vein and the disciples were mesmerised. This was not a way of teaching and thinking to which they were accustomed.

"Yeshua, you said, we have to learn from you how to live our lives and that we need to pray without ceasing, Yeshua, we do not even know how to pray. Will you not teach us to pray?" Mattheus said.

Mattheus, I have already taught the others, but it is good to repeat, "When you pray, do not be like the hypocrites; for they love to stand and pray in the synagogues and at the street corners, so that they may be seen by others. Truly I tell you, they have received their reward. But whenever you pray, go into your room, and shut the door and pray to your Father who is in secret; and your Father, who sees in secret will reward you," Yeshua said.

"Yeshua is that why you go so often into the wilderness or seek out the forests or woods wherever we are and go off on your own?" Nathanael asked.

"Yes, Nathanael. But it does not matter where you go, find that quiet place, where you can be alone and undisturbed. Seek a place, that you feel safe and secure and where you can be alone. It is not always possible to be close to the forest or an isolated patch of seashore, find that quiet place in your home. The real quiet place is of course your inner room, your heart. You can be anywhere and you can shut the door to the noise around you, to the rowdiness of dissipation and madness around you and turn your heart to your heavenly Father who dwells within you." Yeshua continued to teach his disciples about how to pray.

"Yeshua, when we pray, what should we be saying to God, what words should we be using?" Thomas asked.

Yeshua replied, "When you are praying, do not heap up empty phrases as the Gentiles do; for they think that they will be heard because of their many words. Do not be like them, for your Father knows what you need before you ask Him."

Yeshua continued, "Of course, prayer is not only asking God for things that we think we need. Most people see prayer as asking God for what they need or want. And it is only in time of need that the Gentiles turn to God and plead with Him, and if their prayer is not heard immediately and in the way they want, they turn away from God."

"So should we not ask God for what we need?" Lucia asked.

"Of course not, Lucia, God is a loving and compassionate Father and Mother, our Abba, our Immah who loves us more than any earthly father and mother does. When we were children, we sometimes asked for things that our parents knew would not be good for us, so they did not give us what we asked for, but gave us instead what we needed, above all they gave us their love and care and attention," Yeshua said.

Yeshua continued by repeating what he had said to the others, "Therefore I tell you, when you pray, do not worry about your life, what you will eat or what you will drink, or about your body, what you will wear. Is not life more than food and the body more than clothing? Look at the birds of the air, they neither sow nor reap nor gather into barns, and yet your heavenly Father feeds them. Are you not of more value than they? And can any of you by worrying add a single hour to your span of life? And why do you worry about clothing? Consider the lilies of the field, how they grow, they neither toil nor spin, yet I tell you, even Solomon in all his glory was not clothed like one of these. But if God so clothes the grass of the field, which is alive today and tomorrow is thrown into the oven, will he not much more clothe you— you of little faith? Therefore, do not worry saying, 'What will we eat?' or 'What will we drink?' or 'What will we wear?' For it is the Gentiles who strive for all these things and indeed your heavenly Father knows that you need all these things. But strive first for the kingdom of God and his righteousness, and all these things will be given to you as well. So do not worry about tomorrow, for tomorrow will bring worries of its own. Today's trouble is enough for today."

The disciples who were hearing this teaching for the first time were completely engrossed in Yeshua's teaching. The others had heard some of these teachings before; but now alone with Yeshua, away from the crowds, his words seemed to resonate more deeply and have a greater impact.

"So, are we never to ask for anything in our prayers, are we never to petition our heavenly Father?" Thomas asked.

"Of course not, Thomas, but keep in mind, that your Father loves you and wants what is best for you and listens to you. So, I say to you Thomas, as I say to you all, ask with faith, and it will be given to you, search for the truth and you will find it. Search and you will find; knock and the door will be opened to you for everyone who asks receive, and everyone who searches finds and everyone who knocks, the door will be opened.

"Is there anyone among you, who if your child, or anyone's child, asks for bread, will give a stone? Or if the child asks for a piece of fish, will give a snake? If you then, who are evil, know how to give good gifts to your children, how much more will your Father in heaven give good gifts to those who ask Him?"

Yeshua continued to teach his disciples late into the night. He also taught them that prayer was not only about asking God for things but also about thanking God for all the good things we already have and enjoy, and it was also asking for forgiveness whenever we fall into sin, but to remember that when a child stumbles, the father, the mother is there to lift the child up and to comfort the child, and if we do anything wrong, if we confess and repent, we are forgiven. He reminded them of the parable he told of the compassionate Father and his Prodigal Son.

"Yeshua, thank you so much for your teaching but it is getting late, I will go early and speak to the rabbi and inform him you would like to talk to the people," Miriam said.

"Yes, you are right; it is late, time for all of us to rest. We have a full day tomorrow," Yeshua said. They all then retired.

As usual the synagogue was packed. Yeshua had been to their town before and they had listened to him and saw him heal their afflicted. They were back for more teaching and still the sick came from far and wide. Yeshua taught them many things. And he answered all their questions. They were like sheep without a shepherd and they were all so consumed with guilt and weighed down with a consciousness of their sinfulness. They were forever told of how sinful they all are and how much they are in danger of the wrath of God.

Yeshua wanted to remove that heavy burden and show them the love and compassion of God. So, he told them what he had told others, his favourite parable, that of the Compassionate Father and how he forgave his Prodigal Son and then celebrated by killing and roasting the fatted calf. This time Yeshua included the part of an elder son, who was also lost, for the elder son resented his prodigal brother and the preferential and undeserving treatment he got from his father.

Yeshua added onto his former parable with the story of the other son, the 'faithful' son. He said, "Now the elder son was away in the field, and as he came and approached the house, he heard loud music and dancing. He had no idea of what was going on. He was resentful that a party was in process, and he knew nothing about it. Just then one of the servants came out of the house and the son called him and asked what was going on. The servant replied, 'Your brother has come home, and your father has killed the fatted calf, because he has got him home, safe and sound.' The elder son was furious; he became angry and refused to go into the house. The servant went in and reported to the Father, who came out to his elder son to plead with him to come in and join in the celebration. But he answered his father, 'Father, listen to me! For all these years, I have been working like a slave for you, and I have never disobeyed your command; yet you have never given me even a young goat so that I may celebrate with my friends. But when this son of yours came back, who has devoured your property with prostitutes; you killed the fatted calf for him!'

"The father's heart was filled with love and compassion for his elder son, and he said to him, 'Son, you are always with me, and all that is mine, is yours. But we had to celebrate and rejoice, because this brother of yours was lost and has been found, was dead and has come back to life.'"

Yeshua paused as he usually did, to take in the people's reaction to what he was teaching. He could see the bewilderment on their faces, even disagreement with the story; they seem to be identifying with the elder son. Yeshua decided to leave them with that dilemma, to figure it out for themselves, and he would elucidate at another time. He would for now, continue with his theme of being lost and found, so he said.

"What woman among you, who having ten silver coins, and then she loses one of them, will she not search carefully for that one silver coin she lost until she finds it? And when she finds it, does she not call together her friends and neighbours, saying, 'Rejoice with me, for I had found the coin that I had lost.' Just so I tell you, there is joy in the presence of the angels over one sinner who repents."

Yeshua could see the people's agreement with this story, especially the women who were nodding and smiling. It made sense to the others too, for many among those present were tax-collectors, and those regarded as outcasts. All those regarded as outcasts and sinners were present to listen to Yeshua, for they knew he had a high regard and respect for them. He had come and spent time with them, comforted them and healed them and their loved ones. And now they were here listening to him. Even among them were fallen women, from the place at the edge of the town, where Yeshua visited those fallen women. The Pharisees, Scribes, Sadducees and the resident rabbi were not too pleased with the rabble in the synagogue, mixing with the rest of the faithful. Yeshua was aware of who were in the synagogue and that they were not the usual crowd. The Pharisees and the Teachers of the Law could not contain themselves and started grumbling, to those around them, "This man welcomes outcasts, prostitutes and sinners and even eats with them!"

Yeshua heard them. He continued with his theme. And looking directly at the Pharisees and the Teachers of the Law he said, "Take care that you do not despise one of these little ones; for I tell you, in heaven their angels continually see the face of my Father in heaven."

"You all are familiar with David's psalm of the Good Shepherd, 'the Lord is my Shepherd; I shall not want.' Yahweh is the Good Shepherd and we all are his sheep, and he makes sure we will not want. We will not want what we really need for our salvation and for our freedom. He has made sure of that, for he has sent me to shepherd you, his flock. I am the Good Shepherd and I have come to give my life to you, so that you may have life and life to the full."

The people were totally engrossed; hanging onto Yeshua's every word. Yeshua then told them another story, "Which one of you, having a hundred sheep and losing one of them, does not leave the ninety-nine in the wilderness, and go after the one that is lost until he finds it? When he has found it, he lays it on his shoulders and rejoices. And when he comes home, he calls together his friends and neighbours, saying to them, 'Rejoice with me, for I have found my sheep that was lost.' Just so I tell you, there will be more joy in heaven, over one sinner who repents than over ninety-nine righteous persons who need no repentance."

When Yeshua had finished speaking the people came near to him, just to touch him. The Pharisees and their cohort were scandalised at Yeshua allowing all these outcasts and sinners to touch him. The crowd also brought their sick to Yeshua and he healed them all.

Yeshua then went out to villages far away from the town and sought out the outcasts, and when he was there, they brought to him all those who were sick, suffering from all kinds of diseases and disorders; people possessed with demons, and those suffering from fits, and paralytics and all kinds of infirmities and Yeshua healed them all. And all in the crowd were trying to touch Yeshua, for power came out of him, and healed all.

The disciples were absolutely astounded at all that was happening, so many were being healed in these outlying and forgotten places among the outcasts of society. Yeshua spent a long time with these people, listening to their stories and bringing them comfort. Because Yeshua could not speak to them all, many of them approached and spoke to the disciples, who did their best to listen to them and comfort them. Many of the women went to Miriam, for they knew about her, how she was like one of them, for she was possessed of several demons and Yeshua had healed her. She was able to relate to them, and respect them and comfort them. And some of them who could not be with Miriam as she was surrounded by so many women spoke to Rebecca and Lucia. And they were so impressed to hear Rebecca tell them how she grew up with Yeshua in Nazareth and they also listened to Lucia, as she related all she had suffered for twelve years, and how she was healed by merely touching the hem of Yeshua's garments.

Yeshua spent several weeks in the villages and several more in Magdala and the people came from all over to see him, listen to him. His friends from Ziddim, David and his wife, Phoebe and their children, Judah, Yosef, Rachel and Lydia, who were all now grown up with families of their own, came all the way to see Yeshua and listen to him. Yeshua spent some quality time with them all. They all wanted to know how his mother Miriam was and Yeshua had to confess that he had not seen his mother for several months now. He shared with them his sadness of not being with his mother, but told them he would be passing through Nazareth on his way to Tiberias, Caesarea and Jerusalem.

Yeshua's friends from Magdala, Joshua and his wife, Emzara, and their children, Ruth, Orpah, Seth, Japheth and Ham invited Yeshua to their home. They asked Yeshua to bring Miriam with him and Yeshua gladly accepted and he, Miriam, Rebecca and Lucia spent most of a day with them.

Ruth and Orpah were so pleased to see their friend Miriam and just how well she looked. Yeshua enjoyed their company and so did Miriam, Rebecca and Lucia. While they were spending the day with them, the men had gone to visit their own friends and Shimon and Andreus, James and Johanan went fishing and took some of the others with them.

It was late when Yeshua, Miriam, Rebecca, and Lucia returned to their cottages. Only Thomas was there, he told Yeshua that all the rest had gone fishing, and they had been gone for a long time. Thomas was worried about them.

"No need to worry Thomas, Shimon and his brother and Johanan and James are professional fishermen who know the lake like the back of their hands, they are safe and enjoying themselves. Let them be," Yeshua said.

Everyone then retired for the night. About three hours after midnight, Yeshua woke suddenly and realised that Shimon and the others were still not home. He got dressed and walked down to the lake. When he got there the wind was quite strong, not a storm as strong as before when he calmed the winds and the waves, but the wind was strong enough to stir up the sea, enough to batter the boat by the waves, and the boat was far from land, and the wind was against them. Yeshua sensed they could be in trouble again. Yeshua then walked towards them.

When the disciples saw him walking on the sea, they were terrified. Shimon cried out, "It is a ghost." And they were all screaming in fear.

But immediately Yeshua spoke to them and said, "Take heart it is I; do not be afraid."

Johanan cried out, "It is the Master."

Shimon answered Yeshua, "Lord, if it is you, command me to come to you on the water."

Yeshua simply said, "Come!"

So, Shimon got out of the boat and started walking on the water, and came towards Yeshua. But when he noticed the strong wind, he became frightened, and beginning to sink, he cried out, "Lord save me!"

Yeshua immediately reached out his hand and caught him saying to him, "You of little faith, why did you doubt?"

When they got into the boat, the wind ceased and the waves became calm. The disciples were astounded, and they worshipped Yeshua.

Johanan cried out, "Truly, you are the Son of God."

And the others answered, "The Son of God!"

They were in awe; this was now the second time that he saved them from perishing at sea. It was the second time that he calmed the winds and the sea. This time they had seen him walking on water. They knew no one would believe them. They themselves could not believe what they had seen. How could this be? But more and more they came to see the power of Yeshua, power that could only come from God. They were stunned into silence, as they made their way back to the shore.

None of the disciples who were on the boat were able to sleep after their experience. When Thomas awoke, one who had not been on the boat, when they told him, he would not believe what happened. When they all got together for breakfast, Yeshua was not there. He had gone to a lonely place as he usually did first thing in the morning to start his day.

Shimon and the other disciples told the women, what had happened on the sea, how Yeshua came to them, walking on the water.

Thomas then said, "That can't be, he must have been walking on a sandbank."

"Even if there is a sandbank at the lake, it would not be there at full tide and not during that storm last night for sure," Miriam said.

"There was no sandbank there, because I got out of the boat and walked towards Yeshua and I began to sink, the water came up to my head, and I was sinking, and Yeshua reached out and held my hand and rescued me," Shimon said.

"And when Yeshua got into the boat with Shimon, the wind suddenly abated and the sea became calm again," Nathanael said.

"What manner of man is this that walks on water and calms the winds and the waves?" Johanan said.

"Why are you surprised? He makes the blind see and the lame walk, and he cured me after no one else could for twelve whole years, and he raised Jairus' daughter back to life," Lucia said.

Just then Yeshua joined them and they stopped talking about him and what happened on the waters.

"What's for breakfast?" Yeshua asked, rubbing his hands, "I am so hungry I could eat a horse," Yeshua said, full of bonhomie.

"We don't have horse, Yeshua," Andreus said, grinning, "But we do have fish that we caught last night."

"Oh, were you out fishing last night? I am surprised you caught anything, there was a terrible storm," Yeshua said, humouring them.

"Okay, what shall we be doing today," Yeshua said. "All of you who spent the night fishing, I want you to rest up today. We will have an easy day, a day off. Tomorrow, we hit the road again, and visit the poor, the sick and the outcasts. We have not gone to all the villages. Miriam will take us to the leper colony and the house of the women on the outskirts of the town, I want to see how they all are," Yeshua said. "And we can take them some of the fish the gang caught last night," Yeshua said, grinning.

"Yeshua, are you still going to the big cities, Tiberias, Caesarea and Jerusalem?" Thomas asked.

"Yes, Thomas, why do you ask?"

"I think you are wasting your time; they will never accept your teaching about poverty, and giving up their riches and caring for the poor and the needy. They are all consumed by wealth, and power, and prosperity and they believe that is a sign of Yahweh's approval and blessing. They have no time for sinners and the poor and they condemn them as deserving of their condition as a result of their sins and of Yahweh's punishment," Thomas said.

Since Yeshua was using the name Yahweh instead of Adonai with them, his disciples did likewise.

"And the religious leaders, the Elders, the rabbis, the Pharisees, Scribes and Sadducees are all against you, and do not accept what you teach, and will do anything they can against you, and undermine you," Thomas added.

"Thomas, it is not only in the big cities that Yeshua's teaching is not accepted. Even in the smaller towns, wherever we went there were those who even though they saw the wonders Yeshua did in healing all the afflicted, they would still not believe, and not change their ways," Johanan said.

Then Yeshua said, "I hear what you are saying. I too am disheartened when so many listen but do not repent, do not change their hearts, they have hearts of stone. I say woe to them, for if the deeds of compassion, love and power done to them and in their cities had been done in places like Tyre and Sidon, and Sodom, they would have repented long ago in sackcloth and ashes and changed their hearts and their ways."

Yeshua then lifted his eyes to heaven and prayed, "Father, let these you have given me not be discouraged. I rejoice in the Spirit that is with me and with them. I thank you Father, Lord of heaven and earth because you have hidden these things from the wise and the intelligent, and have revealed them to infants, for such is your gracious will."

Then Yeshua turned to his disciples and saying, "Do not be disheartened. All things have been handed over to me by my Father, and no one knows who the Son is except the Father, or who the Father is, except the Son, and anyone to whom the Son chooses to reveal him. Blessed are the eyes that see what you see! For I tell you that many prophets and kings desired to see what you see, but did not see it, and to hear what you hear, but did not hear it. And generations will follow who will wish they had seen what you see, and they cannot see it. Or hear what you hear and cannot hear it. But you will be my disciples and you will tell them what you have seen and heard and learned, and you will make them see and you will lead them out of the darkness into the light."

Yeshua told his disciples many more things that morning, and they absorbed it all. He then left with the women. Thomas remained with all the other disciples. They had been tired from being on the lake all night, and weathering the storm, and they had much to take in of what Yeshua had just told them, but now they were no longer tired. They all dispersed wanting to reflect by themselves.

Yeshua and the women went all over the countryside, to the forgotten places, into the hovels where the poor and the outcasts lived, and they went into the caves where the homeless lived. Yeshua's heart went out to them and they were grateful for all that Miriam and the women brought them, clothing and things to eat, and of course the fish. They ate with relish as Yeshua spoke to them, telling them that Yahweh understands and hears their cries and does not condemn them but loves them and will always love them.

Yeshua felt so helpless in the sight of the plight of these poor, forgotten outcasts. There were enough of this world's goods for all, no one needed to live in poverty. It is greed that drives the rich and powerful to have much more than they need at the expense of those who have nothing or little. A change of heart is needed. The world cannot live with so many hoarding more and more of this world's treasures when so many go hungry. There is so much in the hands of so few and so little in the hands of so many. That is not the way Yahweh intended when he created this world's goods.

Their last stop was the house of so-called fallen women, widows or women who were cast out from their homes for sins they committed. These women were without any income, or anyone to support them so they turned to prostitution. Some of the women had met Yeshua, the last time he visited. But some had since left and new women had come, and they were meeting Yeshua for the first time, and they were overwhelmed. Yeshua spent time with them and listened to them. He did not judge them or condemn them, he felt only compassion. He spoke of Yahweh's compassion and love for them.

As they walked back home, as dusk approached Yeshua's heart was troubled. He felt the pain and the suffering of those forgotten people, and those fallen women. He was walking ahead of the three women. Miriam came up to walk next to him. She had noticed how downcast Yeshua was.

"Yeshua, I see your heart is troubled. I know that you feel the pain of those we have been with. But you have come to change that. The poor are blessed. You have given us your charter, by which we are to live. You said, 'Blessed are you who are poor, for yours is the kingdom of God. Blessed are you who are hungry now, for you will be filled. Blessed are you, who weep now, you will laugh.' They are blessed because they are hated and reviled and cast out as dregs of society, but you told us how Yahweh loves them, and will give them his kingdom," Miriam said.

Yeshua touched Miriam on the shoulder and said, "Thank you Miriam, I needed to be reminded of that. Bless you."

Miriam smiled. Rebecca and Lucia caught up and joined Yeshua and Miriam. And they spoke about the friends they had made, and how overcome they were with the friendliness and how happy the poor were with the little they had. They spoke about how happy they were to spend time with the little children who were all so happy making do with the little they had for their play. The children had nothing or very little, yet they were so cheerful and delighted to speak with them, and to laugh and be funny.

"Yeshua, we went to visit them to cheer them up, to lift their hearts, instead I feel I was uplifted and I was cheered up by my meeting with them," Lucia said.

"It is true, Lucia. They have so little and yet they have so much, they give so much," Yeshua said.

They then continued their journey back home, as the sun had completely disappeared.

Chapter Fifty-One
The Road to Jerusalem Continues

The next day they skirted the coastline of the lake and stopped at Tiberias. "We will spend some time here in Tiberias, it is a big city, and then we might as well go to Sepphoris our capital city. I was born and raised in Nazareth, and lived there most of my life, we were no more than two hundred citizens, how many inhabitants do you think live in Tiberias and Sepphoris?" Yeshua asked.

"Tiberias I think would have over ten thousand people living there," James Zebedee said. "Actually, there are more than fifteen thousand residents in Tiberias and the same in Sepphoris," Mattheus said.

"How do you know that figure Mattheus?" Thomas asked.

"He is the chief tax collector for the whole of Galilee stupid," Nathanael said.

"Oh of course, I forgot; so how many citizens are there in the whole of Galilee?" Thomas asked.

"Over one hundred and fifty thousand," Mattheus replied.

"So, by the number of people you have spoken to Yeshua, I would say, we have only reached less than a twentieth of the population," Andreus said.

"I know, Andreus, we are as they say; only scratching the surface. But word of mouth and above all the deeds of those who heard the Word of God and keep it will spread the message. We are only sowing the seed, lighting the flame, you and all those that follow will have to nurture those seeds and fan those flames," Yeshua said.

"I wonder what those city dwellers will have to say about you, Yeshua; a country boy from the backwaters of Nazareth when you go there, to teach them?" Rebecca said, laughing.

"People in the city have their own problems. More people only multiply the problems that those in the country face. It is easier to get lost and lonely even with so many people around. They all seem so in a hurry, and the people are always moving, moving in all directions, and I often wonder where they come from and where they are going," Nathanael said.

"There are plenty of farmers, farming wheat, barley, all sorts of vegetables, and of course vineyards and olives, and all other sorts of fruit trees, including your favourite Yeshua, figs," Johanan said with a smile.

"And there are cattle farmers as well, sheep and goats and other animals," Phillip said.

"And fishermen of course," Shimon added.

"I have been to Tiberias before, many years ago, when I walked all around the Sea of Galilee," Yeshua said. "And I have a very good friend living there, the blacksmith, his name is Zadok and he was one of my best friends, he lives there with his wife Gadija and their son, Ahijah, you remember Zadok, Rebecca?" Yeshua asked turning to look at Rebecca.

"Oh, I remember Zadok, you and he and Achim were always up to mischief and he was the leader of the pack when you were all still kids," Rebecca said, grinning.

"It will be good to catch up with them. I will go there first. Andreus, you have to look for accommodation for all of us. Mattheus, how is the kitty going, do we have enough for accommodation, or do we have to sleep rough?" Yeshua asked light-heartedly.

"We have enough, Yeshua; people have been very generous in their support. There were some women especially in Bethsaida and Capernaum who gave us a lot of financial help. They also gave me some names of women in Jerusalem they said would be most willing to support you, Yeshua, in your work," Mattheus said.

What Mattheus, did not say to the whole group, he later told Yeshua, that Andreus and Shimon and Johanan and James and their fathers gave a large amount of money to support the work. And Shimon, Andreus, Johanan and James are able to continue to receive part of the share of the profits of their joint family business that will also go into the kitty. Mattheus told Yeshua that Elijah, Miriam' father had also given a large sum of money to support their work. Yeshua was most appreciative.

"Well then, Tiberias, ready or not, here we come," Yeshua said cheerfully.

"Rebecca, would you like to come with me to visit Zadok and his family?" Yeshua asked.

"I'd love to catch up with that scoundrel," Rebecca said, with delight.

"Can Miriam and Lucia come too?" Rebecca asked.

"Of course," Yeshua said. "Zadok, Achim and we were like brothers, and we always said any friends of any one of us, was to be friends of all," Yeshua said with a smile.

Tiberias was not very far from Magdala, so they were there within a couple of hours. It was still mid-morning. And it sure was a bustling city, with people everywhere. No one seemed to recognise Yeshua or the rest of the group.

"What a place, everyone is rushing around like headless chooks," Thaddeus remarked.

"More like dogs chasing their own tails," Phillip retorted.

"Well, while the people are rushing around like headless chooks or senseless dogs chasing their own tails, why don't we take some time to settle in," Yeshua suggested.

"Okay all, while Andreus goes looking for a place for us to stay, we will meet here again, at say, in three hours' time," Yeshua said.

Yeshua thought it would be a good time to go to the blacksmith's shop and see if Zadok was there. Rebecca, Miriam and Lucia decided to visit the markets and go about women's business. Yeshua was so pleased to see them become such good friends, and he thought of Zadok and Achim, his closest friends when growing up, they had made an awesome trio. Yeshua was quite excited to meet with Zadok again. When he arrived at Zadok's work he was intensely engaged over a hot kiln.

"Hey mister blacksmith, I have a horse that needs a shoe fixed," Yeshua said in a gruff voice, trying to disguise his voice.

"I'll be with you in a minute, Sir," Zadok said. After a minute he turned around and instantly recognised Yeshua. His face lit up like the sun. He was so delighted to see his old friend from Nazareth.

"Yeshua! What a surprise! How good to see you and you are looking so well, a bit thinner though. How have you been, how is your mother, what have you been up to, it's been a long time, we have to catch up, how long are you in town?" Zadok asked excitedly.

"Hold your breath, Zadok, I too am excited and delighted to see you, all covered in soot," Yeshua said with obvious delight. "I have just arrived. I will be here in Tiberias for a while, if the people do not throw me out," Yeshua said.

"Yeshua, I have heard so much about you, and what you have been teaching all over Galilee, and all the spectacular feats you have been accomplishing. I hear you are quite the miracle worker. I always knew you had those hidden powers from when we were growing up," Zadok said, smiling. "Gadija, Ahijah and Sofia, our daughter will be so happy to see you. You must join us for dinner," Zadok insisted.

"I will be delighted, as long as you won't be doing the cooking," Yeshua said. "I remember Gadija's cooking and it was out of this world. So, you have a daughter, how old is she?" Yeshua asked.

"She's six now, and of course you know Ahijah, he is almost twelve," Zadok said proudly, and with obvious joy.

"You are looking good, except very sooty," Yeshua said, grinning. "I have Rebecca with me, and two other women, Miriam from Magdala and Lucia from Capernaum. They are my disciples and confidantes and there are also eleven men who assist me and are my disciples as well. They are all from Galilee, some from across the lake, Bethsaida. We have just come from Capernaum and Magdala and will stay here for a while," Yeshua said, "Then we are off to Sepphoris and Caesarea and on to Jerusalem."

"All the big cities, so what are you now that you are no longer a carpenter?" Zadok asked.

"I suppose you could call me an itinerant preacher. More like a teacher. I learned so much from Gamaliel, and now I have been called to teach others." That is as far as Yeshua would go explaining to Zadok. "I will be talking in the synagogue here in Tiberias for some time, if the people wish to listen to what I have to say," Yeshua added.

"I'm sorry Yeshua but I don't have time for the synagogue, these days. I have too much work to do. I only go to the synagogue on special feast days and for the Passover celebrations, like most of my friends and other business people. The Sabbath, I am so exhausted and have so much work at home to catch up on that I don't have time for attending the Sabbath service," Zadok said.

"In any case, Yeshua, the preachers simply put me to sleep. I'm sick and tired of being reminded of how great a sinner I am, and how unworthy I am, and that I have to keep all those ridiculous laws and regulations," Zadok vented.

"I understand, Zadok. There is a time for everything, a time for work and a time for rest, a time to speak and a time to be silent, a time for oneself and one's loved ones, and a time for God. All you have to do is to find time for God, Zadok. Just a simple gaze to the heavens at the beginning of your day, will do. Just to remind you that God sees and knows and loves you with a love beyond compare. I have come not to condemn or to burden people, Zadok; for I know that life already has enough burdens. You work all day at the sweat of your brow. And you do that because you love your family, and you work and sweat and cover yourself in soot, to support them and you are also doing a service to the community. That is a great prayer, Zadok. Your day is a prayer, make it a prayer, at the beginning of the day, simply turn your heart to Yahweh and offer him your day, your work and continue to do your work as you are. And Yahweh will bless you. And at the end of your day, take a moment to be still and silent and give thanks to Yahweh for giving you life this day and all the other blessings he has bestowed upon you, like the love of Gadija and your children. And say a prayer for me Zadok, I need your prayers, and in this way, you too can assist me to do the work that I have been born to do, and now been sent to do," Yeshua said.

Yeshua was so accustomed to speaking of God as Yahweh and not Adonai. He only did so with his close band of disciples but he just seemed okay with doing so with his close friend Zadok.

"Yeshua, thanks for that sermon. Now I don't have to go to the synagogue for a long time," Zadok said, laughing. "So, I see you this evening?" he added.

"Yes, for sure Zadok. I will be there at sunset and remember I will be bringing Rebecca, Miriam and Lucia with me," Yeshua said and then left.

The group of disciples met again as arranged. Andreus had found a place for them to stay a bit out of the city centre but it was clean and much cheaper than in the city centre. They then went there to settle in. There was some forest area close by and Yeshua went there for a walk. The women began to prepare dinner for all. Yeshua had indicated that he and the women were invited to a friend from Nazareth, the local blacksmith.

Yeshua spent a most enjoyable evening with Zadok and his family, as did the women, especially Rebecca who was so pleased to see Zadok again, and to see how domesticated he had become. Zadok had already spoken to Gadija and they offered accommodation to Yeshua. They had extra beds that they could offer to the women as well.

"Thank you Zadok and Gadija, for your kind offer, but we already have accommodation. After a most enjoyable evening, Yeshua and the women thanked Zadok and Gadija and then left and walked back to their accommodation. When they got there, everyone was still up and about and waiting for Yeshua. They wanted to know what the program was for the next day."

"Well, it will be more of the same. I have to get the feel of the place and the people. So far, it doesn't seem like the people here know me. And it is so easy to get lost in the crowd and that is a bit of a relief for me," Yeshua said. "So, for the next couple of days, I just want to move around and get a sense of the people. I will visit my friend Zadok again and speak to him about the people and see if he can tell me of people I could meet and speak to," Yeshua said. "I will of course visit the leaders of the synagogue and introduce myself and ask if I may speak to the people on this coming Sabbath," Yeshua said. "So, for the next two days, leading up to the Sabbath, you too may do as you wish," Yeshua said.

"Well, I'm going fishing, if any of you wish to join me, I'll be up before sunset," Shimon said.

Andreus, James and Johanan said they would come, as did James Alpheus. The rest were noncommittal. The women said they would simply go to the markets and do some sightseeing. After that they all retired for the night.

As planned Yeshua met with Zadok. He recommended that Yeshua meet with Gadija's uncle, Baasha, an elderly gentleman who has lived here in Tiberias all his life. Yeshua followed up on the invitation and found Baasha, who was sitting at the back of his house, under a huge fig tree and eating a fig. Yeshua was absolutely delighted.

"Baasha, Shalom, I am Yeshua from Nazareth, a good friend of Zadok, we grew up together in Nazareth. I have come to Tiberias to preach. I wanted to talk to you to learn a bit about the people and the city. Zadok, speaks so highly of you and your knowledge and love for the city," Yeshua said.

"Yeshua, you are the carpenter, the son of Miriam and Yosef. Zadok had spoken of you often, and I have heard stuff about you, the things you have done, some of it very farfetched. I even heard that you raised a child from the dead," Baasha said.

"First of all, Baasha, may I have a fig. They look ripe and delicious on your fine tree," Yeshua said.

"Well, you have your priorities right, Yeshua, help yourself," Baasha said with a smile.

Yeshua picked one, wiped it on his sleeve and bit into it, skin and all. "Mmm, absolutely delicious," Yeshua said. He was quiet for the next few minutes as he relished the eating of his fig. Then Yeshua said, "Baasha, tell me about yourself."

"Well, I am the brother of Gadija's mother. I was born in Tiberias, seventy-nine years ago. Our city was named Tiberias, not so long ago, eight years ago. Our city was named after Tiberius, the second Emperor of the Roman Empire. He was the step son of Caesar Augustus. As you can see, we are ruled by Rome, with an iron fist. There is a lot of resentment. People are hardworking and many are prosperous with big farms employing several day labourers. But there are many poor and homeless as well. The rich resent having to pay exorbitant taxes and tariffs to Rome that continue to rise and rise, sending many to struggle and some lose their properties. People have a lot of debt and to keep their heads above water and when they cannot pay their debts, they lose their land and their properties. It's what's happening all over Galilee, the Romans are fleecing us, and the rich are fleecing the not so rich, and getting richer and the poor get poorer. As a result, we have a growing crime problem, burglaries, home invasions, and even murders. Everyone has to have dogs to ward off burglars, and also arm themselves with clubs. Many are getting very rich, while many more are becoming poorer, and the rich are getting richer, and the poor poorer. And there is much illness as well, and people dying way before their time. Then we have some zealots among us, who have their moments of uprising, but they are easily squashed by the Roman legions, so many of them here in Tiberias, and the capital Sepphoris. The people are all waiting for a new Moses to deliver them from the Romans. But I think they are waiting in vain," Baasha said.

"Baasha, you paint a dismal picture of your city. But I can understand the bitterness and anger and the suffering of the people." Yeshua listened some more, and had many questions to ask Baasha and he had a wealth of knowledge of the town. Baasha knew the religious leaders but it seemed he had a very low regard for them.

"The religious leaders; the Pharisees, Scribes, Sadducees, while they resent Rome; they work hand in hand with them, and feather their own nests. They keep the people scared of the wrath of God and keep them subservient. And besides Rome fleecing the people, they are also required to pay a tithe, a tenth of all they earn to the synagogue. I And most are fearful of the vengeance of God if they do not pay, they are fearful of eternal condemnation in the fires of hell. So not only is Rome fleecing the poor, but the Temple leaders as well. So, everyone is waiting for a Messiah, the One that will deliver them from the tyranny of Rome," Baasha said.

Yeshua was told that Baasha was an Elder, and Yeshua was surprised, for he spoke of the religious leaders as if they were a group apart, and of which he was not a part. After a couple of hours with Baasha, Yeshua left. With directions given by

Baasha, Yeshua made his way to the home of Jethro, the leader of the synagogue, he too was an Elder. Most of the Elders were well-to-do and of the upper class. Jethro had a fine home. And a slave servant answered the door.

"Please come in Sir, I will call my Master," the servant said, bowing obsequiously to Yeshua. This made Yeshua very uncomfortable. Like all Jews, Yeshua grew up knowing and believing that they were the chosen ones of Yahweh. And owning slaves as servants did not sit right with Yeshua. A time will come he knew, will have to come, when no one will enslave another. How can we have slaves, when we ourselves were slaves in the land of Egypt for four hundred years? Have we not learned? But then, we too are slaves to the Romans, they are our lords, they rule over us. Worse still we are slaves to our fallen natures. I have come to set the people free. Yeshua often had these thoughts come into his mind at the oddest of times, and it was all fruit for what he would say to the people.

A tall, handsome man, with a long white beard and in flowing robes came to the door and greeted Yeshua. "Come in Yeshua," Jethro said in a friendly voice. "So, you are Yeshua, the one I have heard of from the synagogue leaders in Capernaum and Magdala. You are causing quite a stir. What can I do for you Yeshua?" Jethro asked.

"Jethro, I have been travelling all over Galilee on both sides of the lake, and I have been preaching to the people," Yeshua said. "I have come to seek your permission and blessing to talk to the people this coming Sabbath."

Jethro paused for a moment. He then rubbed his face, as if he had just woken from a deep sleep. He then sighed. "Yeshua, my colleagues have expressed concern about your teaching and your example of living. They tell me you have scant regard for our laws and regulations, and that you do not respect the Sabbath and also, they tell me that you are a cause of scandal because you associate with tax-collectors and sinners and even prostitutes, and that you are even seen visiting their house," Jethro said.

"Guilty as charged, Jethro. Jethro, I have been sent not to the righteous like you and your friends, I have come to call the sinners, the poor, the outcasts, the dregs of society, I have been sent to bring them the Good News of the Father's love for them and I have come to bring them hope and salvation," Yeshua said.

Jethro continued to express warnings to Yeshua. But he finally gave permission for Yeshua to preach but with the proviso that he does not turn the people away from the Law and the Prophets. Jethro then called one of the slaves and they prepared and offered Yeshua some refreshment.

Chapter Fifty-Two
The Vine and the Branches

The Sabbath came around and Yeshua was about to address a packed synagogue. All his disciples were there. They were scattered throughout the synagogue on Yeshua's instructions. He did not want them to sit in front. And he wanted them to gauge the reactions of the people, and whether his message was getting through. After each of his teachings to the crowds, Yeshua always had a debriefing and feed-back session with his disciples. He had shared with them his conversations with Baasha and with Jethro, so they were well prepared.

Yeshua was pleased to see Baasha among the people, as well as his friend Zadok. He had seen them coming to the synagogue and greeted them at the entrance, before Gadija and her daughter went to the Women's Court. This too Yeshua found disconcerting, for Rebecca, Miriam and Lucia also had to go to the Women's Court.

Yeshua began by greeting the people. "Shalom. Peace be with you my brothers and sisters and dearest children; the Lord is with you. I am so pleased to be in your city. I have some very good friends here, Zadok, your blacksmith and I grew up together in Nazareth, and I was so pleased to meet with him and his wife Gadija and their children, Ahijah and Sofia."

When he mentioned Zadok and his family, Yeshua looked at Zadok and Ahijah. Zadok was not the least uncomfortable but proud and happy to be acknowledged by Yeshua as his friend. He knew that it would be very good for his business. And his children were giggling with pride, in hearing their names mentioned for all to hear.

"Yeshua continued. I also had the honour of spending some time with Baasha, so I could learn from him about your fine city and its great people," Yeshua said.

Those sitting around Baasha looked and smiled at him. Baasha merely frowned, but was nevertheless pleased to be acknowledged by Yeshua.

"And I am grateful that Jethro has given me permission to address you," Yeshua said. He continued, "I enjoyed some of Baasha's delicious figs, and also the grapes from the fine vineyards you have here in Tiberias. I also noticed people standing around waiting to be hired by landowners to work for them, so they could feed their families. Let me tell you a story," Yeshua said.

"The Kingdom of Heaven is like a landowner who went out early in the morning to hire labourers for his vineyard. After agreeing with the labourers for the usual daily wage, he sent them into his vineyard. When he went out at about the third hour, he saw others standing idle in the marketplace, and he said to them, 'You also, go into my vineyard, and I will pay you whatever is right.' So, they went. When he went out again at about noon and mid-afternoon, about the ninth hour, he did the same. At about the eleventh hour, he went out and found others standing around; and he said to them, 'Why are you standing here idle all day?' They said to him, 'Because no one has hired us.' He said to them, 'You also go into my vineyard.'

"When evening came, the owner spoke to the manager of his vineyard and instructed him what to do and how much to pay the labourers, then the landowner said to his manager, 'Call the labourers and give them their pay, beginning with the last and then going to the first.'

"When those hired at the eleventh hour came, each of them received the usual daily wage. Now when the first came, they thought they would receive more, but each of them also received the same usual daily wage. And when they received it, they grumbled against the landowner, saying, 'These last worked only one hour, and you have made them equal to us who have borne the burden of the day and the scorching heat.'

"But the landowner replied to them, 'Friends, I am doing you no harm; did you not agree with me for the usual daily wage? Take what belongs to you and go; I choose to give this last the same as I give to you. Am I not allowed to do what I choose with what belongs to me? Or are you envious because I am generous? So, the last will be first and the first will be last.'"

There was a gasp among the people, especially by the group of Pharisees, Elders, Sadducees and Scribes surrounding Jethro. There were also murmuring among some of the people, most likely not agreeing with what the landowner did. There were also smiles on the faces on many men who were most likely those who stood in the mornings waiting to be hired. Some of them would have had the experience of standing all day in the marketplace and not having anyone hire them.

The disciples were pondering on Yeshua's words; as usual he always provoked them to reflect more deeply on the truth.

Yeshua allowed time for his words to be digested and the murmuring to stop. He could see that the people were thinking about what he had said. He was simply trying to encourage late starters, and show that God is a generous God, who cares for all. Yeshua was also showing the people the difference between worldly concepts of fairness and justice and those of God. God wants to provide all with what they need, and those working all day and those working for one hour have the same daily needs, and so God, the landowner in this story is thinking about the needs of the workers, all of them. He loves all and wants all to be satisfied and have their needs fulfilled.

"My dear friend, the landowner in this story is God, and God's justice is not the same as worldly justice. God's justice is always tempered with mercy and compassion. He sees the plight and misery of those men, who are standing all day long, waiting, expecting to be hired so they can feed their family, but no one hires them. But God does notice. He has eyes and a heart filled with compassion for their suffering, so he hires them and pays them what they need to feed their families."

The disciples especially were deep in thought; again, Yeshua teaches a radically different philosophy of life and shows that God's ways are not our ways. Yeshua also makes landowners think about the dignity of work, and the rights and needs of their workers.

Yeshua then decided to bring them the truth about who has sent him and why, so he continued, "My dear brothers and sisters, I told you how I admired the fine vineyards in your city. I say to you, I am the true vine and my Father is the vine grower. He removes every branch in me that bears no fruit. Every branch that bears fruit he prunes to make it bear more fruit. Abide in me, as I abide in you. Just as the branch cannot bear fruit by itself unless it abides in the vine, neither can you, unless you abide in me. I am the vine; you are the branches. Those who abide in me and me in them bear much fruit, for apart from me you can do nothing. Whoever does not abide in me is thrown away like a branch and withers; such branches are gathered, thrown into the fire, and burned. If you abide in me and my words abide in you, ask for whatever you wish, and it will be done for you. As my Father loves you, so I love you, abide in my love. If you keep my commandments, you will abide in my love, just as I have kept my Father's commandments and abide in his love. I am giving you these commands that you may love one another. I say these things to you so that my love, peace and joy may be in you, and that your joy may be complete."

With those words, Yeshua stopped talking. The people were aghast. Who is he and what is he saying about himself. Even his disciples had not heard him speak in such a manner about himself. They had of course seen the deeds he had done. And now he was revealing himself in a personal way.

Because it was the Sabbath, the people were not allowed to bring their sick to Yeshua for healing as they would on other days, for it was forbidden to work on the Sabbath and healing was regarded as work by the Pharisees and the other sticklers for the Law.

In the synagogue there happened to be a man with a withered right hand that hung limply and uselessly from him. The Pharisees and the Scribes and the other religious leaders, saw the man approach Yeshua and watched carefully to see what Yeshua would do, whether he would cure the man on the Sabbath, so that they might find an accusation against him. Yeshua knew what they were thinking and Jethro had warned him about healing on the Sabbath. The disciples also knew that Yeshua had been forewarned not to heal in the synagogue on the Sabbath. In fact, Jethro and the others had guards preventing any sick or afflicted to enter. But somehow the man with the withered hand had avoided detection. He was accompanied by some of his friends who helped shield him.

Yeshua said to the man with the withered hand, "Come closer my dear man and stand here." He came closer and stood in front of Yeshua. There was whispering around the synagogue, as the word spread to those who could not see, about what was happening and then there was a hush all over the synagogue.

Yeshua then spoke up and said, "I ask you, is it lawful to do good, or to do harm on the Sabbath, to save life or to destroy it? Suppose one of you has only one sheep and it falls into a pit on the Sabbath, will you not go into the pit yourself and lay hold of it and lift it out? How much more valuable is a human being than a sheep! So, I tell you, it is lawful to do good on the Sabbath." Then Yeshua said to the man, "Stretch out your hand." To the amazement of all who could see, the man, using his good hand, stretched out his withered hand, and Yeshua touched his withered hand, and there before the eyes of all, the man's right hand was restored and he started moving his fingers repeatedly and gaping at them with an open mouth, absolutely astonished. He raised both his hands in jubilation, and moving them repeatedly. He fell on his knees before Yeshua and grabbed hold of his legs. Yeshua immediately took hold of the man and raised him to his feet. The man and his friends left, almost dancing as they left the synagogue.

Yeshua then left immediately after the cured man and his friends, not giving his detractors any opportunity to attack him. And he went to a lonely place to be by himself. He asked his disciples to come with him and he instructed Andreus and Shimon to make sure the crowds would not follow. When they had walked deep into the forest, and arrived at a clearing Yeshua stopped. He turned to his disciples and said, "Pray here with me for a while."

They all found a spot, some stood and some sat down on a fallen log or on the grass. Yeshua stood and turned to the heavens and with his arms outstretched he prayed, "Father, your will be done. I thank you for giving me these friends to accompany me. Bless them Father that they may understand and be filled with your Spirit. Father we are on our way to the city of Jerusalem. And I fear that it will be a trying time. Father give me; give us all the strength we need for what lies ahead." After a while of silent prayer, Yeshua turned to his disciples and spoke to them. "My dear friends, I thank you for being with me, I thank you for your friendship and your support, and your generosity. You have sacrificed so much to be with me. You have left your families, your friends, your businesses, your support systems, your homes, to follow me and learn from me. I thank you. You are indeed the true branches of the vine. You are alive with the Spirit, for you abide in me. You have made your home with me, and for that I am most grateful—now is there anything you wish to say or to ask me," Yeshua said.

"Yeshua, the people were all listening with great interest to what you were saying to them about the vine and the branches. And they were all astounded when they saw you heal that man's withered hand. But among them were some who seem to be against you for healing that man on the Sabbath. To me it seems that they may be a thorn in your side," James Zebedee said.

"My friends fear not. I am well aware of my detractors. They have hate in their souls. I have given them too, the commandment that I give to you, that you love one another as I love you. There can be no place for hate in your hearts. I have come to destroy hate in the world; hate is the work of the devil. My work is to bring love, to spread love. If the world hates me, it will hate you. If you belonged to the world, the world would love you as its own. Because you do not belong to the world, but I have chosen you out of the world—therefore the world hates you. Remember what I told you—'Servants are no greater than their Master,' If they persecute me, they will persecute you. If they keep my word, they will keep yours also. But they will do all these things to you on account of my name, because they do not know Him who sent me. They have heard what I said, and seen what I did, and know that I come from the Father, and yet they hate me. They have forgotten what is written in their own Law—'They hated me without a cause'."

Yeshua was tempted to tell them more, to prepare for the persecution that awaited him and also the persecution they would endure for being his disciples and believers in him and in his word. But he did not want to make them fearful at this time. There was still much to do and so little time.

"Do not be afraid. I say to you again, what I said to the people in the synagogue, this is my commandment, that you love one another as I have loved you. As the Father loves me, so I love you; abide in my love. If you keep my commandments, you will abide in my love, just as I keep my Father's commandments and abide in his love. I say this again to you my friends, that you love one another as I love you. No one has greater love than this, to lay down one's life for one's friends. I do not call you servants, because the servant does not know what the master is doing, but I call you friends, because I have made known to you and will continue to make known to you everything that I have heard from my Father. I chose you and I appoint you to go and bear fruit, fruit that will last." With these words Yeshua continued to speak to his disciples. When he had finished speaking to them in this vein he said, "We will leave for Sepphoris tomorrow, for a short while and then to Nazareth, which is really so close and yet so far from Sepphoris. So let us go now, and have our Sabbath rest."

So, they walked to their base and on their way, they passed through some cornfields. Yeshua and the disciples were hungry, so the disciples began to pluck heads of grain and began to eat. Yeshua and his disciples did not realise that they were being watched by a few men, with them two Pharisees. The group pounced on Yeshua and the disciples and confronted them.

Yeshua and his disciples were surprised not realising they were being followed and watched.

The Pharisees then spoke, "Look, your disciples are doing what is not lawful on the Sabbath."

This was not the first time; the disciples were caught picking corn on the Sabbath and eating.

Yeshua gave them the same reply he gave before, "Have you not read what David did when he and his companions were hungry? He entered the house of God and ate the bread of the Presence, which is not lawful for him or his companions to eat, but only for the priests. Or have you not read in the Law that on the Sabbath the priests in the Temple break the Sabbath and are guiltless? I tell you something greater than the Temple is here. But if you had known what this means, 'I desire mercy and not sacrifice,' you would not have condemned the guiltless, for the Son of God made man is Lord of the Sabbath."

The Pharisees were shocked, but there was nothing they could do, so they left grumbling. The disciples had stopped eating during that altercation with the Pharisees and their band of followers. But when they left, they continued eating.

"Yeshua, it seems like the Pharisees and their spies are following us, we need to look out for them and be more careful in future," Shimon said. The others agreed with him.

Yeshua said nothing. They then continued and the disciples continued to help themselves with the grain.

"We will meet again for supper at where we are staying. Peace be with you all." They then all went their own way.

In the next few days Yeshua and his disciples' worst fears of being spied upon were confirmed. After Yeshua preached in the synagogue, some Pharisees and Teachers of the Law, among them some all the way from Jerusalem, approached Yeshua and said to him. "Yeshua, we have reports that you and your disciples do not wash their hands before eating, contrary to our Laws on cleanliness. And why is that even Johanan the Baptisers fast as we Pharisees do. We fast often, but your disciples don't fast at all."

Yeshua looked at them with frustration for their pettiness. He had to restrain himself, so many times have they complained like this and Yeshua calmly answered, as he usually did, "The wedding guests cannot mourn as long as the bride and the bridegroom are with them, can they? The days will come when the bridegroom is taken away from them and then they will fast. No one sows a piece of unshrunk cloth on an old cloak, for the patch pulls away from the cloak and a worse tear is made. Neither is new wine put into old wineskins, otherwise the skins burst, and the wine is spilled, and the skins are destroyed, but new wine is put into fresh wine skins, and so both are preserved." The Pharisees and Teachers left puzzled by what Yeshua was saying to them. They left scratching their heads.

The next few days in Sepphoris were similar to their Tiberias experience. Sepphoris being the capital of Galilee seemed to have an air about it, as all capital cities do, an aura of superiority over people from elsewhere. Yeshua noticed again the pomposity of the Pharisees, who strutted around with their elaborate dress and their noses in the air. His encounters with them so far had not endeared them to him but he knew they too needed to be saved. He knew how they trusted themselves that they were righteous and regarded others with contempt. He was also aware of the wide gap between the rich and the poor and heard stories of how so many people were spiralling into debt they could not pay and ended up losing their properties and ending in jail. Yeshua had in mind two stories he would tell the people of Sepphoris.

Word had spread to Sepphoris of what had happened in Tiberias and the Pharisees and the Scribes were out in full force in the synagogue, sitting right in front. Yeshua noticed the same men from Tiberias sitting with the religious in front. When Yeshua began to speak, all eyes were on him.

"My dear friends, let me begin with a story. Two men went up to the Temple to pray, one a Pharisee, the other a tax-collector."

Immediately, everyone was alert with attention. They were all aware of the Pharisees present and their reputation as self-righteous with an air of superiority, as if they were the chosen few of Yahweh, and everyone else were inferior and sinners, and had to learn from them. And of course, they and everyone else despised the tax-collectors. The Pharisees regarded the tax-collectors as sinners. And they knew that Yeshua had a reputation of associating and even dining with tax-collectors, and they knew that he had a chief tax collector Mattheus as one of his disciples. So everyone was agog, excitedly waiting to hear this story of a Pharisee and a tax-collector. The Pharisees in the audience were a bit uneasy but Matteus, and the other odd tax-collector in the audience were hoping they would not be the antagonist of the story Yeshua was about to tell them. Everyone though was all ears, they loved Yeshua's stories, even though some of them left them clueless.

Yeshua continued with his story. "The Pharisee went up to the front of the Temple and standing by himself was praying thus, 'God, I thank you that I am not like other people, thieves, rogues, adulterers, even like this tax-collector. I fast twice a week; I give a tenth of all my income'."

The people were aghast at Yeshua's words, a direct confrontation with the Pharisees. Everyone thought as Yeshua did, but no one dared confront the Pharisees as Yeshua was doing right now, here in the synagogue of all places. The crowd were excited and full of attention hanging on Yeshua's every word. The frowns on the faces of the Pharisees, however, were something to see, it seemed their faces were about to crack open. They were fuming at Yeshua's attack on them. They were filled with hatred for this impostor. He was not a man of God, for daring to attack and belittle them.

Yeshua continued, "But the tax-collector, standing far off at the back of the Temple would not even look up to heaven, but was beating his breast and saying, 'God be merciful to me, a sinner'!"

People's mouths were agape. This parable they fully understood. They were shaking their heads in disbelief. They all hated and despised the tax-collectors and were in agreement with the Pharisees that the tax-collectors were indeed sinners of the worst kind. But now in this story they were on the side of the tax-collector. There were also among the crowd some tax-collectors and of course Mattheus. The tax-collectors were smiling, at least for now; they were the heroes of this story. And they also had heard of what happened to Mattheus and how he had become a disciple of this man, and how this man Yeshua is a friend of theirs. The Pharisees' ire went up even more, they were now fuming.

Yeshua concluded his story saying, "I tell you, this tax-collector went down to his house justified rather than the other, for all who exalt themselves will be humbled and those who humble themselves will be exalted."

Yeshua then stopped and paused allowing people time to reflect. Yeshua was well aware of how forthright he was being. The disciples however thought that Yeshua was going a bit too far, for they feared retaliation. The people were all silent, busy with their own thoughts. Yeshua had the habit of allowing times of silence, whenever he had a message to give. He always felt the need to ponder the words of the teachers when they preached in the synagogues, but they would go on with something else or they would chant psalms or lead the people in prayer in preparation for sacrifices and what was said was quickly forgotten. Yeshua instead wanted and allowed time for his story of the Pharisee and Publican to sink in and forever be in their minds.

After some time, when Yeshua thought they all had sufficient time to digest his story he continued, "I am aware of how many of you are in debt and how many of you have lost your livelihoods because of debt and how you are being swallowed up by debts. I want to tell you this story." The story Yeshua was about to tell was not only for the rich, those who people were indebted to, but for all, for Yeshua knew we can all be in debt to someone at some time or other, or we can all be in the position of having someone owing us something or other, someone being indebted to us. So, Yeshua continued, "The Kingdom of Heaven may be compared to a king who wished to settle accounts with his subjects. He called his accountants so he could begin the reckoning. A person, a slave, who owed him ten thousand talents, was brought to him; and as he could not pay, the king ordered him to be sold into slavery, together with his wife and children and all his possessions and the money received to be used as payment for his debt. The debtor fell on his knees before the king pleading with him, saying, 'Have patience with me, and I will pay you everything'. He pleaded so earnestly that the king had pity for him and released him and forgave him the debt."

"This same person, who was forgiven such a big debt, went out rejoicing. And he came upon one of his fellow slaves who owed him a hundred denarii, and seizing him by the throat, he said, 'Pay what you owe me.' Then his fellow slave fell down on his knees and pleaded with him, 'Have patience with me and I will pay you.' But he refused, then he went and had him thrown into prison and in this way had his debt repaid. When his fellow slaves saw what had happened, they were greatly distressed and they went and reported to their lord all that had taken place. Then the king summoned him and said, 'You wicked slave! I forgave you all that debt because you pleaded with me. Should you not have had mercy on your fellow slave, as I had mercy on you?' And in anger the king handed him over to be tortured, until he would pay his entire debt."

The people in the synagogue could relate to Yeshua's story, so many were rich landowners and many were indebted to them. And there were also money-lenders who charged exorbitant interest and went to extreme lengths to extort payment. And of course, there were many who were in debt and who were struggling to pay their taxes to Rome, let alone their debts. So, this story resonated with all.

Yeshua concluded his story with the words, "So my heavenly Father will also do to you, if you do not forgive your brother or sister from your heart."

After Yeshua had allowed his usual time for silent reflection, he called the people to prayer and he led them in the prayer he had taught his disciples, "Our Father, who art in heaven, hallowed be your name, your kingdom come. Your will be done on earth as it is in heaven. Give us this day our daily bread and forgive us our debts as we forgive those indebted to us. And in time of temptation, deliver us from evil."

When Yeshua got outside the synagogue Miriam, Rebecca and Lucia were waiting for him. They were surrounded by a crowd of women. They had lots of children of all ages with them, including small babies in their arms. When the men came out, they had to be content to be on the outside of the crowd. Shimon and Andreus forced their way to the centre and near to Yeshua. The other disciples followed and stood beside Yeshua. The women were pleading with Yeshua to touch and bless their babies and their children. When Shimon and Andreus and the disciples saw what was happening, they sternly ordered the women not to do it and not bother Yeshua. But Yeshua turned to his disciples and said, "Let the children come to me, and do not stop them, for it is to such as these that the Kingdom of God belongs!" Then Yeshua took the babies up in his arms, and smiled at them and touched them. He laid his hands on each of the children and spoke to them, and blessed them, and then he turned to his disciples and the crowd around him and said, "Truly I tell you, whoever does not receive the Kingdom of God as a little child will never enter it."

Yeshua then left with his disciples. The crowd however followed him. But he got Andreus and the others to get the people to go to their homes as it was still the Sabbath. Yeshua and his disciples went to the lake and they found a deserted spot, where they had a simple meal of bread and dried fish, and figs and some wine. After their lunch they went for a walk along the beach, and some of them went in for a swim.

When they had all walked for long time, they came to a stop. There was no one else around, so they sat on the shore and Yeshua spoke to them and taught them. He again touched on the theme of loving one's enemies and forgiving those that hate us.

"Teacher, you speak so much about how to treat our enemies and those who hate us and do harm to us, you speak about us turning the other cheek. This is a hard teaching, how many times must I turn the other cheek before I can respond in the manly way, I am accustomed to," Shimon said, more with tongue in cheek. The others were all smiling, knowing that Shimon was merely baiting Yeshua, but at the same time, they could see that Shimon had a serious aspect to his questioning, for he was not accustomed to turning the other cheek.

"Seventy times, seven times?" Shimon asked.

"Seventy times, seven times, how much times are that Mattheus, you are the tax-collector, you would know that answer," Nathanael said, jokingly.

It seemed they were all having a dig at Yeshua, who simply played along with them. "Well, Mattheus, we are waiting for an answer," Yeshua said.

"The answer is four hundred and ninety times," Mattheus said.

"There's your answer Shimon," Yeshua said.

"So, Simon you can start counting from now, when someone strikes you on the cheek for the four hundred and ninety first time, then you can respond in your usual way and knock the person's block off," Johanan said, laughing out loud. The others joined in.

"That will take a life time, Shimon," James Zebedee added.

"Well, really it won't take long," Yeshua said. "How many times has anyone of you been really struck on the cheek?" Yeshua played along.

There was a moment of silence, "I was once, when I was a teenager, with an uncle who was drunk and obsequious and cursing God. I told him he was displeasing God and should not curse like that, and with that he socked me in the face and gave me the only black eye I ever had," Johanan said.

"You do not have to take me literally," Yeshua said, in a more serious vein. "I just like to use colourful language, it's easier for the people to understand and remember my teaching," Yeshua continues, "That is why I tell the stories, stories that have lessons in them. Stories people will remember and retell over and over again, so it will become imbedded in their minds and hearts," Yeshua said.

"Turning the other cheek is not to be taken only in the odd literal sense but in the symbolic sense. It means whenever anyone strikes you in any way, by their words, looks, gestures, deeds, when they insult you, degrade you, humiliate you, belittle you, curse you or do any kind of evil against you, you are to turn the other cheek. And by turning the other cheek I am not advocating that you not stand up for your rights and what is right and good. You have to challenge any wrongdoing done to you. When I gave that teaching, I was merely responding to our way of responding, the way of our Laws, of an eye for an eye and a tooth for a tooth. We are not to seek revenge, but understanding, forgiveness, love and compassion. You know the saying, 'vengeance is mine, says the Lord.' Do not repay hate with hate but respond always with love," Yeshua said.

By now they were all quiet and serious and appreciated that Yeshua went along with their jollification and then led them into a serious discussion of his teaching.

That night they had a barbecue and roasted a lamb and had a feast. Yeshua had taken up an invitation from Zadok who wanted to entertain Yeshua and his friends. They ate much and drank plenty of wine. When the evening was over Yeshua said to his disciples that they would leave for Nazareth the next day.

Chapter Fifty-Three
The Plotting Begins

The Pharisees, Scribes, Sadducees and Elders at Sepphoris were livid with the way Yeshua depicted them and the story he told about the Pharisee and the Publican. It seemed he was mocking them. They were custodians of the Law, the special ones of Yahweh, chosen to lead and give an example to right living according to the Law of Moses and the Prophets. And Yeshua was upsetting the apple cart, and humiliating them in the eyes of the people. They were furious, so they called together a meeting of their fellow religious leaders from all over Sepphoris and Tiberias, Magdala, Capernaum, and also from the other side of the lake, from Bethsaida. A couple of Pharisees even came from Nazareth.

Jethro chaired the meeting. "My dear friends, we have a serious development all across the land. This itinerant preacher, the carpenter from Nazareth, is going all over Galilee, preaching and teaching a way of life that is contrary to what we are all accustomed to, and contrary to the wishes of Adonai. He is destroying all the good will we have built up over the years, and dismantling the doctrines we have so painstakingly taught over and over again. And we have shown the people how to live, as pleasing children of God. Now this impostor, this servant of Satan, who works miracles in his name, has come and is destroying all we hold dear and precious. He is destroying the work of our God among us. He has to be stopped".

A Pharisee from Bethsaida spoke, "Jethro, I heard that he had cured a man's hand in your synagogue on the Sabbath," he said with disdain.

"Yes, he has absolutely no regard for the Sabbath. Why, he and his disciples were seen picking corn in the corn fields and eating, this very Sabbath. We caught them red handed and he sought to justify their breaking of the Sabbath by misconstruing our Sacred Scriptures," one of the Pharisees said.

"Not only does he have no regard for the Sabbath and other people's property, he and his disciples do not wash their hands before eating," another said.

There was a gasp among those present. Another spoke, "and he and his disciples do not fast at all. He overindulges in food and drink, is forever at feasts and he is a drunkard and a glutton. He associates with loose women," said another.

"As regards all those wonders he is supposed to have performed, I think all those so-called miracles of his, are magic or tricks of sorts. He is a good magician, and a sorcerer, and a trickster, he has it all prearranged to dupe the people."

"It may be so," Jethro said, "but I knew the man with the withered hand, so he definitely has magical powers of sorts, but as you say, they cannot come from God, for he is not a man of God, for as you have all remarked and observed, he has no respect for the Sabbath, or our laws and traditions, he associates with tax-collectors, prostitutes, sinners, and touches the unclean and even dines with them. He even has a tax-collector as one of his disciples, who goes around with him. And he also has three women, one of them a woman who was possessed of seven demons from Magdala, as his disciples. And it has been reported that he cast out several demons from some demoniacs and sent the demons into pigs that went over a cliff in Bethsaida."

"It can only be by the power of the ruler of demons that he casts out demons. I tell you this man is dangerous and must be stopped," Jethro said.

Many others spoke condemning Yeshua, his teaching and example and his way of life. Another spoke, "This man is evil parading as good. He goes around spreading falsehood and living like a sinner and unclean and he is defiling the Temple and dismantling our Laws. He must be stopped."

Another spoke, a Pharisee, "Gentlemen, I am Daniel, and I came all the way from Jerusalem. Our leaders there are as concerned as you are. They have sent me to investigate, and see for myself what was happening here in Galilee. News of this man, this impostor, this carpenter from Nazareth has reached our ears, and we are as concerned as you are, that the very fabric of our faith is being eroded, dismantled by this man's spurious and preposterous teachings. From what I have heard here today from all of you has confirmed our suspicions and our worst fears. We have to stop this man and stop the spreading of his lies, and stop the contempt he shows for our laws and traditions and way of life."

"Gentlemen," Baasha stood up to speak. "I have spent a lot of private time with this man Yeshua. He is a good friend of Zadok, the blacksmith in Tiberias. Zadok is married to my niece. This man Yeshua grew up with Zadok in Nazareth, and he told me so much about him. And Yeshua spent time with us, and I got to know him more intimately. He is not the fake you make him out to be. He is a man of integrity. Some of his methods may be questionable, but I believe his heart is in the right place. We need to engage with him, get him on our side, and not challenge him. He has a strong following. People love him and he has a way with them, speaks their language, tells them all simple stories, stories that are so powerful and have such a lasting impact. I think we, who are the teachers and leaders of the people, have a lot to learn from this man. We have to get him on our side," Baasha pleaded.

The rest of those present ignored Baasha, as an old and demented man. They ignored what he was saying. They wanted to get rid of Yeshua, have nothing to do with him. He was not a man of God, could not be. His contempt for the Sabbath and his breaking of the Laws of the faith they all held dear showed without a doubt that he was not sent by God as he claims. He must be stopped.

After hours of discussion, Daniel finally spoke, "We have our people watching this Yeshua carefully. Watching his every move and listening to all his teaching and all his deeds and reporting to us in Jerusalem. We believe he is in fact on his way to Jerusalem. We will be ready for him. I ask you to continue to watch him and report to us. I thank you gentlemen for organising this important gathering. I will be heading back to Jerusalem in the morning to speak with the leaders there, shalom to you all, my brothers." And with those words, Daniel left.

Chapter Fifty-Four
An Interlude

Yeshua and his disciples arrived in Nazareth. Yeshua sent Andreus and Shimon to Achim and his father, to speak to them about accommodation. Between them, Rebecca, and Gamaliel, who now was quite feeble, Yeshua was confident they could find sufficient accommodation for them all. Rebecca let it be known that she would be able to provide accommodation for Miriam and Lucia at their home.

"We will stay in Nazareth for three days. I will not be speaking here during this time, for a prophet is not welcome in his own hometown. I want to spend some time with my mother," Yeshua said.

When they saw Nazareth in the distance, Yeshua's heart skipped a beat as usual. Rebecca came up and walked next to him. "Yeshua it is so good to be back in Nazareth," she said.

"It sure is Rebecca, it sure is," Yeshua said.

"Oh Yeshua," Miriam cried as she heard her son, Yeshua's voice greeting her, as he entered their home. She ran and hugged her son for dear life. "Oh, Yeshua, I missed you so. How have you been, you are looking so thin, are you eating properly. I must start the fire. Make you some of your favourite food. I have some wine which I kept for you. Have a drink while I prepare something to eat."

"Mother, sit down, don't worry about cooking. I am not hungry. I am so pleased to see you Immah. How have you been, you are looking well," Yeshua said, pleased to see his mother was looking good and healthy.

"I have been hearing such great things about you Yeshua. Preaching and teaching all over Galilee, and healing so many sick people. And Rebecca is travelling with you. Are the two of you becoming close? Will you betroth her Yeshua?" Miriam asked, hopefully.

Yeshua smiled. "You won't give up, will you mother. You know I cannot marry. My time is too short. I will not be around much longer," Yeshua said.

"What are you talking about Yeshua?" Miriam asked with concern.

Yeshua had a sense of the plotting that had already begun. He was conscious of his teaching, as being radical and revolutionary, he had come to change the face of the earth, and that would be a great shock to the existing systems. He had come to spread the truth about Yahweh, about his ways. He had come to lead the people out of darkness and into the light. Moses led the people out of slavery in Egypt, where the people were enslaved for over four hundred years. But they only got themselves enslaved in other ways more sinister, subtle and disintegrating. They have chosen the darkness for the light, the false for the truth, the evil for the good, and the self for God. He had been sent to set them free from the slavery to self and sin.

"Never mind mother. I am home now. I have come to spend some time with you." Yeshua sensed he would most likely not see his mother again, at least not here in Nazareth. He sensed the powers of evil afoot. He placed those feelings aside and wanted to spend quality time with his mother, whom he loved so much and missed so much.

Yeshua shared with his mother all his experiences, the people he met and the friends who were now his disciples. "Mother I would like us to have a feast here in the next couple of days, so you can meet all my friends, my travelling companions, who are assisting me in my work," Yeshua said.

"That will be good, Yeshua. I would love to meet your friends. I will go to the markets early in the morning and get some produce," Miriam said.

"Don't worry Immah, just tell me the things you need, and I will get them for you," Yeshua said. And Rebecca will help, as will my other disciples.

"Yeshua, how many friends are travelling with you doing your work?" Miriam asked.

"Let me see, we are now eleven men, and three women," Yeshua said, "You'll meet them all, Immah. I am so fortunate to have them with me; they are like family to me. Rebecca too, I am so pleased to have her with me. She is a great friend and support."

"Yeshua, how are you managing, how are you supporting yourself, are you still doing woodwork?" Miriam asked.

"Unfortunately, mother, I do not have time for carpentry now, as all my time is doing the work for which I was born, for what you brought me into the world to do. As far as support goes, Yahweh is looking after me, after us. We have lots of benefactors, of support from many people. Some of those travelling with me are fishermen from Capernaum and Bethsaida, who have a thriving business there, and they continue to get funds from their business, and I have our friend, Miriam from Magdala, whom you know, and whose father is well-to-do, owns vineyards and a winery in Capernaum, of course you know all this. He also supports us and there are a number of women who support us and our work as well. And wherever we go people are so eager to support our work. So, you see mother, we are well cared for and you have nothing to worry about. And that is also why I am able to send you what I do," Yeshua said. "And if the worse comes to the worse, I can always find some work to support me. So do not worry mother," Yeshua said.

"And how is Gamaliel?" Yeshua asked.

"He has grown old, Yeshua, and quite feeble. And he is not very happy with the rabbi and the new teachers at the school. He feels they are taking backward steps with what and how they are teaching."

Yeshua later met with Gamaliel who wasn't looking so good. He had aged considerably and Yeshua felt for him. Gamaliel, however, was delighted to see Yeshua, his star pupil.

"Yeshua, you are looking well, a bit leaner than when I last saw you. Are you well?"

"I am fine, my young friend," Yeshua teased his dearest friend, mentor and teacher. "I have never been fitter, walking miles and miles all over Galilee. And now we will be walking all the way to the coast, to Caesarea and then on to Jerusalem. We will most likely then cross the Jordan, at Jericho, and then all the way up to Bethsaida, before we come back to Nazareth, in the far future, which I fear may be my last visit, Gamaliel," Yeshua said. Yeshua didn't think he would be back in Nazareth again, but he didn't want to alarm his dear friend.

"Be careful, Yeshua, that road from Jerusalem to Jericho is very dangerous, full of outlaws, who will harm you and rob you," Gamaliel said.

"Not to worry, Gamaliel, I have eleven strong men with me, four of them fishermen from Capernaum and Bethsaida. The crims won't have a chance," Yeshua said with a smile. "And I and all the men have our staffs with us," Yeshua added.

"And why do you say the next time you visit here, will be your last?" Gamaliel asked.

"I just have that sense Gamaliel. The storm clouds are gathering, and I just have this feeling that there are plotters afoot who are gathering and planning my downfall. Wherever I go I encounter firm opposition from a group, they are mostly Pharisees, Scribes and Sadducees, Elders and they seem to come from all over, and I think they also have spies following me around," Yeshua said.

"I can understand, Yeshua, you are a threat to them. They feel you are knocking them off their perch, from where they have ruled the people with fear, the fear of God. You have come bringing a message of hope and liberation but they want to keep the people enslaved so they can rule over them. They are not even aware of this Yeshua; they are like lords and keeping the people as their slaves, their religious slaves. And they wield power with their knowledge of the Law, which they use to keep the people enslaved. You have come to tear those laws apart and set them free, and they feel threatened. They want to hold on to their position," Gamaliel said.

"You are right, Gamaliel, my friend, but wrong in saying I have come to tear the laws apart, I have come not to destroy thc Law but to complete them, to perfect them, to interpret them for the people, and not scare the living daylights out of them. God is a God of love and compassion, not one wishing to overburden them with superficial and onerous laws. Any law that is without love and compassion is not a right law," Yeshua said.

"Are you going to preach in the synagogue, while you are here, Yeshua?" Gamaliel asked.

"No, I don't think so, last time I was not made welcome. You know the old adage, Gamaliel, 'a prophet is not welcome in his own hometown,' well that seems to have rung true with me. I have come to spend time with mother and just catch up with old friends, with you," Yeshua said.

"Things are not the same here in Nazareth, Yeshua, the new rabbi and Pharisees that are here, are poisoning the people, with the ridiculous minutiae of the Law, and people are so more fearful than before. I no longer teach at the school and I miss that," Gamaliel said.

"I'm sorry to hear that Gamaliel. And I am sure the students miss you, and the people miss your sermons, and your humour, it seems that the God that is preached seems to be a God without humour, a serious, stern and austere God, when in fact God is a God of joy, of humour, of laughter. I am just thinking now, Gamaliel that I have been too serious myself, and need to tell people, show people more of my fun side, and God's fun side, the humorous side of God. This was good talking to you, Gamaliel, as usual, you have inspired my theme for my next sermon, to speak of a fun-loving and humorous God," Yeshua said grinning.

Gamaliel laughed. "You are right, Yeshua, our people are so intense, especially those who are religious, they pray and sacrifice and fast and do good, but with dreary faces and dispositions, they need to lighten up," Gamaliel said. "You need to lighten up their days Yeshua, and lighten up their lives. Unburden them," Gamaliel said, with a smile.

"I shall do that, Gamaliel. I am so glad to see you again and to receive your guidance and wisdom. Are you now an Elder here in the synagogue?" Yeshua asked.

"No, not really, I am not officially an Elder. The rabbi and his crew have made it clear that my services are no longer needed. They have put me out to pasture. And they have discouraged, more like forbade the people to seek my counsel," Gamaliel said.

"I'm so sorry to hear that, Gamaliel, how short-sighted and stupid of them, you are the kindest and wisest man I have ever known, they do not realise how much they are depriving the people of what you have to offer," Yeshua said. "You will always be my guide and mentor, Gamaliel," Yeshua said warmly.

"Thank you, Yeshua. Tell me now of all that has happened with you. I heard so much about you, from people, who heard you speak, and from some of my friends who visited me from around Galilee, who encountered you on your journeys. They related to me the stories you tell the people. I am so glad to hear them, Yeshua. And they have told me of the great miracles of healing you have done, Yeshua, the power of our God is with you. I knew that from the time I first taught you," Gamaliel said.

Yeshua then shared with Gamaliel all that had happened so far and he sought Gamaliel's counsel. Gamaliel was so happy to listen to his star student and to learn all that Yeshua was doing for the glory of God.

"So, Rebecca is with you, as one of your disciples?" Gamaliel said, with delight. "She was always so sweet on you and had eyes for no one else. When you left Nazareth, she was pining for a while and came to see me and we talked. She never seemed to be interested in any of the boys or men around here and she always spoke about you Yeshua. She believed that you two would be together one day. I told her that she would, that you two would be together, but not as husband and wife. She eventually accepted that," Gamaliel continues, "But now it seems that her dream has come true," Gamaliel added.

"It has Gamaliel. She is such a good friend and support and confidante. I have two other women accompanying me and supporting me in my work and providing me with such good counsel, counsel only women can give," Yeshua said.

"You see Yeshua, you are different and enlightened and forward thinking, and may I say radical, you have women travelling with you as your disciples. Men and women travelling together who are not married couples, some of the men even married, and who have left their wives at home; this is unheard of Yeshua, and I can understand why the religious leaders are against you. You are too revolutionary for them. Do carry on, you are a breath of fresh air in this stinking climate of burdensome laws by a supposedly cruel, severe, vindictive and punishing God" Gamaliel said. "You are changing all that and people hate change, especially the powers that be, they do not want to lose the power they have over the people. This is why the Pharisees, Scribes and Sadducees hate your guts," Gamaliel said.

"Tell me about the other women you have as your disciples," Gamaliel asked, with interest.

"Miriam is from Magdala. She had suffered all her life. People believed that she was possessed by several demons. I first met her briefly when I did that trip of mine around the Sea of Galilee more than ten years ago. When I started on my mission and landed in Magdala I caught up with a family of friends that I had made on that trip and I enquired of them about Miriam. They took me to her. She was in a bad way. She was severely depressed and incoherent. I prayed with her and held her hand

342

and those spirits of depression left her for good, never to return. Her father is a well-to-do businessman, who owns several vineyards in Magdala and Capernaum and a winery in Capernaum. They support us in our mission and my home base in Capernaum is on their property. Miriam is such a beautiful person. She has suffered much and is so understanding of the suffering of others, especially women. And wherever we go, the women and girls come to her and she teaches them and counsels them. And she is my confidante too, especially in how I ought to relate to women. I have learned so much from her and from Lucia who is from Capernaum."

Yeshua then related how Lucia had suffered for twelve years from haemorrhaging and was cured and how she is such an asset with Miriam and Rebecca, as his disciples.

"Yeshua, this is a good thing you are doing. We are so backward in the way we treat women as inferior beings, when we are equal, different but equal and we complement each other and can learn so much from each other. I'm afraid, it will take centuries for this male domination to eventually give way to a semblance of equality between men and women, definitely not in our time, Yeshua, but you are making a start," Gamaliel said.

Yeshua and Gamaliel spent most of the day together. They shared a meal and a couple of cups of wine. By the time Yeshua left, Gamaliel was feeling so much better. They hugged each other as they parted.

The next few days, Yeshua spent time with relatives and friends and also with Rebecca's parents. They were so pleased to see Yeshua and to hear him tell of how great their daughter Rebecca was doing, and how much she has been helping to spread the Good News of God's love and compassion. Rebecca's parents were so glad that she was in such good company and that they were doing such wonderful things all over Galilee.

Chapter Fifty-Five
God Is Laughing

Notwithstanding the fact that Yeshua was not made welcome the last time he was in Nazareth, the rabbi did come and invite Yeshua to talk to the people on the Sabbath. Yeshua sensed he was being put to the test and that he would be spied on, but he accepted the challenge.

Yeshua was impressed with the renovations in the hall; it was now looking like a proper synagogue. Yeshua needed no introduction. But the synagogue was overflowing with people, not only from Nazareth, but from elsewhere. There was not enough room in the synagogue, so the overflow of people hung around the entrance and at the windows wanting to listen to Yeshua.

Yeshua looked across the synagogue at the people present. His disciples as usual were scattered around the place. And as usual the men and women were separated to different sides. He saw his mother looking so proud, as was Gamaliel. Yeshua then smiled at the people and began

"My dearest brothers and sisters of Nazareth, and from elsewhere in Galilee and beyond, I welcome you to our little village. I am so proud and so happy to be back with you. It has been a while. I am grateful for the invitation to speak to you. And what I want to speak about was inspired by my conversation with my dearest friend, teacher and mentor, Gamaliel."

The people turned to look at Gamaliel, who was sitting somewhere in the centre. Gamaliel nodded and smiled in appreciation at Yeshua's words. Then Yeshua continued.

"What I want to speak to you about is the Good News. And part of the Good News is that our God is not a cruel and demanding and sour God, who wants to overburden us with countless laws that make no sense to our daily living. Our God is a God of joy, of peace, of love. I want to speak to you today of a God that laughs, a God with a sense of humour. A sense of humour is one of the precious gifts God gives us. God cannot give what he hasn't got.

"We never hear about God laughing, do we, or God's sense of humour. I was thrilled as I was reading a psalm from the Sacred Scroll yesterday in preparation for my teaching today. We are so fortunate to have these beautiful songs, these psalms, written by our ancestor and Prophet, Kind David. I am proud to be one of the line of David. I am a descendent of David, who was a descendent of our Father Abraham. I have checked and discovered, that there are fourteen generations from Abraham to David and fourteen from David to the exile of our people, in Babylon, and fourteen then to my birth, in a stable in Bethlehem. I was born in a stable in Bethlehem more than thirty-one years ago. It so happened when my mother, Miriam, who is here with us today, was pregnant with me, and close to giving birth."

The people then turned to look at Mary, who was smiling, as were all the women around her. Yeshua continued, "Those of you old enough will remember the decree that went out from the Emperor Augustus that all the world should be registered. It was the first registration and was taken while Quirinius was Governor. Everyone had to go to their own towns to be registered. Yosef my father from this town of Nazareth had to go all the way to the city of David in Judaea called Bethlehem, because he was descended from the house and family of David. And while we were in Bethlehem, I was born in a stable, because my parents could find no room in the inn. Of course I don't remember that, but they told me I was quite happy to be amongst the animals," Yeshua said, smiling broadly.

There were many smiles and laughter among the people, especially the women. And they looked towards Miriam, who was also smiling broadly.

Yeshua continued, "Now I didn't mean to give you all that information about my birth, but it simply came to mind as I mention our Father David and the songs, the psalms he wrote. I came across these lines in his second psalm, of God's Chosen King, that made me laugh with our God. David wrote these words."

Yeshua then recited the psalm from the Scroll of Scriptures.

"Why do the nations conspire?
And the peoples plot in vain?
The kings of the earth set themselves
and the rulers take counsel together,
against the Lord and his anointed, saying,
Let us burst their bonds asunder,
and cast their cords from us.
He who sits in the heavens, laughs,
the Lord has them in derision."

Yeshua, while unfolding his theme was also having a dig at his detractors, the Pharisees, Scribes and Sadducees from other places in Galilee, who were sitting up front and listening carefully to his every word.

Yeshua continued, "We do seem to have an image of a stern and serious God, but I would like to correct that image, an image of God smiling often, full of laughter and humour and joy of living. Even when he chides us, it is not with a stern face or a pointing finger, but rather a warm smile, like that of a loving father or mother correcting their child.

"When I was in our capital city of Sepphoris not so long ago, I was walking past the front door of a public eating place. I heard so much laughter that I had to enter the place and see for myself where this laughter was coming from. A group of about six women were sharing a meal and they were so full of happiness and joy, chatting animatedly, and laughing heartily. I looked at them as I passed and felt the joy they shared, the joy of the Lord. They brought a smile to my face and joy to my heart. I went about my business and had to pass that place more than an hour later, the women were still full of humour and joy and laughter. I had to approach them and with a smile on my face, I said, 'you're still at it.' They gave me the warmest of smiles. I walked away with a spring in my step and joy in my heart. Joy my friends, joy begets joy. Humour, fun, joy, is so infectious. I felt the presence of the Lord with them, enjoying their company. I felt the Lord's presence. To witness such incidences and be part of such joy is what our God desires, for he is a God of joy."

Yeshua continued. He took up the scroll and said, "Let me read to you these words from the great prophet Isaiah who describes the coming Messiah as a Man of Sorrows, the Suffering Servant."

The people were puzzled; Yeshua said he was speaking about a fun-loving God, God's sense of humour, why is he reading from Isaiah about the suffering servant.

"I know, you may be wondering why I choose to read these words from Isaiah, but bear with me, and all will be revealed," Yeshua said with a smile. He continued, "Isaiah writes, 'He was despised and rejected by others; a man of suffering and acquainted with infirmity; and as one from whom others hide their faces he was despised and we held him of no account.'

"Yet in the chapter before that, Isaiah tells Zion to rejoice. He writes:

"Put on your beautiful garments, O Jerusalem, the holy city…
How beautiful upon the mountains
are the feet of the messenger who announces peace,
who brings good news,
who announces salvation…
Listen! Your sentinels lift up their voices
together they sing for joy.

"And in the Book of Ecclesiastes, we read that everything has its time:

"For everything there is a season, and a time…
a time to be born, and a time to die…
a time to weep and a time to laugh;
a time to mourn and a time to dance."

Yeshua continued, "In the midst of all the wars, violence, pain and suffering, the Scriptures abound with exclamations of joy and calls to rejoice. Another psalm of David's is about a harvest of joy. Let me conclude this talk by calling Miriam to come forward to sing this psalm to you, for the psalms were written by David to be sung. This psalm encapsulates this spirit of joy."

Yeshua had already asked Miriam to prepare for the singing of the psalm, and at Yeshua's invitation she came forward. The people were surprised but intrigued; women were not allowed in the men's court, let alone in the sanctuary. They looked at the rabbi and the Pharisees and the others with them, they had stern and disapproving looks on their faces. They were livid. The disciples were concerned. They thought that again Yeshua was being provocative. They had warned him about the dangers of provoking the Pharisees and their cohort. Yeshua seemed unperturbed and welcomed Miriam with a warm smile.

Miriam then sang, in an angelic voice that moved the people:

"When the Lord restored the fortunes of Zion,
we were like those who dream.
Then our mouth was filled with laughter,
and our tongue with shouts of joy…
May they who sow in tears
reap with shouts of joy
Those who go out weeping,
bearing the seed for sowing,
shall come home with shouts of joy,

carrying their sheaves."

After Miriam's singing, all was quiet. Some were moved to tears by the singing. Miriam had such a sweet voice. The women especially were beside themselves. Yeshua then left the sanctuary during the silence, without a word. He joined the people for the rest of the service.

Before the service had ended Yeshua rose and walked out, his disciples followed. Yeshua did not want to remain and be attacked by the Pharisees and their group, and spoil the mood of the people. He knew that he had upset the Pharisees and their cohort, and that they would retaliate and seek to undermine him in the presence of the people. He was not frightened of them, or not up to the challenge, but he wanted the people to go on their way with joy in their heart, and the sweetness of Miriam's singing.

As they were well on their way to Miriam's place, Yeshua spoke to his disciples. "Today is a day of rest. So have a good rest. We will have a quiet day tomorrow. I won't be talking at the synagogue. I will let the people reflect on what I had said today, and to continue to relish Miriam's singing and remain with joy in their hearts," Yeshua said. He then turned to Miriam and complimented her. "Miriam your singing was absolutely beautiful, you sing like an angel." The others all agreed and complimented Miriam as well.

The following evening arrived and they had their feast. The women were helping Miriam, Yeshua's mother with the preparations. But Yeshua got the men involved. It was only Yeshua and his disciples present, but Yeshua made Gamaliel his guest of honour. Gamaliel was so overwhelmed and delighted to meet all the disciples and to get to know them, and he was also delighted to meet Miriam and Lucia and he complimented Miriam on her singing.

They feasted well into the night. There was much laughter and fun and they shared experiences that made them laugh and that brought joy into their lives. Miriam, Yeshua's mother shared how Yeshua caused her the greatest sorrow and then the greatest joy, when at twelve he was lost for three days and then found again. "I was beyond consolation. My heart was filled with fear and anxiety and my heart was breaking. Those three days were the worst days of my life. And when I saw Yeshua in the Temple debating with the Teachers I was overwhelmed with joy. All that pain disappeared in an instant and my heart was filled with a joy that I cannot describe," Miriam said.

"Did you or Yosef not want to slap Yeshua for causing you so much grief," Shimon the former Zealot asked.

"No Shimon, I know Yosef was mad for a moment, but then relief just swamped him, as it did for me. The joy then just took over and flooded my heart," Miriam said.

"I will never forget that experience," Yeshua said. "My father never reprimanded or punished me, although I know he had an instant desire to discipline me, not for the grief I caused him, but for the pain I caused mother. It is something I regret. But my only defence, is that I was only twelve, not yet a teenager and had no sense at that age, and thinking only of myself and being thoughtless. I say sorry again Mother, I hope I have made up with the joy I have caused you ever since," Yeshua said, as he went and hugged his mother warmly.

"Yes, you have, Yeshua, yes, you have," Miriam said, as she was being held by her son in his arms.

There was much joy that evening. Yeshua made a request that Miriam sing again that psalm of David's to close the evening. They all sat down and listened as she sang.

Some of the men were staying with Achim, Shimon and Andreus were with Yeshua, and the rest were staying with some of Miriam's neighbours and friends. Yeshua accompanied Gamaliel home, and the women joined them as they were staying at Rebecca's, that was on the way.

Yeshua said goodnight to his friend and mentor, wondering if he would see him again. Yeshua then walked home alone under the stars. He felt good, with joy in his heart.

Chapter Fifty-Six
The Resurrection and the Life

Yeshua and his disciples left Nazareth the next morning after breakfast. It was a sad parting between Yeshua and his mother. "I will be back soon mother," Yeshua said, trying to comfort her.

Yeshua still had the sense that he only had less than a few more years to do the work his Father had sent him to do. Time was of the essence. All the disciples met at his place and from there they headed for the town of Nain, a name that meant 'beautiful' and it was an apt name for the town had a reputation for its beauty.

Nain was just over eight miles south of Nazareth, so Andreus estimated they would be in Nain in time for a midday meal. They were all in a good mood. They had a most pleasant last couple of days in Nazareth, with Yeshua's talk on God's sense of humour rubbing off on them, and it was most appropriate that Yeshua arranged for them to have such a great feast last night. They knew though that tough times lay ahead. But for now, they would enjoy the sunshine.

They walked for about six miles and passed a few little villages tucked away, and a distance from the road they were travelling. They came to a small settlement of people on some level ground at the foot of a beautiful mountain; they knew to be Mount Tabor.

Yeshua and his disciples stopped to rest and spoke with some of the people from the village. They were a small community of only a few families, no more than fifty to sixty people and children who lived there. They were poor; they lived in little homemade huts. Yeshua, decided to stop and rest there for a while. There was plenty of open space to rest. Yeshua then said, "I will like to climb Mount Tabor, it is so appealing and just crying out to me to be climbed, how high you think it is?" Yeshua asked.

"Looks like over a thousand feet, to me, at least a thousand and a half," Nathanael estimated.

"Good, I'll be on my way then; in the meantime, you can get to know the people here." Yeshua then went on his way. While he was gone, the disciples met with the people. They were quite reserved but friendly and surprised to see so many men travelling together and women with them and they were taking the trouble to visit their tiny village and engage with them, for most people would just shun them and pass by. But as they were off the beaten track few people stopped there anyway and the curious ones who did, when they saw them would scamper away immediately. The people wanted to know why the disciples stopped at their village.

"We are disciples of Yeshua, have you not heard of him," Shimon said.

"No, we have not," one of the men spoke.

"My brother and a few others of our group, were disciples of Johanan the Prophet, who was baptising the people in the River Jordan, he was calling us to repentance for the day of judgement would come. Herod had him arrested and he is now languishing in prison," Shimon said. "Have you heard of him?" Shimon asked.

They said they had not.

"Johanan was a prophet who baptised people in the River Jordan. He spoke of one who was to come after him, who is greater than him, a prophet, a man sent from God who would teach us the truth, show us the way, and liberate us from the darkness. We heard from Johanan disciples about Yeshua, what happened when Johanan baptised him, a voice from heaven was heard saying about Yeshua, 'This is my beloved Son, listen to him'."

"We met Yeshua, in Capernaum and Bethsaida, and elsewhere in Galilee. He is our teacher, guide, mentor, he is also a healer," Andreus said.

"What kind of a person is he," the spokesman from the village, asked.

"He is like no other man we have ever met. We were so impressed with Johanan, but Yeshua is a man of such deep wisdom and charity and compassion. He says what he means and speaks the truth without fear. He is not afraid of anyone, and a person's rank or living circumstances means nothing to him, he treats all with kindness, love and compassion. He has a special relationship and love for the poor, and those regarded by our faith, as sinners, the tax-collectors, fallen women, the afflicted, those spurned and cast out by the rest of the people," Johanan said.

"I am a tax-collector, I was chief tax collector for Galilee, and Yeshua simply came up to me and invited me to be one of his disciples. And he dined with my fellow tax-collectors," Mattheus said.

"And he has the greatest of respect for women," Miriam said, "and he called me too to be his disciple. I was much tormented for most of my life, and people believed that I was possessed of several demons, Yeshua befriended me, and cured me and invited me to be his disciple," Miriam said.

"And I had been suffering from a flow of bleeding for twelve years and everyone avoided me for fear of being unclean. I believed that if I could get near to Yeshua and he touched me I would be cured. But I knew no one would allow me near him, so I covered my face and sneaked up behind him, and said to myself if only I can touch the hem of his garment, I would be healed. I managed to do that and instantly I was cured. I later spoke with Miriam and we asked Yeshua if I could follow him and be his disciple, and here I am," Lucia said.

Rebecca told them of her growing up with Yeshua in Nazareth.

The men of the village were in awe, for men to travel around with women, who were not their wives or family members would be frowned upon and regarded with suspicion and disdain. And here were these men and women, disciples of Yeshua on the road with him.

The women of the village were impressed.

Shimon told them about how Yeshua calmed the winds and the sea and the disciples told of how Yeshua cast out demons and sent them into pigs that went hurtling over the cliff at Gergesa.

The people were absolutely enthralled with what the disciples had to say about Yeshua. They were now so eager to meet him. They made the disciples welcome and shared with them the little they had.

It was late afternoon when Yeshua returned. The disciples asked him what it was like and he told them that there was a track to the top of the mountain and it seemed well trodden. The view from there was spectacular and he spent some time in prayer.

"Mountains are sacred places," he told them and spoke of Mount Sinai, where Yahweh appeared to Moses and gave him the Ten Commandments.

"So did you see a burning bush up there, and did you hear the voice of God?" Thomas said, tongue in cheek.

"No Thomas, I didn't see any burning bush but I did hear the voice of God, not as He spoke to Moses, nevertheless I heard him in my heart. Up there on the top of the mountain the air is so clean and pure and sweet and it is so quiet and still that it is so easy to hear the voice of God and feel his closeness."

Yeshua was in good spirits. The disciples told him about their meeting with the people and that they would like to meet him and listen to him speak. There were only about fifty or sixty people and children living in the village. Yeshua was pleased to meet with them, spend time with them and get to know them.

That evening the people gathered around an open fire and prepared a simple meal of soup, bread and figs for Yeshua, for they learned from his disciples, that figs were Yeshua's favourite. Yeshua was most appreciative.

Yeshua sat on the ground surrounded by the people, some widows and orphans among them, men, women and children. Yeshua was touched by the warmth and kindness of these people. They were evidently poor and forgotten, outcasts. But they nevertheless were happy to welcome these strangers into their midst.

Yeshua spoke to them; he repeated some of the Beatitudes that he gave to the people on a much smaller mount in Capernaum. "Blessed are you who are poor, for yours is the kingdom of God. Blessed are you who are hungry now, for you will be filled. Blessed are you who weep now, for you will laugh." Yeshua also told them the story of the rich man Dives and the poor man Lazarus and they delighted and laughed when Yeshua told them of the fate of Dives. He also shared with them, how he was born in a stable in Bethlehem and how his parents had to flee into Egypt as refugees and outcasts and had to go without for the four years they lived in a foreign land.

"Yours is the kingdom of God," he said to the people. "God hears your cries, he sees your suffering, he longs for you, and he loves you and cares for you and is beside you every moment of your day and prepares a place for you. So do not give up hope. I see your children playing. They have so little and yet they find so much to amuse them and they are filled with fun and laughter and happiness. Your love for them is what sustains them and your love for each other is what sustains you. God is love and if you love one another, then God is in you and with you."

The people brought their children to Yeshua and he spoke to them and teased them and tickled them and made them laugh. There were also sick ones among them and Yeshua blessed them.

While Yeshua was up the mountain, his disciples had told the people about Yeshua's power of healing, so they brought their sick to Yeshua. They did not ask to be healed, but Yeshua asked them if they believed they could be healed and when they answered, 'If it is your will, we can be healed. We believe you have been sent by God and God is with you.'

Yeshua healed their sick and there was much rejoicing. Yeshua and the disciples remained with the people for the rest of the day. The people offered their little huts to Yeshua and his disciples and they themselves were prepared to sleep in the open.

Yeshua refused. They lit a fire and Yeshua and his disciples camped around the fire for the night. Some of the women came and offered Miriam, Rebecca and Lucia a place to sleep in their little huts. Miriam, Rebecca, and Lucia thanked them but told them they would sleep with the others around the fire.

Yeshua and his disciples stayed two more days with them, sharing their lives, listening to their stories, bringing them comfort.

After two days the disciples were ready to leave. But Yeshua said they would stay another day. When alone with his disciples on the evening before they planned to leave, Yeshua spoke to his disciples. "These are the people to whom I have come, to whom I've been sent, the lost sheep of the house of Israel, the forgotten ones of history. We hear only of kings and prophets and of the powerful and the rich and famous, but it is these little ones that are dearest to the Father, and to whom I have been sent, and whom we are to serve. These and all who have been wrongly labelled as sinners or unclean are the ones that are dearest to our heavenly Father, and it is to these that I have been sent. Yahweh sent me to bring them hope and consolation and salvation. We have to care for them, and love them, and do what we can for them. So, Mattheus before we leave, I want you to talk to their Elders and give them all of our funds that we do not need to survive for the next while. We have not really known poverty as these people do, so we can live poorly if needs be, until we receive what we need."

"I keep telling you that I have come to make the blind see, the lame walk, the deaf hear. But I have come to save not only people who are physically so, for many are blind to the truth, blind to the plight of the poor and needy. People are walking in the dark and we have to lead them out of the darkness and into the light. We all look up to the rich and famous and the powerful with envy, yet it is not those who we need to envy. We are not to seek wealth, power or prestige. We are to seek and offer love and compassion to those favoured by our father in heaven, all those who suffer in any way; those who are persecuted and cast out because they are considered to be sinners and unclean. They are the lepers, the prostitutes, the tax-collectors, the unclean, widows, orphans and all the others left to fend for themselves. They are looked down upon as sinners and because of their sins people believe that God has punished them. We have to keep reminding ourselves and teach that this is not true. The poor, the oppressed and the outcasts are not so because they have sinned. Sin is not the cause of poverty or the sign of Yahweh's displeasure and likewise riches and success and power is not the sign of Yahweh's blessing. No matter what our forefathers have written about this. I have come to change that way of thinking and for all of us to realise that God is a God first and foremost for the forgotten ones, those who are poor, and all those who are despised by the rest of humankind. These people, with whom we have stayed these past days, have so little, yet they are rich in the eyes of God. They may know little of the Law, but they live its spirit to the full. These people suffer shame and disgrace for they have to beg for a living. So, we must never pass one who begs without stopping and sharing what we have, even if a kind word or a listening ear is all we have." Yeshua continued talking to his disciples in this vein. They listened and learned.

None of them had any questions. What Yeshua was saying to them, he had said before, not in so many words, but here living these last few days among the poor and destitute, and the outcasts they began to understand.

It was now getting late, and all became silent, when a woman approached. She went to Miriam and asked if she could speak with her and the other women. Miriam, Rebecca, and Lucia got up and they went with the woman. When they were a distance from the men the woman spoke.

"Miriam, Rebecca, Lucia, I have heard Yeshua speak, and I have witnessed his healing, but above all his sincerity, his respect and love for us and his deep compassion. He treats us with such love. And I was deeply moved by what he taught us over these past few days. I live here with my mother and father, I would like to join you and follow Yeshua, be his disciple with you all and help him in his work in whatever way I can," she said. "And I want to learn all I can from him," she added.

"What is your name?" Miriam asked.

"My name is Rachel," she responded.

"You are very young, Rachel, are you sure this is what you wish?" Miriam asked.

"Have you spoken to your parents, and what do they think about this," Lucia asked.

"I am nineteen and will be twenty in a couple of months, so I am old enough to make my own decisions. And yes, I have spoken to my parents and they are quite in agreement, in fact they are pleased for me to do this," Rachel said.

"Come then, let us speak to Yeshua," Miriam said.

The woman found Yeshua still awake, as if he was waiting for them. He had observed what was going on and had an idea of what was afoot. So, he rose to his feet and waited as he heard them approaching. He walked towards them and smiled. "What is it you want?" he said to the women, and looking straight at Rachel.

"Yeshua, this is Rachel, she would like to join us, be another of your disciples," Miriam said.

Yeshua responded, "When I was on the top of the mountain, with Yahweh, I spoke to him about more women to assist me in spreading his message, and I asked if he would call one of the women from this place. So yes Rachel, Yahweh and I wish you to join us. Go home now, and say your goodbyes, we leave at first light."

"Rachel was so overcome; she wanted to rush into Yeshua's arms but restrained herself and thanked Yeshua profusely, her heart overflowing, as she ran home."

"Now I think, we can all have a good night's sleep," Yeshua said with a smile.

When the day arrived for them to leave the people gathered around to say goodbye. Their spokesman thanked them for their visit. They thanked Yeshua for all he had taught them. And they thanked the disciples for their friendship and the women thanked Miriam, Rebecca and Lucia for their time with them and for their kindness.

Miriam then spoke to the people. "We are most grateful for your kindness, friendship and hospitality. We have enjoyed out stay with you and we will forever hold you in our hearts. We will never be able to forget you because Rachel is now one of us; she has joined us as one of Yeshua's disciples. I ask for your prayers for us as you will always be in ours."

The village people were overjoyed and proud, especially the women, that one of their own was now a disciple of Yeshua. They all rushed around Rachel and hugged her and kissed her and wished her well.

Yeshua and his disciples thanked the people for their kindness and hospitality and then said their goodbyes. As they were ready to leave, Mattheus remained behind for a few minutes and then spoke to the people and said, "We are fortunate, that Yeshua has many who support him and us as we travel all over Galilee to spread the Good News. Yeshua has asked me to give to you what we do not immediately need, so I give you this with our blessing." He then handed over a bag with money to their leader, who bowed and thanked him. And then Mattheus left and caught up with the rest.

"Our next stop is Nain," Yeshua said. "It's only a couple of miles away, so we should be there within the next couple of hours."

It was an overcast morning and the sun was still not visible, but a few clear blue patches of sky offered some hope for the sun to come out. Yeshua walked on ahead as he usually did when they left a place and when they were approaching another. Yeshua needed the time to reflect and the disciples soon learned Yeshua's ways and moods. He was really a loner at heart, and by nature, more of an introvert, they thought. Although Yeshua loved the company of others and was all for dinners and feasts, for good food and wine, and company, music and dancing and laughter, he would feel tired and drained afterwards and needed to be by himself. And his healing of the afflicted also took a lot out of him, as power went out of him, so they respected his need for being alone.

As they saw the town of Nain ahead, Yeshua stopped and waited for them to catch up with him. "Let us pause for a moment and turn our hearts to our Father in heaven," Yeshua said. He then let them remain in silence for a while and then together they prayed the prayer that he taught them 'Our Father'.

As Yeshua and his disciples approached the gate of the town, a funeral was in progress. A coffin was being carried out of the town to the cemetery. A large crowd was following the deceased. There was much weeping.

Yeshua stopped. As the procession came closer, Yeshua softly asked one of the mourners, who it is that has died.

"He is Benjamin, so young, a good man, and the only son of Joanna. He died of an unfortunate accident. Joanna is a widow and now she is all alone and destitute, poor woman," the man whispered.

When Yeshua saw Joanna, walking behind the coffin and weeping, his heart went out to her; he felt an overwhelming compassion for her. He approached her and said, "My dear Joanna, do not weep, your son shall rise again." Yeshua touched her on the shoulder.

The mourners were surprised to see a stranger touch Joanna, a man, at that. He could only be a relative they did not know, they surmised. And they saw a number of others, men and women with him, and they wondered who all these mourners were, for they had not seen any of them before.

Yeshua went to the front of the bearers and held up his hand and said, to them, "Please stop." And they stopped, a bit perplexed at the appearance of this stranger, telling them to stop. But he seemed to have an air of authority about him, like a teacher or a rabbi, so they stopped. Yeshua then stepped forward and touched the coffin, and said, "Young man, I say to you, rise!"

The mourners were bewildered. Who is this man, and why is he touching the coffin. He is making himself unclean. Is he a Gentile or a Samaritan? The crowd began whispering among themselves, as they watched Yeshua and heard him speak. "Who is he?" one of them asked, and "He speaks with such authority," said another. "He has made himself unclean, he must be driven away," said another. But they all just stood still, mesmerised, by the strange man, who speaks such nonsense. "He must be a lunatic," another said.

All of a sudden, the dead man sat up, and a gasp went all around the crowd and they were gripped by fear and consternation. Yeshua said to the people, "do not be afraid. Adonai is with you."

Then Benjamin, rubbed his eyes, and looked at his white robe and seemed perplexed. He looked around and saw his mother, she was weeping profusely, but they were tears of joy, for her face was radiant with happiness. He looked at the coffin and then he was confused.

"What's happening? Is this some kind of joke?" He asked.

Then one of the bearers spoke up. "No Benjamin, you have died, and we were taking you out to bury you when this man here, touched your coffin, and told you to rise, and you rose," the man said, hardly believing his own words, but his eyes could not deny what he was seeing and what had just happened.

The people were stunned and stood still for an instant and then there was uproar, and cries were heard, "He is alive, he is alive, Benjamin is alive, he has come back from the dead, he was dead and now he is alive."

The people were beside themselves, bamboozled and shaking their heads in disbelief. Some rubbing their eyes and trying to work out what has just unfolded in their presence? Many were shaking their heads; others gasped and were covering their mouths with their hands. Others simply stared in disbelief.

Joanna was overwhelmed. She could not believe what was happening. It seemed like she was dreaming. She rushed to be beside the coffin, as the bearers lowered it onto the ground, so Benjamin could step out. Yeshua took Benjamin by the hand, and then gave him to his mother and said, "He is alive, Joanna. Take your son home now, and give him something to eat, for he is hungry."

Benjamin was still in a daze. But Yeshua looked at him and said, "Benjamin, do not be afraid. Adonai has blessed you and given you back to your mother. Go home now, and live in peace."

Benjamin placed his arm around his mother's shoulder and they began to return to the town and to their home, with the crowd in tow. Fear seemed to grip some of the crowd. But most of them were glorifying God and saying among themselves, "A great prophet has risen among us!" And another cried out, "God has looked favourably on us!"

Yeshua and his disciples joined the crowd as they walked back into the city rejoicing. But everyone was so overwhelmed, some ecstatic, some bewildered, some fearful. The disciples too were overwhelmed, except Shimon and Andreus, and Miriam because they were in Bethsaida, in the room of Jairus' daughter when Yeshua raised her from the dead. The rest of the disciples were not in the room when Yeshua raised Jairus' daughter from the dead, but they were in the house and saw his daughter alive. But they were nevertheless just as mystified as the rest of the crowd. They had seen him cure cripples, made them walk, made the blind see, the deaf hear, the mute speak but raising someone from the dead, this was beyond belief.

The priest, who was officiating at the funeral, was astounded. He could not fathom what had just transpired. The crowd was so rowdy now and they were all rejoicing and moving forward. Yeshua was being swamped as everyone wanted to have a good look at this man, this prophet, this miracle worker, who had raised one of them from the dead. No one has ever been able to do this, and none of them had ever witnessed such an event, God has visited his people, God has visited their town. They were rejoicing and there was a buzz in the air.

Shimon and Andreus and the others surrounded Yeshua lest he got mobbed and injured by the enthusiasm of the crowd. "Who is he?" people were asking the disciples.

"He is Yeshua, from Nazareth; he will speak to you all later. Go to your homes now, and give glory to God," Shimon said.

The people did as Shimon said, but several of them still could not take their eyes off Yeshua. Some of them wanted to touch Yeshua, but the disciples warned them off.

The people went into the town, and back to their lives but the word spread like wild fire, throughout the town. The news spread throughout the town and beyond. And everyone wanted to see for themselves. They went to Joanna's home, to see Benjamin. But the front door was barricaded by relatives. One of them said to the crowd that gathered there. "Go home, Joanna and Benjamin wish to be left in peace for now, you will all see them later."

The people left and told those that were approaching that the house was shut up and that Benjamin and his mother would be stepping out later. So, they all returned to their business, and left Joanna and Benjamin in peace for the time being.

Yeshua in the meantime, led his disciples into a lonely place. He told Shimon and Andreus to go into the town, to the synagogue and speak to whoever was in charge and ask if he, Yeshua, could speak to the people in the morning, and he told them to search for a place for them to stay. Miriam, Rebecca, Lucia, and Rachel, said they would also go and search for a place to stay. Yeshua then told the disciples they could all go and he would meet them at the town gate, an hour before sunset.

When the people heard that Yeshua's disciples were out and about, they all gathered to meet with them. They were hoping to see Yeshua again. But they were told that Yeshua was in the forest praying and that they would be able to hear him speak in the synagogue the next morning. When the townspeople heard that the disciples were looking for a place for them and for Yeshua to stay, the people were vying with each other to provide them with lodging.

The next morning came. The synagogue was packed. When Yeshua entered there was a hush all over the place and people were stretching their necks to get a glimpse of Yeshua.

Yeshua was feeling well rested and refreshed. He cast his eyes all over the synagogue and saw Joanna and Benjamin in the front row. An exception had been made for Joanna to join her son on this occasion. Yeshua nodded to them and smiled; they returned the smile.

"Shalom my brothers and sisters," Yeshua greeted everyone warmly and with a smile on his face. "What a beautiful town you have, so many flowers and plants bring so much delight and your many fine works of art and natural beauty are a joy to behold.

"My disciples and I wish to thank you for your warm welcome, your kindness and your hospitality, especially those who have provided us with food and lodging. We are most grateful. We have been travelling this past year all over Galilee, across the Jordan and the Sea of Galilee and visited every city, town and village on the way. We are now on our way to Caesarea and then on to Jerusalem for the Passover. We hope we will see some of you there."

Yeshua stopped to draw a breath and then continued, "You have witnessed the power and compassion of God in your town. Yesterday morning, you were weeping, especially Joanna, for you were carrying Benjamin out of the town to bury him, but God, our Father has heard your cries, and he has given Benjamin back to you. Life is precious.

"In the beginning the earth was a formless void and darkness covered the face of the deep. But God in his infinite love brought form, and light, and life. He banished the darkness and created all the beauty we see and touch and smell and delight in. The seas, including Galilee, the mountains, including Tabor, are all the work of his hands. But all this he created for us, for you and me. This town of Nain is his gift to you. You all are his gift for each other.

"When he had finished his work of creation, he then created all living creatures in the sea and on the land. Millions of species we are still to discover and encounter. Our God is a God of bountiful love, of infinite generosity and magnanimity. Everything that exists he created for you and me. This beautiful town of Nain is his gift to you.

"Then God said, 'Let us make humankind in our image and like us.' So, God took some earth and breathed life into it, the breath of life, and man was created as a living being. But God's work of creation was not complete. He would hand over to humankind, the carrying on of his creation. So, he caused a deep sleep to fall upon the man, and so we have inherited that, and God continues to cause upon us a deep sleep, at the end of every day, to remind us of his creation of our first man and woman. We cannot survive for long without that sleep, that rest God gives us. While the man was asleep, God took one rib from the man and breathed upon him the breath of life, and the rib formed into that of the first woman, the mother of us all. And God then brought the woman to the man, and when he saw her, his heart stirred like never before. The love of God, was now alive in him and likewise when the woman saw the man, something in her heart stirred, her very first emotion was one of love, love for this man that God had created for her. And so, God continues to give us this gift of love for each other. God gave the gift of love to Joanna for Benjamin and Benjamin for Joanna, and he gave it to each of us for those we love. This is God's greatest gift, love. We are born to love, to love our God and to love one another. Love comes naturally. Everything else we have to learn."

"My dear friends, we are created by God, we are born to love and be loved. And our love for each other is to have no limits. For God's love for us is limitless, boundless, absolute, unconditional and eternal. And so, we have to love one another. Not only those who love us, but even those who hate us, even our enemies. For God is love and who abides in love abides in God."

Yeshua continued, "With love for God, for one self, for others, without exception, we are complete. Unfortunately, the first man and woman that God created in kinship with all of creation wanted more, they wanted to be like their Creator, and so tempted by the evil one they were no longer contented with all they had, with the love for God and one another and God's love for them and all God gave them, they wanted more. They were consumed by pride and greed; they wanted to be like God. They wanted power, and authority, and wealth, and prestige and all that dominion over all. And so, they did the unthinkable and rebelled against God, and so sin and death entered the world. But this is not the way it was meant to be, and now we are all tarnished with sinful desire and we all die. With our first man and woman death entered the world, and now we all must die."

Yeshua stopped. While he was speaking the people were completely silent and hanging on his every word. They all had heard the story of creation, as it was written by their great prophet Moses in his first book of their Sacred Scriptures. But it came alive to them as Yeshua was speaking.

After allowing some time for the people to digest what he had said, Yeshua continued, "Life is a precious gift. It is also so fragile. We can destroy it through sin, through evil. We are all tempted, we all covet riches, wealth, position, power, prestige, yet few things are necessary for life. We can survive on bread and water, but that is not enough, and neither should it be. We have progressed so much as human beings, and the progress we will make will astound us, and will amaze future generations. But the mistake and the fall of the first man and woman will be repeated over and over again. We want to be like God. The quest for power and control, for riches, for prestige, for self-gratification will continue. Power, envy, greed are not born of love. Hatred is not of God; hatred comes from our sinful natures, our fallen human nature. When all that matters, is that we love God, and love one another, as we love ourselves. Any thought or action that is not born of love only harms us and the world in which we live. God is love and who abides in love abides in God. That is all that matters and only love will make us into the persons we were created to be. So, I say to you, cast out of your hearts all hatred, envy, greed, lust, and the desire for revenge and live in love and peace with one another."

Yeshua then stopped. "I have spoken enough. Let us have some time of silence to reflect on what we have heard and turn our hearts to our Creator and loving Father in heaven, who dwells within our hearts."

The priest then continued with the service. When the service was over, the people waited outside for Yeshua. Yeshua however spent some time alone in prayer, and giving thanks to Yahweh. When he came outside the crowd gave a loud cheer. And they surrounded Yeshua. The disciples had their hands full protecting Yeshua from being crushed.

A person in the crowd, yelled out. "Yeshua, who are you, our prophets have done great things but never before has any of them raised someone from the dead," he said.

"That is not true my young man, have you not heard of the prophet Elijah of Tishbe in Gilead? The rains had ceased and there was severe drought all over that land. But the Lord fed Elijah like he fed our forefathers in the desert. He also led him to the wadi from which he drank. But when the wadi dried up God told Elijah to go to Zarephath, which belongs to Sidon, and live there. God said to Elijah, 'Elijah, go now to Zarephath, for I have told a widow who lives there to feed you.' So off he went and when he came to the gate of the town, he saw a widow there gathering sticks. He called to her and said, 'Please bring me a little water in a vessel, so that I may drink.' As she was going to bring it, he called to her and said, 'Bring me also a morsel of bread in your hand.'

"But she said, 'As the Lord your God lives, I have nothing baked, only a handful of meal in a jar and a little oil in a jug. I am now gathering a couple of sticks, so that I may go home and prepare it for myself and my son, that we may eat it and die.'

"Elijah said to her, 'Do not be afraid, go and do as you have said; but first make me a little cake of it and bring it to me and afterwards make something for yourself and your son. For thus says the Lord God of Israel, *The jar of meal will not be emptied and the jug of oil will not fail until the day that the Lord sends rain on the earth.*'

"She went and did as Elijah said, so that she as well as Elijah and her household ate for many days. The jar of meal was not emptied; neither did the jug of oil fail, according to the Word of the Lord that he spoke to Elijah.

"Some time after this, the widow's son became gravely ill and died. She then said to Elijah, 'What have you against me, O man of God?' You have come to me to bring my sin to remembrance, and to cause the death of my son.'

"Elijah then said to the widow, 'Give me your son.' Elijah then took him from her bosom, and carried him up into the upper chamber where he was lodging, and laid him on his own bed. Elijah then cried out to the Lord, 'O Lord, my God, have you brought calamity even upon the widow with whom I am staying, by killing her son?' Then he stretched himself upon the child three times and cried out to the Lord, 'O Lord, my God let this child's life come into him again.' The Lord listened to the voice of Elijah; the life of the child came into him again, and he revived. Elijah took the child, brought him down from the upper chamber into the house, and gave him to his mother. Then Elijah said, 'See, your son is alive.'

"The woman and her whole household were astounded. They could not believe their eyes. Then the woman said to Elijah, 'Now I know that you are a man of God and that the Word of the Lord in your mouth is truth'."

"So, you are a prophet, then?" a voice in the crowd yelled out.

"Are you Elijah come back to life?" another voice cried out.

Yeshua did not respond. But Shimon did, "Yes he is a prophet, and more than a prophet, he is a man sent by God, he is the Promised One, the One that Johanan the baptiser spoke about when he said one greater than he was to appear and he would teach us the truth and show us the way, and give us the life."

Yeshua smiled at Shimon but said nothing. Then Andreus, Shimon and the disciples told the people to leave and let Yeshua alone. "We will be in Nain for some time, so you can see Yeshua again and listen to what he has to say. So go now."

The people then dispersed; they were chatting among themselves animatedly. Yeshua then led the disciples to the edge of the town, and at an open space he sat down and they all sat down around him.

Then Yeshua spoke, "Shimon, I am grateful for what you said to the people. When I am no longer with you, all of you will have to speak out boldly as Shimon had done. You will teach the people all I have taught you." Yeshua then continued to speak to them and taught them many things. He opened the Scriptures to them, and all that was written about the One that was to come to bring salvation to all.

When Yeshua was finished teaching them, he said, "I want to thank you Mattheus, for managing all our finances so well."

"Not only our finances, but managing us all as well," Thomas said, jokingly.

"I cannot manage you mob," Mattheus said, "That is Andreus lot, and duty," he said, with a smile.

Yeshua spoke again. "I also want to thank you Miriam, for leading the women, and for you too, Rebecca, Lucia and Rachel for caring for us all, for accepting the gifts that is given to us, and for making sure we are well fed," Yeshua said smiling.

"And so that you are all kept clean, and not smelling like desert rats," Rebecca said, grinning.

"Yes, for that too Rebecca, thank you for the positive influence you all have on us men in that regard. But sincerely I am also grateful for all the guidance you have given me and the group, your wisdom is much appreciated. Your woman's perspective is enriching to us all. And I have not failed to see how many women have approached you and how you have taught and inspired them. Thank you."

Yeshua had sought a lot of counsel from Miriam, and she with Shimon seemed to be merging into the role as leaders of the group. And by his actions and his time with both of them individually and together, the group soon came to see that Yeshua was grooming them to be their future leaders. But they also came to accept that Yeshua was teaching all of them to carry on his work. He kept reminding them that he would be with them for only a short time longer, but they did not really work out what he was saying. They all believed that he would be with them for a long time. They knew of the opposition that was out there, but they were confident that Yeshua would come to no harm; after all he had the power of God on his side.

They all remained in Nain for several more days. In the meantime, the word about Yeshua and what he did in Nain was spreading beyond the town. Then when the time was right, Yeshua told his disciples they were ready to leave for Caesarea.

When they drew near Caesarea, Yeshua sent them ahead, while he sought a deserted place. He told them to seek for lodgings and he would catch up with them later

Chapter Fifty-Seven
Pontius Pilate

The disciples walked into the centre of the city of Caesarea. It was bustling with activity. Later when Yeshua arrived, he was surprised to see so many soldiers on the streets in their full uniforms, and armed. But the disciples, who had already been in the town for a while, had discovered the reason why.

James Alpheus told Yeshua, "Yeshua, you have just missed a big celebration in the city. The new Prefect Governor, Pontius Pilate appointed by the Emperor Tiberius, had just arrived and was paraded through the streets. He now rules over all of Judaea, which of course includes Jerusalem, and he is also the Prefect of Samaria and Idumaea."

Thaddeus described the activities, "There was much pageantry, Yeshua. Bands were playing loud music, and all the soldiers were marching, and people were lining the streets watching the spectacle and there was cheering all around, but not from the people, but from all the Romans, Pilate's entourage and their families and servants, now living in Caesarea."

Nathanael then spoke, "Yeshua, the people were watching the spectacle but they were not amused. They had not heard about Pilate, what kind of man he is. But if he was put in this important position, it is certain he would be a harsh man, and one who could wield power with an iron fist. Yeshua you should keep clear of this man. Keep a low profile here in Caesarea."

Yeshua listened patiently to what Nathanael was saying, he knew that his disciples were all concerned about his welfare, but he had made it clear to them of what lies ahead. He also had a premonition that somehow, he and Pilate would one day cross paths.

Pontius Pilate would turn out to be a cruel and ruthless governor. He would go out of his way to provoke the Jews and quickly and ruthlessly squash any semblance of an uprising. Pilate would turn out to be harsh, inflexible, in fact criminal, using bribery, calumny, violence to overthrow any semblance of opposition or insubordination. In fact, the first act that Pilate would orchestrate would infuriate the Jews. Pilate would order that the Roman Standards or the Imperial Insignia be taken to Jerusalem. This had not been done before, because it was clear just how much the Jews regarded as idolatrous these insignia which bore images of the emperor and their religious symbols.

Pilate from the start did not endear himself to the people. He lived in a lavish palace, built by Herod, the father of Antipas. This was his official home, and he would only go to Jerusalem for special or official occasions or if there were any danger of insurrection.

"Yeshua, you should steer clear of the Roman governor, and maybe we should not stay at Caesarea," Shimon said.

"Shimon, do not be afraid. Pilate has just arrived and needs to settle in; he won't have time for us. But we cannot avoid coming into contact with Roman authorities. They rule over us and will do so for a long time to come. But their authority and power will come to an end. So many nations will rise up and lord it over others, subjugate others, and rule over others for years, even centuries, but all those powers, authorities and kingdoms will eventually come to an end, but the Kingdom of God will last forever. We are here Shimon, to establish that kingdom, here in Caesarea, and throughout Galilee, Samaria, and Judaea and to the ends of the earth and to the end of time."

Yeshua turned to all of his disciples and said, "I have chosen you to be my disciples. Learn from me for I am gentle and humble of heart. Take up your cross every day and follow me. I will be persecuted and so will you, be brave, be fearless, be courageous, I am with you always, and when I am taken from you, the Spirit of Yahweh will come to you, and strengthen you. Come let us now go to the synagogue."

When Yeshua and the disciples arrived at the synagogue, a number of people were there waiting for him, they were from Nain and the towns and villages that he and his disciples had visited. They found out that Yeshua was on his way to Caesarea, so they followed him, and waited at the synagogue for Yeshua to appear as he usually did. And the word spread far and wide in Caesarea about Yeshua and what he did in Nain. The word spread that a prophet was in town, a carpenter from Nazareth, a man of God, who speaks with authority, and who works great wonders, and even raised the son of a widow in Nain from the dead, and this man is now in Caesarea.

Crowds from Caesarea gathered with those following Yeshua, and waited for him to arrive. Waiting also were the Elders, Scribes and chief priests and their associates. They too were curious to see this man, whom people from Nain claim had raised someone from the dead.

When Yeshua and his disciples arrived at the synagogue, the crowd pressed in on Yeshua. Shimon and Andreus and the others had their hands full trying to protect Yeshua from being swamped.

"Please, stand back, Yeshua is going into the synagogue where he will address you," Shimon uttered.

Usually, Yeshua sought the permission of those in charge of the synagogue before he preached, but he was mobbed and those in charge approached him, and introduced themselves and Yeshua asked for their blessing to proceed. They gave him their blessing.

Yeshua then addressed them all. "My dearest brothers and sisters of Caesarea and elsewhere, I thank you for coming here today, into this sacred place, this Temple of the Lord. This is a place of prayer, and this morning your priests will lead us all in prayer and sacrifice. I will begin to speak with you about my Father in heaven who has sent me to you, to bring you the Good News of his love, the Good News of salvation and redemption for all."

Yeshua continued to exhort the people, saying, what he had told others on his travels, "You are the salt of the earth; but if salt has lost its taste, how can its saltiness be restored? It is no longer good for anything, but is thrown out and trampled underfoot. You are the light of the world. A city built on a hill cannot be hid. So let your light shine before others, so that they may see your good works and give glory to your Father in heaven."

Yeshua noticed the priests, Elders and Scribes who had introduced themselves to him at the beginning, they were right up front, and were listening to his every word. He knew they would judge him for what he was saying. He continued, "Do not think I have come to abolish the Law of the Prophets; all they taught by their teaching, their deeds and their lives. I have not come to abolish any of that. I have come to fulfil all that was taught. Truly I tell you, until heaven and earth pass away, not one letter, not one iota of a letter, will pass from the Law until all is accomplished. Therefore, whoever breaks one of the least of these commandments, and teaches others to do the same, will be called least in the Kingdom of Heaven. But whoever does them and teaches them, will be called great in the Kingdom of Heaven. But I tell you, unless your righteousness exceeds that of the Scribes and Pharisees, you will never enter the Kingdom of Heaven."

Shimon and the disciples were aghast. What is Yeshua thinking? He had started so well but how could he end his talk by saying those words again, and be so provocative, call out the Scribes and Pharisees when he knows some of them are present here, and some of them, or at least their spies have been following them and keeping track of them. They were extremely anxious.

Yeshua continued, "You have heard that it was said to those of ancient times, 'You shall not murder' and 'whoever murders shall be liable to judgement.' But I say to you that if you are angry with a brother or sister, you will be liable to judgement, and if you insult a brother or sister, you will be liable to the Council, and if you by your words or actions demean, insult, belittle anyone with what you say, like calling them, 'fool' because they are not one of you, because they do not believe what you believe, or because they are not of the same race as you, or because they do not live like you do, or because they are poor, or whatever, or if you brand them as sinners simply because of their poverty or sufferings, or if you call them unclean because they do not observe such minor rituals like washing of their hands, you will be liable to the hell of fire.

"Soon we will be offering our gifts at the altar. I say to you now, that when you are offering your gift at the altar, if you remember that your brother or sister has something against you, leave your gift there before the altar and go; first be reconciled to your brother or sister; and then come and offer your gift."

Yeshua paused; his eyes swept across the synagogue and finally came to rest in the front to where the leaders of the synagogue, the religious leaders of the people were sitting. They looked so smug, and Yeshua could see their antagonism smouldering. He continued with his teaching.

"You have heard that it was said, 'You shall not commit adultery.' And that if a woman is caught committing adultery, she should be stoned. But I say to you, that everyone who looks at a woman with lust has already committed adultery with her in his heart. God has created us male and female and he has given us a natural attraction for each other, he has endowed us with beauty and attractiveness. And to see another's beauty and to admire such beauty is not lust, but to entertain selfish and unlawful pleasures, and designs for one's self-gratification, that is lust. And to do this is already committing adultery. So, I say to you, if your right eye causes you to sin, tear it out and throw it away; it is better for you to lose one of your members than for your whole body to be thrown into hell. And if your right hand causes you to sin, cut it off and throw it away; it is better for you to lose one of your members than for your whole body to go to hell."

There was so much more that Yeshua wished to teach the people but he stopped, instead he had this to say to them in conclusion. "Let me finish with an exhortation. I have walked through your city, and through so many other cities and big towns, especially during this past year. And I notice just how so many are downcast, walking around with stern faces, with smouldering looks and stooped shoulders, and oblivious to others around them, and seem so heavily burdened as if they have the whole world on their shoulders, and they seem oblivious to what is around them.

"And I have been in the villages away from the cities, where the poor and outcasts live. They too have their burdens but I have encountered so much warmth and welcome from them, and they seem so more content, joyful and open, and shared with my disciples and I the little they have.

"What is it that burdens you so? What is it that weighs on your mind, the desire for riches, possessions, power, prestige, position, and belonging? We worry and are anxious over so many things, when only one thing is necessary, one thing that will give you peace in your hearts.

"Look at those who have wealth, power, position, prestige, popularity, are they content? They lord over others and many of them are a miserable lot. Seek first the kingdom of God and everything will be yours."

Yeshua ended his teaching and then joined the people for the rest of the service. When he came outside of the synagogue there was a group of men waiting for him. They confronted Yeshua, surrounding him. The crowds gathered around and they saw who it was that was surrounding Yeshua; the Elders, chief priests, Scribes, Pharisees and they had the Sadducees with them; the experts in all aspects of the Law. Then two men dragged a woman into their midst, pushing her into the centre of the circle, and causing her to fall onto the ground where she remained. Her clothes were torn and she was dishevelled and looking extremely frightened and vulnerable. All the men had stones in their hands.

Then in a loud voice for all to hear, one of the Sadducees spoke up. Pointing a finger at the woman he said, "Teacher, this woman was caught in the very act of adultery. Now in the Law, Moses commanded us to stone such women. What do you say?"

The people were now totally engrossed. They were all waiting for Yeshua to reply. The disciples were concerned, for they knew that Yeshua was cornered. The disciples knew that they were putting Yeshua to the test. The religious leaders out of envy wanted to bring Yeshua down, they thought that in one foul stroke they would make him lose his credibility. If he showed the compassion he preached and defended this woman from being stoned he would show no respect and allegiance to the Law. Yeshua was cornered.

Yeshua knew exactly what was happening. He was seething within, but he sighed heavily and tried his utmost to keep his cool. There was a long pause, as all waited for Yeshua's response. Yeshua went to the woman and whispered in her ear, and raised her to her feet. She straightened her hair and her clothes. She was so frightened but Yeshua seemed to have said something to her that calmed her. Then he stooped down and wrote with his finger on the dusty ground.

The accusers and the people in the crowd were straining their necks to see what Yeshua was writing. The accusers continued én masse to repeat their questioning. Yeshua then straightened up and in a voice for all to hear he calmly said, "Let anyone among you who is without sin be the first to throw a stone at her." And once again he bent down and wrote on the ground.

There was a gasp all around the crowd, and open mouths, people gaping and shaking their heads marvelling at Yeshua's astuteness in his answer. Many were smiling and rubbing their hands in glee, and waiting for a response from the accusers.

When the accusers heard this, they were momentarily stunned. They thought they had trapped Yeshua but instead, they now felt trapped. Still with stones in their hands they approached Yeshua, curious to see what he was writing. And as soon as they looked at what Yeshua wrote, they dropped their stones and slithered away. One by one they slinked away, starting with the Elders, and Yeshua was left alone with the woman. Yeshua's disciples and the crowd however remained to the last. They wanted to see the final outcome.

Yeshua straightened up, held the woman's hand in his, and looked her in the eyes, and filled with compassion he said to her, "Woman, where are they? Has no one condemned you?"

The woman finally looked up and saw none of the men with stones. She replied, "No one Sir."

Yeshua then said, "neither do I condemn you. Go your way, and from now on do not sin again."

The woman thanked Yeshua profusely, kissing his hands, and then hurried off, as the crowd parted to make way for her.

Shimon and Andreus assisted by the other disciples then dismissed the crowd. Then Yeshua and his disciples went to their living quarters, for lunch and rest.

Yeshua was walking out front and the disciples following. The disciples were discussing among themselves what had just happened.

"I think the Sadducees and the others were trying to trap Yeshua, after his teaching about adultery. They wanted to belittle him, humiliate him; instead, Yeshua adeptly turned the tables on them," Thomas said.

"I wonder what he was writing in the dust," Shimon Cananean asked.

Johanan said, "Maybe he was writing the sins of all those men and when they saw what was written they slipped away with their tails between their legs."

"I think Yeshua wrote, 'go and fetch the men adulterers first'," Rebecca said, with a smile on her face.

"Miriam, go and ask Yeshua what he wrote," Shimon suggested.

"It's not necessary Shimon, maybe he was just doodling," Miriam said.

The next day Yeshua continued his teaching in the synagogue. And the place was crowded again. He repeated what he taught elsewhere concerning retaliation of the eye for an eye and a tooth for a tooth, and instead to turn the other cheek, and about loving one's enemies, and about giving so that the left hand doesn't know what the right hand is doing, turning the other cheek, and not storing up treasures on earth.

Yeshua continued, repeating his teaching saying, "The eye is the lamp of the body. So, if your eye is healthy, your whole body will be full of light, but if your eye is unhealthy, your whole body will be full of darkness. If then the light in you is darkness, how great is the darkness!"

"I have come," Yeshua said to them, "to bring you out of the darkness. I am the light of the world. Whoever follows me will never walk in darkness but will have the light of life."

Then one of the Pharisees from the front row spoke up on behalf of his associates, "You are testifying on your own behalf, your testimony is not valid."

The disciples were listening intently and looking at the Pharisee as he was speaking, and then they turned their eyes on Yeshua. The people too were caught up in this debate between Yeshua and the Pharisees. No one ever debated with the Pharisees in public. Everyone was too afraid. But they all felt that Yeshua spoke on their behalf, he became known for challenging them, and was willing to debate everything with them. Yeshua was fearless and they loved him for it. They hung on his every word as he responded.

"Even if I testify on my own behalf my testimony is valid because I know where I have come from and where I am going, but you do not know where I come from and where I am going. You judge by human standards, I judge no one. Yet even if I do judge, my judgement is valid; for it is not I alone who judge; but I and the Father who sent me."

The spokesman for the Pharisees then asked, "Where is your Father?"

Yeshua answered, "You know neither me nor my Father. If you knew me, you would know my Father also."

Yeshua continued teaching, speaking to the people, as well as their religious leaders. He warned them against profaning what is holy by saying, "Do not give what is holy to dogs; and do not throw your pearls before swine, or they will trample them under foot and turn and maul you."

Then Yeshua addressed the people saying, "I warn you, beware of false prophets, who come to you in sheep's clothing but inwardly are ravenous wolves. You will know them by their fruits. Are grapes gathered from thorns, or figs from thistles? In the same way, every good tree bears good fruit, but the bad fruit bears bad fruit. A good tree cannot bear bad fruit, nor can a bad tree bear good fruit. Every tree that does not bear good fruit is cut down and thrown into the fire. Thus, you will know them by their fruit."

The people were amazed and taking in all that Yeshua was saying. He taught them as one having authority, and not as their rabbis and teachers did. Everything he said made so much sense and they delighted in the way he taught, using images to which they could relate, sheep, fruit trees, grapes, figs, and thistles and fire, and so much more from life around them, images that were part of their daily existence.

Yeshua was about to end his teaching when one of the Pharisees, to test Yeshua, and again seeking to trap him and embarrass him, asked, "Is it lawful for a man to divorce his wife for any cause?"

Yeshua looked straight at the Pharisee, and the others sitting with him. They were sneering and pleased with one of them putting Yeshua to the test, in the midst of this crowd of people, for the crowd was swelling all the more.

Yeshua answered them, as he so often did, with a question, "What did Moses command you?"

The spokesman for them all said, "Moses allowed a man to write a certificate of dismissal and to divorce her."

The Pharisees and their associates were nodding and pleased with themselves. There were a number of them who had used this Law of Moses, and divorced their wives and married again. And among the crowd there were a number of divorced men too and also women who bore the brunt of those divorces. Everyone had an interest in what Yeshua would have to say about this issue that touched so many of them, if not personally then one of their family or loved ones.

Yeshua was aware of how easily men could divorce their wives, and did so, he sighed, and then spoke, "Because of the hardness of your heart, Moses wrote this commandment for you. But you all know; this is not the way it was in the beginning of creation. God intended a man and a woman to live together as one, for the rest of their lives. God made us male and female and for this reason a male is to leave his father and mother and be joined to his wife, and the two shall become one flesh. Therefore, what God has joined together, let no one put asunder."

Yeshua continued, "And I say to you, whoever divorces his wife and marries, commits adultery against her, and if she divorces her husband and marries another, she commits adultery."

There was an uproar among the crowd, and not only from the Pharisees, Scribes and their associates but from the crowd itself, especially the men. Was Yeshua accusing all of them who had divorced and remarried of living in adultery?

One man in the crowd spoke up for what was on the minds of so many and said out loud, "Teacher, if such is the case of a man with his wife, it is better not to marry."

Yeshua knew this was a hard teaching, so he said to them, "Not everyone can accept this teaching, but only those to whom it is given. For there are eunuchs who have been so from birth, and there are eunuchs who have been made so by others. And there are others who have made themselves like eunuchs in accepting a life of celibacy for the sake of the kingdom of God. Let anyone who can, accept this."

The crowd were not satisfied. This was a hard saying of Yeshua, and Yeshua was fully aware of that, so he said, "I know not everyone can accept this teaching. You have to enter into your conscience and ask for the Spirit of God to guide you and enlighten you. Husbands love your wives always, as you love yourselves. Wives love your husbands, as you love yourselves. Love conquers all. Life is full of crosses to bear; married life is no exception. But I say to you, take up your cross daily and follow me. And in your marriage and in your families, in everything do to others, as you would have them do to you, for this is the Law and the Prophets."

Shimon then stepped in. "That is enough. Yeshua has to leave now. Yeshua is on his way to Jerusalem and has to be there for the celebration of the Passover. I'm sure many of you will be in Jerusalem as well, and you can listen to Yeshua there."

The people were pleased to hear what Shimon was saying, and they dispersed to their homes.

That evening the disciples sat around an open fire in the back of one of their dwellings, they had a meeting chaired by Shimon. They had told Yeshua that they wanted to discuss future strategy. Yeshua excused himself and said he was tired and would have an early night but told them to go ahead. So, the disciples met without Yeshua.

Shimon began, "Friends, we have now been with Yeshua for more than a year. This is the first time we are heading for Jerusalem. I know that Yeshua will want to stop at the villages on the way. But the Passover is now just two weeks away. It will take at least four to five days for us to get there, if we walk our usual four hours a day. Yeshua likes to leave early, before sunrise so that he can be at the synagogues for the morning services. But I am worried about the opposition that seems to be building between Yeshua and the Pharisees, Scribes and Sadducees and all their associates. You have seen the conflict here in Caesarea and the other places we've been. That is mild to what we can expect in Jerusalem, so we have to be very careful, and Miriam you must please try to speak to Yeshua to not be so provocative in the presence of the Pharisees and their associates. And in Jerusalem there will be hundreds of chief priests and Pharisees, Scribes, Sadducees, Elders from all over Judaea, Samaria, and Galilee and elsewhere for the celebration of the Passover."

"And Pilate will be there for sure. His guards will be all over, to keep everything under control. The Roman garrison is in the fortress that overlooks the Temple, so if there is a semblance of anything untoward the guards will be there in a flash. Pilate will want to make sure everything goes peacefully. And he will rely on the religious leaders to help him maintain the peace," Shimon Cananean said.

"How many people do you think will be in Jerusalem?" Andreus asked.

"Thousands, hundreds of thousands," Shimon Cananean said. "Jerusalem has about one hundred thousand inhabitants and that swells more than fourfold with Jews from all over Judaea, Samaria, Idumaea, Galilee of course, and further north from Phoenicia, Iturea, Abilene. And they will come from across the Jordan, from Perea, Decapolis, and Trachonitis and from all other parts of the world. It will be absolute chaos."

"Many of course would not have heard of Yeshua, so it will be easy for him to go around unnoticed and be lost in the crowd," Johanan said.

"But I am sure, Yeshua will want to speak in the Temple and wherever he can. For people will be wanting to hear from the Teachers and the Chief Priests and the Scribes and Sadducees and of course the Pharisees, who will be out in full force," Thomas said.

"And Caiaphas, Annas' son-in-law, is now the Roman-appointed Chief High Priest in Jerusalem," Phillip said.

"There are two powerful courts overseeing law and order, of course the Roman court as Andreus mentioned with legions of soldiers armed and ready for any uprising. And then there is our own Jewish court, the Sanhedrin, that exists to do Rome's bidding, and help to maintain the peace during the festival," Mattheus added.

"And the Sanhedrin has at least eighty officials consisting of Caiaphas and Annas at the helm and other chief priests, Elders, and Scribes, and many of course, of the ubiquitous Pharisees," James Alpheus said.

"We have to protect Yeshua, at all costs," Shimon said.

"Yeshua will want to meet with the people, he will want to speak about the Good News that he has been ordained to do," Miriam said. "And nothing and no one is going to stop him," Miriam added.

"But Miriam, you have to warn him to be careful," James Zebedee said.

"I think we have discussed enough for now, it's time to retire. We rise at sunset. Goodnight to you all and rest in peace," Shimon said to them all.

Chapter Fifty-Eight
Jerusalem, The Holy City

Yeshua was in agreement with his disciples about heading directly to Jerusalem. It would be good for them all to settle into the city before the crowds came from all over and invaded the holy city. It would also be easier to find suitable accommodation.

Yeshua and his disciples walked non-stop to Emmaus and rested overnight. The next day they left early and arrived at Jerusalem at midday. At the gates of the city before entering, they found an open space that was set up with tents for accommodating the influx of people coming for the Passover celebrations.

"Yeshua what do you think about this place. There are lots of other similar campsites all around the city. This is as good as any. Or would you like us to find better lodging in the city?" Andreus asked.

"Andreus, whatever you and the others decide I will go along with," Yeshua said.

"Yeshua, we were blessed again, we received lots of monetary gifts in Nain, and Caesarea," Mattheus said.

"A lot of our funds came from women, both in Nain and Caesarea, Yeshua," Miriam said. "They also offered to provide us with meals and accommodation if ever we returned there," Miriam added.

"You all decide. I am going to Bethany to visit some friends. It's just about an hour's walk from Jerusalem. Maybe we could stay there and walk into Jerusalem every day during the celebrations. It will be good exercise for us at the beginning and end of the day. I will most likely stay with my friends in Bethany for the time being; you all can find lodging in Jerusalem or Bethany, whatever you decide," Yeshua said.

"While you decide, find a place for all to be close to each other in the meantime. You can then find me at Bethany. Just ask for the sisters Miriam and Martha and their brother Lazarus, that is where I will be staying," Yeshua said. "I will most likely stay there for a couple of days and then come to Jerusalem. See you later." With that Yeshua left and walked to Bethany on his own.

"Andreus, we ladies, will find our accommodation in the city, on the outskirts. I think after a couple of days, we might take a walk to Bethany, and catch up with Yeshua and his friends before he comes to Jerusalem. What do you think ladies," Miriam said, looking at the other women.

"Yes, that sounds fine," Rebecca responded, and the others agreed.

"Okay, we will look for accommodation as well, for a couple of days, and meet you all in Bethany. See you then." The men and women disciples then parted ways.

"I wonder how Johanan is doing in prison. Is it possible to visit him," Nathanael asked, as they were entering the city.

"I will make enquiries among my former Zealot friends," Shimon Cananean said.

"Andreus, Johanan and James and I were disciples of Johanan for quite some time, and we have lots of friends here, who were disciples as well. We will catch up with them. I think we can visit them. They may be able to provide us with lodging as well," Shimon said.

"I was thinking, when those of us who were disciples of Johanan, when we meet up with Johanan's former disciples, we might let them know that Yeshua is in Jerusalem, and that we are now his disciples," Thaddeus said. "Johanan spoke so highly of Yeshua, and you all know what happened when Johanan baptised Yeshua in the Jordan," Thaddeus added.

"That's a good idea, in that way we will help spread Yeshua's message. And I will also let all my former Zealot friends know about Yeshua," Shimon Cananean said.

"Okay, let's disperse in pairs. I'll go with my brother, Shimon, and I guess, Johanan and James you will go off together, and the rest of you can pair off. But as we are eleven, there will be three of you in one group," Andreus said.

"Let's say we meet at noon at the Temple," Shimon suggested.

Mattheus handed out sufficient funds to each to tide them over for the next couple of days. They then all went their own way, in twos, with James Alpheus, Thomas and Thaddeus, forming a group of three.

While all this was going on, Yeshua was on his way to Bethany. He was looking forward to catching up with Miriam and Martha. He had not yet met Lazarus, who his sisters had told Yeshua, was an adventurer who travelled to, they knew not where, in search of a fortune, in gold, silver and precious gems. He spent most of the year on his travels to strange lands.

Yeshua had to pass the Mount of Olives. He walked through the Kidron valley to the Mount of Olives and into the quiet and peaceful Garden of Gethsemane. Here he stopped and rested. He found a place, a huge rock on which he sat and inhaled the fresh air, and the smell of the olive trees, and the other wild shrubs and plants. He sat and let himself be embraced by Mother Nature. Yeshua spent some time communing with his Father, and reflected on where he was, and where he was going.

What a beautiful and peaceful place, this garden, so near to Jerusalem and to Bethany, Yeshua thought, and he said to himself that he would spend lots of time here while in Jerusalem. Yeshua spent more than an hour in prayer in his peaceful surroundings and then continued this walk to Bethany.

Yeshua arrived at the home of Miriam and Martha. No one was out front, so Yeshua walked around the house to the back, where he had spent so much quality time with Miriam and Martha, around the fire. When he came to the back of the house, Martha was busy hanging up some washing.

"Martha," Yeshua called to her.

Martha got a start, but turned around, and her face lit up with joy, she rushed to Yeshua and hugged him warmly.

"Yeshua, it is so good to see you. It has been such a long time. Are you here for the Passover celebrations? Miriam will be over the moon to see you," Martha said, excitedly.

"Martha, it's good to see you. Yes, I will be staying for the Passover. In fact, I will be staying in Jerusalem for a long time. I now have eleven men and four women, who are travelling with me, they are helping me in my work," Yeshua said.

"That's wonderful Yeshua. You must tell us all about your work, and them, and what has been happening with you all these years. You are looking well. Miriam has gone to the markets for some produce. She should be here shortly," Martha said.

Martha finished hanging the last pieces of washing, and she sat down with Yeshua. "Yeshua, can I get you something to drink, or something to eat?" she asked.

"Actually, I am rather thirsty and a bit peckish, a couple of slices of bread will do," Yeshua said.

"Sit there Yeshua, I'll only be a minute." Martha rushed into the house. And as she entered the back door, Miriam entered the front. "Miriam, I'm so glad you're back. We have a visitor out back. Go and be with our visitor, while I prepare some refreshments," Martha said, not wanting to give the gender or identity of their visitor. She wanted her sister to enjoy the surprise. She was well aware how fond Miriam was of Yeshua, and how fond he was of her in return.

"Who is it?" Miriam asked, frowning.

"Go and see," Martha said, maintaining a vague look.

Miriam went out back, when she stepped into the back yard, Yeshua had his back turned. He was looking at the trees in the distance. He heard movement and turned around and his eyes lit up, "Miriam, how good to see you," he said, smiling.

"Oh Yeshua," was all that Miriam said, as she rushed into Yeshua's arms and hugged him, not wanting to let him go. Finally, she did. "Yeshua, it is so good to see you. It has been such a long time. How long are you staying?" she asked.

"I will be staying indefinitely Miriam, I am here for the Passover, and to do my work here," Yeshua said. He then repeated what he had told Martha.

"Oh, Yeshua, you must tell me all about what you have been doing. And these disciples of yours who are they?" Miriam asked.

Yeshua then told her. "The first one I called to be my disciple, has your name, she is Miriam from Magdala. A beautiful person, you'll like her. There are three other women disciples too; Rebecca who has been my friend since childhood, she is from our hometown of Nazareth. And then there is Lucia from Capernaum, and Rachel from a village at the foot of Mount Tabor."

Miriam was amazed and thrilled that Yeshua actually had women as his disciples. And that it was a woman he first called to be one of his disciples. This is unheard of. She wanted to know all about Miriam, and the other women.

"Tell me about Miriam, Yeshua, and the other women disciples of yours," Miriam said excitedly.

"I will Miriam, but they will be here shortly, I told them I am here with you, and you will meet them, then, and ask them whatever you wish," Yeshua said.

"How exciting Yeshua, I can't wait," Miriam said.

"Then I have eleven men. Most of them fishermen from around Capernaum and Bethsaida, Shimon and his brother Andreus, Johanan and his brother James, Phillip and his friend, Nathanael, Mattheus, a former chief tax collector for Galilee, Thomas, and his twin brother, James of Alpheus, and another Shimon, who was previously a Zealot, and Thaddeus. I think that's all of them," Yeshua said.

"Wow, Yeshua you sure have an interesting bunch of people as your disciples," Miriam said.

"They are interesting all right. They are all from Galilee and have been with me on the road for more than a year, and have been such a help and support to me," Yeshua said. "In fact, you will meet them all. They are in Jerusalem, setting up lodgings for us all. And I told them to meet with me here in Bethany, before I return with them to Jerusalem," Yeshua said.

"You can stay here, with Martha and me; it is only an hour's walk, less for you, to Jerusalem. Please say you will."

Just then Martha came with a tray of bread with spreads of honey and slices of cake, warm milk, and fruit juice as well as nuts and fruit, including figs. "Please say you will what?" Martha asked her sister.

"I have just asked Yeshua to stay with us while he is in Jerusalem," Miriam said.

"Of course, he will be staying with us, Miriam, I will not take no for an answer," she said, smiling at her sister and Yeshua.

"Thank you for your kind offer. But I was going to ask two of my dearest friends whom I love so much to offer me accommodation."

As Yeshua was speaking, both Martha and Miriam were unsure, if Yeshua meant them or someone else. But by his expression they saw that he was baiting them.

"And whom are these two friends that you love so much may I ask," Martha said.

"Aah, you know them well. They are two beautiful women, and they have a brother, I am still to meet," Yeshua said, smiling broadly.

"So, you are going to stay with us. That's great Yeshua. And you will meet Lazarus. He is in town, back from his travels. He will be staying for the Passover as well. He has his own place now, not far from here," Martha said.

"That looks yummy, thank you, Martha. I'll have some bread with that honey and some of the cake for sure," Yeshua said.

"And the figs, of course," Miriam said, smiling, knowing how much Yeshua loved figs.

Yeshua spent the rest of the afternoon chatting with Martha and Miriam, mostly with Miriam because Martha was busy with many things, including preparing dinner for Yeshua.

Martha went out back and said to her sister, "Miriam, why don't you take Yeshua to meet Lazarus. If he's home, invite him to join us for dinner," Martha said.

"Yes, I will Martha. Is that okay with you, Yeshua, or would you like to rest," Miriam asked.

"I'd love to meet Lazarus the explorer and adventurer," Yeshua said.

Miriam and Yeshua began their walk to Lazarus' place. "I'd be very surprised if Lazarus is home. He is always on the go," Miram said.

"So how long has he been back?" Yeshua asked.

"This has been the longest. He was quite ill when he returned from, I don't know where. He goes to all those exotic eastern places, and eats all kinds of different foods and what not. Some of the places he visits and stays are hot and humid, and they have such spicy foods, so he must have picked up a bug of sorts. He had a fever for a while, and we were very worried, but he is okay now. After that he bought a place, and said he was home for good. But I know he is just recuperating, and once he is feeling fit and strong again, he will be off on his adventures, and his search for another fortune," Miriam said.

"I'm so sorry to hear, he was not well. However, you and Martha must be pleased to have him home with you," Yeshua said.

"Yes, we are. He is the first-born, and when Father died, we were all so young, and he tried to be like a father to us, but he is only a couple of years older than Martha. He was barely out of his teens when he was off to explore the world. When mother died, he was away and we had no way of contacting him. When he returned, he stayed for a while and did not want to leave Martha and me to ourselves. But he was so restless and fidgety, we told him that we had done all right without him all these years and we can do so now. So, he left," Miriam said.

"You and Martha are still single. Have neither of you met anyone with whom you would wish to have a family of your own?" Yeshua asked.

"I haven't met anyone Yeshua. No one I was really attracted to until I met you," Miriam said, laughing and close to elbowing Yeshua in his ribs.

"But seriously. When mother got ill, we both decided to care for mother. And I guess we got used to being by ourselves," Miriam said.

"Well, you are both still young," Yeshua said.

"There's his house," Miriam said, pointing ahead to a fine-looking stone house perched on a little hill, with a winding foot path to the front door.

When they arrived at the front door of the house, Miriam called out, "Lazarus! You home? I brought you a visitor."

To her surprise, Miriam heard her brother's voice, "Miriam, is that you? I'll be there in a second," he called from another room in the house.

Then Lazarus appeared. Yeshua thought he was a handsome man, tall and heavily tanned, more so than the men in Galilee, who worked out in the sun all day. Lazarus was surprised to see Miriam with a man, and a man he did not recognise.

"Shalom, sister, and who is this?" he asked.

"Lazarus, this is Yeshua," was all that Miriam said.

"Oh, so this is the famous Yeshua, whom my sisters never stop talking about," Lazarus said. He then turned to Yeshua and said, "So Yeshua, are you coming to ask for Miriam's hand, do you wish to betroth her?" Lazarus said, smiling.

"No Lazarus, Yeshua has come to Jerusalem to do his work, and he is here with his disciples, who are all in Jerusalem at the moment," Miriam said.

"So, you are Yeshua, one of the disciples of Johanan, who is now in prison, put there by that madman Herod. So are you come to get rid of that mad Herod, and rule Israel," Lazarus said.

"No Lazarus, I will not be able to do that, as you can see, I am but a humble carpenter, and at this moment my army consists of eleven men and four women from Galilee. And most of the men are fishermen," Yeshua said.

"You have four women disciples? Do they travel with you? Well, this is revolutionary. What do the high priests and the Pharisees have to say about that? That must shock them for sure," Lazarus said. "But I have been to faraway lands where the women rule and are the leaders of their tribe, and the men have to obey them. So, I guess that is not so revolutionary, is it?" Lazarus said.

"So, tell me Yeshua, what do you want to accomplish? What is your work? I heard about your baptism by Johanan, and he preached a hard message of repentance and fasting and all that, and preparing for the coming of the Messiah, and the end of the world. Are you the one he kept speaking about who was to come, who is greater than he is, and the one to lead us out of this slavery to Rome, and to free us at last?" Lazarus said.

"Lazarus, Yeshua is here to visit us, and to have some peaceful time. He will be preaching and teaching here in Jerusalem for many days to come. You will have plenty of time to grill him with your questions, so leave him in peace for now," Miriam said.

"Thank you, Miriam. But I will answer Lazarus briefly. Yes, Lazarus, I have come to free the people from the yoke of Rome. We are all enslaved to Rome, and they have caused our people so much pain and suffering. But as you know from our history, we have been enslaved over and over again, for four hundred years in Egypt, until Moses set us free and brought us to the Promised Land. And now we are slaves again to the Romans, but not forever, for the power of Rome, their kingdom will come to an end. And then other powers, other kingdoms will come and rule over us, so that is not the freedom I bring to our people. The freedom I bring is the freedom of God; I bring the Good News of salvation and redemption for all. I have come to bring true and everlasting freedom," Yeshua said.

"Those are fine words, ideals, but what do they mean, Yeshua?" Lazarus said.

"Even if we were not living under the yoke of Rome, our people would still not be free. We are enslaved like the Romans, for we are ruled by the same power of evil that rules over them, the power of Satan. The Romans are not free, the Jews are not free, and no one is free who seeks power, position, prestige, wealth, and rule by greed, for more and more, at the expense of the poor and needy. We are not free if the rich get rich on the backs of the poor, and the rich get richer and the poor get poorer. We are not free if we are consumed with hoarding up riches for ourselves, wanting more than we need at the expense of others. We are not free if we are consumed by greed, power and lust and selfishness and self-interest. We are not free if we are enslaved by ungodly values. We are not free if we believe, wrongly, that wealth and power is a reward from God for a job well done, and that poverty and illness is a punishment from God for one's sins. This is not freedom for the rich or the poor. True freedom is in the mind and hearts and souls of people. True freedom is living content with what one needs and not what we want. There is enough in what nature provides for the needs of all, but not enough for our greed. We are greedy and selfish and hurtful and lord over others and cast out the poor, the sick, the afflicted, when they are the ones, we need to embrace and support and love. My kingdom, Lazarus is a kingdom of Love, Peace, Compassion. Our God is a God of love and compassion, a love that is boundless, unfathomable, generous, unconditional and eternal. And that is the kind of love we need to all have in our hearts for one another, for without it we will never be free," Yeshua said.

"Wow!" Lazarus said. "That was quite a speech. What you say Yeshua, makes a lot of sense. I have travelled all over the world and seen how the rich lord over the poor, exploit them, mistreat them and leave them to live in squalor. I have seen so much injustice and greed and evil, and so much hatred in the world," Lazarus said.

"Excuse my lack of hospitality, Yeshua. May I offer you something to drink, or some refreshment?" Lazarus asked.

"A cup of water will do, Lazarus, thank you," Yeshua said.

"Lazarus, Yeshua is staying with us, while he and his disciples are in Jerusalem. They will be staying for the Passover celebrations, and beyond that. Martha is preparing dinner and you are invited," Miriam said.

"I'd love that," Lazarus said. He was now very interested to hear more from Yeshua. He was different to the other teachers, who preached so much about sin and judgement and a God who was watching and wanting to punish. And that life was all about reward and punishment; reward for those who observed the Law and punishment for those who did not. And he has women followers, disciples. Now that must really upset the apple cart, Lazarus said to himself.

They all gathered for dinner at Martha's and Miriam's place. Miriam had spent so much time sitting beside Yeshua and listening to him, while Martha was busy with so many things. When Lazarus arrived, he was greeted with a familiar scene, of Martha fussing about preparing for their meal, but surprised to see Miriam sitting at Yeshua's feet. Lazarus knew that was the way with disciples, they sat at the feet of their Master, their Teacher. But women were never seen or allowed to sit at the feet of the Teacher, for women were not allowed to be disciples. It was just not condoned. It just didn't happen. And to see Miriam sitting at the feet of Yeshua, and listening and learning from him, warmed his heart, and warmed his feelings for Yeshua.

The four of them ate a hearty meal and the conversation was lively. They drank some good wine and this helped the conversation even more. Yeshua was interested to hear all about Lazarus' adventures into foreign lands.

"Lazarus, I am so interested to hear about those places you visited, and the people you encountered. I have been sent to the lost sheep of the house of Israel, but I am preparing my disciples to go out to those lands, and those people, and bring them the Good News of God's love and compassion. No one needs to be enslaved anymore. They need to be brought out of the darkness into the light, and out of slavery into true inner freedom," Yeshua said.

The hours slipped by without anyone wanting to end the conversation. Eventually Martha spoke up and said, "It is getting very late. I'm sure Yeshua would like to rest now, and have a good sleep," she said.

"Yes, thank you Martha and thank you for this great dinner. And thanks for the wine, Lazarus. I will spend tomorrow with you, just have a quiet day. My disciples will turn up the following day, and then we are off to Jerusalem. We will stay there for the Passover celebrations. I am grateful to you Martha and Miriam for your hospitality and a place to stay. I might not come home every day; it all depends on circumstances. But I will see you shortly after the Passover, once all the crowds have dispersed and gone home," Yeshua said.

"It sure will be pandemonium with people coming from all over to Jerusalem," Lazarus said.

"We'll see you in Jerusalem Yeshua, for we will be there for the Passover Celebrations in the Temple," Miriam said.

They all then said goodnight and retired. The next day was a quiet one, and Yeshua took a walk through some bushland, and he also took a walk to the Mount of Olives, which wasn't too far away, and he spent some time in prayer with his Father in the Garden of Gethsemane. He got back to his place in Bethany late afternoon, and he brought a bag of olives back with him.

At Yeshua's insistence, they had a simple meal of bread and soup. Yeshua said he still felt full from yesterday's dinner. They had a relaxing evening and Lazarus had joined them again. Yeshua grew in affection and friendship with Lazarus, as he did with Martha and Miriam.

The disciples turned up as Yeshua had said, the following day. Martha and Miriam and Lazarus were excited at meeting them all. He especially enjoyed meeting Rebecca, and hearing all about Yeshua and her growing up in Nazareth.

Yeshua noticed Rebecca spending a lot of time with Lazarus in conversation, and it warmed his heart, for he thought they were so well suited to each other, and he hoped the friendship would grow.

The men were enjoying Lazarus' company and the stories of his adventures and the exotic animals he saw, and interesting people. They also spoke of fishing, politics and of course religion, which so intertwined in the lives of the people. Yeshua had not told Lazarus, Martha and Mary anything about his healings. But the disciples when they got the opportunity spoke all about Yeshua's healing of the sick and the incapacitated, making the blind see, the deaf hear, the dumb speak and the lame walk. They spoke of all the miracles Yeshua had done, including his raising of the widow's son in Nain, from the dead. Lucia related to the women and the men how Yeshua had cured her from her illness of twelve years by her simple touching of the hem of his garment.

What really fascinated Lazarus was how Yeshua had cast out the demons among the tombstones, and sent them into a herd of over a thousand pigs that went hurtling over a cliff. "I can just imagine that, what a spectacle it must have been," he said.

Lazarus, Martha and Mary had heard rumours about Yeshua, but now they were sure they were not rumours, and the miraculous signs he had done astounded them and their esteem of Yeshua increased.

What astounded Miriam, Martha and Lazarus was how unassuming and humble Yeshua was in the face of all that he was accomplishing.

And the topic of Johanan the baptiser came up. Some of the disciples, who were disciples of Johanan wanted to visit him and wondered if that was possible. They did not want Yeshua to go as that would be too dangerous. They told Lazarus all about the opposition that Yeshua got at the hands of the Pharisees, Scribes and Sadducees wherever they went, and they were sure that some of them, if not all of them were in Jerusalem now, and that Yeshua would need to be careful.

Lazarus said he had a contact and would see if he could get one or two of them to visit Johanan in prison, if possible. Lazarus mentioned that he knew a man named Chuza, who is a steward in Herod's court. He would speak to him and see if he could arrange for a couple of them to see Johanan.

After the meal, the disciples said they needed to get back to Jerusalem before dark. Yeshua told them he would meet them all at the Temple around mid-morning the following day. The Sabbath and Passover celebrations were still four days away.

The disciples left, and so did Lazarus. Yeshua helped Martha and Miriam clean up and they had a nightcap together. They then all retired for the night.

And so, it came to pass. Chuza orchestrated smuggling the Zebedee brothers, Johanan and James, who were disciples of Johanan until he was arrested, into the prison to see Johanan. They arrived down in a foul smelling, dark and dingy place that had a few cells with iron bars and two guards in attendance. Johanan and James were allowed to see Johanan in his cell but they could only speak to him through the iron bars.

Johanan looked awful. His beard was so much longer than when they last saw him, and he was looking gaunt. However, Johanan was pleased to see two of his former disciples. They told him that they were now with Yeshua, for more than a year.

James spoke, "Yeshua is now in Jerusalem to spread the Good News. We are two of the eleven disciples of Yeshua. Actually, we are a total of fifteen disciples, because we have four women disciples as well."

"Women disciples!" Johanan expressed some dismay. "I had a visit about six months ago from one of my disciples, Judas. I had asked him to find out more about

Yeshua, what has been happening with him. Since that incident in the Jordan when I baptised Yeshua, I have been wondering if he is the One who is to come, the promised Messiah that is to set us free. But what I have heard about him disturbs me. He has scant respect for the Sabbath and some of our Laws, he associates with loose women, even dines with them, and he has a lackadaisical attitude to sin. So, I am not so sure. Ask him if he is the Messiah and let me know," Johanan said.

"We will Johanan. He has never indicated to us that he is the Messiah," James said.

"But by his words and deeds I would say that he is," Johanan said. "But we will tell him you wish to know for sure," Johanan added.

"Thank you. And see if you can contact Judas, he is called Judas Iscariot. He is a fine man. He is from further south of Judaea but stays often in Jerusalem. His father owns a jewellery store not far from the Temple. You can't miss it. He works for his father, in several of his businesses. He is someone who is searching for the truth, so go and see him. And let him join you as disciples of Yeshua. From what I heard of his miraculous powers, Yeshua must be a man of God," Johanan said.

"We will look for him, Johanan," James said, "and we will also ask Yeshua outright if he is the Messiah. I would like to know for sure as well," James added.

"I doubt if you will be able to visit me again. But you can get word to me through Chuza. He and his wife Joanna were good disciples of mine. They are good people, who fear the Lord and walk in his ways," Johanan said.

"We will do that Johanan, and we will pray for you, Peace be with you," James said. They then left.

At mid-morning, around the fourth hour, the disciples came together at the entrance to the Temple. Yeshua came walking towards them. He looked well rested and ready to do his work. "Come let us enter the Temple and speak to whoever wants to listen," Yeshua said.

"Yeshua, I have spread the word to all our friends, former disciples of Johanan, the baptiser," Shimon said, on behalf of Andreus, Johanan and James and the others who were disciples of Johanan. "We told them we are now your disciples and invited them to come to the Temple to meet with you," Shimon added.

"And I have spread the word to all of my former Zealot friends Yeshua, that you are in Jerusalem and they should come to the Temple this morning to listen to you," Shimon Cananean said.

"We met some women Yeshua, and we too spoke to them about you. And we told them too, that you are in Jerusalem for the Passover, and that you would be coming to the Temple this morning," Miriam said.

"That is good work, I thank you all," Yeshua said.

"And Yeshua, I noticed people from Capernaum and Bethsaida," Johanan said. "Many of them are here already for the celebration of the Passover," Johanan added. "And I have told them you would be teaching in the Temple this morning."

"And I think the whole of Nazareth is here, Yeshua, I met several of them. They are staying at their usual campsite just outside the city," Rebecca said, "and I told them as well that you will be here this morning."

"And I have seen a number of people from Magdala and Capernaum," Miriam said, and several of them knew you would be here. They said they would be at the Temple this morning.

"And I have also noticed a lot of Pharisees by their long tassels, and their band of brothers. I recognised a few of them from Caesarea," Nathanael said.

"I'm sure all of these people have already spread the word of your presence here, Yeshua," Johanan said.

"You have to be careful what you say, here in Jerusalem, Yeshua. Because the high priest, the chief priests, the Pharisees, Scribes and Sadducees and all the religious leaders will be out in full force. What you experienced in Galilee is nothing in comparison to what you can expect here," Shimon warned.

"And Pilate is in Jerusalem and his full cohort. And the guards will be out in full force. So, we have to be extra careful," Andreus said.

While the disciples were saying all this, a crowd had already started to gather around as some of them recognised Yeshua and they spread the word.

"Come, let us enter the Temple," Yeshua said.

Chapter Fifty-Nine
Whitewashed Tombs

When Yeshua, followed by his disciples entered the Temple, no service was taking place but there were many people around, who had come to the Temple to pray and just to be there. When Yeshua found the spot from where to speak, the crowd merged and the disciples had to keep a space in front of Yeshua.

Yeshua then addressed the people, "My dear friends, my brothers here with me and my sisters, in the Women's Court; it is good to see you all on this beautiful day in Jerusalem. You have all come to Jerusalem to celebrate the Great Passover, when on that fateful night, the angel of the Lord, passed over the homes of our ancestors, who were enslaved to the Egyptians for over four hundred years. It was the blood of an unblemished lamb on their doorposts that saved them. And our great prophet and Saviour Moses led our people in such glorious fashion out of Egypt, dry-shod through the Red Sea to our freedom, here in this Promised Land."

"But Yeshua, we are not free. We are still slaves to the Romans, have you come to set us free," a voice from the crowd yelled.

"Most likely one of Shimon the Zealot's friends," Shimon whispered to his brother Andreus.

Yeshua had encountered these sentiments so many times and he never failed to respond. "You are right, my friend. We are not yet free. But you are also wrong. For freedom is within your grasp. You can be free. There were some of our brothers and sisters who were living in Egypt in slavery who were free. The hardships they endured, the cruelty they were subjected to, the poverty they experienced failed to take away their freedom, for they believed in Adonai. They believed in his love for them. And they knew that all their suffering was not in vain. They believed in Adonai's great love and compassion for them. They knew they were loved and not forgotten. They knew that God, our heavenly father was suffering with them. And when the rains came, they knew it was the tears that our heavenly was shedding for them, and they stood in the rain and let the tears of God wash all over them. When the sun rose in the morning, they stood and greeted Adonai and let his warmth embrace them. And when they heard the wind rustle the leaves of the trees they sang to the music with delight and sang to Adonai and praised him and thanked him for another day. And when the birds sang, they danced to their music and praised their Father in heaven. They were already free.

"And now, my dear friends, my brothers and sisters, I ask you, before the Romans came, were we all free? If the Romans leave, will we be free? I have come to bring you a freedom that will last forever, a freedom that no tyrant, no worldly power, not even death will be able to take from you. I have come to bring you this freedom, for it I live and for it I am willing to die. And the freedom I bring is freedom from evil, sin and death."

The crowd were absolutely silent. They were mesmerised, never before has anyone spoken to them like this, and with such authority.

Yeshua continued to talk to the people and teach them many things. After he had spoken for quite some time, a person in the front of the crowd stood up and said,

"Teacher, I am one of the chief priests here in Jerusalem. I am also a Pharisee. With me are other Pharisees, many who are Elders and Scribes. I am one of the many members of the Sanhedrin, the highest religious court in our land, a court of the law and of our people and made up of the high priest and several chief priests, Scribes and Elders. I am a proud Pharisee and appointed to teach the Law of Moses and all that our God expects of us as his chosen people. And as a representative of the Sanhedrin and of our Pharisee spiritual leaders and teachers, I ask you Yeshua, by whose authority do you teach?"

"He is surrounded by Scribes and Sadducees as well and there are so many Pharisees among them," Andreus whispered to Shimon.

"Yes, and they are not only from Jerusalem but from all over Judaea and Galilee and elsewhere," Shimon said in return. "And I am sure they are all here to gang up against Yeshua and get rid of him," Shimon added with a heavy heart. He was extremely worried about what would happen with so much concerted opposition to Yeshua, and he knew that the Pharisees would go all out to undermine Yeshua, and put a stop to his teaching.

Shimon was immediately on the alert as he listened attentively to what the chief priest was saying, as were the other disciples.

The chief priest continued, "We have heard about all the supposedly miraculous feats you have done, and heard so much about what you teach and now listened to all that you have to say, tell us by what authority are you doing these things and teaching these matters. And who gave you this authority?"

Yeshua sighed, and the disciples and the crowd were straining their necks, and wanting to hear Yeshua's response.

Yeshua spoke, "I have just one question to ask you in answer to the questions you put to me. If you tell me the answer, then I will also tell you by what authority I do what I do and teach what I teach."

Now the crowd were full of expectation and straining to make sure they too heard the question Yeshua was about to ask his questioners. The crowd knew that Yeshua was not liked by the Pharisees and all the religious leaders. He was so different to all of them in every way.

Yeshua then put the one question to the chief priest, "Did the Baptism of Johanan come from heaven or was it of human origin?"

The chief priest was stumped for a moment. He turned to his associates and, sotto voce, he consulted with his colleagues. And they argued with one another, and after some discussion one of them summed up their deliberations; if we say 'From heaven,' he will say to us, 'Why then did we not believe Johanan?' But if we say 'Of human origin,' we can fear the reaction of the crowd, for they all regard Johanan as a prophet.

The chief priest then spoke on behalf of all of them by saying, "We do not know."

And Yeshua said to them, "Neither will I tell you by what authority I do what I do, and teach what I teach."

Yeshua then directly addressed the Pharisees and their cohort. "Tell me what you think of this. A man had two sons, he went to the first and said, 'Son, go and work in the vineyard today' He answered, 'I will not,' but later he changed his mind and went into the vineyard to work. The father went to the second son and said the same and he answered, 'I go, Sir,' but he did not go. Which of the two did the will of his father?" Yeshua asked them.

They all replied in unison, "The first."

Yeshua then said to them, "Truly I tell you; the tax-collectors and the prostitutes are going into the kingdom of God ahead of you. For Johanan came to you in the way of righteousness and you did not believe him, but the tax-collectors and the prostitutes believed him; and after you saw that you did not change your minds and believe him."

The crowd were smiling. They loved this contest between Yeshua and the Pharisees, who lorded over them and made their lives a living hell with their strict observances of the Law and the burdensome rituals and observances they were supposed to uphold under fear of eternal damnation.

Yeshua said to the Pharisees, "Have you never read in the Scriptures, 'the stone that the builders rejected has become the cornerstone, this was the Lord's doing, and it is amazing in our eyes.' Therefore, I tell you, the Kingdom of God will be taken away from you, and given to a people that produce the fruits of the Kingdom. The one on whom this stone falls will be broken to pieces and it will crush anyone on whom it falls."

When the Pharisees and the Chief Priests and their associates heard his parables, they realised that he was speaking about them. And so did the crowd. The Pharisees, the chief priests wanted to arrest Yeshua there and then but they feared the crowds, because they regarded Yeshua as a prophet.

Yeshua continued his teaching of the people. During Yeshua's talking a few of the Pharisees sneaked out and returned with reinforcements, more experts of the Law. Without any semblance of being surreptitious they burst to the front and joined Yeshua's opponents.

The crowd got more boisterous, forgetting they were in the Temple. They were sensing a battle to the death and it had now become a blood sport for them, between Yeshua and the Pharisees and their army of legal experts.

"Hey, I recognise those men," a voice from the crowd called out. "They are Herodians," he shouted.

"Herodians! They brought in Herodians!" cries went out.

"Who are the Herodians?" Rebecca asked Miriam, sitting next to her in the Women's Court. The two of them with Lucia and Rachel wished they were closer to Yeshua.

"I don't know, followers of Herod I suppose," Lucia answered.

A woman sitting behind them answered, "They are fanatics, Hellenistic Jews who call themselves a political party. They are followers of that rat Herod. They want to restore Herod on the throne, and are diametrically opposed to the Pharisees, who of course say they want to restore the Kingdom of David."

"Thank you for that," Miriam said.

"It's strange then that they should be showing up with the Pharisees, with whom they are so utterly opposed," Rebecca said.

"It is strange indeed," the woman said.

"Not so strange, it's a case of enemies joining forces against a common foe," a woman, sitting with the woman who spoke to them, said.

"Sssh," the women around urged them. They too were engrossed with the spectacle that was unfolding. It was like Yeshua was facing a group of gladiators.

Yeshua was unperturbed with the commotion. He waited patiently for the newcomers to be seated. Some had to stand for lack of seating; they stood up front in the aisles and close to Yeshua.

Once all had settled Yeshua continued, "Let me tell you another story. The Kingdom of Heaven may be compared to a king who gave a wedding banquet for his son."

"My goodness, how could Yeshua know, he is speaking about the kingdom of God, in front of both the Pharisees and the Herodians," Miriam whispered to those around her.

Yeshua continued, "The king sent his slaves to call all those who had been invited to the wedding banquet. But they all turned down the invitation with excuses and would not come. But again, he sent out his slaves, saying to them, 'tell those who have been invited that I have already prepared a dinner for them, my oxen and my fat calves have been slaughtered, and everything is ready, come to the wedding'."

Yeshua continued with the story, "But they all made light of it, and went on their way, one to his farm, another to his business, while the rest seized his slaves and even killed some of them. When those slaves who survived came back battered and bruised, and told the king what had happened, he was enraged. The king sent his troops, destroyed those murderers, and burned their city."

The Pharisees, the Herodians, and their associates were listening, with great intent. They couldn't help being intrigued with the story and wondered how it was going to unfold. The crowd too were mesmerised, hanging onto Yeshua's every word and engrossed with the story, excited about how it would conclude.

Yeshua continued, "Then the king said to his slaves, 'the wedding is ready, but those who were invited were not worthy. Go therefore into the main streets and the highways and byways and invite everyone you find to the wedding banquet.'

"The slaves did as the king commanded them and went out into the streets and gathered all whom they found, both good and bad, so the wedding hall was filled with guests."

Yeshua concluded his story with the words, "For many are called but few are chosen."

The Pharisees, the Herodians and their associates were livid. They knew that Yeshua was criticising them, without really saying so, without explicitly reproving them.

One of the Herodians then stood up and addressed Yeshua with a question. A hush came over the crowd. The Herodian spoke in a deep voice, surprising the people in addressing Yeshua as teacher.

The Herodian, with an air of superiority addressed Yeshua, "Teacher, we know that you are sincere, and teach the way of God in accordance with truth, and show deference to no one, for you do not regard people with partiality."

The disciples were perplexed, if this Herodian was one of the Pharisees reinforcements, then they have lost their battle with Yeshua. He greets Yeshua with such respect and admiration. But Yeshua knew it was merely a ploy.

The Herodian continued, "Tell us, then, what you think. Is it lawful to pay taxes to the emperor or not?"

There was a gasp. Everyone knew this was a loaded question, and that they were now goading Yeshua, setting him up, setting a trap for him.

Miriam had her hand to her mouth. She wanted to be down there with Yeshua, to be with him, support him no matter what. Shimon and the others were engrossed but extremely anxious. How was Yeshua to get out of this tricky situation and be true to his teachings?

But Yeshua was aware of their malice, and he said to the Herodian and all those with him. "Why are you putting me to the test, you hypocrites?"

There was a gasp throughout the crowd. No one had dared insult the Pharisees with such harsh words, and in front of such a big crowd and here in the Temple of all places. Yeshua's disciples both the men and the women were aghast, as well as frightened for Yeshua. But Yeshua seemed as cool as could be.

There was a hush throughout the Temple as Yeshua continued to speak.

Yeshua said, "Show me the coin used for the tax."

The Herodian and his associates were caught off guard, they did not expect this. The people were intrigued. Was Yeshua using a stunt in return?

The Herodian slipped his hand inside his robe and shook his head to his associates. "Anyone got a coin?" he said to them.

And then there was laughter. "Be quiet!" The chief priest stood up and faced the crowd with a stern look on his face.

But people were stifling their smiles. "Here I have a denarius," a man nearby said and handed it to the Herodian who looked at the man with contempt, but nevertheless he begrudgingly took the coin and he brought it to Yeshua, still not knowing what Yeshua was up to.

Yeshua then in a most theatrical manner held the denarius aloft for all to see, and said in a loud voice for all to hear, "Whose head is this on this denarius, and whose title?"

Before the Herodian could answer, the owner of the coin yelled out, "The emperor's," and then there was laughter. The people loved the theatrics. Again, the chief priest stood up and simply looked at the crowd with a stern and disapproving look.

When the murmuring died down, Yeshua then said, in a dramatic voice, for he knew the people were enjoying the drama, and so was he. Yeshua had always loved debating and he grew up debating, and loved the repartee, and while he could be ruthless in a debate, there was never any malice. Yeshua then said, "Give therefore to the emperor, the things that are the emperor's, and to God the things that are God's."

All of a sudden, the crowd burst forth in a sound of clapping. The chief priest got up and yelled, "Be quiet, have you no respect for the Temple of the Lord."

The crowd then became still.

But Yeshua's opponents were not ready to concede defeat. This time one of the Sadducees stood up and addressed Yeshua. "Teacher I am a Sadducee and we are not able to believe in the resurrection, may I ask you a question?"

"Please do," Yeshua said, wondering what the next question could be.

The crowd would not disperse; they wanted to see this contest to the end.

The Sadducee continued, "Moses said, 'if a man dies childless, his brother shall marry the widow, and raise up children for his brother.' Now there were seven brothers among us, the first married, and died childless, leaving the widow to his brother. The second did the same, so also the third, down to the seventh. Last of all, the woman herself died. In the resurrection, then, whose wife of the seven will she be? For all of them had married her."

Yeshua was not perturbed by these efforts to unsettle him or corner him. He was accustomed to tough debates and relished these occasions. But here he knew malice existed. The Sadducee waited, really thinking he had Yeshua in a corner, and he would make him look ridiculous. The people waited for Yeshua's response.

Yeshua answered, "You are wrong, because you know neither the Scriptures nor the power of God. For in the resurrection, they neither marry nor are given in marriage, but are like angels in heaven. And as for the resurrection of the dead, have you not read what was said to you by God, 'I am the God of Abraham, the God of Isaac, and the God of Jacob?' He is God, not of the dead, but of the living."

The Sadducees would not give up in finishing Yeshua. So, one more of them challenged Yeshua, he was a lawyer. He asked Yeshua a question to test him, "Teacher, which commandment in the Law is the greatest?"

Everyone wanted to hear the answer to this question. Yeshua was pleased for the question. He looked at all of those who were sitting there with the Sadducees, the religious leaders and he looked all around the temple, and answered the question, "'You shall love the Lord your God, with all your heart, with all your soul and with all your mind.' This is the greatest and first commandment. And the second is like it, 'You shall love your neighbour as yourself.' On these two commandments hang all the Law and the Prophets."

Yeshua had enough of trading blows with his adversaries, being on the defensive. He turned to the crowd and addressed them, "My dear brothers and sisters."

When Yeshua greeted them like that the women were all attentive for, they knew he was speaking directly to them and including them in all he had to say.

Yeshua continued saying to the people, "The Scribes and the Pharisees sit on Moses' seat; therefore, do whatever they teach you, and follow it; but do not do as they do."

There was a gasp from the Pharisees and those with them. And from the crowd too, then they were quiet and attentive.

Yeshua continued, saying, "For they do not practice what they teach. They tie up heavy burdens, hard to bear, and lay them on the shoulders of others; but they themselves are unwilling to lift a finger to move them."

The crowd was shocked that Yeshua would dare to say these things in the presence of the Scribes and Pharisees and their associates. The Pharisees and those with them were livid. How dare he insult them so?

But Yeshua continued, saying, "They do all their deeds to be seen by others, for they make their phylacteries broad and their fringes long. They love to have the place of honour at banquets, and the best seats in the synagogues."

The Pharisees, Scribes and their cohort sitting in the best seats here in the Temple were shifting in their seats feeling uncomfortable, but the crowd, especially the women in the Women's Court were enjoying themselves. These were thoughts they all had and shared among themselves privately but would never dare say it publicly and here was Yeshua confronting the Pharisees in their presence.

Shimon and the disciples were extremely worried. They wanted Yeshua to stop. But Yeshua ploughed on.

Yeshua continued, "And they expect to be greeted with respect in the marketplaces, and to have people call them Rabbi. But you are not to be called Rabbi, for you have one Teacher and you are all students. And call no one your father on earth, for you have one Father—the one in heaven. Nor are you to be called instructors, for you have one instructor, the Messiah. The greatest among you will be your servant. All who exalt themselves will be humbled and all who humble themselves will be exalted. I have come not to be served but to serve, and give my life as a ransom to many."

There was a hush. The women and the other disciples of Yeshua were left wondering at Yeshua's last sentence. What did he mean about giving his life as a ransom for many?

But they immediately let those thoughts go as they listened to Yeshua continue.

Yeshua then said, "But woe to you Scribes and Pharisees, hypocrites! For you lock people out of the Kingdom of Heaven. For you do not go in yourselves and when others are going in, you stop them. Woe to you Scribes and Pharisees, hypocrites! For you cross sea and land to make a single convert, and you make the new convert twice as much a child of hell as yourselves.

"Woe to you Scribes and Pharisees, hypocrites! For you tithe mint, dill and cumin, and have neglected the weightier matters of the Law; justice, and mercy and faith. It's these you ought to have practiced without neglecting the others.

"Woe to you Scribes and Pharisees, hypocrites! For you clean the outside of the cup and of the plate, but inside you are full of greed and self-indulgence. You blind Pharisee! First clean the inside of the cup, so that the outside also may become clean."

"Wow! I can't believe what Yeshua is saying, condemning the Pharisees and Scribes and all those with them in such a vehement way," Miriam whispered to the women around her.

Shimon and the disciples were shaking their heads in consternation and disbelief. They could not believe what they were hearing. Never before has anyone expressed such harsh words of condemnation to the Pharisees, and the religious leaders, the upper crust of Judaean society in such vituperative terms, and face to face. They were extremely worried about the consequences for Yeshua.

But Yeshua seemed unperturbed. He continued saying, "Woe to you Scribes and Pharisees. Hypocrites! For you are like whitewashed tombs, which on the outside look beautiful but inside they are full of the stench of the bones of the dead and of all kinds of filth. So, you also on the outside look righteous, but inside you are full of hypocrisy and lawlessness."

The Scribes and Pharisees were up in arms, there was uproar. The chief priest spoke on their behalf, "How dare you speak to us like this, who do you think you are. We are the upholders of the Law; we have been appointed to teach and lead the people in the ways of the Law and the Prophets. You are but a simple carpenter from Nazareth of all places, how dare you insult us in this way." They were all seething with anger, and would very much like to take Yeshua away and arrest him, but they feared the people who regarded Yeshua as a great prophet.

The crowd, on the other hand, loved this confrontation, they were lapping it up. For them it was entertainment at its best. At last, someone has come to show up the Pharisees and their ilk, and to speak on behalf of the people, what they all held privately in their hearts.

But the chief priest would not concede, he continued speaking; he wanted to counter what Yeshua had just said about them as whitewashed tombs, so he said. "We are the ones who have built the tombs of the prophets out of respect for them, and we are the ones who have decorated the graves of the righteous. If we had lived in the days of our ancestors, we would not have taken part with them, in shedding the blood of the prophets."

Yeshua responded without letting up, "So you testify against yourselves, for you are descendants of those who murdered the prophets. You snakes, you brood of vipers! How can you escape being sentenced to hell?"

There was a gasp throughout the Temple. The Pharisees and the people too could not believe their ears. Never before had they heard anyone dare condemn the Scribes and Pharisees and the religious elite in such vivid and scathing language.

The Pharisees and those with them were seething, but there was nothing they could do. They were in a state of shock, shocked into silence.

Yeshua continued, "You are descendants of those who continue to kill the prophets. Therefore, I send you prophets, sages and scribes, some of whom you will kill and crucify, and some you will flog in your synagogues, and pursue from town to town, so that upon you may come all the righteous blood, shed on earth, from the blood of righteous Abel to the blood of Zechariah, son of Berechiah, whom you murdered between the sanctuary and the altar. Truly I tell you, all this will come upon this generation."

The Pharisees were at a loss of how to respond. And the people were lost in wonder and disbelief at what had just transpired. Never in their wildest dreams did they expect such outrageous and disparaging words of condemnation come out of the mouth of Yeshua. But they were on his side. He spoke on their behalf; he said what was simmering within all of them. He articulated what they were all feeling. But at what cost? He was putting himself in mortal danger.

Yeshua then concluded his words with a lament, "Jerusalem, Jerusalem, the city that kills the Prophets and stones those who are sent to it! How often have I desired to gather your children together as a hen gathers her brood under her wings, and you were not willing! See, your house is left to you, desolate. For I tell you, you will not see me again until you say, 'Blessed is the One who comes in the name of the Lord'!"

Yeshua then left and the disciples surrounded him. The crowds followed him outside. Miram, Rebecca, Lucia and Rachel caught up with the women who were sitting behind them and talked to them. They introduced themselves to each other. The women were friends with each other and they were from Jerusalem, Joanna, the wife of Chuza, Susanna and Salome.

"We were disciples of Johanan the Prophet, and we were baptised by him in the Jordan," Joanna said.

"You are the wife of Chuza, how uncanny we were just speaking about him, not so long ago, and he had arranged for some of our men, to visit Johanan in prison," Miriam said.

"You mention some of Yeshua's disciples, what do you mean, are you also disciples of Yeshua?" Joanna asked.

"Yes, we are, and not simply disciples like those who listen and believe a prophet, we are disciples in the real sense, for we follow Yeshua wherever he goes. We live with him and learn from him; he is teaching us everything he knows. We travel with him wherever he goes and we are witnesses to all he does, and he in turn seeks our advice and counsel, and we support him with whatever resources we have, and what people give us to do his work," Miriam said.

"All four of you?" Susanna asked.

"Yes, I am from Magdala, Rebecca is from Nazareth, and Lucia from Capernaum, and Rachel from a village at the foot of Mount Tabor," Miriam said.

"That is amazing. May we too be disciples and learn from Yeshua. I will be most willing to follow Yeshua, support him, and we have means, and to learn from him. When Johanan was imprisoned, we were at a loss. We had heard things about Yeshua from Johanan, and what happened when he baptised Yeshua, and Johanan had spoken so highly of Yeshua. And now that Johanan is in prison, we have been seeking a teacher. We heard that Yeshua is in Jerusalem for the Passover, and that he was speaking in the Temple this morning. And what words he spoke. It is a sign for me that God wants me to be his disciple," Joanna said.

"The same goes for me," Susanna said.

"And for me," Salome said too.

"Why don't you come and meet Yeshua. He will most likely be talking to the people right now outside the Temple," Miriam said.

The seven women then went together to see Yeshua. He was surrounded by the people, talking to them. But Yeshua did not speak for long. He sent the crowd away, saying he would be back next day at the same time. So, the crowd slowly dispersed.

When Miram and the women saw Yeshua alone with the men, they approached and introduced, Joanna, Susanna and Salome.

Yeshua was pleased to meet them. They spoke to Yeshua and told him how they had been baptised by Johanan and were his disciples and supported him in whatever way they could.

"Yeshua, we have spoken to Miriam and the women and we too wish to join them in following you wherever you go, and support you in whatever way we can, here in Jerusalem, for we are all from Jerusalem," Joanna said.

"We wish to learn from you Yeshua," Susanna said.

"We have heard of the wonders you have done, and listened to you speak this morning. We want to learn all we can from you, and support your work in whatever way we can," Salome said.

"Let it be so. I am thrilled to have you join us in spreading the Kingdom of God earth. Miriam will bring you up to date," was all that Yeshua said. He would find time to be with each of the women, get to know them and bless them. His band of disciples was growing and he was pleased. He felt the future of his work was in good hands.

"By the way Yeshua, I am the wife of Chuza, he has told me of helping your disciples meet with Johanan in prison," Joanna said. "He is an officer, a steward of Herod's but he was a disciple of Johanan's, and is doing all he can for Johanan while he is in prison," Joanna said.

Yeshua went quiet for a few moments, and then he said, "Come now, follow me, we will go to the Mount of Olives and spend some quiet time in the Garden of Gethsemane, and then have some lunch."

As they were leaving, Shimon pointed to the building of the Temple, saying to Yeshua and the others how fine a building it was.

Then Yeshua said to them, "You see this Temple do you not? Truly I tell you, not one stone will be left here, upon another; all will be thrown down."

The disciples were thrown by Yeshua's words, and did not know what to make of it.

They then continued walking towards the Mount of Olives, Yeshua walking on ahead of them by himself. Miriam and the others were talking to the newcomers, and telling all about what they had so far experienced with Yeshua. They spoke of what he taught them and also told them of all the wondrous deeds he had done. Miriam and Lucia and Rachel shared with them their personal experiences with Yeshua, how Yeshua healed them and made them whole.

And Rebecca told of how she grew up with Yeshua, and she delighted the women in telling how she pursued Yeshua, and was hoping to catch him. She told them how she tried but to no avail. "I persisted and persisted and was most unwomanly in throwing myself at Yeshua. I wanted him so much. There was just no other man like him in Nazareth, in the whole of Galilee for that matter. There was no man like him, and I wanted him for myself. But it was not to be. He speaks of his time being short with us, and that he has to give all his time and energy to spreading the Kingdom of God on earth. So being his disciple, and following him and supporting him is a great joy for me," Rebecca said. "She also told them all about the intimate times she had with Yeshua, walking alone with him in the bushland around Nazareth and him joining in running and racing her."

The women were all envious of Rebecca, and warmed to her, and could understand what she was feeling and experiencing towards Yeshua.

"He would be a great catch for any woman" Salome said.

"He is ruggedly attractive. And his own man. He is fearless. Look how he attacked the Pharisees and their mob, pulling no punches, and telling them like it is," Susanna said.

"Yes, indeed. Imagine him calling them whitewashed tombs beautiful from the outside and full of the stench of dead men's bones within. What powerful and destroying words are those, and he was willing to speak to them to their faces. No one, man or woman would have dared to do what he did," Joanna said.

"And now as people walk past the cemetery and see all those beautiful white painted tombs, they will remember Yeshua's words," Joanna said.

"And the Pharisees and their cronies, whenever they see those whitewashed tombs, will cringe," Salome said.

The men too were discussing what had happened in the Temple. But they were very concerned.

"I bet you the Pharisees and their cohort are gathering together right now, and plotting their revenge, and what they can do to bring Yeshua down. There are so many of them in Jerusalem right now. The Sanhedrin alone has seventy-two members, and now they have chief priests, Scribes, Sadducees, and Elders from all over Judaea and Galilee and elsewhere, here with them. And I'm sure the Sanhedrin is meeting with the high priest Caiaphas and telling him all that has happened. And then there is Herod, I'm sure he will hear of this. As well as Pilate, who is now in Jerusalem," Shimon said.

"I don't think we should stay in Jerusalem, it is just too dangerous," Andreus said. "Shimon speak to Yeshua. Tell him to be more careful and not antagonise the Pharisees anymore," Andreus added.

"He won't listen to me, you know that, he makes up his own mind," Shimon said.

"In any case, I don't think the Pharisees and their mob will try anything, Yeshua has the people on his side, there will be an uprising if they did," Thomas said.

By now the women were also talking about the dangers Yeshua was facing. The women from Jerusalem were very conversant with the likes of the Pharisees, and Joanna, being the wife of one of Herod's officers, knew so much about the goings on in the court. She had a very low opinion of Herod. He had even flirted with her when she had accompanied her husband to a function in the palace.

Joanna spoke, "It is now almost one hundred years since we were colonised by the Romans. And it looks like we will continue to be under their thumb for another hundred years. The Romans made Herod, father of Archelaus, ruler, in name only really, over this colony of theirs. Herod died about thirty years ago, and the Romans divided the kingdom among Herod's three sons. Archelaus of course, we know ruled over all of Judaea and Samaria until he died about fifteen years ago, and Antipas over Galilee and Peraea, and Herod Philip over the other most northerly regions."

"Why did Herod Antipas imprison Johanan?" Rebecca asked.

"Because Johanan dared to criticise him, reprimanding him for marrying Herodias, who was wife of his brother Philip," Joanna said.

"So, he broke up their marriage," Rebecca said.

"And I believe that Herodias is just as ruthless as Antipas," Susanna said.

Joanna then spoke of all the religious groups and sects, among the Jews. "We have of course the much-loathed Pharisees who think they are God's gift to humankind, and whom Yeshua so adeptly brought down to size. And we had the Zealots, who were more of an underground political movement wanting to get rid of the Roman presence, they were like freedom fighters. They really wanted to overthrow the Roman government and rule over the whole of Judaea themselves. But they have been squashed and now almost non-existent, but I think they are still smouldering underground and waiting to strike again," Joanna said.

"And then we have the Essenes, who are even more religiously fanatic than the Pharisees. We think that Johanan the Prophet was one on them but left to do his own thing. I think he became disillusioned with their ways; they became more supercilious, like the Pharisees and also a bit like the Zealots in wanting to overthrow Rome. Then there are the Sadducees, you met and heard some of them in the Temple trying to undermine Yeshua," Joanna said.

"How interesting, Joanna, all these various groups existing, here in Jerusalem," Rebecca said. "What are the Sadducees all about?" Rebecca asked.

"The Sadducees, I think are the opposite of the Zealots and the Essenes. The Sadducees, are more, shall I say, conservative, though a bit like the Pharisees. They cling to all our ancient Hebrew traditions and reject anything new, so you can see why they are so opposed to Yeshua's teachings. They don't believe in any afterlife or any kind of resurrection. So, they were at loggerheads with Johanan, and now with Yeshua. Unlike the Essenes and the Zealots, they collaborate with the Romans to maintain the situation as it is," Joanna continued.

"What other groups are there?" Rachel asked, now very interested to know who Yeshua was up against.

"Many more, we have of course the Chief Priests and the Elders. The chief priests offer the sacrifices like all the other priests but are responsible for the running of the Temple, all the organisation and administration and they were out in full force this morning attacking Yeshua," Joanna said.

"Then there are the Elders, the rich, they are the upper class, our aristocracy if you like, they are the rich landowners, and own most of the land. And of course, we can't forget the Scribes or rabbis, they are the intellectuals, the most learned of the groups, they know the Law inside out, and among them are the foremost Teachers and Lawyers and the like, but they are not priests," Joanna continued.

"But they still proved no match for Yeshua," Rachel said, smiling.

"Tell us about Johanan, the prophet," Rachel asked. "What was he like?"

"He was a great prophet. Different to Yeshua, I would say. He was, is more intense, whereas Yeshua seems more relaxed," Susanna said, for she was also a disciple of Johanan, as was Salome and Joanna.

"Yeshua is relaxed alright. He loves being with people, all kinds of people, rich and poor alike. He treats everyone with the greatest respect and affection. He is full of compassion and generosity and never condemns anyone really, except what happened in the Temple today, really surprised me, it was so out of character," Rebecca said.

"Not really, while Yeshua is kind and respectful, he will not fail to call out any form of injustice or hypocrisy, and the Pharisees got what they deserved," Miriam said.

"I suppose you're right, Miriam," Rebecca agreed.

"So go on telling us about Johanan," Rachel said.

"Johanan, well he was very serious. And he looked a bit wild and scruffy. As you know he was living by himself in the wilderness for so long, living on locusts and wild honey. He preached a harsh teaching, an angry God who was disappointed with the people, and he was going to rain down punishment unless the people repented of their sins. And according to Johanan a prophet would come who would execute God's justice and punishment on the people. One thing he had in common with Yeshua was his criticism of the Pharisees; he also had harsh words for them, but not with so many words as Yeshua did, in the Temple," Susanna said.

"I wonder what is going to happen to him, languishing like that in prison. Will he ever be released?" Rebecca asked.

"We sincerely hope so. But it seems very unlikely. Herod is afraid of releasing him, and it seems, afraid too of executing him. He is afraid of divine retribution because it seems that Herod believes Johanan to be a prophet. We will have to wait and see what Herod does, we can only pray he will release Johanan," Susanna said.

When they all arrived at the foot of the Mount of Olives, Yeshua rested on a rock, and the disciples found places to sit and rest as well. Then Phillip asked Yeshua, "Yeshua you seemed to say that a time is coming when the Temple will be destroyed, tell us when will this be, and what will be the sign of the coming of the end of the age?"

The disciples were glad that Phillip put that question to Yeshua and they all listened with interest to what Yeshua would say.

Yeshua answered, "Beware that no one leads you astray. For many will come in my name saying, 'I am the Messiah!' and they will lead many astray. And you will hear of wars and rumours of wars, and pestilences and worldwide epidemics, pandemics that will infect every nation on the earth, and that will lead to despair and a sense of hopelessness, and people will turn against each other. See that you are not alarmed, for this must take place, but the end is not yet. For nation will rise up against nation, and kingdom against kingdom, and there will be famines and earthquakes and severe and destructive storms in various places, and fires and droughts that will destroy people and their homes and their livelihoods and there will be much despair in various places. All this is but the beginning of the birth pangs."

The disciples were all silent. Then Yeshua told them of future persecutions that awaited them. "There will come a time, when you will be persecuted, and you will be handed over to be tortured, and will be put to death, and you will be hated by all nations because of my name. My name and all those who are my disciples will be ridiculed. And what I have taught and what you will teach will be misunderstood, ignored or misinterpreted, and people will still worship the false gods of power, greed, money, wealth, position, prestige, reputation, popularity and worldliness, and God will be forgotten and sidelined, as people become consumed with consuming this world's goods, and there will be worldwide exploitation of this world's resources by the rich and powerful. There will be the new Herod's and Pilates and Pharisees of the world, and the rich and powerful will become richer and more powerful at the expense of the poor. Rich nations will exploit poorer nations and the poor will become poorer. Then many will fall away, and they will betray one another, and hate one another. And many false prophets will arise and lead many astray. And because of the increase of lawlessness, the love of many will grow cold. But the one who endures in the face of all this, and not lose their inner peace and love and compassion, and endures to the end, will be saved. And the Good News of the Kingdom of God will be proclaimed throughout the world, as a testimony to all the nations, and the end will come."

"Yeshua what you are telling us is scary. How will we know that the end has come?" Thomas asked.

"There is no need to fear Thomas, I will be with you, and I am with you to the end of time. Immediately after the suffering of those days, the sun will be darkened, and the moon will not give its light, the stars will fall from heaven, and the powers of heaven will be shaken. Then the sign of the Son of Man, the Son of God made man, will appear in heaven, and then all the tribes of the earth will mourn, and they will see the Son of God made man, coming on the clouds of heaven with power and great glory. And God will send out his angels, and they will gather his elect from the four winds, from one end of heaven to the other."

The disciples were troubled by what they were hearing. Yeshua was talking to them like he had never spoken to the crowds. What he was saying was similar to the warnings of Johanan, who preached a lot about the end of the world.

"Yeshua, what you are saying is frightening. I know that God created the world and that time then began, and that time will end, but God will never end. And as he created all there is, he can also end all there is. When will this day come?" Thomas asked, still not satisfied with what Yeshua had just said.

"Yes, all of creation will come to an end, but you will not, humankind will not. God has created you to his own image; you all have been endowed with immortality. In this way you are like God, eternal. I have come to bring you life and life to the full. I have come to conquer evil and death. And I will be with you to the end of time and in all eternity," Yeshua said.

The disciples were consoled with these words of Yeshua. Yeshua continued, "In answer to your question Thomas, take a lesson from the fig tree."

There were smiles all around, especially from Miriam and Rebecca, for they all knew how much Yeshua loved figs, relished eating figs. They were now more relaxed and listened to what Yeshua was to teach them.

Yeshua continued, "From the fig tree, learn its lesson; as soon as its branch becomes tender and puts forth its leaves, you know that summer is near. So also, when you see and experience all these things, you know that He is near, at the very gates. Truly I tell you, this generation will not pass away until all these things have taken place. Heaven and earth will pass away; but my words will not pass away. But about that day and hour, no one knows; neither the angels of heaven, nor the Son, only the Father. So, you must be ready for the Son of God, who is also the Son of Man, is coming at an unexpected hour."

Yeshua spoke some more in parables about the end of times and the coming of the Son, and final judgement. The disciples however wanted to change the subject and were glad when Johanan did.

Johanan told Yeshua all about his visit with James, to Johanan in the prison. And then he said to Yeshua, "Yeshua, Johanan told us to ask you, if you are the Messiah, the promised Redeemer, Saviour of the people?"

"Thank you, Johanan and James, for visiting Johanan, I am saddened that he still languishes there. I tell you, among those born of women, no one is greater than Johanan; yet the least in the Kingdom of God is greater than he."

"Yeshua, the people had a great respect for Johanan and listened to him and believed what he preached, and were baptised, except the Pharisees, and the lawyers, refused to be baptised by him," James said.

Yeshua then said, "To what then shall I compare the people of this generation, and what are they like? They are like children sitting in the marketplace and calling to one another, 'We played the flute for you, and you did not dance; we wailed and you did not weep.' For Johanan the baptiser has come eating no bread and drinking no wine, and this generation say, 'He has a demon.' The Son of God become Man has come eating and drinking and this generation says, 'Look a glutton and a drunkard, a friend of tax-collectors and sinners.' And future generation will fare no better. They will laugh at the truth at the Son of God becoming the Son of Man. They will regard him as a figment of the imagination of past generations. They will scoff at the idea that God can become man, and dwell among us. And they will dismiss his teaching of love and compassion, of loving all without exception, of loving one's enemies, loving those who hate us and doing good to those who do us harm."

"Yeshua, what do we say to Johanan, to his question of whether you are the Messiah, or are we to await another?"

All the disciples were now all agog; they wanted to hear what Yeshua had to say.

Yeshua said to his disciples, "Go and tell Johanan what you have seen and heard; the blind receive their sight, the lame walk, the lepers are cleansed, the deaf hear, the dead are raised, and the poor have the Good News brought to them."

And then Yeshua stopped and said, "Come now, I think you all have had enough of me talking today, and I have spoken enough, it is time for us to eat."

"Yeshua, we can offer you and your disciples a meal. And Salome, Susanna and I have plenty of accommodation between us, and we have several friends, also former disciples of Johanan who will be willing to offer lodging for your disciples," Joanna said.

"That is most kind of you, Joanna, we gratefully accept. Speak to Andreus, he manages all that for us," Yeshua said. "So now, we will follow you. A simple lunch will do," Yeshua said.

All eleven men and seven women and Yeshua walked along, chatting with each other and following Joanna. When they arrived at the neighbourhood, they all convened at Joanna's place. Salome and Susanna spoke to Andreus about arrangements, for all of them. It was agreed that Yeshua and Miriam, Rebecca, Lucia and Rachel would stay with Joanna, for she had lots of place. And then Susanna and Salome left to make arrangements for lodgings for the eleven men disciples.

They sat and had some wine while the servants prepared a meal for them all. There was much joviality.

After luncheon, Miriam said, "Yeshua, it has been a strenuous morning for you. Would you like to have a nap and take some rest?"

"I have a spare room all ready for guests. Yeshua, a bed is all ready with clean linen," Joanna said.

"Thank you, Miriam and Joanna, but I am quite refreshed with that lovely lunch. I am reenergised. I would like to visit the people in the outlining areas, the little villages, those who would not come into the city at this time," Yeshua said.

"A lot of them do come into the city, Yeshua, at this time, to beg," Joanna said.

"Yes, you are right; we will talk to them too. But let us go to those cast out because they are considered sinners and unclean, and the poor and the sick," Yeshua said.

So, after all had a wash, they were about to go on their way. By this time, Salome and Susanna had returned, so had Johanan and James who had visited and reported to Johanan what Yeshua had said. Johanan and James returned with Judas, as Johanan had insisted, they go and see Judas and take him to Yeshua.

"Yeshua, this is Judas Iscariot, a leading disciple of Johanan, who is here to meet you," James said.

"Judas, yes, I have heard others speak of you. You are a keen businessman, and you work with your father in his many businesses. What is it you seek of me?" Yeshua said.

"Yeshua, I was a disciple of Johanan. I tried to support him in whatever way I could. He spoke of someone who was to follow him and that the Messiah too was to come and save us all. Johanan spoke to me about you, and told me what happened when he baptised you. And I have heard many other things about you, and what you teach. And your disciples Johanan and James Zebedee have informed me further. I am here to join your disciples, to follow you and assist you in your work," Judas said.

"You are most welcome, Judas. All the men disciples I have are from Galilee, and I am pleased that you are from Judaea. Speak with Andreus, he will bring you up to date," Yeshua said. And so, Judas too became another disciple, making up the twelve men, Yeshua had in mind.

"We are on our way now. You may join us Judas or you may wish to spend some time with Andreus, to brief you on all that I have taught and done so far," Yeshua said.

"That will be good. I will spend time with Andreus, and then speak with my father, and let him know my plans," Judas said.

While Yeshua and the others visited all those in the surrounding villages, the poor and outcasts, Judas spent time with Andreus.

Judas listened and had lots of questions to ask Andreus. Andreus told Judas about Yeshua's encounter in the Temple with his opponents, and that they will most probably be back tomorrow morning when Yeshua will teach again in the Temple.

"They will be sure to return in full force, and with reinforcements, and prepared to attack Yeshua," Andreus said.

When Judas heard that all of them had been travelling all over Galilee and now in Judaea for more than a year and where all they had gone, he was surprised.

"How have you supported all of you, for all that time?" Judas asked.

"Shimon and I and our father have a thriving fishing business in partnership with Johanan and James and their father Zebedee. We continue to receive some income from the business. Miriam is from Magdala and her father owns vineyards and a winemaking plant in Capernaum and she too supports us financially, as do other women. And we have been blessed wherever we travel people make us welcome and provide us with accommodation and food. And here in Jerusalem, Yeshua has three new women disciples, Joanna, Susanna and Salome and they have offered to accommodate and feed us, together with some of their friends who were also disciples of Johanan the baptiser," Andreus said. "And they have already offered financial support as well."

Judas was very impressed. "So, who looks after all your finance?" Judas asked.

"Mattheus, he is, or rather was a chief tax-collector, from Galilee," Andreus said.

"A tax-collector? Really!" Judas said, full of surprise.

"Miriam and the ladies help with all the gifts other than money that we receive. And Miriam is in charge of the women," Andreus said.

"Judas, you have lots of business experience, would you mind being our treasurer and looking after our finances," Mattheus has expressed a desire for someone else to take over our financial affairs.

Andreus was so pleased when Judas agreed. "I will let Yeshua, Mattheus and the others know you will be our treasurer from now on," Andreus said.

"So, you have been with Yeshua for over a year. You have been his disciple so you learned from him. So, tell me, what is the essence of his teaching, the core of his message?" Judas asked.

"The core of his message," Andreus said out loud. "Now no one has ever asked me that. Yeshua gave us Ten Commandments, sort of, not the Ten Commandments of Moses, but more or less which Johanan has now termed for us the 'Beatitudes.' It is like a manifesto, a charter of sorts for all of us to follow. And the very first one is about being blessed if you are poor, for the Kingdom of God belongs to the poor. That seems to be foremost in Yeshua's teaching and it is encapsulated in his life. He has a preferential love for the poor. And he wants us to be poor in spirit, and poor in every way, and to love and care for the poor. When he spoke to us about the Ten Commandments given to us through Moses, he always spoke of the Beatitudes and he summed up all in what I would say is the core of his message and that is to love God with all our heart, with all our soul and with all our strength, and our neighbour as ourselves. The essence of his teaching is that God loves us with an unfathomable, boundless, infinite, unconditional and compassionate love and that we in turn have to love everyone as God loves us, and as we love ourselves," Andreus said.

"So, what would be the second most important of his teaching?" Judas wanted to know more. Judas was hoping for some inkling of Yeshua's teaching about God's justice and retribution against Rome and saving the people.

"The second! Mmm, I suppose the need for compassion and also humility. You should have been in the Temple when he destroyed the pride and arrogance of the Pharisees. He wants us to be humble, and he keeps telling us that the proud will be humbled and the humbled will be raised up. And he tells us that if we want to be the greatest then we must be the servant of all, and that he came not to be served but to serve," Andreus said.

Andreus was glad for the questions put to him by Judas. He had not really been asked these questions before, and it gave him an opportunity to articulate Yeshua's teaching, for he knew the day would come when Yeshua would no longer be with them, and that he and the other disciples would have to carry on his teaching. But he hoped that would be many years in the future.

After they had finished their discussions, Judas excused himself and Andreus told him that Yeshua would be at the Temple around mid-morning, the next day.

Chapter Sixty
The House of Ill Repute

While Yeshua was going about visiting the poor and the outcasts, he also stopped at the house of prostitution. None of the disciples would enter with him, except the women disciples. Miriam was not surprised for she had taken him to the house of prostitution in Magdala where Yeshua had made friends and a number of those women have since left that way of life. The other women accompanied Yeshua as well. The men however knew that Yeshua had a reputation of befriending prostitutes, and that he was condemned for this. But he didn't care. He was full of love and compassion for them.

There were some men there, and when they saw Yeshua, they recognised Yeshua from the Temple, for they too had been present. Yeshua did not condemn them either, he felt only compassion. Yeshua knew that in the beginning only the good existed, that his Father had created all in his own image of goodness but that humankind wanted more, wanted to be like God, wanted power and position and authority and prestige, so they rebelled, and so evil entered the will, and sin and death entered the world. And that prostitution had existed soon after that. Yeshua knew that the spirit of humankind is willing but that the flesh is weak. And that humankind needs to turn to God for forgiveness and for strength to turn away from sin.

The women were awestruck seeing Yeshua, and some women with him, in this house of theirs, on the edge of the town. They knew of him, heard about him and that he was a man of God, a Prophet, and a miracle worker, but they had never met him, and even though they heard that he befriended prostitutes, they never dreamed he would visit them here in Jerusalem, and at this time, their busiest, as men from all over Judaea and Galilee and elsewhere would seek out their services.

Yeshua spent some time with the women. Yeshua did not question them about why they were doing what they were doing. But some of them offered reasons.

"Yeshua, I was desperate. My husband divorced me and left me with two young children and I had no gainful employment and no one would hire me. I was blamed for our marriage breakdown," the woman said.

"Yeshua, I was beaten by my husband, and then when our son was of age, he too beat me often. I could take no more so I left, and everyone condemned me for leaving my husband and I sought refuge here. The women took me in, they did not force me to do anything, they showed me kindness but soon I had to earn a living and support myself, and there was no other way for me."

"I was too proud to beg," another said.

"Yeshua, I was never married. But my parents fought all the time, and finally divorced and my mother left Jerusalem to live with her family, and my dad was a drunkard and she left me with him, I could not live with him like that, so I left and landed up here," another said.

"Yeshua, I had no way of earning a living and I knew this is easy money, so I came here," another said brazenly.

Yeshua listened with love and compassion. Before he left, he said, "I have come not to condemn anyone, and not to condemn you, but to tell you of God's love for you. Only he knows what is in your hearts, and only he is judge of all. For me, for all of us, we are not to judge, for we know not what is in the heart of another. All we are called to do is to not judge one another, but to love one another, as God loves us, and as we love ourselves. God loves you; I can guarantee you that, and he wants you to love him in return and to love one another," Yeshua said.

The women were comforted by Yeshua's words, and his compassion and they were quite heartened to see that Yeshua was travelling with some women.

Miriam and Lucia told them of how Yeshua touched their lives, how he cured them. And the other women also spoke of Yeshua's kindness to them, and that they felt so privileged to follow Yeshua and to be his disciples.

This pleased the women so much. No other spiritual leader had women as their disciples in the way that Miriam and the other women were disciples, on par with the men.

Yeshua spoke of Miriam and the other women disciples with such affection and admiration and told the women of the house how much he appreciated their discipleship, their support, their wisdom, their example, and their counsel.

Yeshua and his disciples left, leaving the women with much to think about. Miriam told them Yeshua would be speaking in the Temple the next day in the morning, and that the women were most welcome to attend.

As they were walking towards the town, a man came running towards them. He went down on one knee and bowed at Yeshua, "Please get up Sir, what brings you here?" Yeshua said.

"Sir, I am a servant of Shimon, he is a Pharisee and he has sent me to invite you to dinner," the servant said.

"Tell your employer Shimon that I accept," Yeshua said, "and tell him my disciples will be with me, we are a group of twenty, if that is, okay?" Yeshua asked.

"That will be fine Sir, my master will be much pleased," the servant said. "You may all meet at the Temple entrance and I will fetch you," he added.

"Good, young man, we should be there around the eleventh hour, tell Shimon we are looking forward to the meal," Yeshua said.

When the servant rushed off, Shimon said to Yeshua, "Yeshua are you sure that is a good idea. It could be a trap. After what you said to the Pharisees in the Temple, I think you should avoid them like the plague."

"Yes Yeshua, I agree with Shimon, it could be dangerous," Johanan added.

And the other disciples agreed.

"It will be okay, my time has not yet come," was all that Yeshua said, and that was settled.

At the eleventh hour, Yeshua and all of his disciples arrived at the Temple, Andreus and Judas included. Andreus had already informed Mattheus that he was relieved of his duties as treasurer, and that Judas was taking over. Mattheus was delighted. Being in charge of the finances reminded him so much of his previous life. He could now give his full attention to the teaching of the Master and support him as best he could. Andreus also informed Yeshua and the rest of the disciples.

When Yeshua and his disciples arrived at the Temple, two servants were waiting for them. They bowed obsequiously to Yeshua and his disciples. Yeshua bowed in return and greeted them. "Peace to you, my friends. Thank you for coming to fetch us, lead the way and we will follow."

As Yeshua and his disciples were walking Yeshua was recognised. And the people hailed Yeshua, and wanted to approach him but Andreus, Shimon and Judas stopped them.

"The Master is off to have his dinner. He will be at the Temple tomorrow morning where you may listen to him there," Shimon said.

The people then left Yeshua and walked away, but still looking at Yeshua in wonder.

Yeshua and the disciples arrived at a grand house, a big stone building with a large front porch. Shimon and some servants were standing at the front door, and they welcomed Yeshua profusely.

"Maybe Shimon wasn't at the Temple, when Yeshua criticised the Pharisees so," Johanan whispered to the others.

They all entered a big room, more like a hall. In the middle was a long table filled with a feast fit for a king. But all around the room were other guests. And the disciples began to feel unsettled.

"They must all be Pharisees, for sure," James whispered to the other disciples.

"Yeshua, gentlemen, ladies, you are most welcome to my home, and to share my table with me. With me are some of my family and relatives and some of my community. You are most welcome to my home. Please help yourselves. The servants will serve you with cups of wine," Shimon said warmly.

Yeshua thanked Shimon and the servants and then he said, "May we begin, with a prayer of thanks to our heavenly Father?"

"Yes, please do," Shimon, their host said.

Yeshua closed his eyes for a moment and then opened them and prayed, "Heavenly Father, I give you thanks for friendship and hospitality. I thank you for giving me so many friends and disciples, and I thank you for Shimon and his friends and family, and I ask you to bless them for their kindness and hospitality, and I ask you to bless all the servants and all who had a hand in preparing this feast for us. We praise you Father and we thank you for the fruits of the earth and for all we are about to receive."

Then there was chatter all around. The disciples were so hungry they forgot all about their anxieties and got stuck into the food. The servants brought the guests cups of fine wine. And they all drank and ate to their hearts content.

After about an hour and a half when they had quite a bit to eat, there was a kafuffle at the entrance and a woman stormed in. She was scantily dressed. Then Judas recognised her, as did some of the other disciples, and Miriam and the women as well. She was one of the women they had met at the house of prostitution.

There was a gasp as the hosts and their relatives and the Pharisees saw the woman. Before they could react, she was already standing close to Yeshua.

Shimon the host yelled, "Get her out of here!"

But Yeshua raised his hand in a gesture, restraining Shimon.

Then the woman spoke, "Yeshua I have searched for you, and was told that you are here at the house of Shimon the Pharisee."

The woman had brought an alabaster jar full of perfume, with her. She knelt down at Yeshua's feet, weeping, and began to bathe his feet with her tears, and to dry them with her long hair. Then she began kissing Yeshua's feet, and anointing them with the perfume.

Now, when Shimon, who had invited him saw this he was appalled, and he said to himself, what the other Pharisees were thinking, 'If Yeshua were a prophet, he would know who and what kind of woman this is who is touching him—that she is a sinner.'

The Pharisees present were murmuring to each other. "Surely he can see what kind of woman that is touching him," whispered one, who knew the woman as he was a frequent visitor to the house of ill repute. "By her dress and her loose hair, he must know she is a sinful woman," said another. "She is one of the prostitutes from the house of ill repute," whispered another. "By letting this woman touch him, Yeshua is allowing himself to become unclean, and he could make us all unclean," whispered another.

Yeshua knew what they were all thinking, and whispering to themselves, so he turned to his host, Shimon, and said, "Shimon I have something to say to you."

"Teacher," Shimon replied, "speak!"

"A certain creditor had two debtors; one owed five hundred denarii, and the other fifty. When they could not pay, he cancelled the debts for both of them. Now which of them will love him more?"

Shimon answered, "I suppose the one for whom he cancelled the greater debt."

And Yeshua said to him, "you have judged rightly." Then turning to the woman, Yeshua said to him, "Shimon, do you see this woman? I entered your house; you gave me no water to wash my feet, but she has bathed my feet with her tears, and dried them with her hair. You gave me no kiss, but from the time she came in, she has not stopped kissing my feet. You did not anoint my head with oil, but she has anointed my feet with perfume. Therefore, I tell you, her sins which were many, have been forgiven; hence she has shown great love. But the one to whom little is forgiven, loves little."

Then Yeshua turned to the woman and took her by the hands and lifted her to her feet, and kissed her on her cheek, and said to her, "My dear one, your sins are forgiven."

The Pharisees were shocked by Yeshua's words and actions, and were now mumbling among themselves. "Who is this who even forgives sins," Shimon their host, said.

And Yeshua said to the woman, "My dear, your faith has saved you; go in peace."

Tears were running down Miriam's cheeks as well as the other women. The other disciples were astounded. They did not expect Yeshua to treat the woman with such a display of affection. But they were not surprised with the compassion he displayed. And it was not the first time he forgave sins.

Yeshua then turned to his host, Shimon and the Pharisees and said, "Do not judge, and you will not be judged. Do not condemn and you will not be condemned. Forgive and you will be forgiven. Give and it will be given to you. A good measure, pressed down, shaken together, running over, will be put into your lap; for the measure you give, will be the measure you get back."

Just then the servants came in with desserts, all sorts of cakes, nuts, delicacies, dates, olives, grapes, and all sorts of fruit, including figs. Yeshua's eyes lit up and he helped himself to the juiciest fig.

Then Yeshua said, not only to the Pharisees but to all present, Shimon and his family and relatives, to Shimon and Andreus, Miriam and Rebecca and all of his disciples; words he had often uttered before, but the sight of the figs brought those words back, "No good tree bears bad fruit, nor again does a bad tree bear good fruit, for each tree is known by its own fruit." Then Yeshua took a second juicy fig and held it up for all to see and said, "Figs are not gathered from thorns." And then he picked up a bunch of grapes, and said, "Nor is grapes picked from a bramble bush." Then looking to his disciples and then to everyone around the room he said, "The good person, out of the treasure of the heart produces good, and the evil person out of evil treasure produces evil; for it is out of the abundance of the heart that the mouth speaks."

Yeshua continued, "Many people call me Lord, Lord, and do not do what I tell them. I will show you what someone is like who comes to me; hears my words, and acts on them. That person is like a man building a house, who dug deeply, and laid the foundation on rock; when the flood arose, the river burst against that house but could not shake it, because it had been well built. But the one who hears and does not act is like a man who built a house on the ground, without a foundation. When the river burst against it, immediately it fell, and great was the ruin of that house."

Yeshua then stopped talking and simply held the fig in one hand and the grapes in the other, deciding which to eat first. The disciples were watching Yeshua and smiling. Philip turned to Nathanael and said, "You want to bet, Yeshua will eat the fig first."

Just then, Yeshua looked at Philip and smiled, he had heard what Philip said, Yeshua looked at the fig and the grapes again, and then looking at Philip and Nathanael, and the other disciples were now also in the game, and Yeshua slowly put the fig down on the table and began eating the grapes, and smiling at his disciples.

The rest of the occasion went without a hitch. But the disciples could feel the air thaw somewhat since the woman came and went and Yeshua's words to Shimon and those with him.

When Yeshua thought it was time, he said to Shimon and his wife and family and the servants and all present. "Shimon, I want to thank you and your wife and all your family for offering us this scrumptious dinner, it was a feast fit for a king. I thank you for your kindness and hospitality." And turning to the servants, Yeshua smiled and thanked them warmly. The servants were surprised for never before had a guest ever thanked them.

Yeshua and his disciples then left, but before they did, Shimon and Andreus told everyone that Yeshua would be teaching in the Temple on the next morning, and he hoped to see them all there. They then left.

Chapter Sixty-One
Losing His Head

While Yeshua and his disciples were feasting at the home of Shimon the Pharisee, a terrible event was taking place in Herod's palace, which would shock so many, and break so many hearts. Herod still had Johanan languishing in prison because Johanan dared criticise him publicly for marrying Herodias, the wife of his brother Philip. But Herod would not have him killed for Herod feared Johanan, knowing that he was a holy and righteous man. He liked to listen to Johanan even though he would be greatly mystified by some of what he was saying.

Today was Herod's birthday. And he gave a great banquet. While Yeshua and his disciples were feasting at Shimon's place, Herod too had a great feast, a banquet fit for a king. All his courtiers, officers, and leaders of Galilee were present. All those that were in Jerusalem for the celebration of the Passover, were present. There was abundance of the best food and wine, and the musicians on the flute and harp entertained Herod and his guests and there were the usual acrobats and jokers and there was much laughter and everyone was letting their hair down, and kowtowing to Herod.

Then the music came on, and there was a hush all over the place, as Salome, his step daughter appeared, in a gorgeous and provocative dress, displaying her curvaceous figure and so much cleavage. Salome was blessed with great beauty and she knew it. The men were gawking, at such a rare sight. Herod too was mesmerised by Salome's beauty and her almost see through flowing attire. His wife Herodias, mother of Salome, sitting next to Herod was delighted. She could see the impression Salome was making on Herod.

"Did you arrange this, my darling?" Herod turned and said to his wife, who had a broad smile. "She looks absolutely stunning."

"Sshh, watch her dance," his wife said.

Herod and all the guests could not take their eyes off Salome, she was an excellent dancer. She was as graceful as a swan, and as provocative as a temptress. Herod was gawking and his wife, Herodias, stole a glance, and was pleased, for she had an ulterior motive in arranging her daughter to dance. She was hoping her plot would work. Herodias hated Johanan for publicly condemning both her and Herod, and Herodias wanted Johanan killed but Herod would not. She was hoping to get him drunk and in a good mood by watching Salome dancing, and then she would strike, like a viper, while his defences were down, and persuade him to have Johanan killed. She wanted Johanan out of their lives forever.

And it worked. Herod and all the guests were so enchanted with Salome's appearance and her dancing. The men were salivating like dogs. Herod too was extremely delighted. And in a compulsive gesture he called Salome to him. She came forward and provocatively, as her mother had coached her, knelt at the feet of Herod, displaying her ample cleavage.

Herod, then for all to hear, said to Salome, "Salome, ask me whatever you wish and I will give it," He was so taken in by Salome that he went even further, and promised her something he would deeply regret. Herod said to her, "Salome I swear to you, whatever you ask I will give you, even half of my kingdom."

As soon as he said those words, Herodias felt like dancing. She was over the moon. This was going to be easier than she had planned, and hoped for.

Salome came up alongside her mother and in a soft voice for no one else to hear, she asked her mother, "Mother, what should I ask for?"

Herodias then in a soft voice as well, so that no one could hear, said to her daughter, "Ask for the head of Johanan the baptiser."

For a moment, Salome was shocked. She did not expect that. She was hoping for something precious and valuable for herself and riches for herself, but she dared not go against her mother's wishes. She was fully aware of how ruthless her mother could be, and in a way, she too hated Johanan, not as much as Herod and her mother did, but nevertheless she hated him, and all he had said and all he stood for, so she went and stood before Herod.

A hush came over the guests as they saw what was unfolding, and an air of expectation hung like a cloud. They had seen Salome consult with her mother, and they wondered what Salome would ask for. They were silent wanting to hear what she was about to ask.

Standing in front of Herod, Salome brazenly made her request. "My King, I want you to give me the head of Johanan the baptiser, on a platter."

There was one almighty gasp, as if everyone was choking on whatever was in their mouths. "What did she ask for?" one of the guests said, not believing his ears.

"She asked for the head of Johanan the baptiser, on a platter," his friend, standing next to him replied.

Everyone was in a state of shock. But then as the minutes passed, they began to realise that it was bound to happen eventually. They all knew that Herod would not set Johanan free and that Johanan would die in prison. But now Herod had to act. The guests waited in heightened expectation to how Herod would respond.

Herod too was in a state of shock. Not in his wildest dreams did he anticipate Salome's request. But then on second thought he saw Herodias' hand in what had just happened. He knew she had hatched this plan, and he was greatly distressed, yet he could not lose face, and had to honour his oath and his guests, so he could not refuse Salome. Immediately he acted. He called a guard to him and ordered him. "Bring me Johanan's head on a platter."

The guests were aghast. They did not expect Herod to act so swiftly. But Herodias was highly pleased. Her plan was coming to perfection. She was smiling. Herod and the guests then continued with the festivity, everyone reaching for their cup of wine. Herod had his silver chalice filled with more wine and he gulped it down without catching a breath, and then requested a refill.

It wasn't too much later, when the gong sounded and everyone knew that the guard was returning. Then he appeared, with extra guards one on either side of him. The guard carried the head of Johanan the baptiser on a large silver platter, the head still dripping with blood. A gasp rippled throughout the room. It was a gruesome sight. Herod himself was aghast. He gulped down his wine and then sat there frozen and speechless. The guests held their breath, some holding their hands to their mouths; others had their mouths agape in disbelief. The guests were stunned; they could not believe what had just happened and what they were witnessing.

Herodias however had a smirk of triumph on her face. Salome sitting next to her had a frozen look; no one could fathom what was going on in her head.

Herod was momentarily thrown off balance. He was briefly in shock, not believing what he was seeing, but he quickly recovered, and then in a bizarre action, Herod took the platter with Johanan's head, and carried it and gave it to Salome.

Salome, seemingly emotionless, as if she were in a trance, gave the platter with Johanan's head to her mother. Herodias, equally and apparently emotionless, placed the platter and Johanan's head on a table beside her. She displayed his head for the rest of the celebration. When Herod eventually had enough, he got up and went off on his own to his quarters, and asked to be left alone. All the guests then left.

Herodias and Salome were the last in the room with the three guards. She turned to the guards and said, "Take this head and throw it in the prison cell with the rest of him and at first light get rid of the body and the head for good, where no one would ever find him."

The guards bowed, took the head on the platter and left.

Chuza who was present throughout the banquet was in a complete state of shock, as he was experiencing what had happened after Salome's dance. He was the first of the guests to leave. He went and told his wife, Joanna, and she in turn went to tell Miriam who informed Shimon and the other disciples. She was too afraid of telling Yeshua.

"We have to get out of Jerusalem. It is now too dangerous. Yeshua could be next," Andreus said.

"We have to get Johanan's body and give him a decent burial," Johanan said, and they all agreed.

"Yeshua is asleep, should we wake him and tell him," Judas asked.

"No let him sleep, he is tired. We will tell him in the morning," Shimon said.

With a heavy heart, they all went to sleep, except Shimon, Johanan and James.

"We better go and see Chuza," Shimon said.

It was pitch dark when they arrived at Chuza's place. They knocked on his front door. After a while a voice was heard from inside the house.

"It's Shimon, and with me is two of Johanan's disciples, we are now with Yeshua. We came to see you about Johanan the baptiser. May we come in?"

Chuza immediately opened the front door. He appeared in his night clothes. He was holding a lamp.

Once inside, Shimon asked about how to get Johanan's body for burial.

"Herodias, Herod's wife had told the guards to bury Johanan where he would not be found."

"Can we get the body and bury him ourselves?" Johanan asked.

"I could bribe the guards, to let us have the body," Chuza said. "At first light I will go to the palace. Everyone will be hung over and asleep," Chuza said.

"On my way, I will stop at some of the homes of a few of Johanan's disciples, whom I can trust, and ask them to spread the word to a few others, and to meet us at the burial grounds," Chuza said.

"We will get Mattheus to reimburse you, for the bribe," Shimon said.

"Judas, will reimburse, he is now in charge of our finances," James reminded Shimon.

"Oh yes, I forgot, Judas," Shimon said.

They then parted and went back to where they were staying.

Before the sun began to rise, Shimon, Johanan and James, woke the others and told them what was happening.

"Should we wake Yeshua?" James asked.

"I think Yeshua would want to be at the burial of Johanan," Johanan said.

Yeshua was shocked when he heard what had happened. He went back into his room and wept. Later that morning all of Yeshua's disciples, many who were Johanan's disciples and many other disciples of Johanan from Jerusalem were at the burial grounds. They had a rabbi with them, who was also a disciple of Johanan, whom Chuza trusted. He officiated at the burial. It was a sombre occasion. Chuza, his wife, some of Johanan disciples and all of Yeshua's disciples were present. There was another burial happening but the mourners were so overcome with mourning a loved one that they paid no attention to the burial of Johanan, the baptiser. The apostles surrounded Yeshua to make sure he was not recognised. Johanan was buried at the edge of cemetery, so they were free to speak freely of him. There was much weeping and mourning. But all were satisfied that Johanan had a decent burial by his friends and disciples.

They all then returned to their homes. Yeshua went off to a lonely place to be by himself. Later that morning they reassembled at the Temple.

Chapter Sixty-Two
Out of the Darkness

The crowds were already in the Temple waiting for Yeshua, for they all knew that he was going to preach. In spite of what happened and what Yeshua had said about them, the Pharisees, Scribes, Sadducees, Elders and their associates were out in full force, in the very front of the Temple, as usual.

There was a buzz about the place, and an air of expectancy. The crowd were hoping for another round of debating, of fighting between Yeshua and the Pharisees and their cohort. There were also two factions among the crowd, those that were captivated by Yeshua and hanging onto his every word, and then there were the supporters of the Pharisees, who still hung onto their every word. There were those frightened of the Pharisees, those that were easily swayed by them, and they were told not to believe everything that this man Yeshua was saying. He was a simple carpenter from Nazareth, and the Pharisees spread all kinds of rumours and lies about Yeshua, seeking to discredit him among the people, and there were those who were swayed and cautious and suspicious of what Yeshua was saying. Nevertheless, they too were enthralled in listening to Yeshua.

Yeshua began to preach, "My dearest brothers and sisters, I greet you in the Lord, peace be with you. This is a sad day. This morning, we buried Johanan the Prophet, the baptiser. He was also my cousin. Many of you were disciples of Johanan; a greater man born of woman has not lived. We are saddened at his death. He is now resting in peace, in the Kingdom of Heaven. He was a true and faithful servant. He was a man of God; he was like a voice crying out in the wilderness, 'make straight the way of the Lord'.

"Johanan lived alone, with God, in the wilderness and many of you went out into the wilderness to meet with him. What did you go out in the wilderness to see? A reed shaken by the wind? What then did you go out to see? Someone dressed in soft robes?"

Then looking at those in the front rows, Yeshua said, "Look, those who wear soft robes are in royal palaces. What then did you go out to see? A prophet? Yes, I tell you, and more than a prophet. This is the one about whom it is written, 'See I am sending my messenger ahead of you, who will prepare your way before you.' Johanan came to prepare you for the one who was to come. Johanan came to lead you out of the darkness."

Yeshua paused. There was silence. The people were hanging onto his every word, and waiting for what he was to say next. The Pharisees and their associates however were listening carefully to find something with which to discredit Yeshua.

Yeshua then looked at all in the Temple and said, "I am the light of the world. I have come to lead you out of the darkness. Whoever follows me will never walk in darkness but will have the light of life."

Then one of the Pharisees stood up, and the crowd stretched to see him, he said to Yeshua, "You are testifying on your own behalf; your testimony is not valid."

Those captive to the power of the Pharisees in the crowd, whispered to those around them, "The Pharisees have a point." But others told them to be quiet.

Yeshua answered the Pharisee, "Even if I testify on my own behalf, my testimony is valid because I know where I have come from and where I am going, but you do not know where I come from or where I am going. You judge by human standards. I judge no one. Yet even if I do judge, my judgement is valid, for it is not I alone who judge, but I and the Father, who sent me. In your Law it is written that the testimony of two witnesses is valid. I testify on my own behalf and the Father who sent me, testifies on my behalf."

Another Pharisee stood up and asked, "Where is your father?"

The heads of those present moved in unison from Yeshua to the Pharisee and then back to Yeshua. They were lapping up this repartee between Yeshua and the Pharisees.

Yeshua answered, "You know neither me nor my Father. If you knew me, you would know my Father also."

He then said to them, "I am going away, and you will search for me, but you will die in your sin. Where I am going, you cannot come."

"Is he going to kill himself?" a person in the crowd said to those around him. "Is that what he means by saying, 'where I am going you cannot come'?"

Yeshua heard and then said, "You are from below, I am from above, you are of this world, and I am not of this world."

One of the Pharisees then yelled out, "Who are you?"

Yeshua replied, "Why do I speak to you at all? I have much to say about you, and much to condemn, but the one who sent me is true, and I declare to the world what I have heard from him."

The Pharisees and those around them and the people in the Temple were at a loss, and did not fully grasp that Yeshua was speaking to them about the Father.

Another Pharisee stood up and spoke, "Stop speaking to us in riddles, speak plainly."

So, Yeshua said to them, "When you have lifted up the Son of Man, the Son of God, made Man, then you will realise I am he, and that I do nothing on my own, but I speak these things as the Father instructed me. And the One who sent me is with me; he has not left me alone, for I always do what is pleasing to him."

Then another one of the Pharisees stood up, pointed at Yeshua and turning to the crowd in the Temple shouted, "This man is an impostor. He is not who he says he is. We are the children of Abraham. We have one father, God himself."

The Pharisees were now trying to stir up the crowd against Yeshua. "This man is an impostor, a fraud, a blasphemer, a liar, and the truth is not in him, he cannot be a man of God, and his claims are preposterous, we have to rid ourselves of the likes of this man."

"Yeah, yeah!" the rest of the Pharisees and their associates yelled.

There were murmurings among the crowd in the Temple; especially by those already captive to the Pharisees, and those who were easily swayed by what the Pharisees were saying.

"How can he claim to be the Son of God made man. We believe he is a man, mere mortal, how can he claim to be the Son of God, his claim is preposterous, as the Pharisees, our real Teachers tell us," a person in the crowd said to those around him.

People were confused. Some believing in Yeshua and some seeming to have been persuaded by the Pharisees, and turning against Yeshua.

Shimon and the disciples were becoming really concerned that the crowd would turn against Yeshua and harm him. They were still reeling from the death of Johanan, they now feared for Yeshua, not from Herod, but from the Pharisees and their cohort, they had been ruling over the people for so long, persuaded them for so long, to their way of thinking, and they were so easily swayed by them. Shimon wanted to get Yeshua out of the Temple.

Then one of the Jews in the crowd, a devotee of the Pharisees, spoke out loud, "Are we not right in saying you are a Samaritan and have a demon?"

Shimon and the others, Miriam and the women too were now concerned that some of the crowd were becoming agitated and confused and that they might turn on Yeshua.

"They are spies planted among the crowd by the Pharisees to stir up the people," Joanna said to Miriam and those around her, in the Women's Court.

Shimon then stood up, and approached Yeshua and said, "Yeshua things are getting ugly, we better leave now."

"Okay Shimon, I have said enough for today, let us go."

Yeshua then walked out with his disciples following him. Miriam and the women also left the Temple.

But when Yeshua came outside the Temple, there was another crowd waiting for him, and they had their sick with them, hoping Yeshua would heal them. All those with various kinds of diseases were brought to Yeshua, and he laid his hands on each of them, and cured them. Those that were in the Temple had also now joined the crowd outside but they could not see what was happening. But they soon found out as they heard the gasps of excitement from the people who had brought the sick to Yeshua, and witnessed them being healed.

There were also some who were possessed of demons. Those that brought them were restraining them and pleading with Yeshua to heal them. Some of those that were in the Temple with Yeshua had now squirmed their way nearer to the front, and they could see what was taking place. One of them yelled out for all to hear. "He has his hands on those possessed of demons. He is blessing them."

As Yeshua laid his hand on those possessed, the possessed began shouting, "Leave us alone, let us be, you are the Son of God!"

Those around were astounded, especially those that were in the Temple, for Yeshua had just claimed that he was the Son of God. And here the demons were saying the very same. But some of the Pharisees who had managed to come nearer and see and hear what was happening spoke up. One of them said, "What did we tell you, it is by the power of Satan, king of the demons that he casts out demons."

Yeshua had heard this accusation before and he knew he would be wasting his breath to argue with the Pharisees. They had closed their minds and their hearts to him, and what he had to say. Yeshua then commanded the demons to come out of the possessed and Yeshua commanded them not to speak anymore, because they knew he was the Messiah. All those possessed were cured and then went away rejoicing.

Then Shimon and Andreus told the crowd to leave, and that Yeshua was remaining in Jerusalem for the final day of the Passover, and that he would be preaching and teaching at the Temple each morning, and they should now go about their business, and let Yeshua be.

Yeshua said to his disciples, "Let us go to the Mount of Olives for a while."

As they were heading in that direction, they saw a blind man.

"That's Reuben, he's been blind since birth," Judas said.

Thomas, sensing what everyone else was thinking put a question to Yeshua, "Teacher, who sinned, this man or his parents, that he was born blind?"

Thomas, as well as the others had heard Yeshua refute this erroneous way of thinking, inculcated by the Pharisees. But they wanted Yeshua to articulate it once more.

So, Yeshua said, "Neither this man nor his parents sinned; he was born blind so that God's works might be revealed in him. We must do the works of him who sent me while it is day; night is coming when no one can work. As long as I am in the world, I am the light of the world."

Then Yeshua approached Reuben and then much to the surprise of the disciples, Yeshua spat on the ground. Even Miriam and the women were surprised at Yeshua's behaviour, and wondered why he was spitting in front of the blind man. After all, this is the worse act of contempt one can show for another. Was Yeshua contradicting all he had taught, they wondered.

They watched mystified as Yeshua made mud with his saliva and then spread the mud on the man's eyes.

Reuben shook, perplexed, not knowing what was happening to him.

"It is okay, Reuben, I am Yeshua, today you will see the light. Do you believe me, Reuben?" Yeshua said.

Reuben, wanted more than anything else to see, so he said, "Yes, I believe."

Then Yeshua said to him, "Go, and wash in the pool of Siloam."

Reuben went to the pool, full of hope. As soon as he washed in the pool, his eyes were opened and he burst into song, singing the praises of God. "I can see, I can see," he cried and all those around him were astounded. How can this be? Reuben was blind from birth and now he can see.

Reuben went past his home, and his family and neighbours were all astonished. He told them that the Prophet Yeshua, had made mud and put it on his eyes and told him to wash in the pool of Siloam, and when he did, his eyes were cleansed, and he could see. Reuben was amazed. He was looking all around him and taking in the sights, like a newborn baby seeing the world around for the first time. He was enraptured by all he was seeing and he praised God. Then he ran off to find Yeshua. He knew they were walking towards the Mount of Olives. He found Yeshua and his disciples in the Garden of Gethsemane at the foot of the Mount of Olives.

Reuben fell down on his knees before Yeshua and thanked him profusely. "You are sent by God, for no one can do what you do, praise you, Yeshua."

"Stand up Reuben, walk now in the light. Go now in peace."

Reuben left, hopping and skipping like a child. The disciples were absolutely delighted to see the joy exhibited by Reuben, and they forgot all about Yeshua's altercations with the Pharisees and their followers at the Temple.

All those who knew Reuben, his family, neighbours, people from around the Temple and elsewhere, where he begged every day, were absolutely amazed. A person who had not known Reuben but who saw him around the place, begging for years, said, what everyone was asking, "Is this not the man who used to sit and beg all over the place?"

"It is him," another replied.

"No, it is not him, but it is someone like him," said another

But Reuben kept saying, "I am the man."

But they kept asking him, "Then how were your eyes opened?"

He answered, "The man called Yeshua made mud, spread it on my eyes, and said to me, 'Go to Siloam and wash.' Then I went and washed and received my sight."

Those who had not yet met Yeshua said, "Where is he? Where is this man called Yeshua?"

He told them that he did not know.

Some of those who did not believe Reuben persuaded him to go with them to the Pharisees. When he got there, the Pharisees also recognised the man who begged for a living, and who had been blind from birth. For them his parents must have sinned for him to be cursed in such a way. To them he too was therefore a sinner. They were contemptuous towards him, and asked him how he had received his sight.

By now Reuben was becoming impatient and annoyed as they would not believe what had happened. So impatiently he said, "He put mud on my eyes. Then I washed and now I see."

The Pharisees were getting exasperated with Yeshua. They did not believe he was genuine or a man of God, so one of them said on behalf of the others. "This man, Yeshua, is a sinner, he does not respect our laws and traditions, he has no regard for the Law of Moses or the Prophets, and he has a very lax attitude to sin, he associates with tax-collectors, prostitutes, the unclean, and sinners, and he has no regard for the Sabbath. He is not a man of God." They were simply regurgitating their points of attack against Yeshua.

But there were some that could not explain what happened, and one of them said, what his colleagues were saying, "How can a man who is a sinner perform such signs?"

They were divided, so they said again to the blind man, "What do you say about him?"

Reuben said, "He is a prophet."

Still there were those who would not believe. They just couldn't accept the power of Yeshua. They had so low opinion of him. So, in their own blindness, they did not believe that Reuben had been blind. They surmised that he was simply pretending, so that he could beg for a living. So, they called for his parents.

Their spokesman asked the parents, "Is this, your son, who you say was born blind? How then does he now see?"

Reuben's father answered for him and his wife. "We know that this is our son, and that he was born blind, but we do not know how it is that now he sees. Nor do we know who opened his eyes. Ask him, he is of age. He will speak for himself."

The parents were intimidated by these Jews for they had already heard that anyone who confessed Yeshua to be a prophet or the Messiah, would be ostracised and put out of the synagogue, that is why they said, 'He is of age, ask him.'

So, for the second time, they called Reuben and they said to him, "Give glory to God! We know that this man is a sinner."

Reuben answered them, "I do not know that this man is a sinner. One thing I do know, that though I was blind, now I see."

They persisted and asked, "What did he do to you? How did he open your eyes?"

Reuben now became exasperated, and he said to them, "I have told you already, and you would not listen. Why do you want to hear it again? Do you also want to become his disciples?"

His questioners then turned on him, with venom, with their spokesman saying, "You are his disciple, but we are disciples of Moses. We know that God has spoken to Moses, but as for this man, we do not know where he comes from."

Reuben had enough, he said to them, "Here's the thing, here is an astonishing thing! You do not know where he comes from, and yet he opened my eyes. We know that God does not listen to sinners, but he does to one who worships him and obeys his will. Never since the world began has it been heard that anyone opened the eyes of a person born blind. If this man were not from God, he could do nothing."

Those questioning Reuben became furious, how this man dare speak to them like that, so then one of them, speaking on behalf of the others said out loud, and with his voice cracking, and the veins on his neck looking as if they were ready to burst. "You were born entirely in sins, and are you trying to teach us?"

And they drove him off, and forbade him to ever enter the Temple.

Reuben was unperturbed by them. He had a new lease of life. He could see. Now they had ostracised him, forbidding him from entering the Temple. "Well, they can go to hell," Reuben said to himself. "Who needs their bloody Temple, those hypocrites? They are the sinners, everyone kowtowing to them, as if they are God's gift to the human race. They are…" Words came to Reuben's mind about the Pharisees, and their band of brothers, those who questioned him, that he could not, would not utter. They are idiots. He had never been foul mouthed before; in spite of the abuse, he had received all his life. But he had also received kindness from strangers who left money in his scarf when he begged and who said kind words to him. Most people though did not have the time of day for him, and many abused him, called him a sinner. But now he could see and they can all go to hell.

Reuben decided to go and look for Yeshua and let him know what had happened to him. Yeshua and his disciples had been on their way to the Mount of Olives when he was cured, so Reuben headed in that direction. He found the disciples in the Garden of Gethsemane at the foot of the Mount of Olives. They were all sitting around, in silence. So Reuben found a spot to sit and sat in silence with them.

After a while, Reuben could wait no longer, he approached one of the disciples, it was Miriam and he whispered in her ear. "Excuse me my lady, I am Reuben, the one who was blind from birth and whom Yeshua had cured and made me see. May I speak to you?"

"Sure Reuben. I am Miriam, I am with Yeshua, come let us go over there," Miriam said, as she led him to a short distance from the others.

"What is it Reuben, what bothers you?" Miriam said. She could see that Reuben was somewhat upset.

Since his altercation with the Pharisees and those that came with them, and their condemnation of him and banning him from the Temple, his mood had changed. He was still on top of the world that he could now see, but he was livid to be treated so poorly and to be banned from the Temple. Now that he could see, he so much wanted to enter the Temple, to praise God and to give thanks for the great gift of sight that has been given to him.

Reuben then related to Miriam what had transpired between him and the Pharisees. She listened patiently and she too was furious at the way Reuben was treated. "You may speak to Yeshua, and tell him what happened," Miriam said.

"I am not worthy to speak to Yeshua. Please Miriam speak to him on my behalf," Reuben said. He was scared that he might swear or disappoint Yeshua in some way, and he felt so inept and unworthy to speak to Yeshua, for he knew that he was a holy man, a man of God.

Finally, Yeshua appeared and immediately he saw Reuben with Miriam and the others. Yeshua went straight to Reuben and greeted him. "Shalom Reuben, how nice to see you, have you come to admire the Father's creation, the Mount of Olives and this beautiful Garden of Gethsemane?"

"Yeshua, up to now I could hear things, people talking, the birds singing, and the sound of the wind rustling the trees. I could feel the warmth of the sun on my face and listen to the roar of thunder and the cry of the sea. I could smell the flowers and the plants and herbs and feel the soft flesh of newborn babies, and hear the laughter of children at play. Lord, I did not feel deprived for I was born this way. I had also heard bad words and received bad treatment of all kinds and abuse at the hand of some, but I have also received kindness. And most of all Yeshua, you have given me a great gift of sight. And I have not ceased to contemplate the wonder and riches of Mother Nature and of all of God's creation. I don't know how to thank you, Yeshua."

"I am happy for you, Reuben. But you are disturbed, what is it that troubles you?"

In spite of Reuben feeling inadequate and that he would not be able to relate to Yeshua his run-in with the Pharisees, he told Yeshua all that transpired.

Yeshua sighed. He rubbed his face in his hands and held it so for a while and then said to Reuben. "Reuben, do you believe in the Son of Man, the Son of God made man?"

Reuben answered, "And who is he, Yeshua? Tell me, so I may believe in him."

Yeshua then said to Reuben, "Reuben, you have seen him, and the one speaking with you, is he."

Reuben then fell on his knees before Yeshua and worshipped him.

Yeshua helped Reuben to his feet and then said to Reuben and his disciples, "I have come into this world for judgement, so that those who do not see may see, and those who do see may become blind."

Yeshua then sent Reuben away, telling him to go in peace.

Yeshua then began walking in the direction of the city and the disciples followed. The disciples were walking a distance from Yeshua. Judas then threw out a question to them, "What was Yeshua saying about those who do not see, making them see and those who see, making them blind?"

Johanan answered, "Yeshua was speaking about spiritual sight and spiritual blindness. He wants us to see with his eyes, so that we won't judge people on their appearances, their physical condition, whether they are blind or lame or whatever."

"And not to judge anyone on what they possess, or do not possess. Not to judge people because they are different; on their looks, their gender, or their nationality, but to see them all as beloved children of the Father. We have to not merely look to the outside but see into the heart of others," Miriam said.

"Well said, Miriam," Rebecca added with a smile.

Shimon then walked faster and caught up with Yeshua and spoke, "Yeshua, it has been a rough day for you and for all of us. Shall we call it a day? It would be good for you to have a rest. And the others as well."

"Yes, you are right, Shimon. Tell the others to go their way, and I will see you all at the Temple tomorrow. The day after is the final day of the Passover and that will be hectic. So, see you tomorrow. I think I'll walk to Bethany and see my friends there. I will stay the rest of the day with them and sleep over and will see you all at the Temple. And go and fetch Reuben so that he may enter the Temple with you all," Yeshua said.

Chapter Sixty-Three
The Good Samaritan

Yeshua enjoyed the time alone. He had spent more than an hour in prayer with his Father, seeking enlightenment for what lay ahead. He also enjoyed walking by himself at his own pace along this pleasant road to Bethany, and the joy of anticipation of spending time, quality time, with his three friends, and especially Miriam. He loved Martha and Lazarus but he was especially fond of Miriam, they seemed to be on the same wavelength.

Yeshua thought of the women in his life; his mother of course, and then Rebecca with whom he had and still has a close relationship. I guess Rebecca is really my first love. And if you Father, had not sent me into the world to do what I am to do, I would most likely have settled down with Rebecca, Yeshua mused. But it wasn't simply musing, for Yeshua was in conversation with his heavenly Father as he walked, nothing was off limits, and he conversed and spoke of everything with his Father.

Yeshua thought about the state of his world. All the political leaders, the religious leaders, had no women amongst them, no women in positions of power or authority. No women were allowed in the ranks of the Pharisees, Scribes, Sadducees, priests and the religious elite. And yet Yeshua had seemed to relate so easily to women, powerful and intelligent women. Yeshua knew that he was looked upon as an oddity, and by many with suspicion, especially the religious elite. Yeshua knew that to be seen with a woman, who was not one's wife or sister, would be viewed with suspicion. But Yeshua did not care. He was not concerned with appearances. What mattered was what was in his heart.

"Father, I hope this will change, and that we accept women in our midst on equal terms. Father the women you have sent me, to assist me in the work you have for me, the women you have given me are such a godsend," Yeshua said, looking upwards and smiling at the pun. He felt his Father was smiling back. "I have learned so much from Miriam, and Rebecca and the other women who are my disciples. And I am grateful. And I am grateful for all the friends I have Father, and I ask you to bless them, especially Miriam, Martha and Lazarus with whom I am so looking forward to see and with whom I will spend some time."

Before he realised it, Yeshua saw Bethany. It was now late afternoon. No one was outside the house, so Yeshua knocked, and he heard footsteps. It was Miriam. She rushed into Yeshua's arms, and threw her arms around him.

Again, Yeshua thought about this; for a man, not married to a woman to be hugged like this would be frowned upon, but Yeshua's friends and disciples knew him and his Father knows what is in his heart. And Yeshua relished being hugged by Miriam, and felt so at ease, and content to be so embraced. It lifted his spirits, and his heart went out to Miriam. "It is so good to see you Miriam, and you are looking well, are you well?" Yeshua asked, as he released her.

"I am well, and all the better for seeing you. Are you well, Yeshua, you look tired, come in and rest. Martha is out back, cooking on the fire. She will be so pleased to see you. Lazarus is gone, to where, we do not know, he said he wouldn't be gone long, a week or two at most," Miriam said, as she led Yeshua to a comfortable couch. "Can I offer you a drink Yeshua, maybe a cup of wine?" Miriam asked.

"A cup of wine would be just what the doctor would prescribe Miriam," Yeshua said with a smile, and with delight.

Just then Martha came in from out back. She saw Yeshua and rushed into his arms and gave him a respectful and brief hug. "It is so good to see you, Yeshua. I had a feeling you would come, so I roasted a lamb, it should be ready in an hour or so," Martha said.

Yeshua licked his lips, smiling. "Martha, you are a gem, a precious gift and a wizard, you have such foresight, and such good taste, and such kindness. I can't wait for some of your roast lamb, it has been a while since I had roast lamb," Yeshua said with delight.

Yeshua spent a most enjoyable time with Miriam and Martha, eating more than he planned and drank a second glass of wine with his meal. It had also been a while since he imbibed. Yeshua helped Martha and Miriam to clean up, and then they sat for a few more hours chatting. Yeshua told them all about what had happened and his experiences with the Pharisees, Scribes and Sadducees and their group in the Temple, and he also spoke to them about Reuben.

Both Martha and Miram listened and enjoyed Yeshua's conversations. But they were concerned about the opposition Yeshua was experiencing at the hands of the Pharisees and some of the religious leaders.

Yeshua also wanted to know everything that had happened in their lives. Martha spoke of her concerns for her brother Lazarus. "He is still not altogether well, Yeshua. But he became so restless and we could not keep him at home. We have to be here for him when he returns," Martha said.

"We told him to be careful where he goes and where he stays and the food he eats, and so on," Miriam said. "We are concerned that his health does not deteriorate while he is away. He needed to stay longer at home and regain his full strength but he became impossible and we just couldn't stop him," Miriam added, expressing her concern for Lazarus.

Yeshua had one more cup of wine and then said, "Martha, Miriam, thank you for a glorious evening. Thanks for that roast lamb, it was most delicious. And I enjoyed the wine, but most of all your company. But I must retire now."

"I have put clean bedding on your bed, and a clean towel for you Yeshua. If there is anything else you need, please let me know," Martha said.

"No, I'll just go out back and have a splash and a clean and then I'm hitting the sack," Yeshua said. "Goodnight. I will be leaving at sunrise, I plan to spend a bit of time at the Mount of Olives, in the Garden of Gethsemane, before heading to the Temple, where I will be giving my last talk, as the day after is the final day of the Passover, and absolute pandemonium in the Temple with all the sacrificing going on. I will most likely spend some more time around Jerusalem or the surrounding villages and might not see you again, before I head back to Galilee with my disciples," Yeshua said.

Yeshua then went out back and washed. When he returned into the house, Martha and Miriam were still up.

Miriam spoke to Yeshua, "Yeshua, Martha and I have been talking. We had not yet heard you preach in the Temple, so we thought we would go with you to Jerusalem tomorrow, if you don't mind."

"Not at all, Miriam, Martha, now I am getting nervous, knowing you will be in the congregation. But I most likely will not see you if you are not out front in the Women's Court. I hope we can have some light lunch together at an eatery before you return to Bethany," Yeshua said.

"That will be fine, Yeshua," Martha said.

They then all said 'Goodnight' and retired.

The next morning Yeshua was up early, at sunrise. He was as quiet as possible so as not to wake Martha and Miriam. He washed his face and rinsed his mouth outside and then remained there in the quiet and silence of the morning. He sat on the stone bench and turned his mind and heart to his Father in heaven. It was quite nippy and a gentle breeze caressed his face. Yeshua thought of the prophet Elijah at Mount Horeb, where he went into a cave, spending the night there. Then the voice of the Spirit moved Elijah to go out and stand on the mountain before the Lord for the Lord would be there and pass by. Yeshua placed himself on the mountain with Elijah, waiting for the Lord to pass by. With Elijah, Yeshua witnessed the howling of a mighty wind, so strong it split part of the mountain and shattered the rocks, before the Lord, but the Lord was not in the wind. Yeshua was lost on the mountain with Elijah, as he waited for the Lord to appear. After the wind came and earthquake but the Lord was not in the earthquake. And after the earthquake came a fire. But the Lord was not in the fire. Yeshua, still deep in prayer, he was completely lost in the moment. He was no longer at the back of the home of Martha and Miriam in Bethany but with Elijah on Mount Horeb, waiting for the Lord to appear. After the fire there came the sound of a gentle breeze. Then the Lord spoke to Elijah asking him what he was doing in that place. And Yeshua heard the voice of his Father in heaven, asking him what he was doing in this place.

Yeshua then went quiet and became conscious of being in the presence of his heavenly Father. Yeshua had his eyes closed and he felt no need to be conversing with words, he was now conversing without words, or rather he was in union with, in communion with, one with his Father in heaven. He was like a child being held in the arms of his mother. Yeshua felt himself being held, being loved by his Father. He remained in that embrace, for how long he did not know. When he opened his eyes, the sun was now up. Yeshua remained in that moment of deep silence and peace and offered himself to the Father, offered the day to his Father, all that he would experience, all that he would teach, he offered himself completely to his Father, to do his will. And he asked for his Father's blessing.

Just then Martha came outside with a towel. "Good morning, Martha, did you have a good sleep?" Yeshua asked.

"Yes, I did, and what about you, Yeshua?"

"I slept like a baby, Martha," Yeshua said, smiling.

"I left some warm milk for you on the table and there is some bread as well. And some figs," Martha said, smiling.

"Thank you, Martha, you are so thoughtful. Now I know this is going to be a good day." Yeshua then went inside. And the aroma of freshly baked bread filled him with delight and transported him back to his home in Nazareth where there was no more pleasant smell than that of freshly baked bread. Miriam was now up and she too went out back to freshen for the day, after exchanging greetings with Yeshua.

After breakfast, Yeshua, Martha and Miriam set out for Jerusalem. On the way they stopped at the Mount of Olives and Yeshua was transported back to Mount Horeb and the experience of meeting the Lord in the gentle breeze. The three of them rested in the Garden of Gethsemane to catch their breath and to spend some quiet time in prayer.

When Yeshua, Martha and Miriam arrived in the Temple, it was packed. As usual the front rows were stacked with Pharisees, Scribes, Sadducees, chief priests, and Elders. This was the penultimate day of the Passover. And this would be the final teaching Yeshua would give in the Temple. Yeshua had now made up his mind to leave Jerusalem, as soon as the Passover was over. There were many places he still needed to go; to bring the Good News of salvation and redemption, and freedom from evil, sin and death. And Yeshua felt his time was running out.

Yeshua in his walks had seen shepherds out in the field tending their sheep and closing the gates so the sheep might not scatter. So, he stood up and began to speak. "My dearest brothers and sisters I greet you in the Lord. The peace of the Lord is with you. In the book of Jeremiah, we read these words, 'Woe to the shepherds who destroy and scatter the sheep of my pasture, says the Lord.' The Lord then says he himself will gather up all the sheep and he will bring them back to the fold. And it is written, 'I will raise up shepherds over my flock who will shepherd them, and they shall not fear any longer, or be dismayed, nor shall any be missing,' says the Lord."

Yeshua took a deep breath and then boldly said, in a loud voice, "I am the Good Shepherd. I know my own and my own know me, just as the Father knows me and I know the Father. The hired hand, who is not the shepherd and does not own the sheep, sees the wolves coming and leaves the sheep and turns away—and the wolves snatches them and scatters them. The hired hand runs away because a hired hand does not care for the sheep. I know my sheep and I care for the sheep. And I lay down my life for my sheep. I have other sheep that do not belong to this fold, I must bring them also, and they will listen to my voice. So, there will be one flock and one shepherd."

The Pharisees and their cohort began murmuring among themselves. One said, "He has a demon, he is out of his mind, how can he compare himself with the Father."

Another said, "But he gave sight to a man born blind, can a demon open the eyes of one born blind."

Some of the people sitting behind the Pharisees did the unthinkable and shushed them.

Yeshua continued talking about his Father as the one who cares for his sheep and raises up shepherds to shepherd his flock, and Yeshua quoted from Ezekiel and Jeremiah to show this and gave an example of David as a shepherd to his flock.

But the Pharisees objected to Yeshua, a carpenter daring to compare himself with these holy men. They were becoming exasperated with Yeshua's claims about himself, so one of them spoke up on their behalf. "How long will you keep us in suspense? If you are the Messiah, tell us plainly."

The crowd were still and quiet, they all had the same question and they wanted to hear Yeshua's response.

Yeshua spoke, slowly and deliberately, "I have told you and you do not believe. The works that I do in my Father's name testify to me; but you do not believe because you do not belong to my sheep. My sheep hear my voice. I know them and they follow me. No one will snatch them from me. No one can snatch them out of the Father's hand. The Father and I are one."

"Outrageous! Unbelievable! How can this man, this mere carpenter, from the backwaters of Nazareth, a Galilean, a person possessed of a demon, dare compare himself to our Father in heaven. We have been appointed to be the shepherds of the people. This man is a fraud, an impostor, possessed of a demon. Do not listen to him."

Uproar ensued. The Pharisees and their cohort had their associates and followers planted all over the Temple, and they joined their voices in condemning Yeshua. "Stone him, stone him," some cried out.

Shimon and the disciples were gripped with fear. Martha and Miriam were overcome with alarm, fearful of what they might do to Yeshua. And so did Miriam and the other women.

Yeshua raised his arm and called for silence and then he spoke, "I have shown you many good works from the Father. For which of these are you going to stone me?"

One from the front row answered on behalf of the others, "It is not for a good work that we are going to stone you, but for blasphemy, because you, though only a human being, are making yourself God."

The crowd was divided between the followers of the Pharisees and their cohort, sitting in the front rows and spread throughout the Temple and followers of Yeshua, and those who accepted what he was saying.

Yeshua continued, "If I am not doing the works of my Father, then do not believe. But if I do them, even though you do not believe me, believe the works, so that you may know and understand that the Father is in me, and I am in the Father."

The people were becoming agitated and the Pharisees and their supporters more boisterous. Shimon went to Yeshua and spoke with him, urging for him to leave. Yeshua could see that was the only way to calm the crowd so he got up and left and all his disciples left with him. The women disciples also left.

But when Yeshua came out of the Temple, as was expected, a huge crowd were there again, with their sick and afflicted. Yeshua stopped and spoke to the crowds and he healed all the sick that they brought to him.

When Yeshua had finished healing those that were brought to him, a well-groomed and well-dressed person, with fine robes, looking like upper class, and with an air of superiority, spoke up. "Yeshua, may I ask you a question?" the man said.

"It's Abel, the lawyer," a person in the crowd said.

"This is going to be good," said another.

"Yeshua is no match for him, he's the best lawyer in all of Jerusalem," said another.

Yeshua responded, "Sure young man, go ahead."

By this time the Pharisees and all those who sat with them in the front of the Temple had joined the crowd, and when they heard Abel speak, they forced their way to the front of the crowd, making sure they would witness this altercation between Abel and Yeshua.

Abel put his question to test Yeshua. "Teacher, what must I do to inherit eternal life?"

Yeshua then responded, as he usually did to questions put to him, he asked the questioner a question in return. Yeshua put the question to Abel. "What is written in the Law? What do you read there?"

Abel gave his answer almost immediately, "You shall love the Lord your God, with all your heart, with all your soul, and with all your strength, and with all your mind; and your neighbour as yourself."

Yeshua smiled and said to Abel, "You have given the right answer, do this, and you will live."

Abel was not satisfied, wanting to justify himself, and still wanting to get the better of Yeshua put a further question to Yeshua by asking, "And who is my neighbour?"

The crowd were murmuring and everyone jostling to see what was happening and to hear what Yeshua would say in response to Abel's question, especially so the Pharisees, now in front of the crowd.

Yeshua replied, "A man was going down from Jerusalem to Jericho."

Immediately all ears piqued, for everyone knew about that road from Jerusalem to Jericho, it was notorious as a road infested with robbers, outlaws, criminals and low life, and no one would dare venture on that road alone and unarmed, especially at night time.

Yeshua continued with his story. "And the man fell into the hands of robbers, who stripped him of all he had, even his clothes, and then beat him, and went away, leaving him half dead."

The crowd were enthused. This story was close to home. They all knew of someone who was waylaid on that road. The Pharisees especially wondered where Yeshua was going with this story.

Yeshua looked at those in the front of the crowd, among them were chief priests. Yeshua then said, "Now by chance a priest was going down that road, and when he saw the man, he passed by on the other side. So likewise, a Levite, when he came to the place and saw the man, lying battered and bruised, he passed by on the other side. But a Samaritan, while travelling came near him."

The crowd, especially the Pharisees, and the others with them, were now sensing what Yeshua was about to say. He was going to pit this Samaritan against the priest and the Levite. He was going to humiliate us, Pharisees and priests and anointed ones. Everyone knew that the Samaritans were looked down upon by the Jews as low life, people of a lesser god, and they had no time for them, and would not associate with them, and would avoid going through Samaria at whatever cost.

And they were right about Yeshua's intentions, for Yeshua continued with his story about the Samaritan saying, "When the Samaritan saw the man lying there helpless, and seeing his condition, he was moved with pity. He went to him and bandaged his wounds, after having poured oil and wine on them. Then he put the man on his own animal and brought him to an inn, and took care of him."

The Pharisees, the priests, the Levites and the religious elite were livid. How dare Yeshua humiliate them like this in front of the people? But while the Jews, who were not one of the elite relished Yeshua's story telling, they too were not too pleased that Yeshua would put a Samaritan over the Jews and put the Samaritans in such a good light. For they all despised the Samaritans.

Before any of them could react, Yeshua continued with the story. "The next day, the Samaritan took out two denarii, gave them to the innkeeper, and said, 'Take care of him; and when I come back, I will repay you whatever more you spend'."

Yeshua looked at the lawyer and said, "Which of these three, do you think, was neighbour to the man who fell into the hands of the robbers, and regarded that unfortunate man as his neighbour?"

Abel could not help but smile, he had tried to outsmart Yeshua, but he conceded Yeshua had outsmarted him. He conceded and said, "The one who showed him mercy and compassion."

Yeshua then looked at the crowd and then at Abel and said for all to hear, "Go and do likewise."

Shimon then approached Yeshua and touched his arm and said, in a soft voice so only Yeshua could hear, "Yeshua I think we should go now. And leave Jerusalem, it is no longer safe for you here."

Yeshua agreed with Shimon. His time had not yet come, he still had people to visit, places to go, to spread the Good News of God's Kingdom. "Yes, you are right Shimon."

Yeshua then took Shimon aside and said, "I will go to Bethany with Miriam and Martha, and spend the night there. Tell everyone to pack and be ready to leave tomorrow. We will attend the Passover and leave just before the Passover celebrations have concluded. There will be crowds and those that wish us harm will be otherwise engaged. We will fetch our things immediately and meet at the Sheep Gate."

Shimon told Andreus and he spread the word among the others. Johanan told Miriam and she told the women.

Yeshua left with Martha and Miriam. They walked briskly but once outside of the city and close to the Mount of Olives they stopped. And they rested for a while in the Garden of Gethsemane.

"Yeshua that was a beautiful story you told about the Good Samaritan. It surely put you at odds with the Priests and the Pharisees," Martha said.

"Yeshua, I could sense that most of the people were on your side and appreciated all you were saying. But I also sensed a lot of opposition from the Pharisees and the Priests and all the religious elite, and from some of the people that were spread among the crowd," Miriam said.

"Yes, Miriam, I know. The Pharisees and the Priests have their spies all over, wherever I go. But I will leave Jerusalem tomorrow, and will not return for a long time. I will let things die down a bit in Jerusalem. I will go to other places to spread the Good News. Tomorrow we will leave and travel to Jericho and then cross the Jordan and up to Bethsaida, where Shimon and Andreus and some of the others are from. We will spend some time in Bethsaida and the surrounds and then cross over to Capernaum, where Johanan and his brother James live. My disciples have been on the road for a long time now and I will give them a break when we get to Capernaum. I won't be back in Jerusalem for at least a year."

Miriam and Martha were saddened to hear the news that they would not see Yeshua in the coming year. But they were used to his long absences, but so grateful for seeing so much of him now. And they knew that whenever he came to Jerusalem, he would spend time with them.

Yeshua, Miriam and Martha left Gethsemane, and walked, for most of the rest of the journey, occupied with their own thoughts. Yeshua was so pleased when they arrived at Bethany, and he was looking forward to unwinding for a bit, and spending some precious time with his two dearest friends for whom his love had grown deeper and deeper. They and Lazarus was always in his prayers and in his heart.

But the time came for Yeshua to leave Bethany. It was a sad farewell. Yeshua told them that he wasn't sure when he would see them again.

Yeshua spent some time on the Mount of Olives on his way to Jerusalem. When it was time for the Passover sacrifices and celebration in the Temple, Yeshua kept a low profile. He kept his face partially covered and had a change of robes; different to the white he always wore. He did not wish to be recognised and the disciples all went by themselves and not in a group. People always saw Yeshua in the company of his disciples, mostly all nineteen of them, men and women, and they would not notice him on his own.

When Yeshua entered, he was disgusted when he saw the Court of Gentiles filled with traders trading livestock, and tables with moneychangers doing a brisk trade. He felt deeply that this was unbecoming, they were defiling the Temple.

Yeshua had witnessed the altar and several added tables with dozens of priests taking turns to slaughter the animals in sacrifice. It was more like a butcher's slaughter house and a money-making affair, than a Temple. This has to change, Yeshua thought.

When the long service was coming to an end, Yeshua and his disciples slipped out. They all then met at the Sheep Gate and left the city.

Chapter Sixty-Four
Jericho and the Sycamore Tree

"We will take the road to Jericho," Yeshua said.

"To Jericho!" Judas said with alarm. "Yeshua, you know the road is not safe and it is too dangerous, especially now when the criminals know there are so many people moving in and out of Jerusalem."

"Judas, we are twenty, thirteen of us, men, and with the likes of Shimon and Andreus, I fear not. And we all have our crooks with us, which we will use as weapons to ward them off, if necessary," Yeshua said.

"They are mostly cowards and won't attack a big crowd," Nathanael said.

They walked along the infamous road, and the disciples thought about the parable Yeshua had told about the Good Samaritan. They were nearing the town of Jericho when a group of people who were coming in from a side road, saw them and they recognised Yeshua. They rushed on ahead and spread the news and a crowd soon gathered and went to meet Yeshua on the road. The news spread throughout Jericho like wild fire, the Prophet Yeshua was coming to our town. He is at the entrance to Jericho. The people were excited, to actually have Yeshua visit their town. When Yeshua came near to the town the crowd had swelled considerably, and they welcomed Yeshua warmly and were thrilled to have Yeshua visit them.

As they were about to enter Jericho, a blind beggar was sitting by the roadside. He asked what was happening, why the commotion. The crowd told him to be quiet. But he pestered them, wanting to know, what could cause such an unusual show in his town. Was there a festival about to take place that he did not know about?

"Who is making that noise," one of the crowd asked.

"It is Bartimaeus, the blind son of Timaeus," one of the crowd responded.

"Tell him to be quiet," said another voice in the crowd.

A person approached Bartimaeus and said, "Bart, will you keep quiet and stop shouting," the man said.

"Tell me what's going on and I will," Bartimaeus answered.

"The Prophet, Yeshua, from Nazareth is here, he has come to Jericho," the man said.

When Bartimaeus heard this, he began to shout, "Yeshua, Son of David, have mercy on me!"

Many in the crowd sternly ordered him to be quiet, but he shouted out even more loudly, "Son of David, have mercy on me!"

Yeshua heard the shouting and he stopped in his tracks and said, "Call him here."

A few of them approached Bartimaeus, and one of them said, "Take heart, Bart, get up, Yeshua is calling you."

Bartimaeus sprang to his feet and the men led him to Yeshua, the crowd opening a pathway for him.

There was an air of expectancy in the crowd. They had heard the stories of how Yeshua worked miracles, healed the sick and the afflicted but most of them from Jericho had never seen any such feats. Yeshua had never been to their town. And they heard how Yeshua had just recently given sight to a man born blind, who lived in Jerusalem, Would he work a miracle here, in our town, would he give sight to Bartimaeus, they wondered.

When Bartimaeus was before Yeshua, the men let go of his arm. Yeshua then spoke to Bartimaeus. Yeshua had heard his name, so he said to him, "Bartimaeus, what do you want me to do for you?"

Bartimaeus was so uplifted to hear the voice of Yeshua addressing him, and he said to Yeshua, "My Teacher, let me see again."

Yeshua, simply said to him, "Go; your faith has made you well."

Immediately, Bartimaeus, looked up to the sky with awe and then to Yeshua, he rubbed his eyes and his mouth was agape, he looked at the people and they were all looking at him, stunned. They were the people he knew only by their voice and the sound of their feet as they approached, and by their smell. He could now see them clearly, and all of creation around him and he gazed with wonder. He could not believe his eyes; he kept blinking to make sure he wasn't dreaming. He looked at Yeshua. Yeshua was an ordinary looking man, slightly above average height, with a rugged look but he had penetrating eyes that to Bartimaeus was as if Yeshua could look into his soul. To Bartimaeus Yeshua's eyes were full of compassion and joy, and he could see Yeshua was happy for him.

The crowd were overcome. "God has visited his people, a Saviour has come to our town, praise the Lord," a voice from the crowd gave sound to what filled all their hearts.

Bartimaeus joined the crowd in following Yeshua into their town. By now more people had swelled the crowd, and surrounded Yeshua.

Yeshua turned to Andreus and spoke to him. "Andreus, I would like to stay here in Jericho for a while, find some accommodation for us all."

People in the crowd heard this, then one of them, spoke up. "Yeshua, I am in charge of our Council, and in charge of the affairs of our citizens. On behalf of our citizens of Jericho, I welcome you and your disciples to our town. We offer you and your disciples' whatever accommodation you need."

"Thank you so much. You are most kind. Andreus, who manages our affairs will talk with you," Yeshua said, gesturing to Andreus, who nodded to the man who spoke on behalf of the people.

Yeshua then said he would like to go to the synagogue for prayer. The crowd followed him in droves, and in their midst, Bartimaeus, who was now like a celebrity, people wanted to be near him, and touch him and speak to him, and look at his eyes.

As they were walking, a man from the town approached the crowd and asked one of them what was happening. The man immediately recognised Zacchaeus, and looked at him with contempt, for he was rich, and the chief tax collector.

"What's going on, what is all the kerfuffle about?" Zacchaeus asked the man.

"It's Yeshua, the Prophet from Nazareth, he has just healed the blind beggar, Bartimaeus, gave him his sight," the man said.

Zacchaeus, had heard about Yeshua, and learned from some of his tax-collector friends about Yeshua, that he was friendly with them, with tax-collectors, and even dined with some. He also learned that Yeshua had chosen the chief tax collector of Galilee, Mattheus as one of his disciples.

Zacchaeus was so eager to see Yeshua, what he looked like. Zacchaeus was jumping up and down, but still could not see Yeshua, because of the crowd, and because Zacchaeus was very short of stature. Zacchaeus was so desperate, so he ran ahead and climbed a sycamore tree to catch a glimpse of Yeshua, for he was heading in that direction, and would pass that way.

No one noticed Zacchaeus in the sycamore tree, but Yeshua did. Yeshua stopped and looked up and smiled. Yeshua thought about how he, Achim and Zadok climbed all those trees around Nazareth when they were growing up. Yeshua was amused and fascinated to see a grown man, up in the tree.

The crowd saw Yeshua looking up, and they then too turned their gaze upwards, and were equally amazed and amused. They were smiling and some were laughing for Zacchaeus cut a comic figure, standing on a branch of the tree, hanging on for dear life. And at the same time, they were hoping he would fall down and break his neck because he was the most despised person in Jericho.

"It's Zacchaeus, the chief tax-collector," a person in the crowd yelled out.

Yeshua took some steps closer to the tree and then looking up to Zacchaeus, Yeshua said, "Zacchaeus, hurry and come down; for I must stay at your house today."

Zacchaeus could not believe what he was hearing. He hurried down, brushed off his garments, and rubbed his hands clean, and said to Yeshua. "Yeshua I am most honoured to welcome you to Jericho, and to my home."

The people began to grumble, they could not believe what was unfolding. Yeshua was actually going to stay with Zacchaeus, and dine with him, a sinner of the worst kind. A person in the crowd could not contain himself and yelled out. "Yeshua you cannot be a guest of this man, he is a sinner."

The crowd all yelled their agreement.

Zacchaeus, felt uneasy, and he did not want to be denied this opportunity to have Yeshua as his guest, so he stood his ground, and overcome with the Spirit, he said out loud for all to hear, "Lord, I give half of my possessions to the poor. And if I have defrauded anyone of anything, I will pay them back four times as much."

The crowd were amazed at this turnaround display of generosity by Zacchaeus. A voice in the crowd yelled, "Yeshua, you have astonished us by giving sight to the blind Bartimaeus, but changing this cheat and sinner, this chief tax collector to one who publicly repents and pledges to recompense all he has cheated is a miracle, I never thought I would ever see," the man said laughing. And all in the crowd joined in the laughter.

"He will be a very poor man, once he has given half of his fortune to the poor, and then recompense fourfold all those who he has defrauded," the man said, still laughing.

The crowd all joined in the laughter, at Zacchaeus' expense.

But Yeshua looked at Zacchaeus and said to him, for all to hear, "Zacchaeus today salvation has come to you and your house, because you too are a son of Abraham. For the Son of God, made man, has come to seek out and to save the lost."

Zacchaeus was unperturbed by the insults and being the brunt of the peoples jokes about him, Yeshua was coming to dine at his home. Zacchaeus was about to lead Yeshua to his home. But Yeshua said to him. "Zacchaeus, I am on my way to the synagogue where I will speak to the people. Can you send your servant to come and fetch me later, say at the eleventh hour? By the way, Zacchaeus, I have nineteen disciples with me, twelve men, and seven women, is it okay if they join me as your guests?"

"Yes, Yeshua, I will be most honoured. I'll see you later then." Zacchaeus then hurried home as Yeshua and the crowd continued on their walk to the synagogue.

In the synagogue, the people quickly settled to listen to Yeshua. Yeshua thought, as he was in Jericho, he would repeat the story he told before he left Jerusalem about the Good Samaritan, as it featured their town. The people enjoyed hearing their town mentioned in Yeshua's parable. Their reaction however was similar to the Jews in Jerusalem, they delighted in Yeshua bringing the priests and Levites down to size, but they were not too pleased that Yeshua made the Samaritan the hero of his story. They too hated and looked down on the Samaritans. They were already not pleased with Yeshua for accepting the invitation by Zacchaeus; in fact, it was Yeshua himself who told Zacchaeus that he wanted to stay at Zaccheaus' house.

The people were two-minded about Yeshua. They could see he was a prophet, he made Bartimaeus see, but he seems to have a soft spot for Samaritans and associates with tax-collectors.

Yeshua sensed the mood of the people, so he retold them the story of the Pharisee and the tax-collector that went into the Temple to pray. The people delighted in Yeshua ridiculing the pomposity of the Pharisees but again they resented him casting a publican, a tax-collector as the hero of his story.

Yeshua also repeated the story that he told elsewhere of the rich man Dives, who lived a good life and feasted sumptuously, while ignoring the poor beggar, not even giving him the crumbs that were falling from his table, giving it instead to his dogs. They both die and Lazarus ends up with Abraham in Paradise, whereas Dives burns in hell for all eternity.

The people liked the story. The poor did, but the rich not so much.

Shimon and the disciples were now accustomed to Yeshua's parables. They saw how his stories were provocative, and divided the crowds. It was no different here in Jericho.

The disciples and the people soon recognised Yeshua's preference for the poor and the despised, like Samaritans and tax-collectors. Yeshua did nothing to alter their perception of him or his reputation.

Yeshua ended his talk by saying, "You are all precious in the sight of God. He made you all because he wanted you to be alive. He wanted you to have life and he has sent me to bring you that life. I have come to give you life and life to the full. God is love, I am sent to bring you God's love, to let you know how much he loves you. He loves you so much that he sent me to you to endow you with his love. And you are truly pleasing in the sight of God if you love one another, without exception. God loves all those he created without exception. We are all made in his image, and to hate one made in his image is to hate God. We were not made to hate; we were made to love. We are the children of love. We are therefore to live in love and to give love to one another."

The people were now warming to Yeshua's teaching and his words, and they all felt uplifted until Yeshua spoke about loving one's enemies, repeating his teaching about turning the other cheek, giving the clothes off one's back, going the extra mile. That they found too much, it was a bridge too far for them. Yeshua knew that, but he did not stop.

Yeshua told them, "Love knows no boundaries. If you love only those who love you, what can you expect? Even the robbers and criminals, who live in the forest and rob people on the road out of your town to Jerusalem, do that, so love one another and care for one another. If you love only those who are your associates, or those who love you, then you are no better than those criminals who rob and assault people travelling between Jerusalem and Jericho."

Yeshua continued, "We all have sinned. We all have done things we are not proud of; we have all done harm to others, but God who sees all, does not stop loving us. He is a God of love and compassion, and forgiveness, and loves all without exception, and yes, he does have a preference for the poor and the outcasts, the vulnerable, the neglected, the suffering. He sees their plight and he hears their cries, and so must we. The Father has sent me to you, I am his Son, as you are his sons and daughters and the least you do unto any of these little ones, you do to me and to my Father."

Yeshua stopped. He just stood where he spoke and looked ahead, and ceased making any eye contact. He wanted them to reflect on his words and to turn their hearts to the Father.

After a considerable time of Yeshua standing still, a deep and peaceful silence spread throughout the synagogue. And it was as if they were gone, in a cloud somewhere, Yeshua's words ringing in their ears, and piercing their hearts.

When Yeshua felt they had enough time of silence and reflection he went and looked through some of the scrolls and picked one that had the book of Ezekiel, which he brought to read to the people.

Yeshua began, "To end our time of prayer and reflection, let me read to you a passage from the Prophet Ezekiel. These words God addresses to you today." Yeshua then held the scroll and read to the people these words: "*I will sprinkle clean water upon you, and you shall be clean from all your uncleannesses, and from all your idols. I will cleanse you. A new heart I will give you, and a new spirit. I will put within you, and I will remove from your body the heart of stone and give you a heart of flesh. I will put my spirit within you, and make you follow my statutes and be careful to observe my ordinances. And you shall be my people and I will be your God.*"

Yeshua then stepped down and walked out of the synagogue. The people followed him outside and as expected more people were waiting for Yeshua there, and they brought their sick to him and he touched them and they were all healed. And there was much rejoicing in the town. Yeshua then told Shimon and Andreus to dismiss the crowd and tell them that he would be in the town for a while and will preach in their synagogue. Johanan, James and the others helped them to disperse the crowd.

Yeshua then told his disciples to do their own thing until the eleventh hour when they could meet at the synagogue and wait for Zacchaeus to send for them. "I'm sure Zacchaeus, will give us plenty to eat, so I think I will just skip lunch," Yeshua said.

They then all went their own way, and Yeshua walked around the town, stopping to talk to the people, the traders, the shoppers, the mothers with their children. Yeshua especially loved chatting to the children and the babies on their mother's arms. The babies were absolutely adorable and Yeshua was able to bring out their warmest of smiles. They appreciated his stopping to talk with them. The mothers too were pleased. Some had heard Yeshua speak, but not all of them. Almost everyone heard that Yeshua was in town, and that he healed Bartimaeus, and their sick, but not all of them had yet met Yeshua. But when they saw this man, and his radiance, and that he was not of their town, they knew. He had a glow about him, a warm and

425

natural smile, and a joy that seem to radiate from him. And he spoke with such warmth and kindness, and showed so much interest in them, and their children. Yeshua also stopped to talk to the beggars in the streets, and sat down with them. Yeshua showed an interest in all the people he met, and those that had already met him, wanted to ask him questions, and Yeshua in an informal and conversational style and intimate manner, spoke of the Good News of God's love and compassion. He told them how much God loves them and wants their love and how much he cares for them.

Yeshua passed a stall selling herbs, vegetables and fruit, which also had plenty of figs. Yeshua stopped and wanted to buy a couple of the figs. The man who served him was overwhelmed that Yeshua stopped at his stall and spoke to him and wanted some of his fruit. He began to wrap some fruit to give to Yeshua, but Yeshua stopped him. "Thank you, my dear man, but I just want a couple of figs. I will be dining at Zaccheaus' house in a short while, so I have no need for your fruit, thank you for your kindness and generosity."

Yeshua always kept a few coins with him, for small purchases, but the man would not take his money. Yeshua then left the market place and walked around the edge of the town and through the streets and past the homes of many of the residents. The children were out in the streets playing, chasing each other and skipping and running and laughing. And Yeshua stopped, sat on the front stoop of one of the houses and watched the children at play. Yeshua thought about his childhood in Nazareth and all the games he, Achim and Zadok played. He also thought of his mother. He missed her, and wondered how she was, and he whispered a prayer for her, asking Yahweh to keep her safe.

Yeshua spent the rest of the afternoon among the people, just being with them, greeting them and speaking with them. He smiled at all of them, and when he noticed someone looking down and forlorn, he sought to bring them some comfort allowing them to talk about what it was that was bothering them.

As the eleventh hour was approaching, Yeshua made his way to the synagogue. Most of the disciples were there, except for Thomas and Judas. Zaccheaus came in person to fetch Yeshua. They waited for a while until Thomas and Judas turned up, they were chatting away, unconcerned that they were keeping everyone waiting.

Yeshua walked beside Zacchaeus, who felt overwhelmed to be walking beside Yeshua. Zacchaeus felt so proud to be walking alongside Yeshua, and for the people of Jericho to notice Yeshua beside him, and conversing with him. The rest followed close behind.

"Here we are," Zacchaeus said, as they approached a huge stone house, all white, with a very spacious frontage and plenty of grounds around the house, with plants and flowers. And to one side of the house there was a vegetable garden, and a few fruit trees. There were some servants attending to the garden.

Yeshua and the disciples entered the house and into a large room, in the centre was a long table with roasted lambs and cooked fish, and plenty of vegetables and fruit. The servants came around and brought cups and served Yeshua and the guests with wine. The servants were astonished to see the women with Yeshua. And when they saw Miriam and Rebecca chatting with Yeshua, they assumed they were related, and wondered if Yeshua was married to one of them.

Zacchaeus had his family and relatives and some of the tax-collectors present. They all heard about Bartimaeus and all the other cures Yeshua had done, and what he said in the synagogue. And they were all so overwhelmed by his presence. But Yeshua quickly put them all at ease. He spoke to them in a most kind and respectful way. The tax-collectors, especially were in awe of Yeshua, and knew of his reputation of having a soft spot for them. He never condemned any of them. Nevertheless, some of them did feel uncomfortable. What people thought of them was true of a lot of them in their profession. Some of them approached Mattheus to listen to his story, and how he came to be one of Yeshua's disciples.

As everyone became more relaxed and comfortable and had a few cups of wine to drink one of the tax-collectors approached Yeshua and asked if he could have a moment.

"Sure, what is on your mind," Yeshua said. Yeshua asked his name and how he was related to Zacchaeus.

"I'm Isaac, and I am a tax-collector. Yeshua, I have heard about your kindness to us. I know we have a poor reputation among the people because of what we have to do. And people resent our wealth, and that we are collecting taxes for the Romans. But we work hard and deserve our wealth. Yet you speak of God's preference for the poor, and you seem to come down hard on the rich. We have always believed that wealth is a blessing from God and poverty a curse. I myself believe that it is also a reward for hard work and industriousness and that many of the poor are lazy and bring their poverty onto themselves. What do you say?"

By this time, the rest of the party had gathered around and were listening to Isaac and now waiting for Yeshua's response.

"It is true what you say Isaac, my Father and I do have a preference for the poor. And for some as you say, they are lazy, but it is not so with all. And who are we to judge their circumstances, and what cause them to be poor. Yahweh, alone is our judge, we are not to judge each other, for we do not know each other, and we can only know a bit, by first walking in another's sandals. We are not to judge, or we will be judged. God is a God of love, kindness, compassion, and generosity. Sure, he is a just judge, more than any of the judges in our courts and tribunals, for he sees all and he knows all, and he sees what is in the heart of all, and he knows of all the extenuating circumstances in people's lives. There is so much that is unknown and not visible to the naked eye. We can only judge by what we see, God judges by what is unseen, what is in the minds and hearts and experiences of us all. And he is full of mercy as well as justice. He knows our weaknesses and that the spirit is willing but the flesh is weak." Yeshua then stopped.

"Now, Isaac, what was it you asked me again?" Yeshua said, as he had a sip from his cup of wine.

"About wealth and poverty, as deserved rewards and punishment, and your seeming harsh words for the rich," Isaac said.

"Oh yes. Yes, I am hard on the rich, for I came to save all. And as I have said, so many times, it is easier for a camel to pass through the eye of a needle, than for a rich man to enter the Kingdom of Heaven."

The disciples, especially the women, found the image that Yeshua construed, of a camel trying to pass through the eye of a needle, so amusing. Isaac however was not amused nor convinced. "So, are we all to remain poor, and is wealth a curse? And what have you to say about us collecting taxes for the Romans? People hate us for doing it, but it is a job, for which we have the skills. Are we all to remain poor to enter the Kingdom of Heaven?"

"Of course not, Isaac, material riches come with hard work, ingenuity, and industriousness, and sometimes with a little bit of luck, with inheritance and so on. There is nothing wrong or sinful with material riches, as long as that wealth was not the result of exploitation, injustice and on the backs of the poor. Civilizations have been built on the backs of the poor, who were and are treated unjustly, who are exploited. The rich get richer on the sweat of the poor who are not paid a just, living wage. What is the purpose of accumulating more and more, more than one needs? You cannot take it with you, and what will it profit you if you gain the whole world and suffer the loss of your immortal soul. The fact that there are so many poor all around us, tells us that there is some imbalance, and something is drastically wrong. Because God gives us all enough for what we need but greed and selfishness, and injustice, and exploitation continue to create this imbalance. Accumulate all you need for yourself and your loved ones, and then give your surplus away, use it for the benefit of those in need."

Still not fully satisfied, Isaac persisted, "What about our profession? We are hated by the people, and we are only doing our job."

"Yes, you are doing your job and doing an honest day's work, so you have to be honest. You receive a wage on the commission for what you collect. So do an honest day's work. Overcharging on the tax is not honest. Skimming off the money collected is not honest. Do your work with honesty, integrity, and compassion. For you know how people struggle and how exorbitant the taxes and tariffs are, and so many become poor because they are over-taxed. Do what you can to bring about fairness and justice and be fair and just in all that you do and know that you too will be treated fairly and justly by the Lord in return. The justice you meet out is the justice you will receive."

"Okay Isaac, that's enough," Zacchaeus came and broke up the altercation. "Yeshua has come here to relax and enjoy himself. We will have some music now, my daughter plays the flute beautifully, and we have an experienced harp player here too, so sit down and have some cake, fruit and nuts or more wine and relax and enjoy the music."

They all sat down, with most of the men opting for more wine, as they listened to the music of the harp and the flute and the two combined. It was beautiful and relaxing.

After the music, there was more animated chatter. The women got together and they all wanted to listen to Miriam and the rest of Yeshua's women disciples. They wanted to know how it was like being Yeshua's disciples, and they wanted to know all about their relationship with Yeshua. They were absolutely intrigued to hear how Yeshua made sure they were treated with respect by the men who were his disciples.

"I grew up with Yeshua, in Nazareth. And he always treated me with the utmost respect. We had such fun times together. We loved to walk together in the woods and I loved to run and Yeshua often joined me," Rebecca told them. The women were fascinated and envied her relationship and friendship with Yeshua.

Miriam and Lucia shared their healing encounters with Yeshua. And all the women spoke of how Yeshua loved them and respected them, and valued them, and listened to them, and sought their counsel, and also how much they were learning from Yeshua.

They were all touched by how they supported themselves going from town to town preaching and teaching and healing and doing God's work. When the women realised that they all pooled their resources and that they had been on the road for more than a year some of them offered to support in whatever way they could. Miriam and the women disciples were most grateful and assured the women, Yeshua would know of their generosity.

"Do you think Yeshua would come and speak to us women on our own?" one of the women asked.

"Now that is something no other group of women have asked. I will ask Yeshua, I'm sure he will be willing to do that," Miriam replied. She and the other women disciples were enthused with the idea.

Miriam sent Rebecca to speak with Yeshua. Yeshua excused himself from the group around him, and listened to what Rebecca wanted to say.

"Yeshua, the women wondered if you would speak to the women on their own, while you are here in Jericho," Rebecca asked.

Yeshua was silent for a moment, and then his eyes lit up. "Now isn't that just a great idea! We have not had such a meeting ever. Yes, I will be most happy to spend time with the women, at a women's only gathering. I promised the people I would speak again in the synagogue tomorrow, so arrange something for the next day. Make it an all-day affair. You and Miriam and the others and some of the women from the town can arrange the day. Maybe we could start in the morning and have lunch and the afternoon together," Yeshua suggested.

"Why not dinner too, Yeshua, let the men fend for themselves for one day," Rebecca said, with a mischievous smile.

"Rebecca, I leave it to you, Miriam and the others, I'll go along with whatever you arrange. I'll make myself free for the day."

Rebecca immediately went back to the ladies and gave them Yeshua's response. They were delighted. Miriam and Rebecca called the others together, Lucia, Rachel, Joanna, Susanna, and Salome and Bathsheba, the woman who suggested the idea. She roped in Tamar, Zacchaeus wife as well.

"What a great idea. You can have our place if you like. It's much more congenial and convenient than the Women's Court in the synagogue or the community hall, and we can have lunch together," Tamar said.

They all accepted Tamar's place as the venue for their meeting.

"I'll make sure Zacchaeus is away and that we are undisturbed for the day," Tamar said.

"I'll just go and tell Yeshua," Rebecca said.

Rebecca relayed to Yeshua the women's deliberations.

"That's wonderful Rebecca. Can they get women to come who really could do with a break, women in need, some of the poor women in the town," Yeshua said. "And maybe you could see how the women could have other arrangements for the care of their children. If they can't then they can bring their children with them, and maybe Tamar can have some of her maids look after them. Some of the maids might also like to join us for the day. In any case I'll leave all the decisions to you and the ladies," Yeshua said. "This is so exciting, Rebecca, I am really looking forward to it," Yeshua said, smiling.

The rest of the evening passed quickly and Andreus then nudged Shimon and told him to prompt Yeshua about calling it a day.

They then thanked Zaccheus and Tamar and all their servants and the guests and then Yeshua and his disciples left for their arranged places of accommodation.

Chapter Sixty-Five
Women's Business

There was much excitement in the air. The day had come for the women's gathering. This was a first for the town of Jericho, and a first in Yeshua's ministry. The women were beside themselves with the joy of anticipation, and looking forward to this gathering. They spent the last forty-eight hours preparing. They had to convince their husbands and men folk to cooperate, and they used Yeshua's authority to smooth the way. They said that it was Yeshua's request. The men were not too pleased. But the women did all the necessary cooking, and cleaning in advance, so the men had no excuse. Child care arrangements were made, with some grandparents helping out, and there was also a room set up for the children and plenty of maid servants to care for them, at Tamar's place.

Cooking began the night before and the women organisers were at Zacchaeus and Tamar's place early to set up everything. Arrangements were made to begin early after everyone had their breakfast at home. They would begin at the third hour. Miriam, Rebecca, Lucia, Rachel, Joanna, Salome, Susanna, were there early to assist Tamar and Bathsheba to get everything ready. There was a buzz in the air.

"This is a day to remember ladies. Something like this has never happened here in Jericho," Bathsheba said.

"Neither in all the time and places we went to with Yeshua," Miriam said.

"Neither in all the time I lived in Nazareth, with Yeshua," Rebecca added.

"Neither in all my time in Capernaum," Lucia said.

"Ladies, we are making history," Tamar said.

The women started arriving a half hour before they were meant to start. There was so much excitement and expectancy. The women felt so uplifted and empowered. It was such a joy for them to have to leave the housework for a day and to concentrate on themselves, and be with other women, and chat about women's business, and to have Yeshua all to themselves for the entire day, they were walking on clouds.

A quarter of an hour before starting time, Yeshua arrived. He was looking fresh and radiant, and all could see Yeshua was happy to be with them, and just as excited as they all were. Yeshua greeted the women warmly and there was much animation in the air.

Yeshua had some water to drink and thanked Tamar for offering to host this gathering in her place. Tamar was only too pleased. Tamar knew how despised her husband was in the community, and no one from Jericho would be seen dead in their place. And it was only their close relatives and the tax-collectors and their families that visited. They were shunned by the people, because of their husbands. But in the past few days, things have changed dramatically. Zacchaeus has changed, and a lot of the people's attitudes had softened towards him, and his family. The people still abhorred the tax-collectors in general, but they had changed somewhat in their attitude to Zacchaeus and his family. And it is all because of Yeshua. Tamar felt so grateful.

Tamar let Bathsheba chair the gathering, as she was the one who had suggested the idea in the first place. Bathsheba called everyone to take a seat that was arranged in rows of semi-circles, starting with a small intimate semi-circle close to Yeshua and then rows of semi-circles, filling the large room, right to the surrounding walls, with seats all around the perimeter of the large room. There were more than seventy women crammed into the room, with some women standing all around the back of those seated, even though there were enough chairs for everyone. They all wanted a good view of Yeshua.

Bathsheba cleared her throat, and with a broad and proud smile, she welcomed everyone. "Ladies, this is history in the making. Never before in my lifetime have such a gathering of so many ladies taken place here in Jericho," she said. "I wish to thank Tamar for her kindness, generosity and hospitality, in hosting this gathering here today. I especially thank all Yeshua's disciples, who are with us here today; you will have a chance to meet them all. And above all I welcome Yeshua, who is our guest speaker and teacher for today. Welcome Yeshua, it is a pleasure to have you with us and thank you for so readily agreeing to this day."

Bathsheba then welcomed Yeshua to take the floor and speak to the ladies. Yeshua went to the front and looked across the large room and the sea of faces and he smiled and said, "I must be in heaven," and everyone burst out laughing. It was a great ice-breaker.

Yeshua continued, "Of course in heaven, we are neither male nor female, we are pure spirits, we are like God and his angels. Of course, now we cannot see clearly, we see like Bartimaeus did, blindly, not at all. We are all like Bartimaeus, as far as seeing the ways of God. Many of us are spiritually blind, and we live in darkness, I have come to bring all out of the darkness and into the light."

Yeshua then stopped to welcome and thank, by saying, "I want to join my sentiments with what Bathsheba had said, and welcome you all, and thank Tamar for her kindness and generosity. She is a most gracious host, and my disciples and I had a wonderful time here only a few days ago, thank you Tamar."

Tamar nodded to Yeshua with a smile, and the ladies all burst into applause and that even uplifted Tamar all the more.

Yeshua continued, "I want to also thank you for inviting me. I hope I can fulfil your expectations, for I am only a man, and you all know and agree we are the weaker sex really," Yeshua said with a smile.

And there were smiles and chuckles all around.

Yeshua continued, "God made us all to his image and likeness. He made us female and male. So, God's nature must have both male and female ingredients in some way, for no one can create what is not from within. What the Creator creates is from within. And you all are the beauty of God, personified," Yeshua said, as he opened his hands and spread his arms in an open gesture to capture the entire audience, who were all ears and eyes and relishing Yeshua's opening remarks.

"Ladies, I learned all about the warmth and love of a woman from my mother, Miriam. She was only sixteen, so young, when she bore me within her womb, and when she nourished me at her breast. There is no greater miracle on this earth and no greater example of God's love for us, than the love of a mother for her child, than your love for your children, if you have children, or your love for your family members and friends and relatives, if you are not a mother. As women, you are all mothers; you were created with a nurturing, caring and loving nature. To see you all, and to see also mothers, who nurse and nurture their children gives us all a glimpse of the love of God for all of us.

"The way you love your children, you sacrifice so much for your children, you go without so they may have, you are full of compassion for them, and you will give your life for them. And if you have no children of your own, we still see your maternal care for all of God's family, especially our little ones. I think of those beautiful words of our prophet Isaiah, that will ring through the ages, let me utter them to you now; Isaiah begins by saying 'Listen to me, O coastlands,' but I would like to add some other places to his opening words, 'Listen to me O coastlands, listen to me women of Jericho, women of Galilee, women of Judaea, women from all over the world.' Isaiah goes on to say, 'pay attention you peoples, from far away! The Lord called me before I was born; while I was in my mother's womb, he named me. He made my mouth like a sharp sword, in the shadow of his hand he hid me, he made me a polished arrow, and in his quiver, he hid me away'."

Yeshua continued, "Isaiah continues to speak of the coming of the Saviour, with these words, 'Thus says the Lord; in a time of favour, I have answered you, on a day of salvation I have helped you, saying to prisoners, 'Come out,' to those who are in darkness, 'Show yourselves.' They shall feed along the ways, on all the bare heights shall be their pasture, they shall not hunger or thirst, neither scorching wind nor sun shall strike them down, for he who has pity on them will lead them, and by springs of water will guide them. Sing for joy, O heavens, and exult, O earth; break forth, O mountains into singing! For the Lord has comforted his people, and will have compassion on his suffering ones."

"These words my friends are addressed to you today; O women of Jericho, of Galilee, of Judaea and all over the world, the Lord comforts you, and has love and compassion for you, especially you who suffer much."

Yeshua paused. The women were touched by what Yeshua was saying to them and about them, and they were lost in the dazzling words of Isaiah, and it was as if they were the words of Yeshua himself, and it was as if Isaiah was prophesising about Yeshua, who was now here with them in the flesh. Yeshua could see the minds of the women, absorbing his words, and he continued to remain silent, to let them continue their reflections.

After a while Yeshua continued, "My dear ladies, Isaiah writes so beautifully about our God, our heavenly Father, about Yahweh, his love and compassion for us. I was inspired to recall Isaiah's words while speaking about us being created in the image and likeness of God, and I see that image so clearly in you women, and in a very special way in the image of a mother and child. This is an image of our God, he is our mother, who gave birth to us, and who nurtures us at her breast. So intimate is God's love and care for us. And Isaiah goes on to say, and these are his words, that I really wanted to say to you. They are such beautiful words that conjure up in our minds and hearts just how dear we are to our God who loves us with an unconditional and eternal love, Isaiah says. 'Can a woman forget her nursing child, or show no compassion for the child of her womb? Even these may forget, yet I will not forget you. See I have inscribed you on the palms of my hands.'"

Yeshua stopped and sighed heavily. He was so moved by these words of Isaiah. Yeshua looked at his open hands, then joined them and put them to his lips as if in prayer. Yeshua was lost in the moment, in the depth of God's great and abiding love. Yeshua lost all consciousness of the women in front of him; he was totally absorbed in the presence of his heavenly Father, in his abiding and undying love, inspired by the words of Isaiah.

The women looked on astounded. Yeshua seemed to be glowing, his face radiant. All the women knew and felt that they were in the presence of a holy man, a man of God, a prophet. He had made Bartimaeus see, so he is also a miracle worker, a healer. They were so astounded to be in the presence of a man like this. Yeshua's disciples were also in awe, Yeshua never failed to move them. They walked with him, all over Galilee, crossed the Sea of Galilee and the River Jordan and now they are travelling all over Judaea and they have seen his human side, his humanity, he could laugh, and shed tears, and joke, and enjoy a drink and tease and loved a good party. And then at times, and like now, they could see that he was more than human. As Miriam looked at Yeshua now, she thought of Moses, as he came down from Mount Sinai, his face was so resplendent that the Israelites could barely gaze on him. Yeshua was now glowing, radiant, and alive with God's presence.

Yeshua seemed to come out of a trancelike state, and looked at the women; they were waiting for him to speak.

Yeshua smiled and continued, "My dear sisters in the Lord. I am so moved to be in your presence. You are the finest image of God amongst us. For too long have you been diminished, banished to the kitchens of the world. And yet you have made of the kitchen, the heart of the home, there all of the family are nourished bodily with the fruit of your fine cooking, your labour of love, and there our souls are nourished with the warmth of your self-sacrificing, generous and abiding love. You are the heart of the world. You are the expression and presence of God's love in our homes and in our midst. I praise you and I honour you."

Yeshua drew his breath. The women were in awe, and for some there were tears rolling down their cheeks. They were so moved by Yeshua's words. Never before has any man, any one spoke so highly and so beautifully and so movingly about them, about all women.

"My dear sisters in the Lord, it pains me, the way you are ill-treated by many, and how you suffer in silence. Mankind has not recognised your worth. You have a unique insight into life, and we are the poorer for not giving you the chance to receive of your wisdom. You will suffer still for years to come, for generations to come, how long suffering you and your sisters have endured at the hands of your brothers, fathers, male rulers, leaders. But there have been great women, role models for us, like here," Yeshua said with a smile. "And like Tamar, mentioned in our Scriptures, like so many women, Tamar was ill-treated and betrayed by men, who controlled her life, her future, but she fought with courage and determination for her right to believe in a loving God. And then there was Rahab, one of the heroines of your fine city of Jericho. She lived here, her spirit lives here; she is with us here, just like when she looked out of her window onto the plains of Jericho. She was a woman of such wisdom, ingenuity and courage, and with an indomitable spirit, she wanted to be treated with dignity and respect, she got her way, but she knew there was more in life, and then God came to her, she learned of the God of Abraham, the God of Isaac and the God of Jacob, of his love for all of humankind, and she wanted his love, and wanted to love him in return. She had a past that was that of all women, looked upon as inferior, and subservient to men, but she wanted and God gave her a future. When she learned about the power of God, and how he saved the Israelites from the most powerful nation on earth the Egyptians in such a miraculous way, and brought them to a Promised Land, she wanted to love and serve such a God. And she did."

Yeshua paused. He wanted to catch his breath and also allow what he had said about Tamar and Rahab to sink in.

Yeshua continued, "And you know the story of Ruth. She lost so much, sacrificed so much, and God blessed her and gave her so much in return. She became the great-grandmother of the mighty King David. Ruth was of a different race and different faith to her mother-in-law Naomi, but she remained faithful to her to the bitter end. Ruth challenges us all, especially the chosen people of God, and all men who tend to view, who tend to look down on women, and all who are different in any way, with suspicion and disdain."

Rebecca was enthralled once again. When Yeshua had first told her the story of Ruth, she was so impressed with her, and now to hear the story again, lifted her soul.

Yeshua continued, "When Naomi was returning to her country and her people, she knew the ill-treatment Ruth would receive because she was a woman, of different faith and race, so Naomi urged Ruth to return to her people, and the practices of her religion, but Ruth would not desert Naomi, and she sings her beautiful song, that continues to ring through the ages."

Yeshua, had prearranged with Miriam that he was most likely going to speak about the heroic women of the past, including Ruth and Hannah and he spent time with her coaching her in the singing of Ruth's Song and Hannah's Song. Yeshua then said to the women. "Ladies, we are fortunate to have Miriam with us, and she has been blessed with such a beautiful voice. And she has prepared and will now sing for us the beautiful Song of Ruth."

Miriam came forward and a bit nervously at first but once she opened her mouth the nerves left her and she sang like an angel, enthralling the women. Her voice rang across the room as she sang:

"Do not press me to leave you
or to turn back from following you!
Where you go, I will go;
where you lodge, I will lodge;
your people shall be my people
and your God my God.
Where you die, I will die—
there will I be buried.
May the Lord do thus and so to me,
and more as well,
if even death parts me from you."

Rebecca's eyes lit up and her heart rejoiced as she recalled Yeshua telling her the story of Ruth, and how she gave up everything, expecting and asking for nothing in return. She remembered how captivated she was when Yeshua first told her the story of Ruth, who gave up everything and God honoured her. And now hearing the story again, and listening to Miriam sing Ruth's song, stirred her soul. All the women were moved, and some had tears streaming down their cheeks.

Yeshua continued, "Thank you Miriam, you sang that beautifully. My dear sisters, the list goes on. And here and now, there are great women, who will be remembered for years to come for their wisdom, their unfaltering spirit, and above all for their love and compassion. I have such women, here with us today, women who have given up everything to follow me, and be my disciples and learn from me, and when I am no longer with you, they will carry on my work of spreading the Good News of God's love and compassion and salvation and redemption for all of humankind."

Yeshua's disciples were taken by surprise; they were not expecting to be singled out. But they appreciated Yeshua's kind words.

"You know these women; they are in your midst. What they have learned from me, and what I have learned from them, they will share with you today. I ask them to stand, so you can see who they are."

Yeshua's disciples were somewhat self-conscious, but proud to be acknowledged by Yeshua as his disciples, and in such an honourable way. They all stood up as Yeshua called out their names, "Miriam from Magdala, Rebecca from my hometown of Nazareth, Lucia, from Capernaum, Rachel from a village at Mount Tabor, in Galilee, and Joanna, Salome and Susanna from Jerusalem."

The women clapped. And were delighted to have Yeshua's disciples with them today, and they were looking forward to spending time with them and learning from them.

"And now, I am dying for some refreshment. We will break for a while and when you are ready, we will reassemble."

The women got up and had their break, and ate all the delicacies set out on the table and there were hot and cold drinks to wash it all down. There was so much chattering and some of the women sought Yeshua for a private chat, and others sought Miriam, and the other of Yeshua's disciples, and the other women of Jericho, caught up with each other. Many had not seen or had not spent time with each other, for a very long time. They were all consumed with their own lives, and it was such a pleasure to meet with other women, and engage in women's business. The place was abuzz. After Yeshua had something to eat, he slipped out back for a quiet moment, to refresh spiritually. Yeshua found this a new experience, and it brought home to him just how important it was for all to appreciate the role of women in society, and to respect their views and cater for their needs. And to realise that they are equal in dignity and worth to men.

When everyone regrouped, Yeshua continued, "I have one more great woman, whose story I wish to share. Her name will live on forever, she will be honoured for all time to come; she is my mother, Miriam, from Nazareth."

The women were all ears, wanting to hear about Yeshua's mother. Yeshua continued, "My mother was just turning sixteen when she gave birth to me. Nine months earlier she was visited by an angel, who told her she was to conceive and bear a son."

The women took what Yeshua was saying in a figurative sense. To be 'visited by an angel' was a common enough expression, like being 'moved by the Spirit'.

Yeshua continued, "The angel told her she was to bear a son, and she was to call him Yeshua, and the angel told her marvellous things about her son, and about his kingdom that would last forever. And that is why I am here today. I am building the Kingdom of God on earth, a kingdom of love, compassion, and forgiveness. My mother has sacrificed so much for me. I was born in a stable in Bethlehem, just over thirty-one years ago, because at that time, my father Yosef had to go to his home town of Bethlehem to register for the nationwide census ordered by the Emperor Augustus. Can you imagine, my mother, almost nine months pregnant and travelling all the way from Nazareth to Bethlehem? And when we got there, she was about to give birth, and as there was no room in the inn, she gave birth to me in a stable, the home of the animals."

The women were attentive and fascinated to hear Yeshua speak of his mother and share the story of his birth. Yeshua went on to tell them of their flight from Herod into Egypt and what life was like in Egypt for the following four years. Yeshua also spoke of how much pain he gave his mother when at the age of twelve he stayed behind in Jerusalem after the Passover and his parents had left and had to return to seek for him, and it took three days before they found him.

The women all put themselves in Miriam's shoes, and felt the anguish she must have felt having lost her twelve-year-old son for three whole days.

Yeshua went on to heap praise on his mother, for all she taught him, sacrificed for him, for all the love and care she gave him, and he told the women just how much he missed her, and could hardly wait to see her again.

Yeshua continued, "Let me tell you how, I met Johanan the Prophet, whom I am sure some of you met, and maybe were his disciples," Yeshua said. "We are saddened that Johanan is no longer with us in the flesh, but he is with us in spirit, and has received his just reward in the Kingdom of Heaven, where he sees our God face to face. When my mother knew she was pregnant she learned that her cousin, Elisheva was also pregnant, six months in fact. Now Elisheva was of advanced age and past childbearing age and had been barren all her life and her husband, Zechariah was even older than her and my mother was amazed but rejoiced, and she went into the hill country here in Judaea to visit her cousin, and my mother told me that when she and Elisheva met and greeted each other, Elisheva told her that little Johanan in her womb leapt for joy."

The women's mouths were agape with delight at this vision of the meeting between Johanan and Yeshua, and their mothers.

Yeshua continued, "My mother told me that Elisheva uttered words of praise on both me and my mother, Elisheva exclaimed to my mother, 'Blessed are you among women, and blessed is the fruit of your womb. And blessed are you Miriam for believing that what had been spoken to you by the Lord would be fulfilled.' My mother told me that she was so moved by what Elisheva was saying to her that she burst into a poetic mood, as words came out of her from nowhere, but she told me afterwards, that they were really inspired by the Song of Hannah. But I remember well the words that my mother uttered on that day, I hold them forever in my heart, these are her words, her Song of Praise:

My soul magnifies the Lord,
and my spirit rejoices in God my Saviour,
for he has looked with favour on the lowliness of his servant,
Surely, from now on all generations will call me blessed;
for the Mighty One has done great things for me,
and holy is his name.
His mercy is for those who fear him
From generation to generation.
He has shown strength with his arm;

he has scattered the proud in the thoughts of their hearts.
He has brought down the powerful from their thrones,
and lifted up the lowly;
he has filled the hungry with good things,
and sent the rich away empty.
He has helped his servant Israel,
in remembrance of his mercy,
according to the promise he made to our ancestors,
to Abraham and his descendants forever."

Yeshua paused for a moment. The women were enraptured with those beautiful words uttered by Yeshua's mother. Yeshua continued, "My mother is great, she is a prophet and all those words she uttered are what I have been sent to do, and am doing here in Judaea, and throughout Galilee and beyond. I am to proclaim the Lord's mercy to all, scatter the proud, bring down the powerful, lift up the lowly, feed the hungry, send the rich away empty, and give a helping hand to all in need."

Yeshua paused again; he wanted the women to relish the words of his mother's Song of Praise. And he too wanted to delight in it himself. Yeshua continued, "My mother, when she related to me these words, I wanted to remember them, and I do and they have a great impact on my life. She did tell me that her Song of Praise was inspired by the song of that other great woman Hannah, which she sang to give thanks to God for the birth of her son Samuel. And now I call on Miriam and we will have her sing to us again, the Song of Hannah." Yeshua gestured to Miriam to come forward.

This time, Miriam had no nerves whatsoever and she was ready and willing to sing Hannah's Song, and she sounded like the voice of an angel, as she sang:

"My heart exults in the Lord;
My strength is exalted in my God.
My mouth derides my enemies
because I rejoice in my victory.
There is no Holy One, like the Lord,
no one besides you;
there is no Rock like our God.
Talk no more so very proudly,
let not arrogance come from your mouth;
for the Lord is a God of knowledge,
and by him actions are weighed.
The bows of the mighty are broken,
but the feeble gird on strength.
Those who were full
have hired themselves out for bread,
but those who were hungry are fat with spoil.
The barren has borne seven,
but she who has many children is forlorn.
The Lord kills and brings to life
he brings down to Sheol and raises up.
The Lord makes poor and makes rich;

he brings low, he also exalts.
He raises up the poor from the dust;
he lifts the needy from the ash heap,
to make them sit with princes
and inherit a seat of honour.
For the pillars of the earth are the Lord's,
and on them he has set the world.
He will guard the feet of his faithful ones,
but the wicked shall be cut off in darkness;
for not by might does one prevail.
The Lord! His adversaries shall be shattered;
the Most High will thunder in heaven.
The Lord will judge the ends of the earth;
he will give strength to his King,
and exalt the power of his anointed."

The women were completely rapt in the Song of Hannah been sung so beautifully by Miriam. It was a long song, but the women felt that Miriam could go on forever. Yeshua and his disciples too were taken in with the singing by Miriam, and also the words of Hannah. They were so meaningful. And Yeshua could see why his mother said she was inspired by the words of Hannah's Song of Praise.

When Miriam had finished singing, the Song of Hannah, one could hear a pin drop, so deep was the silence. The women were moved to the core. Yeshua allowed time for the women to relish and rest in the song they had just heard sung. There was so much to delight in and to ponder. When they came out of their silence, Yeshua continued to speak about Hannah's Song, the power of God over all enemies, God's preference for the poor and the lowly, and above all his love and compassion for us, and our need to trust and turn to God in times of need, but not only in times of need, but always.

"My dear sisters, I spoke a lot about the Father's preference for the poor, I will also say he has a special place for you, and for all women, for he knows just how ill-treated women are, how subjugated women are, how ill-treated women are, how women are abused by men all over the world. He created men and women as equals in dignity and worth, different but equal, and meant us to complement each other, not dominate one over the other. Because men are physically stronger that does not give them the right to use that force to ill-treat and abuse women. Women too have their own strengths; emotionally, spiritually women are by far superior and able to endure so much more. You have suffered in silence for so long, but the Lord does not forget you, he sees all you endure, and he is full of love and admiration and compassion for you, as I am for you."

Yeshua continued speaking in this vein, extolling the strength and virtue of womanhood, and uplifting them all. They listened with such appreciation of what Yeshua was saying, never before has a man of Yeshua's standing spoken so eloquently and forcefully of the greatness of their sex. They were filled with hope. Many had tears streaming down their cheeks.

Yeshua continued to speak to the women, and they wanted to know more and more about his teaching. He taught them his Beatitudes, the charter for all of those who wished to be his followers. He taught them about the need to be humble, and to pray without ceasing, and to take up their cross daily and follow him. He dispelled the false beliefs about pain and suffering, and made it clear that God does not cause suffering, and that poverty and suffering and illness, is not a result of one's sin, nor a punishment from God, and that wealth and good fortune is not a reward from God for living without sin. He spoke of God's justice that is not like humankind's justice, and about God's compassion and mercy, and his readiness to forgive. He made it clear to them that God is not a severe and spiteful God watching and waiting for one to sin, so that he can strike you down. He is a forgiving and understanding God, who will forgive and forget, and lift one up every time one falls into sin. He spoke of a God that not only shares their sorrows and sufferings, but delights in their happiness and shares all those great and happy moments with them, and he loves to laugh with them. He spoke of God's great sense of humour and fun, he created and gave us a sense of humour and that we have the capacity for fun, laughter and merriment.

One of the ladies stood up, and spoke for all. "Yeshua, you have lifted up my soul. I feel ten feet tall. I am so grateful that you have shared so much with us this morning. You have made us believe in ourselves as never before. And yes, we do see God's sense of humour in you. We see God's love and sense of humour in you, in your stories and images. We saw how amused you were with Zacchaeus, up in that sycamore tree," the woman laughed and the others laughed with her with the recalling of the little man Zacchaeus up in the tree, he looked like a little boy with a man's head.

"Sorry Tamar, us making fun of your husband," the woman said.

"Not at all, that was funny even for me. I would have simply loved to have been there and seen my Zacchaeus making a fool of himself, and being the butt of laughter. I would have laughed too," Tamar said with a smile.

Another woman spoke up, "And Yeshua I couldn't help smiling, laughing when you said 'it is easier for a camel to pass through the eye of a needle than for a rich man to enter the Kingdom of Heaven.' It conjured up such a ridiculous image in my mind I could not help laughing, and I felt like sending needles to all those rich and powerful people, who laud over and ill treat all those who slave for them."

Rebecca rose to speak, "I know Yeshua, we grew up together in Nazareth, and I pursued him and wanted him all for myself," she said laughing, and the women joined in the laughter with her. She continued, "And Yeshua had such a great sense of fun and sense of humour, he made me laugh all the time. And his stories and his sayings would have me in stiches, even when he is imparting a very serious lesson. Like when he lampooned the Pharisees for their ridiculous pomposity, likening them to whitewashed tombstones. And when he gave them and the people the lesson on not judging others, ridiculing not only the Pharisees but all of us really by asking, 'why do we see the splinter in our brother's eye and in our sister's eye for that matter, and ignore the plank in our own'," Rebecca said smiling.

Miriam then stood up to speak. "I have been with Yeshua for more than a year now and he often makes me laugh without realising it. I was very ill and forever depressed and he healed me and now I can't stop laughing," Miriam said laughing, and the women laughed with her. "And I agree with Rebecca, Yeshua has a knack of teaching, using simple stories and images and words that does bring a smile to one's face. Even when he was criticising the Pharisees I couldn't help smiling and laughing at the words he used, 'Woe to you, Scribes and Pharisees, hypocrites! For you tithe mint, dill, and cummin, and have neglected the weightier matters of the law: justice and mercy and faith. You blind guides! You strain out a gnat but swallow a camel.'" Again, the women couldn't help laughing. Miriam continued, "'Woe to you, Scribes and Pharisees, hypocrites! For you clean the outside of the cup and the plate, but inside you are full of greed and self-indulgence. You blind Pharisees!'"

The women disciples continued to share their stories with the women. Yeshua then spoke again. "Thank you for that, Rebecca and Miriam, Lucia and Rebecca, I see my methods are working, for you, and you remember what I said. Yes, I try to bring home God's sense of humour, and use his light heartedness in driving home profound truths. We cannot go around with stern and frowning faces, and without laughter and a sense of humour, we would all live a dull life. We never hear about God laughing or God's sense of humour, and not so long ago, I spent my whole teaching in the synagogue on God's laughter and sense of fun, so I was thrilled when I was praying one of David's psalms not so long ago. Let me recite for you a few lines from the second psalm, God's Chosen King:

"Why do the nations conspire?
And the peoples plot in vain?
The kings of the earth set themselves
and the rulers take counsel together,
against the Lord and his anointed, saying,
Let us burst their bonds asunder,
and cast their cords from us.
He who sits in the heavens, laughs,
the Lord has them in derision."

Yeshua continued, "It delighted me so, to read those words of David of God laughing at his enemies and the Lord having them in derision. Even when Isaiah speaks of the coming Messiah and describes him as a Man of Sorrows, as the Suffering Servant, by saying 'He was despised and rejected by others; a man of suffering and acquainted with infirmity; and as one from whom others hide their faces, for he was despised, and we held him of no account.' Yet previously he tells Zion to rejoice with the coming of the Messiah with these words," Yeshua then recited the words from Isaiah:

"Put on your beautiful garments, O Jerusalem, the holy city…
How beautiful upon the mountains
are the feet of the messenger who announces peace,
who brings Good News,
who announces salvation…
Listen! Your sentinels lift up their voices
together they sing for joy."

Yeshua continued, "and the Book of Ecclesiastes tells us that everything has its time:

"For everything there is a season, and a time…
a time to be born, and a time to die…
a time to weep and a time to laugh;

440

a time to mourn and a time to dance.

"And on that note, I will say, it is a time to eat," Yeshua said smiling, and everyone burst into laughter.

And the laughter continued as the women shared a meal and shared funny stories, many at the expense of their husbands and menfolk.

After lunch, the women had split into seven smaller groups led by each of the seven women disciples. Yeshua excused himself, and wanted the women to speak openly about their lives from their perspective, their women's business. Yeshua went for a walk. He came back a couple of hours later to end the day.

The women wanted to share what they had discussed in the smaller groups, and everyone listened and learned, and so did Yeshua.

Yeshua then spoke to the women. "I think we have spoken and listened and learned enough from each other today. We are all older and wiser," Yeshua said with a smile.

"Take courage. And know that God is with you, and knows you, and loves you, and will protect you no matter what. You have been strengthened by the love of God and each other. Continue to love each other and support each other and keep up that sense of humour. Let me conclude this day by reciting another of David's songs, this one is entitled, 'A Harvest of Joy'." Yeshua then recited the psalm:

"When the Lord restored the fortunes of Zion,
we were like those who dream.
Then our mouths were filled with laughter,
and our tongue with shouts of joy,
then it was said among the nations,
The Lord has done great things for them.
The Lord has done great things for us,
and we rejoiced.
Restore our fortunes, O Lord,
like the watercourses in the Negeb.
May those who sow in tears
reap with shouts of joy.
Those who go out weeping,
beating the seed for sowing,
shall come home with shouts of joy,
carrying their sheaves."

"So now, my dearest sisters, go home with shouts of joy. May your mouths be filled with laughter, and your tongues with shouts of joy, and your hearts filled with love, and go home now with shouting with joy, carrying your sheaves with you, the fruits of this day. Carry with you all you have learned and received from God and from each other. Go in peace and may the love of God be with you."

Thunderous applause erupted. The women were filled with the Spirit. They thanked Yeshua and each other and hugged one another. The women hung around, not wanting to leave. They were so filled with the Spirit, and with such indescribable joy.

Eventually, Yeshua said his goodbyes and gave thanks to all, especially Tamar and Bathsheba and Miriam and all who had a hand in the organisation and preparation of this day. Yeshua walked home alone, as Miriam and the others helped clean up, and many of the women still wanted them there. They were the last to leave.

When Miriam and the ladies arrived back at their place of residing, Yeshua was there waiting for them. He needed to debrief. They spent the next couple of hours chatting about the day, and sharing their experiences and their feelings. When Yeshua felt it was time, he left.

"Goodnight, Miriam, Rebecca, Lucia, Rachel, Joanna, Salome, Susanna. It was a most enlivening day, thanks to you all. The Lord was smiling on us all. Have a good night's rest now. And I think it would be good if we all had a day of rest tomorrow. Let Shimon and the others know, I will be going for a walk in the woodlands and will see you all in two days' time at the synagogue."

When Yeshua eventually caught up with his disciples after that brief sojourn, Yeshua and the disciples spent the next few weeks in Jericho. Yeshua went to all the outlying areas, where the poor and the marginalised lived, where the outcasts were banned, and he spoke to them, words of comfort and brought the Good News of how God loved them and cherished them, and that he sees all they suffer, and endure, and he is with them now and always. Yeshua brought them all words of comfort, and healed all their sick.

And then Yeshua told his disciples they were ready to leave Jericho.

Chapter Sixty-Six
Crossing the River Jordan on the Way Home Again

Yeshua and his disciples then headed for Bethabara, where Johanan baptised Yeshua and his disciples. When they reached Bethabara, they rested at the banks of the River Jordan. Yeshua then spoke to them. "It is here, my friends, where it all began, here Johanan baptised me, more than a year ago. This is a sacred place for me, and for so many who were baptised and received the Holy Spirit. This has always been a sacred place. It is around here that Joshua led our ancestors across the River Jordan into the Promised Land. And it is here that Elijah also crossed before he was taken up into heaven. Johanan preached all over these territories, and we will do the same. We will proclaim to the people that what Johanan preached about the Kingdom, about to come, is being fulfilled. We will spend as much time as the Father wants us to, in these territories, and bring the Good News of the Kingdom. We will reach out to all of Johanan's disciples, so they may not lose heart, but be reinvigorated. We will announce to all of them the Good News of God's Kingdom of love and compassion and forgiveness, and salvation and redemption for all."

Yeshua and his disciples spent several months around these territories where Johanan preached. The people gathered in big numbers, some thinking it was Johanan come back to life. But as the people listened to Yeshua, and saw all his great deeds, they began to believe. And many wondered if Yeshua was the Promised One, Johanan had spoken of. Some who were there when Yeshua was baptised fuelled the belief about Yeshua, for they told everyone what had happened when Yeshua was baptised by Johanan.

Yeshua told the people that Johanan was secretly buried with dignity surrounded by his friends and disciples. And that he is here in spirit with them. Wherever Yeshua and his disciples went, crowds gathered. News about Yeshua's time in Jericho also began to filter through, and people heard about Bartimaeus being healed of his blindness and made to see. They also heard about Zacchaeus, the chief tax-collector and his conversion, and Yeshua's association with the hated tax-collectors. And there were also some tax-collectors around the area that were baptised by Johanan and were his disciples.

One of the tax-collectors approached Yeshua and spoke to him. "Yeshua, I was a disciple of Johanan's, as are many of my profession. I and several other tax-collectors were baptised by Johanan, he called us to repent of our sins, and we have, and he told us not to collect more than is legal, and to treat all with dignity and respect, and we have done that ever since."

"I am so pleased for you. Continue to do as Johanan taught you. Treat all with dignity, respect, justice and mercy, as the Father treats us all. Reach out to the poor and needy in your midst in whatever way you can, and above all show kindness and love to all you meet," Yeshua said.

"Yeshua, I heard that you dined with Zacchaeus, the chief tax-collector in Jericho, will you dine with us here too," the man asked.

"I will gladly dine with you, break bread with you, and what is your name?" Yeshua asked.

"I am Josiah, the chief tax-collector here in Bethabara," the man said.

"Josiah I am pleased to meet you and I will willingly dine with you and your friends. But we have just arrived and will be travelling all over this territory and continue to speak with and encourage and uplift all of Johanan's disciples and let them not lose heart or lose hope, for the Kingdom of God that Johanan preached is now in their midst. When we are ready, Josiah, we will take up your invitation. And note that I have nineteen disciples with me, who travel with me, and assist me in my mission of spreading the Good News that Johanan proclaimed. And by the way, I have Mattheus, as one of my disciples; he was formerly a chief tax-collector in Galilee," Yeshua said.

"We know about Mattheus, Yeshua," Josiah said. Josiah then thanked Yeshua and went away exhilarated and looking forward to be able to entertain Yeshua, and his disciples in his home.

Yeshua spent weeks in all the territories around the River Jordan where Johanan preached and baptised, and he brought comfort to the people, and told them the Good News of God's Kingdom, the Good News of salvation and redemption. The people noticed a difference between Yeshua and Johanan. Whereas Johanan was very austere and dressed in rags and was withdrawn from the people and preached with fire, and called all to repentance or be lost, Yeshua seemed more benign, less austere, who preached about love and forgiveness, and kindness and mercy, and spoke of God, not as a severe and punishing judge, but of God as a loving Father, who cares for all, the just and the sinners, and who wants all to be saved, and who loves all with a boundless and infinite and unconditional love. Yeshua's message was so uplifting and encouraging. And what also impressed the people was Yeshua's compassion in healing all their sick and afflicted, and even driving out demons.

After several more weeks around the territories of the River Jordan of preaching and teaching and healing, Yeshua and his disciples took up Josiah's invitation and dined at his place. It was just as grandiose as the time with Zacchaeus, but most welcome as Yeshua and his disciples needed to let their hair down for a bit, as they had been so busy preaching, teaching, healing, comforting all. It was a time for some self-care.

The day after the feast at Josiah's home, Yeshua and his disciples began to travel further north and all over Perea. They stopped at all the outlying districts, and visited the poor and the outcasts living in caves, and little clusters away from the cities and the towns, and Yeshua brought them comfort and the Good News of God's love for them, and Yeshua healed their sick and afflicted, and the disciples shared what they had with them all. Yeshua and his disciples continued to receive gifts, including money from grateful people wherever they went, gifts and money to support them on their mission. And Yeshua always made sure that they kept only what they needed, and gave their surplus to the poor that they encountered along the way.

Yeshua and his disciples passed through Philadelphia, and then crossed into Decapolis and in a north-easterly direction, where they crossed the Jabbok River and on to Gadara. The days, weeks and months flew past, and Yeshua and his disciples were getting tired. It was endless preaching, teaching, healing, comforting and bringing the Good News to all. There were towns and territories where Yeshua and his disciples were made welcome but there were also places where they were treated with suspicion and not made welcome. Yeshua simply passed through those places. And there were places where Yeshua met with plenty of opposition but Yeshua was so used to that, and he was able to combat whatever was thrown at him, and he loved the banter and the debates. He treated everyone's opinion with respect and was willing to argue and debate all aspects of his teaching. Wherever they went, the fact that Yeshua had female disciples travelling with him was treated with suspicion, especially when it was discovered that some of the men disciples of Yeshua were married, and that the women were not their wives. And some of the disciples, men and women were not married. This, a lot of the people found disturbing, and regarded with suspicion.

Yeshua and his disciples had spoken about this and discussed this aspect of his ministry. He wanted to make sure people would not be scandalised, but he would not retreat from accepting both men and women as his disciples. And he made sure they all treated each other with the greatest respect and decorum. Yeshua visited all the ten towns of Decapolis and all the outlying settlements where the poor and outcasts dwelt. After this they were exhausted. They rested up for two full days and Yeshua decided they would head home to Capernaum. They had been on the road for at least eighteen months, which included the Passover celebrations in Jerusalem, which now seemed a world away, a time long past. They were all looking forward to their homes, their families, the familiar sights, sounds, faces and places.

They now crossed the River Yarmouk and stopped at Gergesa. When they passed the cliffs, it brought back memories of over a thousand demonic possessed pigs screaming in a horrifying sound, as they rushed over the cliff. Yeshua was not made welcome. People were scared and many were made to believe that it could only be by the power of Satan, the king of demons that Yeshua could do something like that. But there were those who believed in Yeshua as a man of God, and with the power of God in him. Yeshua decided to spend some time there and speak to the people. But he did not stay long, just a couple of days, as he felt the animosity and those who were against him were stirring up the people.

Yeshua and the disciples then walked along the coast of the Sea of Galilee to Bethsaida, home of Shimon, Andreus, Philip, Nathanael, and Mattheus. Yeshua and the disciples only stayed for one night in Bethsaida. The next morning Yeshua said he had changed his plans. He was going to his home town of Nazareth to see his mother and some of his friends, and he felt everyone should do the same. "We all are in need of a good rest, and some tender loving care, so go home to your loved ones," Yeshua said.

"We have been on the road so long. I am feeling tired and in need of some rest. I am sure all of you must be tired of being on the road, and tired of me and of one another.' Yeshua said laughing. "Go and be with your families and loved ones. We can all meet here in Bethsaida at Shimon's in say three weeks from today," Yeshua said. "We have been spreading the Good News for eighteen months now. So have a good rest for we will spend another eighteen months on the road again, and I feel it is going to get tougher from now on. We have a lot to do and still many places to visit, and many people to whom we have to proclaim the Good News, and we do not have much time left to do it. So, I will see you all in three weeks from now, well rested and ready to go," Yeshua said.

"What about those of you from Jerusalem, Joanna, Salome, Susanna and Judas, what would you like to do for the next while? We will be going back to Jerusalem next time and you may have some time to recover then, or you may wish to find your way back to Jerusalem now, and we will see each other there," Yeshua said.

"Or you can all stay with me at Magdala," Miriam said, and have a bit of a holiday. "We have a place in Capernaum as well, so we can stay there for a while," Miriam offered.

"That sounds wonderful. I won't have any rest if I went home," Joanna said. "And I would love to spend time in Capernaum and Magdala," Joanna added.

"So will I," Salome chimed in.

"Me too," Susanna said.

"I'll cross over to Capernaum. I have a few friends there, whom I haven't seen for years. I will visit them and see you all here back in Bethsaida in three weeks' time, and will have a break when we get back to Jerusalem later," Judas said. "Yeshua what are your travel plans after your break," Judas asked.

"I was planning to go north, this time, before going south. From Bethsaida, I plan for us to go north as far as Caesarea Philippi, and the other towns and villages in Trachonitis. And then cross over into Phoenicia and spend time in all those places and travel all the way along the coast of the Great Sea, through the coastal towns of Tyre, Zarephath and Sidon. And from there we will make our way back to Jerusalem." Yeshua said.

"That's a lot of walking Yeshua," Judas said.

"That's true, Judas, that is why I want you all to have a good rest. We will need all our strength and wits to go to those places," Yeshua said.

"That's settled then. We will all meet here, at Shimon's in three weeks from today. Go now, have a good rest and peace be with you all," Yeshua said.

All the disciples from Capernaum joined Yeshua, the women and Judas and sailed across the Sea of Galilee. Yeshua, Miriam, Rebecca, Joanna, Salome and Susanna, continued on to Magdala. Judas remained in Capernaum, as did Johanan and his brother James, James Alpheus, Thomas, Thaddeus, and Shimon Cananean.

Miriam and Rebecca were looking forward to spending some time with their family and friends. And the women from Jerusalem were looking forward to spending some holiday time with Miriam in Capernaum and Magdala. And Judas was looking forward to spending time with friends he had not seen for a long time. The women enjoyed having Yeshua all to themselves as they walked at a leisurely pace to Magdala. Miriam decided they would go straight on to Magdala first, and then stay a while in Capernaum, on their way back to Bethsaida. Miriam was looking forward to some time with her family and friends; she was in no hurry to part with Yeshua. It has been more than eighteen months that she has been on the road with Yeshua. And she had a feeling that the next eighteen months was going to be even more hectic. There seemed to be urgency in Yeshua's expressions about what lies ahead. And from the itinerary Yeshua had in mind it was going to be tough. She too needed to be well rested, and the ladies from Jerusalem, as well, for what lay ahead.

Yeshua and Rebecca stayed the night with Miriam and her parents and the women in Magdala. It was a great night of feasting and enjoying each other's company and Miriam's parents wanted to know all about what had happened. They missed Miriam so much, and they were so excited to see her. She looked younger and more radiant. They were also pleased to see Yeshua, and meet Rebecca again, and Yeshua's women apostles from Jerusalem.

Miriam's parents, Lydia and Elijah were not at all perturbed about their daughter Miriam travelling all over Galilee and Judaea, and now heading for those Gentile provinces along the coast of the Great Sea. They knew that Yeshua was a prophet sent by God. He had healed their daughter and changed her life forever. She was so different, so alive, so radiant and so happy. They had full confidence and trust in Yeshua. They knew that all would be well with their daughter in Yeshua's company.

Yeshua had to put a stop to Elijah refilling his cup with wine. "Elijah, you make the finest wine I have drunk for a long time. But I had enough to give me a good night's sleep. So, I think I will call it a day now. I will be sleeping in tomorrow and get up when I get up, if you don't mind. And then head straight for Nazareth." Yeshua then said goodnight to all and retired.

Elijah also said goodnight as he had to be up early, because he was heading to work at Capernaum. But Lydia, Miriam, Rebecca, Lucia, Rachel, Salome and Susannah stayed up much later. They had so much to tell Lydia, especially about the women's gathering at Jericho. They also told Lydia, about all the wonders that Yeshua had done and just how much they have learned from Yeshua.

Lydia could see a big difference in her daughter and she was so pleased. And she felt so at ease with the ladies from Jerusalem, and pleased too that Miriam was not alone, not the only woman disciple travelling with Yeshua. It gave her so much more confidence and peace of mind.

Yeshua and Rebecca left early the next morning, as the sun was rising. Miriam and her mother were up to serve them breakfast, and to send them on their way, with food for the journey.

"We have a day's walk before us, Rebecca. Maybe we can stay overnight at Cana. I have some relatives there. Whom I'm sure will put us up for the night. Or we could find some lodgings. Judas has given us enough money to see us through these next few days." .

"Can we rather seek some lodgings, Yeshua? I would really like some time away from people, if you don't mind?" Rebecca said.

"I can understand Rebecca. We have been surrounded by crowds for so long, and.it does overwhelm with time. Yes, I wouldn't mind that at all. Are you sure it isn't because you want me all to yourself?" Yeshua teased.

"Yes, if you must really know. So, I can seduce you," Rebecca joked.

"Rebecca, how are you doing? I mean on the road and not pursuing some man to love and cherish?" Yeshua asked with real concern.

"I can't Yeshua, you are the only person I ever loved, the only man I ever loved, and will ever love," Rebecca said boldly. They were such great friends and so in tune with each other they both felt at ease, teasing each other.

"And I have always loved you Rebecca, and will always love you, and if circumstances were different, you would be the one with whom I would settle down, you know that. But it is not to be. So, we have to put those thoughts and desires out of our minds, okay?"

"Not okay," Rebecca continued her teasing mood. "How can I? It is just so unfair."

"Rebecca, I do not think I will be around much longer. I think maybe a couple of years more before the storm erupts. The powers of evil are gathering. And what they have done to all the prophets before me, will be my fate as well."

"Yeshua are you the one that Johanan the baptiser spoke of or are we to wait for another? Are you carrying on the work of Johanan preparing us for the Messiah?" Rebecca asked.

"All will be revealed soon, Rebecca. It won't be long now. And I will reveal all to all of you my disciples, very soon," Yeshua said.

If Rebecca read between the lines, she would know that Yeshua is indeed the Messiah. In her heart, Rebecca believed that Yeshua is the one to save the people. He is already doing that work. He is changing our world, the way we think and look at things. He is revealing a God we had not really known, a God of so much love and compassion, and a preference for the poor and lowly, the afflicted and the outcast, for sinners.

"Now tell me how are you feeling about continuing carrying on with me?" Yeshua asked.

"Yeshua, you told us to take up our cross and follow you, and I am ready to do that to the bitter end," Rebecca said.

"I am glad to hear that Rebecca, I need you, because it will indeed be a bitter end," Yeshua said.

Rebecca then impulsively stopped Yeshua in the middle of the road. No one was around. She turned and threw her arms around Yeshua and hugged him warmly, joy filling her whole body, soul and heart. She held onto him. She did not want to let him go. She knew she could not display such great warmth, affection and love for Yeshua in the presence of the others or the people, but here alone, on this lonely road, alone with Yeshua, this is what she wanted to do, for a long time. She then kissed him on the cheek.

Yeshua felt the warmth and love of Rebecca, and it filled him with joy and happiness. He then released her and took her hand and they walked hand in hand for some time, as they used to as friends in Nazareth, until they came to a spot filled with trees and bushland where they stopped for some refreshment.

It was so peaceful. Birds were flitting around and chirping and a slight breeze made music with the branches of the trees. And the clouds formed a collage of wondrous art. Yeshua and Rebecca sat against a tree and ate some of the biscuits that Miriam had baked. And they drank some milk while it was still fresh and cold.

"Yeshua, when we were in Jerusalem, and you were getting such a hard time from the Pharisees, Scribes and Sadducees, I went on my own one day into the synagogue to pray for you. And there was a rabbi there with a group of people listening to him. He was reading from Isaiah about a suffering servant. And a cold shiver went up my spine," Rebecca said.

"Why Rebecca?" Yeshua asked.

"I don't know. I went specifically to pray for you, and here was this rabbi reading these awful things that was happening to this suffering servant of the Lord, and I couldn't help thinking it could be you, Isaiah was prophesying about," Rebecca said.

"Rebecca let us not think about that, not now. We do not have to worry about tomorrow, for there is no tomorrow, tomorrow never comes, for it is always in the future. All we have is today, so it makes no sense to worry about tomorrow, each day has enough of its own burdens to bear. And I trust in my Father, he will not ask of me what I cannot bear, and he will give me the strength for whatever lies ahead, and he has given you to me, and the others, to be my support. I do not fear. I trust in the Father, and I trust in those whom he has given me. So, we are on a holiday break, so let's break from all those considerations and enjoy the country side and each other," Yeshua said, as he smiled at Rebecca, who reached out and touched Yeshua on his arm.

After a while they continued on their journey and arrived at Cana in the middle of the afternoon around the eighth hour. They immediately sought some lodgings on the outskirts of the town. They found a cheap place, with clean inexpensive enough rooms. They paid for two rooms for one night. They had a bit of a wash and then decided to head for the bushland close by. They did not want to be recognised. They spent a most enjoyable time walking among the trees and the bushland, with all the sounds and smells and sights of nature. It took them back to their childhood in Nazareth. Yeshua took his staff along, just in case they had some wild animals to contend with. But they were left in peace. They did not speak much, they simply loved to walk in the natural bushland, and enjoy each other's company. After about an hour of walking they turned around and by the time they were back at their lodgings, the sun was setting and it was getting dark. Yeshua and Rebecca had some bread, cake, dates and nuts and berries that Lydia and Miriam had prepared for them. They continued chatting in Rebecca's room, and eventually Yeshua called it a day and went to his own room to sleep.

As Yeshua lay in his bed, he thought of Rebecca up the passage, alone. And for a moment he had the desire to go and be with her, hold her and share a bed with her. But Yeshua immediately dispelled the desire, knowing it was not to be, and that they are already intimate in their love for each other, and that is the way it has to be and remain.

Yeshua lay in his bed and prayed, "Father, what you ask of me, is hard. I desire what every mortal desires the love and intimacy of a woman. But you have called me to give my life to you, to do the work you have sent me to do, and I know that my time is short. Give me the strength to be true to you." Yeshua then slowly drifted off to sleep.

Rebecca was having similar thoughts and desires. But she knew it could only be desires and desires that could not, would not be fulfilled. It would go against everything Yeshua teaches and against his integrity and respect and love for her. She held Yeshua in her heart and slowly drifted off to sleep.

The next day at sunrise, they made their way out of Cana, and were on the road before the townspeople even knew they were there. They enjoyed this last leg of their journey, and their hearts raced as they saw the first glimpses of their hometown of Nazareth. This time Yeshua turned and gave Rebecca a hug and said, "Rebecca, I have enjoyed your company immensely. It was such a delight travelling alone with you and sharing so much with you. I thank you so much for your love and friendship. Now go home, and we'll leave in a couple of weeks, and give ourselves enough time to get to Bethsaida as planned, and meet with the others."

They then walked together into Nazareth and went their separate ways to their homes. Miriam burst with joy and happiness at the first sight of Yeshua, smiling at her. She was overcome and grabbed and hugged Yeshua and would not let him go, until Yeshua had to unwrap himself. "Oh Yeshua, it is so good to see you. And you are looking okay, still lean as ever. How long will you be staying?" Miriam asked, for she knew that Yeshua was not home for good, and that he would be on his way again.

"Mother, I will be with you for the next two weeks. Rebecca is also back home."

Miriam was so pleased to know that Yeshua was home for two whole weeks. "Are you hungry? I'll prepare us something to eat."

"No mother, I'm not hungry. I had plenty to eat on the road. A light supper later, will do. Relax, we have so much to talk about, and I have so much to tell you mother," Yeshua said. "And mother, I will not be doing any preaching or teaching this time. I have come to spend this time with you alone, and also to get as much rest as I can. So maybe it is better if I am not seen, if that's at all possible. At least let people know I am not here to preach or teach, and that I want to be left alone, as I need some rest for the work that lies ahead. My disciples have been travelling all over Galilee, Judaea, Idumea, Perea, Cappadocia, Trachonitis, for more than eighteen months, and we are all exhausted, and now have to rest up for the next phase. So, I really need some rest and quiet. I won't be going into the village centre or the markets at all, and will spend some of my time skirting around the town and into the bushland. And will have plenty of time napping and sleeping, and spending my waking time with you alone, mother," Yeshua said smiling.

Miriam smiled back at Yeshua; it suited her well to have Yeshua all to herself. She would protect him and give him all the rest he needed, and feed him well. They remained together for the rest of the day and shared supper. She had some wine she kept for Yeshua, which he really appreciated. They chatted late into the night, as Yeshua shared all his travels and all that happened over the past eighteen months. But Yeshua did not want to burden his mother with the enemies that were lurking in the shadows. Yeshua also spoke about all of his nineteen disciples. Miriam was pleased to know that her son now had twelve men and seven women disciples to surround him, support and protect him. She felt so much more at ease. They chatted late into the night. Eventually Yeshua said he was tired and ready to sleep. He had one more cup of wine before retiring. Yeshua then kissed his mother goodnight and went to sleep. It was a deep and peaceful sleep.

Yeshua spent two weeks with his mother, avoiding all contact with the rest the people. On the day before leaving Nazareth, he visited Achim and his family, who were pleased to meet with Yeshua after so long a time. They had heard things about Yeshua and all he was doing, and they were pleased to have him as a friend. Yeshua also spent some time with Gamaliel, who was still feeble but seemed to perk up when Yeshua visited, and when he heard all that Yeshua was doing.

On the morning of leaving, Yeshua said goodbye to his mother. She held onto him tightly, not wanting to release him. But she had to let him go. She recalled the words of Simeon at the time when Yeshua as a baby was presented in the Temple. Simeon had spoken of Yeshua as a light to the Gentiles, and bringing glory to God's people, Israel. And Miriam recalled what Simeon had said to her, that 'a sword would pierce your own soul too.' She now felt the tip of that sword and felt it would pierce much deeper into her soul. She also recalled when at twelve years of age, Yeshua went missing for three days, and how they found him in the Temple at Jerusalem and he had said, "Why are you searching for me? Did you not know that I must be in my Father's house, be about my Father's business?"

Miriam felt that she would not see Yeshua again for a long time. She wept as she let him go. Yeshua felt the heaviness he was causing his mother, and it saddened him. He prayed that his Father would comfort her.

Yeshua caught up with Rebecca, spent a short time with her parents and then they were off. "You look well rested, Rebecca; did you have a good time and a good rest?"

"I did Yeshua. And you look well rested too," Rebecca said.

"Yes, I did sleep a lot and avoided the crowds. So, I feel quite refreshed and ready for what lies ahead. We have a long trek, a day's walk to Magdala, but we can stop at the same place in Cana, on our way and reserve our energy. And that is what they did. They left Cana after breakfast the next day, and arrived at Magdala at noon."

There was so much excitement, Yeshua and Rebecca meeting up with Miriam, Lucia, Joanna, Rachel, Susanna and Salome. They felt more like family than friends. There was so much hugging and laughing and sharing of all of the past two weeks. Yeshua and Rebecca could see that the ladies had a very good time indeed. Lydia was also looking so happy, as if she too was one of Yeshua's disciples, and she was so pleased to see Yeshua and Rebecca again. Elijah was not there; he was in Capernaum. They stayed the night and early the next morning they made their way to Capernaum.

Chapter Sixty-Seven
On the Road Again

Yeshua and the women stayed at Elijah's place for one night. Elijah was pleased to see them again. He was a most gracious host again. Before they retired, he said good bye to his daughter and Yeshua and the women, as he would be up and gone before the sun rose.

Yeshua went to bed early as well, but the ladies stayed up late, they had so much to share with Rebecca, and also wanted to hear from Rebecca about her time alone with Yeshua and her time in Nazareth.

They all left after breakfast and got a boat that took them across the lake, the Sea of Galilee, to Bethsaida, where they were scheduled to meet with the rest of the disciples. Shimon and Andreus and their families met them all with great warmth and excitement and it was like a feast with so many of them. The disciples arrived in dribs and drabs with Thomas and Judas the last to arrive, late in the afternoon.

They had their supper together, all nineteen disciples with Yeshua. And he repeated his planned journey again. "We will remain in Bethsaida for the next couple of weeks and preach and teach the people, confirm them in the faith, and minister to the poor and the needy here in Bethsaida and the surrounding villages. It may be a while before we return here," Yeshua said.

"That is good Yeshua, because Shimon and I have been telling the people all about you and what has happened over this past year and a half. And they are all keen to meet you again and hear you speak," Andreus said.

Philip, Nathanael and Thaddeus, who are from Bethsaida also indicated that they had spoken to the people about Yeshua.

"Everyone wanted to hear news about you, Yeshua. And it seems the whole of Bethsaida is excited about your coming to the town again."

"Yeshua, our finances are pretty low, we have not added anything to our coffers, and I had to lay out quite a bit for everyone's expenses over these past two weeks," Judas said.

"That's okay, Judas. Shimon and I have some funds to give you," Andreus said.

"And so have Johanan and I," James said.

"And so have I," Miriam said, "My father has given me quite a lot. He wants me to be taken care of, he said, but he has given enough to care for all our needs for some time," she said.

"Well, that's settled. We thank and pray for all who have and are supporting us so generously. We pray the Father will bless and reward their kindness and generosity," Yeshua said.

"Andreus, can you make arrangements for me to speak in the synagogue, tomorrow morning?" Yeshua asked.

"Can do, Yeshua, the people all know of your scheduled arrival today and they will all be at the synagogue to listen to you tomorrow," Andreus said.

When Yeshua and his disciples arrived at the synagogue it was packed and people were still streaming in. Once all had settled down, the priest in charge welcomed Yeshua back to Bethsaida and asked him to speak to the people.

"My dearest brothers and sisters, I am so glad to be back in Bethsaida. A number of the men from here have been with me for almost two years now. We have been travelling all over Galilee and Judaea on both sides of Lake Galilee to tell all of the Good News of God's love and compassion. The Kingdom of God that Johanan the baptiser spoke about is now among you. It is not like any kingdom that has existed before or any kingdom that exists in our world. In the kingdoms of this world everyone strives for a place of honour, to be first, to have authority over others, everyone seeks wealth, power, prestige, position, honour, and all the riches this world has to offer. Everyone wants to be in a position where they can have slaves and servants to be at their beck and call. Everyone seeks to be served by others and to be above others. Everyone wants to be first and to be the greatest. But in the Kingdom of God, it is not to be like this. He or she who wants to be the greatest, must become the least, must not seek to be served but to serve. The Son of God made man has not come to be served but to serve and give his life as a ransom for many. Very truly, I tell you, unless a grain of wheat falls into the earth and dies, it remains just a single grain, but if it dies, it bears much fruit. Those who love their life will lose it, and those who hate their life in this world will keep it for eternal life." Yeshua then paused.

Yeshua paused because he knew he was using strong language to drive home how important it was for them to realise just how diametrically opposed to worldly kingdoms, the Kingdom of God is. How God turns the world and all it values upside down.

Yeshua continued in the same vein, wanting to drive home his message. "Everyone wants to rise up and be above others but I tell you seek rather to be below others, seek the opposite way, downwards, choose to be poor, rather than rich, choose a lowly place rather than the most prestigious. Whoever wants to be the greatest must become the least of all, like a little child, like a slave, like a servant to all. The rulers in the kingdoms of the world, lord it over the rest, over their subjects, like tyrants over them. It is not so in the Kingdom of God. It must not be so among you. Whoever wants to be first must seek the last, the least. Whoever wishes to be great among you must be your servant, and whoever wishes to be the master, to be first among you, must be your slave, just as I said to you and say to you again, the Son of God, is among you, the Son of God made man comes not to be served but to serve and to give his life as a ransom for many."

The people were in a daze. The disciples were also astounded at the strong words Yeshua was using. They were accustomed to this, to Yeshua's controversial teachings. So diametrically opposed to what they and the people have been taught for so long. The values that Yeshua held and taught challenged their way of thinking and living. They recalled his teaching about loving one's enemies and doing good to those that harm you.

Miriam was listening carefully. She thought, what was Yeshua saying about the Son of Man coming not to be served but to serve, and giving his life as a ransom for many? Was Yeshua speaking about himself? Was he going to sacrifice himself for many? Was he speaking about what was already happening? He had given up everything to go and spread the Good News of God's Kingdom to all. He is already giving up his life as a ransom for many. He could be at home, be married to Rebecca, have a family, he would be such a loving husband and wonderful father, and a gracious friend, but he is already giving up his life, for being on the road, for doing God's work.

Yeshua allowed everyone to wrestle with their own thoughts. He decided to stop his teaching. He wanted the people to remain with their thoughts, wanting what he had said to capture their minds and hearts. He wanted all to learn that God's ways are not the ways of the world.

When Yeshua eventually came out of the synagogue, as usual, many were waiting outside with their sick and afflicted. Yeshua was filled with compassion as he walked among their sick, and he touched them and healed them.

This crowd outside had not been in the synagogue and did not hear Yeshua's teaching. But some of them inquired and were told that Yeshua preached about true greatness. One of the persons in the crowd asked Yeshua, "Master, who is the greatest in the Kingdom of Heaven?"

Yeshua looked at the man, and the people around him, who were waiting for an answer. He had spoken about what makes a person great, in the synagogue. He noticed several women with children among the crowd, so he said, "Let some of the mothers come forward with their children."

There was a kerfuffle among the crowd as space was made for mothers and their children to come forward.

"Let the children come to me," Yeshua said. "And mothers too, so the children will be at ease," Yeshua said. Yeshua then gestured for the children to come forward and they surrounded him and he smiled at them and blessed them, placing his hand on their heads and their shoulders.

Yeshua was smiling at the children and enjoying their company. The crowd were also smiling, including the disciples, especially the women. They forgot the question as they were captivated by this delightful sight of Yeshua surrounded by children.

Yeshua, still with his arms around the children closest to him, said to the crowd, "Truly, I tell you, unless you change and become like children, you will never enter the Kingdom of Heaven. Whoever becomes little and humble like these children is the greatest in the Kingdom of Heaven. Whoever welcomes one such child in my name, welcomes me."

Someone in the crowd then cried out, "Yeshua tell us about the Kingdom of Heaven, what is it like?"

Yeshua said, "The Kingdom of Heaven is like a mustard seed that someone took and sowed in his field. It is the smallest of seeds, but when it has grown it is the greatest of shrubs and becomes a tree, so that the birds of the air come and make nests in their branches."

There were smiles on the faces of many; especially the farmers in the crowd, for some of them had planted mustard seeds and watched it grow. And Yeshua on his walks had seen the mustard trees for himself, and it made him think of this parable.

Yeshua saw the mothers, still standing around him, protective of their children and he thought of his mother and he wanted to speak of the Kingdom of God that would relate to and appeal to the women in the crowd, so he said, "The Kingdom of Heaven is like yeast that a woman took and mixed in with three measures of flour until all of it was leavened."

The women were smiling, and Yeshua was smiling with them, and in smiling with them he was smiling at his own mother.

Yeshua continued, "You have ears, listen to what I am saying. What I proclaim has been hidden from the foundation of the world. You have all been living in the darkness; I have come to bring you out of the darkness and into the light. I am the light of the world."

The people were astonished with what Yeshua was saying. He continued, "The Kingdom of Heaven is like treasure hidden in a field, which someone found and hid, then in his joy, he goes and sells all he has and buys that field."

Yeshua then thought of his friend Lazarus who was gone searching for treasure, so he said, "Again, the Kingdom of Heaven is like a merchant in search of fine pearls, on finding one pearl of great value, he went and sold all that he had and bought it."

Yeshua looked at his disciples close to him, Shimon, Andreus, Johanan and James, and the rugged men in the crowd and he knew that many of them were fishermen, so he said, "Again the Kingdom of Heaven, is like a net that was thrown into the sea and caught fish of every kind; when it was full they drew it ashore, sat down, and put the good into baskets but threw out the bad. So, it will be at the end of the age. The angels will come out and separate the evil from the righteous, and throw them into the furnace of fire, where there will be weeping and gnashing of teeth."

Yeshua ended on the frightening note. People however were accustomed to be reminded of hell fire, by their preachers. Yeshua never sought to frighten people, God was not one to scare the hell out of people, but Yeshua had to now and again remind people of the consequences of their actions, and their need to repent of their sins, and walk in the ways of righteousness. They had the commandments given them by Moses that were to be a guide to their way of living, and Yeshua gave the people his Beatitudes, that is his new charter, for living in the spirit that his Father wanted. His Beatitudes were not only a recipe for good living, but the only way to true happiness.

Yeshua then called on the mothers to collect their children. He spoke with the mothers and blessed them too. He then began to walk away, and Shimon and Andreus and the other men made a pathway for Yeshua among the crowd, who were trying to see Yeshua and touch him. The disciples surrounded Yeshua for his own protection; they did not want him to be crushed.

Yeshua asked Shimon and Andreus and the other disciples living in Bethsaida to take them to the places where no one else goes, to where the discarded ones were, the little ones, where the poor and the beggars and those who were ostracised from society lived, because they were regarded as unclean and sinners and punished by God. Yeshua then spent the rest of the day with his disciples going around to these outlying places, where the poor and outcasts lived, and where he had not been before. He spent time with them, listening to them, speaking to them of the Father's love for them, and that the Father hears their cries.

The next day was the Sabbath and Yeshua decided that he did not want to preach, he felt that he had said enough the day before for people to think about. So, he let their regular preachers, talk to them. The people were disappointed; they could not have enough of Yeshua's preaching to them. But Yeshua wanted what he taught not to be something fleeting, but truths that needed to be pondered on and digested and made part of their lives.

After the service, a crowd followed Yeshua and his disciples. Yeshua walked through the grain fields; his disciples were hungry, so they began to help themselves, plucking heads of grain that they began to eat. Now there were some Pharisees among the crowd and they were scandalised and spoke among themselves and then one of them turning to the crowd pointed to the disciples, eating the grain, and then said to Yeshua, for all to hear, "Look, your disciples are doing what is not lawful to do on the Sabbath."

Yeshua shook his head and stifled his impatience; will they never stop? Yeshua had to again refute this attack about the Sabbath, again and again. What the Pharisees regarded as a weakness, for Yeshua seemed not to be concerned about the restrictions the Law demanded for the keeping the Sabbath holy. Yeshua repeated again, what he had said on so many other occasions, and said, "I tell you, something greater than the Temple is here now. But if you had known what this means, 'I desire mercy, not sacrifice,' you would not have condemned the guiltless. The Sabbath was made for man, not man for the Sabbath, and the Son of God, made man, is Lord of the Sabbath. And if you worship God in your hearts, and show love and compassion to all, on the Sabbath, then that is how you keep the Sabbath holy, but if you go about like policemen waiting to pounce on others for doing something so innocuous, as appeasing their hunger, by plucking a head of grain on the Sabbath, then you yourselves are not keeping the Sabbath holy."

The Pharisees mumbled among themselves. They still refused to hear what Yeshua was saying and would only grab onto whatever they could use to attack him. So, one of them said, for those around him to hear, "what is he talking about, 'the Son of God, made man, is Lord of the Sabbath?' Is he claiming to be the Son of God? This is blasphemy," he cried. And those with him, agreed.

Yeshua simply ignored their cries and walked away. As Yeshua and his disciples were walking away, coming towards them was a group of men; they had with them a man, whom they held by both arms, assisting him on the way. They approached Yeshua and one of the men said, "Master, our friend, Noah, is both blind and mute, and possessed of a demon, please help him."

Yeshua was touched by the faith and compassion of the men. The Pharisees and their cohort were still there and Yeshua knew he would be attacked by them for healing this man of the Sabbath, just how blind and stupid could they be? Yeshua then touched the eyes and the mouth of Noah and prayed quietly.

Suddenly Noah cried out, "I can see, I can see!"

The men that brought Noah to Yeshua, as well as the crowds were amazed that Noah could both see and speak, and by his demeanour they could see he was no longer possessed. One of Noah's friends said what others were saying, "Can this be the Son of David?"

But when the Pharisees saw what had happened and what the crowds were saying, they were outraged, they knew attacking Yeshua about the Sabbath was of no use, so one of them spoke up for the others, "It is only by Beelzebub, the ruler of the demons that this man casts out demons."

This attack and vilification of Yeshua as being a servant of Beelzebub was not new. Yeshua had to contend with this all the time, whenever he casts out demons. Again, he had to reiterate what he said before, and this time added more to his answer, he said, "Every kingdom divided against itself is laid waste, and no city or house divided against itself will stand. If I cast out demons by Beelzebub by whom do your own exorcists cast out demons? But if I cast out demons by the Spirit of God, then the Kingdom of God has come to you."

Yeshua then turned and went on his way. The crowd still followed. He came among some fruit trees and as he was in a different place and among different people, he repeated his lesson about the fruit-bearing trees, pointing to the tree he said, and also took the opportunity to take a swipe at the Pharisees, hoping they would take to heart what he was saying. Yeshua said, "A tree is known by its fruit. Either make the tree good, or make the tree bad, and its fruit bad, for the tree is known by its fruit." Then turning and looking at the Pharisees, Yeshua said, "You brood of vipers! How can you speak good things, when you are evil? For out of the abundance of the heart, the mouth speaks. The good person, like those friends of Noah, brings good things out of a good treasure, and the evil person brings evil things out of an evil treasure. I tell you on the day of judgement you will have to give account for every careless word you utter, for by your fruit and by your words you will be justified, and by your fruit and by your words you will be condemned."

The next day, Yeshua again went about to those most in need to bring them words of comfort, and to simply be with them and listen to them, and heal their sick. The disciples and the people heard about this and saw Yeshua heading to those places, but would not follow him there, although some of the people did.

It was mid-afternoon and Yeshua told his disciples he was going to a deserted place by himself. But the crowds were out and about and waiting for him to appear, to be back from the outcasts, word got out that he was on the move. Yeshua and his disciples had reached a deserted place but still the crowds sought him out and found him and they were streaming in, non-stop. They came in their thousands from all over Bethsaida and the surrounding towns, even from places on the other side of the Sea of Galilee. When Yeshua saw the crowd, he had compassion on them; they were like sheep, without a shepherd. So, he waited for all the people to gather around him. He had to speak in a loud voice for most of them to hear what he was saying, he spoke to them of God's love and compassion, and he healed all their sick. The crowds were in awe, some had come from far and wide with their sick, and some simply to see this great man, this Prophet, this Teacher, this miracle worker and healer that the whole world was speaking about. There were thousands present.

Yeshua then began speaking and they were hanging onto his every word. They were mesmerised by his teaching and his parables and were oblivious to the time. The light was starting to fade. Yeshua, the disciples and the people lost all sense of time. When it was evening, Shimon and Andreus and the other disciples came to Yeshua urging him to send the people away. Shimon spoke on behalf of the disciples, "Master, this is a deserted place, and the hour is now late; send the crowds away, so that they may go into the villages and buy food for themselves."

Yeshua then said to Shimon and the disciples, "They need not go away, you give them something to eat."

"What!" Shimon exclaimed, thinking Yeshua is out of his mind. Shimon replied. "Yeshua, we have nothing here with us, but five loaves and two fish."

Yeshua said to Shimon, "Bring the bread and the fish here to me," And he said to Shimon and the disciples, tell the people to sit down on the grass.

The crowd were wondering what was going to happen. The word spread among them, "The Master's disciples wanted him to send us away to the villages to buy food for ourselves, but he told them to feed us themselves." Some among them,

Pharisees mostly, scoffed at the idea of Yeshua and his disciples feeding thousands of people out here in this deserted place. Another in the crowd said, "He asked the disciples to bring to him what they had, five loaves and two fish." The crowd, who could see, were watching Yeshua carefully and they were passing on the word to the others about what was happening.

Yeshua took the basket with the five loaves and two fish, he looked up to the heavens, and blessed and broke the loaves of bread, and gave the basket to the disciples saying, "Now distribute this among the crowds." All nineteen disciples took a piece of the bread that Yeshua broke and a piece of the fish and walked all over the vast crowd and gave it to sections of the crowd. And then something happened, that could not be explained, as it was unfolding, people were passing on some bread and fish to one another, for everyone was eating and ate to their full. They were eating, for they were hungry, and they were chatting among themselves. Some did bring bread with them, but not enough to feed such an enormous crowd, but those that had brought bread, shared what they had, and it seemed that the bread and fish just would not run out.

When the people had enough, Yeshua said to his disciples, "Do not let us litter, or waste anything, go and pick up all the broken and discarded pieces of bread and food. We will take them to our friends in the outlying villages."

The disciples then walked among the crowd and were able to get some baskets, that some of the people had with them. There was much chatter and joviality among the crowd, as if they were one happy family. They passed on all the scraps of bread and pieces of fish that were over. Because of the vastness of the crowd, the people were not yet aware of what was happening. The disciples took a while to go throughout the crowd as there were thousands of people present. They finally found their way back to Yeshua, where a few people were surrounding Yeshua and chatting with him, they were mostly Pharisees and they seemed seriously intent on what was being discussed.

When all the disciples finished their task of collecting the leftovers, it amounted to twelve baskets full to the brim.

"It's a miracle, it's a miracle, it's a miracle," a lone voice in the crowd shouted. "Yeshua has worked a miracle, he has fed us all with five loaves of bread and two fish," And the chorus rang out as others repeated what the lone voice had exclaimed. The crowd were in awe. They had already witnessed Yeshua's power of healing and now they saw something so spectacular and they knew they had a story to tell.

Once the crowd calmed down, Yeshua then had a final word to the crowd. He told them to find their way home and that he would be leaving Bethsaida the following day after speaking to them in the synagogue. They finally then slowly dispersed and went on their way home, filled bodily and spiritually.

The apostles stood around Yeshua, spellbound, with twelve baskets full of leftovers.

"What are we going to do with all this food?" Thomas asked.

"We can take it with us tomorrow, at first light, and give it to the homeless and the poor people living in the caves. Andreus and Judas, can you organise this, it would be wise to go first thing in the morning, so that what we have is still edible," Yeshua said.

"I will need all of you, we have twelve baskets," Judas said.

All the men and women agreed to accompany Judas in taking the food to the people living in the caves. Yeshua said he would go with them as well.

As usual, Yeshua was walking ahead by himself. The rest were trailing, and then Thomas asked the others, "How many people do you think were present here today?"

"I'd say, about five thousand," Judas said.

"Much more than that, I think, I would say five thousand men alone, not counting women and children," Mattheus said.

"Well, the businessman and financier and the tax-collector have given their estimates of the numbers, we have to accept that," Shimon Cananean said, laughing, which caused laughter all around.

"Yeshua was walking on ahead of the disciples. No one really spoke about what had just happened. How was it possible that over five thousand people had been fed, out here in that deserted place? All we had were five loaves and two fish," Thomas said.

"It is one of those signs again, that is hard to explain. I think some of the people did have food with them, but they were only a few. People did not expect to stay out here and listen to Yeshua for so long a time. And they did not expect to stay so late," Miriam said.

"It was a miracle. Another sign of Yeshua's powers," Rebecca said.

At the beginning of their discipleship, now so long ago, when they were all getting to know each other, the men and the women kept apart as two distinct groups. They felt they had to, to avoid any misconception or be the cause of any scandal. But as time went on, they intermingled and became as one, and the people came to accept this as well. And because of the women, a lot of the women came forward to meet with the women disciples to ask questions.

The next morning early, before the sun was beginning to rise, Yeshua and the disciples were on their way to the caves, carrying the twelve baskets of bread and food.

The people in the caves were already stirring, and they heard people approaching and one of them, filled with trepidation, went to see who it was. He immediately recognised Yeshua and his disciples, and they were carrying baskets with them. He called out to the other cave dwellers that Yeshua was here, and they all got up immediately.

It was quite a sight. The people were astonished to receive so much food. "Here, distribute this among yourselves. And if there is any over, take it to others who need it. It has to be eaten today, the bread can last for a few more days, but not the fish," Shimon said.

The people immediately got stuck into the bread and the fish. Yeshua and the disciples could see they were hungry. They were so appreciative and thanked Yeshua and the disciples profusely.

Yeshua then told the people they would see them again, but then left them to enjoy their meal.

As they were walking Yeshua thanked his disciples for what they had done. And then he said, "It is pleasing to Yahweh that we seek out and serve the poor and the needy. But do you not see how much they serve us, they have so little and are so poor, but whenever I am with them, I feel so content. There is serenity among them, most of them. The children have nothing but make do with what they have, and are always smiling and happy. The poor will share the little they have and suffer so much and yet seem so much happier than everyone else who has so much of this world's goods. We receive more from them that they do from us." Yeshua then walked ahead of the disciples, as he was wont to do.

When they finally came near to the synagogue a crowd had already assembled outside. They had heard Yeshua say that he was leaving Bethsaida today, so they came out in their thousands, must have been most of them that experienced the miracle of the day before when they all ate and were fed out in that deserted place. They were hoping to see more wondrous signs from Yeshua.

Yeshua however addressed the crowd, and said, "My friends you have come here, not because you have seen signs, but because you ate your fill of the loaves and the fish. Do not work for the food that perishes, but for the food that endures for eternal life, which the Son of God, made man will give you. For it is on him, that God the Father has set his seal."

Then someone in the crowd yelled, "What must we do to perform the works of God?"

Yeshua answered, "This is the work of God that you believe in him whom he has sent."

There was murmuring among the crowd, and one of the Pharisees spoke on their behalf, "What sign are you going to give us then, so that we may see it and believe you? What work are you performing? Our ancestors ate the manna in the wilderness, as it is written, 'He gave them bread from heaven to eat'."

"Why is he asking for a sign? Was he not there in that deserted place where Yeshua fed over five thousand people with five loaves and two fish?" Miriam said to Lucia and the other women around her.

The crowd were now listening intently, rapt in what Yeshua would say.

Yeshua answered, "Very truly I tell you, it was not Moses who gave you bread from heaven, but it was my Father who gives you the true bread from heaven. For the bread of God is that which comes down from heaven and gives life to the world."

Then someone in the crowd voiced what people were thinking, he yelled, "Sir, give us this bread always."

The crowd were totally engrossed in this altercation. They were grateful to the man for asking that question, and they now waited for Yeshua's response.

Yeshua answered, "I am the bread of life, whoever comes to me will never be hungry, and whoever believes in me will never be thirsty. I have come down from heaven to do my Father's will, and this is his will, that I should lose nothing of all that he has given me, but raise it up on the last day. This is indeed the will of my Father that all who see the Son and believe in him may have eternal life; and I will raise them up on the last day."

A hush spread all over the crowd, they were stunned by what Yeshua was saying about himself. The Pharisees and their followers in the crowd began murmuring among themselves, they were complaining, but they found an opening, something new with which to attack Yeshua, so one of them spoke up on behalf of all.

"Yeshua, we have a complaint because you said that you are the bread come down from heaven. We know that you are the son of Yosef, we know of your father and mother, who are from Nazareth. How can you now say, that you have come down from heaven and that you are the bread that came down from heaven?"

The crowd were now totally engaged in this argument. This was a new teaching; they had not heard these words before that were uttered by Yeshua. They hung on Yeshua's every word.

Yeshua responded, "I am the bread of life. Your ancestors ate manna in the wilderness, and they died. I am the bread that came down from heaven. Whoever eats of this bread will live forever, and the bread that I will give for the life of the world, is my flesh."

There was uproar, not only from the Pharisees but from the people as well, they were saying, 'how can this man give us his flesh to eat.' The Pharisees could see what was happening, and they stoked the flames. So, one of them spoke and asked Yeshua outright, what everyone in the crowd was asking, "How can you, a man, give us your flesh to eat?"

Yeshua instead of giving a clear answer, even confused the crowd more, and went even further and said, "Very truly I tell you, unless you eat the flesh of the Son of Man, and drink his blood, you have no life in you. Those who eat my flesh and drink my blood have eternal life, and I will raise them up on the last day, for my flesh is true food and my blood is true drink. Those who eat my flesh and drink my blood abide in me, and I in them. Just as the living Father sent me, and I live because of the Father, so whoever eats me will live because of me. This is the bread that came down from heaven, not like that which your ancestors ate, and they died. But the one who eats this bread will live forever."

Yeshua dropped a bolt from the blue. The people were confused. They did not understand what Yeshua was saying. "He's gone mad," some were saying. "How can we eat his flesh and drink his blood, we are not cannibals, he is crazy," others said.

"We told you, this man is not from God," the Pharisees told the people. "He has a devil, he is possessed," another Pharisee said.

The people were murmuring among themselves, many were confused, and the Pharisees stoked their confusion. "We told you he is a demon, he is crazy, he is not a man of God, now he talks of us eating his flesh and drinking his blood, he is crazy, he is mad," one of the Pharisees said, as loud as he could, and his words spread like a wildfire.

Slowly the people started dispersing, until only Yeshua and his disciples and a small group of people remained. Besides the twelve men and seven women disciples that had left everything and given up everything and dedicated their lives to be Yeshua's disciples, living with him, learning from him, travelling with him, there were many other disciples, more than a hundred at least that were also disciples of Yeshua. They were from Galilee, and they were always present wherever Yeshua went and they assisted Yeshua and his disciples in whatever way they could. And Yeshua spent time with them too and got to know them and appreciated their support and loyalty. And he gave more time and teaching to them, for they were eager to learn and assist in his work. And the same number of disciples seemed to gather when he was in Judaea. Now only a few of them remained for many of them too, found this teaching of Yeshua's just too farfetched and unreasonable to accept and they started to doubt Yeshua.

The small crowd also eventually left, disappointed with what had happened. And all Yeshua's words and all the great deeds he had done, seemed to have vanished, blown away like feathers in the wind. In the end only Yeshua's nineteen disciples remained and Yeshua said to them, "Let us leave this place now." So, Yeshua led his disciples away. Yeshua walked ahead. He seemed unconcerned about the turn of events, of the people turning away from him. As they were walking the disciples too were nonplussed.

"What was he thinking, saying such things?" Thomas said.

"I couldn't believe my ears; did he really say that he was giving us his flesh to eat and his blood to drink?" Judas said. "I really hoped that Yeshua would be the one to free us from the bondage of Rome, but now he has turned the people away, they will now no longer follow him," Judas added.

"I think Yeshua was speaking in a spiritual sense, of himself as spiritual food and spiritual drink, as spiritual nourishment," Johanan said. "Do you recall when Yeshua said to us, that man does not live on bread alone, but on every word that comes from the mouth of God? I think, his teaching today is the most profound he has taught to date. I think we need to stay and be patient, I'm sure what Yeshua has told us today will become clearer with time," Johanan said.

"This teaching is difficult, who can accept it?" Thomas said.

"Why did he have to alienate the crowd like that?" Philip added.

Yeshua, who was walking ahead, was however hearing everything that was being said and listening to all their complaints, so he stopped and spoke to his disciples. "So, what do you believe? What have you to say about what I told the people?"

Thomas spoke first, and he was ventilating what all the others were thinking and saying, as they walked along, "Yeshua, what you taught is difficult, who can accept it?"

Yeshua then spoke to them, "Does what I said, offend you? It is the spirit that gives life; the flesh is useless. The words that I have spoken to you are spirit and life."

The disciples were still unsure and uncertain, but they thought of what Johanan had said, about taking what Yeshua said in a spiritual sense.

Yeshua continued, he had been with the twelve men and seven women for more than a year and a half and he got to know them intimately, he knew their moods, their ups and downs, and their own internal struggles. They all came and spoke to him at times, with their difficulties. And he knew that they had their own discussions among themselves, and that some of them still doubted him, so Yeshua said, "Among you there are some who do not believe. For this reason, I have told you, that no one can come to me unless it is granted by the Father." Yeshua looked at Judas, for Yeshua had his one-on-one chats with Judas, and Yeshua had trouble convincing Judas that he was not seeking to build an army to overthrow the Romans.

Yeshua continued, "All our disciples are now gone, and only you nineteen remain. Do you also wish to go away?"

A silence followed, no one wanted to answer, or speak on behalf of all. After an uncomfortable silence, Shimon spoke up, and said, "Lord, to whom shall we go? You have the words of eternal life. We have come to believe and know that you are the Holy One of God."

Then Yeshua made a shocking statement that dumbfounded his disciples even more.

Yeshua said, "Did I not choose you, all twelve of you men, and seven of you women? Yet one of you is a devil."

Yeshua knew he had caused great shock. He knew what was in the hearts of all of them. And he was sending out a warning. He needed them all to believe in him, and be in tune with him, or it could drastically disrupt and undermine his mission.

"Come now, we will stay here today, and then leave this place, in the morning. We have left much for the people to think about. We will then make our way to Caesarea Philippi."

Chapter Sixty-Eight
Who Do You Say I Am?

Yeshua and his disciples were on the road to Caesarea Philippi. They stopped at villages and wherever there were settlements of people, and Yeshua spoke to the people, bringing them the Good News of God's love and compassion. In some of the outlying areas far away, where a few clusters of people lived, Yeshua spent time with them, befriending them, and bringing words of comfort and sharing what they had. It would have taken most of the day simply walking to Caesarea Philippi but it took Yeshua and his disciples more than a week, for Yeshua stopped and stayed with the poor people he met along the way. Yeshua simply wanted to be with them and befriend them and offer them friendship and kindness and speak to them of his Father's love for them.

When Yeshua finally came into the district of Caesarea Philippi, he turned to his disciples and asked them, "My friends you have been with me a long time now, you have listened to all I have taught, and you have seen what I do, tell me, who do people say that I am, I who am a son of man, like all of you, who do people say I am?"

Yeshua asked this of the disciples, for he knew and heard about how people were talking about him in their families, at their community and social gatherings, at their work places, around their dinner tables, in the market squares, in all places where they gathered. He knew that he was discussed in Jerusalem, Capernaum, and especially when they were in Bethsaida. There the people had questions about who he is, after he told them he was the Son of God and when he said he was the bread that had come down from heaven. Many of his disciples left him in Bethsaida. Yeshua had not really discussed what happened there with his nineteen closest disciples. So now he put the question to them. He wanted to gauge what the thoughts of the people were about him and also what they themselves thought about him. He knew that he was a sign of contradiction. He had scant respect for the Law as it was being taught. His preaching was like no other, he portrayed God not as a powerful king or ruthless judge but as a loving father or mother, a meek and gentle person, forgiving and understanding and overflowing with a generosity and love unheard of and his teaching was so diametrically opposed to what they and every Jew was being taught about God.

Johanan was first to speak, he said, "Some say that you are Johanan the baptiser."

His brother James then said, "Others say that you are the prophet Elijah, come back from the dead."

Andreus added, "Many think you are one of the prophets."

Yeshua then asked his disciples, "You have been with me now for close to two years. Rebecca has known me for most of my life, but she too has only been my disciple the same length of time as all of you and listened to what I taught and what I did. So, I ask all of you, who do *you*, say I am?"

There was silence. They all looked to Shimon, and the women looked to Miriam; they were both now regarded as the ones who spoke on their behalf. Shimon looked at them and they all urged him to reply.

Shimon drew a long breath and said, "You are the Messiah, the Son of the living God."

There was a silence, as they all waited for Yeshua's response to Shimon's declaration. This was the first time anyone had said this directly to Yeshua. In all their travels there were people who had asked them if Yeshua was the Messiah, but they had not answered but now Shimon had spoken on behalf of all. This was a huge declaration.

Yeshua then broke the silence, looked at Shimon and said, "Blessed are you Shimon, son of Jonah! For flesh and blood has not revealed this to you, but my Father in heaven. So, tell me what do you understand about the Messiah, what do you know about Him?" Again, Yeshua wanted to test his disciples, to gather what they thought.

There was a silence again. Yeshua had never claimed to be the Messiah and even in his response to Shimon, he left it open ended. The disciples were accustomed to Yeshua putting all kinds of challenging questions to them, provoking them, allowing them to come to their own conclusions, and at the same time he taught them great truths.

Yeshua spoke again, "What does our Sacred Scriptures record, what have our prophets said about the Messiah?" Yeshua asked them.

The disciples were at a loss, so Yeshua began to teach and said to them, "At the beginning of creation and of humankind, all was in total equilibrium between God and us. Humankind lived in the presence to God, saw Him face to face. Humankind was living in a state of innocence. But then they wanted more, wanted to be like God and rebelled, gave in to the temptations of the evil one, for power, position, prestige, wanting to be equal to God, and as a result of their sin, they separated themselves from God, and sin and death entered the world.

"But ever since that separation all of humankind has yearned once again for that life with God our Creator, our Father, yearned for what was lost. Imagine you were taken away from your father and mother as a little babe, and given out in adoption. Once you got to know you were an adopted child how would you feel, what would you do? Would you not search and yearn to know your true parents, your real mother and father, and would you not do all you could to find them, to be reunited with them? Would you not be restless until you found them? Would you not want to know if your parents still loved you and wanted you?"

"Yes, we would," Miriam said immediately, and they all agreed.

Yeshua continued, "David the psalmist encapsulates this truth beautifully in his song, of Longing for God, he writes:

"As a deer longs for flowing streams,
so, my soul longs for you, O God.
My soul thirsts for God,
for the living God.
When shall I come and behold
the face of God?

"David sings so much more in this song of his about how the soul longs for the living God. We shall have a look at his words in the Sacred Scrolls, which I am sure the synagogue here in Caesarea Philippi, will have a copy. I recall other words in his song." Yeshua continued to recite:

"My tears have been my food
day and night,
while people say to me continually,
'Where is your God?'"

"David feels so deeply this longing for God, this loss, this absence of God, for he continues in this song, lamenting," Yeshua said, and he continued with David's song:

"I say to God my rock,
why have you forgotten me?
Why must I walk about mournfully?
because the enemy oppresses me?
As with a deadly wound in my body,
my adversaries taunt me,
while they say to me continually,
'Where is your God?'"

"David ends this song, with words of hope, he writes:

"Why are you cast down, O my soul,
and why are you disquieted within me?
Hope in God; for I shall again praise him,
my help and my God."

"That is absolutely beautiful, Yeshua, that song of David's. It has touched my heart," Lucia exclaimed. And they all agreed.

"Yeshua, you must teach Miriam that song of David's so she can sing it to us," Rebecca said.

"Yes, I will, Rebecca, I will. We can all learn those words together," Yeshua said.

"But," Yeshua continued, "as much as all of humankind longs for God, so God longs for humankind even more. In fact, it is Isaiah who says this about God's desire for us, He writes, 'The Lord called me before I was born, while I was in my mother's womb he named me' and then he also writes those loving words of his about how God will never desert us," Yeshua said.

"Do you know those words, Yeshua?" Phillip asked.

"Yes, I do, Phillip. I learned all of what Isaiah wrote from my teacher and mentor, Gamaliel in Nazareth and then also at the Advanced School of Learning in Jerusalem, many years ago. And whenever I had access to the Sacred Scrolls I would read and reflect on Isaiah's words as well as the psalms," Yeshua said.

"So, what else does he write about God yearning for us?" Nathanael asked.

Yeshua looked heavenward as if to recall Isaiah's words and he said, "I have quoted you these words of Isaiah before, but I can never tire of repeating them, Isaiah writes these touching words, 'Can a woman forget her nursing child, or show no compassion for the child of her womb? Even these may forget, yet I will not forget you. See I have inscribed you on the palms of my hand,'" Yeshua looked at his hands while saying this.

All the disciples were enthralled listening to Yeshua and it was as if the prophet Isaiah himself was speaking to them.

"You remember what I already told you about what Isaiah has written about the coming of the Messiah, Isaiah actually puts these words onto the lips of the Messiah himself, when he writes, 'Listen to me, O coastlands, pay attention, you people far away! The Lord called me before I was born; while I was in my mother's womb, he named me. He made my mouth like a sharp sword, in the shadow of his hand he hid me, he made me a polished arrow, and in his quiver, he hid me away. And he said to me, *You are my servant, Israel, in whom I will be glorified*'."

The disciples recalled Yeshua citing these particular words of Isaiah on other occasions.

Yeshua continued, "Isaiah then writes about how the Messiah will be deeply despised, abhorred by the nations and treated like the slave of rulers but then he goes on to say, 'Kings shall see and stand up, Princes, and they shall prostrate themselves, because of the Lord, who is faithful, the Holy One of Israel who has chosen you'."

The disciples were enthralled by Isaiah words. Isaiah's words were so poetic and deep and touched them deeply.

Yeshua continued, "Let me conclude with these words that I remember from this chapter in Isaiah, where he writes about the coming of the Messiah, he writes, 'I will give you as a light to the nations, saying to the prisoners, 'Come out,' and to those who are in darkness, 'Show yourself. They shall feed along the ways, on all the bare heights shall be their pasture; they shall not hunger or thirst, for he will lead them to springs of water. And I will turn all my mountains into a road, and my highways shall be raised up. Sing for joy, O heavens, and exult, O earth, break forth, O mountains, into singing! For the Lord has comforted his people, and will have compassion on his suffering ones.'"

Yeshua stopped. The disciples were in awe. They were astounded at Yeshua's knowledge and grasp of the Scriptures. Who was Isaiah speaking about? The disciples had just heard Shimon respond to Yeshua's question and saying that Yeshua is the Messiah. So, is Yeshua the Promised One that Isaiah writes about and that Johanan the baptiser spoke about? They were still unsure. But all the signs seemed to confirm Shimon's declaration about Yeshua, yet Yeshua does not confirm it.

Johanan then spoke up, "Yeshua, my brother and I and Shimon and Andreus were disciples of Johanan and we were all baptised by him in the River Jordan. And we spent time with him in the wilderness and he taught us all that has been prophesied about the coming of the Messiah." Johanan then also recited parts of Isaiah about the coming Messiah and said, "I recall us learning that the Kingdom the Messiah was coming to establish, was to be a Kingdom of Peacefulness."

"Johanan, do recite for us what you recall," Miriam said, and the others all urged Johanan do so.

Johanan cleared his throat and began, "These are the words of Isaiah that I recall hearing, 'A shoot shall come out from the stump of Jesse, and a branch shall grow out of his roots. The Spirit of the Lord shall rest on him, the spirit of wisdom and understanding, the spirit of counsel and might, the spirit of knowledge and the fear of the Lord. He shall not judge by what his eyes see, or decide by what his ears hear; but with righteousness he shall judge the poor, and decide with equity for the meek of the earth."

"Isaiah writes so much more about the Messiah that is to come, and Johanan taught us so much," Johanan said, "and now you Yeshua have continued to teach us as Johanan said you would."

"Yeshua, Shimon has spoken on our behalf, and he has said that you are the Messiah, the Son of the living God. What is your response to Shimon," James Zebedee asked.

All eyes turned to Yeshua with anticipation.

Yeshua then looked at Shimon and said, "Shimon, I repeat what I said; you are blessed because my father in heaven has revealed all to you. And I now call you Peter, the Rock, and on this rock, I will build my church, and the gates of Hades will not prevail against it. I will give you Peter, the keys of the Kingdom of Heaven, and whatever you bind on earth, will be bound in heaven, and whatever you loose on earth will be loosed in heaven."

Yeshua knew that he had again, dropped a bolt from the blue on his disciples. He could see them all trying to fathom what he had just said, what he had taught them about the Messiah, and what Shimon had said and what he himself had said in reply to Shimon and his talking about his church, and his changing Shimon's name to that of Peter, which means rock. Yeshua felt he needed to give his disciples time and space to digest and dissect what they had just heard, so he excused himself and decided to seek a lonely place.

Yeshua then said to them. "What I have said to you about me, I want you to keep to yourself for now. There will come a time, when all this will be revealed and you will be the ones to reveal all about me, and all I have come to teach and accomplish. And I will be with you always. We will meet at this place again in an hour or so. I will see you then." Yeshua then left them and went off on his own.

"Shimon, I mean Peter, are we now to call you Peter, the Rock," Thomas asked. "What was all that, which Yeshua said to us, all that about the Messiah, was he really referring to himself?" Thomas added.

"Thomas, did you not hear what Yeshua had just said, he warned us not to tell anyone he is the Messiah," Johanan said.

"But how can we be certain that he is, he might be telling us because he isn't," Thomas said. "I know you will tell me about all that Yeshua has said and done, and all the miracles of healing he has performed. But if he is the Messiah, if he is to establish his kingdom on earth and save us from the Romans, where is his army, where are his soldiers, what weapons does he have?" Thomas added.

"Thomas, do you still not understand, Yeshua has told us often that his kingdom is not of this world?" Miriam said.

"But we live in this world, and we are enslaved to the Romans, and there can be no salvation for us as long as we are enslaved to them," Shimon Cananean said. "I have many Zealots friends in Jerusalem. If Yeshua is ready to form a rebellion, then I can get word to all of them," Shimon added.

"Shimon, I thought you were finished with that way of thinking. Have you learned nothing all this time as a disciple of Yeshua?" Johanan said.

"Friends, that's enough. We have to take Yeshua at his word. There can be no doubt that he is the One that Johanan the baptiser spoke to us about, he is the Promised One, he is the One Isaiah speaks of, he is the Messiah, there can be no doubt. He has asked us not to tell anyone, and I expect you to respect his wishes. Let us now go into the city and find accommodation. Judas what are our funds looking like?" Peter asked.

"We have enough for now, but not for long, Shimon, I mean Peter," Judas said.

"This is going to take some time getting used to, Peter," Andreus said smiling, and drawing out the pronunciation of Shimon's new name of 'Peter.' "All my life, since we first learned to speak, I have been calling you Shimon, and now I have to call you Peter, Peter, Peter, this is definitely a challenge for me," Andreus said, smiling.

"Friends, we will now go into the city," Andreus then said, "And I will seek out accommodation for us all."

"And we will meet here again, as Yeshua asked, in a couple of hours," Peter said.

"Rebecca, Lucia, Rachel, Susanna and I will seek our own accommodation, for all the women," Miriam said.

"Try the outskirts of the town, there will be cheaper accommodation there," Andreus said. "If the worse comes to the worst, we can always seek out caves, as Yeshua tells us," Lucia said.

They all then went together into the city, and then the men and the women went their own ways.

Two hours later, they reunited at their meeting place and Yeshua was still nowhere in sight. But it wasn't long when they saw Yeshua. He looked radiant. He was smiling as he approached. "Come let us go to Caesarea Philippi," Yeshua said. "We have much to do. We will stay in Caesarea Philippi and the surrounding areas, as long as the Spirit wants us to, then we will head for the coast of the Great Sea as I had said, and spend time in Phoenicia. After that we will again make our way to Jerusalem."

"Yeshua, it is not safe for you to go to Jerusalem. Herod had Johanan in prison for such a long time and then had him killed in such an atrocious manner. If he did that to Johanan, he will not spare you," James Alpheus said.

Yeshua replied, "I must go to Jerusalem and suffer much from the Elders, the Chief Priests and the Scribes, the Teachers of the Law. I will undergo great suffering, and be killed, and on the third day I will be raised."

They were all in shock and disbelief with what Yeshua was saying. These bolts were coming in rapid succession from the mouth of Yeshua. Peter took Yeshua by the arm and led him a distance from the group, but still near enough for all of them to hear. And Peter then remonstrated with Yeshua, saying, "God, forbid it Lord! This must never happen to you."

But Yeshua looked Peter straight in the eye and said, loud enough for all to hear, "Get behind me, Satan! You are a stumbling block to me, for you are setting your mind not on divine things but on human things."

Then without another word, Yeshua returned with Peter to the disciples, and said, "If any of you want to become my followers, let them deny themselves and take up their cross and follow me. For those who want to save their life will lose it, and those who lose their life for my sake will find it. For what will it profit them if they gain the whole world but forfeit their life?"

Peter was in shock at Yeshua's vehement outburst. He was deeply hurt and confused. The disciples too were bewildered by Yeshua's harsh reprimand of Peter.

Yeshua continued, and seemed to be looking at Thomas when he spoke, he said, "For the Son of Man, the Son of God made man has, and is to come with his angels in the glory of his Father, and then he will repay everyone for what has been done. Truly I tell you, there are some standing here who will not taste death before they see the Son of Man, the Son of God made man, coming in his kingdom."

The disciples were stunned. They were in shock, not only on the outrageous words Yeshua used to reprimand Peter, but all he was now saying about his suffering and death. And they found all his talk about suffering and death distressing.

Yeshua then walked ahead into the city and his disciples were following, still in shock and trying to decipher and digest all that they had just heard Yeshua saying to them.

Peter was walking by himself, downcast. Miriam noticed how his shoulders stooped and how perturbed he looked. She went up to him and touched him on the arm. "Peter, Yeshua had called you to lead us, you are to be the Rock on which he is to build his church, his kingdom on earth. I know what he said to you was severe, but he is toughening you up Peter, for what lies ahead. We have to take Yeshua at his word; he will suffer and die, when, we do not know. But whatever happens he wants us to be strong, and we are to carry on his work, and he is preparing us for the worst. And he is preparing you Peter for the worst. He wants you to lead us, he wants you to be strong, so be strong," Miriam said.

Peter looked at Miriam and his stooped shoulders visibly lifted and straightened and he smiled at Miriam. "Thank you, Miriam, I needed to hear that. Come them let us follow him," Peter said.

Andreus was observing his brother, he had noticed the terrible shock he got with Yeshua's reprimand, he had decided to give Shimon some space and time, before he would talk to him, but then he saw Miriam approach and talk to Shimon. He still could not get the name Peter in his mind. He noticed the visible change in Peter while Miriam was talking to him and he was glad.

Andreus then went to Peter and spoke, "Peter, Yeshua has put a heavy cross on your shoulders, upon you he is going to build his kingdom. I know what he said to you, cut you to the core. He wanted to make you aware of the presence of Satan, Peter. Earlier he commended you and told you that it was the Spirit of the Father that revealed to you that he was the Messiah, and he said you were to be the Rock on which he will build his church, and then he said, the power of Hades will not prevail against you, or against his church. He just wanted to remind you to be careful, to be watchful, for you will have to do battle with the powers of Satan," Andreus said.

"Thank you, brother, you and Miriam have brought me great comfort, and I will depend on your support in what lies ahead."

Andreus, stopped Peter, stood in front of him, looked him in the eyes and placed his hands on Peter's shoulders and said, "Peter, you can depend on me and Miriam and all of us, we will support you in whatever you are called to do," Andreus said. They then embraced each other and then walked ahead in silence.

In the meantime, Miriam had caught up with Yeshua, and asked to have a word. She said, "Master, what you said to Peter, cut him to the quick, calling him Satan was very harsh and hurt Peter deeply."

"Yes Miriam, I know. I am sorry. I am becoming more conscious that my time is fast approaching. We will be going to Jerusalem soon, as the Passover is not far off. And I tremble as I sense the suffering that I will have to endure, and that my life is in mortal danger. When Peter remonstrated with me, I was so full of mixed emotions that I blurted out those words, and called him Satan, for he reminded me of Satan, who tempted me at the very beginning of my public ministry." Yeshua then told Miriam of the three temptations he endured at the hands of Satan, who tempted him to use his divine powers to save himself from all harm, and from all suffering.

"I understand Yeshua. I will let Peter know, of your sorrow for the hurt you caused him and what you were experiencing at the time," Miriam said.

"Do that, Miriam, and let Peter know, that I am sorry. And that I love him," Yeshua said.

Miriam spoke to Peter, shared with him what Yeshua had said and what Yeshua was experiencing and his own bout with Satan, and Peter's soul lifted, and he was most grateful, to Yeshua and to Miriam.

Chapter Sixty-Nine
The Gentiles

Yeshua and his disciples arrived in Caesarea Philippi; none of them had ever been in this city before. It had a different feel to the other cities and towns of Galilee and Judaea. It was quite a cosmopolitan city, and people spoke different languages. Yeshua and the disciples recognised the Aramaic, even though it was a different dialect to theirs. Yeshua always spoke in his Galilean Aramaic, whenever he travelled and spoke throughout Galilee. Aramaic was also the common language throughout Judaea, but Jerusalem had its own Aramaic dialect, in which Judas was the only one who spoke it fluently. Although he was from the southern part of Judaea, Judas spent a lot of time in Jerusalem, and was living there for a long time, before he met Johanan and became his disciple, and was still there when he met Yeshua.

Yeshua too became conversant with the Jerusalem dialect, as he travelled there quite often, and became quite fluent in the dialect during the time he was at the Advanced School of Learning in Jerusalem, where all his lessons and talks were in the Jerusalem brand of Aramaic. Yeshua also became familiar with Hebrew, which was really the preserve of the priests and religious scholars and the language used for writing, like the Sacred Scriptures. Yeshua also picked up some Greek, but was not fluent in Greek. Yeshua wished he could speak Greek more fluently, as he heard the language being spoken by some people here in Caesarea Philippi. And Yeshua also noticed some symbols of the Greek gods.

As they walked through the city, the people noticed Yeshua and the disciples. It wasn't all that strange, because the residents often saw groups visiting their city, and the locals recognised that Yeshua and his disciples were conversing in a brand of Aramaic, different to their own. They were surprised to see these thirteen men and seven women walking together. Men and women were usually separated in groups. The townspeople knew they were foreigners, but simply ignored them.

Yeshua knew a bit about the city and wanted his disciples to know, so he asked them "what do you know about Caesarea Philippi?"

The disciples were unresponsive, but Judas, who was the most educated of them all, spoke up, "Caesarea is named after the Emperor Caesar, of course. We all know that. Philip, one of Herod's sons, who is the half-brother to Archelaus, and you all know about the other half-brother, the cruel Antipas, governor of Galilee. He has a palace in Jerusalem, built by Herod, everyone calls Herod the Great. It was of course Herod Antipas who imprisoned and had Johanan killed. Antipas married Philip's first wife, Herodias. And that was the catalyst for Johanan's arrest because he spoke out publicly about Herod. Philip is now married to Salome."

They all turned to look at Salome who gave them a shake of her head and a grin.

"Go on Judas, this is interesting," Philip said. "Of course, you would find it interesting to hear about this namesake of yours, Philip." Judas smiled at Philip and continued, "Philip is the tetrarch of all of the territory east of the Sea of Galilee, which includes Ituraea and the whole of Trachonitis. Philip founded this city of Caesarea, and has his palace here. This city has always been called Caesarea Philippi, after Phillip of course, but also to distinguish it from that other city called Caesarea, on the coast of the Great Sea."

"Thank you for that history and geography lesson, Judas," Thomas said.

"What about the people, what do they believe," Salome asked.

This time Yeshua spoke up, for he had learned somewhat from Gamaliel and also at the School of Advanced Learning in Jerusalem. "I sensed the Greek presence, and like the Romans they have many gods, with Zeus, who is their god of the sky, and like our Yahweh, he is also the king of the gods. We of course, only have one God, and he is King of kings and the one and only God. You all know the story of Noah, Yahweh in his frustration with the people for turning away from him and embracing evil; purged the earth with a flood, and only Noah and all those with him in the Ark were saved. So too according to the Greeks, Zeus was angry with the people for they were turning away and no longer praying, so he sent floods, and droughts, and all kinds of hardships, to bring the people back to prayer and the gods. They have many gods, with the main ones, Zeus of course, and Poseidon as their god of the sea, and Hades, their god of the underworld."

As they were walking into the city, Yeshua and the disciples continued their walk towards the city square. They came across a temple and discovered that it was dedicated to the Greek god Pan. "I have never heard of the god, Pan, does anyone know of this god?" Yeshua asked.

Another group had been standing beside Yeshua and his disciples, and one of them interrupted, "Excuse me gentlemen and ladies, I can see you are not from here, and are Jews, not Greeks. I couldn't help overhearing you speak of our gods, Zeus, Poseidon and Hades. I am of Greek descent, and I can tell you something about Pan."

Yeshua looked at the man, with affection, interest and delight. "Thank you so much, that is very kind of you. So, who is Pan, and of what is he the god?" Yeshua asked.

"I heard you speak of Zeus, Poseidon and Hades; they are our main gods. We also have the god of earth, Mother Earth; she is Gaia, and several other gods. Pan is not very well known of our gods, and one of the lesser gods, but we here in Caesarea have a great affection and reverence for him," the man said.

"Why is that so?" Judas asked.

"Well, it's because Pan has enormous strength. He is the god of the wild, and we are a bit wild here in Caesarea," the man, an elderly man, grinned mischievously, revealing a gap in his front teeth.

"So, something like Hercules, the Roman god," Mattheus said.

"What else is Pan famous for?" Judas asked.

The elderly man continued, evidently delighted to be instructing these ignorant Jews about the Greek gods, and Pan in particular. He said, "Pan can transform objects, and he transports himself between Mount Olympus and earth. And besides being the god of the wild, he is also god of the shepherds and their flocks, and the god of nature, of the mountains," the man said.

"I see that statue over there, is that symbol of Pan?" Phillip asked.

"Yes, we depict Pan with his top part as that of a man, and his bottom half as that of an animal, a goat," the man said. "And, oh, yes, he is also the god who is good at running long distances," the man said. "And as I get older, I pray to him, for some of his powers, to just keep walking," the man said, grinning and then laughing.

Yeshua and the disciples couldn't help laughing with him.

"Thank you so much for that, Sir," Peter said. "We are, most of us from Galilee, and some are from Judaea and Jerusalem. We have with us Yeshua, from Nazareth, he is our teacher and prophet, and he has come here to speak to those of the God of Israel, and to all who would like to listen to him."

"Especially the lost sheep of the God of Israel," Lucia said.

"The lost sheep!" the man said, not quite understanding.

"Like those who turned away from Zeus, they were like lost sheep, so our God uses whatever means to bring them back into the fold," Peter said.

"We respect all your gods," Peter said. "We have come to speak of Yahweh, who is the one true god and the king of all the gods, including Zeus and all the gods, the Greek gods, the Roman gods and all gods. Our God, Yahweh, is God of the sky, sea, and the earth, He is the Creator of all that exists and without him, nothing exists," Peter added.

Yeshua was so pleased to listen to Peter speaking, and the disciples were equally impressed. Since Yeshua had changed his name to signify his position and his future, Peter seemed to grow in stature and confidence.

"I would very much like to hear about this god of yours," the man said. The people surrounding him were also engrossed in the conversation.

"Is there a Jewish synagogue in your city," Andreus asked.

"Yes, there is, not a very big one, but there is one," the man said.

"Good," Andreus said, "our teacher here, Yeshua, will be speaking there every morning, and he will be speaking to anyone who wishes to listen and to learn about the one true God."

"I would be very interested, as would these people with me," the man said, and the people around him nodded. "I will let the people around here know," he added.

Yeshua thanked the man and went on his way, with his disciples.

As they were walking away, Rebecca said, "what a delightful and funny man. I think I like Pan, for he is the god of running long distances, and because I like running, and Yeshua and I used to run long distances in Nazareth. And we might not be running long distances now, but we sure are walking long distances, like no one else," Rebecca added with a grin.

When they had all settled in, the next day, Yeshua and his disciples found their way to the synagogue, but there was a crowd of people waiting outside. The old man with the gap in his teeth was there grinning, and he had quite a crowd with him, and there were others there as well, who were chatting in Aramaic, and some in Greek.

The man with the gap in his teeth spoke, "Sir, I have with me some of my friends. We have come to listen to you speak about your great god, who is the king of all gods. We want to know if he is perhaps Zeus you speak of," the man said.

Yeshua spoke, "It is good to see you all here, this fine morning. I am a Jew from Nazareth. My people, the people of Israel, have one God, Yahweh, he is the Creator of all that exists, of nature, of humans, animals, the sky, the sea, the mountains, the trees, the plants, the wild life, all that grows and flourishes, everything that nourishes our bodies. He is the Creator and Father of all, and we are all his children."

"Your god is indeed a powerful god. So, who first told you about your god and how he created all that exists, or are you just making it up? Is your god mightier than our Zeus?" a man in the crowd asked.

Yeshua answered the man, "You ask a good question, Sir. We Israelites were enslaved to the Egyptians, under the Pharaohs for four hundred years. But Yahweh heard our cries and he raised up a Saviour for us, a man called Moses. Yahweh chose this man to lead us out of the bondage of the Egyptians, and he did this with great signs. So great were his signs and such catastrophes were wrought on the Egyptians that they eventually let our people go, and it was a day of great rejoicing, an exodus like no other. But as our people were on their way Pharaoh and his army gave chase, pursuing us. By now our people, the Israelites were at the shore of the Reed Sea, and we had no way of crossing the sea. But Moses lifted his staff and he gazed into the heavens and parted his arms and immediately the Reed Sea parted and came to rest leaving a great passageway for all the Israelites to pass through dry-shod. Pharaoh and all his men and their chariots gave chase into the pathway and when they were in the middle, the sea suddenly returned to its place, and Pharaoh and all his armies were drowned."

"That is amazing, but that does not answer the question I had put to you, who told you about this god of yours, and how he created all that exists," the man asked.

The people were interested in this fascinating story, and Yeshua had such a captivating way of telling the story. Even the Jews in the crowd listened with interest, as did the disciples. They never tired of hearing the story of Moses and their great Exodus.

Yeshua answered the man, "thank you for your question. I told that story, because it is Moses who told us all about how Yahweh created all that exists. Our ancestors, the Israelites, wandered for forty years in the desert and settled at the foot of Mount Sinai. And Moses one day went up the mountain and there he encountered Yahweh, who spoke to him from a burning bush that was burning but not being consumed. Moses spent a lot of time with Yahweh, listening to him, and Yahweh gave him Ten Commandments for us to live by to be saved, and to enter his Kingdom. It is this Moses who had recorded all, and has written the first five books of our Sacred Scriptures, which begins with the story of creation."

"What did he write?" someone asked.

"I will give you briefly what Moses wrote about creation," Yeshua said and continued, "Moses wrote, 'in the beginning Yahweh, God, created the universe. The earth was a formless void and darkness covered the face of the deep. Then God let light appear. He then put some order into what he created. And God named the light 'Day' and the darkness, 'Night', and the dome, 'Sky'. He then continued separating his creatures and named the land 'Earth' and the water that he brought together, 'Sea'. He filled the sea with countless creatures and the sky with numerous birds. Then God created all kinds of animals. Then God made us humans, according to his own image. He took some soil from the ground and formed a man out of it; He breathed life-giving breath into his nostrils and the man began to live. And while the man was sleeping God formed a woman out of the man's rib. God did all this grandiose work of creation in seven days. At the end God looked at everything he had made, and he was very pleased. And then God rested.'"

The people were totally engrossed. Storytelling was the way they learned, and they all knew and remembered stories, that were handed down from generation to generation.

"That is a beautiful story, Sir, your god is indeed a powerful god," a woman in the crowd said.

Yeshua continued, "It is indeed a beautiful story. In a nutshell, it speaks of God's great love, power, and generosity, his wanting to share all of himself with us, all of us, without exception, and his wanting to shower on us his goodness, and his beauty. We are still discovering more and more each day of the wonder and beauty of what God has created for us, and has given us, and continue to give us."

"So, who are you, Sir, what authority do you have to teach?" a man in the crowd asked.

"I am Yeshua, son of Miriam and Yosef from Nazareth. I was born at the time of Herod and I am the child whom Herod wanted to kill when he killed all those innocent newborn babies in Bethlehem. He was told of a newborn king who would be the King of Kings. I am that newborn child and I was spared because an angel appeared to my father in a dream and told him to take me and my mother and flee into Egypt where we lived until Herod died, and then we went and lived in Nazareth," Yeshua said. "I was born to teach, to bring you the Good News of God, who has sent me to tell you all the Good News of his unfathomable love for us, his love that is eternal, boundless and unconditional, and he wants you all to have true happiness and to be with him now and for all eternity."

"Yeshua, you say that your god is also the god of the sea, is he greater than Neptune our god of the sea?" another man in the crowd asked.

Peter then addressed the crowd, "I am Peter, and one of Yeshua's disciples and have been with him for two years now and travelled with him all over Judaea, Galilee and now all over Trachonitis. One night my friends and I, disciples of Yeshua, were sailing on the Sea of Galilee, Yeshua was asleep at the rear of our boat, when suddenly a severe storm erupted, the waves were slashing against either side of our boat and tossing us about, and we had to hang on for dear life. The wind was so fierce and the waves so wild we were fearful for our lives. I woke Yeshua and I knew that he could save us, and I asked him to save us or we will perish. Yeshua stood up, stretched out his arms and said to the sea, 'Be still!' And immediately the winds ceased and the sea was all calm again."

The crowd were mesmerised by Peter's story.

"So, he is a magician, he can calm the winds and the waves, what else can he do?" the man asked.

"He can heal the sick, he can make the blind see, the deaf hear, the dumb speak, and cast our demons, and even bring the dead back to life," Johanan said. "I am Johanan from Capernaum, and I too have been a disciple of Yeshua's, and I have witnessed all this," he added.

The crowd were overawed with what Johanan was saying, some shaking their heads, others scratching their heads not knowing what to make of all they were hearing.

"Come now, let us go, into the synagogue," Yeshua said.

Some of the people, the Jews in the crowd followed Yeshua into the synagogue and the rest went on their way.

Yeshua spoke to the people in the synagogue. He told them what had happened outside. And then he said, "You are the chosen people, the ones chosen by God; you are to be the light to others, to bring them out of the darkness and into the light. So let your light shine brightly. Let your light of kindness to all without exception shine; let your days be filled with good works. You live with those of other faiths, respect them and their beliefs but be bold and humble in speaking of our God, of the one true God. I have been sent to make him known and loved and to let all know of his great love. You too must do all you can to know and love our God and make him known and loved. And you do this by keeping his commandments, and above all by loving God with all your heart, with all your soul, with all your mind, with all your strength and your neighbour as yourself. And your neighbour is all who live here in your city, but also all you encounter, without exception."

Yeshua and his disciples stayed a couple of weeks in Caesarea Philippi and spoke to the Greeks and the Jews. Yeshua spoke to people outside of the temple of Pan, and he spoke of their belief of Pan being the god of shepherds and flocks and then spoke about God as the Good Shepherd, and all Yeshua had taught about the Good Shepherd who leaves the ninety-nine sheep in the fold and goes and looks for the one that is lost. He spoke how God knows them personally and intimately and he has a preference for the poor and the suffering, the vulnerable and ostracised, and that he knows all and cares for each person, and he loves all without exception. The people were interested to hear about a god that had this intimate interpersonal relationship with his creatures. They were used to gods of power, who were distant and above them and all powerful and to be feared. They liked the God Yeshua was telling them about, a God of love and compassion.

Yeshua also visited all the surrounding villages and settlements and also the caves where the homeless lived and he spent time with them, shared what they had with them and spoke to them of God's love for them. They were so taken with the preacher, no one of their religious leaders and teachers had ever come near them. This teacher came to them and touched them and spoke with them and befriended them and respected them and spoke of his love for them and God's special love for them.

When Yeshua felt that they had spent enough time in Caesarea Philippi they left and headed west.

Chapter Seventy
The Canaanites

Yeshua and the disciples left early in the morning. There was a slight drizzle and the air was nippy. Yeshua was walking ahead on his own, as he usually did.

"It looks like it will rain soon," Susanna cried out for Yeshua to hear.

"Yeshua, we better find some shelter soon or be drenched," Miriam called out.

Yeshua stopped and waited for them all to catch up with him. "Yes, we need to find shelter soon, and wait out the rains," Yeshua replied.

"Master, where exactly are we going?" Peter asked.

"Peter, I told you, we are going all the way to the coast, to Phoenicia, this road we are on will take us to the town of Tyre, where we will stay," Yeshua said.

Yeshua then went further ahead of his disciples to continue his walk on his own. Yeshua did this for some private time to gather his thoughts, to pray, talk to his heavenly Father and prepare for what lay ahead, and he also made himself available to any of his disciples who wanted a one-on-one talk with him. And most of his disciples made use of this, and in this way, Yeshua also got to know his disciples and what they were thinking, in a more personal and intimate way.

"What is Yeshua thinking?" Judas asked the rest of the disciples, making sure Yeshua could not hear.

"Why do you ask, Judas? What's on your mind?" Peter asked.

"Why is Yeshua going to Phoenicia, it is a territory of non-believers, Canaanites, why waste time going there?" Judas said.

"I have never been to Phoenicia," Susanna said. "I have never been near the Great Sea, it would be nice to visit the coast and see the mighty ocean, and walk along the beach," Susanna added.

"It would be nice," Rebecca agreed, as did the others.

"But the territory around Tyre and Sidon where Yeshua wants to go is not part of our people?" Judas said. "And they are not like our people, they are not a pure race," Judas added.

"Who are they then?" Thomas asked.

Judas answered, "They are made up of many different racial groups. They are a mixed race, with migrants who came from the east, thousands of years ago. They are a race of people who displeased Yahweh. They used to sacrifice sons and daughters in fire, to their gods."

"Surely they don't do that now, in this day and age, Judas," Miriam said.

"Oh, there are races that still have human sacrifices, Miriam," Judas retorted.

Judas continued expressing a deep-seated hatred the Jews had for the Canaanites' that lived there, because of their race and their beliefs and looked down upon them as children of a lesser god. The Jews would not associate with them in any way.

Judas continued, "They practice divination, sorcery, and engage in witchcraft and cast spells on people, and all sorts of practices that are detestable to Yahweh."

"Sounds ominous, Judas. Peter, maybe you better speak to the Master and get him to change his mind about going there," Thomas said.

"Yeshua did say, his work is to the people of Israel," Nathanael said.

"That is true, but he does not turn away any one who approaches him and seeks his teaching and his blessing. Remember he even healed a centurion's servant," Miriam reminded them.

"That is true, but he has not gone to territories populated by heathens, gentiles, non-believers, why is he going to Phoenicia?" Judas said, sounding frustrated.

"Maybe Yeshua simply wants a change of scenery, or some respite, along the ocean. You know how he likes walking on the seashore. And we are heading to the open sea, an ocean, not a lake, like Lake Galilee, even though we all call it a sea, the Sea of Galilee," Miriam said.

"Well, it sure behaves like a sea, and can whip up quite a storm," Peter said, seeking some light heartedness, as he sensed some tension arising among the disciples. "Remember the storm we experienced on that night on the Sea of Galilee when Yeshua calmed the waves and the wind," Peter added.

"Who can forget how scared you were Peter," Thomas said, laughing.

"We were all scared," Phillip added.

"Whatever Yeshua wants to do, wherever he wants to go, we follow. We are his disciples and he told us to take up our cross and follow him. So, Judas, if you feel going to Phoenicia is a cross, then you just have to grin and bear it and carry your cross," Peter said, with a smirk.

"So, what do these Canaanites believe?" Lucia asked.

Judas answered, "They are like the Greeks and the Romans, they believe in many gods. They are big on venerating the dead. They believe in Elohim, while at the same time, believing in and venerating other gods and goddesses, like Baal, El, Asherah and Astarte. They regarded Baal as one of their most important gods," Judas said, proudly displaying his knowledge.

"Thank you, Judas, we sure are lucky to have you with us, you have a wealth of knowledge," Phillip said. "But tell me, we are going to the province of Phoenicia, are the Canaanites and Phoenicians one and the same or different races altogether," Phillip asked.

"No, not really, the Canaanites are Phoenicians and the Phoenicians are Canaanites," Judas answered.

By now the rain started to come down more heavily. Luckily, they came across some caves, where they sought shelter from the rain that was now in full force. The sky was overcast.

"Yeshua, it looks like we are stuck here for the day, it doesn't look like it is going to let up," Thomas said.

"You're right Thomas; we will camp here for the day. See if you can find some dry wood around, and start a fire," Yeshua said.

When they eventually settled with a fire going, they sat around and Yeshua broke some bread which they all ate, with some dried fish.

Yeshua then spoke to them. "Little children, I am with you only a little longer."

The disciples were surprised by the way Yeshua addressed them as 'little children,' he had never addressed them like that before. It was an intimate and endearing expression. They listened intently, sensing something different to come from the mouth of Yeshua.

Yeshua continued, "You have all been with me for more than two years now. I am most grateful for your love, your friendship and your support. I am with you only a little longer. You will look for me but where I am going you cannot come. I remind you of the new commandment I have given you that you love one another. Just as I love you, you also should love one another. By this everyone will know you are my disciples, if you have love, one for another."

Peter then said to Yeshua, "Lord, where are you going?"

Yeshua answered, "Where I am going, you cannot follow me now, but you will follow afterward."

Peter then said to Yeshua, "Lord, why can I not follow you now? I will lay down my life for you?"

Yeshua answered, "Will you lay down your life for me Shimon Peter? Very truly, I tell you, before the cock crows, you will have denied me three times."

"I will never deny you, Master, never!" Peter said vigorously, he was perplexed that Yeshua would say this to him.

Yeshua continued speaking to his disciples, who were thankful for the rain, for they looked forward to having Yeshua spend time speaking to them and teaching them.

Yeshua then said, "Do not let your hearts be troubled. Believe in God, believe also in me. In my Father's house there are many dwelling places, and if I go and prepare a place for you, I will come again, and will take you to myself, so that where I am, there you may also be."

Thomas said to Yeshua, "Lord, we do not know where you are going, how can we know the way."

Yeshua then said to Thomas and to all of his disciples, "I am the way, the truth and the life. No one comes to the Father, except through me. If you know me, you will know my Father also. From now on, you do know him and have seen him."

The disciples were somewhat puzzled by what Yeshua was saying. They were accustomed to Yeshua speaking in parables, but they knew that what he was telling them was not a parable but the truth. They were grateful to Phillip, who put a request to Yeshua.

Phillip said to Yeshua, "Show us the Father, and we will be satisfied."

Yeshua said to Phillip, "Have I been with you all this time, Phillip, and you still do not know me? Whoever has seen me has seen the Father. The words that I say to you, I do not speak on my own; but the Father who dwells in me does his works. Believe me that I am in the Father and the Father is in me; but if you do not, then believe me because of the works themselves. Very truly I tell you, the one who believes in me will also do the works that I do and, in fact, will do greater works than these. If in my name, you ask me for anything, I will do it."

The disciples were alarmed, and at the same time overcome with amazement, at what Yeshua was predicting would happen to them. Yeshua often spoke about his time on this earth being limited, and there was always urgency in what he wanted to do. Some of the disciples thought that Yeshua might be suffering from an unknown illness or disease that none of them knew about, and that Yeshua kept to himself what he knew would shorten his life. But Miriam and the women sensed it was something else. They sensed the danger that lay ahead for Yeshua. Yeshua was a revolutionary in his teaching, his way of living, his example and he openly and fearlessly criticised the Pharisees, Scribes, Sadducees, chief priests, Elders; the religious elite and recognised leaders of the people. They resented how Yeshua was influencing the people, and they were envious of his popularity. Yeshua did not seek fame or fortune or power or popularity, but fame and popularity seemed to follow him.

The women knew that Yeshua was not doing what he was doing to gain prestige or popularity; he was simply telling the truth.

Yeshua knew that he was unsettling his disciples. But he was preparing them for what lay ahead. So, he said to them, "As the Father has loved me, so I have loved you, and continue to love you, and will always love you. I say these things to you, so that my joy might be in you, and that your joy may be complete."

Yeshua's words about joy that they would receive lifted the spirits of the disciples. They all remained in the cave for the night. It was now pelting down and getting cold. They had made the fire as close to the cave entrance as possible without being put out by the rain but they couldn't feed the fire anymore or else it would fill the cave with smoke, so they had to put it out. They dressed as warm as they could for the night.

The disciples had put out containers and whatever they found that could capture some of the rain water. Miriam sang some songs, to the light of the dying embers, and Lucia played the flute and they had a sing-song and told stories well into the night. Eventually they said goodnight and went to sleep.

The rain had stopped during the night and it was cool and fresh when they all rose from sleep. They washed in the water they had captured, then had something to eat, and were on their way. They were feeling well rested, and it was a good night of camaraderie, and they all got to know more about each other.

While everyone was packing up Yeshua was out and about taking a short walk by himself. When he returned, they were ready to leave.

They walked mainly in silence. The women, to keep the proper decorum, walked together as a group separated from the men, but out in the wilderness, away from the cities and the towns, they felt freer to mix, as they did now. Not all of the men or the women felt comfortable to cross those social boundaries, even out in the privacy of isolation, but some did. Miriam was chatting to Peter. At first Peter had kept his distance, but since Yeshua had placed such a responsibility on him, Miriam sought to give Peter all the support he needed and Peter appreciated her support, friendship and counsel. Rebecca, when she thought Yeshua had enough private time would walk with him and they would chat about Nazareth, their loved ones, and the people they knew, and wished they could go for a run through the bushland in Nazareth again.

After walking for about two hours, Yeshua and Rebecca stopped and waited for the rest to catch up.

Yeshua spoke to them, "It will take a couple of days for us to reach the city of Tyre, but we will soon be approaching some villages that may be off this road, we will stop at all the villages and settlements along the way and talk to the people there. In Capernaum and Bethsaida, we had lots of disciples, who had gone around with us. In Caesarea many gathered around us as well, but they turned away when I spoke to them about my giving myself to them as food for their souls. And in Jerusalem we have lots of disciples from all over Judaea who follow us when we are there. It is time to gather these disciples with us and for us to teach them more intensely, so they can already go out before us and spread the Good News of God's love. You all have to help to teach them all. I have taught you, and now you must begin to teach the other disciples, so they can help spread the Good News, now already, while I am still with you, and help you when I am no longer with you."

Peter felt like remonstrating with Yeshua again, and was depressed for a while, after Yeshua said that he would deny him three times before the cock crows. What was Yeshua saying? Was he predicting that I would deny him, three times? Peter was greatly disturbed but he dismissed it as Yeshua having a slip of the tongue, a momentary lapse.

The disciples also did not really want Yeshua to speak about him leaving them. But he mentioned this more often but they still believed it was far in the future.

The disciples then saw a well-trodden path that broke off from the main path they were travelling, and Yeshua led them down that path. They walked for about an hour and arrived at a small village. The people were surprised to see such a large group of men and women, who seemed officious, coming to their village. They hoped they were not tax-collectors or officials sent by the Romans to take the little they had from them.

Yeshua saw their trepidation so he greeted them warmly. "Shalom, peace be with you, do not be afraid, we come in peace and we come to bring you the Good News of Adonai's love for you. I am Yeshua and these are my disciples, we have travelled all over Judaea and have now come from Trachonitis, and on our way to Phoenicia but we wish to be here with you, to speak with you about Adonai, and the Good News he has for you."

"Yeshua, you are the carpenter from Nazareth, I heard about you," one of the village people said. "You are a healer. We have some sick people here, who are badly in need of medical treatment, and we have no way of getting them for the help they need, and no doctor will come out here to us, can you come and make them well," the man said.

"Take me to them," Yeshua said.

The man and those with him took Yeshua and his disciples to the sick. All the people in the village who saw this unusual gathering of outsiders being led by one of their own, joined the group, when they were told that it was Yeshua, the healer, and he was going to visit their sick, they became quite animated and were delighted to have Yeshua visiting them. There were sick babies, and a few young children and some elderly and Yeshua took pity on them all, and healed them. And there was a lot of rejoicing, and the people shared with Yeshua the little they had.

Yeshua and his disciples spent the day talking to the people. Because they were not a big crowd Yeshua spoke to all of them, about God's great love and compassion and his special love for them. He made them realise and feel how close God is to them, and loves them, and will never forsake them, and has prepared a place for them. The disciples were also engaged in speaking with smaller groups throughout the day. The women sought out Miriam and the other women disciples to speak with them about their own issues. There was a buzz throughout the village, and the villagers were so appreciative to have such knowledgeable and respectable people to be with them, and to talk to them, and teach them, and especially to have Yeshua with them, who healed all their sick.

Yeshua and his disciples were fully occupied all day, and went late into the night, people could not have enough of them and they did not want Yeshua and his disciples to leave, so Yeshua stayed three more days with them.

Eventually, Yeshua said to the people, "We thank you all for your kindness to us over these days. We have great friends here. We are so pleased to have brought you the Good News of God's great love for you. We will always pray for you and always carry you in our hearts, and whenever we pass this way again, we will spend time with you. But we must leave now for there are others to whom we have to bring the Good News. God bless you all and we leave you, our peace." And with those words Yeshua and his disciples left with the whole village seeing them off.

"What a great bunch of people," Salome said. "They have so little and they seem so rich in so many ways," she added.

They all agreed with what Salome said.

"These are the people that are dearest to my Father's heart, and they are the ones that have to be dearest to our hearts, we are never to forsake them or forget them but always to reach out to them in whatever way we can," Yeshua said. It was a message he never tired of inculcating into the minds and hearts of his disciples.

The disciples felt so uplifted by these people and the time they spent with them. They walked for another two days and came across settlements of people off the beaten track and spent time with them too, and befriended them, spoke to them about the Good News, and ministered to them, and Yeshua healed all their sick.

It was weeks by the time Yeshua and his disciples finally arrived at Tyre; they were quite tired and needed to have some rest.

"Andreus, Judas and Miriam, will you arrange lodging for us. I want to take a walk along the beach," Yeshua said, smiling. He was so excited about going for a beach walk and feeling the sand and the water beneath his feet. All the disciples were also excited about going to the beach. It was as if they were going on a holiday, after all this was the Great Sea that stretched for miles to the horizon that seemed endless. And the disciples had been so busy assisting Yeshua in his ministry and walking so much, that they welcomed this break.

Yeshua sensed they needed some rest so he said, "We will take a couple of days to rest before we seek out the people here to minister to them," Yeshua said.

Unbeknown to Yeshua and his disciples, word had spread from the surrounding villages that the prophet and healer Yeshua, the Nazarene was heading for Tyre. As the disciples were on their way to the beach, a Canaanite woman approached them and she had a group of women with her.

The woman forced her way close to Yeshua, before Peter or any of the others realised it. If they did, they would have restrained her. They knew Yeshua wanted to have a rest from the crowds, and he needed the rest.

The woman was already close to Yeshua, and she called out, in a loud voice, "Have mercy on me, Lord, Son of David; my daughter is tormented by a demon."

But Yeshua was intent on getting to the beach, looking forward to feeling the sand under his feet, and to walk along, in the water along the seashore, and he might even have a swim, it had been such a long time since he had a swim. So, Yeshua seemed to ignore the woman and kept on walking, without saying a word to her.

But the woman was unperturbed. She followed them and cried out again in a loud voice, "Yeshua, have pity on my daughter, she is tormented by a demon, who will not leave her."

Peter and Andreus kept the woman at bay, and prevented her from coming close to Yeshua, and Judas stood in front of the woman, blocking her access to Yeshua.

Yeshua continued his walking to the beach apparently ignoring the woman. Miriam and Rebecca who were walking alongside each other were surprised at Yeshua's lack of compassion for the woman.

"What's going on, what's with Yeshua, this is so uncharacteristic of him, ignoring this poor woman," Miriam said, to the other women.

"Yeshua is tired and he was so excited about going to the beach, and looking forward to a walk on the beach, and most likely a swim," Rebecca said. She knew Yeshua.

The woman continued to follow Yeshua, and the disciples continued to block her access but she persisted and would not stop yelling at Yeshua, "Yeshua, Lord, Son of David, have pity on my daughter, she has been tormented by a demon, which will not leave her. Lord, have pity on her, Lord have pity on her," the woman cried out.

Peter came next to Yeshua and said to him, "Master, send this woman away, for she keeps shouting after us."

Yeshua then stopped and turned around and said to the woman, "I was sent only to the lost sheep of the house of Israel."

The disciples reflected on the discussion they had about Yeshua going to Gentile territories, and recalled how they discussed Yeshua healing Gentiles, even a Centurion's servant. Is Yeshua now limiting his healing, only to those of the house of Israel, they wondered.

But the woman was unperturbed, she forced her way right up to Yeshua, and fell on her knees before him and pleaded, "Lord, help me."

Yeshua looked at the woman; he did not lift her to her feet, as he usually did when people knelt before him. He simply said to the woman, "It is not fair to take the children's food and throw it to the dogs."

Miriam and Rebecca gasped, as did the other women disciples. Never before had they heard Yeshua speak to anyone, let alone a woman, in such a demeaning way. They were perplexed.

Judas, however and some of the men, were agreeing with Yeshua. Judas was also well aware of the debasing names he and his Jewish mates used when talking about the Canaanites, and calling them 'dogs' was a common name they used when speaking of the Canaanites. Judas thought that Yeshua could have heard of this term for the Canaanites.

But this feisty woman would not take 'no' for an answer, and she said, "Yes, Lord, yet even the dogs eat the crumbs that fall from their master's table."

Yeshua was amazed. He stopped in his tracks, shaking his head. The thought of the beach evaporated from his mind, like thin air. The disciples, especially the women were all stunned, as was Yeshua.

Yeshua, instead of being annoyed by this woman, now smiled at her. He said to the woman, "Woman, great is your faith! Let it be done for you, as you wish."

Yeshua then bent down, stretched out his hands, wanting to lift the woman off her knees, but she grabbed both his hands and kissed them profusely, saying, "Thank you, Lord, thank you!" She got up and then ran off, with some women following her, trying to keep up.

When the woman was coming near to her home, she could see her daughter was waiting for her outside their home with her husband and surrounded by her three other children and their servant. They were all smiling broadly, as was their daughter.

When they saw the mother running, and some people running with her and some walking fast, further back, they knew that they knew. The daughter ran to meet her mother, and they embraced, and the daughter said, "Mother I am cured, I am cured, I felt as if I was being touched by an angel, and I felt something happened, there was a loud frightening cry, as the demon left me, but then a warmth and a peace filled my whole being," the daughter said.

The father and the family and the servant were able to testify to what happened. "We all heard the screeching sound as the demon left our daughter," the man said.

The whole family and all those with them were astonished, and they told all their neighbours, and the word spread about what had happened to the daughter they all knew was possessed by a demon. People then all went to look for this man, whom the woman called Lord and Son of David, who had cured her daughter, who has power to cast out a demon from afar. What manner of man is this they wondered? As they went on their way in search of Yeshua, they told others along the way, and the crowd grew and grew.

In the meantime, Yeshua and his disciples made their way to the beach, and Yeshua immediately ran into the water and splashed himself. And they all wet their feet, and walked at the water's edge. The sun was out now, and there was no trace of the rain. Yeshua and his disciples had walked for a while, when they saw the crowd, lots of people, coming towards then, almost running, and with them was the woman and her daughter.

Yeshua stopped and waited for the people to come near to him. When they were close the people were all staring at Yeshua, in wonder. Some wanted to touch him but Peter, Andreus and the others protected Yeshua.

The woman then came forward with her daughter and her other children. "Lord, here is my daughter, Tabitha, and I am Esther. I am so grateful to you for healing my child; she wants to meet you and thank you."

Yeshua was delighted to meet Tabitha. He took her hand and said, "Tabitha, shalom, I am pleased to meet you, and so pleased to know that you are well."

"Yeshua the people heard what you did for my Tabitha, and they have come to meet you and listen to you, we believe you are a man of God, will you speak to us," Esther said.

Yeshua then walked towards a nearby sand dune and climbed a few feet up the dune, and then told the people to sit on the sand. The people immediately and excitedly sat down to listen to Yeshua. Never before had such a man of God come to their shores.

Yeshua addressed the people. "My name is Yeshua, I am a carpenter from Nazareth, and with me are my disciples, men and women from Galilee and some from Jerusalem. They have travelled with me for two years now; we had been in Jerusalem for the last Passover celebrations. And have travelled all up the east coast of the Sea of Galilee as far as Caesarea Philippi, and made our way from there to your beautiful seaside city. We are all Jews, children of Yahweh, the one true God. We know you believe and worship the same God, whom you call Elohim, but you have many other gods. But I come to tell you that there is only one God, Yahweh, he is the God and Father of us all, and I have been sent to bring you the Good News of his boundless love for you. He has shown you his power and his compassion and his love for you by healing Tabitha, who is here with us; she will always be a reminder to you not only of God's power but of God's love and compassion for you."

Yeshua continued, "God is love. He made the world and all in it because he is love. He created the first of our human family and told us to love each other and to bring forth the fruits of that love, and so we are all here today, the fruit of God's love, and the love of our mothers and fathers, and all those around us. We are the children of Love, and we are created to love God and to love each other, and to bring peace and love to one another, to live in peace with each other. God is light and in him there is no darkness, and if we walk in that light, then we will be children of light. All that is not of God, all the sin and evil in this world is done under cover of darkness. I call you to come out of the darkness and live in the light, the light of Life, the light of Love. Love God and love one another. And let there be no exceptions to your love. We are all children of God, who makes his sun shine on us all, good or bad, Jews or Canaanites, Greeks or Romans; he made us all and loves us all. We deplore the evil that men and women do, and we have to do all in our power to fight for what is right and true and just, but never with any hatred, always with love in our hearts. We were born to love and not to hate. Hate kills, love gives life. Life is the fruit of love, and the greatest gift anyone can give is to lay down his or her life for another. I have come to bring light to the world, to bring the world out of the darkness and into the light. I have come to give my life to the world; I have come to bring love to the world, God's love. For this I live and for this I am prepared to die. So, I say to you, love one another, as God loves you, love God with all your mind, with all your strength, with all your heart, with all your soul, and your neighbour as yourself."

Someone in the crowd, yelled, "Sir, my neighbour is a devil, he is a pain in the neck, he causes my family so much trouble, how can I love him?"

Yeshua smiled at the man. "I know, we are all weak at times, and we do not always agree with each other. But do not fight hate with hate, for you will destroy not only your neighbour but yourself, and all you love, in the process. Act always with love." Yeshua then repeated his teaching about loving one's enemies, and doing good to those who hate us, for he told them again, that God loves us all and makes his sun shine on the good and the bad, and if we love only those who love us, what reward can we expect because even pagans do that, people who do not know of a God of love, do that.

Yeshua spoke for a long time. The people pleaded with him to stay in their town and to speak some more with them.

"I will stay with you as long as you wish me to. We will seek lodgings. As I told you, I have several of my disciples with me, twelve men and seven women. They are here with me, and you may speak with them too, for I have taught them all the Father has taught me. I will introduce you to them."

Yeshua then called Peter, Andreus, James, Johanan, Phillip, Nathanael, Mattheus, Thomas, James Alpheus, Shimon Cananean, Thaddeus and Judas, to come forward. This was not the first time Yeshua had formally introduced them to the crowds. But this time the disciples knew that this was Yeshua's gesture of telling them they were ready to teach the Good News that he has been teaching. The people were impressed to see all these men, and then they were even more so, when Yeshua called the women to come forward, Miriam, Rebecca, Lucia, Rachel, Joanna, Salome and Susanna. The women in the crowd were in awe that this man of God would have women disciples. This was unheard of.

Yeshua then told the crowd to go home. "I will be here tomorrow, at this place, at the same hour, if you wish to hear some more of the Good News that I bring. Go now in peace and love one another."

The crowd began to disperse, but some of the women approached Miriam, and the women disciples, to speak with them, and they offered lodging for them. Some of the men also approached Peter and Andreus and Judas and offered accommodation for the men as well.

Yeshua and his disciples remained in Tyre for two more weeks, preaching and teaching and bringing to them the Good News of God's compassion and love and exhorting them to love one another. The disciples were also approached by small groups of the townspeople wherever they went, who sought to hear from them all that Yeshua teaches. And this happened with the women as well, wherever Miriam and the women disciples went, the women from the town would approach them to ask them questions, and hear all about Yeshua.

After two weeks Yeshua was ready to move on, but the people were so enraptured with Yeshua and his disciples, and they wanted to hear more and more, and Yeshua had also healed all their sick. They just could not have enough of this man of God, and his troupe of followers. They wanted to hear from them too about Yeshua. And the apostles shared all their experiences of the power, compassion and love that Yeshua has for all, and his preference for the poor, and how he detested all forms of hypocrisy and control.

So, Yeshua and his disciples spent another week with the people of Tyre and on the final day with them he told the people that he and his disciples had to go to Sidon and the other villages along the way.

Yeshua gave his parting words to the people on the beach, "My dear brothers and sisters, my disciples and I thank you for your kindness, generosity and hospitality. Let me leave you with the story of Moses who led the Israelites out of Egypt where they were slaves, for four hundred years. One thousand and three hundred years ago, they walked through the desert and first settled at the foot of Mount Sinai. And it was on Mount Sinai, where Yahweh spoke to Moses, the same Yahweh, who you worship as Elohim. Yahweh gave Moses Ten Commandments that we need to adhere to, if we wish to gain eternal life. The first of these is, *I am the Lord your God, you shall have no other gods before me. You shall not make for yourself any idol, and you should not bow down to them or worship them for I am a jealous God, punishing children for the iniquity of their parents to the fourth generation of those who reject me, but showing steadfast love to the thousandth generation of those who love me and keep my commandments.*"

Yeshua paused for a moment and then continued. As God appeared to Moses, and spoke to him from a burning bush when he gave him the Ten Commandments, so God too spoke to me, in the River Jordan, when Johanan baptised me. When I came out of the water, suddenly the heavens opened and we all saw the Spirit of God, descending upon me like a dove, and God's voice from heaven could be heard saying, "'This is my beloved Son, with whom I am well pleased.' I have with me disciples of Johanan, who can testify that I speak the truth."

Yeshua continued to speak to a silent and rapt crowd, "As Moses handed down to us the Ten Commandments, so I too, on a mount not far from Capernaum, handed down to the people, new commandments, and blessings, and a new way of worshipping, loving and serving God, and a way to true happiness. They are now known as Beatitudes, and I give them to you this day, learn them, and live by them, and you will find true happiness, happiness nothing in the world, no possessions, position, power, prestige, popularity or anything else, can give you."

Yeshua then gave them the Beatitudes:

"Blessed are the poor in spirit, for theirs is the Kingdom of Heaven.
Blessed are those who mourn, for they shall be comforted.
Blessed are the meek, for they shall inherit the earth.
Blessed are those who hunger and thirst for righteousness, for they shall be satisfied.
Blessed are the merciful, for they shall obtain mercy.
Blessed are the pure in heart, for they shall see God.
Blessed are the peacemakers, for they shall be called sons and daughters of God."

Looking at his disciples, who had heard these before, Yeshua continued with the Beatitudes that were specifically directed to his disciples:

"Blessed are those who are persecuted for righteousness' sake, for theirs is the Kingdom of Heaven.
Blessed are you when men revile you and persecute you and utter all kinds of evil against you falsely on my account.
Rejoice and be glad, for your reward is great in heaven, for so men persecuted the prophets who were before you."

Yeshua concluded with these words, "All of the Ten Commandments and the Beatitudes can be found in this Greatest of all Commandments, 'You shall love the Lord your God with all your heart, with all your soul, and all your mind, and with all your strength, and you shall love your neighbour as yourself'."

With these words Yeshua stopped, he and his disciples then left. Earlier on, some townspeople had invited Yeshua and the disciples to a dinner; they now came to Peter and Andreus and gave direction where to go.

Yeshua and his disciples arrived, hungry and thirsty and in the mood for a feast. They always enjoyed such feasts from time to time. They ate and drank quite a bit. When they finally left the party, Yeshua told his disciples he was looking forward to a sleep-in and he told the disciples to do the same. They would all meet at the beach at noon the next day.

At noon the disciples all began to arrive in dribs and drabs. Yeshua was sitting on the dune and looking out to the sea. It was a cool day, but not cold, although it was cloudy, there was still a lot of the blue sky visible. The seagulls were making a racket. Yeshua loved the sea and was enjoying being here at the shore of the Great Sea.

When all the disciples were gathered, Yeshua was pleased to see they all looked well rested. Yeshua then said to them. "I thank you all for all the work you have done in spreading the Good News to the people here in Tyre. We will continue along the beach as far as we can and then find the main road to Sidon, and stop at all the villages along the way."

"Yeshua, the next big town on the coast is Zarephath; it is about halfway to Sidon, will we stop there?" James asked.

"Yes, James, we will. How far is it to Zarephath?" Yeshua asked.

"I think it is only about fifteen miles at most, maybe a bit more," James said.

"So, we have a good walk ahead. But we will stop wherever there are people living," Yeshua said. With that they were on their way.

It took over two days, as Yeshua spent time at little villages along the way, and wherever clusters of people appeared. He stopped and spoke with the farmers, and the labourers, the shepherd and goatherds, as he always did. Some of them had not heard of Yeshua and his message, so he spent a lot of time with them.

The people who worked on the land and the farms, who did not know about Yeshua, were intrigued by this group of men and women travelling preachers, and they were happy to have a break and listen to what they had to say.

Yeshua spoke about the Good News using all the agricultural images, such as the Good Shepherd, and workers in the field. About faith as small as mustard seed that could move mountains. And about the pearl of great price that someone found and hid in a field. And when he came to workers in the vineyard, he spoke of himself as the vine and his followers as the branches. And to the day labourers on the farms, he told the parable of the landowner who paid the labourers who worked for one hour just as much as those who toiled all day. This really fascinated the day labourers and they wanted to hear more. And to those farmers who happened to listen he spoke of the rich man consumed by wanting more and more and building bigger and bigger barns for all his grain and that very day when he had built these huge barns he was called by God, and Yeshua spoke of the emptiness of seeking riches, for riches sake, and power and authority to lord over others and what does it profit a man if he gains the whole world and loses his immortal soul. And Yeshua also repeated the parable of the sower who went out to sow corn, and some fell on rocky ground, and some among thorns and some on fertile grounds.

The disciples also spoke to smaller groups who had questions about what they heard and they wanted to know more about who Yeshua was.

At one of the places where the landowners of wheat farms and their families and labourers were listening to Yeshua, he told them the story, a parable of weeds among the wheat, he said, "The Kingdom of God, may be compared to someone who sowed good seed in his field; but while everybody was asleep, an enemy came and sowed weeds among the wheat, and then went away."

The farmers and labourers were captivated, wanting to listen to the rest of the story. Never before had they heard anyone speak about the Kingdom of God like this, in a way to which they could relate.

Yeshua continued, "So when the plants came up and bore grain, then the weeds appeared as well. The labourers went to the farmer and said, 'Master, did you not sow good seed in your field? Where then did these weeds come from?' He answered, 'An enemy has done this.' The labourers said to him, 'Do you want us to go and gather them?' But he replied, 'No, for in gathering the weeds, you would uproot the wheat along with them. Let both of them grow together until the harvest, and at harvest time I will tell the reapers, collect the weeds first and bind them in bundles to be burned, but gather the wheat into my barn.'"

After this, Yeshua felt it was time to move on.

***

Yeshua and his disciples eventually arrived at Zarephath, where they spent several weeks, preaching and teaching, and healing the sick, not only in the town, but in all the surrounding villages. They then made their way to Sidon, there again Yeshua and his disciples spoke to the people on the beach.

The weeks flew by. Yeshua had often said, he was sent to save the lost sheep of the house of Israel. But he spent so much time here in Phoenicia. When the disciples questioned Yeshua about this, he said, "Yes, I did not intend to stay so long, here in Phoenicia. I had never come to this part of our land, and I was curious, and I love the Great Sea. I had been to Caesarea at the sea and I loved the ocean. I thought it would be good for all of you, to see this coastline, and I knew I would never have another chance, I will not return here again. And the Canaanite woman, whom I so poorly insulted, by her faith, so inspired me, and I thought she was such a fine example for the rest of her people that I had to spend time here and spread the Good News of God's love to them," Yeshua said. "But now it is time for us to return to Galilee. We will head straight for Capernaum. We will leave the coast and travel all along this side of Mount Lebanon, and past Chorazin to Capernaum."

"Yeshua, that is a long walk, it will take us a whole week for sure," Thomas said.

"Yes, I know Thomas. So let us rest up tonight. Light up a fire and we can have our own feast before we leave for Capernaum in the morning. We will all have a long night's sleep and leave when the last one awakes," Yeshua said.

"That will be Nathanael, he will sleep forever, if I don't wake him," Phillip said, laughing, and the others joined in, for they all knew about how Nathanael loved to sleep, and so easily would find a tree and nod off.

They had a great feast of what they had received from the people, a feast just among themselves. It was a kind of debriefing too, as they started sharing and reminiscing about all that happened from the time they arrived at Tyre and the encounter with Esther, the Canaanite woman. But then they ate and drank and told stories and jokes and Miriam sang and Lucia played the flute.

It was a great night and they slept way past sunrise. And when Nathanael finally awoke, they went on their way.

Chapter Seventy-One
From Capernaum to Jerusalem

They were walking for a couple of hours, and Yeshua was hungry, as he had nothing to eat since their feast last night. Seeing a fig tree by the side of the road, Yeshua's eyes lit up. He went to the tree and was completely disappointed because he found no figs on it, except leaves. Then he spoke to the tree.

The disciples stood around, they were not fazed, for they saw how Yeshua spoke to the trees. He loved trees, and touched them, nestled in them, and was forever stopping to admire them in all their diverse beauty. But then the disciples were surprised by what happened next.

Yeshua said to the tree, "May no fruit ever come from you again!" And all at once the fig tree withered away before their eyes. When the disciples saw this, they were amazed, and Thomas spoke what they were all thinking, "How did the fig tree wither at once?" But some of them, especially the women were puzzled by why Yeshua would use his power in this way. There were a couple of times when Yeshua used his powers in a bizarre way, a way they could not understand, and this was one such occasion.

Yeshua was aware of what they were thinking, so he said to them, "Truly I tell you, if you have faith and do not doubt, not only will you do what has been done to the fig tree, but even if you say to this mountain here, 'Be lifted up and thrown into the sea,' it will be done. Whatever you ask for in prayer, with faith, you will receive."

Still Miriam and the women discussed this bizarre miracle of Yeshua's. Finally, Miriam concluded for all of them, "Maybe Yeshua was simply trying to reinforce his teaching about a tree that has to bear good fruit for if it does not bear fruit, it will be cut down."

When Peter and the others joined the women, they related what Miriam had said about Yeshua cursing the fig tree. Peter then related what he thought was the most bizarre miracle of Yeshua's he had ever witnessed. They were all interested to hear Peter's story, so he told them. "It was a long time ago; I was still called Shimon then. It happened in Capernaum. The collectors of the Temple tax came to me and said, 'Does you Teacher not pay the Temple tax?' I told them, yes, he does. And when we got home, I told Yeshua and then Yeshua said to me, 'What do you think Shimon? From whom do kings of the earth take toll or tribute? From their children or from others?' I said, "From others." Then Yeshua said to me, 'Then the children are free. However, so that we do not give offence to them; go to the sea and cast a hook; take the first fish that comes up, and when you open its mouth, you will find a coin.'"

"And did you find a coin?" Thomas asked with scepticism; he thought Shimon was just pulling their leg.

"I chide you not Thomas, it happened just as Yeshua had predicted, and he told me to take the coin and to give it to the Temple tax-collectors, from him and me," Shimon said.

"How bizarre," Lucia said, and they all agreed. They then continued to share stories about their encounters with Yeshua, especially those ones they could not fully understand when it happened but came to understand later.

It took more than two weeks when Yeshua and his disciples finally arrived at Capernaum. As they were approaching the city, Yeshua spoke to his disciples. "We will have a week's rest, before we continue our work. Go to your homes, your families and your loved ones. Judas, Joanna, Salome and Susanna, it has been a long time since you have been with your loved ones. We will soon make our way to Jerusalem again, for the Passover, and you can spend an extended time with your family and loved ones, in Jerusalem," Yeshua said.

"Yeshua I will be going to Magdala and spend the week with my mother. Father, will most likely be in Capernaum, and we can all stay there, of course. And, Rebecca, Salome, Joanna, and Susanna, you are most welcome to spend the week with me in Magdala if you wish," Miriam said. "Lucia, I'm sure you would like to go home, to your family," Miriam said.

The women said they would love to spend time again with Miriam.

Lucia said, "I will go home, it has been a long time, and I miss them."

"What about you, Rachel, do you wish to go home to your village for a while?" Miriam asked.

"I'm not so sure. I would not like to travel on my own. I will stop there for a while when we next pass that way on our way to or from Jerusalem," Rachel said.

"You are most welcome to stay with me in Magdala, if you wish Rachel," Miriam said.

"I'd love that Miriam, thank you so much," Rachel said with a smile.

"What about you Judas, would you like to go to Jerusalem, as well? We will be going there for the Passover, which is not too long away," Yeshua said.

"Actually, I might just go now and I will see you all in Jerusalem, for the Passover," Judas said.

Peter then took Judas aside and spoke to him. "It's good that you are going to Jerusalem ahead of us, Judas. Have a good look, and take the pulse of the people there. See how they feel about Yeshua coming to Jerusalem for the Passover. And you may wish to arrange our old accommodation spots with our friends there in Jerusalem. Let them know Yeshua is coming. But keep it low profile for now," Peter said.

Judas had his own thoughts. He was growing impatient with Yeshua. He wanted Yeshua to show his power, not only to the Jews and the Gentiles but to the Romans. Yeshua had shown such great power, and to Judas, Yeshua needed to use his power to conquer and get rid of Rome, once and for all. However, Judas, kept his thoughts to himself, and simply said, "I will, Peter."

They all spent the day together in Capernaum. Miriam's father, Elijah, was in Capernaum, busy at the winery when Yeshua and the disciples arrived. Miriam sent one of the servants to tell her father. He was eager to see his daughter again. It had been a while. When he finally caught up with his daughter, he was so pleased to see how well she looked. She seemed so much more mature and self-confident.

Elijah arranged a sumptuous meal for Yeshua and his disciples. It was much appreciated. When they finished, the dinner, and as the darkness approached, they all retired, for the night.

The week passed quickly and they all, except for Judas, reunited in Capernaum, and Yeshua began his routine of preaching and teaching in the synagogue and at the shore of the Sea of Galilee. The people knew that when Yeshua was not in the synagogue, he could be found at the seashore. Over the next two months, great crowds came to him, from all over Capernaum, Gennesaret, Magdala, even from as far as Tiberias on the shore of the Sea of Galilee, and they came from Chorazin, in the north, and even the other side of the River Jordan and the Sea of Galilee, from Bethsaida, and Gergesa. They did not realise that Yeshua intended crossing over the Sea of Galilee after he had finished ministering in Capernaum.

Yeshua taught them all and brought them great words of comfort, assuring them of God's boundless compassion and love for them all. And the crowds brought with them the lame, the maimed, the blind, the mute, and many others. They simply put them at Yeshua's feet, while he was talking to them, and Yeshua cured them all. And the crowd never ceased to be amazed when they heard the mute speaking, and when they saw the maimed made whole, the lame walking, and the blind seeing, and they all praised the God of Israel.

As usual the Scribes and Pharisees and their cohort, wore blindfolds. They just simply could not fathom how a man like Yeshua, could be given the adulation he was receiving; he who seemed to be living a loose life and a law unto himself. So, they continued putting Yeshua to the test but he continued to outwit them all.

When it was time to leave Capernaum, one evening, Yeshua got all his disciples together and as he often did, when he thought it was time, he told them to take the next couple of days off, to unwind, for they would then cross over to Bethsaida and continue their work there only for a short while, as many had come from Bethsaida to Capernaum. He said that they would then head to Jerusalem in time for the Passover.

Peter said to the others, "I think I will go fishing. I think there should be one of our boats here."

"If not, Peter, we could use one of our boats," James said. "And I will join you."

"So will I," Johanan said.

Andreus, Philip, Nathanael, Thomas, James Alpheus and Shimon also said that they would join them. Yeshua however decided to retire. But something woke him in the middle of the night; he had a strange feeling about Peter and the others on the sea. And it was not only because the wind had started howling. He remembered the time when he was asleep on the boat and Peter and the others were so scared and he had to calm the winds and the waves. Yeshua got up. Yeshua thought it could be any time between three and four hours after midnight. He walked towards the shore. By the direction of the wind, Yeshua could see that the disciples would have difficulty coming to the shore, for they would be rowing against the wind.

Instinctively, Yeshua simply took off and began walking on the sea. But as he approached his disciples, they did not recognise him, and they were terrified. "It is a ghost," James shouted. They all agreed that it could only be a ghost that could walk on water, and they all cried out in fear.

Yeshua realising their terror, immediately said, loud enough for them to hear, "take heart, it is I; do not be afraid."

Peter, instinctively, answered him, "Lord, if it is you, command me to come to you on the water."

Yeshua simply said to Peter, "Come."

Peter then, without thinking, got out of the boat and started walking on the water, and came towards Yeshua.

The disciples were amazed; they could not believe what they were seeing. First Yeshua and now of all people, Peter too, was walking on the water.

But when Peter noticed just how strong the wind was, he became frightened, and beginning to sink, he cried out, "Lord, save me!"

Yeshua immediately reached out his hand and caught Peter, saying to him, "You of little faith, why did you doubt?"

When they both got into the boat, the wind ceased. The disciples were astonished, even though they had already witnessed Yeshua's power over the winds and the waves before, but this incident of Yeshua and Peter walking on the water, astounded them more than ever, and they worshipped Yeshua, saying, "Truly, you are the Son of God."

After a couple more days in Capernaum, Yeshua and his disciples sailed across to Bethsaida, where they planned to stay for only a short while. When they arrived in Bethsaida, Yeshua told the disciples that he would be gone for the next couple of days; he was going into a deserted place and would then meet with them.

Yeshua went by himself to a lonely place. But word soon got out that Yeshua was in Bethsaida, and that he was not staying long and will be leaving for Jerusalem. The people from Bethsaida and the surrounds, sought him out, and found him and followed him into the deserted place. Yeshua spoke to the people; they were still so hungry for all he had to say. He brought them so much hope.

As the day proceeded, the crowds kept coming to be with Yeshua, in the lonely place. The stream of people arriving seemed endless. Yeshua spoke to the people. They would not leave him. It was late afternoon, and Yeshua decided it was enough. Yeshua had intended staying in this deserted place and Yeshua knew the crowd would not leave, unless he did. He called Peter and Andreus, Miriam and the other disciples and said to them, "I have compassion for the crowd, because they have been with me now all day and have nothing to eat; and I do not want to send them away hungry, for they may faint on the way."

The disciples thought, saying to themselves, 'not again.' So, Peter said to Yeshua, "Master, where are we to get enough bread in this deserted place, to feed so great a crowd?"

As he did before, Yeshua asked them, "How many loaves have you?"

They said, "Seven, and a few small fish."

"Tell the crowd to sit down on the ground."

The disciples did as Yeshua had ordered and when everyone was seated, Yeshua took the seven loaves and the fish, and after a prayer of thanksgiving, he broke the bread and the fish into smaller pieces, and gave them to his disciples, and the disciples started distributing it to the crowds.

Once again, the inexplicable happened. Everyone ate to their hearts content, until they were all satisfied. How, no one knew, but they were all astounded and would speak of this for many months, if not years to come. But the disciples were even more amazed. For they had already witnessed Yeshua feeding more than five thousand people with nothing more than five loaves and two fish.

Again, Yeshua told them not to waste and to gather up the broken pieces and this time they collected seven baskets of left over pieces of bread and food that the disciples would distribute the next day to the poor.

At the end of the day, as they were on their way home, Thomas asked Mattheus. "Mattheus, Judas has gone already, so it is up to you to tell us the size of the crowd this time. How many people did Yeshua feed this time around?"

"I think this time was a bit less than last time, more like around four thousand," Mattheus said.

After his two days by himself, Yeshua caught up with his disciples in the city of Bethsaida. They then decided to leave immediately, and they travelled along the east coast of the Sea of Galilee, and re-visited all the places and people they had visited before. Everyone was so excited to see Yeshua and his disciples again, after so short a time. Yeshua engaged his disciples in preaching and teaching the people. After travelling all along the east of the Sea of Galilee, Yeshua decided to cross the River Jordan, so that they could visit Mount Tabor, and allow Rachel to spend some time with her loved ones.

Yeshua had initially planned to cross the River Jordan once they arrived close to the Dead Sea, and visit Jericho before going to Jerusalem. But Yeshua changed his mind, as he recalled that Rachel was the only one of his disciples who had not had some time with her family and loved ones. And it gave him and the disciples the opportunity to minister to the people there.

Yeshua also recalled the time he had spent time in Caesarea Philippi and Phoenicia, among Gentiles; those whom the Jews thought as less, and beneath them, but Yeshua was impressed by how open they were to his message, and how strong their faith was. So, when he crossed at Mount Tabor, he thought after spending time in the village there, he would visit towns in Samaria.

After two weeks in the village, Yeshua left with his disciples. They continued for the next couple of days, all along the western side of the Jordan River, until they reached the Samaritan town of Scythopolis near Mount Gilboa. As they were approaching Scythopolis, Yeshua sent his disciples ahead of him, to make things ready for him. But the townspeople were unwelcoming; they did not want Yeshua to stay in their village.

James and Johanan approached Yeshua and said, "Lord, do you want us to command fire to come down from heaven and consume them?" They did not realise what they were saying.

Instead, Yeshua rebuked them, and decided to go directly to Jericho.

The people of Jericho were over the moon, especially Zacchaeus and his family, and more so the women of the town. Meetings were arranged for women with the women disciples of Yeshua's, once again. Yeshua and his disciples stayed a week in Jericho, preaching, teaching, confirming the people in their faith, and then they headed for Jerusalem.

Judas met with them all, and had organised all their accommodation at the same places they stayed the last time, at the homes of Johanan's former disciples, who were now wanting to be disciples of Yeshua. Judas had also arranged a meeting with over two hundred disciples, who had surrounded Yeshua the last time he was there. Yeshua was pleased that Judas had done that, for Yeshua knew it was time for others to help spread the Good News to more distant places. Yeshua knew his time was short, how short, he did not know.

When Yeshua arrived at the meeting with his nineteen disciples, there were more than two hundred present. Yeshua was a bit disappointed to see that those whom Judas had invited were all men. Yeshua took Miriam aside and said to her. "Miriam, with the other women from Jerusalem, make sure we have more women join us for the next gathering."

Yeshua spoke to the large gathering about why he has been sent by the Father. He spoke to them at length about the Good News. And he thanked them for their support. And told them, soon they would be going out to other towns and villages.

"Every time, I've been in Jerusalem, you have been with me, surrounded me with your affection and support, and I am most grateful. You have heard of the Good News I have preached, and soon I will send you to spread this Good News to others." With his disciples, led by Peter and Miriam, Yeshua wanted to make a point, by mentioning Miriam as one of his leading disciples as well, to remind them all that the women have just as important a role to play in spreading the Good News to all. Yeshua continued, "Peter, Miriam and the others, will spend some more time with you, share with you all that I have taught them, before we leave Jerusalem, then I will send you to all the surrounding towns that we plan to visit."

And so it came to pass, Yeshua and the nineteen had several gatherings with his growing number of disciples to prepare them for spreading the Good News, to go to the places they had not yet visited, and to far-flung places he would not have the time to visit.

Yeshua also spent his time in Jerusalem taking part in all the Passover ceremonies. But Yeshua found the crowds overbearing. Everyone though, was in a festive mood. Yeshua did manage to speak in the Temple during the seven days of celebration. But when the last day came, and all the sacrifice of the animals took place, the pandemonium in the Temple, with the sale of livestock, and moneychangers sitting at tables in the Court of the Gentiles of the Temple doing their business, worked on Yeshua's nerves. It was like a marketplace and Yeshua could not stand it. Yeshua left with his disciples, and they celebrated the Passover Meal at Joanna's place.

Yeshua spent several more weeks in Jerusalem and the surrounding areas and continued to preach and teach in the Temple. One Sabbath, Yeshua and his disciples were walking near the Sheep Gate, where there is a pool, called Bethsatha, which has five porticoes and the Jews believed it had healing powers. In the porticos there lay many invalids—blind, lame and paralysed. And they all believed that the first one, who got into the pool when the water is stirred up, will be cured.

Yeshua approached the invalids, he was full of compassion for them, and spent time with them, speaking with them. The only people around were invalids, with a few carers. Yeshua encountered one man, named Obadiah. Yeshua heard from the man how he had been an invalid, for thirty-eight years.

Yeshua spoke to the man, "Obadiah, do you want to be made well?"

Obadiah replied, "Sir, I have no one to put me into the pool, when the water is stirred up, and while I am making my way, someone else steps down ahead of me."

Yeshua filled with compassion, said to the man, "Obadiah, stand up, take your mat and walk."

At once, the man was made well. He took up his mat and began to walk. Everyone was amazed. And Obadiah was jumping with joy. He could not believe that he was able to walk, for the first time, after thirty-eight years. He thanked Yeshua profusely.

As Obadiah made his way home carrying his mat, some pious Jews accosted him, saying, "It is the Sabbath, it is not lawful for you to carry your mat."

But he answered them, "the man who made me well, said to me, 'Take up your mat and walk'."

Later on, Obadiah went to the Temple and he met Yeshua there, and thanked him once more. And Obadiah could not contain his exuberance and told everyone that it was Yeshua who had healed him.

The Jews, who had seen Obadiah breaking the Sabbath, reported to Pharisees and the Scribes and Elders that it was the preacher, Yeshua, that had cured Obadiah on the Sabbath and made him carry his mat.

The Pharisees and the religious leaders, when they encountered Yeshua, attacked him for what he did on the Sabbath.

Yeshua simply answered them, with the words, "My Father is still working, and I also am working."

Now they all were even more determined to get rid of Yeshua, because not only was he breaking the Sabbath, but he was also calling God his own father, thereby making himself equal to God.

Peter and the others were becoming more agitated and concerned for Yeshua's safety and they finally convinced Yeshua to leave Jerusalem. The disciples heard that there was actually a plot to get rid of Yeshua, to kill him. They were scared that the Jews might report him to Herod or even Pilate on some trumped-up charges to have him killed, and Yeshua could have a similar fate as Johanan, the baptiser.

Before Yeshua and his disciples left Jerusalem, of the about two hundred other disciples that the Yeshua and the disciples had spent time teaching and preparing to send out to pave the way for Yeshua, Yeshua appointed seventy-two of them as disciples, who would not join the nineteen, but who would go out on their own, in twos, to spread the Good News, to all the surrounding towns. Yeshua told them he would return to those places later, when the crowds had left Jerusalem and things have quietened down.

Chapter Seventy-Two
The Woman at the Well

It was now more than two years, since Yeshua began his public ministry and he had this feeling it was going to be his last. He sensed the animosity from the religious leaders of the people and he knew they were out to get him, and would stop at nothing to see him stopped, and silenced. He had a strong feeling that his life was in mortal danger. What had happened to the prophets of old, he felt would now soon also happen to him. But Yeshua had complete trust in his heavenly Father.

Yeshua told his disciples they would return to Galilee, to their base in Capernaum and continue and consolidate their work there. The Jews in their despising of the Samaritans usually skirted around Samaria and took a longer and roundabout route from Judaea to Galilee and vice versa, simply to avoid any contact with the Samaritans, whom they despised so much. This time Yeshua said they would take the direct route through Samaria.

Peter was about to remonstrate with Yeshua again, but thought otherwise. The disciples were surprised, because when they had last crossed the Jordan River from the east, into Samaria, and entered the town of Scythopolis, the Samaritans did not welcome them, in fact they practically threw them out of their town. And the disciples knew of the animosity that existed between their race and those of the Samaritans.

Yeshua knew what was on the minds of his disciples, so he spoke to them. "This is ridiculous, us going back to Galilee, taking such a longer route, just to avoid Samaritan territory, when we can take a much shorter route through Samaria." Yeshua knew what they were thinking, so he said, "we will head directly north and pass through Ephraim and stop at the Samaritan town of Sychar." Yeshua then said, "I know that I have said that my ministry is to the chosen people, and especially to the lost sheep of Israel. But God, my Father in heaven, is father of all of humankind, and he wants all to hear the Good News of his love, and he wants salvation and redemption for all. And when I am gone, you must go to every corner of this earth and spread that Good News. So let us make a start. We saw the faith of the Gentiles, the Centurion, the Canaanite woman, faith greater than I have ever seen. So let us change." Yeshua then walked ahead.

"I am really concerned for Yeshua. He seems downcast. And this time in Jerusalem, I sensed a growing animosity and ferocity in the way Yeshua was being attacked by the Pharisees and the other religious elite in Jerusalem. And now we are going into Samaritan territory?" Peter said.

"At least, I don't think Yeshua will be under attack from the Samaritans, he is no threat to them," Judas said.

"Why do we Jews harbour so much animosity for the Samaritans," Rebecca asked. "They are no different to us," she added.

"But they are different," Judas said. "They are not a pure race, but a blend of all kinds of people," Judas added.

"So, what!" Rebecca retorted. "We are all mixed in some way. There is no pure race, ever since Adam and Eve left Paradise and populated the earth," Rebecca said.

"And especially when our people were captured by the Assyrians and taken into captivity to Babylon, and intermingled with them, all those centuries ago," Miriam said.

"But the Samaritans, adhere to a different Torah to us Jews. They have their own Torah, which they falsely claim to be the original, unchanged Torah, as opposed to our Torah, handed down to us by Moses himself," Judas said.

"Anyhow, we will most likely have a hostile reception and get thrown out again," Thomas said.

"Maybe not, we are on a different route and it seems that the Samaritan town on this road we are taking is the town of Sychar. I have never been there before. It would be interesting to visit," Johanan said.

"It is quite a distance. It will take us at least three days, as Yeshua does not want us to walk for more than four hours on any day," Judas said.

"And of course, we will stop at any villages along the way," Rebecca added.

Four days later, Yeshua and his disciples were approaching the Samarian town of Sychar, near Mount Gerizim. They had slept rough, in caves along the way. They arrived at a well, just outside the town. Yeshua said to his disciples. "We will stay here for a day or two, go into the town and buy some food and seek some decent lodgings for the next couple of days. I will stay here at this well until one of you returns."

The disciples walked into the town, and left Yeshua at the well outside the town. "I think, I'll only book accommodation for one night, I'm sure the people will throw us out, as they did at Scythopolis," Judas said.

It was now noon and Yeshua sat down at the well. After a short while, Yeshua was surprised to see a Samarian woman coming to draw water. Why would she be coming to draw water in the middle of the hot day, outside of the town by herself, it was customary for the women to draw water for the day's use at the beginning of the day.

The woman too was surprised to see a man, sitting by himself at the well, at this time of the day, and from his features she could see he was a Jew, which surprised her even more. What would a Jewish man be doing sitting here by his lonesome self in the middle of the day, here in their town? Jews would not have a bar of us Samaritans. She looked contemptuously at Yeshua, ignored him, and went on with her business.

Yeshua then spoke to the woman, "Lady, please give me a drink."

The woman was startled. He is a man, a Jew at that and he talks to me, a Samaritan and a woman, she thought. She said to him, "How is it that you, a Jew, ask a drink of me, a woman of Samaria?"

Yeshua answered her, "If you knew the gift of God, and who it is that is saying to you, 'Give me a drink,' you would have asked him, and he would have given you living water."

"Humph!" the woman sneered and with a smirk, she said, "Sir, you have no bucket, and the well is deep. Where do you get that living water? Are you greater than our ancestor Jacob, who gave us this well, and with his sons, and his flocks, drank from it?"

Yeshua then said to her, "Everyone who drinks of this water will be thirsty again, but those who drink from the water that I will give them will never be thirsty. The water that I will give will become in them a spring of water gushing up to eternal life."

The woman was now somewhat intrigued by this stranger, who seems to speak in riddles, but like a preacher, talking about eternal life. So, she says to him, with a hint of sarcasm, "Sir, give me this water, so that I may never be thirsty or to keep coming here to draw water."

Yeshua then said to her, "Go, call your husband and come back."

The woman was taken by surprise. She answered Yeshua, "I have no husband."

Yeshua said to her, "You are right in saying, 'I have no husband;' for you have had five husbands, and the one you have now is not your husband. What you have said is true!"

The woman was taken aback. She thought to herself, how can this man, this stranger, know all this about me? We have never met. Then she said, "Sir I see that you are a prophet. Our ancestors worshipped on this mountain, but you Jews say that the place where people must worship is in Jerusalem."

Yeshua said to her, "Woman, believe me, the hour is coming when you will worship the Father neither on this mountain nor in Jerusalem. You worship what you do not know; we worship what we know, for salvation is from the Jews. But the hour is coming, and is now here, when the true worshippers will worship the Father in spirit and truth, for the Father seeks such as these to worship him. God is spirit, and those who worship him must worship in spirit and truth."

The woman now lost all her sneering and was beguiled by this stranger, this Jew, who knew all these private things about her, and who spoke like a prophet. She then said to Yeshua, "I know the Messiah is coming. When he comes, he will proclaim all things to us."

Yeshua's heart went out to this woman. And he then said, what he had not said to anyone before, he now said to her, "I am he, the one who is speaking to you."

Just then the disciples returned with some food for Yeshua. They were just in time to hear what Yeshua was saying, 'I am he, the one who is speaking to you,' but had no clue of what it meant. And they were surprised that he was speaking with a woman, a Samaritan at that. But on second thoughts, they were not really surprised because Yeshua spoke to women all the time; it was just that he was all alone, and with this Samaritan woman, in this lonely spot.

In the meantime, the woman was so overcome at what Yeshua had known about her but most of all what he had said, what he had claimed to be, the Messiah. She was so excited that she forgot all about her water jar and ran back into the town.

She spoke to the people in the marketplace about her encounter with Yeshua. She told them how he knew everything about her. The people knew that Photine would not lie about such matters. She said to them, "he is a Jew, he is not from here, yet he knows all about my life, everything I have ever done. When I told him that we are waiting for the Messiah, he told me that he is the Messiah. Come and see for yourselves. He cannot be the Messiah, can he?" she said.

While this was going on between the Samaritan woman and the townspeople, the disciples brought food for Yeshua and urged him to eat. But he said to them, "I have food to eat that you do not know about."

The disciples thought that maybe the woman or someone else had given Yeshua something to eat.

But Yeshua said to them, "My food is to do the will of him who sent me and to complete his work. Four months more then comes the harvest. But I tell you, look around you, and see how the fields are ripe for harvesting."

Yeshua then said to them, once again, "The harvest is plentiful, but the labourers are few; therefore, ask the Lord of the harvest to send labourers into his harvest."

While Yeshua was speaking, a crowd came from the town with Photine, who pointed out Yeshua to them. One of them, their spokesman, said, "Sir, Photine, has told us all that has transpired between you and her and your claim to be the Messiah."

When the disciples heard this, they were astonished. Yeshua, for reasons of his own, had never before publicly and explicitly claimed to be the Messiah, and here he has publicly said this to this woman, who must be some sort of woman not in good standing, to have gone to draw water by herself, in the middle of the day, and in the heat of the day, outside of the town. They would later learn the truth about her.

"Do tell us more about yourself and what it is you wish to say to us," their spokesman said.

Yeshua then said, "My name is Yeshua, I am of the line of David, and I am from Nazareth but I was born in Bethlehem."

"In Bethlehem?" the spokesman said, with obvious excitement. "Why it is written by our prophet that the Messiah would be born in Bethlehem and that the Messiah would be a shepherd king who would rule over all peoples."

"Yeshua will you not stay with us, and tell us more?" the spokesman pleaded, and all the people agreed.

Yeshua and the disciples stayed in their town for two more days and many came to believe in Yeshua and what he had to say. The people also met with Peter and all the disciples, and the women met with Miriam and the other women disciples. They all accepted the Good News Yeshua and the disciples brought them. When Yeshua was ready to leave, all of the townspeople gathered in the town square, to farewell Yeshua and his disciples. They gave offerings of money and gifts and food for their journey. Yeshua thanked them. Peter and Miriam also spoke and thanked them on behalf of all the disciples.

Yeshua and his disciples then made their way to Capernaum. They crossed over from Samaria into Galilee at Nain, but did not dwell there; they had arrived under cover of darkness and carried on well out of the town before resting for the night. When they eventually arrived at Capernaum, after a night and a full day's rest, Yeshua called together all of his disciples.

Chapter Seventy-Three
What Lies Ahead?

Yeshua led all nineteen disciples with him, into a lonely place in the woods. It was early in the day, after all had something to eat. Yeshua had said he had something important to tell them. The disciples were anxious, it sounded ominous.

When they came to an open spot, Yeshua spoke to them. "My dearest, brothers and sisters, my friends, you have been with me now for more than two years. You have left everything to follow me; your reward will be great in heaven. I will not be with you much longer. So, you will now journey all over the land with me, and re-visit every place we have been before, to confirm the people in their faith. We will visit every city, town, and village where we have been. We will begin by going north, stay at Chorazin, then cross the Jordan River, head for Caesarea Philippi one more time, then return to Bethsaida and circumnavigate the Sea of Galilee, returning to Capernaum and then head west and visit every place in Galilee, Magdala, Tiberias, Cana, Nazareth, of course, then on to Nain, from there we will cross into Samaria, visit our friends in Sychar, then on to Arimathea, Ephraim, Jericho, and all of Judaea; Emmaus, Bethany, and Bethlehem and of course, we will spend time in Jerusalem. It will be our third visit to Jerusalem, but this time it will not be during the Passover. We will then cross over into Perea, and visit Gedara, travel all along the eastern bank of the River Jordan, through Decapolis, onto Gergesa, and end up at Bethsaida, before crossing over the Sea of Galilee and back to Capernaum, where we will rest."

"Yeshua, this will be an exhausting year for us all, are you sure you want to cover all that territory?" Peter said.

"Yes, Peter, my time has come; soon I will be handed over to the authorities, and they will seek to annihilate me. They will succeed, they will take my life from me, but on the third day, I will rise again."

The disciples were shocked. What Yeshua was saying perplexed them. But he had said something like this before. Was he now predicting his death? And what is he saying that on the third day he will rise again? Is he speaking figuratively, or is this some kind of riddle of his, some statement with a hidden meaning? They could not, would not accept literally, what Yeshua was saying.

Thomas spoke up, articulating the thoughts of the others, "What are you saying Yeshua, I do not understand."

"You do not understand, but all will be made clear. The Son of God, made man, is destined to suffer and give his life for many. The power of evil will seem to have triumphed, but when I am raised up, I will raise up all of humanity with me."

"Yeshua, we will follow you, no matter what," Johanan said.

"We too will follow you, Yeshua," Miriam said.

"So, you will, Johanan, and you Miriam, but most of you will flee and abandon me, in my darkest hour."

"Lord, I will never abandon you," Peter said, vehemently.

"Peter, dear Peter, I said this before, before the cock crows you will deny me three times"

Peter was outraged, "Never Lord, never! I will never deny you," Peter said adamantly.

"We will stand by you, Lord, no matter what," James added.

"James, you all will also abandon me, but I will never abandon you, and my Spirit will come to you, and bring you back to me, and you will be my apostles, you will spread my word all over the earth," Yeshua said.

"We will go with you Lord, we are ready," Peter said.

And so began the third year of Yeshua's ministry. The disciples sensed it could be their final year as disciples of Yeshua. It seemed different somehow, more intense and yet more peaceful, it seemed everywhere Yeshua went he was saying goodbye, not really telling the people that they would not see him again, but it seemed that was what he was hinting.

The time was passing quickly and Yeshua seemed relentless, as they moved from town to town. People were so excited to see Yeshua again, and they did not want him to leave. But Yeshua spoke to them of dark days ahead but that they needed to remain strong and trust in Yahweh. He had come to bring them out of the darkness and into the light.

"Do not fear the powers of darkness. I am the light of the world, trust in me, and I will bring you out of the darkness. Even when I am no longer with you, in the flesh, I will be always with you in Spirit; I will never leave you, and where I am you too will be."

They had visited all those places Yeshua had mentioned and they were now heading further south and arrived at Nain, where Yeshua visited the widow and her son, whom he had raised from the dead. They were so happy to see Yeshua, and they did not want him to leave, as did the people of Nain, but Yeshua said he had to go, there were others who needed to hear the Good News and to be confirmed in their faith. "Love one another, as I love you," was Yeshua's parting words.

After leaving Nain instead of continuing south, Yeshua led his disciples west towards the River Jordan and then set up camp at the foot of Mount Tabor.

Once they reached the foot of Mount Tabor, there was much level ground, so they set up camp. Yeshua then asked them to sit down.

Yeshua spoke to them; this time more explicitly than he had done when they were about to leave Capernaum. He said, "The Son of Man, the Son of God made man, must undergo great suffering, and be rejected by the Elders, the chief priests, and Scribes, the Teachers of the Law, and be killed, and on the third day be raised."

They heard similar words in Sychar, but there was a gasp among his disciples. They could not believe what they were hearing. They heard it before but would not, could not process what he was saying. They knew of the dangers Yeshua faced, but they all knew of his powers. Often before when his enemies wished to do him harm, he simply disappeared from their sight.

Judas especially was taken aback by Yeshua's words about being killed. He expected Yeshua to use his powers and triumph over his enemies. Judas could not, would not accept what Yeshua was saying.

Yeshua was aware of what they were thinking, so he continued, and repeated his words, wanting it to enter their psyche, he said, "If any want to become my followers, let them deny themselves, and take up their cross daily, and follow me. For those who want to save their life will lose it, and those who lose their life for my sake will save it."

Yeshua had spoken like this before, but now it struck home more deeply, and the disciples listened with their hearts racing.

Yeshua continued, to repeat, what was important for them to hear again and to take to heart, he said, "What does it profit you if you gain the whole world, but lose or forfeit yourselves? Those who are ashamed of me and of my words, of them the Son of God, made man will be ashamed when he comes in his glory, and the glory of the Father, and of the holy angels. But truly I tell you, there are some standing here who will not taste death before they see the kingdom of God."

Yeshua then left Andreus and Miriam in charge. Yeshua knew there was much they would wish to discuss. But Yeshua called Peter, James and his brother Johanan and asked them to accompany him up the mountain, Mount Tabor, to pray.

After a while of climbing the steep mountainside, they came to some level ground, and Yeshua stopped to rest. He told the three disciples to remain where they were and rest, while he went a bit further on and began to pray.

The disciples were resting but were watching Yeshua. All of a sudden, a change was happening to Yeshua. He was being transfigured before their eyes. His face now shone like the sun, and his clothes became dazzling white. Suddenly there appeared two men, who looked like prophets of old, and they were talking with him.

"Who are those men, talking with the Lord," Peter asked.

"From what they seem to be saying, I think one could be Moses, and the other Elijah," Johanan.

"Moses and Elijah, really!" Peter said to Johanan.

"Remember Moses on Mount Sinai, when God spoke to him from the burning bush and gave him the Ten Commandments and Moses' face was so radiant, people could not gaze at him? Peter, Johanan, I think we are having a similar moment, a similar experience. I can barely gaze at Yeshua's face, it is so dazzling," James said.

Suddenly and impetuously, Peter approached, and as soon as he was near enough for Yeshua to hear, Peter blurted out, "Lord it is good for us to be here; if you wish, I will make three dwellings here, one for you, one for Moses, and one for Elijah."

While Peter was still speaking, suddenly a bright cloud overshadowed them, and from the cloud a voice was heard, saying, "This is my Son, the Beloved, with him I am well pleased. Listen to him!"

When Peter and James and Johanan heard this, they fell to the ground, and were bent over, with their heads almost touching the ground, overcome by fear.

But Yeshua came and touched them, saying, "Get up and do not be afraid."

And when they looked up, they saw no one, except Yeshua himself, alone.

"Come let us go back down the mountain," Yeshua said.

As they were coming down the mountain, Yeshua ordered them, "Tell no one about the vision until after the Son of Man, the Son of God made man, has been raised from the dead."

Peter, was bamboozled. He asked Yeshua, "Master, Why then do the Scribes say that Elijah must come first?"

Yeshua replied, "Elijah is indeed coming, and will restore all things, but I tell you that Elijah has already come, and they did not recognise him, but they did to him, whatever they pleased. So also, the Son of Man, the Son of God made man, is about to suffer at their hands."

Yeshua then walked ahead of them, as they began their climb down to the foot of the mountain.

"What did Yeshua mean, about Elijah having already come, and us not recognising him?" Peter asked James and Johanan.

"I think, Yeshua was speaking about Johanan, the baptiser," Johanan said.

Peter and James accepted what Johanan said to them. They then climbed down in silence, still enraptured by what they had seen and experienced. Then before they reached the base camp, Johanan said to Peter and James, "You know the voice that said, 'this is my beloved Son, and with him I am well pleased. Listen to him,' is exactly what I was told was what was said by a voice from heaven, when Yeshua was being baptised by Johanan in the River Jordan." Peter and James heard what Johanan was saying but they were in a daze, unable to process what had happened on the mountain.

Yeshua and the disciples camped for the day, at the foot of Mount Tabor and then found a more protected place in a cave and slept for the night. In the morning, they were on their way and continued their journey. They traversed all of Samaria, stopping again at Sychar. The Samaritans were overjoyed and would not let Yeshua leave.

Yeshua was pleased to meet with Photine, who had become quite a celebrity in the town. When they eventually managed to leave Sychar, Yeshua said to his disciples. "Did you see what Photine is accomplishing in Sychar? She is doing what we are doing, she is spreading the Good News and leading and inspiring the people, confirming all we have taught. So, we have to let the seventy-two go out from Jerusalem and spread the Good News to all." Of the hundreds of followers of Yeshua, they had picked and gave further teaching and instruction to the seventy-two, who with the nineteen would have to carry on what Yeshua had started. Yeshua said again, "And when I am no longer with you, you will have to carry on what I have started."

Yeshua and his disciples finally arrived at Jerusalem. As it was not the Passover, there was a different feel to the city. It was more relaxed and not so crowded and boisterous as it is during the time of the Passover, when the city could expand more than fourfold. Yeshua caught up with the disciples in Jerusalem and with the seventy-two and spent more time with them, fortifying them in the faith, and encouraging them to continue their work of spreading the Good News.

The disciples stayed a week in Jerusalem, and Yeshua rarely spoke in the Temple, which was not so crowded. The enemies of Yeshua also seemed to be taking a hiatus, for they did not bother much with Yeshua at this time.

At the beginning of their stay in Jerusalem, Yeshua got Peter, Andreus, and Judas to convene a meeting with the seventy-two disciples. And Miriam and the women disciples from Jerusalem were also involved as there were also women disciples among the seventy-two. Yeshua spoke to them and anointed them, and sent them out to all the places he was still to visit.

Chapter Seventy-Four
Yeshua Celebrates Thirty-Three Years

Yeshua and his disciples had spent another year on the road; they were now back, at Capernaum. Yeshua was exhausted, as were his disciples. Judas, and the women from Jerusalem had remained in Jerusalem, this time, for Yeshua had told them he would return soon, for the Passover, which was only a few months away.

That evening, at a dinner provided by Elijah, especially for Yeshua, who was celebrating his thirty-third birthday, Yeshua spoke to his disciples, in a very solemn manner. "My dearest friends, I cherish your good wishes, and your friendship and companionship, and your love. This is it; my time is come. You have been with me for three years now. And we have traversed these lands for so long, and so many times, spreading the Good News and healing the sick. You have helped me to bring the people out of the darkness. But now dark clouds are gathering for me and for you. Together, we had been to Jerusalem, three times, we will go there one more time, for the Passover celebrations. So, I want you to go home now. Spend some quality time with your families and loved ones, and we will meet here in Capernaum, in two weeks from today, when we will head for Jerusalem, one more time."

The disciples were perplexed. Was Yeshua disbanding the group? Is this the end? Is he now going it alone?

Yeshua knew what they were thinking, so he put them at ease. "Do not be afraid, I will never leave you, and you will never leave me. You are stuck with me, whether you like it or not," Yeshua said, laughing. And they all laughed with him.

And there was much laughing for the rest of the evening, as they indulged in good food, excellent wine and each other's company, and they were relishing some time for being with their families and friends and engaging in their pastimes.

The next day everyone went their own way. Yeshua and Rebecca again had the joy of travelling together from Magdala, where they parted ways with Miriam. It was so good to be back in Nazareth for two whole weeks.

The two weeks passed so quickly and the disciples all gathered again at Capernaum. Everyone was looking so refreshed and so glad to be back again, with Yeshua. Yeshua too was looking good and re-energised and ready to go. The disciples forgot all about the ominous words Yeshua had spoken a few weeks ago, when they were last together.

Yeshua's main objective was to be in Jerusalem for the Passover. So, they remained in Capernaum for a week, and Yeshua continued his ministry of spreading the Good News and visiting the poor and sick, and confirming everyone in the faith. He continued to preach and teach in the synagogues, at the seashore, in open places, wherever people came to seek him out. And he continued to heal their sick. And then the time came to head for Jerusalem, for the Passover.

After a couple of days in Jerusalem, Yeshua went to visit his friends in Bethany, Miriam, Martha and Lazarus. This time Lazarus was home and Yeshua noticed that he wasn't looking as healthy as before, he was looking gaunt. After a while, Lazarus excused himself.

"Lazarus is not looking well," Yeshua said.

"Yes, Yeshua, we are worried. When he returned from his travels a week ago, he started losing his appetite. And he has to rest a lot. We are giving him all the medicine the doctors have prescribed, and giving him lots of honey, and lemon, and plenty of rest. We hope he gets better soon," Martha said.

"Miriam and Rebecca are on their way, they were keen to meet you both," Yeshua said.

"Will they be staying here for the night, with you?" Martha asked.

"No Martha, not this time, we have to move on," Yeshua said.

"Then at least stay for dinner. I will just go to the markets quickly and get some vegetables and then prepare for dinner," Martha said, and then rushed off.

Miriam however remained with Yeshua, and sat listening to him speak of all their travels and all that happened to him and his disciples.

"Miriam, my time is coming; I will not be around much longer."

Miriam was a bit sad, to hear Yeshua speak so. But she listened and Yeshua shared so much with her, and spoke of the sadness he felt about what was to happen with him, and also how afraid he was of what lay ahead.

"Do pray for me, Miriam that I remain strong, that I do not lose faith, for I fear the worst will happen to me. I will be cut down and killed but on the third day I will rise again."

Miriam was shocked; she could not believe what she was hearing. She was sickened by what Yeshua was telling her. Yeshua seemed so vulnerable. She went across to him, where he was seated on his favourite chair, and knelt before him and kissed his hands. "Yeshua, I will pray for you every day. You will not falter. I know the Father is with you, and will give you the strength for whatever lies ahead." She then kissed Yeshua's hands.

Yeshua placed his hands on Miriam's head. "Thank you, Miriam, I am so grateful for your friendship, and your love and your prayers, they sustain me."

Just then Martha arrived with her arms full of parcels of vegetables to go with the roast lamb that she immediately went about preparing to roast for dinner. Miriam continued to sit with Yeshua; she felt Yeshua needed her company.

Martha started the fire at the back of the house, from the embers, and then spiced up the lamb with all sorts of herbs, and put it on the spit above the flames. She then came to prepare the vegetables to cook. While she was doing this, she was also cleaning up the house and preparing beds, just in case Yeshua and Miriam and Rebecca did all sleep over, even if Yeshua did say they were not going to sleep over. And she tidied up the house to make it look better and during all this she also set up the table for herself, her sister Miriam and her brother Lazarus, and Yeshua, and his two disciples Miriam and Rebecca.

Martha was getting a bit flustered with all the running around, and looking at her sister Miriam sitting at Yeshua's feet and listening to him, and conversing with him, she got annoyed and a bit envious too, she also would love to do what Miriam was doing, sitting with Yeshua, and listening to him, but they had more guests coming, and she was preparing the house and a meal for six of them, with the three guests, surely Miriam could see how busy she is, and give her a hand. So, Martha approached them and she addressed Yeshua, "Lord, do you not care, that my sister has left me to do all the work by myself?"

Yeshua looked at Martha, with great love, but instead of acquiescing to Martha's request for Miriam to help her, Yeshua could see how much Miriam was engrossed in his company and just how much she loved him and loved all he had to say and was hanging onto his every word and Yeshua also knew how much Martha loved him, and how kind and caring and loving she is to her brother and to all she comes into contact with, and just how busy she was, but he wanted to teach her more, so he said to her, with great love and compassion in his heart, "Martha, Martha, you are worried and distracted by many things; there is need of only one thing. Miriam has chosen the better part, which will not be taken away from her."

Martha was taken aback. She was hurt that the Lord would not come to her aid. She felt resentful and bitter towards her sister. Yeshua could see the pain his words caused Martha and he thought it was time to put her out of her misery, so he said to Miriam. "Okay, Miriam, it is time for us to help your sister." He lifted Miriam to her feet and approached Martha and spoke, "Martha, Martha, you are so efficient and we have taken you for granted. Here we are, how can we help, how can we make it up to you," Yeshua said with a smile.

"Sorry sister, I got so involved with all that Yeshua was saying to me, it was remiss of me not to have given you a hand, do forgive me."

Martha smiled, "Okay you two lovebirds, here place these plates and cups on the table. And then go and attend to the roast outside, make sure it doesn't burn and go up in flames. And Miriam you can prepare a salad," Martha said.

About an hour later, Miriam of Magdala and Rebecca arrived. Martha and Miriam had tidied themselves, and had a wash and were ready for their guests. They had also woken Lazarus, who was now feeling a bit better after his rest. Martha, Miriam and Lazarus were so pleased to welcome Miriam and Rebecca.

They all sat down to a lavish roast dinner, with cups of wine. The conversation flowed so freely. These six people were so in tune with each other, and they were five of the dearest friends of Yeshua. He loved them and held them so close to his heart, and whenever he was in Jerusalem, he always tried his best to spend time with them. His heart ached now though, because he knew he would not be with them much longer, and that they would suffer at his absence. But on this night, with these dearests of friends, Yeshua wanted to put all of that out of his mind, and enjoy this feast but above all, their company.

Martha was glad she had the foresight to prepare enough beds and bedding for Yeshua, Miriam and Rebecca, because they chatted late into the night, without realising just how much time had passed. It must have been well past midnight and they were still chatting.

"It is too late for you to go to Jerusalem, now, Yeshua, especially with Miriam and Rebecca, it is not safe so much after dark, you must stay her for tonight," Lazarus insisted.

"You're right, Lazarus. I didn't realise just how much time was passing. We gladly take up your offer." They continued talking for another couple of hours, even while they all helped to clean up, they continued their conversations. It must have been three hours after midnight when they all retired. Yeshua could not remember when last he had such a good time and enjoyed so much conversation, and neither did the rest of them.

After a week in Jerusalem, the seventy-two returned, as was prearranged, and they met again with Yeshua and his troupe of close disciples. The seventy-two returned with great joy. They were all bubbling over, and their leader, a man named Matthias, spoke on their behalf, "Lord, when we spoke to the people and told them we came in your name, they would listen. We told them that you were soon to visit. And Lord, in your name, even the demons submit to us!"

Yeshua was pleased and spoke to them. "Praise the Lord Almighty." He then continued, "I watched Satan fall from heaven like a flash of lightening. See I have given you authority to tread on snakes and scorpions, and over all the power of the enemy, and nothing will hurt you, but rejoice that your names are written in heaven."

"Lord, there were some places, where we were rejected, and they would not make us welcome," Matthias said.

"Expect that, and do not be disheartened. But whenever you enter a town and they do not welcome you, go out into its streets and say, 'Even the dust of your town that clings to our feet, we wipe off in protest against you. Yet know this; the Kingdom of God has come near you.' Yeshua added, I tell you, on that day it will be more tolerable for Sodom than for that town."

Yeshua continued speaking to the seventy-two and his nineteen closest disciples, confirming and affirming them, and strengthening their faith and their resolve. He said to them, "Whoever listens to you, listens to me, and whoever rejects you, rejects me, and whoever rejects me, rejects the one who sent me." Then looking up to heaven, Yeshua prayed, "I thank you Father, Lord of heaven and earth, because you have hidden these things from the wise and the intelligent and have revealed them to infants; yes Father, for such was your gracious will."

Yeshua then looked at all of them present and said, "All things have been handed over to me by my Father, and no one knows who the Son is, except the Father, or who the Father is, except the Son, and anyone to whom the Son chooses to reveal him."

Yeshua then dismissed the seventy-two. And when they had left, he said to the nineteen, "Blessed are you! Blessed are the eyes that see what you see! For I tell you that many prophets and kings desired to see what you see, but did not see it, and to hear what you hear, but did not hear it."

The Passover was still a couple of weeks away so Yeshua and the nineteen disciples left Jerusalem and headed east.

Chapter Seventy-Five
Lazarus, Come Forth!

Yeshua and his disciples were not gone long, and barely out of the city, when two messengers came running to them, out of breath, they wanted to speak to Yeshua.

"What is it you want?" Peter asked them.

"We have a message for Yeshua, from the sisters, Martha and Miriam from Bethany."

When Peter and the others heard this, they immediately urged Peter to speak with Yeshua, who was walking ahead of them.

When the men came to Yeshua they said, "Lord, Martha and Miriam have sent us. They ask you to come, for Lazarus has taken a turn for the worse. He is gravely ill and they are asking for you to come to him," one of the men said.

"Thank you, for your message," was all that Yeshua said, and it didn't seem like he was greatly concerned, as he then sent the two messengers on their way, and didn't seem to be turning around and heading for Bethany. The messengers were perplexed, but they had delivered the message, and that was all they could do.

The disciples too were mystified, because they knew just how much Yeshua loved Martha and Miriam and their brother Lazarus. And they expected Yeshua to immediately dash off back to Bethany.

Yeshua knowing their confusion, said to them, "This illness of Lazarus' does not lead to death, rather it is for God's glory, so that the Son of God may be glorified through it."

And although Yeshua loved Lazarus and his sisters, he spent two more days on the road, stopping at villages along the way.

After the two days, Yeshua suddenly stopped in his tracks on the road, and said to his disciples. "Let us go to Jerusalem again."

The disciples were puzzled. Why return to Jerusalem? He had finished all he wanted to say and do there, and had said his goodbyes to his disciples, and said they would only see him again at the Passover. And the Pharisees, Scribes, Sadducees and Elders, were just beginning to mobilise against Yeshua for they got word about Yeshua forming a band of seventy-two, men and women, and giving them authority to do his work, of undermining the faith of the people.

Peter then spoke for all, "Lord, the religious leaders were just beginning to mobilise against you, and we got out of Jerusalem just in time. We heard rumours that they were out to stone you."

Yeshua seemed completely dismissive of Peter's warning, he said, "Are there not twelve hours of daylight? Those who walk during the day do not stumble, because they see the light of this world. But those who walk at night stumble, because the light is not in them."

Seeing the concern on the faces of his disciples, Yeshua said, "Our friend Lazarus has fallen asleep, but I am going there to awaken him."

The disciples were somewhat puzzled and Peter spoke what they were all thinking, "Lord, if Lazarus has fallen asleep, he will be alright."

As they clearly misunderstood Yeshua, he said it bluntly, "Lazarus is dead. For your sake, I am glad I was not there, so that you may believe. But let us go to him."

Thomas said to his fellow disciples, "Let us also go, that we may die with him."

By the time Yeshua and his disciples neared the town of Bethany Lazarus, had already been in the tomb for four days. And many had come from all over to console Martha and Miriam.

When Martha heard that Yeshua and his disciples were coming and that he was nearby, she rushed to meet him. Miriam on the other hand, stayed at home, buried in her grief. When Martha met up with Yeshua, she said to him, "Lord, if you had been here, my brother would not have died. But even now I know that God will give you whatever you ask him."

The disciples were astounded by Martha's words. Some of them had witnessed Yeshua's power, even over death. He had raised three other people from the dead, over the time they had been with him; the Centurion's servant, Jairus' daughter, and the son of the widow at Nain. Would he now also do the same for Lazarus? But this was different, Lazarus was dead and buried for four days now.

Yeshua then said to Martha, "Martha, your brother will rise again."

Martha responded, "Lord, I know that he will rise again in the resurrection on the last day."

Yeshua then said to her, "I am the resurrection and the life. Those who believe in me, even though they die, will live, and everyone who lives and believes in me, will never die. Do you believe this?"

Martha replied, "Yes, Lord, I believe that you are the Messiah, the Son of God, and the one coming into the world."

The disciples were boosted in their belief about Yeshua; he has now more frequently accepted others acknowledging him as the Messiah. Peter, James and Johanan especially, they recalled how Yeshua was transfigured in the presence of Moses and Elijah, and they heard the voice of God. But Yeshua had told them to say nothing until he had been raised from the dead. But now will he be raising Lazarus from the dead, after four days?

In the meantime, Martha dashed off, and ran home, to tell her sister. She took Miriam aside and said to her, "Miriam, Yeshua is on his way. He is close by."

Immediately Miriam got up and ran out of the house. All those that were with Miriam, consoling her, saw her get up and run off. They too got up and followed Miriam because they thought she was going to the tomb to weep there.

When Miriam arrived where Yeshua was on the road, and as soon as she saw him, she knelt at his feet, and said to him, "Lord, if you had been here, my brother would not have died."

When Yeshua saw her weeping, and all those who came with her also weeping, he was greatly disturbed in spirit and deeply moved. He took hold of Miriam's hands and raised her to her feet and he said, "Where have you laid him?"

Miriam said, "Lord, come and see."

Immediately Yeshua began to weep. Yeshua stopped in his tracks, he could not move, as grief got the better of him. His hands went up to his face and his fingers were buried in his moist eyes, and then he wiped away the tears from his eyes with the tips of his fingers.

All those that were there with Miriam were amazed, and several of them said, "See, how he loved him!"

Yeshua then put his arms around Miriam. This was not proper custom for a man to do, unless he was a close relative, even in these circumstances. But they all knew how close Miriam, Martha and Lazarus were to Yeshua. Whenever he came to Jerusalem, he would not fail to visit them, and stay with them, and they were like close family.

But one among the mourners verbalised the thoughts of many, by saying, "Could not he, who opened the eyes of the blind man, have kept this man from dying?"

Eventually Yeshua and the crowd arrived at the tomb. Yeshua was again greatly disturbed, as he saw the tomb. It was a cave, and a stone was lying against it. Yeshua said, "Take away the stone."

Martha was immediately alert and solicitous of Yeshua's well-being and said to Yeshua. "Lord, already there will be a stench because he has been dead for four days."

Yeshua said to her most gently, "Martha, did I not tell you, that if you believed, you would see the glory of God?"

The men present began to roll away the stone. All present were in awe. They stood like statues, not knowing what to expect. Yet they were expectant of something, what, they did not know. His disciples who had witnessed him raise people from the dead before wondered if he would do so again. Would he raise Lazarus from the dead, he who has been in this grave for four whole days?

Yeshua looked upwards and said, "Father, I thank you for having heard me; I knew that you always hear me, but I have said this for the sake of the crowd standing here, so that they may believe that you sent me." Then Yeshua cried out with a loud voice, "Lazarus, come out!"

The dead man came out; Lazarus came out, his hands and feet bound with strips of cloth, and his face wrapped in a cloth.

Martha and Miriam were in shock, as were the disciples and the people witnessing what was happening. They could not believe what was unfolding before their very eyes. Never before had they ever witnessed anything like this. For some it sent a shiver up their spines, for others the hair at the back of their head stood up. Some were so astounded that they fell on their knees. Others were stupefied, their mouths wide open and their hands covering their gasps.

Yeshua, as calmly as ever, said to them, "Unbind him, and let him go."

The disciples began to unbind Lazarus. When Lazarus' face became visible, he looked at the crowd of people staring at him, in puzzlement. Why were they staring at him so? Then he saw Martha and Miriam, and there were tears streaming down their cheeks. "Martha, Miriam, why are you crying?" he asked, as he went to them and threw his arms around them.

The rest of the crowed were dumbfounded. They could not stop staring at Lazarus. Martha and Miriam held their brother tightly. Then Lazarus saw Yeshua, and he gently released his sisters, and went to Yeshua. "Yeshua, what is going on, why am I here, in front of this tomb?"

The disciples and the other people were still thunderstruck, looking on, staring at Lazarus. And now they were waiting to hear what Yeshua would say to Lazarus.

Yeshua spoke, "Lazarus, you have fallen asleep. But now you are awake."

Lazarus replied, "Yes, but it is a sleep like I have never had before. It was so deep and so peaceful. I saw this deep light and kept being carried, as if by angels into this light, and then I heard your voice, and I woke," Lazarus said.

"Lazarus, you have died. But now you have come back to life. Come let us go home, you must be hungry," Yeshua said.

"What are you saying Yeshua. I have died? Of course, this is a tomb. No wonder, I felt like I was in such a peaceful state. How long have I been in the tomb?" Lazarus asked.

"Four days, Lazarus," Martha said.

"Four days! No wonder I feel so hungry," Lazarus said. And the whole crowd laughed. Lazarus's laughter and that of those present broke the ice, and brought them back to earth.

They walked, some chatting and reliving the experience, others in silence, others gawking at Lazarus and at Yeshua. But some of them went to the Pharisees and told them what Yeshua had done.

With haste the Pharisees got together as many of the Council as they could, which was instigated by Caiaphas, the high priest. They met with only one item on the agenda, 'Yeshua of Nazareth.' There were forty members present, more than half of the full Council.

Caiaphas began the proceedings, "What are we to do? This man is performing many signs." Caiaphas could not bring himself to mention the raising of Lazarus from the dead.

One of those present said, "If we let him go on like this, everyone will believe in him, and the Romans will come and destroy both our holy place and our nation."

Caiaphas then spoke again, "You know nothing at all. You do not understand that it is better for you to have one man die for the people, than to have the whole nation destroyed." And so began the sinister plot to have Yeshua eliminated, to have him killed.

Now among those present at the Council meeting was Nicodemus, a Pharisee and his friend Yosef of Arimathea, they met afterwards by themselves. Nicodemus said, "Yosef, what do you think. God, man, this man, Yeshua, I have heard such incredible stories about him, and now this, raising Lazarus from the dead, surely, we need to meet with him and find out more about him. He must be a man of God, to do such things."

"Yes, we must meet with him. But we have to do it secretly, for there is danger afoot," Yosef said.

"Okay, I will meet with him. I will seek out his disciples, there are so many of them now, here in Jerusalem. And then I will get in touch with you, so we can see how to proceed from here," Nicodemus said.

Nicodemus made inquiries and found out where Yeshua was staying, so he went there at night time, and knocked on the door. Andreus came to the door. Nicodemus greeted him and gave his name, but did not mention that he was a member of the Council, he said, he wanted to speak with Yeshua.

Then a voice came from inside, it was Yeshua's, he said, "Andreus let him in."

Nicodemus came in, a bit apprehensive, but also excited to be meeting this man Yeshua at last. After exchanging greetings with Yeshua, Nicodemus asked if he could speak with Yeshua privately. Yeshua then led him into his private room. He got an extra chair for Nicodemus.

Yeshua could see that Nicodemus was a bit nervous, so Yeshua put him at ease. "Nicodemus, tell me about yourself, and what brings you here?" Yeshua asked.

Nicodemus was not too eager to reveal to Yeshua all about himself. Being a Pharisee and a member of the Sanhedrin, and knowing how critical Yeshua was of the Pharisees, he was reluctant to divulge his personal details, so he began by saying, "Rabbi, I am a teacher, we know that you are a teacher who has come from God; for no one can do these signs that you do apart from the presence of God"

Yeshua gazed at Nicodemus with affection. He then answered him, "Very truly, I tell you, no one can see the Kingdom of God, without being born from above."

Nicodemus did not quite grasp what Yeshua was saying, so he said, "How can anyone be born after having grown old? Can one enter a second time into the mother's womb and be born?"

Yeshua simply replied by saying, "Very truly, I tell you, no one can enter the Kingdom of God without being born of water and the Holy Spirit. What is born of the flesh is flesh, and what is born of the Spirit, is spirit," Yeshua continued. "Do not be astonished that I said to you, 'You must be born from above.' The wind blows where it chooses, and you hear the sound of it, but you do not know where it comes from or where it goes. So, it is with everyone who is born of the Spirit."

Nicodemus said to Yeshua, "How can this be?"

Yeshua answered him, "Are you a teacher of Israel, and yet you do not understand these things?" Yeshua continued, "No one has ascended into heaven except the One who has descended from heaven. And just as Moses lifted up the serpent in the wilderness, so must the Son of Man, that is the Son of God who took on the form of man, and representing all of humankind, so must this Son of Man be lifted up, so that whoever believes in him may have eternal life."

Yeshua could see that Nicodemus was eager to hear more. So, Yeshua continued, "For God so loved the world that he gave his only Son, so that everyone who believes in him may not perish but may have eternal life. Indeed, God did not send his Son into the world to condemn the world, but in order that the world might be saved through him. Those who believe in him are not condemned; but those who do not believe are condemned already, because they have not believed in the name of the only Son of God. And this is the judgement, that the light has come into the world, and people loved darkness, rather than light because their deeds are evil. For all who do evil hate the light and do not come to the light, so their deeds may not be exposed."

Nicodemus asked so many questions about Yeshua and how he came to the knowledge of the truth. Yeshua shared with him the circumstances of his birth and how his parents fled into Egypt to escape the wrath of Herod.

"So you were that child. I heard of those stories. They said the child that Herod sought was alive, like Moses, he was saved. So, you are like a new Moses to our people," Nicodemus said.

Nicodemus spoke of Johanan the baptiser with great sorrow and regret. "I should have spoken up, in defence of Johanan. He did nothing to deserve imprisonment. What he said about Herod was right; he was breaking the Law of God, given to us by Moses. We are the religious leaders, we should have supported Johanan and challenged Herod, instead, we remained silent and let Herod have his way. Yeshua there is much that I do not agree with what is happening with our people, and the way our faith is being governed. What you are teaching is a breath of fresh air. I want to learn more from you."

Yeshua could see the goodness of Nicodemus' heart, and so he spoke openly and at length all about what he had been teaching these past three years. He showed

Nicodemus how diametrically opposed the ways of God were to the ways that was been promulgated by the Pharisees, the Scribes, Sadducees, Elders and all of the religious leaders. He spoke of God's preference for the poor and the need for not seeking power, position, prestige, wealth, to be first, but instead to seek the opposite, poverty, the lowest place, and he told Nicodemus, "Learn of me, for I am gentle and humble of heart and you will find rest for your soul."

"I want to Yeshua, I want to, and I want to learn, all you have to teach," Nicodemus said.

Yeshua could see the hunger in Nicodemus eyes, and in his heart, and he continued to teach. They spoke for hours, without realising the time, in fact they spoke throughout the night, and only realised that the night had passed when the disciples awoke and disturbed them.

The disciples were astonished to see that Nicodemus was still with Yeshua. They did not inquire, and thought maybe he had left last night and had returned early this morning, for he did come under cover of darkness. Judas recognised him, and told the rest of the disciples his name and his position, he was a member of the Council, the Sanhedrin, and he was a Pharisee. The disciples were alarmed. Why would a member of the feared Sanhedrin come to Yeshua, and why would Yeshua speak with him?

The next night, Nicodemus was back, and this time he brought with him Yosef of Arimathea. They did not stay the night, but did stay many hours. There was so much they wanted to know.

The disciples did not disturb Yeshua and left him to spend the time with Nicodemus and Yosef.

Nicodemus and Yosef warned Yeshua. "Yeshua, the Council has met and they want you dead. It is not safe for you in Jerusalem. And Herod too is worried. He is going crazy. He has heard about you raising Lazarus from the dead, and he thinks that you are Johanan come back to life."

Both Nicodemus and Yosef came to believe in Yeshua, believe that he is the Anointed One, the true Messiah that they had been waiting for. And they now recognised what salvation and redemption was all about, and they believed that Yeshua was not a temporal king, who was gathering power and troops to lead a rebellion against Rome, but that his Kingdom is a Kingdom of Love, Peace. Joy, Justice, Mercy, Compassion, Forgiveness and Hope for all.

When Nicodemus and Yosef left, the disciples were curious and wanted to know what they wanted. Judas had informed the disciples that Nicodemus and Yosef were members of the Council.

Yeshua told the disciples that the Council is plotting to kill him. The disciples were alarmed. "Yeshua, you have to leave Jerusalem immediately!" Peter said. All the others agreed.

"Maybe, you are right. Let us leave for now. We can return when the Passover begins," Yeshua said.

"Yeshua is right. The Council won't dare touch Yeshua, with more than a million people in Jerusalem, for fear of a riot," Judas said. Judas did not want Yeshua to leave Jerusalem altogether, he too had his own plans. He wanted to get things on the move, and Yeshua to play his hand, use his power against the might of Rome. Judas was hoping in some way to precipitate this confrontation, and for Yeshua to show his might and triumph over Rome.

Chapter Seventy-Six
The Anointing

Yeshua and his disciples were just about to leave Jerusalem, when there was a loud knock on the front door and everyone jumped. They were all on edge, and wondered who it could be. A smallish man, burnt brown from overexposure to the sun, stood there, and asked for Yeshua.

"I come from my master, Shimon, an important man in Bethany. I have come to tell Yeshua and his disciples that my master wishes to honour them for what they did to Lazarus and the town, he invites you Sir and all your disciples, to a grand feast at his place. Will you come?" The servant pleaded.

Peter answered at once. "Tell your Master; Yeshua cannot accept the invitation, as he is leaving Jerusalem, today."

The servant was crestfallen, he did not want to disappoint his master, nor everyone else in the household, for they were all excited about having Yeshua for a guest, and Lazarus too. They were keen to just see what Lazarus looked like, now that he had died and come back to life. He pleaded with them, "Please, my Master is a good and generous man, he wants to honour Yeshua and Lazarus and the sisters Martha and Miriam, and others from the town will be there. Please come!"

But Peter would have none of it, and was about to force him to leave. The servant was about to leave, when Yeshua heard the servant's plea and when he mentioned that Martha and Miriam would be attending, he stopped Peter from sending him away.

Yeshua then addressed the servant, "Go, and tell Shimon, we gladly accept his invitation. It is very kind of him. Tell him we will be there at noon, six days before the Passover."

Peter was not too pleased. Neither were the others, except Judas. The messenger, pleased he had succeeded with the task, set by his master, hurried back to Bethany.

Yeshua and his disciples then left Jerusalem and headed north to the town of Ephraim in the region near the wilderness, and remained there until it was time to return to Jerusalem.

When they eventually left Ephraim, less than twenty miles from Jerusalem, they arrived in Jerusalem, at evening time, a week before the Passover. Jerusalem was pandemonium and Yeshua and his disciples were lost in the crowd. Peter and Andreus had decided that it would be better that they do not move around in Jerusalem as one, but break up into smaller groups, so as not to draw attention to themselves.

But people were looking for Yeshua. Word had spread about what he did at Bethany. And many people went there to have a look at Lazarus, so much so that Lazarus had to go into hiding.

The people went to the Temple hoping to find Yeshua there, and were disappointed that he was nowhere to be found. They were asking one another as they stood outside the Temple. "What do you think? Surely, he will not come to the festival, will he?" someone said. He had heard the word put out by the Pharisees and the Chief Priests, who had given orders that anyone who knew where Yeshua was, should inform them, so that they might arrest him.

In the meantime, Yeshua kept to himself with his disciples. But as the six days before the Passover were fast approaching and the crowds had swelled, Yeshua moved around more freely. He met with some of the seventy-two disciples and spoke with them, warning them of hard times ahead. Yeshua told them he would be going to Bethany for an engagement and then come to Jerusalem. He spoke of how saddened he was with what has been going on in the Temple during the Passover and the other great feasts during the year. He spoke to them and said, "I will be going to Bethany for an engagement, but then will come to Jerusalem. I want you all to meet me at the Temple; I want to send the traders and money-lenders on their way, to let them know that we will not tolerate them turning the house of God into a market place. I want your support, to make sure the traders are blocked from returning to the Temple."

Judas met with Shimon, who was formerly a Zealot, urging him to get in touch with his former Zealot friends as well, and get ready to be at the Temple when Yeshua goes there in the next days. Judas also met with his friends who were of a same mind as him, and told them that Yeshua was about to play his hand, use his powers to begin the destruction of Roman power. Judas was pleased. It seemed to him, that Yeshua was now mobilising his forces, and that he would somehow display his power in the Temple itself.

It was six days before the Passover, and as Yeshua had said, they all came to Bethany. Yeshua went first to visit Martha and Mary and Lazarus. He sent Peter and Andreus to Shimon's house to let him know they are in Bethany, and to find out when the feast will begin.

In the meantime, Yeshua spent time with Martha, Miriam and Lazarus. They were so pleased to see Yeshua. They too had heard about the danger that Yeshua was facing, and they pleaded with Yeshua not to return to Jerusalem. But Yeshua put them at ease and told them not to fear.

Peter and Andreus arrived sometime later at Martha and Miriam's place and told Yeshua that Shimon is putting on the dinner and that they are all expected an hour before sunset.

"Andreus, we will leave after the dinner and go straight to Jerusalem, to our usual lodgings, let everyone know," Yeshua said.

Martha and especially Miriam were alarmed to hear that Yeshua was going back to Jerusalem, because they knew his life was in danger.

The time came for the dinner. Shimon's palatial home was packed with important people from the town and of course many Pharisees. The Pharisees knew of how Yeshua had criticised them, but they also knew that he had many Pharisee friends and had dined with many of them. He still showed them respect. And here he was in the home of Shimon, a Pharisee. And they knew that he had already dined once before with another Pharisee, also named Shimon, right here in Jerusalem. And they also knew about Judas, one of his disciples, and he was a Pharisee.

Shimon's home was packed. Martha was busy serving, and Lazarus sat at the table with Yeshua and Shimon and some other important people from the town. The party was in full swing, when Miriam appeared, what seemed out of nowhere. Martha saw the bottle that Miriam had with her, and knew it contained a pound of costly perfume made of pure nard. Martha and all the guests were astonished to see

Miriam kneel down at Yeshua's feet. Everyone stopped talking and watched Miriam, wondering what was going on. Then they saw her open the top of a bottle. She then emptied the entire bottle of perfume, and anointed Yeshua's feet with the pure nard. The house was filled with the sweet aroma, with the fragrance of the perfume. Everyone was taking in deep breaths to inhale the beautiful aroma that filled the room.

Judas surprised everyone when he spoke, he said, "Why was this perfume not sold, it could fetch three hundred denarii, and the money could be given to the poor."

Johanan especially was shocked at Judas's attempt to debase what was unfolding. Johanan knew that Judas was saying this not because he cared about the poor, but because he was a thief. Johanan had seen how Judas, who kept the common purse, stole from it. He had spoken to Peter about it, but nothing was done. Peter had told him they could not confront Judas unless he was caught in the act by at least two of them.

Yeshua however confronted Judas and said, "Leave her alone. She anoints me in preparation for what lies ahead. She bought it so that she might keep it for the day of my burial. You always have the poor with you, but you do not always have me."

Judas remarks had put somewhat a damper on the celebration. But Shimon got out his musicians who played uplifting music and called on the stewards to serve more wine.

Word soon spread that Yeshua was in Bethany and visitors to Jerusalem flocked to Bethany, which was only a couple of miles away. They came not only because of Yeshua but also to see Lazarus, whom Yeshua had raised from the dead.

So, the chief priests planned to put Lazarus to death as well, because it was on account of him, that many of the Jews were deserting and believing in Yeshua.

The feast went on late into the night. Martha and Miriam convinced Yeshua to sleep over at their place. Yeshua accepted and all the disciples did the same, Shimon found places for all of them to spend the night.

Chapter Seventy-Seven
Yeshua Weeps Over Jerusalem

The next day as Yeshua and his disciples were walking towards Jerusalem, and arriving at Bethpage, near the Mount of Olives, Yeshua sent James and his brother Johanan and said to them, "Go into the village ahead of you, and immediately as you enter it, you will find there a colt that has never been ridden; untie it and bring it to me. If anyone says to you, 'Why are you doing this?' just say this, 'The Lord needs it, and will send it back here immediately'."

James and Johanan went on their way. "How strange, Yeshua's instructions. How does he know that there will be a colt tied up, as soon as we enter Bethpage? And how does he know that the colt has never been ridden?" James said.

"James, it's time that we just accept these things we can't explain. But then we know that Yeshua often spends time at the Mount of Olives by himself and on our way to Bethany he stopped at the village, didn't he?" Johanan said. "Maybe he had spoken to the owner of the colt, who knows," Johanan said, with a shrug of his shoulders.

When they arrived and entered the village, it was exactly as Yeshua had predicted, they found a colt tied near a door, outside in the street. As they were untying the colt, one of the bystanders looked at them in amazement and gruffly said, "What do you think you're doing, untying the colt?"

James spoke and told them what Yeshua had said, and then immediately everything went calm and they allowed James and Johanan to take the colt.

As they left, "Bizarre!" was all that James said, shaking his head.

Johanan responded to James, "You have just witnessed Yeshua raise Lazarus from the dead, four days after he was buried. And you exclaim after this little episode, 'Bizarre'? Really James!" Johanan said with a chuckle.

"Yep, I guess, you are putting things into perspective, Johanan. But Yeshua does surprise me with the bizarre at times. We were just discussing that not so long ago, remember."

"You have a point James, what was most bizarre for me was what Peter told us that when Yeshua got him to go and catch a fish, and telling him that the first fish he caught would have a coin in its mouth, and then Yeshua told Peter to pay the tax, with the coin," Johanan said.

"I remember when Peter came home, after going to pay the Temple tax, with the coin taken out of the mouth of a fish. Do you remember how we were all stifling our laughter, and even Yeshua, seemed to be having a problem hiding his amusement. Peter seemed so at a loss. He didn't want to put his foot in it again and embarrass himself so he did what Yeshua said. Really, Johanan, I thought Yeshua was pulling Peter's leg; I was stupefied to find out that Peter really got a coin to pay for the Temple tax out of the mouth of a fish. Wonders will never cease with Yeshua," James said with a grin.

As they walked along with the colt, they knew that Yeshua was going to ride on it. In all their travels, they had insisted that Yeshua ride a colt or a donkey, but Yeshua preferred to walk. He always said that the donkey would slow them down, and that there were many of them to share the load of the meagre stuff they carried with them.

But this time, for some unexplained reason, Yeshua said he was going to ride on the colt. The disciples could not believe their eyes, seeing Yeshua riding on a colt. It was a common enough form of transport; it is just they had never seen Yeshua on one. James and Johanan had put their cloaks over the colt for Yeshua to sit on.

As they were approaching Jerusalem, crowds that came to Jerusalem for the festival of the Passover heard that Yeshua was coming to the city, and was in fact on his way from Bethany. So, they went out to meet Yeshua. On the way they broke off branches from palm trees to use to wave at Yeshua on his approach.

"There he is!" A cry went out.

The crowds of people swooped on Yeshua, and surrounded him on the road. Yeshua was still sitting on the colt and it moved slowly, Yeshua didn't want to frighten the colt. Then the people did a strange thing, they removed their cloaks and spread them on the road, and others spread leafy palm branches that they had cut in the fields, across the road. Others with branches of palms were waving them as Yeshua was passing. Then some went in front of Yeshua and some followed in procession, and they were spontaneously crying out in a loud voice:

"Hosanna!
Blessed is the One who comes in the name of the Lord!
Blessed is the coming Kingdom of our ancestor, David!
Hosanna in the highest Heaven!"

When Yeshua and the boisterous entourage entered Jerusalem, the whole of the city was in turmoil. Everyone wanted to know what was going on. "Who is this man, that comes riding on a donkey, being revered as if he were a king?" someone in the crowd yelled. Another in the crowd yelled back, "This is the Prophet Yeshua from Nazareth in Galilee."

Another in the crowd amazed everyone by quoting one of the prophets and crying out loud, "People of Jerusalem, what is unfolding, has been spoken by the prophet, saying, 'Tell the daughter of Zion, look, your king is coming to you, humble and mounted on a donkey, and on a colt, the foal of a donkey'."

Eventually Yeshua got off the donkey and handed it back to James and Johanan. The nineteen disciples surrounded Yeshua to protect him from being mobbed by the crowd. Peter and Andreus restored some order and got the crowd to give Yeshua some space, as he entered the city.

As Yeshua entered the city, a flush of sadness gripped him, and he was overcome, tears began rolling down his cheeks. People were amazed as they saw Yeshua weeping. He wept over the city of Jerusalem, saying, "Jerusalem, if you, even you, had only recognised on this day the things that make for peace! But now they are hidden from your eyes. Indeed, the days will come upon you, when your enemies will set up ramparts around you, and hem you in on every side. They will crush you to the ground, you and your children within you, and they will not leave within you one stone upon another, because you did not recognise the time of your visitation from God."

Miriam was moved to tears herself at the sight of Yeshua weeping. Rebecca too and the other women were deeply moved. They could sense the sadness overcoming

Yeshua. Peter and the others were also troubled, but they were unsure what Yeshua was saying. What enemy was he speaking of that will crush Jerusalem to the ground?

Judas however was elated. "At last Yeshua is going to show his hand, use his power to crush Rome," he said.

"Judas, what are you saying, have you still not understood," was all that Johanan said, because he knew nothing else would convince Judas otherwise.

Yeshua however continued with his lament over Jerusalem, he spoke, "Jerusalem, Jerusalem, the city that kills the prophets and stones those who are sent to it! How often have I desired to gather your children together as a hen gathers her brood under her wings, and you were not willing! See your house is left to you desolate. For I tell you, you will not see me again, until you cry, 'Blessed is the One who comes in the name of the Lord'."

Yeshua headed directly for the Temple, with the crowd following him. Eventually they all arrived at the Temple. As soon as Yeshua entered the Temple at the Court of the Gentiles, he came across lots of merchants doing a roaring trade with live animals, cattle, sheep and doves. And close by were several tables with moneychangers. Every male Jew, of the thousands upon thousands who were arriving every day, was supposed to spend a certain portion of their income in Jerusalem, and also support the upkeep of the Temple. And they came from all over Israel and every part of the Roman Empire, and the Greek world, and they all carried foreign currency that had to be changed. Of course, it was common knowledge that they were being ripped off by the money changers, who were lining their own pockets.

Every time Yeshua came to Jerusalem, he was enraged by what was taking place in the Temple. This time he was determined to do something. As soon as Yeshua entered the Temple at the Court of the Gentiles, and saw the merchants trading live animals, sheep and doves, he took out a whip that he had with him, a whip that he had made of cords, just for this occasion. He held the whip for all to see, and then raised it above his head and swished it in front of the traders, who jumped out of the way. Yeshua then continued whipping and then shouted at the traders to get out and he drove them out, with their sheep and cattle.

Judas, who was standing close by with his confreres, was jubilant; at last, the Master is showing his power. But Peter and Miriam and the other disciples were deeply concerned.

They have never seen Yeshua this angry. This would get to the Pharisees and the Roman authorities who would both come down hard on Yeshua and all of those with\him.

Yeshua however seemed unperturbed. He then went across to the moneychangers who were shell shocked, as they experienced what was unfolding. Yeshua approached the moneychangers and poured out their coins from their containers, and overturned their tables and sent them scampering for cover.

Yeshua said to them, "It is written, 'My house shall be called a house of prayer,' but you are making it a den of robbers." And with his whip raised Yeshua drove them out of the Temple.

Judas and Shimon and their friends who came prepared blocked off the traders and moneychangers from coming back into the Temple. Judas, who was standing close to Yeshua, during all of this, he and his confreres, were jubilant, at last the Master is showing his power. But Peter and Miriam and the other disciples were deeply concerned. This would get to the Pharisees and the Roman authorities, who would both come down hard on Yeshua, and all of those with him.

Some of the Pharisees, who had witnessed all that was unfolding, were livid. Eventually one of them spoke up, saying, "On whose authority are you doing this? What sign can you show us for doing this?"

Yeshua answered them, "Destroy this Temple, and in three days I will raise it up."

They were bamboozled, what was he saying, they wondered. And their spokesman with obvious contempt for Yeshua, said, "This Temple has been under construction for forty-six years, and will you raise it up in three days?"

All the Jews in the Temple were amazed. While all this was happening many brought to Yeshua their sick, some blind and lame and he cured them all. But the Chief Priests and the Scribes and the Pharisees, who were extremely annoyed at witnessing what Yeshua did with the traders and the moneychangers, and now saw the amazing things he did, and heard the children crying out in the Temple, "Hosanna to the Son of David," they became even angrier. And one of them said, "Do you hear, what these are saying?"

Yeshua said to them, "Yes, have you never read, 'Out of the mouths of infants and nursing babies, you have prepared praise for yourself'?"

During these days of the festival, many came to believe in Yeshua, they were swayed by his words and the miracles they witnessed. But Yeshua would not entrust himself to them, because he knew all people, and needed no one to testify about anyone, for he himself knew what was in everyone. Yeshua just knew what was in everyone's heart. And he knew what was brewing, and he knew what was in the heart of Judas and those who followed him.

For the next few days, Yeshua came to teach in the Temple. The chief priests, the Scribes and the leaders of the people kept looking for a way to arrest Yeshua, but they could not find anything they could do, for all the people were spellbound by what they heard and saw.

Yeshua then told his disciples that they would all now return to Bethany, where they would stay for a few more days. On their way, Yeshua stopped at the campsite, where the people from Nazareth usually stayed and there, he found his mother.

Yeshua spent some time with his mother. It was a sad meeting for Yeshua, but he did not let his sadness show. In his heart he knew this would be the last such meeting with her. He knew now that his hour had come. His mother though, was overjoyed to see him. But she too was greatly troubled by what she was hearing. She sensed that things would not turn out well for her son. She prayed for him as soon as he left, asking the Father to protect him from all harm.

While they were there, Miriam Zebedee, who was also in Jerusalem for the Passover approached Yeshua with her two sons, James and Johanan. When she had the opportunity to and saw Yeshua alone, she pounced and approached Yeshua and fell on her knees before him. Yeshua knew Miriam; she too was one of his disciples and supported him in his work. Yeshua reached out and helped her off her knees.

Yeshua smiled at her, he was pleased to see her, the mother of two of his favourite disciples, with whom he shared so much, and especially Johanan, whom he loved most of all of them. "Miriam it is so good to see you. Are you well?"

"Yes, Yeshua, very well, thank you. Yeshua, I have a favour to ask of you," Miriam said.

"What is it you want, Miriam?" Yeshua asked.

"Yeshua, declare that these two sons of mine will sit, one at your right hand and one at your left, in your Kingdom."

Yeshua was taken by surprise but he quickly recovered and said to her, "You do not know what you are asking, Miriam." And turning to James and Johanan, who looked somewhat perplexed, they had no idea that their mother would make such a request. She had simply told them that she wanted to have a word with Yeshua. Yeshua, when he turned to them, said, "Are you able to drink the cup that I am about to drink?"

They, somewhat mystified, said to him, "We are able."

Yeshua then said to them, "You will indeed drink my cup, but to sit at my right hand and at my left, this is not mine to grant, but it is for those for whom it has been prepared by my Father."

Miriam then left. The ten other men disciples, who were close by, were curious at what was happening and they were listening in. They did not realise that James and Johanan had not planned this at all. However, they were really angry with them. Yeshua noticed what was happening, so he called them to himself and said, "You know that the rulers of the Gentiles lord it over them, and their great ones are tyrants over them. It will not be so among you; but whoever wishes to be great among you, must be your servant. And whoever wants to be first among you must be your slave; just as the Son of God, made the Son of Man came not to be served but to serve, and to give his life a ransom for many."

Yeshua and his disciples then headed for Bethany where they spent a few days with Martha and Miriam. He knew it would be his last time with them. And Miriam too, sensed likewise. Lazarus was not there. Martha told Yeshua, "Lazarus, got sick of all the attention. He said, he wanted to go to a place where no one knew him and where no one knew his name."

And Miriam added, "He said, we will see him, when we see him."

"Do not fear. Lazarus knows how to look after himself. And you will see him again," Yeshua said.

It was now the fourth day of the week, and three days before the end of the Passover. Yeshua and the disciples were accustomed to have a Passover Meal at this time every year, and when in Jerusalem, he usually had the meal on the fifth day of the week, two days before the Sabbath.

That evening when they were all together. Thomas put a question to Yeshua, "Yeshua you seem to have spoken of the destruction of the Temple, you said that not one stone will be left upon another, all will be thrown down. Tell us, when will this be, and what will be the sign of your coming, and of the end of the age?" All of the disciples were glad Thomas asked those questions; for it was somethings they all wanted to ask.

Yeshua answered, "Beware that no one leads you astray. For many will come in my name, saying, 'I am the Messiah!' and they will lead many astray. And you will hear of wars and rumours of wars; see that you are not alarmed; for this must take place, but the end is not yet. For nation will rise up against nation, and kingdom against kingdom, and there will be famines, and earthquakes, and floods, and droughts, and fires, and diseases and epidemics in various places, and all kinds of deadly plagues and viruses, and even a pandemic that will threaten the entire world, killing millions. All this is but the beginning of the birth pangs. But do not be afraid, for with birth pangs there comes new life. The whole world will suffer birth pangs before new life is born. I am that new Life. Trust in me and you will live. I have come that you might have life and life to the fullest."

When Yeshua had finished speaking to the disciples, Peter asked him, "Lord, where do you want us to go and make the preparations for you to eat the Passover?"

Yeshua replied, "Peter and Andreus, go into the city, and a man carrying a jar of water, will meet you; follow him, and wherever he enters, say to the owner of the house, 'The Teacher asks, where is my guest room where I may eat the Passover with my disciples?' He will show you a large room upstairs, finished and ready. Make preparations for us there."

Peter and Andreus went as Yeshua instructed. This time they were surer of themselves and that as Yeshua predicted it would happen. Nevertheless, Peter spoke, "Andreus, this is weird, how can Yeshua know a man carrying a jar of water will meet us?"

"Peter, have you ever seen a man carrying a jar of water, that's a woman's job?" Andreus said, with a giggle.

"You're right Andreus. I forgot. With Yeshua the differences between what men and women can do have changed somewhat," Peter said.

Peter and Shimon, smiled, looking at each other, as they found the man and followed him to a grand two-storey house, evidently belonging to a rich man. He did everything that Yeshua told them and the man said, "I will prepare the room, how many of you will be coming for the Passover Meal," he asked.

"With the Master, we are twenty, thirteen men and seven women," Andreus said.

"Yeshua's mother, and some others will be there as well," Peter added, not quite sure who else would be there, but somehow, he felt that Miriam, Yeshua's mother would be there and maybe Miriam and Martha from Bethany as well, and maybe some of the seventy-two disciples.

"Good, I will have my servants, prepare the meal. Shall we say at the twelfth hour? Do tell the Master, I will have everything ready by then," the man said.

In the meantime, Judas, who was disappointed that since the Temple incident, Yeshua had no further displays of his power, or of his intent. Judas wanted to precipitate events, he wanted Yeshua to now seize the moment, he had the momentum, the people are now with him, now is the time for him to unleash his power and display his might against the Romans. So, Judas slipped away and went to the chief priests.

When Judas found some of them, he spoke to them and said, "I am one of Yeshua's disciples, I have been with him now for almost three years. I can hand him over to you. What will you give me, if I hand him over to you?"

The chief priests were delighted. They saw this as the hand of God, for they had, together with the Scribes and Officers of the Temple Police, just been discussing how to arrest Yeshua, but had decided not to do it during the festival, as it would cause a riot. But now this betrayer is willing to deliver Yeshua into their hands. One of the chief priests took a moment to consider and then he said to Judas, "We can offer you thirty pieces of silver."

Judas was pleased. He would be killing two birds with one stone. Handing Yeshua over to them, but really putting Yeshua in a position to use his power and bring them all down, and at the same time, he would be making a good haul of money in the process. Judas left, with a spring in his step, and was now determined to get things moving, and look for an opportunity to hand Yeshua over to the chief priests, and then Yeshua will have to unleash all his almighty power. Judas was not really concerned, for he had seen how Yeshua, when he was under threat of harm from the crowd, like when they wanted to hurl him of a cliff, just disappeared from their sight.

Chapter Seventy-Eight
The Last Supper

Evening came, and about two hours after sunset, Yeshua and his disciples went to the Upper Room. Yeshua wanted only his nineteen disciples to be with him on this occasion. When they arrived, all was prepared as the man had said. Yeshua sat down, surrounded by his nineteen closest disciples, with whom he had shared so much, and now from whom much is expected. They are to carry on what he had started, so he said to them, "I have eagerly desired to eat this Passover with you before I suffer; for I tell you I will not eat it, until it is fulfilled in the Kingdom of Heaven." They then had the meal. There was an eerie feeling in the air, after the disciples heard what Yeshua had said. Yeshua seemed to indicate that this would be the last supper that he would share with them.

Then during the meal, Yeshua asked for their attention. They put down what they were eating. Yeshua then looked at each of them, his eyes meeting them; he was filled with love for each and every one of them. He knew he would be leaving them, all nineteen of them, but he wanted to leave them something of himself. He looked up to heaven and his eyes were moist, but filled with the Spirit he prayed silently, and then taking a loaf of bread, he broke it and gave a piece to each of his disciples saying "This is my body, which is given for you, take and eat. Do this in remembrance of me." The disciples took the piece of bread and ate it in silence. They somehow sensed this was a new ritual that Yeshua was giving them, teaching them.

When everyone had consumed the portion of bread he gave them, Yeshua then took his cup, and poured some wine in it. He then quietly prayed with his eyes cast heavenwards, and then he said, "Take and drink from this cup. This cup that is poured out for you is the new covenant in my blood. Do this in remembrance of me."

The disciples solemnly drank from the cup, in silence.

Miriam whispered to Rebecca, sitting next to her. "Remember, when Yeshua spoke about himself as food and drink, as nourishment for our souls, giving us his flesh to eat and his blood to drink, and when everyone who heard his words, found it hard to grasp and left him, I think, that what Yeshua has just done is somehow connected."

Rebecca listened, without saying anything. She was feeling too heartbroken; as she too felt in her heart that this was to be the last supper she would share with Yeshua.

When they had finished eating the main meal, Yeshua, knew that this was to be his last supper with them, for he sensed his hour was near when he would be handed over to the powers of darkness. He looked at all of his disciples, the twelve men, and the seven women, and he was filled with love for them, and gratitude for all they had sacrificed for him. His eyes fell on Judas, who looked unusually nervous and fidgety. He was blinking, biting his nails, and covering his mouth with his hands. Yeshua knew then, that Judas was about to betray him.

Yeshua then got up from the table, took off his outer robe, and tied a towel around his waist. The disciples wondered what Yeshua was up to.

Yeshua told them to turn around on their stools. Then he poured water in a basin and approached his disciples, starting with Miriam. He placed the basin next to her and then with both his hands took hold of Miriam's feet, and placed them in the basin, and then with a wash rag and with his hands he began to wash her feet. Miriam was taken aback, and reacted almost wanting to draw away, but Yeshua raised his hand and simply looked at Miriam, and she saw the love in his eyes, and she acquiesced, and let her feet be washed. He then took the towel and dried her feet. And then he went to all of the other women and finally came to the men, starting with Peter.

Peter immediately rebelled, no way, was Yeshua going to humiliate himself like that, do what was something reserved for slaves and the lowest of servants, so Peter moved his feet to the side and said to Yeshua, "Lord, you are not going to wash my feet!"

Yeshua then said to Peter, "Peter, unless I wash you, you have no share with me."

Peter immediately changed his demeanour and said, with his usual candour and exuberance, "Lord, then wash not my feet only, but also my hands and my head."

Yeshua could not help a faint smile, and said to Peter, "Peter, one who has bathed does not need to wash, except for the feet, but is entirely clean. And you are clean, though not all of you."

The disciples were taken aback by Yeshua's comments, about not all of them being clean, what did he mean? He had hinted at this before. They were all silent, while Yeshua went from one to the other, washing each other's feet. This is something they had not witnessed ever before. No one of such stature and standing as Yeshua, he whom they now all believed to be the Messiah, would stoop so low and perform such a menial task. And here was Yeshua, on his knees before them, washing their feet. They were all deep in concentration, busy with their own thoughts.

When Yeshua reached Judas, he paused, and it was as if he was taking a deep breath. He looked at Judas with sad eyes. Judas was so uncomfortable, he could not look into Yeshua's eyes, and he averted his gaze. And again, Yeshua noticed the nervous twitches on Judas face. And as Yeshua was about to take Judas' feet in his hands, he saw how Judas knees were shaking up and down. Judas seemed unable to stop the shaking. So, Yeshua placed his hands on Judas knees, and looked at him with love. Judas knees stopped shaking. And Yeshua proceeded to lovingly wash Judas' feet.

After Yeshua had washed all of their feet, he washed his hands, and then put on his robe and returned to the table and all the disciples turned around and gazed at Yeshua. Yeshua then said to them, "Do you know what I have done to you? You call me Teacher and Lord—and you are right, for that is what I am. So, if I, your Lord and Teacher have washed your feet, you also ought to wash one another's feet. For I have set you an example, that you also should do as I have done to you. Very truly, I tell you, servants are not greater than their master, nor are messengers greater than the one who sent them. I tell you, whoever receives one whom I send receives me; and whoever receives me, receives him who sent me."

Yeshua then stopped. His demeanour changed, he seemed troubled in spirit, and declared, "Very truly, I tell you; one of you will betray me."

The disciples were shocked and could not believe what Yeshua was saying. They looked at each other, unable to imagine any of them doing such a thing. Peter whispered in Johanan's ear, "Johanan, ask Yeshua, of whom he is speaking."

Johanan, who was sitting next to Yeshua, leaned over and he too whispered, asking Yeshua, "Lord, who is it?"

Yeshua answered, "It is the one to whom I give this piece of bread, when I have dipped it in the dish."

None of the other disciples heard exactly what Yeshua was saying to Johanan. But they then saw Yeshua dip a piece of bread in the dish of olive oil and give it to Judas. But they heard what Yeshua then said to Judas, "Do quickly what you are going to."

None of the disciples knew why Yeshua said this to Judas. Thomas, sitting next to Andreus asked him, "what was Yeshua telling Judas to do quickly?"

Andreus replied, "I don't know, maybe because Judas has the common purse, Yeshua asked Judas to buy what we need for the festival."

"Or maybe, that he should give something to the poor," Lucia said.

But as soon as Judas received the piece of bread, he immediately went out into the night. It was pitch dark, must be close to midnight.

When Judas had gone out, Yeshua spoke to his disciples, with a heavy heart. He addressed them as he did on rare occasions as 'little children,' as he did now. He said, "Little children, I am with you only a little longer. You will look for me, and as I said to people, so now I say to you, 'Where I am going, you cannot come.' I give what I gave you before, I give you now again, once and for all, a new commandment, that you love one another. By this everyone will know that you are my disciples, if you have love for one another."

Yeshua continued to speak to his disciples, it almost sounded to them, like a farewell speech. He said, "No one has greater love than this, to lay down one's life for one's friends. You are my friends if you do what I command you. I do not call you servants, because the servant does not know what the Master is doing, but I have called you friends, because I have made known to you, everything that I have heard from my Father. You did not choose me, but I chose you. And I appointed you to go and bear fruit, fruit that will last."

Peter asked Yeshua, what they all wanted to ask, "Lord, where are you going?"

Yeshua answered, "Where I am going, you cannot follow me now, but you will follow afterward."

But Peter said to him, "Lord, why can I not follow you now, I will lay down my life for you."

Yeshua looked at Peter, with so much love in his heart for Peter, but he said, with a hint of sadness in his voice, "Will you lay down your life for me?" And then Yeshua said to Peter, what he had said before, "Peter, I tell you, before the cock crows, you will have denied me three times."

Peter was deeply hurt, and he had nothing to say. Yeshua had said this to him before, this was now the third time, but this time it sounded imminent. Did Yeshua mean, before the cock crows tomorrow? Peter wondered.

Yeshua then said to them, "Do not be afraid. If you love me, you will keep my commandments. And I will ask the Father, and he will give you another Advocate, to be with you forever. I have said many things to you, but the Advocate, the Holy Spirit, whom the Father will send in my name, will teach you everything, and remind you of all that I have said to you. Peace, I leave with you, my peace I give you. And you will spread my peace, my love, my joy, to the whole world. I have come to spread peace. In the midst of wars, and evil, you must bring peace, peace to live forever in the hearts of men and women. I wish my peace to reign supreme in the hearts of all, so that no matter what happens in their lives or the world around them, they will always be at peace. You, with the help of the Spirit, will spread peace to the world. You will, by your teaching and your lives, spread my love, peace, and joy into the world, to all of creation, to all creatures, to all with whom you come into contact."

Yeshua stopped. The disciples were stunned into silence. Peter was still reeling to what Yeshua said about him denying him three times. The rest too were silent, saddened by what Yeshua was saying, they all felt he was saying goodbye.

Yeshua then said, "Do not let your hearts be troubled. I will be with you forever. I will not leave you orphans. The Spirit, the Spirit of my Father and me, will come to you and comfort and strengthen you. Tomorrow is the eve of the Passover. You need your sleep now. But I will go to the Garden of Gethsemane to pray. Peter, James, and Johanan, will you come with me." With that Yeshua left for the Garden of Gethsemane.

Chapter Seventy-Nine
Gethsemane

Often before, Yeshua had stopped here, in this garden to pray. It was just across the Kidron valley, a mile long ridge slightly to the east of the city of Jerusalem. This time, Yeshua felt deeply saddened, troubled and afraid. He could feel it in the air. Judas had been gone for a while, and Yeshua could almost sense what he was doing. He was plotting with the powers of darkness. This is what I have come for, Yeshua said to himself; to bring all out of the darkness and into the light. I have come to be the light of the world.

Yeshua said to Peter, James and Johanan, "My heart feels as if it is being pierced. I am feeling really sad, and greatly troubled, my soul is sorrowful unto death. Please stay here with me. I will go yonder and pray."

James was the only one with a lantern, he wanted to give it to Yeshua, but Yeshua refused and went a bit further on into the darkness. Fear began to grip Yeshua's very entrails. Yeshua then fell on his knees and began to pray. "Father, is this it, is this the night of nights. Is my hour finally come? Is this the beginning of the end for me?" In his heart, deep within his soul, Yeshua heard his Father's voice, 'No, my Son, this is but the end of the beginning. You have done what I have sent you to do. Be brave, for great suffering awaits you.'

Yeshua continued with his prayer, "Father, I am greatly troubled. Judas is gone off into the night, and I know he is now with those who seek my downfall, who seek to destroy me, but Father I trust in you, I pray for strength to endure whatever lies ahead."

Yeshua sighed. He still felt anxious and afraid. He prayed, "Father, I know, when they strike the shepherd, the sheep will scatter. Father, I am unsure what lies ahead, but I put my full trust in you. I pray Father for Peter, he will deny me three times, that I know, but Father, I have chosen him to be the leader, when I am gone, give him the strength to not lose all hope. And all the others too, they will all abandon me in my hour of need, except the women. Father, I need them now more than ever. Father, I feel so alone, in this hour. Father, is this my final hour with them, whom I have chosen, who have been my friends, who have been so close to me these past three years. Father bless them; send your angels to protect them from all harm, until the Spirit comes to them."

Yeshua then threw himself flat on the ground, and pleaded with his Father, "Father if it is possible, let this cup pass from me." Yeshua lay there motionless in the dirt; he was now gripped with fear and sorrow, and drops of sweat that seemed to be like blood were dripping from his forehead. But then he prayed, "Yes Father, your will be done, not what I want, but what you want." And again, Yeshua heard the voice of his Father deep in his heart, it was the same words that he heard not in his heart, but from the heavens, when he was baptised by Johanan in the River Jordan, what seemed now like a century ago. It was the moment when he began his public ministry.

And now he heard that voice again, in his heart, 'You are my beloved Son, and in you I am well pleased. I sent you into the world, not to die, but to live, to live life to the full, and dying is part of life. Your life, your death, your teaching, your example, will live on forever. I have sent you into a dark world, and you will now enter even more deeply into that dark world. But by your life and your death, will bring all out of the darkness. You will bring light to the world. All that you have done will lead them all out of the darkness and into the light. Be not afraid my son, I am with you.'

Yeshua continued to pray silently, he was oblivious to the time, an hour must have passed and Yeshua got up, his eyes were now accustomed to the darkness, and he walked towards his disciples. The lamp was standing on the ground, and the three disciples were fast asleep. Now, when he needed them to be awake, to pray with him, to be a comfort and strength for him, he found them sleeping. He bent down and shook Peter, who was now snoring loudly.

"What! What!" Peter woke up suddenly, not knowing where he was, and he instinctively grabbed for his sword. Peter had surreptitiously armed himself with a sword. He had sensed Yeshua speaking so much of danger ahead, that he wanted to be prepared, and armed, just in case. Peter's shouts also woke James and Johanan, who rubbed their eyes.

Yeshua spoke, "Peter, it is alright." And when Peter got his bearings, Yeshua chided him and Johanan and James, "So, could you not stay awake with me one hour? Stay awake and pray that you may not come into the time of trial" And Yeshua then added, "The spirit indeed is willing, but the flesh is weak."

Yeshua then went back to his place of prayer and continued to speak with his Father. Yeshua prayed for Peter, James and Johanan and all the rest of his disciples, including Judas. He prayed that they may be kept safe, until the Spirit comes to them. He thanked the Father for giving them to him; they were such strength and a comfort to him. And he thanked the Father for everything, his life so far, and he prayed once more, "Father, if this cannot pass unless I drink it, your will be done." Again, Yeshua went into prayer, praying the prayer of silence, the prayer of the heart, where words did not mater, where two hearts became united, his and the Father, they became as they are, one, and one with the Spirit. Yeshua was lost in the silence, in the prayer of the heart. Another hour must have passed.

Again, Yeshua went to the three disciples, but again he found them asleep, for their eyes were heavy. But Yeshua also realised that they had just had a big supper and had quite a bit to drink. He could understand them feeling drowsy, so he left them and went back and prayed some more.

Then Yeshua heard sounds in the distance. He got up and went to his three disciples and found then still sleeping. He shook them awake and said to them, "Are you still sleeping. Wake up now! See the hour is at hand, and the Son of Man, the Son of God made man, like all other men, is betrayed into the hands of sinners. Get up, let us be going." Yeshua then saw figures in the shadows, and said, "See, my betrayer is at hand."

James lifted his lantern, as he saw a group of men approaching. It was quite a large crowd, they had lanterns, so Yeshua, Peter, James and Johanan could see some were Temple guards and many of them, the guards, and the others with them, held clubs in their hands and some were brandishing swords.

The disciples were horrified and afraid. Peter immediately grabbed his sword, but still in the scabbard. One of the men spoke up, "We have been sent by the Chief

Priests and the Elders of the people to arrest Yeshua the Galilean, the man from Nazareth."

The disciples were gripped with and frozen in fear. They then saw Judas with the mob, and then all became clear of what happened while they were having supper and what Yeshua had said to Judas. Then they watched incredulously, as Judas, flanked by guards with swords approached Yeshua. They were however somewhat confused as they saw Judas approach Yeshua. Judas had given the guards a sign, saying, 'The one I will kiss is the man, arrest him.'

While they were sleeping Judas had gone to the Upper Room while the mob waited in the shadows, and not finding Yeshua there, he had asked where Yeshua was. But the disciples were suspicious, and they told Judas, they did not know where Yeshua was. But Judas, noticed that Peter, James and Johanan were not with them, and surmised that Yeshua was not far away, and immediately concluded that Yeshua must be in the Garden of Gethsemane, because Yeshua often came to Gethsemane to pray.

Now as Judas was next to Yeshua, he said, "Greetings Rabbi!" and kissed him.

Yeshua was filled with sadness, and looked at Judas with longing and compassion, but he said, "Judas, do you betray me with a kiss?"

The three disciples were aghast when they saw what was unfolding, and what Judas did, and Yeshua's response.

Yeshua then looked at Judas and said, calmly, "Friend, do what you are here to do."

Judas then stepped aside and nodded to the soldiers, who immediately came forward and laid their hands on Yeshua. Peter was appalled and James and Johanan were in shock. Peter, immediately drew his sword and struck one of the men nearest to him, and cut off his ear. Blood squirted from the side of the guard's face, and he screamed, as his hand instinctively reached for the side of his face. He was shrieking. Peter was now wielding his sword above his head, and took the guards by surprise, and they momentarily stepped back to prevent themselves from being struck down by Peter.

The guard continued, screaming in pain, with blood oozing from the side of his head, "My ear, my ear, he cut off my ear," the man screamed.

"It's Malchus, the slave of Caiaphas the high priest," a man in the crowd yelled. "That man cut off his ear," he shouted, pointing at Peter, who stood there in front of Yeshua, with his sword drawn and ready to strike again.

Yeshua immediately touched Peter on his free arm and said, calmly but firmly, "Peter, put your sword back in its place; for all who take the sword, will perish by the sword. Do you not think that I cannot appeal to my Father, and he will at once send me more than twelve legions of angels? But how then would the Scriptures be fulfilled, which say it must happen in this way."

Yeshua held firmly onto Peter's arm, and looked into his eyes and pleaded. Peter, reluctantly put his sword back in its scabbard. James and Johanan were both shaking in fear. Judas, however was not swayed, he seemed gratified. In fact, Judas was smiling to himself. The words that Yeshua had just uttered about his power to summon twelve legions of angels, was exactly what Judas was hoping Yeshua would do. But he knew Yeshua would have to be taken under guard and then unleash all of his power and might against Rome and in the presence of the multitudes in Jerusalem, for all to see. Judas was optimistic and full of pride with what he was setting in motion. He would be remembered forever for the part he played in the downfall of Rome, and the freedom of Israel. Judas was gloating.

As soon as Peter had cut off the man's ear, Yeshua had immediately picked up the bleeding ear and then spoke to the man, who was screaming for dear life. "It is okay, it's okay," Yeshua said, touching the man on his arm and saying, "Do not be afraid, you have your ear back." And with that Yeshua who had picked up the guard's ear, placed it back onto the side of the man's face, and it was as perfect, as if nothing had happened.

Malchus touched his ear, again and again, he could not believe it. Those around him were amazed as well. Malchus left Gethsemane immediately, and some that were around him left with him as well.

"Don't bother what you see," one of the chief priests that was part of the group, said, "He does all these things by the power of Beelzebub. That is why he must be stopped."

As they were about to grab Yeshua again, he said to them, "Have you come out with swords and clubs to arrest me, as though I were a bandit? Day after day, I sat in the Temple, teaching, and you did not arrest me. What is happening is the Scriptures of the prophets being fulfilled."

When they arrested Yeshua, Peter immediately disappeared. He ran, gripped with fear and went to the Upper Room. The owner of the house had already arranged beds for Yeshua and all of his disciples. All of them were already asleep, except for Miriam and Rebecca. "We couldn't sleep. Yeshua seemed restless and unsettled at the end of our supper, and when he left for the Garden, he seemed troubled, so we just couldn't sleep until he returned. Is he alright, Peter?" Miriam asked.

Peter told them that Yeshua had been arrested, and that Judas had betrayed him. Peter retold everything that he had witnessed. "Wake everyone, we must tell them what happened."

And so it happened, the disciples, most of them in their night clothes came into the Upper Room and Peter told them what had happened.

"We must go to him," Miriam said.

"Yes, we must," Rebecca agreed.

Miriam and Rebecca ran off and headed for Gethsemane.

"We better stay here," Peter said, "It is not safe out there. I will go and see what unfolds and come back to report. Lock all the doors, our lives are in danger," Peter said.

"I will talk with Isaiah, the owner, and let him know what is happening. And I'm sure he will let us stay here, until it is safe to go outdoors," Andreus said.

Peter pulled down his hood further over his head and went out to see what was happening with Yeshua.

On the way, he met James, who was terrified. "Where is Johanan?" Peter asked.

"I don't know. After they arrested Yeshua, some of them came towards Johanan and me. We ran, one of them grabbed Johanan's robe and he ran, half naked into the night," James said.

Just then, Johanan appeared, all flustered. He was shivering. "Go to Isaiah, and ask him for a robe," Peter said, and remain with the others, and keep the doors and windows bolted, until I return.

"No Peter, wait for me, I'll be back in a minute," Johanan then ran off and returned covered with a new robe. They then went off in search of Yeshua.

Yeshua was taken to the Tribunal, the Sanhedrin that were already gathered at Caiaphas's place. When the guards went to arrest Yeshua, word had spread among the families and friends, of all those working for Caiaphas. And many witnesses were rounded up, and were on standby to be called on when needed. Even the spouses and close friends of the Council members knew what was afoot, even though they were told to keep everything under wraps. Some of the Council members could not resist telling their families and the friends what was happening. So, when the Council members turned up at Caiaphas' place, many of their family, friends and acquaintances turned up as well. They all stood outside the gate and were let in by the servants, into the courtyard. The word-of-mouth communication spread all over Jerusalem like a tidal wave. This was spectacular news; not only for the residents of Jerusalem but for all the thousands of visitors as well. Many knew of Yeshua and they shared all they knew and all that has happened in their city, including Yeshua's cleansing of the Temple. The news about Yeshua spread, that he was Prophet, Teacher and miracle worker and that he was now arrested, for what no one seemed to know. Now so many knew what was taking place and they turned up, and were let into, and filled the courtyard.

Chapter Eighty
The Arrest

This is what happened before the Judas kiss, that betrayed Yeshua into the hands of his enemies. Early in the day, before Yeshua had his Last Supper with his disciples, Judas approached the Chief Priests and the Elders, telling them he could hand Yeshua over to them. Caiaphas, the high priest, who had earlier said, 'it is better for one man to die than for the whole nation to perish,' was delighted. He seized the opportunity with both hands.

Caiaphas first called on Annas, his father-in-law, from whom he inherited the role of high priest. Caiaphas walked into Annas' home, without knocking. He knew that the trial of the Impostor, Yeshua, was important; the future of the faith of the people, and their position was in peril. This man Yeshua had to be stopped at all costs. Caiaphas wanted, needed, all the help he could get, so he went to his father-in-law.

"Caiaphas, good to see you, what can I do for you," Annas got right down to business. He had already warned Caiaphas time and again, about Yeshua, that he must be eliminated or there would be dire consequences for all. Annas knew that it could only be to discuss the Yeshua question that would bring Caiaphas to his door on this day, the eve of the Passover.

"Annas, one of the disciples of the man Yeshua, his name is Judas, I know of his father, a very successful businessman here in Jerusalem. This Judas though, was formerly a disciple of that other radical, Johanan, whom Herod had beheaded. This same Judas has been a disciple of Yeshua, he says for the past three years. He came to us, willing to betray his Teacher, hand him over to us. He wanted a reward, and we handed him thirty pieces of silver."

Annas was thoughtful; he stroked his grey beard and then said, "He must be crucified. Not beheaded behind closed doors, like Johanan. He should be crucified, like a common criminal, for all of Judaea to see his disgrace. So, he can be forgotten forever, and his followers must be threatened that they will receive a similar fate if they continue to adhere to his teachings, and follow him."

"Annas, he has lots of followers, and at least a hundred disciples, here in Jerusalem, who already are spreading his teachings."

"Get rid of their leader and they will fizzle away," Annas said.

"According to Judas, he has eleven men, who are close to him, and have been with him for more than three years, and they are led by a fisherman from Bethsaida, a big brawny oaf, according to Judas. Most of them are fishermen from Galilee, all simple, uneducated men. Judas is the only one from Judaea, and the most educated and sophisticated of the lot, according to what I gather. And oh yes, the Nazarene also has women disciples, that with the men, have been following this Yeshua for the past three years. They have been traipsing all over the land, all over Judaea, Galilee and across the Jordan, even as far as Phoenicia on the coast and up to Caesarea Philippi on the east of the Jordan."

"Women disciples, really, how many women are there?" Annas asked.

"Judas told me that there are seven women, four of them are from Galilee and three from here in Jerusalem," Caiaphas said.

"Okay, that is good information. We must first focus on their leader, this Yeshua, cut off the head of the snake and the body will eventually die," Annas said, making a slicing gesture with his hand, and gritting his teeth.

"How should we go about this?" Caiaphas asked.

"Convene an urgent meeting of the Council," Annas said.

"It will be difficult to organise a full Council meeting till after the Passover," Caiaphas said.

"You must strike while the iron is hot, Caiaphas. This is a golden opportunity. You don't have to convene a full Council, get at least more than half and meet today, this night, and hopefully, this Judas will let this happen this night, when this Yeshua will sure to be meeting for a Passover Meal with his followers," Annas said.

"I will do that right away," Caiaphas said, and he showed that he was ready to rush off and organise such a meeting.

Annas stopped him and said, "Make sure the meeting is stacked with members who will go along with whatever you decide. Make sure you and your closest associates lobby the members and let them know the importance of Yeshua being condemned and executed. He can be made an example during this time, when the whole world seems to be here in Jerusalem. And oh yes, make sure your legal experts are there, the Scribes, ones you can rely on to follow your lead," Annas said.

"Will do, will do," Caiaphas said and rushed off.

Caiaphas got together his closest associates before the others started arriving, and together they organised the meeting. Caiaphas was banking on the possibility that Judas would reappear before the night was over, and hand this Yeshua over to them, so they could try Yeshua this very night. Judas had already been paid thirty pieces of silver, and he was told to do it quickly, so Caiaphas was confident that Yeshua would be brought to him, this night.

As soon as Caiaphas left Annas and met with his cronies, they arranged for messengers to be sent out to all of those they wanted at the meeting. Caiaphas and his closest allies also sent men out to find people who would witness against Yeshua, if they got him to trial tonight. It was a busy day and a busy night, to get together forty members of the Council. There was so much activity afoot, for arranging of a trial that would normally take weeks and even months to organise; they had to do it within hours.

And although it was the day before the eve of the Passover, when all the Council members were home, celebrating with their families, Caiaphas had urged them, ordered them really; informing them that it was an important meeting of life and death, as they were to question Yeshua, the Nazarene. Caiaphas bypassed the protocol. By their own laws, Yeshua should have been taken by the guards and locked in the Temple stockade, until the full Council of seventy-two members could hear his case.

Although Caiaphas had a palatial home, it was not big enough for a full Council meeting, but could easily accommodate an extra forty members, which is more than half of the Sanhedrin, as the Council was known. Caiaphas satisfied himself that was enough of a quorum to make matters legitimate and lawful. He was of course side-stepping the law, and it would make any trial against Yeshua illegal, unlawful. But he didn't care.

And so it came to pass, the forty members came in dribs and drabs to Caiaphas place, and they were served light refreshments and cups of wine. There was a buzz in the air. This was highly unusual, and they were all made to realise just how important this meeting was, their future and the future of the faith of the people of Israel, depended on it. They were there to find this Yeshua guilty, and have him condemned. But guilty of what some of them were thinking.

Caiaphas had refreshments available, and allowed the members to catch up and informally discuss the matter of Yeshua, the Nazarene. After an hour, Annas arrived and Caiaphas called the meeting to order, and he chaired the meeting. For the next hour Caiaphas brought them all up to date of the state of play, and about Judas, who was to play an important role in bringing Yeshua down.

Just then there was a knock on the door, Caiaphas thought it might be Judas, instead he was displeased to see that it was Nicodemus and Yosef of Arimathea. Thorns in his side and members who seemed to be going soft on this Yeshua.

"Shalom, Caiaphas, we heard there was to be a special Council meeting on the future of Yeshua, so we came along," Nicodemus said.

Caiaphas had no option, but to let them in, in any case, they were only two, among so many others, he was sure they could be over ruled.

After the Council was discussing how they would conduct the Tribunal, once Yeshua appeared before them, Caiaphas spoke, "Gentlemen, I thank you all for coming on this bleak night. It is important for you to be here, on this night of nights. I apologise for taking you from your families on this night, and now that it is midnight, it is already the eve of the Passover, I apologise for robbing many of you of your precious sleep," Caiaphas said with a laugh, and the rest laughed with him.

Just then a guard rushed in and blurted out. "Sir, there is a man here; he says his name is Judas, and he needs to see you urgently, and that you are expecting him."

Caiaphas was delighted. "Gentlemen, this is the hand of God. He has brought this man to us who will take us to the impostor. Those of you that have been allotted to fetch the witnesses, do that right now, for we will need them soon. A few of the members rushed out."

Caiaphas brought Judas in and introduced him to the members present. "Gentlemen, this is Judas, the only wise one among the close followers of Yeshua. Well, Judas, what have you to say?" Caiaphas said.

Judas spoke, "I have just come from a place, close to Gethsemane, where Yeshua was having the Passover Meal with the disciples. I know it is late, very late. I had intended to come to speak with you at first light, but as I walked the streets, I noticed the lights on in your place. And I thought I may as well knock on your door now, and I can now see how opportune that is, as this must be a Tribunal meeting. Now is a good time for you to arrest Yeshua. I will take your guards to him. I will kiss him on the cheek as the sign it is he, so your guards can take him."

"We have to send some of you with the guards." Caiaphas then nominated several members of the Sanhedrin to go with Judas and the guards. And so began the bleakest night of Judas' life, and that of the Sanhedrin.

Chapter Eighty-One
The Peter Denials

All of this manoeuvring and plotting by Annas and Caiaphas happened before Yeshua was betrayed with a kiss. The Judas kiss would from this day forward be imprinted in the psyche of all of humanity, as the worst act of betrayal ever perpetrated in the history of humankind.

The mood of the Council changed, as they were now waiting for the return of Judas and the guards, and the accused. The members were all chatting when a loud knock made them all jump. Immediately, Caiaphas himself went to open the door. It was Judas, and the guards and they had Yeshua with them, his wrists were tied with rope. The guards roughly pushed Yeshua into the house.

"Okay, that is enough," Caiaphas said. "We'll have two guards here, to guard this man and the rest of you, stay out front and guard the house, and let no one in," Caiaphas said.

And so began the trial of the century that would be the trial of all time and that would affect people of all time.

Caiaphas and Annas sat at two elaborate chairs, and the other forty members sat all around the sides of the room right to the back, in a semi-circle, and they made Yeshua stand in the middle, close to Caiaphas and Annas.

When Yeshua was taken to the Tribunal, word had spread among the families and friends, of all those working for Caiaphas and the many witnesses who were rounded up and were on standby to be called on when needed. Even the spouses and close friends of the Council members knew what was afoot, even though they were told to keep everything under wraps. Some of the Council members could not resist telling their families and their friends what was happening. So many turned up outside the gate and were let in by the servants, into the courtyard. The word-of-mouth communication was in full swing. Now so many knew what was taking place, and they turned up, and were let into the courtyard by the servants. They filled the courtyard. Late night passersby were curious and when they found out what was afoot, they too were let into the courtyard that was now filled to full capacity.

When Peter, Johanan, Miriam and Rebecca had gone to the Temple, to find out if Yeshua was perhaps locked up in Temple stockade, all was quiet and there was no one around the Temple, even though there were lots of people, walking around and having a look at the Temple, and just enjoying the sights and sounds of the night. After all it was festival time, and Jerusalem had people everywhere. The population quadrupled at this time, and was more than a million that invaded Jerusalem, so there were people everywhere, mainly visitors, who were out walking the streets at this late hour.

Peter, Johanan, Miriam and Rebecca kept together for safety, and they too gravitated towards Caiaphas house, with others heading that way. There were now so many little groups milling around the gates of Caiaphas' place, curious to see so many people in the courtyard and wondering what was happening. It was now well past midnight, and not too far off, only a matter of hours when the sun would rise again. But there were still so many people around, as it was festival time. But especially because word had spread that the Nazarene was arrested in the early hours of this day, and was now at this very hour, being tried by the Sanhedrin, the highest Religious Tribunal of the land. So, people came and came, and waited to see what would unfold.

Peter, Johanan, Miriam and Rebecca, were by no means conspicuous in the crowds, and finding the Temple all locked up and quiet, they went to the home of Caiaphas. The huge wrought iron gates were closed. Many visitors to Jerusalem were still walking past and staring at Caiaphas' palace and having a chat.

In the courtyard, in front of Caiaphas' home, Peter, Johanan, Miriam and Rebecca saw some guards standing at the entrance to the house. And there was a buzz outside, with servants around as well, and the whole house was lit up. And they knew that Yeshua must be there. They had no idea what was unfolding.

"Johanan, it looks like Yeshua must be in there. Nothing seems to be happening at the Temple. Can we get into the courtyard, without being noticed" Peter said.

"If I can catch the attention of one of the servants, moving around, I might be able to get us into the courtyard," Johanan said.

"Do you know them, Johanan?" Miriam asked.

"Some of them know me," Johanan said, and this surprised Peter, Miriam and Rebecca.

Johanan explained, "None of us were aware of this, but when we first arrived in Jerusalem, Caiaphas had sent out some of his scouts to seek out one of us, Yeshua's disciples. They picked me and privately brought me to his house. I had foolishly thought it would be an opportunity to spread the truth about Yeshua, and to the highest religious figure in Jerusalem, so I seized the opportunity. But I wanted to be cautious, for I knew the danger, so I accepted the challenge, but said nothing to any of you. I did not want to implicate, or endanger any of you," Johanan said.

"So, what really happened at your meeting with Caiaphas," Peter asked.

"It soon became clear to me, that Caiaphas' intentions were not good. Under the pretence of wanting to learn more about Yeshua, Caiaphas really tried to get me to spy on Yeshua and to betray the Master. So, I never went back," Johanan said.

As they stood outside the gate, Johanan recognised one of the servants. He called out to him. The servant came, and Johanan said, "I am Johanan, remember, I had a meeting with Caiaphas a few days ago, right here in his home, you served us."

The servant held up his lantern, to have a better look. "Oh yes, I remember you Sir," the servant said.

"Can you let us in, it is cold out here, and I see they are starting a fire, over there," Johanan said.

"Sure, come in, come in," the servant said, as he opened the gate and let them into the courtyard.

"I think it is better, if we split up in here, just in case," Peter said. So, he and Johanan went to opposite sides of the courtyard. Miriam and Rebecca stayed together, near the fire, to warm themselves, as it was getting quite chilly.

The crowds were milling around, for hours, waiting for news of what was happening to the man Yeshua. For word had got out that he was appearing before the highest Tribunal in the land, the Sanhedrin. And they were curious to know what he was been charged with, and what the outcome would be.

Peter was feeling tired and afraid. He sat down on a step at the side of the courtyard. And then after a while, as he stood up, a tiny sized servant girl happened to be passing, and she looked up at Peter, and immediately recognised him. She recognised the tall, big and swarthy, Peter, his big frame towering over her. She blurted out, "you also were with Yeshua, the Nazarene." The people standing around, close to Peter, looked at him.

Peter, was terrified, at once he blurted a response to the servant girl. "You are mistaken. I do not know the man, have never met him." Peter immediately left his spot and went to stand around in the forecourt, away from the tiny servant girl. As Peter was walking away from her the cock crew for the first time, announcing the approaching dawn.

Johanan, Miriam, and Rebecca were huddled around the fire that was still packed with people, standing shoulder to shoulder, waiting for news about the trial, happening inside.

The tiny servant girl, on seeing Peter again, cried out for all the bystanders to hear, "This man is one of them. He is a follower of that man who is being tried."

Again, Peter immediately denied what she was saying. "You are highly mistaken; I am not one of his disciples. You are mistaking me for someone else." Seconds after Peter spoke, the cock crew a second time. Peter, who was so terrified for his own safety, hardly heard the cock crow, nor did he remember what Yeshua had predicted.

Peter was now joining the crowd around the fire. After a while, some bystanders came up to Peter and pointing a finger at him, one of them said to Peter, "Certainly you are also one of them, you are a Galilean, aren't you, why even your accent gives you away."

This time Peter began to curse. "In the name of God, I do not know this man, I have never met him, and you are all highly mistaken." At that very moment, the cock crowed a third time. It was only then that Peter remembered what Yeshua had said to him, on three occasions, "Before the cock crows, you will deny me three times." Peter burst into tears, and ran from the crowd and into the darkness of the night. He did not know where he was going, his heart was pounding. He felt so ashamed of what he had just done. He was shaking, fearing to be struck down by God Almighty for the evil deed he had just done. "Oh God, Oh God, Oh Yeshua, Oh Yeshua, forgive me, forgive me, please forgive me, I am sorry, I am so sorry, I am not worthy of you." Peter came to the Garden of Gethsemane and he went to the very spot that Yeshua had prayed and he threw himself, face down and wept bitterly. There were no more words of sorrow and contrition that he could utter, he just lay there in the dirt, where Yeshua had knelt and prayed. He lay there motionless and with tears not wanting to cease.

After, how long Peter had no idea; he got up and walked to the Upper Room, where the rest of the disciples were still boarded up. He knocked three times, paused for a moment and then knocked once, and immediately the door opened as they recognised the signal they had decided on for the opening of the doors.

"Peter, you look awful, what happened?" Lucia asked, what all of them were thinking. None of them could sleep, and they were all waiting for Peter's return and news of Yeshua.

"Your eyes are all swollen and red, Peter. Let me get a cloth and some water," Joanna said. She went and fetched a damp cloth and gave it to Peter, to dab at his eyes.

Peter spoke. He did not tell them about his triple denial of Yeshua, he was just too ashamed. "Yeshua is at this moment standing trial before the Sanhedrin. Johanan, Miriam and Rebecca are still out there, with servants, guards and onlookers, waiting for an outcome. They all know that Yeshua is standing trial before the Tribunal, the Sanhedrin. What he has been charged with, I have no idea," Peter said. "Let us pray for the Master, who needs us now more than ever. Lucia, will you lead us in prayer?" Peter asked, surprising Lucia and all the others.

Lucia prayed, "Heavenly Father, you sent your Son into the world, as our Messiah, our Saviour, to save us from ourselves. He went about doing good. There is nothing evil, bad or criminal deed with which he can be charged. He is the light of the world; he came and brought us out of the darkness. Father, protect him from the forces of darkness and evil. And Father, give us the grace to remain strong in this darkest of hours, let us not lose hope. We place our trust in you."

The disciples all had their heads bowed in prayer. Peter still had his head bowed in shame. He could no long bear it, so he confessed, "Friends, I have something terrible to confess. You must remember, how I protested so often that I would follow the Master to the ends of the earth, and that I would die with him, and how he said before the cock crows I would deny him three times. You remember, how vehemently I protested, now I confess before you all, the Master was right, this very morning, before the cock crew thrice, I denied the Master, I denied him three times, denying ever knowing him, for fear of being arrested as well." Peter hung his head in shame, but there were no more tears, he had no more to spill. His heart was broken.

Immediately, Lucia, Rachel, Joanna, Salome and Susanna surrounded Peter and held him. The men too surrounded Peter. Then Peter found some more tears, as they rolled down his cheeks.

Chapter Eighty-Two
The Trial

Judas, after he had betrayed the Master, had gone home. His Father, who was awakened by the front door being unlocked, got up. He was surprised to see his son on this night of nights; surely, he would be with his band of brothers and sisters, with the Nazarene. "What brings you home tonight, at this early hour, Judas?" His Father asked.

"Father, they have arrested our Teacher," Judas said.

"They, who do you mean?" Judas' father asked, but he knew it could only be the Sanhedrin, but then it could also be Herod or Pilate, they were all interested in the affairs of Yeshua, who seemed to be stirring up the crowds, and so many people are following him and listening to him, and his teachings are so radical.

"It's the Sanhedrin Father; he is being tried as we speak," Judas said. "But don't worry, Father, there is nothing they can do to him, he has the power of God on his side," Judas said.

"Father, I think I will go and see what is happening," Judas then said. He then found his way to the house of Caiaphas and mingled with the crowd that was now gathering in big numbers outside the house of Caiaphas. It seems the whole of Jerusalem were now privy to the Great Trial that was unfolding. Judas was still waiting to see Yeshua unleash his power against Rome, and he would not let the Sanhedrin get in his way. Freedom was going to happen, and Yeshua would be the one to make that happen.

Meanwhile, inside Caiaphas' house, the trial was in full swing. Caiaphas was putting all sorts of questions to Yeshua about his teaching and his disciples to which Yeshua answered, "I have spoken openly to the world. I have always taught in synagogues and the Temple, where all Jews come together, I have said nothing in secret. Why do you ask me? Ask those who heard what I said to them; they know what I said."

As soon as Yeshua finished his sentence, a guard standing nearby struck Yeshua with the back of his hand, and then with the palm of his hand several times, while saying, "Is that how you answer the high priest?"

Yeshua looked directly at the guard and said, "If I have spoken wrongly, testify to the wrong. But if I have spoken rightly, why do you strike me?"

"Oh, don't you worry about that," Caiaphas then said. "As a matter of fact, we do have witnesses here tonight, who will testify to what you have done and said. Bring in the first witness," Caiaphas said.

The two guards stepped outside the room and instantly returned with the first witness. The witnesses were all bribed, given money to come and testify against Yeshua.

"For the record, state your name and your date of birth," one of the Scribes said.

The man who was in his senior years gave his name and date of birth, he was scruffily dressed, and was someone who clearly was living on the streets. The man felt intimidated appearing before the high priest and all of the Council. He spoke softly.

"Speak up, man," Caiaphas commanded.

The man spoke louder. Pointing to Yeshua, he said, "I saw this man, cure a man possessed by the devil, and he invoked Satan before doing so, and the man came out shouting all sorts of obscenities. He only sets those demoniacs free that Beelzebub so permits, he is a servant of Satan," the man said.

"So, Yeshua, what have you to say to this?" Caiaphas asked.

Yeshua, who had already answered this accusation so many times, remained silent. He had made his defence. All they needed to do was to bring in witnesses who heard the truth that he had spoken. But Yeshua knew that Caiaphas and the Council were not interested in the truth, they wanted to condemn him. So, Yeshua remained silent.

Several witnesses were brought in, one after the other and they all gave false and conflicting evidence.

Nicodemus and Yosef of Arimathea could no longer remain silent, in the face of all the false testimonies that were being given. Nicodemus stood up. "Gentlemen, I have something to say, in defence of this man, Yeshua, you see before you."

Caiaphas wanted to immediately silence Nicodemus, but he thought otherwise. He had to let matters unfold, and not appear to be biased, so he allowed Nicodemus the floor.

Nicodemus continued, "All these witnesses are liars. I wanted to learn from this man Yeshua, all about his teachings, so I spent a night with him. And all he taught was in keeping with our Laws. It was clear that what he said is true; he did not come to abolish our Law, but to perfect it. And what he said in his defence is valid. There are others who can testify against all that is being said by the witnesses who have spoken here, so far. I testify to the fact, that they have all not spoken the truth, either outright lies or distorted what Yeshua had taught."

Caiaphas immediately intervened; he felt Nicodemus had said enough. "Okay, Nicodemus, you had your say. We all know of your leanings to every new preaching, preachers and teachers who keep appearing with new highfalutin ideas, always looking for something spectacular. Sit down and let us continue."

But before Caiaphas could continue Yosef also rose to his feet. He felt he could not let Nicodemus alone stand on the side of Yeshua, so he said, "I must in all conscience, agree with what Nicodemus has said, and I can find nothing in this man, Yeshua that warrants our displeasure, he speaks only the truth and he goes about doing only good."

"Sit down, Yosef, how dare you speak without first seeking permission," Caiaphas yelled.

Yosef sat down. And Caiaphas continued, "We heard those for the defence of this man before us. Let us bring in further witnesses." Many more witnesses came in and it was clear that they were coached beforehand, but they all messed up matters as they got carried away by the grandeur of the occasion, and the important people present in the room. They began improvising and embellishing and contradicting each other.

Caiaphas was not pleased at all with the way matters were preceding, the witnesses were a fiasco, but he had one more ace up his sleeve. "We have one final witness, bring him in," Caiaphas said. He was putting all his bets on this final witness. They had prepared him to be the last to testify, for they believed it would be the winning blow.

This witness was a well-dressed man, definitely upper class. And he spoke as someone who was sophisticated and learned. He gave his name as Midas and he said he was a philosopher and a teacher. He testified to an expectant court, "Gentlemen, this man before you is a fraud and an impostor. He has hoodwinked the masses. We have Abraham, Isaac, Jacob, Moses and all the great prophets who have brought us the Law of Adonai and for thousands of years their teaching has stood the test of time. This man is dangerous, for he is dismantling our Laws," he said, pointing to Yeshua. "This man must be stopped or there will be a catastrophe unheard of. This impostor said, many times, 'I will destroy the Temple that is made with hands and in three days I will build another, not made with human hands.'

"This is the man who had taken whips into the Temple and with his band of misfits and criminals had overthrown the tables of those doing legitimate Temple business, during this time of the festival, and he threatened worse things to come." Midas then took a deep breath and seemed to be enjoying the attention and with a sweeping gesture, he continued, "This man is a mere carpenter from the backwoods of Galilee. Nazareth, of all places, and he dares to make himself equal to God. He claims to be one with God, equal with God, equal with the Father. He says he is the Son of God, become man. Yet he is a mortal, like you and me. And he is a sinner beyond all sinners, he shows no regard for our Sabbath or the Temple, he is a womaniser, associates with prostitutes, and touches the unclean, and dines with tax-collectors, he is a party animal, who overindulges in food and drink, and he is both a glutton and a drunkard. How can such a man dare to equate himself with God? What more can I say?" And with that, he stormed out of the Council.

Caiaphas looking pleased then stood up and looked directly at Yeshua and said, "What have you to say?" But Yeshua said nothing. Again, Caiaphas addressed Yeshua, "Have you no answer to what is being testified against you?"

But Yeshua was silent and did not answer.

Then Caiaphas asked him the question he knew would bring Yeshua down, "Tell us plainly, are you the Messiah, the Son of the Blessed One?"

This time, Yeshua did answer. He said, "I am, and you will see me, I who am the Son of Man, the Son of God made man. I who am like all other men, yet remaining the Son of God, you will see me, seated at the right hand of the Power, and coming with the clouds of heaven."

Caiaphas was jubilant, he knew he had struck the fatal blow, in a gesture of triumph, and finality, he gripped his robe with both hands and tore it down the middle, and said loudly for all to hear, "You have heard his blasphemy! What is your decision?"

With one voice, they all cried out, "He has blasphemed! He is guilty! He deserves death!"

Only Nicodemus and Yosef cried out in Yeshua's defence, but their cries were drowned by the clamour of forty voices, shouting condemnation.

Then there was pandemonium as the Council members went crazy. They approached Yeshua and struck him in the face, and some even spat on him and called him all kinds of names. Then one of them blindfolded Yeshua, and then struck Yeshua in the face and tormented Yeshua, saying, "Prophesy, you false prophet. Prophesy, who hit you then?" he laughed.

The guards also got into the act and began beating Yeshua, punching him all over. Blood was now streaming down the sides of Yeshua's mouth.

It was now past midnight, in the early hours of the morning. Caiaphas then said to the guards, "Take him to the temple stockade and lock him up securely until you have clear instructions from us."

The guards then roughly grabbed Yeshua and took him away. By this time, there were not many in the courtyard. People had grown tired of waiting and many had left. In any case, the guards went out the back door and found their way to the Temple and the stockade, where they left Yeshua, without water or any sustenance. Yeshua did have his supper, and at least that helped sustain him against all the physical abuse he endured.

The Sanhedrin was still assembled. Caiaphas then said, "Gentlemen, I thank you for a fine night's work. We have finally succeeded in our objective. But as you know, although we have the power to convict someone to death, we do not have the power to put anyone to death. That power resides only with Rome. So, our next task is to reach that objective. At first light we must take the Nazarene to Pilate and get him to order an execution. By now word will begin to disperse about what is afoot. So go home, help spread the word.

"On your way home, whoever you meet tell them to be at the Praetorium, where they will see Pilate condemn a man to death. Everyone will want to be there. Before you go, we have to arrange to let the other Council members know what has transpired. So, among you, share out the task. And at first light, no earlier than that, wake up your neighbours and friends and spread the word. I want the courtyard in front of the Praetorium to be packed, and for everyone to see the condemnation to death of the Nazarene. Jerusalem is packed with tourists and pilgrims, so spread the news about the trial and the sentence we have pronounced on the Nazarene. I want the whole of Jerusalem to be in the Praetorium.

"Also, approach all Pharisees, Sadducees, other Elders and Scribes, and all the chief priests; they all have to be informed and briefed. Council members must then take one other member and spread out among the crowd. We need to stir them up, and to get them to persuade Pilate to condemn Yeshua to death."

"How are we going to do that, what charge are we going to put before Pilate?" one of the Scribes asked.

"You heard all that was aired tonight. We can charge him for sedition, with stirring up the people, with planning a rebellion, and uprising, and with blasphemy," Caiaphas said.

"I don't think that will get us the death sentence from Pilate," the Scribe responded.

"If that doesn't, we will shout out that he is against Rome, and that he declares himself as King, the King of the Jews, that will do it. We will let Pilate know that Yeshua is against Caesar, is not for Caesar and force Pilate's hand, and tell him if he doesn't, he is no friend of Caesar's. That will scare the hell out of him. He wants to keep the peace at all costs, otherwise Rome will come down hard on him. We'll get him to cooperate, don't you worry, just follow my lead and stir up the crowd to frenzy. Bribe some people, and spread them among the crowd to help stir up everyone. And brief the rest of the Council members, about what has transpired and what their duty is at the Praetorium." The members then all left in a hurry.

Judas had been hanging around, hoping to find out what was happening and still waiting and hoping for the moment when Yeshua would unleash his power. How, Yeshua was going to do that, Judas had no idea. But he had seen Yeshua's power, and with him all things are possible. Maybe he would let lighting strike down Caiaphas place, for a start.

It was well past midnight when members of the Sanhedrin started coming out and making their way home. When that flow stopped, Judas went up to the door of Caiaphas house, but the guard stopped him.

"Who are you and what do you want?" one of them asked Judas.

"I am Judas. I am the one who has handed over Yeshua to Caiaphas. I have to speak to him," Judas said.

"Okay Sir, you may enter," the guard said, and then accompanied Judas inside. Caiaphas and Annas and their inner circle of advisors were still chatting, plotting, making sure everything would go to plan.

Caiaphas was surprised to see Judas. "Judas, what do you want, we have no more need of you. You may go," Caiaphas said, frowning.

"I just wanted to know what you have planned," Judas asked.

"It's for us to know, but you will find out soon. Be in the Praetorium this morning and you will witness the final downfall of this Yeshua. Go now, and leave us alone."

Ah, right what I wanted, Judas said to himself, as he left. *Appearing before Pilate, the head of the Roman presence and power here in Judaea, this will be the moment when all of Jerusalem will see the power of God, unleashed through his Messiah, our Saviour. The time of our freedom is at hand.* Judas then left, full of hope, that what he had initiated would finally come to fruition, that in the Praetorium, in the presence of Pilate and all the people, Yeshua would unleash his power and begin to annihilate the power of Rome.

Word got to Peter and the others in the Cenacle, the room where they had their Last Supper with the Lord. It was now their home. Isaiah, the master and owner of the large house had given permission for them to stay and to use the Cenacle for their meetings. They had informed him of what had happened to Yeshua. Isaiah told them that his home was now their home, as long as they needed it. That is what he wanted Yeshua to have. And there were plenty of rooms for them to bed down. Isaiah had several servants to make sure that they were all comfortable and had all their living needs met. The disciples were most grateful. None of the disciples knew Isaiah that well, he kept to himself, and did not disturb them, but they all surmised that he must be a believer, a follower of Yeshua, for he spoke with the highest regard of Yeshua and made it clear that all he had was at Yeshua's disposal and for his work, and now available for them.

"So, the Sanhedrin has found the Master guilty of what I have no idea. But they now appear to have condemned him to death. But we all know only Rome has the power to execute anyone, so that is why they are taking him to Pilate. We must be there in the Praetorium and do what we can to prevent that," Peter said.

"Peter, Pilate will have his Roman guards out in full force, there will be hundreds of them in the Praetorium for sure, and hundreds, if not thousands on standby just in case of any uprising. But it will be safer, if we spread ourselves around the crowd," Peter said.

"Peter, I don't think we should be there at all. If we are recognised, we will suffer the same fate as the Master. I think we should stay here, until all this blows over. Yeshua can take care of himself. You see the power he has. I'm sure he would not want us to put ourselves in danger needlessly," Thomas said.

The others agreed, and persuaded Peter that they remain locked up, until all this was over, and that Yeshua was freed, either by Pilate, or he would simply disappear from their midst as he had done on occasions during the past three years. It was decided that they stay locked, with all the doors and windows bolted.

Miriam and the women however had decided that they would go to the Praetorium. They wanted to be there to support Yeshua, in whatever way they could.

Chapter Eighty-Three
Before Pontius Pilate

At sunrise, Caiaphas and Annas and their closest advisers appeared at the door of Herod's Palace where Pilate, the Procurator, the Roman governor, was staying, with his wife and daughter. Pilate had his own palace, in Caesarea on the coast of the Great Sea. Pilate only came to Jerusalem during the different Festivals, and especially for the Passover Festival, when over a million Jews and visitors from all over the world, from all over the Roman Empire, would descend on Jerusalem. Pilate had to make sure to keep the peace; with such big numbers anything could ignite an uprising of sorts.

When in Jerusalem, Pilate had two options; he could stay at the Antonia Fortress at the north-west corner of the Temple Mount that was also erected by Herod's father but now belonged to the Roman authorities.

Herod, the Tetrarch of Galilee and Perea, used the palace as his palace here in Jerusalem, where he spent most of his time.

The Antonia Fortress served as the Roman garrison, with barracks for all the hundreds of Roman guards and personnel and servants. But Pilate always preferred the more palatial, comfortable, spacious and grandiose Palace of Herod's, especially to please his wife Claudia, and their daughter, Procula. And Pilate's quarters, the west wing, were completely separate from that of Herod's that was on the east wing. Herod made sure he was not in Jerusalem at the same time as Pilate. On the odd occasion when he was, he kept away from Pilate, even though they shared the palace. So, they seldom saw each other and that was what they both preferred.

Guards stood at the door of Pilate's quarters, and stopped Caiaphas and Annas, but as soon as they identified themselves and gave their titles as high priests, they were ready to let them in, even though it was so early in the day, the sun was just beginning to rise. Caiaphas told them that it was urgent business, matters of life and death, and that they had to see Pilate immediately.

Pilate was just rising from his slumber and he was told that the high priests, Caiaphas and Annas were in the lobby wanting to speak with him, and that the matter was urgent and they apologised for the early hour. Pilate was by no means pleased to be disturbed at such an early hour.

They waited for Pilate to come. They had to wait for a while, because Pilate had just risen from his slumber and was busy with his morning ablutions. He had a mind to first have his breakfast but he did not want to spoil his breakfast, with the thought of them waiting. And he was curious, wondering what the urgent business was that brings them to him at this ungodly hour.

"Good day to you, gentleman, what is your business?" Pilate went right down to business, which suited both Caiaphas and Annas.

"My Lord," they recoiled inwardly, loathing having to address Pilate in this way, but they were willing to kowtow and eat humble pie in order to get their way with Pilate. "Last night, our whole Tribunal met," Caiaphas blatantly lied, as it wasn't the entire Sanhedrin. But he could not jeopardise their quest in any way. He continued, "Last night, we put on trial this man Yeshua, who is stirring up the people and spreading all kinds of lies and making spurious claims, and he is a danger to the stability of our nation. We tried him and found him guilty of death. But as only you my Lord, are the only one who has the power to execute anyone, to order any one to be put to death, we wish to bring this Yeshua to you, to ratify what we have concluded."

Pilate stroked his clean-shaven chin and considered for a while. He could hear noise from people outside, who were gathering and coming from every corner of Jerusalem.

Caiaphas struck again; he didn't want Pilate to dither. He said, "The people are gathering in the courtyard. They know that we the Sanhedrin, the highest of our courts, have found Yeshua guilty of the vilest of crimes, and he must be put to death, and they want you to make that official," Caiaphas said.

The noise from the courtyard outside was increasing. Pilate told them to wait as he went upstairs and walked out onto a balcony to have a look. He was amazed to see the size of the crowd in the courtyard, at such an early hour, and he looked beyond and saw people coming from all directions. He knew he had no option but to address the crowd. So, he went back to Caiaphas and Annas and said, "Gentlemen, I have considered what you have said. I will examine your prisoner and give you my verdict. Bring him to me later, in an hour's time, as I still have to have my breakfast."

Caiaphas and Annas felt like punching the air. They were jubilant. They rushed off. Their cronies spread the news, which went like air waves across the multitude, as people spread it from one to the other, "Pilate will appear soon at the Praetorium, the place from where he will pronounce judgement on the Nazarene." People remained, not wanting to miss the spectacle and also to see both Pilate and the Nazarene, especially those who had not yet had a glimpse of either of them.

Before the sun rose, Miriam and Rebecca and all the women got dressed and quickly had something to eat and drink and then were on their way. They knew it would be a long day. Miriam and Rebecca hastened to the campsite of the people of Nazareth, to inform Miriam, Yeshua's mother, of what was unfolding. As they walked the streets it was not the usual quiet for this time of day; people were up and about and as the sun was now making its presence felt, crowds of people appeared, filling the streets and alleyways, all heading in the same direction, towards the Praetorium. When Miriam and Rebecca arrived at the Nazarene campsite, people were up and about and some were already on their way into the city. Miriam and Rebecca found Miriam, Yeshua's mother.

"Miriam, I presume, you heard what is happening to your Yeshua?" Miriam of Magdala said.

"Yes, Miriam, I have," Miriam said sadly. "I am just about ready to leave and be with him," Miriam added.

"We will go with you, Miriam, and stay with you," Rebecca said, she was at a loss of what to say to comfort Miriam, who was like a second mother to her. The three women then made their way with the rest of the crowds all converging on the Praetorium at Herod's Palace. Crowds had swelled and the place was packed, and overflowing.

Pilate seemed unperturbed by the noise coming from the gathering crowds outside, as he sat with his wife and teenage daughter at the table having breakfast. "Father, what are you going to do, are you going to condemn that man, Yeshua, the Nazarene? I hear their priests want him to die. What has he done?" Procula asked.

"Father, my friends and I have been talking about him, and we have heard only good things about him, and that he has supernatural powers and can heal people," Procula said.

"Procula, these are strange people and they have strange beliefs, they believe in only one god, they call him Yahweh. This Yeshua, I am told, claims he is the son of this god come down to earth," Pilate said.

"Pontius, you must have nothing to do with this man Yeshua, you must set him free, I had a terrible dream about him," Pilate's wife Claudia said, with great concern.

"Tell us the dream, mother," Procula said, lighting up; she was curious to hear what her mother had dreamed about the Nazarene.

Claudia began to relate her dream, "In my dream, we were asleep and these massive snakes appeared and slid over each of us as we lay sleeping, and in my dream, I woke and screamed but you both could not hear me. And then I smelt smoke and flames started creeping into our room, and I shouted and still you both slept. And I could not move as the flames were all around us, but it would not consume us. And then I was at this hill and on the top of the hill was the Nazarene standing on a cross, he didn't seem to be hanging but standing, and he was dressed in fine gilded garments, royal attire, and on his head was a crown, a kingly crown. And all around, the hill was on fire, but the Nazarene, Yeshua, was not being consumed, and he was smiling.

"And then the fire began to spread, it seemed like a river of fire flowing from the foot of the cross, and then it flowed into the city and then I saw their Temple go up in flames, and then, I don't know how, this Palace of Herod's was burning, and burning, and I was shouting my lungs out, but you both slept. And then in my dream we were back in Rome, and on the top of the Seven Hills of Rome, stood the Cross and it was in flames, but not being consumed. And then I saw the flames consume and burn to ashes all our monuments to our gods. And then I woke up. Pontius, you must let this man go, have nothing to do with him," Claudia insisted.

"It is only a dream, my love. I have to do what I have to do. But I know it is only out of envy that the high priest and his cronies want me to condemn the Nazarene to death. They are envious of him because all the people are following him. On the other hand, he could be a threat if he has such power over the people. He could lead a revolt against Rome. I have to keep the peace at all costs, you know that dear, that is why I am here and what Rome expects of me," Pilate said.

During this time, Caiaphas and Annas and their advisors were busy refining their plans and making the arrangements for Yeshua to be brought to Pilate. Caiaphas had a quick bun to eat and a glass of wine. It was early and he never had a drink at this hour before but he just felt he needed one now. Then he was on his way. He and Annas and his closest allies, went to the Temple stockade and had Yeshua brought out, bound with chains.

Yeshua looked terrible. His hair was dishevelled and his clothes torn and it looked like he did not have any sleep. "Clean him up and give him some water, we can't make it look like we have abused him," Caiaphas ordered the guards before they led Yeshua out to Pilate.

Pilate knew that Yeshua would have been ill-treated by the guards. He did not bother about that, whoever landed in the stockade deserved what they got. But Caiaphas and Annas wanted to make sure that nothing went wrong and they did not want anything to backfire, so they allowed Yeshua to have some water, and to wash the blood and dirt from his face. And then they were on their way.

When they arrived at the Praetorium and the people saw them with Yeshua, now bound with chains, the people began to shout, "It's the Nazarene! It's Yeshua! He is here!" Yeshua was then led up the steps of the Praetorium and made to stand on a dais for all to see. And Yeshua stood in front of an elaborate and stately chair, which had already been put out for Pilate to sit on. It was on a high platform, on the top of five steps, all draped in rich carpets. Two armed Temple guards stood on either side of Yeshua, as they waited for Pilate to appear.

And then he appeared and there was a mixture of cheers and boos. Pilate gave a stately wave and gestured for the people to quiet down. He looked at Yeshua with great interest as if he was inspecting a precious commodity. So, this is the man, a humble, uneducated man, from the boondocks of remote and little Nazareth, who is causing such a stir. He seems so innocuous, Pilate thought. Pilate then turned to Caiaphas and his group and said, "What accusation do you bring against this man?" Pilate spoke as loud as he could, and although the place was built with such good acoustics, not everyone could hear. So, the people passed on to each other what was being said, so that everyone in the crowd could know what was being said, and what was unfolding.

To Pilate's question, Caiaphas answered, "If this man were not a criminal, we would not have handed him over to you."

Pilate said, "Why don't you go and judge him yourselves according to your Law?" Pilate knew they had already done that, but he wanted to let the crowd see he was doing his job.

Caiaphas spoke for all, "We have judged him and found him guilty and deserving of death. But we are not permitted to put anyone to death. That is why we have brought him to you."

Pilate then addressed Yeshua and asked, "Are you the King of the Jews?"

Yeshua answered, "Do you ask this on your own, or did others tell you about me?"

Pilate replied, "I am not a Jew, am I? Your own nation and your chief priests have handed you over to me. So, tell me, are you a king?"

Yeshua answered, and his answer was being relayed throughout the crowd, that was now silent, hanging onto every word being uttered. Yeshua said, "Yes, I am a king. My kingdom is not from this world. If my kingdom were from this world, my followers would be fighting to keep me from being handed over to the Jews. But as it is, my Kingdom is not from here."

Judas was in the crowd and right up front, because he wanted to hear everything first hand and he was full of expectancy and waiting for Yeshua to show his power in front of this enormous crowd. But on hearing what Yeshua had just said, about his kingdom not being of this world and about his followers not being of this world either, Judas was confused and greatly disturbed. Things were not happening as he had expected. Great distress now began to invade his mind.

Pilate then asked Yeshua, "So you are a king?"

Yeshua answered, "You say that I am a king. For this I was born, and for this I came into the world, to testify to the truth. Everyone who belongs to the truth listens to my voice."

Pilate asked him, "What is truth?"

Pilate didn't really wait for or expect an answer from Yeshua. Caiaphas and those with him were getting anxious; they could see that Pilate was being swayed in the wrong direction by Yeshua and that Pilate was vacillating. So, Caiaphas struck and pointed at Yeshua and made accusations, saying what he knew would resonate with Pilate, "We found this man perverting our nation, forbidding us to pay taxes to the emperor and saying that he himself is both King and Messiah."

Pilate had already questioned Yeshua about his kingship and was satisfied that he was no real threat, but this Messiah thing could be a problem. Pilate wasn't sure if he should acquiesce to Caiaphas' and the chief priests' demands. He knew they were just envious of his popularity and because so many people were now his followers. Pilate was inclined to let Yeshua go for now, so he said to the chief priests and the crowd, "I find no basis for an accusation against this man that deserves the death penalty."

Caiaphas struck back immediately, "He stirs up the people by teaching throughout all Judaea, from Galilee where he began, even to this place."

When Caiaphas mentioned Yeshua being from Galilee, which Pilate already knew, he saw a way out, because Galilee was in Herod's jurisdiction, and Herod just happened to have arrived in Jerusalem, so Pilate said, "Herod is the rightful tetrarch of Galilee, and it is only right that he examine this case against a Galilean. Take him to Herod." And with that Pilate got off his chair and went into the house. Claudia, who was listening through an open window, was relieved; she didn't want Pilate to be the one to pronounce the death sentence on this Yeshua.

Although Pilate was living here in Herod's Palace, he and his family remained cut off from Herod's quarters and they never met and did not really associate with each other, except very rarely for official business. Pilate and Herod really abhorred each other, it could be said they were enemies rather than friends.

Caiaphas told the crowds that a verdict would soon be made, and that they were going through the procedures and will be taking Yeshua to Herod. Caiaphas was confident that Herod would play ball and that this was just a slight hiccup. They would go through the motions but be back with Pilate for only he had the power to put Yeshua to death.

Herod was quickly informed by his advisors, that Yeshua was being brought to him. And they briefed him on what had transpired, and what was expected of him. Herod was still unsettled, he still had nightmares with what happened to Johanan, and the sight of his head on a platter kept reappearing in his dreams, causing him to awake in a sweat. Herod had heard of this Yeshua, and heard of his powers and Herod was hoping to see Yeshua perform something spectacular.

Herod questioned Yeshua at length, according to a list that his advisors gave him, but Yeshua remained silent and would give Herod no answer.

Caiaphas and some of the chief priests and Scribes stood by and vehemently repeated the accusations they laid before Pilate. But Yeshua was unperturbed and remained silent, which infuriated Herod, and all the accusers, so they treated Yeshua with contempt, and mocked him. And Herod's soldiers also treated Yeshua with contempt and joined in mocking Yeshua. Then Herod just gave up, and for some reason only he could explain, maybe to confuse Pilate, put an elegant robe on Yeshua, or maybe he was just mocking Yeshua, and he then sent Yeshua back to Pilate.

The crowds were getting restless but no one left the Praetorium. They were all waiting for an outcome. Miriam, Yeshua's mother, Miriam of Magdala, and Rebecca were huddled together amidst the crowd, they too were waiting and hoping that somehow Yeshua would be set free, but they did not have high hopes. Judas too was in the crowd but he, on the other hand, was still entertaining some hope that Yeshua would somehow unleash his power and his glory would be revealed. But Judas was starting to have uneasy feeling in the pit of his stomach.

The people cheered and jeered as they saw Yeshua, still in chains being brought back, surrounded by the high priest and chief priests and guards. They waited until Pilate finally appeared. Pilate was briefed on what had transpired with Herod because his advisors had gone with Caiaphas and his mob to witness for themselves the proceedings with Herod. Claudia had again warned her husband not to have anything to do with Yeshua.

Pilate then addressed Caiaphas and the accusers with him and he spoke loudly for all to hear, "You brought me this man as one who was perverting the people; and here I have examined him in your presence, and have not found this man guilty of any of your charges against him. Neither has Herod, for he sent him back to us. Indeed, he has done nothing to deserve death; I will therefore have him flogged and release him."

Miriam of Nazareth, Miriam of Magdala, and Rebecca, on hearing Pilate's words, were horrified, yet were hopeful, and they prayed to Yahweh to save Yeshua from the hand of his enemies. By this time the rest of the women disciples had met up with them, and they found great strength and comfort in their numbers. Peter and the rest of the men were still cooped up and locked up in the Cenacle, except for Johanan, who was somewhere in the crowd.

Pilate then stood up, went closer to the crowd, ignoring Caiaphas and all of the accusers. Pilate was hoping to sway the crowd, and appeal to their common decency. He said, "This is a great festival for all of you, a time for rejoicing and feasting. As you can see, I have found nothing to condemn this man to death, so for whatever he is being accused of, my sentence is that he be flogged and then released. He will be brought out to you and as is my custom, of releasing a prisoner to you during the festival, I have a mind to release Yeshua to you."

Caiaphas and his associates, and all of the Sanhedrin had been prepared for this. They executed their plan, and shouted for all to hear, "Release Barabbas, not this man." And then in a chorus of voices that resounded throughout the Praetorium, the people shouted, "Barabbas! Barabbas! Release Barabbas!"

Miriam, Yeshua's mother, and Miriam and Rebecca and all the other women's cries for Yeshua to be released were drowned in the thunderous sounds of the voices yelling for Barabbas to be released. There were others in the crowd that would also want Yeshua released, Johanan was one of them, but they were too afraid that the crowd might turn on them. Judas on the other hand was now getting very worried. He could now sense the tide turning completely against Yeshua, and it didn't seem like Yeshua was going to use his powers in any way.

Pilate then spoke to the guards, "Take him away and flog him as I have ordered, and then bring him back, and fetch Barabbas and bring them both back to me."

And so, the soldiers took Yeshua away. More soldiers had been sent for, and there were now many of them surrounding Yeshua. They took him into a basement in Herod's palace, and there they bound him to a pillar and prepared to flog him, as

Pilate had ordered. Caiaphas and some of his associates were with them. They wanted to witness everything. The guards started stripping Yeshua of all his clothes. The Lord of Lords and the King of Kings was naked and exposed, humiliated before these coarse soldiers who began mocking him, slapping him, and some were spitting on him.

"How many lashes?" the soldier with the whip in his hand asked the rest of them.

"The usual," another soldier replied.

"We don't want to reduce him to a corpse yet, Pilate wants him back alive," the Centurion in charge of them all said.

"What about you, Sir?" the soldier with the whip addressed Caiaphas. "How many lashes do you think this criminal of yours deserves, fifty, seventy or a hundred?"

Yeshua was terrified. He had never been whipped in his life, and he thought of the many poor prisoners who went through what he was about to experience. The cruelty of the Roman guards was common knowledge, they were barbaric and reduced criminals to a pulp, before they were mercilessly crucified. Thousands of them could be seen in agony, hanging on a cross, wasting away all over the country side. Pilate condoned the atrocious torture and agonising deaths, for he wanted to create fear among the populace so they would not rebel in any way.

Caiaphas knew that the soldiers would whip Yeshua to within inches of his life. He did not want that to happen yet, so he said, "He must be kept alive. Our law has a limit of forty, less one lashes, so give him thirty-nine." Evidently, that lashing law was created because it was deemed that forty lashes would cause death to the victim.

The soldier then began to whip Yeshua with all his might. Yeshua screamed in agony as the first lash whipped his bare back. And then it came in waves and the pain grew and grew until he was almost numb. He cried out to his Father to save him. And then he almost blacked out and was as if he was in another world, and that nothing else existed except excruciating pain.

Caiaphas and those with him left after six lashes, they could not look on any more or listen to Yeshua's screams. The soldiers continued, and as Caiaphas and his entourage walked away from that dungeon, they no longer heard Yeshua's screams, just slight whimpers, but the sound of the whip on torn flesh made them shake.

The soldiers stopped at thirty-nine strokes. They untied Yeshua from the pillar and Yeshua dropped to the floor, rolled limply to his side and lay still, as if he was dead. Yeshua was in terrible pain, but slowly the pain seemed to subside somewhat, as if the body was getting accustomed to the pain.

The soldiers then proceeded to mock Yeshua. "So, this is their king, the King of the Jews. Come on, guys, let us do homage to the king," one of the guards said, laughing out loud.

"Yes, let us seat him on his throne," said another, as he got a stool and roughly shoved Yeshua onto the stool. Yeshua was still naked, and he felt the humiliation, but even that was numbed by his aching limbs. Yeshua was now starting to breathe more heavily. He was fearful of what further torture awaited him.

"Wait, we cannot worship a naked king; he must wear his regal robes." So, they clothed Yeshua in a crimson cloak. Then one of the soldiers put a reed in Yeshua's right hand. "Look at that beautiful golden sceptre of our king. Let us pay homage to our king." They came before Yeshua and bowed before him and mocked him, and some came up and slapped him in the face, and some spat on him.

"Honourable gentlemen, my lords, we have a king without a crown. Our king must have a crown. Quick, let us get some thorns and weave a glorious crown for our celebrated king."

The soldiers were laughing and taunting Yeshua, while some of them went outside and found some thorns which they brought back in their gloved hands. And then together, they quickly wove a crown of thorns. Then, in a mock ceremony, one of them walked up solemnly, with the crown of thorns on a platter, while the rest cheered as the soldier came up to Yeshua and placed the crown of thorns firmly on his head, and a new kind of pain swept through Yeshua's body as he cried out. Blood was now also seeping down his forehead and the side of his face. Yeshua was feeling faint, as if he was about to black out.

The soldiers then came before him and bowed and they began saluting Yeshua, shouting, "Hail, King of the Jews!"

The soldiers were now in a rage and were like madmen, but the Centurion intervened, "Okay, that is enough. We better take him back to Pilate." They then took off the purple cloak and put Yeshua's own clothes on him, for which Yeshua was grateful. They then led him back to Pilate.

Pilate was shocked to see the state Yeshua was in, he wasn't accustomed to see the effects of the torture dished out by his soldiers. "Take him outside. Put him on the dais, and then get Barabbas to stand on the other dais." And so, it was done.

Pilate then went outside and the swelling crowd was now getting impatient, they were jeering and were like animals baying for blood. Before them was the accused, the Nazarene, the troublemaker, and also Barabbas, the murderer, who committed murder during an insurrection. While some of the crowd sympathised with Barabbas, after all he had the guts to rise up against the might of Rome, they did not think that Yeshua's crimes, were anywhere near that of Barabbas. But they were being primed by the almost seventy Sanhedrin members spread throughout the crowd, as well as so many Pharisees, Scribes, Sadducees, Elders and chief priests. They were telling the people they must pick Barabbas and not Yeshua. The Law and Yahweh demand it.

Pilate then presented Yeshua to the people and pointing at Yeshua, still wearing a crown of thorns, he said, "*Ecce homo*! Here is the man, look at him!" Pilate was hoping that the people would show some sympathy, would see what Yeshua was reduced to and let him go, and choose him to be released over a murderer. So, Pilate said to them, "So, who would you want me to release to you, the King of the Jews, who has done nothing to demand death, or this vile criminal, and murderer you see before you, Barabbas?"

Immediately, a roar came from the crowd, "Barabbas! Barabbas! Barabbas! Release Barabbas!"

Pilate was shocked. His wife, standing at the window, with her daughter, was in shock as well, and Claudia was terrified. How could these people be so stupid, so blind and so gullible?

Pilate then asked the crowd, "What then do you want me to do with Yeshua, your king?"

With one voice the crowd, stoked by the Sanhedrin members and others, roared, "Crucify him! Crucify him! Crucify him!"

Pilate was bamboozled. He had failed in his endeavour to release Yeshua. His wife's dream came back to haunt him. "Bring this man Yeshua to me, I wish to have one more word with him, alone," Pilate said.

Pilate then got up and walked inside flanked by his two guards, and two other guards who were standing beside Yeshua, escorted him into the palace.

Once inside, Pilate sat down and began to speak with Yeshua. Claudia was now in the far end of the room, with her daughter beside her. Pilate indicated to the soldiers to give Yeshua a stool. Yeshua was grateful for the reprieve, he had been on his feet for so long and he was feeling extremely weak and fragile.

Pilate then asked Yeshua, "Where are you from?"

But Yeshua gave him no answer.

Pilate then said, "Do you refuse to speak to me? Do you not know that I have the power to release you and power to crucify you?"

Yeshua then chose to speak and answered Pilate, "You would have no power over me unless it had been given you from above; therefore, the one who handed me over to you is guilty of a greater sin."

Pilate sighed. He rubbed his face with his right hand and rested his hand over his mouth as he looked at Yeshua. There was something about him; he just couldn't put his finger on it. *But here he is, he had used a whip and drove traders out of the Temple, telling them they were desecrating a holy place, claiming it to be his father's house. He is purported to be a healer, and he associates with the poor, with our tax-collectors, who are abhorred by the rest of the populace. I have never heard of him speaking out against Rome or being seditious in any way. And I hear reports of him curing people of all kinds of illnesses and even of raising a man in Bethany from the dead, who had been dead for four days. Of course that could only be a fabrication, by some of his fanatical followers.* Pilate was confused. He looked at his wife, and her looks said to him, 'Release the man.'

Pilate then ordered Yeshua to be brought before the crowd again, and made one final attempt, "Here is your king, I shall release him," he said.

There was an orchestrated uproar, and Caiaphas cried out loudly, "If you release this man, you are no friend of the emperor!" And in unison, the others repeated Caiaphas' cry that then reverberated throughout the crowd, shouting "No friend of the emperor! No friend of Caesar's!"

Caiaphas gestured for the crowd to stop, and then he cried out to stoke the crowd even more, for he felt that the tide was turning his way, "Anyone who claims to be a king sets himself against the emperor, against Caesar!" And the crowd echoed his words.

When Pilate heard these words, he was terrified. *These crafty, meddling priests, they know just how to stir up the crowd and get their way.* He looked at his wife with a look of defeat. Pilate then went and sat on the judge's stone bench, called the Gabbatha, the bench of Judgment. Now it was the day of Preparation for the Passover, and about mid-morning, almost the third hour, and Pilate said to all present, "Here is your King!" It was one final attempt to bring them to their senses.

But prompted by Caiaphas and all his accomplices, the crowd cried out, "Away with him! Away with him! Crucify him!"

Pilate could not believe that they wanted this Yeshua to be crucified, so he asked them, "Shall I crucify your King?"

Caiaphas and those with him answered, "We have no king but the emperor!" And these words reverberated through the crowd like a deafening echo. And cries went out for Yeshua to be crucified.

Pilate now saw that he could do nothing more and that a riot was beginning. He called a guard to him and said, "Bring me a bowl of water and a basin and a towel." The guard obeyed and brought the water to Pilate. Then Pilate ostentatiously washed his hands in front of the crowd and said in a loud voice, "I am innocent of this man's blood; see to it yourselves."

Then the people, prompted by the leaders, answered as one, "His blood be on us and on our children."

Pilate then released Barabbas and handed Yeshua over to be crucified.

Chapter Eighty-Four
The Pathway to the Cross

Yeshua, surrounded by guards and the crowds, was taken to the Antonia Fortress, on the northwest corner of the Temple Mount. The cross on which Yeshua was to be crucified was there, and the soldiers who would do the crucifying had to fetch all that they needed, ladders, rope, and their tools of death; nails, hammers, spears, and clubs, in case they needed to break Yeshua's legs. Two other criminals, who were to be crucified with Yeshua, were already on their way to Golgotha, ahead of Yeshua. Three crosses and lots of hammers and nails and all else needed for the crucifixion, had to be carted to Golgotha. Donkeys were used. However, it was decided, at the prompting from Caiaphas, that Yeshua would carry his own cross through the streets of Jerusalem. They wanted the people to witness his humiliation and demise.

The crowds followed. They were accustomed to see people hanging on a cross all over the land. They were the worst of the scum of society and deserved to die. But this crucifixion they all felt was different. This man was different, he wasn't the typical low life, the barbaric criminal, he was a preacher, a do-gooder, and purported to be a miracle worker, and who claimed to come from God, and to be the Messiah. They all wanted to see it right through to the bitter end, and see how it would all end.

Caiaphas and all of his cronies, the Pharisees, Scribes, Sadducees, Elders, chief priests, and all their supporters were jubilant, rejoicing that they had finally succeeded in achieving their objective, 'it is better for one man to die, than for the whole nation to perish.' They were gloating and blind to the greatest injustice in the history of humankind, in condemning this innocent man, this man who said, he is the Messiah, the Son of God, and the Saviour of the world and the Redeemer of humankind. The tragedy is that they did not believe him, for he is all that he claimed to be. But they were blinded by their arrogance, their envy, their lust for power, position, prestige, popularity, and their living in the darkness, and refusing to be brought out of the darkness, by him who said of himself, and who is, 'the light of the world', and that he had come to give humankind, 'life to the full'.

Yeshua, because he was fully human, was feeling most depressed, disheartened, discouraged, to see all that he had taught being so blatantly rejected. He felt an overwhelming sadness and sorrow. He was mourning a death, not his own, but the death of the people. He loved them all, and this is what they are doing to him. His battered and bruised body was aching in every part, and he was totally exhausted, and could barely stay on his feet. It was now almost six hours since he was arrested, and all of that time, he had been on his feet, except when he was seated on a stool and mocked and crowned with thorns.

Before the Sanhedrin, before Pilate and before Herod, he had been kept standing. His stomach was now aching, as he had had nothing to eat since that last supper with his disciples. And no one gave him a single drop of water to quench his thirst. His thirst made him lick his lips, in an effort to find some liquid, but even his lips were dry and he was feeling so weak and dehydrated. He just felt like falling down and curling up into a ball.

Then he prayed, "Father, I need your strength. Father send your Spirit, our Spirit to lift me up, and give me the strength I need, to carry my cross. Come Holy Spirit, fill my heart and the hearts of all those who remain faithful. Enkindle in them the fire of your love. Father, send forth your Spirit, to come to all of humankind, and they will be created, and let your Spirit touch all here today, all who have had a hand in my sentence, I pray for them all, that you Father, send your Spirit on them all and you will renew the face of the earth."

Yeshua felt renewed and strengthened and reminded of why he came to this earth, to give life and life to the full. He was sent by the Father, to show the way, to teach the truth, and to give that life to the full, and for that he has lived, and for that he is now ready to die.

Miriam, Yeshua's mother, when she heard Pilate's final words, was on the verge of collapsing. She felt faint, but Miriam of Magdala noticed the change that came over her and put her arm around her and held her up. Rebecca too supported her from the other side. The two of them, were holding back their tears, their deep, deep sorrow, for they wanted to be there for Yeshua's mother, they could not begin to imagine what she was going through, what she was suffering at that moment.

The whole of Yeshua's life was flashing through Miriam, Yeshua's mother's mind, as if in an instant, and she could not believe what was unfolding before her eyes. She wanted to go to her son, to comfort him, as she always did. She prayed in her heart for him.

All the women were quietly weeping. They were sorrowful unto death. Johanan's heart too was aching. He felt so ashamed of himself, and of the rest of the twelve, and especially of Judas, the traitor. Johanan was seething. But his heart was broken, and he prayed the prayer the Master taught them, and said that part over and over again, "Father, forgive us our trespasses, as we forgive those who trespass against us. And lead us not into temptation, but deliver us from evil."

Judas, when he heard Pilate's final word, was stunned into a state of shock, disbelief and horror. He stood motionless for a while. The full implication of his actions hit home like a ton of bricks. *What have I done? What have I done?* In that instant, Judas had complete clarity. He realised the fullness of the meaning of Yeshua's life and teaching. All he had half-heard, half-heartedly heard Yeshua say, now came back to him, and now he realised what Yeshua was trying to teach, about his Kingdom, not being of this world. Judas was overcome with emotion. He felt a deep shadow come over him and he felt completely engrossed in darkness. "My God, my God, I have betrayed the blood of an innocent man," he cried.

Caiaphas and Annas, and some Elders, on their way to the fortress, stopped at the Temple and went inside for a moment. Judas had been following and saw them enter the Temple. He saw his opportunity and followed them inside the now empty Temple. Judas approached and called out, "Caiaphas!"

Caiaphas turned around, as did those with him, and they were all surprised to see Judas. "What do you want?" Caiaphas said impatiently, he wanted nothing more to do with Judas.

Judas then said, "I have sinned by betraying innocent blood."

But Caiaphas spoke for everyone, "What is that to us? See to it yourself."

Judas then took the thirty pieces of silver from a pouch and threw it down on the floor of the Temple, in front of Caiaphas and the Elders' feet, and then Judas disappeared.

Caiaphas and the others were momentarily thrown off balance. They collected the thirty pieces of silver. Caiaphas then said, "It is not lawful to put this money back into the treasury, since it is blood money."

"What shall we do with it then?" one of the Elders asked.

"We have been talking about a burial place for foreigners for a while; we could use it for that. We had thought of considering purchasing the Potter's Field for that purpose, maybe we can use this money now for that," another said.

"That's a good idea, that's settled then, we will use this money to buy the Potter's Field as a burial place for foreigners," Caiaphas said. They all agreed. After they had finished their brief business in the Temple they went to catch up with Yeshua and the soldiers.

Judas left the Temple, he was in a very dark place, and he felt as if he had fallen into a deep dark pit from which there was no way out. He was gripped by a deep, dark and dangerous fit of depression, the likes of which he had never experienced before. He had suffered anxiety before but nothing like this. He was feeling like he was being strangled, and he felt so alone and so scared. He went home, walking, as if in a daze. "What have I done! What have I done!" he kept repeating to himself. A dark cloud seemed to be enveloping him. He went searching and found some rope, which he hid in a bag. He then went out looking for a place, a place of execution, execution for himself, for he felt he deserved to die. He found a place, a row of trees along a high ridge. Then Judas committed the ultimate act of despair, he tied the rope around a branch of one of the trees and hung himself.

It just happened that there were strong winds blowing along the ridge. Judas did not take long to die a lonely and miserable death. The winds grew stronger, it caused the rope to slip off the branch and from such a great height Judas' dead body fell among the rocks below and the impact caused him to burst open in the middle of his body and all his bowels gushed out. And that was the sad end of Judas.

Chapter Eighty-Five
Via Dolorosa—The Way of the Cross

Yeshua was still standing, surrounded by guards, as they waited for his heavy wooden cross to be brought out. Yeshua saw the cross and he trembled. Fear never left him, ever since he was first arrested in the garden of Gethsemane. He had seen so many other unfortunate souls hanging on crosses spread around the countryside, and now he would be one of them. He prayed for strength to carry his cross.

The soldiers dropped the heavy wood onto his right shoulder, and Yeshua staggered and almost fell, the cross was so heavy. He had to steady himself and draw on the last vestiges of his strength to prevent himself from falling under the heavy weight, and being crushed by the cross. The soldiers helped steady him. Once Yeshua caught his breath and steadied himself, a soldier whipped him like a beast and shouted, "Get moving, we haven't got all day!"

Crowds were swelling, many of them visitors to the city for the Great Festival, and now they were witnessing a crucifixion, something they could talk about when they got home. The guards had their hands full, keeping the crowds at bay. Among the crowd, somewhere at the back were the women, Miriam, mother of Yeshua, Miriam of Magdala, Rebecca, Lucia, Susannah, Joanna, Salome, and Miriam Cleopas and Miriam Zebedee, who had lately joined the ranks of Yeshua's disciples, and followed and supported him. There were several other disciples, those of the seventy-two that Yeshua had sent out to spread the Good News. Many of them were in a state of shock and disbelief. Many could not fathom how it was possible that this could happen to the gentle and also all-powerful Yeshua. But there were other disciples who knew this would come about, as Yeshua had told them so, and for them it now made sense, but it still filled them with overwhelming sadness and sorrow. For some, they were filled with fear; they feared they too would be targeted and hunted down and have the same fate as their Lord and Master. They tried their best to be as inconspicuous as possible.

All of the members of the Sanhedrin, the entire membership of seventy-two, were scattered among the crowd, they had been there all along as soon as Yeshua was arrested. Some of them were miffed that they were not part of the assembly that had convicted Yeshua to death. They coveted the fame. Also among the crowd were Nicodemus and Yosef of Arimathea, the only two members of the Tribunal who spoke up for, and defended Yeshua. They felt a deep shame, to have even been part of the Tribunal that condemned this innocent man, the true Lord and Messiah to death. But now their lives could no longer be the same, they both knew this.

The crowd continued to swell, and get noisier. The guards sent for reinforcements to keep control, as everyone was pushing and shoving in order to get a better view of Yeshua.

Yeshua walked from the steps of the Antonia Fortress. He was moving so slowly, because the weight of the cross made his steps uneasy. "Move along!" a soldier shouted and whipped Yeshua, causing him to begin to fall. Yeshua had no option but to let go of the cross and try in some way to prevent falling, but there was nothing else he could do but to abandon himself, and just fall and protect himself as best he could. The cross fell on top of his bruised and battered back and all that pain returned and sent a shiver up his body.

"Get up!" a soldier shouted, as he again whipped Yeshua's lacerated body, causing more pain to course though his body. "Get up!" another guard shouted, as he kicked Yeshua in the side of his body. Yeshua groaned and then drew on the last vestiges of his strength to struggle onto his feet.

Miriam, his mother, together with Miriam of Magdala and Rebecca at her side now managed to wiggle their way through the crowd in order to get nearer to Yeshua, and to give him some comfort. "Please let us through, this is his mother, Yeshua's mother," Miriam of Magdala called out.

"It's the Nazarene's mother! It's Yeshua's mother, let her through, let her through," the people around them responded, especially the women. The people made way and allowed Yeshua's mother and Miriam and Rebecca to pass. They were now right in front of the crowd. Miriam saw her son slowly and painstakingly approaching with the cross over his shoulder. Before the guards realised it, she made her way into Yeshua's path, with Miriam and Rebecca by her side.

"Get out of the way!" a guard yelled at them.

"She's his mother," Rebecca yelled back with fire in her eyes and her voice. The guard relented and allowed Miriam a moment with her son.

"Oh Yeshua, oh son, what have they done to you!" Miriam cried, and then touched Yeshua on his bloodied face. It was all she could do, she so much wanted to hug him and hold him, and caress him, and take his pain away.

Yeshua looked at his mother through misty eyes. He whispered, "Mother, it is okay. Do not weep. This has to be. Be strong, mother. Comfort my disciples." Then Yeshua's eyes fell on Miriam and Rebecca, and Yeshua forced the slightest of smiles, and nodded and whispered, "Thank you, thank you."

"Okay! That's enough!" one of the guards yelled and forced the three women out of the way, and pushed Yeshua on, causing him to fall a second time under the weight of the cross. Miriam and the women instinctively rushed to help Yeshua but the guards blocked them and ordered them backwards. He then struck Yeshua with a whip and shouted at him to get up. But Yeshua lay motionless. He had no more strength left. One of the guards looked at the nearby crowd and saw a man who stood out because of the colour of his black skin. "Hey you, come here," he yelled pointing his whip at the man. "What is your name?"

The man was startled to be picked out, but he answered, "My name is Shimon."

"Shimon, where are you from?" the guard was curious.

"From Cyrene, Sir," Shimon answered.

"Shimon from Cyrene, come here and give this man a hand with his cross," the guard ordered.

Shimon came forward and lifted up the cross and put it on his shoulder.

The guard then roughly helped Yeshua to his feet. If he had not done that, Yeshua would have remained in the dirt; he had felt a moment of reprieve lying down, even though his whole body was still riddled with pain. Now he felt the rough hands of the guard helping him to his feet.

"Thank you," Yeshua whispered to Shimon.

The route from the Antonia Fortress to the Hill of Golgotha where Yeshua was to be crucified was only a distance of about half a mile, but to Yeshua who was walking so slowly and painstakingly, it felt like a hundred miles. He was at the end of his strength, and he was grateful for the slight reprieve, as Shimon carried his cross for him.

A woman in the crowd somehow avoided the guards and rushed towards Yeshua, she had with her a damp towel. And before the guards could stop her, she was wiping Yeshua's face with her towel. The guards, when they saw what was happening, allowed the woman a moment.

"Thank you, Veronica," Yeshua said softly, forcing a smile.

"Okay, that's enough, get out of here!" The guard yelled.

Veronica stepped back, in awe of Yeshua. *How did he know my name?* She wondered. She kept the towel close to her heart. It was only later, when she left the hill of Golgotha that she happened to look at the towel and was overcome to see the image of Yeshua's bloodied face on her towel.

Yeshua continued his painstaking walk. "Okay, Shimon of Cyrene, that's enough, hand the cross back to this man," one of the guards ordered. As gently as he could, Shimon replaced the cross on Yeshua's shoulders. The weight seemed to have doubled, and Yeshua staggered and then fell a third time. Immediately, the guards whipped him, ordering him to get up. But Yeshua could not, he had no more strength. He was thirsty and dehydrated and his head was aching and his whole body writhing with pain. The guards had no option but to help Yeshua to his feet, and putting the cross once more on his shoulders.

Yeshua steadied himself and continued his slow walk to Golgotha. A group of women were standing at the front of the crowd behind the row of guards. The women were weeping as Yeshua came nearer to them. Yeshua stopped and looked at the women and although he was almost out of breath, and so weak, he was full of compassion for them, and spoke to them, softly, "Daughters of Jerusalem do not weep for me, but weep for yourselves and for your children. For the days are surely coming when they will say, 'Blessed are the barren, and the wombs that never bore, and the breasts that never nursed'."

The women were alarmed at Yeshua's words of doom. But Yeshua spoke to them of even more atrocious things to come, "Then they will begin to say to the mountains, 'Fall on us', and to the hills, 'Cover us.' For if they do this when the wood is green, what will happen when it is dry?"

"Move on! Move on!" the guards pushed Yeshua ahead. They were now close to the hill of Golgotha, the place where Yeshua was to be crucified.

Chapter Eighty-Six
The Crucifixion

And so, they came to the hill of Golgotha, which means 'The Place of the Skull'. Two criminals were already about to be lifted up, one named Dismas, on the right-hand side of the spot where Yeshua was to be crucified, and the other named Gestas to Yeshua's left. They were both cursing from the pain. But no one was really interested in them; they were all here for the crucifixion of the one who claimed to be the Messiah. When Yeshua stood on the hill, he saw the two men already hanging on their crosses and he knew he was about to join them. He trembled with fear. He whispered a prayer to his Father for strength.

As soon as Yeshua was on the spot where he was to be crucified, the guards stripped him of his clothing. And Yeshua stood naked, except for his loincloth. He was grateful they at least gave him that bit of cover. The soldiers were mocking him and slapping him. One of them though, offered him a drink of wine, mixed with gall, but when Yeshua tasted it and realised it wasn't water, he refused the drink.

When Yeshua was stripped and all the nails were in place, they shoved Yeshua backwards and he fell on the cross; luckily, his back connected with the cross beam, otherwise he would have been more seriously injured. But the fall sent pain throughout his bruised and battered back, where his lacerated flesh left open wounds.

The crowds were waiting, as if they were at an open-air concert. They were chatting among themselves. Miriam, his mother, and all the women and Johanan were among the crowd, as were some of his other seventy-two disciples, but most of them were in hiding, fearful that a similar fate would befall them. Shimon and all the rest of the men disciples, except for Johanan and of course, Judas, were holed up, with fear, in the Upper Room.

They now had Yeshua in place across the crossbeam of the cross and the crucifixion began in earnest. Two soldiers grabbed at Yeshua's right arm and yanked it towards them, over the spot where the nail was to be driven. Yeshua instinctively tried to go along with them but his other arm was also being held down by two other guards. And when they had his wrist in place over the partially prepared hole, they placed the large, thick nail over his wrist and then the soldier hammered down the first blow. The pain was unbearable and shot throughout Yeshua's body, and he cried out, unable to stifle the excruciating pain he felt. The sound of that first blow was like a sledgehammer to Miriam, his mother, and those with her. Miriam, his mother, could not bear to look, she dropped her face into her hands, and Miriam of Magdala and Rebecca, who were themselves overwrought and both weeping, held Yeshua's mother in their arms.

The crowd was stunned. As the hammering continued, they went silent. They heard the first cries of pain from Yeshua, and then it seemed as if he got used to the pain, as his cries grew softer and softer. When the soldiers had finished nailing his right wrist to the cross, they tackled his left wrist. Again, there was a loud cry of pain, which subsided with each deafening blow. By this time, the crowd was getting restless. They wanted to see Yeshua raised alongside Dismas and Gestas.

Now the soldiers tackled Yeshua's feet, which was a more difficult procedure. There was no footrest, so they allowed for a bending of Yeshua's knees so the feet could more easily be nailed to the vertical beam of the cross. And so, they hammered one foot and then the other, until they were satisfied that he was securely nailed. And now, with ropes, a ladder, and several soldiers, Yeshua was slowly being raised up in place, into the hole already prepared. The cross slipped into the hole, with a thud that jolted Yeshua's whole body that was writhing with pain. And now, after the soldiers had secured the cross so that it would stand up straight and secure and not topple over, they stood back, as if admiring the work they had done.

The crowd went wild, cheering and jeering. Caiaphas and his mob were now up front. Caiaphas now noticed the sign on the cross above the head of Yeshua; it read 'Yeshua of Nazareth, the King of the Jews'. Pilate had ordered it to be written in Hebrew, Latin and Greek. He wanted the whole of Jerusalem to be able to read and understand the inscription. Caiaphas and his inner circle were furious, they quickly stomped over to Pilate and complained that they wanted the inscription taken down or changed immediately. They said to Pilate, "You should not have written 'The King of the Jews', but 'This man said I am King of the Jews'."

Pilate merely said, "What I have written, I have written." And with that, he dismissed Caiaphas and his entourage. They quickly went back to the scene of the crucifixion, furious with Pilate, but there was nothing they could do.

When they got back, they quickly became part of the crowd, stirring them up against Yeshua. In spite of that hiccup with Pilate, Caiaphas felt a great sense of satisfaction and accomplishment. He had delusions of grandeur, he relished the thought that he would be admired and forever known as the one that saved Israel, the one that put a stop to the false Messiah, Yeshua the Nazarene. Now, he looked up at Yeshua with hatred in his eyes.

The soldiers in the meantime were finished with Yeshua; they took his clothes and divided them into four parts, one for each soldier, like dead stone killers, taking souvenirs of their victim. They also took Yeshua's tunic which was seamless, woven in one piece from the top. So, one of them said to the others, "Let us not tear this fine garment, but let's cast lots to see who will get it." And that was what the soldiers did.

People now came closer, as the guards began to disperse from around the hill. Some guards still remained on the hill, to make sure that no one came to take the bodies down. Those close by were jeering and shaking their fists and one of them, who happened to be one of the members that condemned Yeshua said what was on the minds of all of them, "You who would destroy the Temple and rebuild it in three days, save yourself if you are the Son of God, come down from the cross."

In the same way, the chief priests, along with the Scribes and Elders, were mocking Yeshua, and one of them spoke on behalf of all, "He saved others, he cannot save himself. He is the king of Israel; let him come down from the cross now, and we will believe in him. He trusts in God let God deliver him now, if he wants to; for he said, 'I am God's Son'."

The soldiers also mocked Yeshua. But one of them came close offering him sour wine, saying, "If you are the King of the Jews, save yourself!"

Yeshua refused the drink. Yeshua saw them all through blood-soaked eyes. He felt an overwhelming pity for them all, but he prayed in as loud a voice as he could, saying, "Father forgive them; for they do not know what they are doing."

Dismas and Gestas both saw what was happening and heard Yeshua forgiving all his executioners and all who were cursing and ridiculing him. Gestas joined the curses and screamed, "Hey, are you not the Messiah? Save yourself and us!"

But Dismas rebuked him, saying, "Do you not fear God, since you are under the same sentence of condemnation? And we indeed have been condemned justly, for we are getting what we deserve for our deeds, but this man has done nothing wrong." Then he said, "Yeshua, remember me when you come into your Kingdom."

Yeshua then slowly turned his head to face Dismas and said, loud enough for Dismas to hear, "Truly I tell you, today you will be with me in Paradise."

The Centurion, who was in charge of the proceedings, was stunned. He had witnessed this man throughout the proceedings, and he did not react like anyone else, like any of the riffraff and criminals whose executions he had witnessed, and he had witnessed so many. *This man has not cursed his God, his persecutors, his executioners or anyone; in fact, he forgives us, forgives me, and forgives this dying thief. Who is this man? What manner of man is he?*

Miriam, Yeshua's mother, and the women now surrounding her came closer. Only the Centurion and a few guards were on top of the hill, continuing to make sure no one came and removed the crucified. The condemned had to be guarded until they died, which in some cases could go on for days. They all died of asphyxiation, or simply loss of blood, or the results of the torture they endured. But to survive on the cross they had to raise themselves up on their feet and at the same time drag themselves up on their crucified hands, in order to breathe. When they could no longer do this, when they had no strength left, they simply suffocated to an agonising death.

Yeshua looked down from the cross and saw his mother standing there with the women. And then he saw his beloved disciple Johanan approach them as well. When Johanan was standing beside his mother, he said to her, "Woman, here is your son." Then he said to Johanan, "Here is your mother."

And from that moment, Johanan was determined to look after Miriam, Yeshua's mother, as if she were his own mother.

Yeshua was now at the end of his endurance. He was arrested in the Garden of Gethsemane, in the early hours of the morning, just after midnight, when it was still pitch dark. Then he was hauled before the Sanhedrin, which condemned him to death, in the early hours of the morning, when most of Jerusalem was asleep, way before the rising of the sun. At the first semblance of daylight, Caiaphas and his mob dragged Yeshua before Pilate, who dilly dallied in his deliberations, whether to cave in to the demands of the Sanhedrin to have Yeshua crucified, or to set him free. He passed the buck by first sending Yeshua to Herod, who after having his fun with Yeshua sent him back to Pilate.

Pilate tried again to have Yeshua freed and sent him off to be flogged instead. Yeshua was then whipped to within inches of his life and ignominiously mocked and crowned with thorns, and sent back to Pilate who tried one more time to free Yeshua by parading Barabbas before the crowd, but even that failed, and Pilate had no option but to acquiesce to Caiaphas and the Sanhedrin's demands. All this took a matter of about six hours, but all that Yeshua endured seemed like six hundred hours.

Yeshua was nailed to the cross early in the day, three hours before midday. He was now on the cross for more than two hours, and still alive, barely. The crowds were still hanging around, waiting for him to die. Some were leaving, they had seen and heard enough, but others, who were otherwise engaged, now began turning up to see the spectacle that the whole of Jerusalem was now speaking about.

Yeshua felt a deep dryness in his mouth and his body was crying out for a drink. He then cried out, "I am thirsty!"

A guard then took a sponge, tied to a branch of hyssop and held it to Yeshua's mouth. Yeshua took a taste, but then turned his head away.

It was a bright sunny day, the eve of the Sabbath, in the first week of the fourth month of the year, and Yeshua was thirty-three years of age, as he now hung on the cross, dying. It was now noon. The people were coming and going, but still a big crowd were standing at the foot of the hill of Golgotha waiting for Yeshua to breathe his last. All of a sudden, the sun began to slowly disappear behind what seemed like someone covering it with a dark cover, it was disappearing from sight, even though there were no clouds in the sky. The people could not look directly into the sun, but they could see the sky becoming darker, and then slowly but surely, they were all enveloped in the darkness.

And then panic took over. "Oh my God, what's happening? What's happening?" People were shouting. They were terrified. It sounded like a cacophony of bells and wild beasts and the elements all wrapped in one, as people were crying out in alarm and fear, and some began running and bumping into each other and falling, and feeling their way into the dark. Others were screaming and huddling in small groups, as the day became pitch dark. People held onto each other; they had no idea what was happening.

Even Caiaphas and his colleagues were bewildered. "Don't be afraid," Caiaphas cried out, "it is the work of the demons. Stay calm. This is the work of him who hangs on the cross. He is a sorcerer. Stay calm, it will pass." But it seemed like it would not pass, because people stayed and waited but it did not pass. Although with time their eyes adjusted to the darkness, and it was no longer pitch black to them, yet they were still filled with terror, waiting and praying for the sun to come out.

When the sun had disappeared and the darkness overcame Jerusalem, Pilate, Claudia and Procula were in the palace. They were shocked and stunned. They could not fathom what was happening. Pilate shouted for the servants, who answered from the dark. "Yes, Master."

"Light the lamps!" Pilate commanded. The servants felt their way around in the dark and eventually one of them managed to light one of the lamps, and then the others lit up from there. Pilate sat down with his wife and daughter, completely perplexed and somewhat fearful.

"I told you not to have anything to do with the Nazarene; this is his work, for sure," Claudia said. Procula, frightened, snuggled up to her mother, who held her in her arms. They both found comfort from each other. Pilate sat at the table and poured himself a big cup of wine, even though it was the middle of the day.

All over Jerusalem, there was panic and pandemonium, and people were shouting out, wondering what was happening. Eventually people found their lamps and the lamp lighters came out and lit up the streets. The middle of the day had turned itself on its head, and it was now as if it was the middle of the night. People were scared and hoping that the light would come and they would come out of the darkness. But two hours had passed and still the darkness prevailed.

Some people now came with their lamps to the hill of Golgotha, to see what was happening, word was spreading that the Nazarene had caused the sun to disappear, and the sky to turn black. They were coming, some repentant, some fearful, but all wanting to be brought out of the darkness.

Day has turned into night. Never has this ever happened. Is this something to do with this man hanging on the cross, the people wondered? They had heard all kinds of stories about miracles he had wrought; now people were saying he can even raise people from the dead. He is also said to cast out demons. And the chief priests and their Tribunal has condemned this man to death, and Pilate has given the order. Some people were wondering about this man hanging on the cross, what manner of man was he?

But the chief priests and all their associates disillusioned the people. They had to maintain their stance. They made their thoughts known to the people, 'This man is not a man of God, he is a false Messiah, he is a blasphemer, he who is a common human, whose morals are suspect, who has no regard for the Law and the Prophets, who is a sinner and associates with sinners, who does not keep the Sabbath holy, who is a drunkard and a glutton, a womaniser, who associates with prostitutes and dines with tax-collectors, such a man cannot be as he claims to be, the Son of God, equal to the Father.'

The people, who kept the Jewish faith, were so accustomed to listening to and believing their chief priests, rabbis and Teachers of the Law and the Prophets that they had to believe them now, at this time of darkness, when the whole world seemed upside down.

Still the darkness remained; still the people remained, hoping that when this man died, so too would the darkness disappear from the face of the earth.

It was close to three hours since darkness came over the land, the crowd were now quiet and huddled together, holding onto each other to make sense of what was happening to their world, and waiting for this man on the cross to breathe his last.

Yeshua too was experiencing the darkness, but not like that of those surrounding him, he felt a deep darkness in his soul, he felt so alone, and so lost. His eyes were dim and he could no longer see clearly, he could no longer see his mother and his beloved disciple and his friends and disciples, standing nearby. He was so weak, and his spirit was weakening too, he felt absolutely abandoned. Then he cried out, as if what felt like his last gasp, "*Eloi, Eloi, lema sabachthani?*"

"What's he saying? What's he saying?" One of the bystanders shouted.

"He is calling for Elijah," someone else responded.

But Johanan said, "No, he is praying to his Father in heaven, he has cried out to him with the words of our Father David's psalm, 'My God, my God, why have your forsaken me?'"

Johanan was right; in his heart, Yeshua continued praying, and with his last breath he was internally praying the lengthy song of David. Even internally, he struggled to pray, the words could barely arise from this heart. He prayed the first and third verses:

My God, my God, why have you forsaken?

Why are you so far from helping me,
from the words of my groaning?
O my God, I cry by day, but you do not answer,
and by night, but find no rest.

But I am a worm, and not human;
scorned by others, and despised by the people.
All who see me, mock me;
they make mouths at me; they shake their heads;
commit your cause to the Lord, let him deliver—
let him rescue the one in whom he delights!

Yeshua, who had such a phenomenal intellect and graphic memory, and who knew all the psalms by heart and prayed them regularly, sang them day and night, now he struggled to remember the words; part of the fifth verse sprang to his now feeble mind:

I am poured out like water,
and all my bones are out of joint;
my heart is like wax;
it is melted within my breast,
my mouth is dried up like a potsherd,
and my tongue sticks to my jaws;
you lay me in the dust of death.

Yeshua could recall no more of the eleven verses, but the last few lines came to mind:
Posterity will serve him;

future generations will be told about the Lord,
and proclaim his deliverance to a people yet unborn,
saying that he has done it.

Yeshua was now past the darkness and the feeling of abandonment. He knew he was dying; he knew he was close to death. He then whispered silently, slowly in his heart to his Father. "Father, you sent me into the world, to show all of humankind, how much you love them all. You sent me to lead them out of the darkness of hate, power, greed, domination, cruelty, and every evil, into the light of goodness, kindness, gentleness, mercy, forgiveness, humility and above all love. Father, I have come; to show them the way, to teach them the truth and to give them the life, real life, life to the full. For this Father, you sent me, for this I came, for this I have lived, and for this Father, I now die."

Then Yeshua cried out with a loud voice, "Father, into your hands I commend my spirit." And having said that, he breathed his last.

At that very moment, the curtain in the Temple was torn in two, from top to bottom. And all of a sudden, as Yeshua breathed his last, the earth shook violently, like an earthquake no one had experienced before. And rocks were splitting open. The people were screaming and scampering in all directions, while some were frozen in fright, and overcome with fear they huddled together, holding onto each other for dear life.

No one living in all of Judaea had ever experienced an earthquake in their life time. And it was the first week in April, the end of the cool and rainy winter and the beginning of the warm spring and hot summer, not a time for the earth to quake.

Those who were running past the cemetery saw in the semi-darkness, tombs being opened and the spirits of the dead coming out of their graves. The people who witnessed this screamed in panic and fear and ran to their homes. Later, all kinds of stories would circulate of the spirits of those who had died, visiting their loved ones and then disappearing from sight as soon as the sun reappeared.

The earth did not quake for long, but to the people it seemed like an eternity. Panic had gripped the whole of Jerusalem. Panic had already started when the day had turned into night, but now was reaching fever pitch. People were telling each other that it had something to do with the Nazarene that was being crucified, and many made their way to Golgotha, while others remained huddled at home, waiting for the darkness to disappear, and the earth to stop quaking. When the earth began to quake, the terror and fear increased a hundredfold, and then there was immense relief when the earth became still again, and the sun began to slowly reappear, and shine and light up the day.

During all of this time, Pilate was sitting in the darkness, pondering on what it all meant. "You see, I told you, you wouldn't listen. I had warned you to have nothing to do with this man. This is all his doing," Claudia said once again.

Pilate merely rubbed his face with his hands and sighed. He had an uneasy feeling about what was happening in Jerusalem under his watch, and that he had made the biggest mistake of his life.

At Golgotha, or Calvary, as it was called in the Roman language of Latin, since it was the day of Preparation for the Sabbath, Caiaphas and the chief priests did not want the bodies left on the cross during the Sabbath, especially because this one was of special solemnity. So, they went and asked Pilate to have the legs of the crucified broken, and the bodies removed. Pilate, who seemed like a broken man, acquiesced to their requests.

The soldiers came and broke the legs of the two men who were crucified with Yeshua, thus hastening their death. But when they came to Yeshua, they saw that he was already dead. But to make sure, instead of breaking his legs, one of the soldiers pierced his side with a spear, and at once blood and water spilled out. It showed that Yeshua had spilled every drop of his blood.

Then the Centurion stood there, a complete metamorphosis occurred in his mind and in his heart. He was convinced that he had just witnessed and been part of the greatest travesty of justice of all time. He knelt down on one knee, removed his helmet, and took his sword from its scabbard and laid his helmet and sword at the foot of the cross on which Yeshua hung, and for the first time he prayed, not to any of the Roman gods, but to the God of this man hanging on the cross. "Forgive me, God, of this your servant Yeshua. Forgive me for what I have done." Then looking at Yeshua, he prayed, "May your God forgive us all for the evil we have done." His underlings and those still around, including Caiaphas heard him utter, "Certainly, this man was innocent. Truly, this man was God's son." And then leaving his helmet and his sword at the foot of the cross, he walked away.

Many of the people were also taken by what they had experienced, and went on their way repentant and remorseful for being part of the death of this innocent man.

Chapter Eighty-Seven
The Pieta

Now all was quiet. The crowds walked away in silence, all occupied with their own thoughts. Some were mumbling and beating their breasts, others shaking their heads. Many walked with eyes cast to the ground, with shoulders stooped, and faces creased with frowns. No one wanted to speak to another.

As the soldiers were now satisfied that Yeshua, and the two crucified with him, were dead, they too left the hill of Calvary. Only Miriam, Yeshua's mother, and three other women, also named Miriam were there too; Miriam of Magdala, Miriam Cleopas, and Miriam, the mother of James and Johanan of Zebedee. And with them was Rebecca, she was overcome, and could not stop weeping. She had known Yeshua since they were little, and she had always loved him, and she knew that he loved her too, and that they both loved each other to the end. She went up to the cross and touched his feet, and kissed them. Miriam his mother had already held Yeshua by his feet too, and kissed his feet, as she had so often kissed his cheeks. All the women did the same; one by one they came up and bowed before the Lord, and silently spoke to him, and kissed his sacred feet.

Three men were present, and they too followed the women and did what they did, kiss the feet of Yeshua. They were Johanan, the beloved disciple, Nicodemus, and Yosef of Arimathea.

There were also several other women, who stood at a distance, they wanted to give the time and space to Yeshua's mother, and those closest to him. These women were also followers of Yeshua, who ministered to him and supported him in his ministry. They came up and paid their respects to, and offered their words of comfort to Yeshua's mother.

"Mother, I will go to Pilate and ask if we can take Yeshua down from the cross, so we can bury him," Yosef of Arimathea said. He addressed Miriam as mother, for he felt that she was now his mother, and mother of all of Yeshua's followers and disciples. "I have a new tomb, hewn out of a rock, in which no one has been laid, and it is close. Mother, I have come to know your son, Yeshua, and although I, and Nicodemus here are both members of the Tribunal that condemned your Son, we want you to know that we did all we could to set him free." Nicodemus nodded his agreement, with what Yosef was saying.

Miriam, in all her sorrow, managed a slight smile, and looked at both Yosef and Nicodemus with great affection and said, "Thank you so much Yosef, and Nicodemus, Yeshua did tell me about both of you, and he had such great love and respect for you."

Yosef and Nicodemus were deeply touched.

"And yes, Yosef, do go to Pilate and ask for my son to be taken down from the cross, so we can bury him."

Yosef and Nicodemus left. The rest all waited at the foot of the cross. They all sat down on the ground at the foot of Yeshua's cross. They sat in silence, as they waited for Yosef and Nicodemus to return.

When Yosef and Nicodemus were ushered into Herod's palace and stood before Pilate, Yosef spoke, "I am Yosef of Arimathea and this is Nicodemus, we are both members of the Sanhedrin, but we had no part in Yeshua's condemnation. We now humbly ask you, my Lord, if you would allow us to take down Yeshua's body for burial. His mother Miriam is at the cross, with some close friends of hers and Yeshua's, and they await your permission."

Pilate was surprised that Yeshua was already dead; no one had yet brought him that information. So, he sent one of his guards to go, and hurry, and get confirmation. The guard ran to Calvary and back. When the guard came back with confirmation that Yeshua had indeed died, Pilate gave permission to Yosef for the body of Yeshua to be taken down and buried.

Yosef and Nicodemus fetched two ladders and plenty of rope, and hammers and other tools to be able to remove the nails, and take Yeshua safely down from the cross. They also brought a little wooden stool for Miriam, his mother to rest on.

And so began the work of taking Yeshua down from the cross. They made sure Yeshua's body was securely fastened around his chest and under his arms to the vertical beam of the cross, before they started removing the nails. Johanan, who was the youngest and strongest, stood on one of the ladders that were placed close to Yeshua, facing him. Johanan held his arm around Yeshua's chest, while Nicodemus held the rope that held Yeshua to the cross. Yosef then began the operation of removing the nails first from both hands and then from his feet. And slowly and painstakingly, they gently brought Yeshua down from the cross and laid him in the arms of Miriam his mother who was now seated at the foot of the cross that served as a back support, as she held her dead son in her arms.

Everyone took a few steps backwards and remained silent, as they allowed Miriam to hold her son. They heard soft sobs coming from Miriam, and they saw tears flowing down her cheeks. Miriam's heart was breaking. She held her dead son, her only son, whom she loved more than herself. Now both men in her life are dead. She recalled old man Simeon in the Temple when she presented Yeshua as a babe; she recalled his words, that a sword would pierce her own heart. She felt as if a sword was at that moment, piercing her heart.

After a while, Miriam of Magdala approached to comfort Yeshua's mother. Rebecca was about to approach but she recalled Yeshua's words to Johanan, and she gestured to him to go with Miriam of Magdala. Miriam of Magdala and Johanan Zebedee, the two beloved disciples of Yeshua's, sat down next to Yeshua's mother and gently placed their hands on each of her arms in comfort. Miriam was grateful for their touch. Then after a while, Rebecca and the other women also approached, and simply laid a hand on Mother Miriam's shoulder, and touched Yeshua's feet.

As all this was happening, the rest all knelt down around Yeshua and his mother. The women were all tearful and sobbing quietly.

As soon as Yeshua had been taken down from the cross, Nicodemus rushed into the city and bought a mixture of herbs and aloes, weighing about a hundred pounds, and he also bought a linen burial cloth, which would be used to wrap Yeshua together with all the spices. He returned and all was ready for Yeshua to be carried to the burial site. Miriam thanked Yosef and Nicodemus, and all the others for the help and support she was receiving. The men carried Yeshua's body, now wrapped in the linen cloth. They would add the spices once he was in the tomb, according to their Jewish burial custom.

Yeshua had to be buried on this day, because it was the Preparation Day, the day before the Sabbath. Miriam walked directly behind her dead son, and all the women, walked behind her. They would surround her and comfort her, once they arrived at the tomb.

And so, they arrived at the tomb that was situated in a garden, belonging to Yosef. It was a beautiful and appropriate burial place for Yeshua, in the heart of a rock and surrounded by nature, by natural beauty, and in a place where no one else is buried.

They slowly carried Yeshua into the rock tomb. Then everyone followed Miriam into the spacious interior of the tomb. As there was no priest or rabbi, Miriam asked Johanan to say a farewell prayer.

Johanan was taken by surprise. It should have been Peter, the Rock, who should be here now, praying over the dead Master. It should have been Peter, the one to give them strength and comfort, instead Peter had denied the Master three times, and now he is holed up in the Cenacle, terrified that he would have a similar fate as the Master, and with Peter were the other nine disciples. It was only the women disciples present here with Yeshua and his mother. But Johanan did not condemn his brothers; he remembered how he too fled in fear for his life. Johanan prayed.

"Heavenly Father, you sent us your Son, Yeshua, to teach us your ways. Your ways are not our ways. Father, you know what is in our hearts. You know how much we love your Son, Yeshua. He came to bring us out of the darkness into his wonderful light. He came to show us just how much you love us all, and just how infinite and boundless and unconditional your love is for us all, each and every one of us, without exception. Your son taught and showed us how to love each other, as you love us. Your son came to give us life and life to the full. For this he lived and now for this he has died. His is the ultimate sacrifice that takes away all of our sins, all the sins of the world. He is now with you, Father, but he has promised us that he would not leave us orphans. We continue to trust him and believe in him. Father into your hands we entrust your Son."

"Amen!" all present prayed in response to Johanan's words.

"Thank you, Johanan," Miriam said. She then went up to her dead son's body and touched it one more time, which was not really the custom, for it would make one ritually unclean. But now, all that meant nothing. Miriam bent over and kissed Yeshua on his forehead. The others came and did the same. And then Yosef and Nicodemus, helped by Miriam and Rebecca, covered Yeshua's body with the spices. Then they covered Yeshua's body with the linen cloth and left in silence.

Chapter Eighty-Eight
Mourning the Death of the Messiah

It was now about the eleventh hour, the sun was beginning its downward slide to end its work for the day. It was an eerie feeling all over Jerusalem and beyond. The three hours of darkness was still haunting the populace. Pilate, Caiaphas and all their associates were consulting their wise men, and seeking answers for the astronomical event. No one could explain how the earth could be pitched into total darkness for three whole hours.

The people came to simply believe that it was the power of darkness. And many believed that it was the Nazarene, whom they crucified, who caused the darkness. They knew the stories about him, his miraculous powers; he must have had something to do with this phenomenon.

Caiaphas, the chief priests and all the religious leaders told the people it was through the power of Satan that the man Yeshua brought darkness over the earth. It was the work of the devil, of Beelzebub, but that people need have nothing to fear, it would never happen again. They told the people to trust Yahweh.

When the high priest, Caiaphas and his associates arrived at the Temple to prepare matters for the Sabbath, they were shocked to see the curtain hanging in the Temple, torn in two from top to bottom. Caiaphas was frozen in fright, confusion and alarm. This was a sacrilegious act of the worst kind. The curtain hid the inner chamber of the sanctuary, which is reserved for the Holy of Holies, for God's presence. It enshrines the Ark of the Covenant, the greatest gift, and symbol of the people of Israel's special relationship with Yahweh. Caiaphas was the only one who entered the Holy of Holies, and only once a year, on the Day of Atonement, when he burns incense and sprinkles the blood of an animal in sacrifice to expiate the sins of all of the people of Israel. Who could do such a despicable and sacrilegious act?

Caiaphas stood there in absolute shock, disgust and anger. He was ready to explode. "It can only be the disciples of that Nazarene!" He shouted. "They will pay for this!"

"Caiaphas, we have to repair the curtain. Or get a new curtain. I will send all these people out and lock the Temple," one of the chief priests said.

"Get a new curtain and take this one down," Caiaphas yelled, as he stormed out of the Temple, fuming.

There were some people in the Temple and they were scandalised by Caiaphas shouting. And they too wondered about the curtain, but they were too afraid to gaze inside the sanctuary for fear of being struck down by God. They were all still reeling over the day's proceedings and the three hours of darkness. They were praying to Yahweh to protect them from the powers of darkness. They were shunted out of the Temple.

After the burial of Yeshua, Miriam his mother and all of those that were there at his grave went together to the Upper Room. There they found Peter and the rest of the disciples. Peter sat alone, in a far corner of the large room. The others were scattered around the room, some were in their sleeping quarters. But when they heard

Johanan's voice, they all convened in the Upper Room, the place where they were last with the Messiah.

Peter sat down in the corner, looking so forlorn and lost. He had his arms clasped around his knees and his head was bowed. He was too ashamed to even look up, to see the eyes of scorn that would surely be there.

Miriam, Yeshua's mother, saw Peter sitting there, like a child who had done something seriously wrong. She walked over to Peter and touched him on the shoulder. "Peter, it is alright. Yeshua is buried. Yosef, here with us, had got permission from Pilate to take Yeshua down from the cross, and we buried Yeshua in a fine tomb, situated in a beautiful garden, owned by Yosef. He and Nicodemus have been so kind and helpful and strength to us all. Peter, you must get up. Yeshua has made you the leader; you must now lead us all," Miriam said, with a firmness in her voice.

Johanan was now next to Miriam. "Peter, we are all sorry for being so weak and scared. But the Master, while he was hanging on the cross, forgave us all. He even forgave those who crucified him," Johanan said. "Be assured that he has forgiven you, and forgiven us all," Johanan added.

"I am hungry," Thomas said, and that broke the ice, as they all were just as hungry, as none of them had eaten since the Last Supper with Yeshua. They had told Isaiah, not to prepare any meals for them; they could not eat while Yeshua was being crucified. But now Andreus and Thomas went to Isaiah and told him, they were ready for a meal.

The gloom in the room began to slowly recede. As they sat around the table, they began to share stories about Yeshua. Johanan spoke, "You know, when Yeshua had been on the cross, he never thought about himself. He forgave one of the criminals crucified with him, who appealed for his mercy. And the Master even forgave all his executioners. And when the darkness came at midday, and remained for three whole hours, and then the earth shook and rocks split open when the Master died, I was thinking of that dark night that we were on the Sea of Galilee being tossed about by the wind and the waves, and Yeshua was sleeping. And you Peter, went and woke the master, who was sleeping like a baby through it all. And the Master, with the wave of his hand and a few words made the winds and the waves calm again."

They all shared stories about Yeshua. The disciples, they were now apostles, so named by Isaiah, their benefactor, who now gave them full use of the Cenacle, the Upper Room, and a place for all of them to stay. He was seldom seen, or heard, but now he had said to them that they were now no longer disciples, but apostles. They now had to continue the work of the Master.

The apostles spoke about how Yeshua, first called them to follow him. Miriam, his mother, shared stories of Yeshua's childhood. She retold the story of his birth, their flight into Egypt, Yeshua being lost and found, teaching in the Temple when he was a mere twelve-year-old child. They spoke of Yeshua's love for children, his preferential love for the poor. Mattheus spoke about Yeshua's many meals with tax-collectors, and reminding them all, that he too was one of them, and yet the Master called him to follow him and be his disciple. And Miriam and Rebecca told of his many visits and befriending of prostitutes, to whom he spoke with such ease and affection and never a word of condemnation. Yeshua spoke to them only of the love, mercy and forgiveness of a loving God. Peter spoke about how he walked on the waters of the Sea of Galilee, in the middle of the night.

"You didn't walk, Peter, you were sinking, and had the Master not caught you by the scruff of your neck, you would have drowned that night," Thomas said, laughing, and they all couldn't help suppressing their own laughter.

Rebecca spoke of how she grew up with Yeshua, and how they enjoyed walking in the bush, and she spoke how she and Yeshua used to race each other, as young teenagers. They all shared their favourite stories about Yeshua, and spoke of his teachings, his many parables and miracles.

It was now getting very late; they did not realise it was already past midnight. And time to retire. And while they were all feeling somewhat refreshed, their mood changed, as they prepared to bed down for the night. As they were left on their own, they again felt the deep sorrow at the loss of the Master, their Teacher, Guide, Friend and Messiah. A dark cloud of sadness once again enveloped them all. They could not believe that Yeshua was dead. But they were all exhausted. The wine they drank did help them too, to fall asleep.

The next day, they all met to talk about their future. They all agreed that they should stay indoors for the day. It was now the Sabbath, so all premises would be closed Peter spoke first. "I think we should stay here, and not go out, unless disguised or under cover of darkness. Our lives are in danger now. We have to let matters die down a bit, before we venture out."

"Peter, we are still mourning for the Master, who is still in the grave. But remember what he predicted on a number of occasions?" Johanan said.

"Remind us, Johanan," Miriam of Magdala urged Johanan.

"I think of the time in Caesarea Philippi, after you, Peter, were still called Shimon, and your declaration about Yeshua, as the Messiah and the Son of the living God. After that, Yeshua changed your name to Peter, the Rock. And the Master said he was to give you the keys of the Kingdom of Heaven. You remember it was then that he foretold of his death. He had said then, that he must go to Jerusalem and undergo great suffering at the hands of the Chief Priests and the Elders and Scribes, and be killed. And remember, he said that on the third day he would rise again?" Johanan said, and stopped.

"Maybe we should remain until the third day, before we leave Jerusalem, and wait to see what happens," Nathanael suggested. They all agreed to stay in Jerusalem for three more days.

"Rebecca, will you accompany me, first thing tomorrow morning? We need to buy some more spices, to do the proper anointing of Yeshua's body. We did not do the full anointing of Yeshua's body when we buried him, as we were in a hurry to bury Yeshua before the Sabbath. We can then go to the tomb and anoint his body," Miriam of Magdala said.

"I will," Rebecca replied. The other women said they too would accompany them.

The Sabbath was a quiet day. It seemed everyone had said all they needed to, during yesterday and during last night. Now they wanted to be alone, alone with their memories of Yeshua. They were now deep in mourning. And all the sadness and sorrow returned. The sense of loss was overpowering. They were however not cooped up in the Cenacle; they were able to walk around the big private grounds and gardens at the back of the house.

Isaiah was a wealthy Jew, a rich farmer, who farmed sheep and goats and grew fruit trees and planted all kinds of vegetables. But as it was the Sabbath, only a few of his servants and labourers were around. And the spacious grounds at the back of his house were just for his enjoyment and the enjoyment of his guests. It was filled with beautiful plants and trees. It did help the disciples with their mourning the loss of Yeshua.

Miriam, Yeshua's mother, was filled with sadness and sorrow. She still could not believe that Yeshua was dead. She felt dead herself. She had nothing of Yeshua. She wished she was back in Nazareth, where she could touch something that belonged to her son. She felt so alone, and lost. Oh why, why did she have to lose both the men she loved? She should have been the first to die, not her son; he was only thirty-three years of age. "Why did he have to die? Why did he have to die?" she cried out in her soul. Tears continued to flow down her cheeks, as the images came flooding back of her son carrying his cross, and his slow agonising death, and the sword piercing his heart. It was as if a sword was piercing her heart. Pain was sweeping throughout her body, and as the image of her son breathing his last, returned, she gasped and felt as if she too were dying.

This Sabbath was like no other. There were no celebrations. Everyone wanted to keep to themselves. They wanted to live with the memories, and be with the Master. They could not believe that he was dead.

And for Caiaphas, the chief priests and the Pharisees, this particular Sabbath, the day after they had Yeshua crucified, was like none other too. They, who so vociferously condemned Yeshua for not respecting the Sabbath, they now too broke the Sabbath by going to see Pilate, with what they believed to be very important business, that was urgent, and could not wait. Pilate was not too pleased to be disturbed on this day, after all the events of the day before. And he had enough of these meddling priests. What in the name of the gods did they want now, the thorn in their side is dead?

"Gentlemen," Pilate said curtly, "what is it you want?"

Caiaphas spoke on behalf of the others, "Sir, we remember what that impostor said while he was still alive. 'After three days, I will rise again.' Therefore, command the tomb to be made secure; otherwise, his disciples may go and steal him away, and tell the people, 'He has been raised from the dead.' And the last deception will be worse than the first."

Pilate was exasperated. But he recalled the stories about Yeshua having raised a man from Bethany who had been in the tomb for four days. He had dismissed that as fabrications. But some little voice in his head told him to go along with what Caiaphas and his cronies were requesting. Pilate said to them, "I give you guards, soldiers; go, make it as secure as you can." And with that he dismissed them.

Caiaphas and the Chief Priests with Pilate's permission went to fetch some of the guards, and took them to the tomb, on this Sabbath, when no such movement or work should be done. They who had condemned Yeshua for not respecting the Sabbath were now themselves breaking the Sabbath. None of them criticised what any of them were doing. They went with the guards to watch, as the guards made the tomb secure. It was already secure as it had a huge rock to seal its entrance. But they placed more rocks on either side of the huge rock.

Caiaphas then said to them. "Make sure that three of you are here at all times, and do not leave this tomb unguarded at any time, not for a moment. You can take three-hour shifts, and then one of you can fetch three others for the next shift. This is of the utmost importance. You must make sure that this man's disciples do not come in the middle of the night and steal this impostor's body."

"Yes Sir!" one of guards said, as the three of them stood to attention on either side of the tomb. As soon as Caiaphas and those with him were out of sight, the guards sat down on rocks close to the tomb. "What in the name of the gods is happening? Why are we to stand guard over a dead man?" They were completely bamboozled, but sat down and made themselves comfortable for their three hours' shift.

Chapter Eighty-Nine
He Is Risen!

The day after the Sabbath, the first day of the week, it was still dark, not yet dawn, when Miriam of Magdala, who had not slept all night, got up. Everyone else was fast asleep, but Miriam could not wait to go to Yeshua's tomb. She went by herself, walking through the deserted streets, and knocked on the door of the merchant, who came down in his nightclothes, expecting the worst, and was surprised to see a woman, all by herself, standing at his door.

"What is it you want, woman?" he growled.

"Sir, I have come to purchase spices to anoint a loved one who was hurriedly buried on the eve of the Sabbath, without our prescribed anointing. I have enough money to pay you."

"Are you talking about the Nazarene?" the merchant asked. When Miriam told him, it was, the man then softened, and told Miriam to come inside. He disappeared and quickly returned with the spices. Miriam paid him and then hurried to the tomb where Yeshua was buried.

***

During the night, the three guards were guarding the tomb. They were bored out of their wits. They saw no sense in guarding the tomb of a dead man. But they had heard rumours about this man and his powers. He could work miracles and it was even reported that he raised a dead guy from Bethany back to life after he was in the tomb for four days.

"Justus, I hope we are not having to guard this dead fellow for four whole days. Let's play some games." And that's what they did for a while. Then Justus brought out a wine bag and the two other guards eyes lit up and they started drinking. After they finished drinking, they decided to take turns to guard while two could sleep. Justus offered to take the first shift. But it wasn't long before he also nodded off and was soon fast asleep.

After a while, they heard a strange noise, they woke up with a start. And they could not believe their eyes. They saw the stone being rolled away. No one was there, it was if an invisible being was rolling the heavy stone away. It rolled and rolled and then came to a stop close to where they were. They were terrified. Then they saw a bright light come from inside the tomb which terrified them all the more. They were now hugging each other like babies in complete terror. Then the light was gone from the tomb and all was darkness again. They lit their lanterns and together and with fear in their hearts they walked together and peered inside the tomb. There was no one there. He was gone!

Frantically, they took flight and decided to go first to Caiaphas and report to him what had happened.

***

When Miriam arrived at the tomb, she found the stone rolled away. She was puzzled. Who could have done this? And why? Instinctively, she felt like running to tell Peter and the others. But it was still dark. She decided to wait a while, until the dawn appeared. So, in the meantime, she wanted to stay here, in this place, where she last saw her Lord. So, Miriam stood there, then dropped onto her knees, weeping outside the tomb. As she wept, she bent over to look into the tomb, and was startled as she saw two beings that looked like angels in white, sitting where the body of Yeshua had been lying, one at the head, and the other at the feet.

Immediately, they spoke to calm her, and one of them said to her, "Woman, why are you weeping?"

Miriam, through her tears, replied, "They have taken away my Lord, and I do not know where they have laid him."

Miriam was still kneeling at the entrance to the tomb, when she heard faint footsteps, she turned around and saw a man standing there, and she did not really bother to have a good look at the man, thinking he could only be the gardener.

Miriam then heard the voice coming from the supposed gardener, it had a familiar ring about it, but still she did not fully recognise the man, as she listened to him.

The voice said, "Woman, why are you weeping? Who are you looking for?"

Miriam replied, "Sir, if you have carried him away; tell me where you have laid him, and I will take him away."

The voice replied, "Miriam!"

And then it was unmistaken. Miriam fully recognised the voice. It was Yeshua; she cried out in Hebrew, "Rabbouni!" meaning Teacher, and then she rushed into his arms, throwing her arms around him; she was overwhelmed with an indescribable joy. She could find no words to say to Yeshua, she simply held onto him, pouring out her love for him.

Yeshua stood there, allowing his beloved Miriam to hold him for quite a while. Then he said to her, "Miriam, please release me, for I have not yet ascended to my Father. But go to my brothers and sisters, and say to them, I am ascending to my Father and your Father, to my God and your God." And then Yeshua was gone.

Miriam looked at the tomb; the stone was still rolled away from the entrance to the tomb. And she could see that the two men, or were they angels, were no longer there. Did she really see the Lord, did he really come to her, did she really hear his voice, and did she really hold him in her arms? She did not doubt for a moment that she had met the risen Lord.

It was now dawn, and Miriam was running, excitedly, on her way to tell Peter and the disciples, when she met the other women, walking towards her.

"Miriam, we thought you would have already gone to the tomb. Have you purchased the spices?" Rebecca asked.

"Yes, I have," Miriam said, holding up the bag containing the spices. Miriam decided not to tell the women what had happened. She was sure that Yeshua himself would let them know that he has risen from the dead, as he had said. So, Miriam joined the women, as they walked towards the tomb.

The women, now with Miriam of Magdala, were Rebecca, Salome, and Johanna. Miriam Cleopas had left with them but parted ways as she decided to catch up with her husband who was living with relatives in the city. As the women were approaching the tomb, it was only then that Rebecca said, "Ladies, who is going to open the tomb for us? Who is going to roll away the stone? I don't think we can do that." No one answered.

As soon as the women arrived at the tomb, they were amazed, stunned into silence. The mighty stone sealing the tomb, had been rolled away from the entrance. There was now a gaping opening to the tomb.

Miriam could still not explain her meeting with Yeshua. She felt incapable of sharing what she had experienced and still wondered if it really happened, but deep in her heart she had no doubt that she had embraced the risen Lord.

Then, all of a sudden, a mighty earthquake shook the earth all around the tomb and around them. The women, feeling the earth tremble beneath their feet, instinctively held onto each other. They had experienced an earthquake on the day Yeshua had died, and now they were experiencing another.

Then the women, still trembling with the earth, saw an apparition. They could not believe their eyes. A being that they could only describe as an angel of the Lord was descending. Miriam however was not at all surprised, in fact she was elated. For now, others too were seeing an angel of the Lord. The angel was dressed in a flowing white robe. The angel stood at the entrance to the tomb. And was now smiling at the women, and that put them immediately at ease.

The angel spoke to the women, "Do not be afraid, I know that you are looking for Yeshua who was crucified. He is not here, for he has been raised, as he said. Come, see the place where he lay. Then go quickly and tell his disciples, 'He has been raised from the dead, and indeed he is going ahead of you to Galilee, there you will see him.' This is my message to you." And with that the messenger of the Lord vanished into thin air.

The women seemed as if they were in another world, in a kind of dream state, and walking on a cloud. They peered into the tomb and gazed on the slab where they last saw Yeshua and where they had kissed his lifeless being. He was not there. Immediately, they rushed back to the Cenacle to tell Peter and the disciples that He is risen, as he said he would.

The three guards that were supposed to be guarding the tomb, were waiting for Caiaphas to wake from sleep. They were now at their quarters at the garrison. They were babbling, struggling to make sense of what happened, and what to tell Caiaphas.

"What happened? Where did he go?" one of the guards, trembling, spoke, "This is strange. Did you see anything?"

"He is gone! The One they buried is gone. What are we going to do? No one will believe us," said the other guard.

"We'll just have to tell Caiaphas exactly what happened. The rest is up to him," Justus, their leader, said.

The other two guards breathed a sigh of relief. They hoped that they would not lose their jobs and hoped that Caiaphas would believe them. But they were not so sure. They knew that Caiaphas and his mob wanted this Yeshua out of the way. He was stealing their thunder.

"Well, even in death, this man is stealing their thunder," Justus exclaimed, bringing a smile to his colleagues.

The women were also hurrying to report what happened, to Peter, and tell him what the angel had said. They felt somewhat uneasy and fearful, yet at the same time, filled with joy, as they hurried along. No one spoke to each other; they were all overwhelmed with their own thoughts and feelings.

Suddenly, Yeshua appeared on the road in front of them and lifted up his right hand and said, "Greetings!"

There was no mistaking. It was Yeshua, and he was radiantly alive. If there was any doubt, the wound in his wrist, where he was nailed to the cross, dispelled that. It was Yeshua alright. The women were overcome as Yeshua approached them. They fell on their knees and worshipped, holding his pierced feet.

Yeshua, bent down, and lifted them up, and said, "Do not be afraid; go and tell my brothers and sisters to go to Galilee; there they will see me." And then Yeshua was gone. They women were overcome with emotion, tears of joy rolling down their cheeks. They seemed to be flying as they hurried to bring the rest of the disciples their news.

When Justus and the two other guards approached Caiaphas and related all that happened, Caiaphas was astounded and was shocked into silence and disbelief. Could this be? No! It couldn't! Caiaphas could not accept what he was hearing. But he soon recovered. "Stay here, don't move, until I tell you," Caiaphas commanded them. He then sent his messengers to Annas and his inner circle of chief priests and Elders. They met quickly and Caiaphas briefed them on the report by the guards.

"Really, Caiaphas? So, he has risen, as he said he would. What are we to make of this?" one of the Elders commented.

"Could he then be all he claimed to be, could he really be the Messiah?" one of the chief priests said.

"No, he can't! He is dead! He is dead! We saw him die on the cross!" Caiaphas was enraged. The veins in his neck looked like they were ready to burst. Caiaphas had to sit down to regain his composure and once he did, he said, "we do not really know what happened. It is impossible for someone to raise himself from the dead. He was most likely not dead, when his disciples took him down from the cross. And they pretended to bury him, or maybe the guards were asleep, while the disciples came and stole the body. Yes, that is what happened. He did die on that cross. We all saw that. And he was dead and buried. But then his disciples came, while the guards were asleep, and rolled away the stone and took his body away."

Caiaphas' mind was racing, seeking some plausible explanation. "In any case, we have to devise a plan to contain this falsehood. I propose that we give some money to the three guards who were there and get them to spread the news that his disciples came by night and stole his body while they were asleep." They all agreed with Caiaphas' hasty plan.

They called for the three guards. Caiaphas spoke to them. "I know what you three witnessed are confusing to you. But it is absolutely important that you speak to no one, what you saw, do you understand? Your careers depend on it. Your life depends on it. Do you understand?" Caiaphas insisted.

"Yes Sir," all three guards said in unison.

"Now, we don't know what really happened at the tomb. We are relying on your word. So, whatever happened there, this is what you must do. And you will be paid handsomely to do this. Here is a large sum of money, to divide equally among you," Caiaphas said, handing the bag to one of the guards. "What you must do is to go and spread the news, and say to everyone, 'His disciples came by night and stole his body while we were asleep,' and don't worry, if it comes to Pilate's ears, we will satisfy him and keep you out of trouble. Do you understand?" Caiaphas said.

"Yes Sir!" the three guards said, and nodded.

"Go now, and do as you have been commanded," Caiaphas said.

The soldiers then went on their way, and did as Caiaphas and his counsellors had instructed them. And this story was to take hold and remain among those who were against Yeshua.

In the meantime, the women had gone to Peter and the disciples and told them what happened and how they saw the Lord on the way from the tomb. Miriam still kept quiet about her encounter with the Lord. It all seemed so strange but she had no doubt that she had indeed met her Lord, and held him in her arms.

When Peter heard the news, he immediately dashed off, and Johanan followed him. The two of them were running like seasoned athletes, but Johanan soon overtook Peter and reached the tomb first. He bent down and saw the linen wrappings lying there, but out of respect for Peter, he did not go in, but waited for Peter to arrive.

Peter arrived, out of breath. He stood for a moment, bent over and with his hands on his knees, taking some moments to regain his breath. And then he entered the tomb. Peter approached the slab on which Yeshua was laid. He instinctively touched the cold stone and then the linen cloth that covered Yeshua's body, lying there. He also saw the cloth that had been on Yeshua's head, over on a small stone table, by itself and rolled up. He went over and touched the cloth, but left it there.

By this time, Johanan too had entered the tomb and saw what Peter saw. "So, Peter, it is true, what the women said. The Lord is risen, as he said he would, and the women have said they had seen him."

"Yes Johanan. I think we should take the linen cloth and the head covering with us, and return to the Cenacle. We have much to talk about." They then left the empty tomb, and walked back to the Cenacle in silence.

Peter reported what he and Johanan had seen in the empty tomb. And they showed them the linen cloth and the head cloth to the others, which they now laid on a side table. They all went to have a look and to touch both the cloths; it made them feel close to Yeshua, something that touched his body. It would be safeguarded as a precious relic of the Lord and Saviour.

Then Peter asked the women to report what they had experienced. They did so. Still Miriam of Magdala kept silent about her experience. She was alone, and felt it was between her and her Lord, and she did not for some reason want to speak about the Lord having appeared to her before everyone else.

"We must go and tell Miriam, Yeshua's mother," Johanan said.

"I heard she is staying at Bethany. She went there after we buried Yeshua. She is staying with Martha and Miriam," Rebecca said. "I'm not sure whether Lazarus is home. He left a while back and wasn't sure when he would return to Bethany," Rebecca added.

"I will go there," Johanan said.

"I will go with you, Johanan," Miriam of Magdala said.

"I would like to go too," Rebecca said.

"That's okay, but no one else, we must be careful. I think we are now all in danger, and must keep out of sight," Peter said. "The rest of us must go out in twos, and go and spread the word among the other disciples, especially the seventy-two, so that they know that the Lord is risen as he said he would." And so, they did this.

Johanan, Miriam and Rebecca, keeping their faces covered, went to see Miriam, Yeshua's mother.

When they met and told her that her son Yeshua was alive, that he had risen from the dead, Miriam said, "Yes, I know, he had come to me, as soon as he rose from the dead. He said he would soon visit you all."

Miriam of Magdala told Yeshua's mother about her experience with the women and how they saw Yeshua on the road, but she still did not divulge her personal encounter with Yeshua.

"Miriam, Yeshua told the women that we must go back to Galilee and that he will meet us there. I think we will most likely head that way in the next couple of days. Miriam, Yeshua had asked me to care for you. So, I am going to care for you. You are most welcome to come and stay with us in our home at Capernaum, when we return to Galilee," Johanan said.

"Thank you, Johanan, that won't be necessary. I prefer to return to Nazareth. I have good friends there, I will be okay," Miriam said.

"And I will return with you, Miriam," Rebecca said.

Johanan was pleased that Rebecca would return with Miriam to Nazareth. "Well, Miriam, I will let you know when we are heading back to Galilee, and you can travel with us," Johanan said. And so, it was arranged.

On their way back to the Cenacle, Miriam thought it would be a good opportunity to tell Johanan and Rebecca about her encounter with Yeshua. She could no longer bear to keep it to herself, and was bursting to tell someone. And moved by the Spirit, she began, a bit tentatively, "Johanan and Rebecca, I have something to confide with you, for your ears only."

Johanan and Rebecca both stopped for a moment. "We can walk and talk," Miriam said. She then told them all about her encounter with Yeshua, and how she had embraced him and he had disappeared from her sight. "After, Yeshua was gone, it seemed like it was a dream, but a dream from which I didn't want to wake. And when I did open my eyes, I saw the empty tomb. But I was in no doubt that the Lord had risen and that he came to me, that I encountered Yeshua, and that he spoke to me and that I embraced him," Miriam said.

"Miriam, that is wonderful, and I am sure you were not dreaming or hallucinating. Yeshua wanted you to experience that precious moment with him. He always had such a tender spot for you Miriam. You are indeed blessed," Rebecca said, as she stopped and hugged Miriam, and now they were both sobbing.

There was nothing Johanan could do but stop and let the two women have their moment. He did not know what to make of what Miriam had recounted, but he was sure she *did* encounter the Lord.

After that, they continued to walk on in silence until they arrived back at the Cenacle. Because they had spent a couple of hours with Miriam at Bethany, most of the others were now back in the Cenacle, having spread the word around about Yeshua's resurrection from the dead.

"Peter, the Master told the women that we must return to Galilee, and that we would see him there. Should we not leave Jerusalem now?" Johanan said.

"Yes, Johanan, we should. You just told Miriam, Yeshua's mother, she can return with us to Galilee, so you can go to Bethany in the morning and find out when she would want to return to Nazareth," Peter said.

When they had finished supper and sat around the room on cushions, Miriam said, "Peter, remember what happened when the Master had supper with us?"

"What are you referring to Miriam; a lot happened at that supper. He washed our feet—"

"I don't mean that, Peter, I'm talking about when he took bread and broke it and gave it to us and said that it was his body and he did the same with the cup of wine saying we should drink it, for it is his blood."

"Yes, I remember that Miriam," Peter said.

"We all remember that Miriam," Andreus added.

"After he had done that and said those words and we ate the bread and drank from the cup he said, 'do this in remembrance of me.' Do you not think it would be good for us to do as he said," Miriam responded.

"Yes, Peter, I agree with Miriam. We heard that at the moment when Yeshua died, when the earth did quake, that the veil in the Temple was torn in two from top to bottom. What was Yeshua trying to tell us?" Johanan said.

"What are you trying to say, Johanan?" James asked.

"Well, the curtain separated the Holy of Holies, the presence of God from all of us, except for the high priest, and he could only enter in the sanctuary once a year on the Day of Atonement when he burns incense and sprinkles the blood of an animal to expiate for all our sins, for all the sins of Israel. The Master often referred to himself as the Lamb of God, who takes away the sins of the world. He is the Lamb of God who died on the cross, and his blood is now the sacrificial blood poured out for all of us on the cross of Calvary. We no longer need the blood of animals to be shed for the forgiveness of our sins, Yeshua has shed his blood once and for all and by what he did at the Last Supper he instituted, as a way to repeat this, for time immemorial. Peter, we can do it now," Johanan said.

There was silence all over the room as everyone listened intently to what Johanan was saying. It all made sense. "Yes, Peter, what Johanan says makes perfect sense. We are to do what Yeshua did, in memory of him. But more than a memory, through the blessing of the bread and the wine, those substances become his body and his blood, which we consume and become one with him," Miriam said.

"I remember, what I heard about when Yeshua was baptised by Johanan in the River Jordan," James said. "Johanan's disciples told me that when Johanan first saw Yeshua coming forward to be baptised," Johanan exclaimed, pointing at Yeshua, "Here is the Lamb of God, who takes away the sin of the world."

"Exactly!" Miriam said. "Yeshua, by his life and death and when he died on the cross, took away the sin of the world. Wiped away the first sin and all sin from the world once and for all," Miriam added.

"Remember what Yeshua said to the crowds at Capernaum, after he had fed the multitude of over five thousand people with five loaves and two fish?" Johanan said. "When the people returned the following day, Yeshua told them, that he is the bread of life. I now remember his words clearly, he said, 'I am the bread of life. Whoever comes to me will never be hungry, and whoever believes in me will never be thirsty'," Johanan added.

"Yes, I remember," Phillip said. "I also remember on that occasion Yeshua saying, 'This is the bread that comes down from heaven. Whoever eats of this bread will live forever, and the bread that I will give, for the life of the world, is my flesh'," Phillip added.

"He said such profound words at that time, and it is only making sense now," Nathanael said. "He said that unless we eat his flesh and drink his blood, we will not have life in him."

"Yes, and I remember everyone walked away, for it was a difficult teaching to grasp at the time. But now it makes sense. What he did at the Last Supper was to give us a way to be united with him in a most intimate way, through the simple act of eating bread and drinking wine, which through his power we become one with him, just as food and drink becomes part of us when we consume and drink," Johanan said.

"Well then, let's do it," Peter said. "We will sit around the table."

As everyone found their place around the table, Yeshua's place was empty, and Judas's. "Peter, you must now take Yeshua's place at the table," James said. They all agreed.

Peter began. "We have that small loaf still over, it's enough for our purpose, hand it to me."

Lucia handed it down the table and it reached Peter. Peter then took the loaf of bread, which was on a small platter. Peter looked at the bread. He wasn't quite sure how to proceed. He wasn't a priest, but now he was to perform a priestly duty. The Master appointed me as head of his church, and said of me that I am to be the Rock on which he is to build his church. I guess this is the beginning; these were the thoughts that were now milling around in Peter's mind.

Peter took the platter with the loaf of bread and stared at it. Then he looked at the expectant faces of the others sitting around the table, and then he began. "My friends in Yeshua, our Lord and Master, our Saviour, our Redeemer, our Messiah, I take this bread. On the night before He suffered and died for us, he took bread in his hands after giving thanks, he gave it to us saying, 'Take and eat for this is my body,' so now let me give thanks. Heavenly Father, we give you thanks for sending us your Son to show us the way, to lead us out of the darkness into his wonderful light. You sent us your Son, to give us life and life to the full. You sent your Son to also come and forgive us our sins. For all this we give thanks. We also give thanks for this bread we are about to consume, no longer bread but the body of your Son, Yeshua. We give thanks for this bread, work of human hands, and we ask your blessing on all who had a part in bringing this bread to us for our nourishment which will now through your power and that of your Son and the Holy Spirit become nourishment for our souls."

The apostles, that's the name they now accepted, instead of disciples. They were still disciples, even though Yeshua was no longer with them in the flesh, even though he was and always will be with them in spirit, but now they knew they were to be the messengers, to spread the message of the Good News that Yeshua had brought, to the world. The apostles' eyes were all glued on Peter, and they were all amazed at his words. And he looked resplendent as he held the bread in his hands.

Peter, with the loaf of bread in his hands, touched it with a silent blessing and then he broke it and placed sixteen pieces on the platter, for missing was Judas, and Thomas, who was nowhere to be found, and no one of them knew where he was.

Also missing was Miriam of Cleopas who was with her husband in the city. Then Peter took a piece of the bread and ate it in silence, and then passed the platter around. Each took a piece of bread and ate it in silence, and passed the bread around.

When everyone had consumed the now sacred bread, Peter took a large cup in his hand; he took some wine, and poured it into the cup. Peter was about to pray again, when Johanan spoke, "Peter, when Yeshua hung on the cross, and his side was pierced, blood and water flowed from his side. We remember how precious water is to us, and how great were our experiences with Yeshua on the waters of the Sea of Galilee. And we remember the waters of the River Jordan, where we, and where Yeshua was baptised. So may I suggest we drop a drop of water into the cup of wine, to remind us of these waters?"

"Yes, I think that is a great idea, Johanan, and the drop of water can also represent us, we become immersed and lost in the wine, and in drinking of this cup we become one with Yeshua," James added.

Peter then took the cup filled with wine and again said a word of thanks, "Almighty Father, we give thanks for this wine, fruit of the vine and work of human hands. Your Son once described himself as the vine and us as the branches, as we consume of this chalice, may we truly become one with your Son, may we share in his divinity as he shared in our humanity." Peter then took the cup and raised it and said, "Take and drink for this is the blood of the Son of God, we do this in memory of him." Peter then took the cup and drank and then passed the cup around, and they all drank.

Silence ensued. Everyone knew that they had just created a new ritual that they would repeat again and again, for it brought them into such close intimacy with their Lord and God.

To end their prayers, Miriam led them in the singing of the psalm, "The Lord is my Shepherd."

Chapter Ninety
The Encounters

Now, on this first day of the week, the day after the Sabbath, one of Yeshua's disciples, Miriam and her husband, Cleopas were on their way home, walking the seven miles west of Jerusalem, to the town of Emmaus. They had heard the news about Yeshua rising from the dead, and his appearing to the women, and that he said he would meet them in Galilee. Cleopas and Miriam were married for a long time, and their two children had left home. Cleopas was busy with his business affairs, and he was quite content for his wife Miriam to have gone off to be with Yeshua, as his disciple, when he came to Jerusalem. But now he is gone, and it was good to have her home.

While Cleopas and Miriam were talking and discussing the appearance of Yeshua to the women, they were surprised by a stranger who caught up with them. They did not recognise Yeshua, just like Miriam of Magdala didn't at first recognise Yeshua, when he had risen from the dead, mistaking him for the gardener. Even if they did have a good look at Yeshua, they might still not have recognised him immediately, for he was changed. He was more radiant, with a glorified body. Cleopas and Miriam however, mistook the man now walking beside them, as a stranger, who said to them, "What are you discussing with each other while you walk along?"

They stopped, standing still, looking sad and lost. Then Cleopas answered, "Are you the only stranger in Jerusalem who does not know the things that have taken place there in these days?"

The stranger asked them, "What things?"

Cleopas replied, "The things about Yeshua of Nazareth. My wife here, Miriam, has been his disciple. When he came to Jerusalem, she has travelled with him all over Judaea, and witnessed all he had said and done."

Miriam then spoke, "He was a Prophet, mighty in word and deed, before God and all the people. And our chief priests and leaders handed him over to be condemned to death, and crucified him," she said, still with sadness in her voice, and feeling tears wanting to flow again.

Cleopas noticed what was happening, so he continued, "But we had hoped that he was the one to redeem Israel. Yes, and besides all this, it is now the third day since these things took place. Moreover, some women of our group astounded us. They were at the tomb early this morning, and when they did not find his body there, they came back and told his disciples that they had indeed seen a vision of angels who said that he was alive. Two of the men, who were leading disciples, went to the tomb and found it just as the women had said, but they did not see him."

Then the stranger spoke to them. "Oh, how foolish you are, and slow of heart to believe what the prophets have said about such a man, about the Messiah. Did you not know that it was necessary that the Messiah should suffer these things and then enter into this glory?" Then the stranger, beginning with Moses and all the Prophets, interpreted to them the things about the Messiah in all the Scriptures.

Cleopas and Miriam were totally engrossed in all the stranger was telling them. From their sadness, they felt uplifted, but still, they did not recognise the risen Yeshua. But his words touched the depths of their soul.

As they were about to turn a corner to their nearby village, Yeshua walked ahead, as if he were going on.

Miriam and Cleopas urged him strongly, to come with them. Cleopas said, "Stay with us, because it is almost evening, and the day is now nearly over."

Yeshua acquiesced, and went to stay with them. While they allowed Yeshua to freshen up, they prepared a meal. When Yeshua was at table with them, he took bread, blessed and broke it, and gave it to them. And then, like a flash, he vanished from their sight. It was only then that Miriam had recognised Yeshua, in the Breaking of the Bread. She had previously heard from Miriam and Rebecca all about the Last Supper, and how Yeshua broke bread with them. Miriam could not contain her exhilaration, "Cleopas, it was Yeshua, it was the Master, all along, as soon as he broke the bread, in an instant, I recognised him. Oh Cleopas, how honoured we are, the Master, who has risen from the dead, as he said he would, has appeared to us. We must hurry back to Jerusalem and tell the others."

Without further ado, they set off to walk the seven miles back to Jerusalem. While they were walking, Miriam said, "Were not our hearts burning within us while Yeshua was talking to us on the road, while he was opening the Scriptures to us?"

"How come we did not recognise him, Miriam?" Cleopas asked.

"I don't know, Cleopas. We were so engrossed in our sadness and our mourning, I guess, and Yeshua was the last person we expected on the road. Why would he appear to us, I am the least of his disciples. But when he broke the bread and I recognised him for the first time, he was the same Yeshua, but yet, different. He seemed even more resplendent," Miriam said.

"When he was speaking, I was wondering who this stranger was, he was so erudite, never before had I heard someone unfold the Scriptures to me, about the coming of the Messiah, as he did," Cleopas said.

"Me too, Cleopas, my heart was burning within me, when he spoke of the Messiah, and I was so deep in thought, thinking about Yeshua, and all he did, that I failed to recognise him before me."

The two of them then went silent as they hurried along, excited to be able to tell the others the good news of them having seen the Lord, that he is indeed risen.

When they got to the Cenacle, they found only seventeen of the apostles there, Peter and the women, and the other men, minus Judas, and Thomas. Miriam and Cleopas excitedly related all that had happened, how Yeshua walked with them for most of the way to Emmaus, without them recognising him, and they spoke of all Yeshua had told them about the Messiah, and they told of how they recognised the Lord, in the Breaking of the Bread.

The rest of the apostles listened with joy in their hearts. Miriam of Magdala and Rebecca came over and hugged Miriam, after she had finished speaking. Then Peter told Miriam and her husband what had happened, how they, after breaking bread, the Lord appeared to them all as well. There was so much rejoicing, as they recalled and listened to each other.

While they were talking about all this, Yeshua himself stood among them. They jumped with fright, all of them, even Miriam and Cleopas and the other women who had already seen Yeshua on the road. Miriam of Magdala was the only one who was calm and recognised the Lord. Because Yeshua now had a glorified body, although it was the same Yeshua, he shone with brightness and newness, the likes of which they had never seen. And the doors were locked, and Yeshua suddenly appeared in their midst, they were startled and terrified as if they were seeing a ghost.

But Yeshua put them at ease, he greeted them, "Peace be with you! Why are you frightened, and why do you have doubts arise in your hearts?" Yeshua then opened his hands and revealed the wounds from the nails that pierced through his wrists. "Look at my wrists." Then he pulled his outer robe to expose his bare feet and the wounds where the nails had been hammered through his feet, and said, "And look at my feet. See that it is I, myself."

The apostles were mesmerised. They stood there gaping and in awe. Yeshua said to them, "Touch me and see, for a ghost does not have flesh and bones as you see that I have." But none of them dared touch his wounds.

The apostles were overcome, with wonder and joy, but still not fully believing, so Yeshua said to them, "Have you anything here to eat?"

Peter handed Yeshua a piece of broiled fish and Yeshua took it and ate it in their presence. When he had finished eating the fish, Yeshua washed his hands and then spoke to the apostles. "Everything that is written about me in the Law of Moses, and the Prophets, and the psalms, had to be fulfilled." Then, like he did to Miriam and Cleopas on the road to Emmaus, he opened their minds to understand the Scriptures, and he said to them, "Thus it is written, that the Messiah is to suffer and to rise from the dead on the third day, and that repentance and forgiveness of sins be proclaimed in his name to all nations, beginning from Jerusalem." Yeshua then raised his hands over them all, and he said, "Receive the Holy Spirit, if you forgive the sins of any, they are forgiven them; if you retain the sins of any, they are retained." Yeshua continued, "You are my witnesses of all that I have done with you. And see, I am sending upon you, what my Father promised. So, return to Galilee, but then come back to Jerusalem in time for the Feast of Pentecost, when you will be clothed with power from on high." And with that he vanished from their sight.

Thomas who was missing, no one knew where he was. He was conspicuous by his absence during the ritual that the apostles celebrated of the Breaking of the Bread, and during the news from Miriam and Cleopas, and now the appearance of Yeshua in their midst.

"Does anyone know where Thomas is?" Peter asked.

They all shook their heads. "He just said he had enough, that he needed a break and some fresh air, and he left without saying a word about where he was going," Nathanael said.

The week after Yeshua appeared to them, the apostles remained most of the time in the Cenacle, locked behind closed doors and windows shut. Isaiah, the owner of the house where they were staying, was an important man in the city, so Caiaphas and his associates would not think of knocking on his door. And it was kept a secret that the apostles were holed up there. They did venture out in twos but camouflaged and disguised, and they avoided all the crowded places. Every day, they began with morning prayers, with the main feature being the Breaking of the Bread. Now they added prayers of repentance, some readings from the Scriptures and singing of psalms before Peter or one of the others performed the Rite of the Breaking of the Bread. It became something very special and dear to them all, and made them feel so close to their Lord and Saviour.

Six days after Yeshua had appeared to them all and showed them his wounds and ate the fish, the apostles were all gathered together for an evening meal, when the three knocks and then a single knock was heard. They opened the door and were surprised to see Thomas, looking hale and hearty and deeply sun-tanned.

"Thomas, how good to see you," Rebecca yelled. The others all approached Thomas to greet him and to hear what happened.

Thomas however was noncommittal. He simply told them he needed a break and needed to get his head straightened out. The apostles brought Thomas up to date, with everything that had happened in his absence, and they told him about how the Lord had appeared to them six days ago, here in this very Cenacle.

But Thomas said to them, "Unless I see the mark of the nails in his wrists, and put my finger in those marks of the nails, and my hand in his side, I will not believe." However, Thomas decided to pick up where he left off and remain with the apostles.

The next day, a week after Yeshua had appeared to the apostles, they were again gathered together in the Upper Room. This time Thomas was with them. Although the doors were shut, Yeshua again came and stood among them and said, "Peace be with you." Then Yeshua looked straight at Thomas. Thomas however, was bamboozled. Was this the Master here before him, or was he hallucinating, were they all in a trance. This man indeed looked like Yeshua, but he was so much more resplendent, sparkling in fact. His face was so radiant and he seemed to be from another world.

Then Yeshua said to Thomas, "Thomas, come, and see my hands." Yeshua then stretched out his hands and wrists for Thomas to see the marks where the nails were driven through his wrists. And then he said, "Thomas, put your finger here." And at the same time, Yeshua opened the slit on the side of his robe and exposed the wound from the spear that pierced his side, and said, "Reach out your hand and put it in my side. And do not doubt, but believe."

Thomas felt so embarrassed and ashamed and overwhelmed. He did not reach out to touch Yeshua's wounds, instead he fell onto his knees and confessed, "My Lord and my God!"

Yeshua gently reproached him with the words, "Thomas have you believed because you have seen me? Blessed are those who have not seen and yet have come to believe." And then Yeshua disappeared from their sight.

Thomas was still on his knees; this time he was overcome. He was weeping like a child. Miriam and Rebecca went to him and held him, and helped him to his feet. "It is okay Thomas; the Master appeared just for you, to confirm you in your faith, and to confirm us in our faith."

Thomas wiped his eyes with the back of his sleeve and thanked Miriam and Rebecca and the others who came and surrounded him and let him know that he is still one of them, an apostle of the Lord.

After Yeshua had left, Peter spoke to them all. "We have to go now, go to Galilee as the Lord has told us to. He wants us to stay safe and have some normality in Galilee. And when things have quietened down, we will return to Jerusalem, in time for the Feast of Pentecost, as he told us to. So, Johanan, make arrangements with Mother Miriam, and we will leave within two days from today. Let all the disciples here in Jerusalem know, that we will be gone, and will be in Galilee, for at least the next four weeks and then we will come to Jerusalem for the Feast of Pentecost." And so, it was done.

Chapter Ninety-One
The Ascension

The eleven men and seven women apostles of Yeshua now travelled to Galilee. They had decided to stay together for a start, for they needed the strength of the group and they had grown accustomed to being with each other, and now that the Master was no longer with them, there was much they needed to discuss, and much each of them wanted to learn from each other. They were all so unsure what lay ahead of them, and what the Master expected of them. Were they to continue his work; that is what he seemed to tell them?

When they finally arrived in Galilee, they decided to all stay at Capernaum, at Miriam of Magdala's family place, for a start. They arrived at midday and settled in, and rested, some sleeping until it was time for supper. At supper, as they sat around the large table, their minds went back to the Last Supper they had with Yeshua.

They were not saying much, they were all busy with their thoughts, and they were still very tired and recovering from their long walk home. They had walked practically non-stop, walking most of the day. They did not stop at villages along the way, like when they were with Yeshua, preaching the Good News to all. They avoided the people, and simply focused on getting to Capernaum. They walked almost a hundred miles, took them five days, as they walked most of the day, just resting to eat and of course for some hours of sleep during the night. They were all reasonably fit, because of all the walking they did with Yeshua, over the past three years, but they had to rest along the way, each day, as the road was long and parts of the terrain quite tough, so Peter insisted they rest enough each day to sustain their energy for the long walk home.

Thomas finally broke the silence. "What are we supposed to do now? We do not have the depth of wisdom and eloquence of the Master. And we do not have his miraculous powers, how will we get the people to listen to us, if we are to continue the Master's work?"

"Thomas, Yeshua said he would be with us, and so he will; his Spirit will sustain us," Johanan said.

"The Master, told us to return here to Galilee, where we would see him. We can ask him outright, what he expects us to do now, when we see him," Andreus said.

"Anyhow, I am so exhausted, I can't think about anything except to have a good and long night's sleep in a comfortable bed, tonight," Thomas said.

"Amen to that!" they all agreed.

"We will have a good sleep, and spend the next few days relaxing and recovering. We can all do our own thing for the next couple of days," Peter said.

"Can we go back to our homes in Bethsaida?" Phillip asked.

"I think we better just all remain here in Capernaum for the time being, as the Lord said we would see him here," Peter said.

The next day, after they had their 'Breaking of the Bread' in the evening, Peter said, "I am going fishing."

"I'll go with you, Peter," Andreus, James and Johanan said in unison. It had been a long time since they had been on the Lake of Galilee, fishing, and they relished the thought of being out there; it would be a perfect way to recover fully.

The four of them were surprised when Thomas said he would join them, and so did Phillip and Nathanael. The seven prepared to set out to fish and enjoy being on the lake, it was a perfect still night. They enjoyed being out on the still waters, except for the gentle lapping of the waters against the sides of their boat, and the feeling of the slight cool fresh breeze caressing their cheeks, and breathing in the fresh, clean air. Even though they fished all night, and caught nothing, they weren't too disappointed, as the main reason was to get away and to enjoy the silence, the stillness, and the peace and tranquillity of being on the lake.

Just after daybreak, as they were nearing the shore, they saw a man, standing on the beach; from the distance they did not recognise that it was Yeshua, the Master. Yeshua called out to them, "Children, you have no fish, have you?"

None of them took offence to being called 'children' by this stranger, because that is how they felt, fishing all night and catching absolutely nothing. They answered in unison, "No."

Yeshua then said to them, "Cast the net to the right side of the boat and you will find some."

Peter thinking the man on the shore must be seeing some fish from where he stood, so Peter told them to cast the net to the right side of the boat, and in no time, the net was teeming with big fish, swimming frantically, and filling the net so much so that they could scarcely haul it in because there were so many fish.

As this was happening, Johanan immediately realised that it was Yeshua on the shore, so he said to Peter, "Peter, it is the Lord!"

When Peter heard what Johanan was saying, he immediately put on some clothes for he was bare-chested and almost naked, except for loincloths, and then fully clothed, he jumped into the sea. But those on the boat steered the boat to the shore, dragging the net full of fish, for they were not far from the shore, only about a hundred yards off.

When they all got to shore, they saw Yeshua standing at a charcoal fire, with fish on it, and with some bread on a cloth beside the fire. Peter recalled a time on that fateful night when he had warmed himself beside a charcoal fire, in Caiaphas' courtyard, while the Sanhedrin was condemning Yeshua to death. He wondered if Yeshua was recalling that now, too.

Yeshua said to them, "Bring some of the fish you have just caught." So, they brought some of the fish, and as it was cooking, Yeshua was smiling as he said to all of them, "Come and have breakfast."

Now none of the seven apostles had the gumption to ask him, "Who are you?" Because they all knew it was the Lord.

Yeshua then took the bread and broke it and gave it to the seven. And then he gave them some of the fish. They continued to eat their breakfast in silence. They were all waiting and expecting Yeshua to speak.

When they had finished breakfast, Yeshua said to Peter, "Shimon, son of Johanan, do you love me more than these?"

Peter was surprised that Yeshua was now addressing him as 'Shimon'. And he was puzzled by what Yeshua was meaning by 'more than these'; was he referring to just the six of those around the fire, or the fish, or for all of humankind? These thoughts flashed through Peter's mind as he heard these words of the Master. Peter answered, "Yes, Lord; you know that I love you."

Yeshua then said to Peter, "Feed my lambs." A second time, Yeshua said to Peter, "Simon, son of Johanan, do you love me?"

Peter replied, "Yes, Lord; you know that I love you."

Yeshua said to him, "Tend my sheep." Yeshua then said a third time, "Shimon, son of Johanan, do you love me?"

Peter felt hurt, because Yeshua said to him the third time, "Do you love me?" But then Peter recalled that fateful night when around that charcoal fire, he had three times denied the Master. Was the Master now putting that all right, giving him the opportunity to right that wrong? Was the Master telling him, that all is forgiven and that now he must carry on his work, and feed his little ones and his sheep? Deep in his heart, Peter was grateful and he said, "Lord, you know everything; you know that I love you."

Yeshua said to Peter, "Feed my sheep." Then Yeshua added some words that Peter could not fully grasp, Yeshua said, "Peter, very truly, I tell you, when you were younger, you use to fasten your own belt and go wherever you wished. But when you grow old, you will stretch out your hands, and someone else will fasten a belt around you and take you where you do not wish to go."

Johanan and the others were watching and listening. While Peter made no sense of what Yeshua was saying; Johanan knew that Yeshua was prophesying about Peter's future. That Peter will be suffering, that others will harm him and have control over him.

Then Yeshua spoke to them all, "You will not see me for a while now. But stay here, it is not safe for you in Jerusalem. Go to Jerusalem later, and be there two weeks before the Feast of Pentecost. Ten days before Pentecost go to the Mount of Olives, at the ninth hour, and I will meet you there. You will receive the gift I told you about, the gift my Father promised. Johanan baptised with water, but you will be baptised with the Holy Spirit. Go now in peace." And with those words, Yeshua disappeared from their sight.

The apostles felt uplifted and full of hope and with a bit more clarity. They would see the Lord again, in Jerusalem. He will then make clear to them what they are to do. Johanan and James went and fetched some of their father's workers, the fishermen; to come and take the fish. The men counted the fish; they amounted to one hundred and fifty-three fish. "Father, will be pleased with the catch," Johanan said to James.

"He sure will," James, replied, and then said to Peter and Andreus, "Peter and Andreus you may like to get some of this fish to your father and his fishermen, and you can tell them how we came by them."

The rest took some fish back with them to where they were staying. When they got there, they told the rest of the apostles of their encounter with the Lord, and also about their catch of fish. They all felt so uplifted and full of joy and praised God.

During the rest of their stay, those from Galilee spent time with their families and loved ones. The women from Jerusalem, as they now knew that Yeshua was to meet with them there again, ten days before Pentecost, they made their way back to Jerusalem. They all arranged to meet at the Cenacle two weeks before Pentecost and then go to the Mount of Olives on the day and at the time Yeshua had told them to.

The next four weeks in Galilee seemed for the apostles as if they were living in a twilight world of semi-darkness. They had Yeshua on their mind all the time, from the moment they awoke in the morning to the time they went to sleep. It seemed like they were just biding time, waiting until they could see the Master again.

The time finally arrived for them to go to Jerusalem. They were all so excited, like children going on their first camping expedition. They felt so energetic and the five to six days they would normally take to walk non-stop to Jerusalem, they did in four days. The anticipation of meeting with the Lord seemed to have given them wings.

They arrived at the Cenacle, twelve days before Pentecost. They had two whole days to settle in before going to the Mount of Olives for their rendezvous with the Master. There was a different mood in Jerusalem, a different aura. The festive crowds were gone, but it wouldn't be long before they came again for Pentecost. They spent the next two days walking the streets of Jerusalem, but not all together in one big group, but in twos, with seven of the men accompanying the seven women, so as not to draw too much attention to themselves. Peter, Andreus, Johanan, and James, went about on their own. Individually they visited the places where Yeshua had been, Caiaphas palace where he was first tried and convicted, and they then went to Herod's Palace. Neither Herod nor Pilate was there, Pilate was in his usual place of abode, his palace in Caesarea by the Great Sea, and Herod for a change was in Capernaum, in part of the territory for which he was responsible, Galilee and Perea. The apostles were glad that both the Tetrarch and the Governor were not in Jerusalem. It made them feel safer and at ease, but they still had to avoid Caiaphas and his associates.

Johanan was the only one who was among the crowd as Yeshua carried his cross to the hill of Calvary. And the other three arranged for Johanan to show them the way and together they relived that Way of the Cross that Yeshua walked. It was a solemn walk for the four of them.

Finally, the day arrived, it was ten days before the Festival of Pentecost and a day before the eve of the Passover, the day Yeshua told them to meet with him at the Mount of Olives. They all went there in the twos they had moved about in Jerusalem, with Peter, Andreus, Johanan and James, making their own way there. The time of their scheduled meeting was the ninth hour, three hours after midday. They all started arriving from a half hour before the time.

At the ninth hour, Yeshua appeared. "Peace be with you!" Yeshua greeted them. He was smiling and he let his gaze take in each and every one of them. He then said, "This is the last time we will see each other in this way. I will leave you and go back to my Father that sent me. But as I said before, I will not leave you orphans. My Spirit will be with you forever. I want you to go into the world and proclaim the Good News that I have taught you and brought to you. I want you to proclaim it to the whole creation. The one who believes and is baptised will be saved, and the one who does not believe will be condemned. And these signs will accompany those who believe; by using my name they will cast out demons; they will speak in new tongues. They will lay their hands on the sick, and they will recover."

Thomas took it upon himself to speak on behalf of all, and he asked, what the others were thinking in some way or other; he asked, "Lord, is this the time when you will restore the Kingdom of Israel?"

Yeshua replied, "It is not for you to know the times or periods that the Father has set by his own authority. But you will receive power when the Holy Spirit has come upon you; and you will be my witnesses in Jerusalem, in all Judaea, Samaria and Galilee, and to the ends of the earth. And I say unto you one last time, 'All authority in heaven and on earth has been given to me. Go therefore and make disciples of all nations, baptising them in the name of the Father and of the Son and of the Holy Spirit, and teaching them to obey everything that I have commanded you.' And remember, I am with you always, to the end of the age."

When Yeshua had said this, as they were watching, he was lifted up, and a cloud appeared out of nowhere and took him out of their sight. And while they were gazing at the cloud, not wanting to stop looking, hoping they would continue to see a glimpse of their Master. But he was gone. Suddenly two beings, in white robes stood before them. They were getting accustomed to the sudden apparition of heavenly beings, for that is what these creatures looked like; they were resplendent and dressed in flowing snow-white robes. Then one of them said, "Men and women of Galilee and Judaea, why do you stand looking up to heaven? This Yeshua, who has been taken up from you into heaven, will come in the same way as you saw him go into heaven." Then they were gone.

When the angels disappeared, the apostles left that place. They were rejoicing, but they were all still unsure what lay ahead.

Epilogue

Out of the Darkness is a novel about a boy genius who lived over two thousand years ago and became a man who changed civilisation and humanity, as no other individual has from time immemorial, and time still to come. We have still only grasped an iota of who he is, what his message is, and how to apply it to our civilisation and our survival.

He said of himself that he is the Light of the World and that he is The Way, The Truth and The Life. Everything we are searching for is in plain sight if only we would come out of the darkness into the light.

He identified us with himself when he said, "I am the light of the world. Anyone who follows me will not be walking in the dark." In his famous manifesto, *The Sermon on the Mount*, he said, 'You are the light of the world.' And he asks us to let our light shine and not put it into a closet, but on a place where it will give light to all. He invites us to let our light shine before others, so they may come out of the darkness and so that they may see our good works and give glory to our Father in heaven.

We need no longer live in darkness, for he calls us out of the darkness and to stop living in the land of shadows and doubt and come out into the light that lightens up the whole world.

> The people who sat in darkness have seen a great light,
> and for those who sat in the region and shadow of death
> light has dawned

I hope you enjoyed the story of Yeshua, the carpenter from Nazareth. Of course, the story did not end with his ascending into the heavens. What happened when his apostles—those ordinary men and women who had followed him and learned from him—left the Mount of Olives after the Master had ascended into the heavens? Well, that's another story!